THE

Matchmaker

BRIDES

COLLECTION

Nine Matchmakers Have the Tables of Romance Turned on Them

THE
Matchmaker
BRIDES
COLLECTION

Kim Vogel Sawyer, Amanda Cabot,
Diana Lesire Brandmeyer, Lisa Carter,
Ramona K. Cecil, Lynn A. Coleman, Susanne Dietze,
Connie Stevens, Liz Tolsma

BARBOUR BOOKS
An Imprint of Barbour Publishing, Inc.

Published by Barbour Books, an imprint of Barbour Publishing, Inc., P.O. Box 719, Uhrichsville, Ohio 44683, www.barbourbooks.com.

Our mission is to publish and distribute inspirational products offering exceptional value and biblical encouragement to the masses.

 Member of the
Evangelical Christian
Publishers Association

Printed in Canada.

Contents

The Homegrown Bride

By Diana Lesire Brandmeyer

Dedication

For my husband Ed, my homegrown groom

Chapter One

Trenton, Illinois, 1887

Emmie Mueller wore her favorite floral dress to the July wedding. She hoped the skirt wouldn't wilt in the humidity. Two old bachelors down and two to go, and then she and Granny would be on their way to Kansas to be with their family.

Orville Tinze, the first bachelor she made a match for, had bluebonnet eyes and soft manners, which made him attractive to several older widows. In less than a month, he said his vows.

Getting today's happy couple together had been the most difficult task. A nigh impossible endeavor. But with God's help, she'd found a wife for George Henderson. One Sunday, she noticed the church organist, spinster Louise Wheeler, sending longing looks toward George. The surly old man would never have picked up on those subtle glances, but Emmie did, and she took action.

With a little coaxing, she managed to get George looking quite dapper before she put the two of them together at the church voters' meeting. He took to Louise like rain on a parched garden.

Finding the other two boarders a spouse couldn't be as tiresome. Her cheeks hurt from smiling.

"Do you take…"

She brought her attention back to the vows. This had to be the best part of the wedding, when two people in love promised to be together forever. And to think, God used her to bring this about. This must be God approving her plan to find matches for the other gentlemen boarders.

Hylda Mueller, Emmie's grandmother, nudged her in the side and leaned close to her ear. "Someday that will be you."

A rush of heat rose to her face. "Shh, Granny." Sometimes her grandmother spoke too loud, and when Mrs. Thompson snickered behind them, Emmie feared this was one of those times.

Granny patted her leg and nodded.

The couple faced the congregation, and the pastor introduced the newlyweds. Both of them beamed through their wrinkles. Satisfied everyone had their attention on the couple, Emmie slipped out the side of the pew. The finishing touches for the reception being held in the side yard of the church needed to be readied.

◆ ◆ ◆

Landon Knipp left the building he was considering renting in Lebanon, Illinois, thankful his father had come along with him to inspect it. This one, unlike others they'd explored, appeared to be the right size for his specialty market and in the right location on the corner of Main and Spruce.

Mr. Knipp brushed dust particles from his jacket sleeve. "You don't need to move. Why not stay in St. Louis and work with the family? It's a headache to start a new place where you aren't known."

"Father, whether you believe it or not, as the youngest I'll never have a chance to be the boss. I've spent my entire life being ordered around by my brothers. I'd like to try being the one in charge." Landon stepped back to inspect the front overhang. "No light peeking through."

"Where do you plan to live?"

"Maybe above the store. That would give me a bit more money to put into this place, maybe on better display cases." Landon shaded his eyes and peered down the busy street crowded with farm wagons and buggies. Another good indication that his store would have customers.

Church bells jangled in an unordered tune, as if a few schoolboys had control of the rope.

"Is it the top of the hour already?" His father checked his pocket watch. "No, not even close. There must be something happening at the church."

"Sounds like it's around the corner. Let's walk in that direction. This building is only one part of my life. I'll need to find a church. Worshipping is important as well."

And finding a wife.

All six of his married brothers had at least one child. When he'd returned from Europe, he'd been surrounded by infants and toddlers. Each one brought a distinct desire in him to have a family of his own. And to stay in one town. No more traveling for him.

If the bells didn't lead them to church, the steeple would have. The redbrick building was simple in appearance except for the stained-glass, circular window above the double entry doors. Though it wasn't as grand as those in Europe or back East. Even St. Louis had more impressive houses of worship.

The side yard contained tables decorated with many different cloths and flowers. "I'd say it's a wedding." Landon stopped at the bottom of the steps.

The door flew open. A blond-haired beauty hurried through it and down the steps.

"Do you suppose that's the bride?" His father snickered.

◆ ◆ ◆

Emmie's narrow-skirted dress hindered her movement. Now she regretted wearing it, instead of the wide skirt she wore at home. Going slow down the stairs wasted time she needed to uncover the food.

On the last step, she stumbled.

Her ankle twinged.

She grasped for something to steady her but found air.

Someone grabbed her by the waist, and she fell into the arms of a man. One she'd never met. Emmie swallowed. Was her embarrassment from the fall? Before she could sort out her feelings, he righted her, and then tipped his hat.

"Landon Knipp."

"Thank you for saving me, Mr. Knipp. I'm afraid my mind was on getting the tables ready for the wedding guests." She smoothed the skirt at her waist.

"Then you aren't the bride?"

She hadn't noticed the older man standing next to Mr. Knipp.

"Father. Excuse him, Miss. . . ?"

"Miss Mueller." She turned to the older gentleman. "No, sir, I'm a helper today."

"My father has an odd sense of humor."

"I see. Well, if you don't mind, I need to get busy." She took a step and winced. "Ow."

He grasped her by the arm. "Here, lean on me, and I'll get you to the tables. You can sit and rest and direct Father and me on what needs to be done."

"I couldn't, shouldn't. . ."

"She's right, son. We aren't guests at this wedding."

"We won't stay. With the two of us, we'll get things shipshape in no time. Miss Mueller?"

If they hurried, there might be a chance. And she did want George and Alice to have a beautiful day. "Please, that would be kind of you, and then you can be on your way." They would have to finish before Granny saw him, or there'd be wedding suggestions before they made it home. Having a new man in town would ignite the fire under Granny, and the pressure to marry would be upon her once again.

Chapter Two

Landon uncovered the third dish of potato salad and moved it down a table next to the other two bowls. That was the last one. He stepped back to inspect the display. Finished and grouped like with like. He and his father did a decent job of making the tables appealing. A feast for the stomach and the eyes. Would Miss Mueller think so? He glanced at her. She rubbed her ankle. It would be blue and purple by evening.

A loud cheer rose from the front of the church. The newlyweds and their guests would be coming this way soon. He headed over to Miss Mueller. "We're finished. Is there anything else you'd like us to do?"

"You've done a marvelous job. I wouldn't have considered placing the foods the way you have. We usually let the person bringing something set it where they want it."

"It makes more sense to have all the potato salad in one place, doesn't it?" He scratched his chin.

She wrinkled her forehead and chewed her lip.

"Unless there is a reason?"

"There is. It's a tradition passed down from generations. If one has all the bowls together, someone might get their feelings hurt if their bowl isn't touched. And sometimes people forget to put something on their plate, and they have a second chance of doing so as they move down the row."

"We should move them around then. I'll get Father—"

Her eyes widened, and she looked past him.

"Emmie, who is this?"

He turned to find an older woman standing behind him. "I'm Landon Knipp, ma'am. My father and I helped Miss Mueller set out the food."

"They aren't staying, Granny. They offered to help when I misstepped and twisted my ankle." She stood, wobbled, and caught the edge of the table to steady herself.

"Nonsense. You helped my granddaughter, and you must stay. There's plenty of food." The older woman beamed. "We love having new people attend our church. Where are you from?"

"St. Louis." His father stepped next to him. "My son is looking at a building to open his new business."

"What do you do, Mr. Knipp?"

"If I decide to settle here, my store will carry items you can't find at the mercantile. My father owns Knipp Emporium in St. Louis. And I'm opening our second one."

"What does that mean? Things I can't find at the mercantile?" Emmie narrowed her eyes.

Landon's heart stuttered. He'd insulted her town and her. "Items from all over the world. Fine china, exotic spices from India, that sort of thing. When a customer walks in, we want them to be wide-eyed and speechless while they take in the displays."

"Followed by excitement. Don't forget that, Landon. Lest the ladies think you want them to be as quiet as a church mouse while they shop." His father chuckled.

"You won't be competing against the mercantile, then?"

"Not at all. Our intent is to have different choices. Not everyone gets to travel around the world purchasing items to decorate their homes or give as gifts. Like this." Landon pulled a handkerchief stitched with embroidered birds from his pocket and handed it to her.

She traced the stitching. "It's beautiful. You're right. I haven't seen anything like this before."

"Our store will be filled with items like this."

"Look, Granny, isn't this exotic?"

Mrs. Mueller held it in her hands and rubbed the fabric between her thumb and finger. "The fabric is soft as down."

"You will do well with a store in this town. When will you decide?" Mrs. Mueller cocked her head. "And where do you plan on living?"

◆　◆　◆

Emmie knew what was coming before Granny asked. She wanted a boarder to fill George's room. "Granny! That's none of our business."

"It certainly is. Did you forget we run a boardinghouse?"

She squirmed like a little girl under Granny's glare. "No, but remember—"

"This is not the time or place to discuss this." She turned to them. "If you are in need of a place to stay, please come see us. We have plenty of rooms available."

Rooms she'd worked hard at emptying of boarders. She knew Granny didn't want to leave this town, but it wasn't fair of her to expect Emmie to stay here. She wanted to be with her family, and that included Granny. Yes, she did want to marry and have children but not here. No, she did not. She wanted to be near her momma. But Momma wouldn't approve of her pouting. She gathered her emotions and tucked them away.

"Mr. Landon, it would be an honor if you'd stay with us for a short time." *Please turn down the offer.*

"Thank you, but Father and I will return to St. Louis this afternoon. I have some decisions to make. I've seen several towns that fit my needs."

His words were like warm butter, and the tension in her shoulders dissolved. A problem diverted, though looking at him again, it wouldn't be hard to find him a wife if he did stay. Handsome, with those Jersey-cow eyes framed with long, dark lashes. Yes, there would be a few women in town that would want to sit at his table every night. Good thing he was leaving, because she might be tempted to get his attention and that would mess up her plan.

◆　◆　◆

There were quite a few people at the reception. Landon listened in on conversations as he filled his plate, hoping to get a feel for the people of the town.

"Something's going on, Walter. I think Emmie is up to some shenanigans."

Hearing Emmie's name, he whipped around and took note of the two older men behind him in line.

"Milton, I'm telling you. Orville getting married didn't surprise me. He still has all his hair. But George? Didn't you notice how Miss Emmie got him to slick down his hair and make sure his mustache didn't have food in it every Sunday?"

"You might be right. Do you think she's trying to match us up, too?"

"We best keep an eye on her. I like things the way they are." Milton plopped potato salad onto his plate.

"Landon?" His father spoke into his ear. "You listening in on conversations again?"

"Yes. You can learn a lot about the culture of a place when you do that."

"You're in Illinois, son, not a foreign land. Not much different from where you grew up. Let's look for a place to sit."

Under a young tree, they found a spot that hadn't been claimed and settled beneath it with their packed plates. From here, Landon observed Miss Emmie Mueller undetected. Her delicate fingers piano-key danced through the air while she chatted with another woman.

"She's a pretty one with that blond hair." His father wiggled his fork in her direction. "Are you thinking this town might offer you more than a place to sell wares from abroad?"

"You know me too well. But it's not just her. I know nothing about her. It's the townspeople that will be the key to having a successful business. Like those celebrating this wedding. I should think them to be an indication of the type of people I'd be selling to."

Miss Mueller filled her own plate even with an injured ankle. He noticed. Yes, he did. He'd been watching for a beau to offer her assistance, but none came. Maybe she didn't have one. Curious that one so beautiful wouldn't have a group of bachelors hanging around trying to capture a smile from her.

"—and you'd need furniture, too." His father's words broke into his thoughts.

"Pardon? My mind drifted somewhere."

"I thought as much. I've been observing your keen interest in the young Miss Mueller. Your fork has been hovering over that piece of ham for quite some time." His father raised his eyebrow. "What interests you the most about her?"

He stabbed the piece of meat and stuck it in his mouth, debating whether to answer his father's question.

"You're stalling, son." He laughed loud enough for a group to turn and stare.

Landon tipped his hat at them. "She must be a member of this church as she is talking to everyone. One of my high priorities. I desire a marriage such as my brothers' and yours. This might be the best town we've seen to open the store." And Emmie Mueller, the possible matchmaker, was the first woman he wanted to get to know.

Chapter Three

Emmie held a bowl of green beans as she settled in the rocker between Milton Taylor and Walter Hoffman. She picked one up and snapped it, the ends falling onto her apron. "What did you two think of the wedding?"

The rockers creaked against the wooden porch floor.

Emmie stared at Milton.

He stopped rocking. "Did you say something?"

"I asked what you two thought of George getting married?"

The rocker resumed its motion at a quick pace. "Don't see what that old grump needed a wife for."

Walter leaned forward. "Me either, Milton. Mrs. Mueller takes good care of us, and we don't have to do anything. Now George will have to do everything his wife wants."

"That's not nice. George is happier than both of you. Did you see him smiling at the wedding?"

"Of course, he was. There were tables of pie waiting for him after the ceremony."

Emmie ignored Milton. "Just think, he will have someone to listen to him at dinner."

"We heard everything he said." Milton snorted. "Even when we didn't care to."

"Never said much worth hearing." Walter nodded. "No sir, that man is going to run out of interesting things to say before next Sunday."

The door opened, and Granny leaned out. "Emmie, can you run and get me some baking soda? I'm plumb out, and I need it to make the biscuits for dinner."

"Yes, ma'am, I'll be happy to." She gathered the hem of her apron in her hand as she stood. "Sitting with these two makes me sad. They don't have a romantic bone in their bodies." She shook her apron over the porch railing.

"We're too old for that foolishness. Set in our ways." Walter settled back against the rocker. "But you're not, missy."

Emmie spun on her heel. "I have plenty of time once I get to Kansas." But did she? Her age was creeping up fast. What if she didn't find someone to love there? *Dear God, is it Your plan for me to be a spinster?* Her stomach sank. If it was, could she follow it?

◆ ◆ ◆

Landon's gut instinct was right four weeks ago when he'd first visited this town. It would be a good place to open his store. And a lovely blond woman had something to do with it as well. He closed and locked the door to the new store and pocketed the key. His stomach growled. He needed to find a place for breakfast. Last night convinced him he had no desire to sleep above the store. The old bed creaked with every breath he took and disturbed his sleep until his body gave up and he drifted off.

This morning, the sun broke through the dirty upstairs window waking him. He missed the smell of coffee wafting up to greet him. Not to mention a plate of eggs and a muffin. He hadn't noticed the lack of a kitchen before he bought the place, and the idea of buying a stove and all that went with it didn't appeal to him. Plus, his cooking wasn't fit for hogs. He could purchase a new bed and eat his meals out, but the cost would add up fast. It might be best to find a boardinghouse.

The scent of bacon tugged him down the street to the Silver Creek Café. As he entered, several diners turned in his direction. Some nodded, others went back to their conversations. He slipped his hat from his head and relaxed his shoulders, happy that his first foray into his new world wasn't going to be confrontational.

"Find yourself a place to sit, and I'll be there directly to take your order." The waitress pointed at a few empty tables and went back to filling coffee cups.

Finding the table close to the window appealing, he settled in to watch the comings and goings of people. He hoped he'd picked a community who would enjoy and purchase unusual gifts possessing novelty and individuality. But if he chose wrong, he would be back on a train to St. Louis to spend the rest of his days being the low man, bossed by his older brothers until he died.

A woman walked past, he noted her plain clothing and decided she wouldn't be a likely customer. A few more people strolled by, heads bent and in a hurry to get to work. What if they couldn't afford what he planned to sell. He would need to place an order for some of the less expensive trinkets. This wasn't St. Louis where he could count on selling to one class of people. He wanted everyone in this town to be able to purchase at least one or two special things from him.

He'd send a telegram this morning after his first shipment was delivered.

"What would you like this morning?" The waitress plunked a coffee cup on the table.

"Scrambled eggs, bacon, and toast to go with the coffee. I'm looking for the boardinghouse that the Mueller's run. Do you happen to know if they have a room open?"

The waitress nodded as she filled his cup. "Yes, I do. A gentleman left last week, and I don't think the room's been let yet. You might want to get yourself over there early today as the Muellers are known for their spread. Guess that means we won't

17

be seeing you here once you taste her granddaughter's muffins."

Miss Emmie Mueller, the girl who haunted his dreams, the one who made him choose this town to settle down in.

"Anything else?"

The waitress pulled him away from the blond-haired beauty in his mind. "Just the address of the boardinghouse."

Chapter Four

Emmie, at her grandmother's insistence, had the afternoon to go play with her friends. She giggled. Imagine, being told at eighteen to do that. The problem was, there weren't any schoolmates to play with. Except for Alice, all of Emmie's school friends had married or moved to other towns.

Her friend lived on the opposite side of town from the boardinghouse. Emmie delighted in the walk, because the late-July weather somehow found a bit of coolness to share. It was nice to be away from the boardinghouse. Since her parents left for Kansas, she and Granny worked harder to keep everything cleaned and polished. Kansas would be a relief for both of them.

And they wouldn't have to take care of Walter and Milton. She stopped walking and turned back to the store she'd passed. She might as well get a spool of thread as they were almost out. Before breakfast, Walter brought down two shirts that needed buttons sewn on. She nor Granny could figure out how he managed to break the threads that held them. Every week he brought down a shirt, buttons in his hand, and delivered it to Granny for repair. Emmie watched him for a week to no avail to see if he was twisting them off while he rocked on the porch.

While she was in the mercantile, she picked up a pack of needles. Since her parents left, she'd been purchasing small supplies to take to Kansas. With her mind on her ever-growing packing list, she stepped out of the store and bumped into a man hard enough to knock her off balance.

Hands steadied her.

"Miss Mueller. I didn't expect to be catching you again."

It was him. Mr. Knipp. Her body heated. It must be from the July weather and not him. She searched for words.

"My apologies. I suppose that wasn't the correct thing to say."

"No. No, it's fine. I'm surprised to see you, and yes, thankful once again that you saved me from a fall. You decided to open your store here?"

"I did. After meeting so many kind people at the wedding picnic, I couldn't think of a better place to reside. May I walk you somewhere?"

"I'm on my way to a friend's home. It isn't far. She just got married a few months ago. I'm running late." Goodness, she sounded like a fool. The man didn't need to know how long Alice had been married.

"Good day then. I hope to see you around. Sunday at church, perhaps?"

"Yes, I'll be there."

"Sunday then. My pleasure to catch you today." Mr. Knipp smiled and headed down the street. She let go of the breath she didn't know she'd held and quickened her steps. Alice would know what to do about these unexplained feelings she had when Mr. Knipp caught her.

"Miss Mueller, how is your mother?"

Emmie paused. She hadn't noticed Mrs. Diekman leaning against the picket fence.

"Have you had a letter from her? I miss seeing her at church."

"I'm sure she misses you, too. We had a letter last week. Father is scouting the land while they stay in town. Mother says it's quite delightful to be the boarder for a change, though she feels guilty about sitting around and not waiting on others."

"I imagine she does. I don't remember her sitting still often. Are you off to visit Alice?"

"Yes, it's been a while since we've spent time together." Because Alice was married and she wasn't?

"Make time for your friendships, dear. You never know when one of you will move."

Emmie bit her lip. She would be leaving soon. Would she ever see her friend again? Or Mr. Knipp?

◆　◆　◆

Landon helped carry heavy, wooden crates from the wagon into the storefront. He intended to sort them as the boxes came in, placing each in the area designated for the type of merchandise inside. Except the driver arrived without any help. Landon slipped off his coat and rolled up his sleeves. It wasn't the first time he'd unloaded a wagon, and owning a store meant it wouldn't be the last time either.

"That's all of them." The driver set down the small trunk he carried and rubbed his back. "What do you have in these crates anyway?"

"Unusual items that can't be found in this town." Landon surveyed the store. The wooden display shelves across both walls would hold a lot. Then there were the cases with glass shelves. Did he order enough to fill the empty places?

"What kind of items?"

"Imported parasols and silks from China, along with other quality pieces."

"Sounds pricy. Don't know how well that sort of thing will sell around here. Mostly farm folks live here, and they aren't likely to buy fancy pieces of material."

"I'll place an order for some less expensive things." He'd do it right away because once word got out that his wares were costly no one would come in to look. He scratched his head. He could make certain pieces look more expensive by displaying one or two things on a shelf. He'd suggested that to his father once, and his brothers laughed. "Why not display everything?" became the taunt of that summer. That's when he'd decided to be the buyer, leaving home, traveling to Europe for the best things. And to get away from her.

◆ ◆ ◆

Breathing hard, Emmie banged on Alice's door.

"What's wrong?" Alice pulled her friend inside.

"He picked our town."

"Who? I'm lost."

"Mr. Knipp. The man who kept me from falling down the church stairs at George's wedding. And today, today I ran into him coming out of the mercantile."

"That's nice that you saw him again."

"No, not saw. Crashed into him. I lost my balance, and once again he saved me from disaster."

"Why does this matter to you?" Alice guided her into the parlor and sat on the sofa. "Sit and tell me what the problem is."

"He's handsome, and when he had his hands on my waist. . ." Oh glory, her face was on fire.

Alice giggled. "You like him. That's wonderful!"

"But I'm moving."

Alice poured tea into a cup and handed it to Emmie. "Yes, you've said that for months now."

Emmie knew where Alice would go next. She took a sip of tea from Alice's delicate wedding china cup. She needed to change the subject fast. "This is beautiful. Are you happy with this pattern?"

Alice traced the rim of her cup. "I think so. It was hard to pick one I wanted to live with the rest of my life. Still sometimes, I think about my other choices. I'll admit to that. Mother says eventually, I'll forget about them."

"I think you did well both in china and husband picking." A twinge of jealousy pricked her mind, but she banished it. After all, what good would a set of pretty china thin enough to see through be in Kansas? It would break before they arrived.

"When are you leaving to meet up with your family?"

"Soon, I hope. Once I find matches for Mr. Hoffman and Mr. Taylor, Granny and I can pack the house and leave."

"Are you traveling alone?" Alice scrunched her face. "I wouldn't care for that at all. It's so much nicer to travel with a man."

"I'm capable, as is Granny, of getting on and off of a train. Father will meet us with a wagon. Granny says not to anticipate problems."

Alice shook her head. "Does she ever worry?"

"I've not seen any sign of it, except for getting the meals on the table on time. If she has concerns about other things, she keeps it between her and God."

"I wish I could be more like that. I can't stop worrying about everything." She stared into her cup.

"Is something wrong?"

"No. It's that I want a family." Her face reddened. "I shouldn't talk of these things with you."

"So society would dictate. But I'm your friend. Tell me."

Alice set her cup in the saucer. "We've been married for three months, and I should be expecting by now."

"Have you talked with your mother?" Emmie had no idea how long it took for such things to occur.

"Yes, she said it takes a while for some, and for others it doesn't. I'm not supposed to fret about it but enjoy my time without children because they will come soon enough, and I'll never have a moment's peace."

Emmie gasped. "She said that?" A giggle bubbled up and broke through, followed by more. "I'm sorry."

Alice joined her. They laughed until their eyes teared and tea sloshed over Alice's cup.

"I'm going to miss you so much. You will write to me, won't you?" Emmie set her cup and saucer on the table.

"Of course, but you must answer. I want to know everything about your new life. Do you suppose we'll see each other again?"

"I'll see you this Sunday at church."

"I meant after you leave." Alice's lip trembled. "Why don't you marry and live here? Our children would be friends, and we would never complain about not having a moment's peace."

"I've told you why. It's hard to leave, but I want to be with my family. Besides, I don't even have a beau."

"It's because you're too picky."

"I'm not. God hasn't put the right person in front of me, that's all." For a brief moment, the concern in Mr. Knipp's eyes tugged at her heart. He'd been in her path twice now. She pushed it away. "The boys we went to school with are still boys in my mind. I don't want to find a toad on my table or my chair covered with honey."

"The honey on the chair never happened. You do understand they are now men, and most aren't mean. They regret calling you Monkey Arms. Some even apologized to you, including my husband."

"I know, but I can't forget how they made me feel. No, I think I'm supposed to marry someone I don't have a history with." *Right, God? That's what you've put on my heart isn't it? That's the reason the rest of my family moved so far away. My husband is waiting in Kansas, right?*

Chapter Five

Landon walked the few blocks to the boardinghouse the waitress recommended. A wide wraparound porch skirted the redbrick building. Its chairs and rockers beckoned him to sit and relax. White shutters hugged the windows, secure enough to withstand a tornado. He knocked on the door and stepped back when it opened.

"It's you, Mr. Knipp. The young man who helped my granddaughter set up for the wedding. How delightful to see you again. Please, come in." Mrs. Mueller stepped aside and wiped her hands on her apron.

He slid his hat from his head. "I've come to see if you have a vacant room to let."

"It just so happens we do. My Emmie wants to empty this place out, but not me. I like having boarders. How long will you be staying?"

"Once I get the store open, and it's running well, I intend to buy a house. So, I'm not sure. A month? Maybe two? Depending on the cost."

Mrs. Mueller gave him a price. It was cheaper than buying a bed and the cost of meals. "I'll take it."

"You look tired. Haven't you been sleeping well?"

She reminded him of his grandmother. Caring for others and seeing to their needs was her way of life. "I spent last night above the store on an old creaky bed. I couldn't find a moment of silence to slide into sleep." He rubbed the back of his neck where the muscles from moving boxes were making themselves known.

"That settles it, then. You'll get your things and be back here by dinnertime. Tonight, you'll rest and wake ready to tackle setting up your store. Before you go, let me get you a few of Emmie's cookies to take with you. She's quite a good baker."

While he waited, his curiosity took over. He inspected the part of the home he could see. Nothing exotic or imported in the parlor.

"Here you are, Mr. Knipp. You snack on these. They should perk you up. Be back here by five. That's when we serve dinner. You can meet the other boarders then."

The scent of vanilla and butter from the cookies smelled of home. The only thing that would make them better was if Emmie was here herself.

◆　◆　◆

Emmie let the screen door bang behind her. She unpinned her hat and hung it on a peg, then grabbed the apron next to it. "I'm so sorry for being late, Granny." She took a paring knife from the drawer and picked up an empty bowl.

"Slow down. You'll cut yourself." She carried a bowl of washed potatoes to the table. "I've scrubbed them clean for you."

"Thank you. You shouldn't have had to do that." She sat in a chair and spread the apron over her lap.

"I'll sit and watch you peel those while you tell me all about your visit." Granny poured two glasses of tea and set them on the table.

Emmie took a drink. "That tastes good. It's so hot today, and I walked fast." Her grandmother gave her the familiar look that often put Emmie in her place when she was small. "I didn't run, but I did work up a thirst. Thank you for the tea."

"I'm glad to know on Sunday I won't hear about you running like a boy to get home."

"I'd not embarrass you. Alice is doing well. She likes having her own home." Emmie set to work on the potato skin. A thin brown ribbon spiraled to her lap. "We promised to write when I go to Kansas."

"I don't imagine you'll need to put pen to paper soon. I took on another boarder this afternoon. The poor man wore his tiredness in his face."

"A new boarder?" Emmie could lay on the table and cry. Now she had three wives to find. *Why God? Why are you keeping me from my family?*

"Why would you take in a new boarder? Don't you want to be with everyone in Kansas? Don't you miss them the way I do?" She gathered the peelings into the center of her apron and dumped them in the bucket by the door.

"I do, but my life is here. St. Mary's is where your grandfather is buried and my parents. I'm not comfortable walking away from my past into an unknown future. That's for young people, not me." Granny rose and touched Emmie on the shoulder. "Look at me, please."

Emmie did as requested. When had her grandmother aged? Her hair held more white strands than brown, and her forehead had more furrows than Emmie remembered.

"I know how much you want to be with your mother and father. If you want to go, I'll write them tonight and get you a train ticket. I'd miss you, but keeping you here for my sake is wrong. You might be missing out on meeting your husband if you don't go."

"No. I'll not go. I promised to stay until you sell the house. When that happens, please say you'll come with me. Even if for a short visit. You could return if you don't like Kansas."

"I'll consider it, but this town has always been my home. I can't bear to leave it behind."

"I understand, but the family won't be complete until we're all together." She sat back in her chair and picked up the paring knife and a potato.

"Honey, we aren't now. Your grandfather isn't here, and the brothers you lost are in heaven. When we all get through those gates and see our Father's face, we will be together again, but not until that happens."

"I hope it's not for a long time. I want us to be a family here forever." She missed her mother and father so much she could weep. If only she hadn't promised her parents that she would help Granny with the boardinghouse until she sold it. "Let's not talk about this anymore. It makes me sad." She popped a thin potato slice into her mouth, enjoying the crunch but wishing she'd sprinkled it with salt first.

"Agreed. Now, remember that handsome young man that helped you at the wedding?"

Emmie's heart skipped.

"Well, seems Mr. Knipp needs a place to rest his head. He is our newest boarder. I let him the room for the same amount as Milton and Walter. He's trying to get his feet under him and looks like he hasn't slept in a week."

"Why would you do that? You don't charge those two hardly enough to cover their food. We agreed we wouldn't take any more boarders."

"I have my reasons, dear. This is still my boardinghouse, and besides, maybe God is nudging me to help that man. Or maybe He wants you to be in close proximity and generate some fondness for Landon."

Emmie touched her hair and found a loose strand. She tucked it behind her ear.

Granny laughed. "You'll have time to freshen up before he gets here for dinner."

"It doesn't matter. I'm not looking for a husband in this town, and I believe he intends to stay here a long time since he is opening a store." She rose and carried the bowl of peeled potatoes to the stove. "I'm going to pray for all of the boarders to get married and for you to change your mind about Kansas." She hadn't counted on Mr. Knipp showing up. He could take care of finding his own wife.

She could only hope she was long gone when he did.

Chapter Six

Landon propped the broom handle against the wall. The air around him swirled and sparkled as sunlight hit the dust. He was grateful he remembered to tie a cloth around his head, cowboy style, covering his nose and mouth. Nothing could be done for his glasses. He slid them off and wiped them clean with a cloth he carried in his pocket, careful not to pull on the gold rims.

He surveyed his work. The broom bristles left streaks, but he didn't intend for the first round to be perfect. This building had been vacant for quite a while. It would take more turns around the floor with the broom, followed by a good mopping, to rid the place of the dust still circulating in the air. For now, this amount of cleaning would do.

He chose the nearest crate to unpack. He pried at the lid with a crowbar. It didn't budge. He took a deep breath and pushed. The nails gave way with a screech. As he pulled the lid away, the packing straw sprang to life and settled with a soft swish on the floor. He dug through, retrieving small bisque porcelain figurines from Germany. These would go into the case closest to the door. They would bring customers farther inside. Who could resist a girl holding a kitten?

He pushed the crate nearer to the case and removed the contents, placing the pretties, as his mother called them, on top. He arranged them by size, the smallest items on the top shelf. Or, they would be as soon as he found the crate with the velvet he needed to line the shelves. Black fabric made the figurines look impressive, but not if covered in dust.

He pulled out his watch to check the time. He had precious little of it to spare. Snapping the cover of the watch closed, he trotted to the stairs where he'd left his packed valise. No time to brush the dust from his hair, or he would be late for dinner at the boardinghouse. He wanted to make a nice impression on the younger Miss Mueller. After all, he'd picked this town because of her.

He flew out the door, tripped on the stoop, and landed face-first in the street.

Chapter Seven

If Emmie came to dinner dirty, then so be it. She wouldn't do more for Mr. Knipp than she did for the other men in the house, despite how handsome she found him back in July. Instead, pulling weeds from the garden would be a better use of her time. She yanked one. The root broke free, and she fell backward. She glanced around to see if anyone noticed. Walter and Milton were nowhere around. She relaxed her shoulders. This was not a tale she wanted retold over dinner tonight.

Back on her knees, she picked a few ripe tomatoes. She wiped the sweat from her brow, and then collected some salad leaves for dinner. Did her parents have a garden? Probably not, as they would have arrived too late to put it in. Where were they getting their food? Did they have kindly neighbors who were sharing? She'd have to ask Granny if they could bring along the peaches they'd soon can. They would be a special treat this winter.

Her grandmother's desire to stay in Trenton troubled Emmie's heart. Should she leave her or stay? Her father insisted that she stay until Granny was ready. But Granny would never leave Trenton willingly. "God, why can't our family be together? And what about Walter and Milton, Lord? Can you show me which women in town would like to be married to them? They are old as Moses, but they would make good companions for someone."

"Emmie!"

She jumped at her grandmother's shout. Had she been praying aloud again? And when did Walter and Milton come out in the yard? Had they overheard her? They sent nasty looks her way. She ducked her head and studied the ground.

"Coming, Granny." She stood and grabbed the handle of the garden basket filled with today's offerings. Agnes Gray recently lost her husband, she would do for one of them, but that still left her one.

Chapter Eight

Are you okay, sir?"

Fancy-stitched boots stood mere inches from his face. "I'm okay." Landon pushed off the dirty sidewalk. "Bruised pride is all."

"Are you sure? You took quite a tumble from what I saw." The man waited for an answer.

"I'm thankful it wasn't a customer that fell. I'll need to get that threshold fixed right away." He brushed off his pants and the front of his coat, pausing at the pocket. His spectacles. Had they survived the impact?

He retrieved them. And shook his head. "That's not good." The frames were bent and one lens cracked. "Do you know where I can get these repaired? And a good carpenter as well?"

"Sure do. Mr. Carr at the pharmacy can help you with those spectacles, and ask for Terrance at the lumberyard. He'll get someone over here to fix your doorway tomorrow morning."

Landon offered a handshake. "I'm much obliged. I'm Landon Knipp."

"Clyde Myeberger. Glad to meet you. I'm down the street at the livery. If you need a horse, stop by."

"I will, and hope you return the favor when I open the store."

"What kind of wares are you offering here?"

"Knipp Emporium will be stocked with unusual and exotic items from around the world. Perfect for gift giving and decorating your home."

"My wife will be excited when she hears that. She misses the big stores in Saint Louis. We might have to trade you horse rentals for what she'll add to her account." Clyde slapped his leg and laughed. "Won't be the first store I've had to do that with. Where were you off to in such a hurry?"

"The boardinghouse. I'm staying there for a while. I'd better get there, or I'll miss dinner."

"You don't want that. Those women are known for their meals. I am surprised they took you on as a boarder. The young one has been telling everyone they're leaving for Kansas soon."

"Then I'm grateful for the chance." How could he keep Miss Emmie Mueller from leaving before he got her to fall in love with him?

◆　◆　◆

"Emmie, answer the door. That's got to be our new boarder." Granny drew her lips in a thin line. "And be nice."

"I will." Emmie untied her apron and laid it across the back of the kitchen chair. When she approached the screen door, she stifled a chuckle. Mr. Knipp looked nothing like her memory. Gone was the well-dressed gentleman. The man in his place wore dust in his hair and on his clothing.

"Difficult trip from town, Mr. Knipp?" She opened the door for him.

"Ah, it's you, and this time I didn't have to catch you." He rotated his hat in his hands.

Would he ever forget her clumsiness? Had he thought about her, too? The words in her mouth dried like glue, keeping her from speaking.

"Mr. Knipp, come in." Granny came up behind Emmie. "After today, you must think of this as your home. There'll be no need to knock."

"Move aside, Emmie. Let him pass through. Why don't you get the bread out of the oven, and I'll show him upstairs?" She nudged Emmie to the side. "This way, Mr. Knipp. You'll be staying in room seven at the top of the stairs on the left."

Mr. Knipp grabbed his valise. "Yes, ma'am."

Emmie blinked twice. That man with his dark brown eyes struck something deep inside of her. She didn't have a name for the warmth running through her. She felt her forehead. Maybe she'd spent too much time in the garden during the hottest part of the day. Yes, that must be the reason. A cup of water was all she needed. She scurried into the kitchen well aware of his pleasant scent.

◆　◆　◆

Landon surveyed the room he'd be living in for a while. He dropped his valise by the armoire, intending to unpack later. He eyed the bed with delight. And sat on it. Soft and not a single creak or groan. Tonight, he would sleep well. The washstand had a pitcher of water, and the mirror alerted him that he needed to use that water. The dust from the shop must have resettled all over him. He glanced at his knees. They, too, were dirty from his fall. He brushed away the dirt.

At a knock on the door frame, Landon turned.

"Thought I'd introduce myself before dinner. Walter Hoffman. The other boarder is Milton Taylor."

He stood. "Landon Knipp."

"Planning on staying long?"

"At least six months, maybe a year. I'm opening Knipp Emporium and decided it would be easier if I didn't have to cook and clean on top of that."

Walter touched his finger to pursed lips and took one step back, looked both ways and reentered the room.

How odd. Why was the man telling him to be quiet?

"Good, Miss Emmie is downstairs. You'll have to watch out for her."

"Why?" Had he made a mistake moving here? Was the woman out of her mind? Dangerous?

"Milton and me figured out what she's doing. She's trying to find wives for all of us."

"Why would she do that?"

"Once we move out, she and her grandmother can go to Kansas to be with the rest of the family. I don't think her grandmother wants to go."

Landon scratched his head. "I don't understand why you must marry for that to happen."

"Because Mrs. Mueller won't sell the house unless we have homes and someone to take care of us." Walter's face reddened. "She likes us. We like her. Why would we want to marry and leave her cooking? We have it good here. Getting hitched would be a lot of hard work. Wives need tending to, and they ask too much. Milton and I have always been bachelors, never envious of our friends who married."

Walter said something about checkers on the porch, but the words circulating in Landon's mind were about Emmie moving to Kansas. Foolish. That's what he'd been. He'd rushed to this town without asking God if Emmie was the one for him. After all, what did he even know about her except she was pretty?

Chapter Nine

In the kitchen, Emmie fanned her face. Mr. Knipp must think her a fool. She'd talked to him twice before, but now, faced with him on her doorstep, all of her vocabulary dissolved like sugar in the rain. It was the dimple in his cheek. It had to be. Most of the men she knew had beards, but not Mr. Knipp. When he smiled at her, the evening sun highlighted that small indent making him look most charming. She was getting heated again. Was she sick? She splashed a bit of cool water onto her face.

"Emmie, did you check the bread? I won't be serving burned food to anyone." Granny pushed past her and opened the oven. The heat blasted through the kitchen.

The oven, of course. That's why she was so warm. "Let me get that for you, while you refill the pitcher with tea."

"Don't be telling me how to run this kitchen, young'un. You only get to boss others when you have your own place."

"Granny! I wasn't!"

"Never mind. I'd rather do the tea than that hot oven anyway."

Emmie stared at her grandmother as she walked away. Was that the problem with moving? Did Granny worry about losing her place in the kitchen since they would all be in the same house?

Granny turned. "Get that bread on a plate and bring it in. The men are waiting."

"Yes, ma'am." Emmie filled the plate and then followed her grandmother into the dining room. She stopped so fast the bread came close to flying off onto the floor. No one was in the right spot.

Walter and Milton had moved from where they'd been sitting for five years. Walter slid out of his chair and took the tea pitcher from her grandmother and set it on the table.

"Mrs. Mueller, allow me." Walter yanked out an empty chair, and Granny slipped into it.

"Thank you."

Emmie stared at the arrangement. There was only one space left. Next to Landon. She took a step.

He hopped up and grabbed the bread plate from her and repeated the actions of Walter.

Walter and Milton sported wide grins. They were up to something.

◆　◆　◆

The next morning, Landon smiled all the way to work. Miss Emmie Mueller had no idea the older gentlemen had figured out her plan, and it seemed they'd decided to match her with him. If they succeeded, the men would be able to stay unwed and waited upon by Emmie's grandmother.

A dog barked from behind a picket fence and startled him. Glad for the jolt of reality, he pushed Emmie from his mind and returned to his massive list of things to achieve at the emporium. Several townspeople nodded at him as he passed and his spirit lightened. Today, he would visit the owner of the mercantile and assure him that their businesses would not compete for customers.

As he approached, he saw a youngster sitting on the stoop of his store. When he drew close the boy jumped to his feet.

"Sir, do you have any work for me?"

The boy wore clean clothes and combed hair. Not small in stature. Muscular. "I might." Landon inserted the key into the lock and turned. It didn't budge.

"You have to rattle it inside the lock to make it work. Most of the stores on this street have the same problem."

Landon twisted the key back and forth, and the tumbler clicked. "Thank you for that tip. You're already proving your value. What's your name?"

"Duck."

"Duck?"

"That's what they call me. My real name is Cyrus."

Landon pushed the door open and motioned the boy to follow him. "How did you get that nickname?"

"My ma says I liked to say the word over and over when I was little, so they started calling me that because I would say it back and laugh."

"Interesting. Do you like being called that?" Landon grimaced at the dust-covered floor.

"I don't mind, but I'd like to be Cyrus when I get older. Probably won't happen as long as I live here. That's why I have to earn money so I can move away. I have five older brothers. They work for my dad. I could, too, but they won't let me do any of the fun stuff. I always have to clean the stalls, and they never call me Cyrus."

Landon understood Cyrus's place in life. "I think I'll call you by your given name. Then maybe others will follow. I, too, have older brothers, and it can be difficult to break their idea of who you are. They tend to think of you as the little brother forever. Do you mind if I call you Cyrus?"

"No, sir." He stood straighter. "Does that mean I get to work here?"

"You're the first to ask. When can you start?"

"Right now."

"Then let's open a few of these boxes and see what's inside."

◆　◆　◆

Emmie carried a bucket with a scrub brush, rags, and Kirk's Castile soap. "Granny, I don't see why we need to help Mr. Knipp. He didn't ask us to." The wind whipped at her skirt hem.

"He's living with us, and he has no family nearby. It's the right thing to do." Granny tugged the basket she carried into the crook of her elbow.

They were almost to the store. It had been vacant for quite some time, and she imagined there would be plenty of dust and dead bugs to remove. "What if he doesn't want our help?"

"Then we will leave the cleaning tools if he needs them, along with these blue-berry muffins."

"Maybe we'll get a peek at some of the specialty items he's planning to sell. Maybe we can buy a few things to take with us to Kansas."

"Your mother won't need any frippery on the prairie. You best save your egg money for winter boots, and a thicker coat." Granny took a ragged breath. "The wind is stirring up something. As sticky as the air is, maybe a storm."

Emmie's shoulders sagged. Granny was right. Pretty things were not needed out West. It might be better if she bought a shovel. Still, she wouldn't give up on the idea of something for her mother. Something that would survive the train trip, small enough that it wouldn't take precious space in her trunk, and something special to bring a smile to her mother's face. Her heart ached. She wanted to be with her family. She missed them so. Why did God continue to make it difficult to leave? She would have to pray harder.

Chapter Ten

Crate lids rested on the floor. The door opened. Straw swirled and crept across the wood planks. "Sorry, we aren't open yet," Landon yelled.

"We aren't here to shop, Mr. Knipp. We came to help."

The sunlight behind Miss Emmie cast a golden glow around her. Stunned by the sight, Landon was rooted to the floor, searching for air.

Cyrus returned from the back room. "Mr. Knipp, I—"

"Duck, I didn't know you were working for Mr. Knipp." Granny held out her basket. "I brought muffins. Come get one."

Cyrus took a giant step then stopped and looked at Landon for permission.

"Go ahead. We've decided to call him Cyrus from now on since that's his given name."

"That's a splendid idea. I'll try to remember to call you that." Emmie waded through the straw. "You have quite a mess here."

"We have, but it's better than it was." Landon shoved two empty crates to the center of the store. "It's not as nice as the boardinghouse, but please, have a seat."

"Nonsense." Granny put her basket on one of the crates. "Grab yourself a muffin, and Emmie and I will get to liberating this room of all that straw."

"You don't need to. That's my job." Cyrus scrunched his eyebrows.

"Humph. Duck, are you afraid if this gets done you won't have a job tomorrow?" Granny stared at him hard enough to make a grown man yell, "Uncle!"

"Yes, ma'am."

"Mr. Knipp, are you going to have more work for the boy, or is this it?"

Landon squirmed. He hadn't thought that far ahead. Once the store was clean and set up would he need Cyrus? There were inventory sheets to be filled out, and he could use help for that. "Cyrus, I'll keep you on. I broke my glasses, and until they are repaired, I won't be able to do any of the paperwork."

Silence filled the room.

"Sir. I can't read or write." Cyrus stared at the floor.

"That's because you ducked out of school so much. Maybe that's why they call you Duck." Granny shook her head. "Regrets are hard to leave behind. Mr. Knipp, Emmie will help you with the books until you can see again."

"Granny!" Her face pinked.

"I'd be obliged, Miss Mueller, if you would help me." They would be together every day for at least a week. His heart quickened. Maybe he'd be able to find a way to make her stay in Trenton. He squeezed Cyrus's shoulder. "No excuses, Cyrus. If you want to be a man in this world, you need to learn to read and write. If you want, I can teach you."

"That's a nice offer," Emmie said. "Cyrus, you need to take this opportunity to learn. Mr. Knipp, I can see you're a kind soul." Her face pinked.

"Please understand, you won't be working for free. You'll be earning a wage."

Her eyes widened. "I'll come help you when Granny doesn't need me."

"I won't need you tomorrow." Mrs. Mueller nodded. "Yep, you two can walk here together in the morning. Now, I insist everyone grab a muffin. We've got some cleaning to do, and we might as well have happy stomachs while we do it."

Landon couldn't believe how fast the pieces of his life were falling together. Could this be God's plan despite his lack of prayer on the matter?

◆ ◆ ◆

A week later, Emmie's neck and shoulders ached. She had no idea how much work it took to set up a store. Landon's spectacles hadn't arrived yet, so she spent hours printing merchandise names, the quantity, and the costs to buy and to sell. She picked up a figurine. Her mother would love this one of a woman surrounded by children. It was too heavy to take to Kansas. With a sigh, she held it high and slid it onto the display shelf.

Landon came up behind her, breathing hard. "I thought you were going to drop it, but I see you have very long arms."

Emmie nodded. Face burning and tears stinging, she couldn't speak. She whirled away from him and went back to the ledgers.

"Did you hurt yourself?"

"No, but I think you need to help Cyrus." His words scraped an old scar raw. She peeked between her eyelashes as he went to the end of the counter where Cyrus practiced writing his letters on the slate Landon provided. Watching Landon work with the boy filled her heart with feelings she didn't want. She couldn't get attached to him, no matter how much she thought he'd make a wonderful husband. Even if she was staying in Trenton, which she wasn't, he'd be just like all the other boys, now men, in this town. No one wanted Monkey Arms for a wife.

In fact, she needed to get back to her purpose. Finding wives for Milton and Walter. Working with Landon slowed down her progress. She'd eliminated the Geis sisters once she'd discovered they didn't eat pork after growing up on a pig farm. That would never work, not the way those two liked their bacon.

"Say the letter name as you write it, Cyrus. You know I can't see the board well, so Miss Emmie will check it later."

"I know my ABCs."

"Yes, but you can't write them, and that means you can't recognize them in words. Your choice. Do you want to be Cyrus or Duck?"

Emmie straightened at Landon's tough words. "Landon, do you think—"

"Miss Emmie, would you be so kind as to run to the pharmacy and see if my spectacles have arrived. Not being able to do half of my job is making me cranky."

She closed the ledger and set the pencil next to it. "Yes, of course, but that's no excuse for being mean to Cyrus."

"It's okay, Miss Emmie. I want to learn. Mr. Knipp is right. I mean, correct. I have to do the baby work if I want to be a learned man, like him."

Emmie smiled at the word change. Cyrus didn't realize he also received multiple vocabulary lessons when he worked with Landon. She slid her hat on her head and secured it with pins. "I'll be back shortly. Is there anything else I should get while I'm out?"

"Keep working, Cyrus." He walked over to Emmie and whispered in her ear. "Bring back some licorice whips, please. This boy deserves a reward."

The words tickled her ear. She shivered. Mercy, she needed to stop working here soon, or she'd be wanting to stay in Trenton. She took a step away. "Should I put everything on your account?"

"Yes, and take your time. I know how hard it is to write numbers all morning. Maybe this afternoon, we'll have a customer or two wander in."

"Don't fret. Tomorrow, everyone will be in town. Saturday is when people come from the small towns around us. You'll sell so much that an order will need to be placed on Monday. I'm sure of it." She picked up her reticule.

"I hope they do purchase, but most will be lookers."

"And there will be those that remember they want to return here when they have extra money. I'll pick up the lunch Granny promised while I'm out. Cyrus, there will be food for you, too, so don't go running off."

Emmie prayed her prediction of sales would be so as she left the store. Landon's store had beautiful things, but costly. Rugs from India, china from England, and parasols from France weren't everyday items. She'd love a lace parasol but couldn't see a use for it on a homestead in Kansas.

◆ ◆ ◆

Landon checked his pocket watch. Emmie should be back by now. He peered out the door. No sign of her coming up the sidewalk. Quite unlike her. He stepped inside. He studied the merchandise displays and didn't see anything to change. He chose the right building. With the big display windows on the corner, his wares couldn't be ignored.

But why weren't the customers coming? His skin itched. He could almost feel the red welts popping up on his back. *Please, God, not hives. I'm stepping back. You are in control.*

Cyrus sat at a small table writing the alphabet. "I wish Miss Mueller would come. I'm hungry."

"Why don't you run down to the boardinghouse and help her carry back the basket. I'm sure she has a reason for being gone so long."

"Maybe she's waiting for a pie to cool." Cyrus licked his lips. "I hope it's a peach crumble. Those are the best." He pushed his slate and chalk to the corner of the table. "I'll be back soon."

Landon watched as Cyrus left, shirttail flying through the door after him.

"Sorry, ma'am."

Cyrus bumped into someone. Maybe a customer? Landon brushed the front of his coat and prepared to greet whoever entered.

A cloud moved, and the sunlight hit the door, blinding him as a woman entered. He squinted and took a step forward. "Welcome to Knipp Emporium."

"Landon?"

It was a voice he never expected to hear again, one that had smashed his dreams and destroyed a friendship. One he'd vowed to never again hear.

No. It couldn't be her.

Chapter Eleven

"Not now, Rooster." Emmie scooted away from the rooster attempting to snuggle with the hem of her skirt. She had Landon's spectacles in one hand and a letter from her mother in the other. Rooster would have to wait. "I'll bring you some corn when I leave." She bolted through the screen door, letting it bang behind her. Granny and Walter sat at the table slicing peaches.

Walter pushed back the chair and popped up.

"Emmie, you know better than that. I've taught you not to let the door slam." Granny's face held a tinge of pink.

What did that mean?

"I think I'll see if Milton feels like a game of checkers." Walter sped past Emmie.

"I'm sorry. I stopped at the post office, and there is a letter from Momma. I rushed home so we could read it together." She set her reticule and Landon's glasses on the table.

"Looks like Landon's eyesight is not as important to you."

"No, not now. He's gone two weeks without them and a few more minutes won't matter. We have a letter from the family." She handed the envelope to her grandmother. "Hurry, open it and see what it says."

"Not so fast, missy. Things like this must be savored. How about you pour us a glass of tea? Then, we'll go sit on the porch, and see what's happening in the great state of Kansas. Though, it might be even more exciting to make you run back to town and give Landon his spectacles first." Granny set her knife next to the bowl.

"No, please don't. He'll be all right. Cyrus is there, and not one soul has come into the store today." She folded her hands together in a prayer position. "Please, don't make me wait."

"All right. Get the tea."

Emmie, holding the tall glasses, followed Granny through the front door and set them on the small wicker table between two rockers. Her heart raced. Would her mother have good news?

Granny settled in her chair. "Stop fidgeting and sit down."

She doubted that would stop her toes from tapping, but she did as ordered.

Granny ripped the end of the envelope with care and pulled out the paper. She unfolded it, then smoothed it against her apron and read aloud.

> *Dear Mama and Emmie,*
>
> *We all miss you! Living in the city at first was entertaining, but the fun ran out. Knowing I wouldn't be living here, I haven't made close friends. I miss those I have in Trenton more than I thought. Postage money for letters must be used to purchase other items. Please tell Mrs. Diekman I haven't forgotten about her and will write.*
>
> *Robert has been working hard to prepare a place for us, and we'll be moved in by the time this letter reaches you. We're hoping our letters cross in the mail, and you have sold the boardinghouse by now. It would be best if you could be here before September to enjoy some of the fall season before winter arrives.*
>
> *Emmie, there is little room to store clothing, so please give away some of yours. Anything you wear for social occasions won't be needed here. Mama, there is no need to bring all your aprons. Two would be best.*
>
> *Father says he thinks he has found a good man for Emmie to marry but will respect her decision after they meet. He has the adjoining farm. He is a widower and has six children that need a mother. It would be best, Emmie, if you found you could look upon him with favor as we have so little room, and it is time you were married. You'd make a good mother.*

◆　◆　◆

Six children. The words repeated themselves as Emmie walked back to the store. Was that the life she wanted? It certainly wasn't the one she'd been working so hard to achieve. In her dream, the family would be together, planting crops and building their house. Marriage, yes, but not right away. Mother's letter made it sound like the minute she put foot on Kansas soil, she'd be whisked off to the church and back home in time to make dinner for six children and a husband. Did he have a home big enough to hold her clothing if she brought it?

"Miss Mueller."

Emmie stopped mere inches in front of Alma Pickens.

"Is everything all right?" Alma arched her eyebrow.

"Yes, I'm sorry I almost knocked you down. We had a letter from Mother. . ."

Alma had married a man with children and, as far as Emmie knew, she loved being their mother. Maybe this was God's way of telling her not to worry.

"Is everything okay with them? Roy and I were surprised to hear they'd left to start over in Kansas."

"Yes, they're fine. Mother misses her friends, of course. There is no stopping my father when he decides to do something. This time, he said Trenton had grown too big. He wanted to walk miles before seeing anyone."

"How sad for your mother, she being sociable and all."

Mother must be lonely. She'd always enjoyed her friendships and knowing almost everyone in town. So did Emmie. Moving to Kansas appealed to her far less today than ever. "Have you been to the Knipp Emporium yet?"

"No, I heard it has unusual items for sale."

"Our newest boarder owns the store. You would like it. Why—"

"Miss Mueller!"

Cyrus ran up to them. "There you are. Do you have pie? Is that why you're late with our lunch?"

Emmie laughed. "No, no pie today, Cyrus, but I'll bring some tomorrow. Why don't you take the basket and head to the store?

"Cyrus?" Anna looked closer. "Isn't your name Duck?"

"No, ma'am. And now Mr. Knipp says people need to start calling me by my real name. And that's Cyrus." He took the basket. "I need to get back. A customer came in when I came out the door. I hope it's not to complain because I almost knocked her over."

"Go, then. Hurry up, and tell Mr. Knipp I'll be along in a little while." He ran off. The milk in the jars might turn to butter the way the basket bobbed in his hand.

"Mr. Knipp must be a good influence on the boy. I'm glad he's using his name. It always felt odd calling him Duck."

"Mr. Knipp is teaching him to read as well. Why don't you walk to the store with me? I have some questions, if you don't mind answering."

"I'm on my way to my father's, but I'll pop in soon when Roy is with me. What do you have on your mind?"

"What's it like to take care of children when you've never had any? My father has a husband picked out for me. He is a widower with six kids. I don't even know his name. Mother didn't think to include it." Emmie couldn't swallow. A new home in a new state and now, marriage. "I don't know what to do."

◆　◆　◆

"Julia?" Landon forced her name past his lips. "What are you doing here? Did Harry send you?"

"I had to get away for a while. I saw your mother at church, and she told me about this town, that you liked it." She did a slow turn. "It's not as big as your father's store, but I like it. Simple surroundings for extravagant things."

"But, why come here?" His mind processed thoughts like boots wading through the mud. The woman he once loved now stood in his store wearing black. Black. Gone were the colorful satins she'd preferred. "Julia? Harry?"

"He passed a month ago. I thought your mother would have let you know."

Her words punched his lungs. His breath escaped. Harry, his best friend until he'd stolen Julia from him, now gone. "What—what happened?"

"Runaway carriage. Please, I don't want to talk about it. I'm lost without him. I'm sorry, I know that hurts you, but he was my everything." She sniffed.

Landon pulled a handkerchief from his pocket. "Here."

She took it and wiped tears from her eyes. "I know you're angry, and you don't want to see me. I had to go somewhere. I knew if I came here, I could be assured to know one person that I could trust if I needed help. I knew you would look after me."

"Julia—"

"Only as a good friend, Landon. My heart still wants Harry."

Her eyes filled with tears and snared him. He would take care of her. He wished he hadn't been so angry with Harry. He thought there would be time once he had a wife of his own for him and Harry to be friends again.

"Where are you staying?"

"I checked in at White Hotel yesterday, but it's lonely eating by myself, strangers giving me sideways glances and wondering where I came from. And saying how sad it is that I'm a widow."

Feelings he thought dead now sparked. Should he fan them? They had a history together. She'd always hated that he traveled, but maybe now that he was staying in one place? But what about Emmie? Her sunny smile tugged at his heart.

Chapter Twelve

Emmie rolled Alma's advice around in her thoughts. Alma insisted on Roy courting her before they married, despite the attempt of her father to have them marry within days of meeting each other. Could she do the same? Months ago she might have thought it possible, but then Landon arrived.

Confused by her feelings, Emmie stepped inside the mercantile to purchase the licorice whips he'd requested. In her excitement about the letter, she'd forgotten to buy them. Landon's kindness to Cyrus touched her heart.

What would Kansas be like? Would she be able to shop as she did here? She would miss this store and the family who ran it. She gazed at the shelves. How long would she be able to remember the coolness of this store after she left. It didn't seem important compared to being with her family, but as the weeks crept by, she noticed the small things she'd taken for granted forever. Her friends, of course, but then there were the townspeople, like Mr. Rutherford at the post office. And did they have a confectioners store where she was going?

"Afternoon, Miss Mueller. Have you heard from your parents?" Widow Beckett held a basket.

"We had a letter today. Mother is missing her friends."

"As we miss her, too."

Widow Beckett's sparkling eyes caught her attention. Didn't she have a sister? "Why don't you come for dinner tomorrow evening? Ask your sister, too. Granny would love to share what she knows with you."

"I'm sure Dorthea would enjoy getting out. We're both so set in our ways that we've become quite boring." Widow Beckett smiled and straightened her posture. "Can we bring something? I've picked up some cornstarch to make a pie. I wouldn't mind sharing it."

"Granny will be thrilled to have company and insulted if you bring a dish. I know she's working on peaches today, so there will be an abundance of peach pie tomorrow. I'll see you then." At least, Emmie hoped her grandmother would approve. She'd forgotten about these two older women. Sisters. Perfect for Walter and Milton. She almost skipped to the counter where the licorice whips tempted the little children from their glass jar. But once she found brides she'd leave town.

Leave Landon.

◆ ◆ ◆

Landon battled back his feelings of attraction for Julia. Grasping for the reasons she'd chosen his best friend over him. Despite her saying she couldn't get past her grief, he was dubious. There wasn't a real reason for her to come to Trenton. She had relatives in many places across the country. In fact, her sister lived in Collinsville.

He backed away from her as Cyrus tromped through the door. "No pie today, but Mrs. Mueller will make some for tomorrow. Miss Emmie sent me on without her. She's yacking with Mrs. Pickens."

"Whoa, Cyrus. We have a customer."

"S–Sorry, sir." Cyrus set the basket on the floor. "Welcome to Knipp Emporium. Can I show you our newest selection of gloves?"

"Thank you, but I've seen the store and not found what I've wanted." She gave him a sour-grape frown.

"Mr. Knipp says we can order anything. Would you like me to get you a catalog?"

Landon choked back laughter watching Cyrus's salesmanship.

"Again, thank you. You're a bit young to work the sales floor, aren't you?"

"No, ma'am. Mr. Knipp is teaching me how to run a store."

Julia turned toward Landon. "I thought you didn't like children." She shrugged. "I'll be off. Maybe you can meet me for dinner this week?"

"He can't. He has to eat at Mueller's boardinghouse every day because that's where he lives and meals are included." Cyrus grasped the basket handle. "We even get our lunch from there. If you're leaving then, we can eat it, right, Mr. Knipp? Because we don't eat in front of customers."

"That is store policy." He could change it, of course, but seeing Julia left his mind in a jumble. "Let me escort you to the door."

"Come back anytime. We'll have new things arriving daily." Cyrus set the basket on the counter and emptied it.

◆ ◆ ◆

Emmie blinked in the bright sunlight. Then blinked again. Landon stood outside the emporium with a woman dressed in black. The woman moved her hands fast enough to stir up a breeze. Why did she stand so close to Landon? Who was she?

He bent down close to her. Emmie held her breath. He was close enough to kiss her. Did he know her? She strangled the licorice whips in her hand. Cyrus would want them, but Emmie couldn't get her feet to move forward. Why was she upset? She knew nothing about this woman. Except that the woman didn't mind when Landon touched her arm. She couldn't explain why that bothered her, but it did.

Heartsick, she turned and went back into the mercantile. She'd wait until the woman left to take Cyrus his treat. Then she was going home, because Granny could use her. There were floors to scrub and dusty front windows to wash. Yes, she'd been spending far too much time with Landon.

Chapter Thirteen

"Emmie, this was not a good day to invite the Widow Beckett and her sister to dinner. I wanted to get the sheets washed. And you promised Cyrus peach pie. Why didn't you invite him to dinner, too?" Granny measured the flour and plopped it into the bowl. "Hand me the vinegar."

"Yes, ma'am." Emmie racked her brain. She would have to help Granny today if the plan was going to work. "We can do it together. I'll strip the sheets and wash them. You work on the pie, because you make the best in the county. Anyone can wash up sheets."

"Stop trying to butter me up. Hurry upstairs then and get to work. Walter and Milton went for a walk. You know how they like to inspect the town in the morning. The old fools. Don't know what they expect to find out of place."

"At least it gives us a chance to tidy." Emmie bounded up the steps. In no time, she had the sheets off of Milton and Walter's beds. She wanted to be done before they returned, otherwise she'd have to listen to multiple stories of their youth. She paused at the entrance to Landon's room. It smelled different. Much nicer than the older men's rooms. Intoxicating, with the scent he wore. She took a deep breath. What would it feel like to be in his arms?

If she was affected this deeply by Landon's cologne she would get some for the bachelors. It wouldn't hurt their chances of attracting Widow Beckett and her sister's attention. But what did he use? She couldn't ask him. She moved to the dresser to search for the bottle. Once she knew the name she could purchase it.

His carpetbag sat unpacked on the dresser, his shaving items next to it. She reached for a bottle and brushed the side of the luggage. It crashed to the floor. Horror flooded through her. Once again Monkey Arms flew forefront in her mind.

She knelt to repack the items that spilled from the valise. She grabbed a picture frame. Maybe it was a photo of Landon's family. She flipped it over. Instead, it was the woman at the store. She pushed it to the bottom of the bag along with a few other things, set the bag on the dresser, and then yanked off the bed sheets hard enough to tear them.

◆　◆　◆

"Miss Emmie, what's got you so excitable this evening?" Milton drew his eyebrows together into one long brow.

"I enjoy having guests for dinner, don't you?" Emmie placed the fork and knife on the table. She stood back. "It looks nice, doesn't it?"

Walter nudged Milton. "Who did you invite?"

"The Widow Beckett and her sister. I ran into the Widow Beckett yesterday, and she seemed so sad. I thought an evening dinner with all of us would cheer her." She turned away so they wouldn't see her face. She might give her plan away.

"Milton, it's going to be a long night. Miss Emmie, we like it when it's just us around the table. There's no need to put on our best behavior." Walter sighed.

"It's good for both of you to keep those skills your mothers taught you." The front door opened. Good, Landon had returned. He could help her with these two. They could learn quite a bit from him.

"Emmie, I hope you don't mind, but I brought along a friend."

The woman in the photograph stood in the doorway. Emmie forced a smile. "Of course not. Granny always says the boarders should treat this home like their own."

"Thank you. This is Mrs. Julia Crump. Julia, this is Miss Emmie Mueller."

"Pleased to meet you, Emmie."

The use of her first name took Emmie aback. Did the woman think she was a servant? "Please, take her to the dining room, Mr. Knipp. We'll be serving as soon as the others arrive."

◆　◆　◆

Landon had noticed the way Emmie had turned frosty when Julia wrapped her arm through his as if she belonged to him. He wanted to refuse to bring Julia to the boardinghouse, but she'd been waiting on the boardwalk when he locked the shop door.

There was no time to explain before Emmie ushered them into the dining room.

"Who's this?" Walter scrunched his face. "It's not the sisters we were expecting. Milton fetch a chair from the kitchen."

Milton nodded and in his ghostlike way disappeared through the door. Come to think of it, that man didn't speak much ever. Landon introduced Julia to Walter. "What sisters are coming?"

"Miss Emmie invited some from the church. I imagine—"

Emmie stepped into the room. "What do you imagine, Walter?"

"Thinking about dinner. When are we going to eat?"

"Don't be such a curmudgeon. We have guests tonight." There was a soft knock on the door. "And there are the rest of dinner guests. I'll let them in and, Walter, behave. Where is Milton?"

"He went for another chair. If he was smart, he kept on going out the door."

"Walter!"

"I apologize, Miss Emmie. I'll let the women in and get everyone seated while you help your grandmother."

"Thank you." Emmie hurried toward the kitchen. Granny would not be happy about having another guest at the table tonight.

"Another person?" Granny grabbed Milton's arm before he took the chair from the kitchen. "Get that in there and come back for another place setting. Tonight, you're family, and family helps out."

"Yes, yes, ma'am." Milton's face reddened as he rushed from the room.

Granny rested her hands on her cheeks. "I'm getting too old for this kind of entertaining."

"Nonsense." Walter entered the kitchen with Milton shadowing him. "Let's start carrying out the food."

"Bless you, men. I never thought I'd let that happen in my house, but today I'm grateful for the help."

Emmie shrunk into the corner. Why hadn't she considered how much work this would be for Granny? She was old and tired. All the more reason to move to Kansas with the family once she got Milton and Walter married, if she could get Granny to go.

Following her grandmother to the dining room with the bowl of peas, she almost dropped it when she saw the seating arrangement. Milton or Walter, probably the latter, had put all the women on one side of the table and the men on the other. And somehow, he'd managed to put Julia in front of Milton, leaving empty seats in front of himself and Landon. Before she could move, her grandmother slid into the chair across from Walter.

Somewhat befuddled, Emmie sat, trying to corral her thoughts as to how this happened before Walter quit blessing the food.

Chapter Fourteen

Miss Emmie, could you run over to Knipp's and pick up some of that nice-smelling hair stuff he has?" Walter stepped off the last step and groaned. "I'd go, but my feet are hurting today. It'll do me good to sit on the porch for a spell."

"Why didn't you ask Landon to bring some home for you tonight? I planned on staying home to help Granny." And every day after. Last night embarrassed her. Those rascals stole her plan and twisted it. Neither of them said more than two words to the sisters. They might as well have put their faces on their plates. Once the prayer was said, they remained silent for the meal except for the occasional, "Pass me some more potatoes."

And Landon. Why had he brought Julia? He didn't talk to her either. The only conversations taking place had been among the women. By the time dessert was served, Emmie and Granny were sniping at each other.

"I didn't think about it. There was so much noise from all of you women talking I couldn't think, much less come up with a question. And I didn't see him this morning at breakfast. So are you going?" He took a step on the porch and winced.

The poor man really did hurt, and besides, if they smelled as good as Landon, it would be easier for women to fall in love with them. "I'll let Granny know, and then I'll be off. But next time, try and ask Landon when he is here." She hadn't seen Landon either. He must have awakened early and gone in to the store.

◆　◆　◆

By the time she arrived at the store, she had steeled herself against seeing Julia. The woman probably even wore Emmie's apron while she worked. She should be happy for Landon, but she wasn't. She couldn't come up with a single reason that he should marry Julia. She'd tried. Yes, she did. All night. And not one thing felt right about those two being together.

She stepped inside.

"Miss Emmie! You're late. Did you bring muffins or something?" Cyrus trotted across the floor and skidded to a stop. "You don't have a basket."

"I'm sorry. I'm on an errand for Mr. Hoffman, or I wouldn't be here."

"But you have to be. Mr. Knipp is having a terrible time with those numbers today. He can't even help me with my studies."

"What do you mean?" She glanced around the room. Landon stood in the darkest corner covering his eyes. "Landon, what's wrong?" Her skirt swished across the floor as she rushed to him.

"The spectacles are the wrong strength. My eyes feel like they've been scratched by a cat. I came back last night and worked on the books too long. Then this morning, I couldn't stand to be in the light."

"You stayed here all night?"

"Yes. I walked Julia back to the hotel and then came here. It seemed too late to return to the boardinghouse. I didn't want to wake anyone."

"You have a key, and Walter and Milton can sleep through anything. Where did you sleep? On the floor?"

"There's an old bed upstairs, and I slept there, or rather tried to."

"You need some cold compresses on those eyes. Cyrus, run to the café and get a few ice chips." She opened the drawer with the delicate handkerchiefs and took out two.

"What are you doing?" Landon stared at her through his fingers.

"Making you feel better. When Cyrus gets back with the ice, I'll wrap the pieces in these, and you can put them over your eyes."

"But those are costly."

"You only get one set of eyes. Where's Julia this morning?"

"At her hotel, I suppose. Why?"

"I thought she would be working with you."

"No, I would never allow her behind the counter at my store."

That stung. Landon thought more highly of Julia. She pushed the handkerchiefs into his hands. "When Cyrus gets back, put the ice in them and hold them on your eyes. I'm going home."

◆ ◆ ◆

"Emmie?" Landon squinted. The film in his eyes moved, and he caught sight of her fleeing the store. "What just happened?"

Cyrus burst into the shop with earth-pounding steps. "Boy, oh boy, Miss Emmie sure seems all fired up about something. She was racing down the street. I bet she gets in trouble from Mrs. Mueller for walking fast. Why is she mad anyway?"

"I don't know. Women puzzle me."

"Did you poke her in the back? They don't seem to like that much." Cyrus handed Landon a cup with ice chunks in it. "Did you call her Monkey Arms? My brother told me they called her that in school. Made her really mad."

"No, of course, I didn't. Why would they do that anyway?"

"My brother said she was always knocking things over with her arms. He said they should never have called her that. It wasn't a nice thing to do."

"He's right. And, no, I didn't call her any names." But he had mentioned her long arms earlier in the week. She hadn't reacted well to that. Now he understood why.

"I have to take the cup back right away. They only let me take it because they said they knew you would return it. How'd you get people to respect you like that?"

Landon folded the ice into the expensive handkerchiefs. He couldn't sell them now. "Time, Cyrus. Being true to your word is the best way to earn respect. If you say you're going to do something, then that's what you do.

"Even if you don't want to?"

"Sometimes." His stomach curled as he remembered a promise to Harry they'd made as kids to always be family. Harry broke the promise first, so did that let him out of fulfilling his side? Did he have to take care of Julia?

◆ ◆ ◆

Emmie couldn't wait to get home. In fact, if she could, she'd start packing her bags and hop on the train for Kansas tomorrow. Julia was too good, too sweet, too special to work at the store, but not Emmie. No, with her monkey arms, she was perfect to work behind the counter. Didn't even need a step stool or a ladder.

Walter and her grandmother were in the kitchen.

"Did you get it?" Walter took a step back from the counter where he'd been stealing a cookie.

"No. I didn't. You'll have to ask Landon tonight."

"What's wrong, Emmie? Are you coming down with something? Come over here. You look flushed." Granny settled her palm against Emmie's forehead.

Granny's touch felt cool and comforting. She would love to cuddle up on her lap and tell her how she felt about Landon and how he had made her feel today. But Walter hovered nearby, dropping crumbs on the floor, and besides, she was too big to get comfort from her grandmother's lap. After all, she was the one supposed to take care of Granny, not the other way around.

"Nothing is wrong." At least, nothing Granny could fix. She was more determined than ever to find a match for Walter and Milton by the end of the week. Maybe the man that waited in Kansas with his six children wouldn't mind the way she looked.

"I'm glad you're back from the store. I felt so bad about Julia living at the hotel that I sent Milton to tell her there is a room for her here. You'll have to pack your things up and move in with me. She'll only be here for a little while, but a grieving woman should be surrounded by people who care for her."

Emmie choked back furious words. How could Granny ask the beautiful, most perfect Julia to move in? Now Emmie would be faced with watching Landon and Julia make butterfly eyes over breakfast and dinner every day.

The situation was now intolerable.

Chapter Fifteen

Heavyhearted, Landon went through the motions of helping Cyrus recite his sums. Was it his place to take care of his best friend's wife? Julia was becoming a thorn in his side.

The day he caught Emmie on the church steps anything he might have felt for Julia evaporated. He and Julia were never meant to be together, and he wished he would've learned that before his friend passed away. He would tell her today to return to St. Louis or go to her family in Collinsville.

"Mr. Knipp, I'm going to promise you that I will learn my sums by this time next week." Cyrus, with his big brown eyes, looked at Landon intently. "Do you think I can do it?"

"I believe in you, Cyrus. This time next week, you will be proficient in your sums, and then we can start with subtraction."

Cyrus sighed.

"Buck up. You didn't think you could do this, and subtraction will be easy now that you know addition. It's just doing the math backwards."

The bell on the door jangled. Landon looked up. A woman customer. His heart beat faster. "Welcome to Knipp Emporium. Please feel free to look around, or if you're looking for something special I will be happy to assist you."

"Thank you. My husband will be here in a moment. I wanted to take a few moments to survey your wares. Miss Mueller told me I would enjoy this store. She made it sound so exciting that I had to come and check it out for myself. Is she here today?"

"She left early." And the way she left, he wasn't sure she would be back. He wished Cyrus were older so he could be left alone with the store. He'd like to find Emmie and figure out what he'd done wrong.

"Mrs. Pickens likes to paint, mostly kittens, Mr. Knipp."

"Cyrus, I didn't see you back there." Mrs. Pickens ran her hand over a silk wrap that lay on the counter.

"You remembered!" Cyrus's wide toothy grin touched Landon. If he accomplished nothing else in this town, he could be proud of helping this boy.

"I did. How about you show me something you think I would like to see."

Cyrus hustled around the counter. We have some very nice china cups with drawings of birds, ma'am. Perhaps those would interest you as we don't have any with kittens?"

Landon held back a laugh. Cyrus was a natural-born salesman.

◆ ◆ ◆

Emmie's stomach hurt, but it did no good complaining to Granny, who'd sent her right back to the emporium. The last thing she wanted to do was cross that threshold, but facing her grandmother's wrath? Now that was something she wasn't willing to do.

"Emmie, you are here. Mr. Knipp told me you left for the day."

Alma. *Thank You, God, for sending this sweet person here today*. It was just what she needed. "I had to come back. I'd forgotten to pick up something for one of the boarders. What do you think of the store?"

"It's amazing. I found at least a dozen things I'd like to get for the girls. Roy will have something to say about that. I'm afraid I'll be baking a mess of pies to make him forget about the purchases."

Emmie gulped. She hadn't considered the fights married people sometimes had. "Does he get rough with you, Alma?" She lowered her voice. "Just tell me and you can live with us, or maybe you can go back to your father's house?"

Alma giggled. "No. Roy doesn't know how to be mean. He does, however, seem to have a different idea about what is essential for little girls."

"Miss Emmie, I showed Alma the painted bird cups. She's thinking about those. Should I put them on the counter just in case she quits thinking?" Cyrus finger-combed his slicked-down hair.

"That would be nice. Then she won't have to go looking for them again."

He crept across the floor with the two cups.

"I think he's afraid he might break them." Landon spoke behind Emmie. "Please don't feel you must buy them. It gives him a chance to practice his store behavior.

Where had he come from? The heat from his breath blew against her shoulder, right through her blouse. It warmed her from the inside. She forced herself to move away from him. "Have you met Mrs. Pickens?"

"I have. You have a delightful friend. I believe I'll help Cyrus. It seems he doesn't quite understand the concept of thinking about a purchase, as he is wrapping the cups."

Emmie pressed her palm over her heart as he walked away.

Alma touched her arm. "I think you best forget about that man in Kansas, Emmie. Someone else has claimed your heart."

◆ ◆ ◆

Could Alma be right? Had Emmie given Landon her heart? What would it be like to call him husband? To make him breakfast and to have his children? Her heart galloped. She fanned herself.

"Are you hot, Miss Emmie?" Cyrus asked. "'Cause I sure am. My friends are going to the pond after lunch to fish and swim."

"Mr. Knipp, did you hear that? Cyrus is giving up his afternoon with friends to work. That's a very grown-up thing to do."

Cyrus cast his eyes to the slate full of math problems.

"Perhaps he should take some time to be a boy today. Do you think you can help me the rest of the afternoon, Emmie?"

Cyrus jumped off the stool. "Could you, Miss Emmie? Please? I've been working so hard, and before you know it, winter will be here."

Emmie laughed. "I'm sure I can handle working here while you have fun. But if you catch a mess of fish, would you bring some to the boardinghouse? Granny would delight in fresh fish for dinner. Come to think of it, we don't have anyone to fish for us anymore."

"You could fish if you wanted to."

"I could, but it wouldn't be proper, and you know it. Will you do it?"

"Yes, ma'am. I hope I catch some, but it's hot and sunny and well, you know fish. They don't like to be caught this time of day." His eyes widened. "I mean, some do like to snag the hook."

"Go on with you." Landon shook his head. "You see where those words took you, correct? You almost talked your way out of being able to go. Run along, and have a good swim."

"Thank you." Cyrus put his slate and chalk behind the counter. "See you tomorrow."

A hush fell over the store. Cyrus took up a great deal of space with his active body and general noise. Now she could hear Landon's every movement.

"Emmie, do you like working here?" He strolled over and leaned against the counter.

"Yes, I do. I'll miss it when I'm in Kansas. I've never had so much money of my own, except for the egg money, but that's never much." He was so close she could count his thick fringed eyelashes.

"What are you going to do with it?" He reached for the ledger resting on the counter and brushed against her hand.

Heat leaped from his hand to hers. She ached, wanting more of his touch. "Buy some warm clothes good for working on a farm, I suppose." The words clunked in her mouth. She didn't want to spend money on those items. No, farming didn't appeal to her. She liked being surrounded by the beautiful things in Landon's store. If she purchased the blue silk and made a dress, would Landon notice her as much as she did him?

Chapter Sixteen

Emmie followed the breeze beckoning from her bedroom window. She'd packed her things and would take them into Granny's room in a moment. This might be the last time she would call this room her own. She plunked down on the window seat where she'd spent time talking to God and reading. A puff of wind graced her like a kiss. Voices floated through the window. She peered out. Landon stood on the front walk close to Julia. They leaned in to each other, talking.

He pulled something out of his pocket and gave it to her. That's when Emmie knew it was over. She hadn't even had a chance with Landon, and until today, she hadn't known how much she wanted one.

She ought to look away but couldn't. When Landon reached out and wiped something from Julia's face, his hand stilled against her cheek. Julia reached her arms around him, and he followed suit, hugging her back.

Emmie's heart shattered. She flung herself on what used to be her bed and stared at the crack in the ceiling. Days ago, she wondered how long she would remember this room, and now all she wanted to do was forget it.

She wanted out of this town. Maybe she would go to Kansas alone. It was obvious to her that Granny's beloved boarders meant more to her than her own family.

◆　◆　◆

"Landon, I'm sorry I rushed here expecting you to save me." Julia fingered the golden locket. "This is so special."

"It's all right. I thought you might like a photo of Harry, and I had one. We promised to look after each other's families when we were younger. While you and I were once close, it was more of a brother and sister relationship. At least on your part."

Her sorrow-filled eyes shimmered.

"I meant that it was better for you to marry Harry. It may have been a short marriage, but I heard from my family you were happy."

"We were, and Harry didn't run all over the world to avoid his family. That's where you and I fell apart."

"Maybe we should thank God He intervened. I wasn't ready to settle down. I had to do some growing up before moving back. Even now I've managed to put the

Mississippi between my brothers and me."

"You had to. They were never going to let the youngest son be more important than them. What do they think of you opening a store here?"

"There's been some grumbling and mention of one of them taking it away from me if I fail."

"You won't. Harry always said you were the best of the Knipp brothers."

His heart warmed. "Harry was a good friend. He would want you to marry again."

She offered a weak smile. "Maybe someday, but I'm not ready yet. I thought I would be if it was you, but to be honest, I would have been miserable pining for Harry. What about you and Emmie? I've seen how you look at her."

"I'm hoping to convince her to stay here and not run off to Kansas."

"What if she won't?"

Landon's throat constricted. What if she didn't choose him? Twice rejected, he'd die a lonely man before he took another look at a woman.

◆ ◆ ◆

"Emmie, can we take a walk after dinner?" Landon took the serving tray from her. He'd been waiting for her, for the chance to talk to her alone.

"I don't think so. Granny will need help cleaning up."

Milton appeared behind Emmie. He winked at Landon. "Walter and I will help her."

"But you've never—"

"It's about time we stopped be so lazy around here. You and your grandmother have been kind to treat us so well. So take the evening stroll with your fellow."

"He's not my—"

"I'll let Walter know." Milton left before Emmie could finish her sentence.

Landon straightened. He had the men on his side. Now, all he had to do was convince this blond beauty to stay in Trenton and marry him. Or for tonight, take a walk with him.

"What about Julia? Shouldn't you be asking her?" Her lips tightened into a straight line, and she looked away from him.

"It will be fine. I don't desire her presence with us for this conversation."

"Come on and sit down." Mrs. Mueller brushed past them with a plate of rolls.

"Yes, Granny. We'll be right there." Emmie turned to Landon. "I'll go with you, but only if you tell Julia at dinner that we're going for a walk."

"I will, and I promise it won't be a problem for her."

Chapter Seventeen

The warm golden glow of the sun setting spread over the town and Emmie, making both stunning to Landon. Emmie was already beautiful, and downright angelic in the sunset colors.

"Does this walk have a purpose, Landon?"

"Yes. There is a house I discovered on the way to the store that I'm considering purchasing, and I wanted to know what you thought of it."

She shot him a quizzical glance.

"You've lived here all of your life, and I thought you could tell me the history of the place." And he wanted her reaction to it before he made an offer. It wouldn't do if she hated it.

"I can try to be helpful. Even though I have lived here a long time, I don't know everything about this town."

Landon stopped in front of the Victorian house that he wanted. The place with its green, rose, and blue painted accents struck him as happy. "This is it. I like the big porch, but it needs a swing and a few rocking chairs like you have at the boarding-house. What do you think?"

"In primary school, I had a friend who lived here. One day, I spent the afternoon with her. It's a splendid house with a lot of rooms. I don't remember many details about the inside. I do know there is a large pantry because we played hide-and-seek and I hid in it."

"When did they move?"

"It was the oddest thing. One day she was at school and the next day she wasn't. Overnight they moved and no one knew where they went. After that, a lot of people have lived here. There are rumors of it being haunted."

"Do you believe that?" This was something he didn't expect from her.

"No. I do believe in houses where windowpanes are not glazed properly, and the wind is able to send sounds through the cracks. That's probably what happened here a few times."

"That's something I'll check before making an offer."

"Why do you need such a big house to begin with? Most of my friends who are married start with smaller houses."

"I have no intention of ever moving. My parents lived in the house I grew up in since they were married. It's a great tradition to carry on. Putting down roots in this town is important to me."

"Why? When so many leave the places they were raised, why would you want to stay?"

"The world is not as exciting as one would think. I traveled all over while purchasing items for my father's store. I missed home. Because of that, I decided I would marry, stay in one town, and have a large family. That's why I need a big house, so everyone will be comfortable."

"But you don't even have a wife—"

"Not yet. But I soon will. That is if she will have me." He moved closer to her and touched her arm.

Emmie's bottom lip trembled, her eyes watered. She broke away from him. "I need to get back. They're lighting the lamps and Granny will need me." She took off at a fast clip.

"Wait up. Do you think the house will work?" He scurried to catch up. He'd done something wrong. Again.

"I'm sure you and your new bride will be happy in the house."

◆　◆　◆

It's not fair, God. Why did Landon have to have such lovely brown eyes? When had Emmie fallen so deeply in love with him? And now, she couldn't have him. Julia would live in that wonderful house while Emmie settled in Kansas with the no-name farmer and his children.

She rolled in bed and kicked her grandmother.

"What's wrong with you tonight? If you're going to be like this to sleep with, you'll be on a pallet on the floor." Granny yanked the sheet straight.

"I'm sorry. I can't sleep. I've been thinking about Mother's letter. Granny, did you love Grandfather right away, or did you come to love him?"

Granny sat up. Her gray hair shined like silver in the moonlight. "I knew that man was the one for me the moment I laid eyes on him. He had the deepest laugh. It settled in and claimed my heart."

"What if I never feel that way about the man father has picked out for me?" She swung her legs off the bed and stood. "I don't know what to do."

"You don't have to marry anyone you don't love. That's not how this family works."

Emmie crossed the small room to the window and stared at the moon. "What about the commandment to honor thy parents?"

"Your father isn't going to demand you marry the farmer. If you wrote and said you wanted to stay in Trenton, he'd give you his blessing. He wants the best for you. That's what a good father does for his children."

"Not go to Kansas? I don't know. I would miss my family."

"Think about it. They've been gone several months, and I haven't seen many tears streaking down your cheeks. Now, get back in bed, and be still. The morning will be here soon enough."

As Emmie crawled under the sheet, the thought of Rooster crowing under her old bedroom window made her smile. Would Julia appreciate the wake-up call? She fell asleep thinking about Landon and his house.

◆　◆　◆

Emmie woke up with a headache. She'd overslept. Rooster hadn't woken her. That's right. She wasn't in her own room. She rolled over in the empty bed. Granny wasn't in the room. She must have let Emmie sleep. At least she hoped she hadn't been told to get up and then rolled over.

She pushed back the sheet and jumped out of bed. In a flurry, she took care of her morning routine despite the fact nothing was normal. Her brush sat on Granny's dresser, not her own. *Father, I need to get this grumpiness out of me before I leave this room. Please help me.* A sense of peace settled over her. Last night, she'd been shown the house of her dreams with the man she'd fallen in love with, but he wasn't meant for her.

In the morning, light illuminated last night's foolishness over Landon's behavior. Crying to Granny wouldn't change things, but her advice was sound. Once Emmie arrived in Kansas, she could decide on her own to marry the widower or not. Now that Landon would be moving into a big house with Julia, she'd ask him if he'd take in Walter and Milton. They could learn to pick up their rooms and eat in the café. Surely, Landon would understand her need to leave, and she wanted herself and Granny on that train by next week.

She tried hard to ignore the rock-crushing ache in her heart as she stepped into the kitchen.

There was her grandmother snuggled in Walter's arms.

"Granny!"

Walter stepped back from her grandmother as if Emmie had struck him with a burning log.

"Now, Emmie. Settle down. I've something to say to you." Granny took her by the hand and navigated her to the kitchen chair. "You see, Walter and I are in love. I'm not leaving Trenton. He's asked me to marry him, and I said yes. You're welcome to stay here with us or catch a train to Kansas. It's up to you."

Emmie sprang to her feet. Tears stung her cheeks as she ran from the kitchen, the screen door banging behind her. It wasn't fair. After all she'd done to marry Walter off, he'd fallen in love with Granny right under Emmie's nose.

Chapter Eighteen

Emmie made it to the church steps. In her haste she'd left her hat behind. She'd lost a few hairpins on her flight and strands tickled her chin. She perched on the stone steps to think. Nothing had really changed other than she was now free to leave. Emmie's father wouldn't worry about Granny living in the town she loved once she was married.

That meant Emmie could leave tomorrow if she wanted.

But she didn't want to. Now that the barriers to leaving had been removed, she didn't want to go. Even if she never found someone to love her, this was her town. She stood and smoothed her skirt. She'd wander to the side of the church and think about what to write to her parents. It would be cool under the tree, and she wouldn't be in plain sight.

Her mother would be heartbroken, or at least Emmie thought she would be. She didn't want to cause her mother pain, but how could she leave? Granny might not need Emmie any longer, but she still had a home. Maybe Landon would hire her to work for him all the time, if she could stand being around him after he married Julia.

"Emmie?"

She turned. Landon stood at the edge of the yard. Almost as if by thinking of him he'd appeared. Did he have to be so attractive? So perfectly kept?

He strolled toward her. "I missed you at breakfast."

"How did you find me?"

"Your grandmother knows you well. I'd like to know you even better." He stopped inches from her.

"But Julia wouldn't care for that."

"She doesn't matter. You do. Last night, you ran off before I could ask you an important question." He stepped closer.

"About the store?"

"No. Emmie." He reached for her hands.

She let him take them, enjoying the way they swallowed hers.

"Emmie Mueller. I'd like to kiss you, but first, I want to know if you'll marry me?"

Emmie swayed, then caught her balance. "Yes, please."

Landon pulled her close and kissed her. White sparks flashed behind her closed eyes. She'd heard her friends say they'd seen fireworks when kissed, but she hadn't believed it until now.

After the kiss, she couldn't catch her breath. "That was lovely."

"Yes, it was. I've wanted to do that since the first day I met you."

"Landon, I don't want to move to Kansas. I want to live in that big house and have a family of our own."

"Then we shall."

Epilogue

Rooster crowed under Emmie's window. She'd miss him. After today, she'd wake up in the house Landon bought for them. The weeks had flown by as she decorated the inside of the house with lovely things from the store and waited for her mother and father to arrive for the wedding. And now the day was here. She shivered. In a few short hours, she'd be Mrs. Knipp.

Thunder blasted the sky apart. How could it rain on her wedding day? She moaned. She wanted it to be perfect, and now it would be a muddy mess.

Her bedroom door creaked as Granny peered inside. "Just because it's your wedding day doesn't mean you get to sleep in. Come on, child. Slip on your wrapper and have breakfast with your parents and me. I've sent Walter and Milton on an errand. They'll be back in time for the wedding, but for today, the boarding-house is for the bride's family only."

"But, Granny, you and Walter are married. He's family now."

"Pshaw. He'll be fine. He's got his shadow with him. Come now, get a bite to eat, and we'll get you into that beautiful dress."

"But the rain! My dress will be a sodden mess during the reception."

"Let's not borrow trouble. It will work out, you'll see. God can dry up the ground if He wants."

◆　◆　◆

Landon's chest swelled with joy as his stunning bride, holding on to her father's arm, walked down the aisle toward him. He'd made the right choice coming to this town. God knew long before he did that he'd find the wife he longed for in Trenton.

The rain drummed harder on the tin roof.

Emmie looked up and met his eyes.

He smiled, and she grinned back. Their reception wouldn't be the one she'd dreamed about in the church's side yard. But he knew his bride. He could almost see how happy she would be when they arrived at the store, and she saw how they had transformed it. This time, she wouldn't be in charge of setting up the dinner. Instead, he, Cyrus, Milton, and Walter had decorated, even pulling out imported linen tablecloths to cover the cases for the many bowls and platters of food. They'd moved shelves, put trinkets away, and hung streamers, all to transform his store into a place of celebration.

Nothing was too special for his homegrown bride.

Christian author **Diana Lesire Brandmeyer** writes historical and contemporary romances about women choosing to challenge their fears to become the strong women God intends. Author of *A Mind of Her Own; A Bride's Dilemma in Friendship, Tennessee;* and *We're Not Blended We're Pureed, a Survivor's Guide to Blended Families.* Sign up for her newsletter and get free stuff at www.dianabrandmeyer.com.

The Unmatched Bride

by Amanda Cabot

Chapter One

Deborah Johnson stared at the note her landlady had just delivered. She'd promised herself a month without assignments, and yet the sight of that firm, almost bold handwriting on the heavy ivory vellum made her pause. Her reputation was secure. So, too, were her finances. She didn't *need* this assignment, but she couldn't deny that part of her *wanted* it.

"I would like to discuss engaging your services," the note read. "Please contact me at your earliest convenience."

The words were ordinary. What was not was the signature. Robert Carmichael was no ordinary man. As president of one of Cheyenne's largest banks, he was one of the most influential men in the city, perhaps in the whole territory. Matching the well-known widower would be a feather in Deborah's cap, a jewel in her crown, a... The image didn't matter. What did was the realization that finding the perfect wife for Mr. Carmichael would be a challenge, and today that challenge felt good.

Deborah read the note one final time before nodding. She'd do it. She'd meet Mr. Carmichael and, if all went well, she would spend the next month or so searching for his perfect mate. But first she needed to prepare for the meeting.

Returning to her bedchamber, she removed her morning gown and donned the deep blue walking suit Madame Charlotte had made for her, knowing the color flattered her complexion and highlighted her eyes, then reached for the matching hat that added a couple inches to her height. Deborah's smile was rueful. Nothing would make her tall—she'd stopped growing when she was only two inches above five feet—but the extra height added to her confidence. A woman meeting with Mr. Carmichael needed every ounce of confidence she could muster.

Half an hour later, the butler, who'd introduced himself as Bradford, escorted her through her potential client's home. The house, one of the mansions on the section of Ferguson Street that townspeople called Millionaire's Row, was what Deborah had expected from a man of Mr. Carmichael's position. Its exterior was impressive, not only because of its size but also because of the beautiful architectural details that made it stand out from its neighbors.

The imported marble flooring in the entry hallway was not a surprise. What was a surprise was that the illumination appeared to be by electricity. Although most of the homes in the city still used gas or oil lights, ever since the Brush-Swan Electric Company brought arc lighting to Cheyenne, stores and some homes had converted to what was being touted as the greatest modern convenience.

Deborah made a mental note of Mr. Carmichael's progressive attitude. Though other matchmakers might not believe it important, she knew such information was a key element in choosing the right wife for him. He would want a woman who appreciated his forward thinking.

"Miss Johnson to see you, sir," Bradford announced as he opened the pocket door and ushered Deborah into her client's study.

Robert Carmichael rose from behind the desk. Though Deborah kept a smile on her face, her mind began to catalog details. He was even more handsome than she'd realized. Prior to today, she'd only seen him from a distance. Though she knew he was tall and distinguished, she hadn't known just how appealing his features were. The combination of dark brown hair, eyes the color of warm chocolate, a chiseled nose and a firm chin made him stand out from other men the way his house stood out from its neighbors. Between Robert Carmichael's wealth and his undeniably good looks, it would not be difficult to find a woman interested in marrying him. The question was, what did he seek in a second wife?

"I'm pleased to meet you, Miss Johnson." The smile that accompanied his words startled Deborah. Men had smiled at her before—hundreds, perhaps thousands of times—but never had a man's smile made her feel as if her insides were melting like butter left out in the sun, as if she and Robert Carmichael were the only two people on Earth.

How strange.

◆　◆　◆

She was prettier than he'd expected, Rob reflected as he took a step toward her. The matchmaker wasn't a beauty like Rachel. Miss Deborah Johnson was half a foot shorter than Rachel, a blond rather than a brunette, with blue eyes rather than green. She didn't possess the kind of beauty that took away a man's breath and scrambled his brains, and yet when she smiled at him, Rob felt as if the sun had come out after a long absence. He couldn't identify it, but there was something special about Miss Johnson.

"Everyone tells me you're the best matchmaker in the city," he said as he gestured toward one of the two chairs in front of his desk. When Miss Johnson had taken her seat, he settled onto the one next to her, angling himself so he could watch her. If this were an ordinary meeting, he would have sat in his usual spot behind the desk, but this was not an ordinary meeting. He needed to gain Miss Johnson's support, and the best way to do that was to establish a friendly relationship. Besides, something about her drew him toward her.

"Your reputation is stellar," he said. "That's why I'd like to hire you."

The matchmaker nodded slightly, acknowledging the compliment. "It's true that I've had my share of success," she admitted, "but you need to know there are no guarantees that I'll be able to find the ideal wife for you."

"For me?" Blood drained from Rob's face at the thought of another wife. That was not what he had in mind. Not at all.

Miss Johnson appeared confused. "Isn't that what you meant? You said you wanted to engage my services."

"I do." Rob cringed as he pronounced the same words that played such a key role in a marriage ceremony. "For my daughter, not me." He needed to ensure that Miss Johnson understood. "When my wife died, I knew I would never marry again." He wouldn't discuss the reasons; no one needed to know about his life with Rachel.

The matchmaker gave him a long, appraising look, as if she'd somehow sensed the story he hadn't shared. There was no way she could know the details, but if she'd seen beneath his carefully constructed façade, Rob knew that same insightful nature would play an important role in choosing Emily's husband.

"I see," Miss Johnson said slowly. As she tipped her head to one side, he caught a whiff of her perfume, a delicate scent that reminded him of spring, even though autumn was just around the corner. Rob couldn't recall the last time he'd noticed a woman's perfume, but then again, he could not recall the last time he'd met a woman like Miss Johnson.

She straightened her neck and looked directly at him. "So it's Emily who'll be my client."

He wasn't surprised she knew his daughter's name. After all, it wasn't as if he and Emily were strangers in Cheyenne. "You look surprised."

"I am. It was my understanding that your daughter has a bevy of suitors."

Rob couldn't suppress his sigh. "She does. That's the problem. She doesn't seem interested in any of them, and I can't tell who would be the best husband for her. That's why I need you."

He didn't want to consider the possibility that she would refuse to help him. Not only was this woman reputed to be the best matchmaker in the city, but the few minutes he'd spent in her company had convinced Rob that she was the only one he could trust with Emily's future.

"Will you help me, Miss Johnson?"

There was no hesitation, and as she nodded, he felt the tension that had twisted his insides begin to subside. "Certainly," she said, "although I have to admit this is one of the more unusual assignments I've ever taken. Normally I have to find suitors, not eliminate them. But it intrigues me."

What intrigued Rob was the woman sitting only a foot away from him. He owed much of his success at the bank to making rapid judgments of people, knowing who would be a good risk for a loan and who would not. The same instincts that had increased the bank's profits told him not to underestimate Miss Deborah Johnson. There was more to her than simply matchmaking. Much more. And so, though he hadn't intended it to be part of his agreement, he found himself saying, "I'm not sure how you normally proceed, but I'd like you to consider living here."

When her eyes widened, Rob knew he'd have to use the same persuasive skills he'd employed to convince several of the territory's cattle barons to move their accounts to his bank. "If you're worried about propriety, I assure you that my housekeeper's presence will keep people from gossiping. The reason I think it's important is that being here would give you a better opportunity to get to know Emily than if you simply saw her occasionally."

Though Miss Johnson nodded, Rob did not know whether she was agreeing to his stipulation or simply indicating that she understood his reasons. Hoping it was the former, he continued. "Once you find the right man for her, Emily will need someone to help with the wedding plans." Rob hadn't planned to ask the matchmaker to become a substitute mother of the bride, but somehow Miss Deborah Johnson's presence made him consider things that had never crossed his mind.

"Can you do all that?"

The matchmaker smiled, one of those smiles that turned her face from pretty to downright beautiful. "Yes, I can, Mr. Carmichael."

As she extended her hand to seal their agreement with a shake, Rob shook his head slightly. "Let's forgo the formalities. Since we'll be spending a lot of time together, surely you can call me Rob."

Her smile broadened and for the first time, he found himself wondering if Emily was right and he ought to consider remarrying. His daughter had been haranguing him about that ever since her first suitor had come to call. Each time she'd mention marriage, Rob had shaken his head, hoping she believed his reluctance was due to lasting grief over Rachel's death. He'd categorically refused his daughter's suggestions, just as he'd sloughed off the less than subtle efforts of a number of widows to gain his attention, yet somehow the idea no longer seemed so preposterous. How strange.

He raised an eyebrow, waiting for the matchmaker's response.

"All right, Rob," she said. "And I'm Deborah."

"Deborah." It was just a name. There was no reason it should feel so good tripping off his tongue, and yet it did.

How strange.

Chapter Two

Deborah smiled as she returned four hours later, a small trunk filled with enough clothing to last her a week in the back of the carriage Rob had insisted she take. The two of them had agreed that her services would not be required on Sundays, and so she planned to spend that day in her own home, leaving the Ferguson Street mansion Saturday evening and returning Monday morning in time for breakfast.

Each week, she would exchange some items of clothing so that it did not appear that she had only six outfits. The reason was more than simple vanity. If Deborah was going to be part of the Carmichael household, she needed to dress appropriately, for Rob had made it clear that she was not a servant but rather a business associate who'd be treated like a valued guest.

"Miss Emily is waiting in the morning room." Though no smile crossed the butler's face, Bradford's expression softened ever so slightly, as if he held a special fondness for the daughter of the house. He slid the pocket door open and ushered Deborah into a small but elegantly furnished room. With its eastern exposure and french doors leading to the backyard, this was clearly a place to enjoy the morning sunshine. Even now, in the middle of the afternoon, it was a room that invited a person to sit and relax.

Emily Carmichael was not relaxing. Deborah could see that the moment she entered the room. Her client rose and took a step forward, her tense expression announcing that she was assessing the woman who'd been hired to find her a husband.

"You're not what I expected." Emily's words were clear and well modulated, although the greeting was unconventional.

Deborah returned the scrutiny, forming her initial impressions of her client. Like her father, Emily had dark brown hair and eyes, but her features were less chiseled than his. While she wasn't a classic beauty, her looks were striking. That combined with her father's wealth guaranteed her more than her share of suitors.

"Just what did you expect?" Deborah wasn't certain whether Emily was testing her or whether she was always so direct.

The young woman tipped her head to the side, as if considering. "Someone much

71

older and. . .well. . .grayer." Deborah had her answer: Emily was indeed outspoken.

"Some of my clients have done their best to turn me gray, but so far none have succeeded. Is it your intention to be the first?" Two could play this game.

If she hadn't been watching carefully, Deborah might have missed the almost imperceptible widening of Emily's eyes. "Why would you think that?" The question sounded innocent, but the young girl's expression said otherwise.

"Your greeting was hardly conventional, and you've yet to offer me a seat."

A slight flush colored Emily's cheeks as she gestured toward the room's most comfortable chair. When they were both seated, she leaned forward. "I don't see any value in wasting time on meaningless platitudes, but if you insist. . ." Emily fixed a patently false smile on her face and simpered. "It's a pleasure to meet you, Miss Johnson. Isn't the weather glorious today? We'd best enjoy it while it lasts, because before we know it, the cottonwoods will be dropping their leaves."

Though Deborah was tempted to smile, she did not. The girl was lovely, intelligent, and more than a little pampered. If she was like this all the time, it was no wonder Rob wanted Deborah to live here. Though he hadn't said it, it was possible he sought someone to help soften some of his daughter's rough edges.

"Social amenities have their purpose, but I will admit that I have almost as little patience for platitudes as you do." Deborah smiled at Emily, wanting to ensure the girl understood she was her ally, not her enemy. "Tell me, though. Which side do you show to your suitors?"

Emily blinked, as if disconcerted by the question. "Why, the sweet one, of course. Not one of them seems to realize that I'm poking fun at them. They think I'm nothing more than a silly, brainless chit who'll one day inherit a fortune."

But, while Emily would indeed become an heiress, she was neither silly nor brainless. Deborah welcomed the surge of excitement that accompanied the confirmation of her initial belief that this assignment would be a challenge. Neither Rob Carmichael nor his daughter was a typical client, and that was good.

Fixing her gaze on Emily, she said, "The first thing you want from a potential husband is the ability to see behind your mask."

Once again Emily appeared surprised by Deborah's assessment. "Was I that obvious? Papa likes it when I put on my sweet face, and so do the men who come to call."

"But that's not the real Emily. You deserve a man who appreciates you for who you truly are." Deborah tried not to frown as she thought about what might happen if Emily married a man who believed her to be a meek, brainless girl only to discover that she was bright and had a mind of her own. She could end up like Clara.

Try though she might, Deborah could not repress the shudder that swept through her at the thought of Emily suffering her sister's fate, and she took a deep breath, vowing that would not happen.

"What appeals to you in a man?" she asked Emily, keeping her voice low and even.

"How important is his physical appearance?" Many of her clients had had definite ideas of what their husbands should look like. "Do you prefer light or dark hair?"

Unbidden, Rob Carmichael's image flitted through Deborah's brain. Though she had always been partial to blond, blue-eyed men, she had to admit that Emily's father's dark hair and eyes were attractive. Very attractive. She brushed the thought aside. It was ridiculous to be entertaining such ideas. She was here to match Emily, not search for a husband for herself.

Emily dipped her head, leaving Deborah unable to see her eyes. "I hadn't really thought about that." The combination of her posture and the false notes in her voice told Deborah she was lying. "All I know is that none of my suitors make my heart beat faster." This time Deborah had no doubt of the girl's sincerity.

"That only means you haven't met the right man yet. You will." Deborah was confident someone in Cheyenne would recognize and appreciate Emily's strengths. It was her job to find that man. And she would. Oh, yes, she would.

"Maybe." Emily appeared unconvinced, but she straightened her shoulders and looked directly at Deborah. "Tell me why you decided to be a matchmaker."

Though she wouldn't divulge the details, there was no reason not to tell Emily the basic story. "I saw women in bad marriages and wanted to save others from the same fate."

"Did you?" Emily's dark eyes sparkled with interest.

"Yes." Deborah had kept in touch with all the women she'd matched and knew they were happy. "Every marriage has its difficult times, but love makes those times bearable. And the rest of the time. . ." Deborah smiled, thinking of some of the couples who invited her to family celebrations so she could see how happy they were. "The good times are simply glorious."

Nodding slowly, Emily fixed her gaze on Deborah. "Then why haven't you married?"

It was far from the first time someone had asked her that. "Because God hasn't sent the right man my way." She'd had her share of suitors, particularly once she became established as a matchmaker and men realized she would be able to contribute to the family's finances, but not one had touched her heart.

"You shouldn't give up." Emily flashed a mischievous smile at Deborah. "After all, you're not old and gray yet." She paused for a moment, obviously considering something. "Let's make a deal. You find a husband for me, and I'll find one for you."

"So you fancy yourself a matchmaker?"

Emily shook her head. "No, but I like you, and I think you deserve to be happy. You believe the right man is waiting for me. Why shouldn't one be waiting for you?"

As Rob Carmichael's face flitted through her mind again, Deborah shook her head. Absurd! But, though she thought she'd long since outgrown the tendency to blush, she could feel color rising to her cheeks. Absurd!

◆　◆　◆

"I can see you two ladies have gotten acquainted." Rob helped himself to another slice of roast beef and smiled at his dinner companions. Emily seemed happier this evening than he could recall, and the smile she'd given him when they all sat down at the table had been almost playful—a welcome change from the normally serious daughter she'd become.

"Miss Johnson and I made a deal." She gave the matchmaker a look that could only be called conspiratorial.

"And what's that deal?"

"It's not for me to tell." Now Emily was back to being coy. "If Miss Johnson wants you to know, she'll tell you."

Rob turned his attention to the woman whose pale blue gown highlighted her eyes. "Well, Miss Johnson . . ." He used the formal salutation deliberately, hoping it would encourage Deborah to divulge whatever it was she and Emily had cooked up between them.

But the matchmaker didn't take the bait. "It's nothing that should concern you," she said firmly. As she buttered a roll, she changed the subject. "Emily gave me a list of the men who've come calling. It was even more extensive than I expected and made me realize that my normal approach might not be appropriate here. I have several ideas I'd like to discuss with you."

"Am I included in this discussion?" Though phrased as a question, Emily's words sounded like a veiled demand.

"Do you want to be?" he countered.

"It's my life, isn't it?" Rob hadn't been mistaken in thinking that something had happened to Emily today. Not only were her smiles different, but her response to his question was far more assertive than normal. In the past, she would have simply acceded to whatever he suggested. For a second, he missed his biddable daughter, but he had to admit that if she was going to marry, she needed to assert her independence.

"Yes, it is your life." Rob wouldn't dispute that, but the decision about including her wasn't entirely his. "Is it all right with you if Emily joins us?" he asked Deborah.

While a part of him recognized the importance of involving his daughter, another part had been looking forward to time alone with the matchmaker. It was silly—downright silly—to be disappointed that that would have to be postponed.

"What do you think?"

"It makes sense to include Emily." The smile Deborah gave him generated more warmth than the new stove Rob had installed in the dining room. "I'd thought you and I might discuss the ideas after dinner, but there's no need to wait."

Deborah cut a piece of meat and chewed it carefully before she continued. "I usually begin by meeting potential suitors individually, getting to know them before I introduce them to my clients. Since you and Emily have already met the men, that doesn't seem necessary this time. Instead, I thought we'd hold a series of social events—dinners, parties, dances—so I can observe them there."

He hadn't expected that, but then again, Rob wasn't certain what he had expected. When he'd heard about Miss Johnson, he'd had no preconceived notions of how she would operate other than that he'd expected to have minimal involvement. It appeared that he'd been mistaken.

"What will dinners and dances show you?"

Her response was instantaneous. "How they treat others as well as you and Emily. I want to see beneath the masks people sometimes wear."

As Emily snickered, Rob turned to stare at her. Perhaps he'd been mistaken, for she appeared perfectly solemn, and yet he was almost certain of what he'd heard.

"Is something wrong, Emily?"

"No, no, Papa. I think Miss Johnson's ideas are good." But the almost imperceptible look she darted at Deborah told Rob he hadn't been mistaken. Something was definitely going on between the two of them, and his daughter had no intention of divulging it. He'd have to ask the matchmaker.

For the remainder of the meal, the three of them discussed the details of the social gatherings Deborah had in mind. Then, when coffee was served, Emily excused herself, leaving Rob alone with the woman whose presence had had such an effect on his daughter.

"I like your approach," he said as he stirred sugar into his coffee. "I want you to know there's no need to spare any expense. All I care about is my daughter's happiness."

"I know, and I agree with you. Emily is a very special young woman. I want to see that she has a husband who'll treat her the way she deserves."

The shadow that crossed Deborah's face was fleeting, yet unmistakable, leaving Rob to wonder what had caused it. He wouldn't ask, for that would be prying, and he was the last person who would pry into someone's private life. But there was one question he couldn't resist asking.

"What was the deal you and my daughter struck?"

"Nothing, really. Just a joke." But the heightened color in her cheeks gave lie to her words.

"Emily didn't act as if it were a joke. What's involved?"

Deborah was silent for a moment, and he could see the indecision on her face. Just when Rob was certain she would refuse to answer, she said, "Emily wants to find me a husband."

A husband! Rob felt as if he'd been blindsided. It was foolish, of course, to feel that way. Deborah Johnson was a lovely, cultured woman. She ought to be married. Why, then, did the idea make him feel as if he'd been punched? That was ridiculous.

Chapter Three

"Deborah! I didn't know you were coming downtown today."

She turned, smiling at both the surprise in Rob's voice and the warmth radiating from his eyes. In the three days that she'd been living in the Ferguson Street mansion, Deborah had shared meals with him, but other than the first evening, they had had no time alone. Instead, she had been fully occupied with Emily. Though that was as it should be, Deborah could not suppress the jolt of pleasure Rob's smile brought.

"Emily is having a fitting with Madame Charlotte," she explained, giving thanks that her voice did not betray her excitement. "They won't need me for at least an hour, so I thought I'd go for a stroll."

She would not tell Rob that she felt the need for a break from his daughter's chatter. Once Emily had decided she could trust Deborah, it had been as if floodgates were opened, and she'd regaled Deborah with tales of the housekeeper's well-meaning but misguided attempts to choose clothing for her.

"It was so awful, even Bradford noticed." Emily had tipped her head to one side, a calculating look in her eye. "You know, Miss Johnson, Bradford is a good man. He might be the one for you."

But he wasn't. Deborah knew that, just as she knew there was no point in telling Emily she had no need for a matchmaker.

She smiled at Rob. "It's too nice a day to remain indoors."

"It is, indeed. May I accompany you?" He bent his arm, waiting for her to put her hand on his forearm.

"But you're working." Though Deborah had known that this particular route would take her past Rob's bank, she hadn't expected him to be outside.

Rob's smile broadened. "One of the advantages of being president of the bank is that I can set my own schedule. The truth is, I was a little hungry, so I thought I'd see what Esther has to offer."

"Esther Hathaway, or rather Esther Snyder?" Though the woman who made some of the most beautiful cakes in Cheyenne had been married for more than half a year, Deborah still had trouble remembering to refer to her by her married name.

"That's the one," Rob agreed. "I've been a loyal customer since she took over the bakery. The woman is a genius with pastries."

As they walked slowly east on Sixteenth Street, Deborah nodded, grateful that the mundane subject helped keep her mind off how good it felt to have her hand on Rob's arm, to be part of a couple, if only for a few minutes. "And her husband is the city's finest painter. Shall we have Jeremy paint Emily's wedding portrait and Esther bake the cake?"

"I didn't realize you were thinking that far ahead. Are you certain you can find the right man for Emily from all those suitors?"

"Not necessarily."

Rob paused and gave Deborah a puzzled look. "Then why are we discussing wedding cakes and portraits? The last time I checked, a groom was an essential part of a wedding."

"That's true, but the right man may not be one of those who've come calling. That's why you hired me, wasn't it? My job is to determine whether any of them would make Emily happy."

"That's correct. It is your job. I don't mean to interfere, but I want you to know that nothing is more important to me than seeing my daughter happily married."

Though his words were matter-of-fact, Deborah sensed a sadness behind them. It was the same sorrow she'd seen flit across his face occasionally, and while she wouldn't probe for its cause, she suspected it was related to his wife's death. Rob must have loved her dearly if he was still mourning her so many years later. Perhaps most men would have remarried, if only to provide a mother for their daughter. The fact that Rob did not was a testimony to the love he'd shared with his wife.

"That's what every father wants for his daughter," she reassured him. "For most girls, and I believe Emily is one of them, marriage is the route to lifelong happiness. Others find happiness in the single life."

He slowed his pace again and turned to face her. "Like you?"

Deborah nodded. "I find great satisfaction in my profession." She wouldn't admit that the longings she'd thought she had buried had resurfaced. Perhaps it was Emily's declaration that Deborah needed a husband. Perhaps it was simply being with Rob and Emily and witnessing their love that made her once again dream of a husband and children. But those were things she wouldn't admit to anyone, especially Rob.

Fortunately, Rob did not question her words, and within a minute they had reached the Mitchell-Hathaway bakery.

As they entered the shop, the proprietor emerged from behind the counter, her increasing girth and slower pace leaving no doubt that she was with child. "It's good to see you both again," Esther Snyder said with her trademark warm smile. "I'd heard you two were working together."

Rob shook his head. "It's Deborah who's working. I'm only paying the bills."

"That's important, too." She gestured toward an empty table, waiting until they were seated before she asked what she could offer them.

When they'd agreed on gingerbread and coffee and Esther's assistant had returned to the kitchen to prepare the food, Rob rose. "Will you excuse me for a moment? I want to see what Jeremy's painting."

Esther took the chair he'd vacated. "The city's buzzing with the news that you're going to find matches for both Carmichaels."

Deborah shook her head. "Once again, the rumors are incorrect. Emily's my client. My only client."

"I was afraid that might be the case, but I was hoping that for once the rumor mill was accurate." The genuine concern coloring Esther's voice was one of the things Deborah admired about her, that she saw her customers as people, not simply a source of revenue. "Rob's a good man. He'll be lonely when Emily marries."

"Lonelier. I suspect he's been lonely for a long time." The sorrow he was still unable to hide told Deborah that while Rob Carmichael did not want for anything material, his life was not completely happy.

Nodding, Esther reached across the table and laid her hand on Deborah's. "You've been lonely, too. Don't deny it. I know the signs, because I was in the same situation. Running the bakery and raising my niece brought me satisfaction, but there was an empty place in my heart. Fortunately, Ecclesiastes is right. There is a season for everything. I thank God each day for bringing Jeremy into my life."

And no one who'd seen them together could doubt that they were meant for each other. They were such an obviously happy couple, each of whom had been given a second chance at love. Was it possible Rob could find happiness a second time? He certainly deserved it. As for herself, Deborah couldn't help wondering if God had a first love in store for her. But she wouldn't think about that now. Her immediate concern was finding a husband—a kind, loving husband—for Emily.

◆　◆　◆

It was late afternoon by the time Deborah and Emily returned to the mansion on Ferguson Street. As Deborah had expected, the fitting had taken a long time, in part because Emily kept being distracted by the bolts of fabric in Madame Charlotte's shop. When Deborah had arrived, the dressmaker had enlisted her assistance in convincing Emily that silver was not a flattering color for her, no matter how fashionable it might be. Though Emily wasn't happy, she had deferred to the older women's judgment and had selected a pale green silk for one of her ball gowns.

Deborah and Emily were walking the three blocks home when the bells from one of the three churches on what the townspeople called Church Corner pealed five times. To Deborah's surprise, Emily flinched, the blood draining from her face as she said, "I didn't realize it was so late."

"There's still plenty of time for us to dress for dinner," Deborah assured her.

"Yes, but. . ."

"But what?"

Emily shook her head. "Nothing." Yet when they entered the house, she did not rush upstairs as Deborah had expected. Instead, she headed toward the morning room, claiming she had left a book there. It made no sense to be searching for a book if she was feeling rushed, but Deborah saw no reason to tell Emily that. The girl was looking frazzled enough without Deborah's gentle chiding.

Instead, Deborah climbed the stairs to her own room, intending to rest for a few minutes before dressing for dinner. As she entered the large room that faced the backyard, she felt a draft from the open window and realized one of the maids must have chosen today to air the room. Though the sun was still shining, the breeze was cold.

Tugging the window down, Deborah glanced at the yard, then stopped when she spotted a woman strolling in the garden. There was no doubt about it. Emily was the woman, and she was walking more slowly than Deborah had ever seen, apparently inspecting each piece of shrubbery. As far as Deborah knew, Emily had no interest in trees or shrubs, and she'd claimed to be in a hurry to reach home. Why, then, was she dallying in the yard?

◆　◆　◆

"So you've approved my loan."

"What?" Rob stared at the man, trying to make sense of his words. Loan. Approval. Of course. That was the reason Cyrus Black was in his office. He'd applied for a substantial loan to expand his restaurant, telling Rob he was certain the presence of the new train depot and capitol building would bring even more business to Cheyenne.

"Yes, we have approved it," he said. "I have the papers ready for you to sign." As he slid a folder from one side of his desk to the center, Rob forced himself to think of nothing but the man in front of him and the loan application.

It was annoying the way his thoughts had wandered the past few days. Though he couldn't understand it, he found himself thinking about Deborah at the oddest times. While he was dressing one morning, he'd wondered whether she would have suggested he wear gold or silver cufflinks. As he'd taken the carriage out of town to meet with a rancher who wanted a loan to acquire more cattle, he'd wondered whether Deborah had ever traveled this road and whether she found the sight of the Snowy Range in the distance as beautiful as he did. Today, when he should have been thinking about nothing other than Cyrus Black's mortgage papers, he'd been remembering the way Emily deferred to Deborah.

Had Deborah noticed that Emily had begun to arrange her hair in the same style she favored? Was she aware that Emily had started putting a single lump of sugar in her tea rather than the three she used to consume? The changes were subtle but unmistakable, at least to Rob, and though he was glad to see his daughter's obvious affection for the matchmaker, he wondered at the reason. Was Emily simply searching for a substitute mother? Would any woman of a certain age have received the same reception, or did she appreciate Deborah for the unique qualities that made her Deborah Johnson?

Rob hoped it was the latter.

Chapter Four

I t was a disaster." Rob's eyes darkened at the memory, and a frown deepened the creases at the corners of his mouth.

Deborah refused to agree. "I wouldn't say that." The two of them were seated in his study, reviewing all that had—and hadn't—happened at the dinner they'd hosted this evening. Unlike the morning room with its feminine elegance and light colors, Rob's study was masculine, featuring mahogany furniture as well as a deep maroon rug. It was a somber room, mirroring its owner's current mood.

"If it wasn't a disaster, what would you call it?"

"A disappointment." Deborah wouldn't minimize that. "I had hoped one of the men we invited to dinner would have been a possible suitor, but it was obvious they were all. . ." She paused, searching for the correct word, finally settling on "unacceptable."

On the surface, the evening might have been deemed a success. The guests all seemed to enjoy the meal, and—with only a few exceptions—the conversation had been pleasant. Deborah had thought she was the only one who'd felt undercurrents, but Rob's blunt assessment told her otherwise.

"I've never seen my daughter so unhappy," he said, settling back in the chair after taking a long swig of his coffee.

The man was even more astute than she'd realized. Not only had he felt the same things she had, but he'd noticed the subtle changes in Emily's demeanor. Deborah hadn't expected that.

"Emily did her best," she said softly. "I doubt any of the guests realized how she felt."

For the first time since they'd entered the small room where he handled all the household affairs, Rob smiled. "She wasn't shy about telling us, was she?"

"Indeed, she was not." As soon as the last guest had left, Emily had turned to Deborah and her father, fisting her hands on her hips as she said, "I won't marry any of them. If you try to make me, I'll run away." Not seeming to notice that her father flinched as if she'd struck him, Emily had continued. "They were awful. Do you hear me? Awful!" And on that note, she'd stormed upstairs.

Deborah met Rob's smile with one of her own. "I wouldn't say the men were all awful, but they were unsuitable."

"Tell me what you found wrong with each of them," he said as he accepted a refill of his coffee cup. Bradford, in his efficient, unobtrusive manner, had appeared with a coffee tray only seconds after Emily had left. Apparently he knew his employer well enough to know that the evening was not over.

Deborah closed her eyes for a second, visualizing the dinner table and its guests, then started with the man she considered the least offensive of the candidates. "Herb Langford was too quiet. Emily would be bored with him."

"I agree. I should have realized that, but every time I saw him, he was with his father. I thought he was simply deferring to him. What about Milt Brendan?"

The answer was easy. "Too self-centered. Did you notice how he tried to turn every conversation to himself and his accomplishments?"

As Rob nodded, a lock of his dark brown hair tumbled over his forehead, giving him a surprisingly boyish look. "Milt became predictable pretty quickly, didn't he?"

They continued their discussion of the men and their failings until Rob said, "That leaves only Frank Fisher. He seemed to be the best of the lot."

Deborah shuddered, remembering the handsome blond man with the cold gray eyes. "He was the worst."

"Really? Why do you say that?" Rob's voice mirrored the surprise she saw in his expression. Apparently he'd been fooled by Frank's genial appearance. Deborah wasn't surprised by that. Most people—men and women—would find Frank charming, but they lacked Deborah's perspective.

"Frank has a cruel streak. Every time someone said something he didn't like, his eyes narrowed. And when Emily smiled at Herb Langford, Frank gripped his knife as if he wanted to throw it at one of them." Taking a deep breath to calm her nerves, Deborah waited a second before she put her fears into words. "Emily wouldn't be safe with him."

"That's a rather strong statement." Rob set his cup back on the desk and shook his head slightly as he looked at Deborah. "I've never heard anything bad about Frank. I wouldn't have let him set foot inside this house if I had."

Deborah wasn't surprised. "Men like that are good at hiding their true nature until it's too late. My job is to make sure that the women I match don't end up with men like Frank." So far, thanks to God's guidance, she had succeeded.

"Is that why you became a matchmaker?" Rob appeared to have accepted her assessment of Frank and was moving on to what he probably thought was a less distressing subject. Little did he know that the two were intricately entwined.

"Yes," she admitted. "Women deserve better husbands than my mother and sister had." She hadn't planned to say that, but the words had popped out, seemingly of their own volition.

Rob was silent for a moment, his eyes solemn as he studied her. At last, he asked, "Do you want to tell me about it?"

Though she started to shake her head, Deborah stopped. It was true she never spoke of her past or the events that had led to her choice of a profession, but she found that she wanted Rob to understand. Somehow, it was important that he know what had made her the woman she was today. That must have been the reason she'd mentioned Ma and Clara.

"It's not a pretty story," she warned him. When he nodded, encouraging her to continue, Deborah said, "I grew up in a house without love." The words were stark, and yet they only hinted at what her childhood had been like. "Our mother pretended that Pa loved us all, but Clara and I knew better." When Rob's eyes lit with a question, Deborah explained that Clara was her older sister.

"We both recognized that Pa had no love to give anyone. I'm still not sure why he married Ma. Maybe it was infatuation. At any rate, his coldness affected us all. Ma withdrew into her shell, and I couldn't wait to escape. Clara wanted marriage, but she said she wouldn't marry a man who didn't love her."

"It sounds as if she did."

Deborah shook her head. "I believe Adam loved her, but it was a strange kind of love. He wanted complete control of her. When she didn't do exactly what he expected, he'd shout at her." Deborah closed her eyes, not wanting to continue, but knowing she couldn't stop now that she'd come this far. "Soon shouting wasn't enough."

When she opened her eyes, Deborah saw the glint of understanding on Rob's face as he picked up his cup. "He hit her?"

"Yes. Each time I saw her, Clara had more bruises than I could count. One time he even broke her arm. I begged her to leave him, but she wouldn't. She said Adam loved her and couldn't live without her." Deborah shook her head again, meeting Rob's gaze as she said, "The days after he hurt her, Adam was always sorry about the bruises and would promise it wouldn't happen again."

"Yet it did."

Deborah nodded. "I was afraid he would kill her, but it turned out that diphtheria did that."

Rob drained his cup then remained silent for a moment while he appeared to be assimilating all that she'd told him. "And now you're alone, with no family."

He made it sound awful, but it wasn't. "There are worse things than being single."

"I know."

The pain that flitted across his face left Deborah with no doubt that Rob was thinking of his wife. Though she wanted to lay her hand on his to comfort him, she did not. Rob was her client, and that meant she needed to be professional in everything she said and did.

"It must have been difficult to lose someone you loved so dearly."

To her astonishment, her words were met with a harsh laugh. "Is that what you thought I meant?"

"Why, yes. The rumor mill says the reason you haven't married again is because you're still mourning your wife."

Rob shook his head, his eyes darkening with emotion. "What I'm mourning is the marriage we could have had if we hadn't been so foolish." When he reached for the coffeepot and poured himself another cup, Deborah suspected Rob was buying time, composing his thoughts, much as she had done earlier.

He took a sip of the coffee then said, "Rachel and I married too young and for the wrong reasons. I was blinded by her beauty." Once again, his laugh was a harsh parody of true mirth. "I thought I was the luckiest man alive when she seemed to favor me. I didn't realize that she didn't want me, just my money. Rachel loved beautiful things, and I was a man who could give them to her."

The reality was so different from what she'd imagined that Deborah felt as if she'd been bludgeoned. She had known Rob was still suffering, but she had been wrong about the reason. Knowing that listening was a form of comfort, Deborah sat silently, waiting for Rob to continue.

"Neither of us was prepared for the reality of marriage," he said. "We both tried, but we failed. Rachel hated being a mother. Fortunately, we had a housekeeper who cared for Emily, leaving Rachel free to visit her friends and buy whatever caught her fancy. She seemed happy for a while, but when she discovered she was expecting a second child, there was no consoling her."

Deep furrows bracketed Rob's mouth as he frowned. "Rachel told me she couldn't bear being married any longer. The next day she ran away." He stared at the wall for a moment before he spoke. "I was frantic. No matter how bad our marriage was, I couldn't bear the thought of her being alone and vulnerable. Luckily, it wasn't hard to find her. I brought Rachel back and did everything I could to make her happy, but it wasn't enough. She was miserable, and so was I."

Rob reached for his cup again, taking a long slug before he finished his story. "And then she died in childbirth, taking our son with her."

"Oh, Rob." Deborah felt her eyes begin to mist, and she blinked furiously to keep the tears from falling. Rob needed comfort, not tears. But what could she say to comfort him other than that she understood why he had no desire to marry again?

"What happened to you and Rachel was tragic," she said as calmly as she could. "But not all marriages are like that."

"I know that," he admitted. "My brain knows that, but my heart is harder to convince. That's why I'm so worried about Emily finding the right man. I can't let her make the same mistakes I did."

"She won't." It might be foolish, and she might regret it in the morning, but Deborah reached out and laid her hand on Rob's, squeezing it as tightly as she could in an effort to show him that he wasn't alone. "She has us," Deborah said. "We'll protect her."

Chapter Five

Deborah's thoughts were still tumultuous when she woke the next morning. Sleep had been late in coming, and when it did, it had been accompanied by dreams that left her both drained and dismayed. Though she could blame her disturbed sleep on the change in her routine, since she had not returned to her own home yesterday, that would be sidestepping the real reason: Rob. Before last night, she had thought she understood the reason for the sorrow he was unable to disguise, but she had been wrong.

Deborah dressed quickly then began to draw a brush through her hair. It was a motion that never failed to soothe her, but this morning it took far longer than normal to feel the expected relief.

The gossips were partly right. Though he might deny it, Rob was mourning his wife. But grief was only part of the equation. The fact that guilt mingled with his grief deepened his emotions and made them more difficult to overcome. Time softened the sharp edges of grief—Deborah knew that from firsthand experience—but it had no such effect on guilt. Instead, the passage of time often intensified guilt. That, Deborah suspected, was what had happened to Rob. Knowing there was no longer any way he could receive Rachel's forgiveness, he refused to forgive himself for his part in their mistake of a marriage, and so even though it had been more than a decade since Rachel's death, he had not been able to put the memories of their marriage behind him.

Deborah winced as the brush caught on a snarl. Rob considered his marriage a mistake. He'd made that clear. But it wasn't a total mistake, for it had given him his daughter. Though her eyes still watered from the pain of the snarl, Deborah began to smile. She had sought a way to help Rob, and she might have found it. She would tell him his marriage and Emily's birth were an example of Romans 8:28. Things had worked for the good.

The thought energized Deborah, driving away the doldrums that had plagued her when she'd first wakened. Glancing at her watch, she nodded. If she hurried, she could talk to Rob before Emily joined them for breakfast.

But when she reached the breakfast room, it was empty. While she waited for him to arrive, Deborah glanced outside, expecting to see nothing more than the carefully tended garden. But this morning the garden was not empty. Instead Emily stood next to a young auburn-haired man, her face more animated than normal as she gazed up at him. Though they were not touching, there was no mistaking the longing on Emily's face. Whoever the man was, he was not a casual acquaintance.

As Deborah watched, the man glanced at the sky, his expression anxious as he shook his head and headed toward the back of the house. Seconds later, Emily entered the breakfast room through the french doors. Though she was humming, she broke off abruptly at the sight of Deborah.

"Oh, Deborah." She sounded breathless, or perhaps it was only that she was startled. "You must be hungry," she said. "Breakfast isn't for another ten minutes."

If she hadn't been so concerned about Emily's apparent rendezvous, Deborah might have smiled at the way the girl had taken the offensive. Though the army wouldn't admit her to its ranks, Emily had the makings of a good general.

Instead of smiling, Deborah gave Emily a stern look. "It seems I'm not the only person who's early. I saw you in the garden."

To Emily's credit, she did not flinch. "Yes. . .well. . .I wanted a breath of fresh air."

As excuses went, it was weak. "And you just happened to meet a young man there. Which one of your suitors disregarded etiquette enough to come calling at this hour?"

"He's not a suitor," Emily insisted, although the faint blush that stained her cheeks gave lie to her words. "He's Noah Chapman. He delivers our batteries."

The timing made sense. Deborah knew that the electric lights that had impressed her on her first visit to this house relied on batteries. The electric company delivered and reconnected those batteries each afternoon before the sun set and lighting was required, then retrieved them the next morning, taking them to the main plant for charging.

It was a simple and yet interesting process, but unless Deborah was mistaken, Emily's interest was not in the batteries but in the young man who delivered them. That could have been why she had been so concerned about being home before dinner the other day.

"I see." What Deborah saw was that there was more to this story than Emily was admitting. Though her flushed face and sparkling eyes might have been the result of the cool morning air, Deborah suspected that was not the case. She wouldn't pressure Emily—not today, at any rate. The girl deserved a few minutes of respite, especially after the less than pleasant evening she had had with her would-be suitors. Besides, the meeting with Noah could have been innocent. Deborah wouldn't say anything more, but she would keep a sharper eye on Emily.

"Your hair is a little mussed," she told the girl. "You might want to fix it so your father doesn't ask why you were outside." And that would give Deborah the time alone with Rob that she sought.

Emily flashed her a grateful smile. "Thank you."

She'd been gone only a few seconds when Rob entered the breakfast room. Knowing she'd have a couple of minutes before Emily returned, Deborah greeted him, then said, "There's something I want to talk to you about."

When his eyes registered concern, she assured him it was nothing bad, and then as Deborah explained the ideas that had come to her this morning, Rob's expression changed. His eyes cleared, and a smile lifted the corners of his mouth.

"You're right," he said when she'd finished speaking. "I never thought of it in those terms, but whatever mistakes Rachel and I made, Emily was not one. She was a gift from God."

Rob took a step toward Deborah, extending his hand as if to touch her, then apparently reconsidered, for he dropped it to his side. But though he remained the approved distance from her, his voice was warm as he said, "Thank you. What would I do without you?"

◆ ◆ ◆

Rob stared at the newspaper in front of him, realizing he'd looked at the same article for at least five minutes without a single word registering. Instead, his thoughts continued to whirl. Without a doubt, this had been the best Sunday he could remember. It had started with Deborah's reminding him that his marriage had not been a failure. He'd known he'd been carrying a heavy burden of remorse, but he hadn't realized just how heavy that burden was until her simple words had lifted it.

Feeling freer than he had since the day he learned why Rachel had married him, he'd entered the church, ready to give thanks to his Lord for turning bad into good. What he hadn't expected was a sermon that seemed tailor-made for him. As if the minister knew his heart, he spoke of forgiveness and pointed out that sometimes the most difficult—and the most important—task was to forgive oneself. When the service ended, Rob had felt as if his spirit had been renewed. He would always regret that he'd been unable to make Rachel happy, but the feeling of guilt was gone. He had done his best. God knew that, and now Rob did, too.

He folded the newspaper, recognizing the futility of even trying to read. Today had been a good day, a very good day, and it wasn't over. In half an hour, he and Deborah would go for a stroll in City Park. The sun was shining, and the perpetual Wyoming wind had turned into little more than a gentle breeze. It was the perfect afternoon for a walk with the woman who'd become such an important part of his life.

"Can I talk to you, Papa?" Emily entered his study, a tentative expression on her face.

Rob rose and gestured her toward a chair. Though she'd been her usual cheerful self at lunch, now she looked as if something was bothering her. "Of course. Have you changed your mind and decided to go to the park with us?"

"No." She wrinkled her nose. "Have you forgotten that two of our guests invited me to walk in the park and I refused? I can't go, even with you and Miss Johnson. That would be rude."

And, no matter how much she disliked the would-be suitors, Rob's daughter would not be rude. "Fine. So, what's on your mind?"

"You. I'm worried about you."

Rob suspected he knew where this conversation was headed. Though she hadn't broached the subject since Deborah had arrived, Emily had a familiar look in her eye.

"What troubles you today?" It was ironic that Emily had chosen this day to speak of her worries when Rob's had been eased.

His daughter pursed her lips. "The same thing that always bothers me. I don't know what you'll do when I marry. I hate the idea of you spending the rest of your life alone."

Rob wouldn't tell her that he'd had similar thoughts, fearing the loneliness once Emily had her own home. He would do nothing—absolutely nothing—to discourage her from marrying and having a family of her own.

"I'll miss you, Emily. Of course I will, but your marrying and moving away is a natural part of life."

Her expression turned defiant. "That may be so, but you don't have to be alone. You could marry again." Fixing her gaze on him, Emily added, "I think you should."

Marry again? It was a thought he'd rejected each time she had raised it, and yet as his daughter's words registered, an image of Deborah seated across the breakfast table from him floated through his brain. Was his daughter right?

◆　◆　◆

"Are you all alone today?" Esther asked as Deborah entered the bakery and looked for an empty table.

Deborah nodded. "Emily's visiting a friend, so I thought I'd take advantage of the free time to have a piece of gingerbread. No one in Cheyenne makes gingerbread as good as yours."

"I appreciate the compliment, but it wasn't Emily I thought might be with you," Esther said as she poured a cup of coffee for Deborah. "I hear you and Rob have been spending a lot of time together."

Deborah took a sip of the steaming beverage as she composed her thoughts. "Of course we have. We're trying to find a husband for Emily."

"And that involved walking through the park on Sunday." Esther seasoned her words with mild sarcasm. "I thought that was your day off."

"Normally it is, but this week was different. We hosted a dinner Saturday night, so I stayed at the mansion."

That didn't explain the afternoon walk. Deborah could easily have returned to her home, but when Rob had suggested visiting City Park, she hadn't hesitated to accept. The time they'd spent together had been wonderful. They'd walked for close to an hour, exploring each of the paths that crisscrossed the park, talking about everything and nothing. And while they'd walked, Deborah couldn't help noticing that Rob seemed different. She couldn't pinpoint the difference other than to say that he appeared happy. Deborah hoped that meant he was accepting the reality of his marriage and that he'd done the best he could.

"I see." Esther's words reminded Deborah that she'd said exactly the same thing to Emily yesterday morning. She only hoped Esther hadn't seen as far beneath the surface as she had.

"You've been good for my business," Esther continued. "It seems as if half of Cheyenne has come in, wondering whether I'd seen you and could confirm the rumor."

"What rumor?" Deborah wasn't sure she wanted to know the answer, but she had to ask.

"That the matchmaker has been matched. The grapevine is speculating that you and Rob will marry by the end of the year."

It was as Deborah had feared. The fact that she, a single woman, was seen in the company of one of the city's most eligible men was bound to raise speculation. There was only one thing to do: deny it.

"You can assure anyone who asks that that won't happen." She took another bite of gingerbread, savoring the rich blend of flavors. "You don't need to share this with anyone, but the truth is Rob was too badly hurt by his marriage to consider another." All Deborah could hope was that he'd find peace.

"What about you? If he asked, would you consider marrying him?"

Would she? The time she had spent with Rob had shown her that he was a good, honorable man, a man who loved his daughter, a man who would never hurt a woman, a man who made Deborah's spirits soar simply by smiling at her. As a frisson of excitement at the thought of spending the rest of her life with such a man made its way through her veins, she nodded.

Chapter Six

Rob looked around the room, trying not to let his annoyance show. The furniture had been moved out to provide space for dancing. Deborah had hired the best musicians in Cheyenne. The food had been excellent. The guests all looked as if they were having a good time. He ought to be satisfied, and yet he wasn't.

Thanks to Deborah, he had watched each of Emily's would-be suitors carefully and had seen beneath the veneer. Though they appeared to be polished, successful men—the kind of men who would be good husbands for Emily—he'd seen the way they'd looked at her. It was as if she were a horse or an expensive painting, something they wanted to acquire. That wasn't what he intended for his daughter. Emily deserved better. She deserved a man who loved her, who valued her for herself, not the fortune she would one day inherit. Though he wished it were otherwise, not one of tonight's guests had treated her that way.

If only the evening were over. Unfortunately, there was still more to be endured. Somehow he had to get through another hour of dancing before dessert was served. Only when the guests had eaten their fill of Esther's cakes and pies would they begin to leave.

Rob knew his duties as a host: keep smiling, keep pretending he was enjoying the evening. In truth, all he wanted to do was usher the men who now seemed like intruders rather than honored guests out of his home, telling them there was no way he would consider letting one of them court much less marry Emily. Less than two more hours to continue the charade. He could do it. He *would* do it for Emily's sake.

As his gaze reached the far corner of the room, a genuine smile crossed Rob's face. For once, Deborah wasn't engaged in a conversation with anyone, and that sparked an idea that turned his smile into a grin. It might not be proper etiquette. Rob wasn't certain, but he also didn't care. After all, this was his home, his party. As quickly as he could, he made his way across the room.

"May I have this dance, Miss Johnson?" he asked when he reached her.

The raised eyebrow followed by a smile told him Deborah was surprised by the invitation but would not refuse. "It would be my pleasure, Mr. Carmichael." She mirrored his formality.

As the music began, Rob drew her into his arms, savoring the sweet scent of her perfume and the warmth of her hand in his. It took a few seconds to adjust to having such a tiny woman in his arms. Though they'd walked together, her hand on his arm, this was different. As they moved to the strains of a Strauss waltz, he soon forgot everything except how good it felt to have Deborah so close to him. Her nearness brought him a sense of comfort, a sense of homecoming, sweeping away the anger and annoyance that had plagued him all evening.

Dimly, he became aware that others were talking and realized he was supposed to carry on a conversation with his partner, not simply move around the ballroom, relishing the sensation of having this wonderful woman in his arms.

"This was a good idea." It wasn't much of a conversational gambit, but it was all Rob could manage. Inexplicably, he was as tongue-tied as a boy who'd finally mustered the courage to talk to the prettiest girl at school, only to discover that he couldn't force a single word past his vocal chords.

"I'm surprised to hear you say that. Earlier, you looked as if you couldn't wait for the guests to leave." Deborah, it seemed, did not suffer from the same malady he did, for she had no trouble expressing herself.

Though Rob had been referring to dancing with her when he'd mentioned the good idea, Deborah's thoughts had moved in a different direction. He decided to follow her lead.

"I hadn't realized my feelings were so obvious," Rob admitted. "The more I watched the men with Emily, the more I could see how wrong they were for her. I just wanted them gone." As he guided Deborah across the ballroom floor, he smiled. "Once again, your method of evaluating suitors has proven effective. In one evening, I've eliminated another six." His smile faded. "I'm worried, though. There are only four more who've approached me. What happens if none of them are suitable?"

She shrugged as if it were of no account. "That's when I really earn my fee. At that point, I start looking for men who would be good for Emily. That's how I usually work."

Rob nodded. "If anyone can find the right husband for my daughter, it's you." His momentary uneasiness disappeared as he thought of all that Deborah had accomplished so far. "I trust you."

As the words emerged from his mouth, Rob was struck by the magnitude of his admission. It was true that he trusted men at the bank, but that was business. This was different. Until tonight he had believed that Rachel had destroyed his ability to trust anyone with what was dearest to him. He had never intended to give Deborah carte blanche with Emily's future, but now... Now he knew he would trust her with his own life and what was even more precious to him: his daughter's.

Deborah was not like Rachel. She was a woman of great integrity, a woman who could and would lavish love on those fortunate enough to have won her heart. She was a one-in-a-million woman.

◆　◆　◆

Deborah took a deep breath as she opened the french doors and walked into the garden. The last guest had left, Emily had gone upstairs, and Rob. . . Deborah wasn't certain where Rob had gone, perhaps to his office. All she knew was that she needed to get out of the house for a few minutes.

While the night air was cool, it felt good after the warmth of the house. Perhaps it would allow her to understand what had happened, why she had been so overheated. It was true that having all those people in one room had raised the temperature, but that was nothing compared to what had happened during the dance she'd shared with Rob.

It had felt so good to be in his arms, gliding around the floor as if they'd done it before and would do it again. That had been good, but what had sent heat rushing through her veins was his expression when he'd told her he trusted her. Though he'd been speaking of Deborah's matchmaking abilities, the tender look he'd given her had made her believe he meant something very different. For the first time, Deborah felt as if Rob was seeing her as more than a matchmaker, more even than a friend. That had felt so good and yet. . .

Before she could complete the thought, Deborah heard footsteps on the stone path behind her. The footsteps were heavy, leaving no doubt of who was approaching. As her pulse began to race, Deborah took a deep breath, trying to calm herself.

"There you are," Rob said as she turned to face him. "I wondered where you'd gone."

"I wanted a bit of fresh air." Somehow, the excuse sounded lame, and Deborah hoped he wouldn't guess that she'd come here to sort out her feelings for him. There were times when he was almost too perceptive. She could only hope this was not one of them.

Rob took a few more steps forward, coming so close she could almost feel the heat radiating from him. "Isn't it too cold? You should have brought a shawl."

"I'm fine." Just having him this near was raising her temperature again.

In the moonlight, she could see the doubt in his eyes. "If you're sure, let's walk for a minute. There's something I want to show you."

He reached out and took her hand in his, its warmth sending shivers up her arm as he laced his fingers with hers. This wasn't the way they normally walked, with her hand nestled on the crook of his arm. This was more intimate, as if they were courting. Deborah hoped Rob did not feel the way her pulse continued to race as they strolled toward the back of the yard.

"Have you seen the gazing ball?" His voice was as calm as ever, telling Deborah he was not affected by their clasped hands. And yet, he'd been the one who had reached for her.

"Only once," Deborah admitted, remembering how it stood flanked by two benches. "Emily gave me a tour of the garden one morning." She wouldn't tell Rob that she suspected Emily had been looking for Noah, the battery man, as she'd escorted Deborah around the backyard.

"It looks different at night," Rob said, "especially with a full moon."

Deborah didn't doubt that. Everything seemed different to her tonight, but she couldn't credit the moon for that difference. It was being with Rob, having her hand in his, walking so close to him that she could smell the faint aroma of the coffee he'd drunk that made tonight a night unlike any other.

When they reached the gazing ball, Deborah drew in a deep breath. As Rob had said, it looked very different than it had during daylight. The moon reflected off the shiny surface, leaving the features of what she'd always called the man in the moon slightly distorted by the ball's shape yet still clearly distinguishable.

"It's beautiful," she said softly, not wanting to disturb the peaceful moment.

"So are you." Rob dropped her hand, leaving Deborah feeling momentarily bereft. A second later, her pulse began to soar as he slipped his arms around her shoulders and drew her closer. For a moment, he did nothing but gaze into her eyes, his lips curving into a smile. And then, ever so slowly, he lowered his head and pressed his lips to hers.

Chapter Seven

Deborah's heart began to race, and the shivers of delight that made their way down her spine were so intense she wondered if she was going to faint. She had read about kisses, dreamt about them, but nothing she had read or imagined could compare to the reality. Being held in Rob's arms, feeling his lips on hers, was more wonderful than she had thought possible. While they were so close, Deborah felt special, she felt cherished, she felt loved. And that was something she had never expected.

Afterward, she wasn't certain how long the kiss lasted. All she knew was that she did not want it to end. But it did. A minute, an hour, an eternity later, Rob broke the kiss and took a step backward, his lips curving into the sweetest of smiles.

"There's so much I want to say," he told her as he took her arm and led her toward the house, "but it's late. We'll talk tomorrow."

When they were once more inside, he pressed another kiss on her lips, then smiled again as she began to climb the stairs. Her heart lighter than she could ever recall, Deborah returned the smile. Without a doubt, this had been the most wonderful day of her life.

When she woke the next morning, she realized that she was still smiling. Had she smiled all night? Perhaps. She closed her eyes for a second, recalling the way the evening had ended. What a special time that had been! It wasn't simply the kiss, although that had been extraordinary. What had made the time so memorable was Rob himself.

He had been angry last night. Deborah had seen the signs. But unlike her brother-in-law, he had not vented his anger on anyone. He'd treated the would-be suitors with more courtesy than they deserved, never stepping out of his role as the perfect host, his restraint telling Deborah he was a man no woman need ever fear. Rob was kind and loving, a man she could trust. A man she could—and did—love. And, unless she was mistaken, today would be the day they admitted their love to each other.

"Only two places?" she asked when she entered the dining room half an hour later.

Bradford nodded. "Just you and Miss Emily. There was a problem at the bank. Mr. Carmichael asked me to tell you he wasn't sure when he'd be back."

The disappointment that swept through her startled Deborah by its intensity. She'd literally been counting the minutes until she saw Rob again, and now their meeting would be delayed. Giving herself a mental shake, Deborah reminded herself that she and Rob had the rest of their lives in front of them. A few hours would make no difference in the way they felt. But, despite the reminder, she could not shake off her disappointment. She wanted—oh, how she wanted—to see Rob again and recapture the wonder of last night. But that was not to be.

Pasting a smile on her face, Deborah greeted Emily as the girl entered the breakfast room. No matter how she felt, Deborah would not inflict her mood on Emily. But it seemed as if Emily was in a world of her own. The meal was quieter than normal, not only because of Rob's absence but also because Emily appeared preoccupied.

"Would you like to go for a drive today?" Deborah asked as she buttered a piece of toast. "It looks as if it'll be another sunny day." Not only had Emily mentioned that she enjoyed riding outside the city limits, that she found the rolling prairie beautiful, but getting away might make the time pass more quickly for Deborah.

"No." The answer was brusque, even for Emily.

"Then perhaps we should go to Minnehaha Park. We could rent a boat and explore the lagoons." Cheyenne's newest park, built on the eastern side of the city, featured a lake and lagoons that were popular destinations for the residents.

Emily shook her head. "I'd rather stay home. I have a new book to read."

"All right." Though Deborah doubted Emily intended to read, she wouldn't argue. That would accomplish little.

Half an hour later, she heard footsteps on the stairs and the sound of a door opening. It wasn't spying, Deborah told herself as she drew back the draperies in the morning room. Watching over Emily was part of her job. And watch she did as the girl rushed toward Noah Chapman, then wrapped her arms around him. There was a moment of hesitation before he drew her closer, but as Deborah watched, the young man lowered his lips to Emily's.

Another couple. Another kiss in the garden. Remembering how wonderful it had felt to be in Rob's arms, Deborah hated to interrupt them, and yet she knew she must.

"Will you introduce me to your friend, Emily?" she asked a minute later as she entered the garden.

The couple broke apart. Though Noah appeared embarrassed to have been caught kissing Emily, her expression radiated defiance.

"This is Noah Chapman," she announced. "He's the man I love and want to marry." Though her words were firm, her face softened as she turned toward him. "Noah, this is Miss Johnson. She's probably going to tell you we can't marry."

Deborah shook her head. "It's not my place to make that decision. Only your father can give or withhold permission."

"And he'll say no. I know he will." Emily's bravado began to crumble, and in that moment Deborah saw the vulnerable girl she'd once been. "He won't understand that Noah is the only one for me."

Before Deborah could reply, Noah took a step toward her. The lips that had been pressed against Emily's were now straight, as if he was trying to control his emotions. "I know my job isn't as important as Emily's father's."

Deborah could only imagine how painful it must be for a young man to admit that. "I wouldn't say it was less important," she told him. "It's simply different. The people of Cheyenne need electricity just as much as they do loans from the bank."

Noah didn't appear convinced. "I know I can't give Emily the luxuries she's used to."

When he gave her a look so filled with longing that it wrenched Deborah's heart, Emily clasped Noah's hand in hers. "I don't need luxuries. All I need is you."

It was time to inject some practicality into the discussion. "It's not easy to live without servants when you're used to them," Deborah cautioned Emily.

The girl shook her head. "I can learn to cook and keep the house clean. I'd be happy to do that if it meant I could be Noah's wife. What good are servants if I'm married to a man who doesn't love me?"

Deborah shifted her gaze from Emily to Noah. While Emily had declared her love for him multiple times, the young man had not pronounced the word.

"Do you love her?" Deborah asked him.

He nodded vigorously, and his lips curved into a smile. "Yes, I do, Miss Johnson. I love Emily, and I'll do everything I can to make her happy."

There was no mistaking the sincerity in his eyes. With instincts honed by more than a decade as a matchmaker, Deborah knew this couple was meant for each other. Though on the surface they might appear to be mismatched, the love they shared was strong enough to carry them through the inevitable problems they would face.

Deborah knew that, but she also knew Rob would be unlikely to give them his blessing. He wanted his daughter to marry someone of the same social standing, a man who could give her the kind of life she had always known. It would take every bit of persuasion Deborah possessed to convince Rob that Noah was the only man who could give Emily something far more valuable than material possessions.

"I'll talk to your father." Deborah wished she could assure Emily and Noah that she would be successful, but she had no such assurances to give.

That didn't seem to bother Emily. Dropping Noah's hand, she rushed to Deborah's side and hugged her. "Thank you, thank you, thank you. If anyone can convince Papa, it's you."

◆　◆　◆

Rob tried not to frown. Today had not turned out the way he'd expected. He'd been so caught up in thoughts of Deborah and the kisses they'd shared that he'd had trouble getting to sleep last night. He hadn't planned the kiss. Indeed, he had not. But the combination of the moonlight and being so close to her had been more than he could resist. She'd been like a magnet, drawing him ever closer. And then when he'd touched his lips to hers, he'd been filled with a sense of rightness. In that moment, he'd known what he wanted the rest of his life to hold—days and nights with Deborah.

He'd spent most of the night trying to find the right words to tell her how much she meant to him, how much he cared for her, and by the time he finally fell into a restless sleep, he believed he'd found them. He would take her aside after breakfast, opening his heart to her and praying that he hadn't been mistaken, that she did indeed care for him the way he did for her.

That plan had been derailed when Bradford woke him with the news of an attempted robbery at the bank. Two men had broken in and were trying to open the vault when the night watchman discovered them. Though the robbery had been foiled, as the bank's president, Rob was the one who had to file charges against the men.

It had been an unpleasant way to begin the day, and unfortunately that had been only the start of what seemed like more than the normal number of problems. All of that had left Rob feeling both disgruntled and disappointed. Now he had to tell Henry Clay that his loan had been declined.

"What do you mean not approved?" the burly man demanded. "You told me you didn't think there'd be a problem."

As his customer's fists clenched, Rob tried to soothe him. "That's true," he admitted, choosing not to tell Henry that the misrepresentations he'd made on his loan application were one reason it had been denied. "I didn't expect a problem, but when our auditors checked your records, they learned you're behind with payments to all your suppliers. I'm sorry, Henry, but the bank can't take the risk."

Henry's response was immediate. His face turned red with anger and he leaned forward, shaking his finger at Rob. "You're a fine one to talk about not taking a risk. You're risking everything you own with that matchmaker in your house. The way I figure it, she's angling for a wedding ring. Once she gets it, she's gonna spend every penny you've got. Women like her are after only one thing: money. You're a fool if you let her get away with it."

As Henry finished his diatribe, Rob felt blood rush to his head. The man was wrong. Completely wrong. But a man like Henry Clay didn't understand words. He only understood force. Though Rob wanted nothing more than to plant his fist on Henry's face and demand that he retract his accusations, he knew he couldn't do that. He was the bank's president, an esteemed member of Cheyenne society. He couldn't simply slug a customer, no matter how much that customer provoked him.

Instead he rose and gestured toward the door. "This meeting is over, and if you can't keep a civil tongue in your mouth where Miss Johnson is concerned, the bank does not need your business."

As Henry stormed out of the bank, muttering curses under his breath, Rob wondered what else would go wrong today. He pulled out his watch and nodded when he realized it was almost time to leave. Once he was back home, everything would be fine. Of course it would.

◆ ◆ ◆

"What do you mean, you think he's the right man for Emily?"

Deborah stared at Rob, shocked by the vehemence of his reaction. She hadn't expected him to be happy when she explained about Noah, but she'd thought they could have a civil conversation. Instead, Rob's face had turned red, and his eyes blazed with anger. He looked like. . . She broke off the unwelcome thought. Rob wasn't like her sister's husband. He was kind, caring and reasonable.

"You hired me to find a husband for Emily," she said as calmly as she could. "We both agreed that she deserved a man who would love her and treat her well. I believe Noah Chapman is that man."

Rob shook his head and continued pacing around his study. Though Deborah remained seated in the hope that he'd calm down and take a seat near her, he strode from one side of the room to the other, his posture leaving no doubt of his anger.

"He's a battery boy," Rob said, emphasizing the final word. "My daughter will not marry a battery boy."

"Then I won't marry anyone at all."

Deborah swiveled her head at the sound of Emily's voice. The last time she'd seen the young woman, she'd been upstairs.

"What are you doing here?" Rob demanded. "This is between Deborah and me."

Emily marched into the room, her posture mirroring her father's. "It's my future you're discussing. You have no right to make decisions about it without me."

Coming to a stop in front of his daughter, Rob took a deep breath, his rapid exhalation leaving no doubt of his frustration. "You're too young to know what's best for you," he told her.

Though customers might have cringed at his tone, Emily did not. "How can you say that when you were younger than me when you married?"

As Rob blanched, Deborah knew that Emily had unwittingly hit a raw nerve. "We're not talking about me," he said firmly. "We're talking about you. I won't let you ruin your life."

Though Deborah wanted to intercede, she knew that would accomplish nothing. Rob needed to listen to his daughter. Feeling at a disadvantage being seated when the others were standing, she rose and took a step toward Emily, wanting to be close enough to comfort her if needed.

"How could I ruin my life by marrying the man I love?" Emily demanded.

"He's only interested in your money."

Emily shook her head. "That's not true. Noah loves me—*me*, not your money."

As Rob glared at his daughter, Deborah knew it was time for her to speak. "Noah is a hardworking young man who's well respected by his customers and his employer." Deborah knew, because she'd spent most of the day investigating Noah and learning what she could about his reputation.

Though Emily appeared grateful, Rob was not convinced. "That doesn't make him the right man for my daughter."

He turned toward Emily, his voice as cold as steel, though his eyes were filled with fury. "I will not let you waste your life. You may think you love him, but you don't. This is nothing more than infatuation."

As he spat the final word, Deborah knew he was remembering his feelings for Rachel and assuming that Emily's were as shallow. Somehow she needed to convince him he was wrong, but before she could speak, Rob continued.

"I forbid you to ever see that boy again." As if anticipating Emily's reaction, he added, "To make sure that you don't try to defy me, I'm going to see that he leaves Cheyenne. There is no place for Noah Chapman in this city."

For a second, Deborah was speechless. Though she knew Rob was angry at the thought of someone he considered unworthy of his daughter wanting to marry her, this reaction was extreme. The Rob she knew, the Rob she loved, would not have done that. But the Rob Deborah knew had never looked like this, his face set in lines of cold fury. Had she been wrong to believe he was a man she could trust? Was he like Adam, wearing a mask in public but revealing his true self in private? Which was the real Rob?

As Deborah struggled to find the words to convince him to reconsider his actions, Emily pounded her fists on the desk.

"I hate you!" She punctuated the words with another blow to the desk. "If you send Noah away, I'll never forgive you."

When Emily started to storm out of the room, Deborah hurried to her side and put an arm around her. Turning back to Rob, she said, "I suggest we all take some time to calm down."

Rob's lips were tight with anger. "Time isn't going to change anything." He looked around the room. "Where's my hat?"

There was only one reason he'd need a hat, and Deborah didn't like it. "Where are you going?"

"To ensure that the battery boy stays out of my daughter's life."

Chapter Eight

Deborah stared at the door, feeling as if every hope she had cherished had been destroyed by Rob's exit. The slamming of the door had shattered her hopes as surely as a hammer shattered glass, leaving nothing but shards with edges so sharp they could slice a finger or a tender heart.

She had her answer, and it hurt more than anything she had ever experienced. When he'd stormed out the door, determined to ruin Noah Chapman's prospects of a life in Cheyenne, Rob had shown his true self. The kind, caring man Deborah had believed she loved was only a mask. The man who'd bellowed at his daughter was the real Rob.

"I hate him!" Tears streamed down Emily's face. "I thought he loved me, but he doesn't. If he loved me, he'd understand how much Noah and I love each other."

Though she wanted nothing more than to leave this house and never again see the man who'd destroyed her illusions, Deborah could not desert Emily. The girl needed her, perhaps more than she ever had. Somehow Deborah had to find the words to comfort her, though her own heart had been splintered.

"Your father loves you," she said as she tightened her grip on Emily's shoulders. "Never doubt that."

"Then why was he so angry?" Emily's eyes were filled with a mixture of pain and confusion. "I've never seen him like that."

Nor had Deborah. Rob had never exhibited the telltale signs of anger just waiting to erupt. That was part of the reason why his behavior today had been so shocking. Something had triggered the explosion, and Deborah suspected she knew what it was.

She fixed her gaze on Emily as she struggled for the right words. Emily needed to understand why her father might have reacted as he did, but Deborah could neither betray Rob's confidence nor destroy Emily's belief that her parents' marriage had been happy.

Taking a deep breath, she prayed for guidance. "I think he's afraid you're making a mistake. Your father only wants you to be happy." Deborah had no doubt of that.

Emily brushed the tears from her cheeks, her eyes still wary. "I *would* be happy if I married Noah. He's better than all those other men combined."

Though Deborah agreed, now was not the time to say that. "Unfortunately, your father doesn't know him." And that was the problem. Rob had been so angry that he'd refused to even consider meeting the young man who'd captured his daughter's heart.

"And now he never will. He's going to run Noah out of town." This time as tears began to stream down Emily's face she made no attempt to staunch them. "I'll never see Noah again. Oh, Miss Johnson, what am I going to do?"

Wishing she had an answer but knowing she did not, Deborah led Emily upstairs and persuaded her to lie down. Though it was too early for bed, perhaps a nap would soothe her. When the girl fell asleep, Deborah rose, torn between what she wanted to do and what she knew she should do. Though the thought of remaining here and facing Rob again made her shudder, she could not abandon Emily.

As she entered her room, Deborah realized she needed to follow her own advice and take some time to calm down. She needed time to think. More than that, she needed time to pray. And that would be best done at home. Quickly, she wrote notes for both Emily and Rob, then descended the stairs. She would not return until she knew what God wanted her to do.

◆　◆　◆

Rob strode down Ferguson Street. He could have taken a carriage—perhaps he should have—but he needed to vent his anger, and pounding his feet against the street might do that. A battery boy! If the situation hadn't been so serious, he might have found the thought ludicrous. But there was nothing even remotely amusing about the idea of his daughter being caught in the snares of a man who was like Rachel. Rob knew his type. This Noah Chapman had no genuine feelings for Emily. He only wanted what she could give him.

As he felt his anger rise, Rob took a deep breath, trying to tamp down his fury. Soon he'd meet the boy, and when he did, he'd ensure that his daughter did not make a monumental mistake. Though he had found himself trapped in a loveless marriage, that was not going to happen to Emily.

He was her father. It was his job to protect her, and he would. He couldn't let Emily ruin the rest of her life. He *wouldn't* let her do that. He would take care of the Noah Chapman problem, and then. . . Rob clenched his fists as he realized that he had no idea how to end the sentence.

And then the bells began to chime. Rob's footsteps faltered. He'd reached the corner of Ferguson and Eighteen Streets, what residents called Church Corner. It was a corner he'd passed countless times, just as he'd heard the bells hundreds, perhaps thousands of times. There was no reason to stop, and yet something about the pealing made him pause.

Rob's glance moved from one church to the other, and as it did, he noticed that the door of one was open. It wasn't the church he usually attended. There was no reason to linger, no reason to have even noticed it, but the sight of that open door beckoned him as surely as if a hand were reaching out to him, drawing him closer. That was ridiculous. He had no intention of going inside a strange church. Of course he didn't.

Rob stood motionless as the bells fell silent. And then, compelled by a force greater than himself, he walked toward the open door.

◆　◆　◆

Deborah took another sip of tea, savoring the aroma of chamomile. Though it rarely failed to soothe her, today it did nothing to calm her turbulent thoughts. Was she wrong? She had spent an hour in prayer. At first nothing had relieved the turmoil deep inside her, but gradually the agitation that had made her heart ache had faded and she'd felt peace begin to invade her spirit. Though the peace was welcome, it brought with it the question of whether she had overreacted to Rob's anger.

Yes, he'd been angry, but knowing what she did about his past, Deborah could understand why he'd responded the way he did to the idea of Emily marrying Noah. Yes, she'd seen fury in his eyes, and his expression had been as hard as stone, but unlike Adam, he had not vented that anger physically, other than slamming the door. A door was an inanimate object; it could not be hurt the way a woman's soft flesh could. No matter how angry he'd been, Rob had done nothing to threaten either Deborah or Emily.

Perhaps she had been wrong in believing he was like her brother-in-law. Everyone had moments of anger. It was how they handled it that mattered.

Deborah took another sip of tea as she reflected on all that had happened today. She had focused on Rob's anger, but the truth was, she had been angry, too. She had dealt with her anger by fleeing. At the time, she had believed that was the best response, but what if she was wrong? Perhaps she should have stayed and tried to make Rob understand why she believed Noah was the right man for his daughter. Perhaps she should have. . .

Before Deborah could complete the thought, a knock on the door interrupted her thoughts. Though she hadn't been expecting anyone, her address was no secret. She rose and opened the door, her heart clenching when she saw a tearstained Emily standing outside. In that moment, Emily looked so much like Clara had after Adam had hit her that Deborah's worst fears were revived. What had Rob done?

"What's wrong? Did he. . . ?" She couldn't pronounce the words.

Her lips twisted with grief, Emily bit her bottom lip. "He wouldn't listen to me. I told him I didn't care what Papa said. I begged him to elope with me, but he refused."

The relief that surged through Deborah left her knees ready to buckle. It was Noah, not Rob, who was responsible for Emily's distress. *Thank You, God.* She offered a silent prayer of gratitude.

"Come in," Deborah said, drawing Emily into her apartment. She gestured toward one of the chairs. "Sit down. Let me get you a cup of tea."

Emily shook her head. "I don't want tea. I want Noah." Her lips were set in the stubborn expression Deborah had seen when Emily's wants were thwarted. "I love him, but he says he can't go against Papa's wishes." She stretched out her hands, beseeching Deborah to help her. "Oh, Miss Johnson, what am I going to do?"

Chapter Nine

Something was wrong. It was true that Rob felt different, but he hadn't expected that the house would, too.

He'd lost track of time when he'd been inside the church. When he'd first stepped into the sanctuary, his only thought had been that he needed to overcome his anger. It had been more difficult than he'd imagined. At first he'd felt as if he were being torn apart by a force he could not identify. The pastor might have called the force Satan. Rob wouldn't dispute that, for he knew that whatever the force was, it was evil. He also knew that the anger he'd unleashed on Emily and Deborah had been wrong. Though he'd experienced anger more times than he could count, Rob had never lashed out like that. That had been wrong, oh so wrong.

Rob had hung his head in shame, begging for forgiveness. Gradually as he'd prayed for strength, he'd felt the anger subside. In its place had come the conviction that he had to undo the damage he'd done. Instead of continuing downtown to confront Noah Chapman, Rob had returned to the house that now felt empty.

When he'd come through the front door, Bradford had greeted him normally. It was only when he'd given his hat to the butler that Rob had sensed that something was awry. "Where is. . . ?" He broke off the question when he realized that Bradford had returned to the servants' quarters. Though he could call him back, there was little to be gained by that. Rob would soon discover whatever was causing his discomfort.

As he entered his study, his eye was drawn to the envelope placed in the middle of his desk. It hadn't been there when he'd left, of that he was certain. Slipping the sheet of paper from the envelope, Rob frowned. There was no salutation, just blunt words.

I need time to think, Deborah had written. *I cannot do that here, and so I have returned to my home. I do not know when or whether I will reside in your home again, but I assure you I will do everything I can to meet the other terms of our agreement.*

Rob's frown deepened at the realization of what he'd done. He'd driven Deborah away. As he'd knelt in the church, he'd known that he'd hurt both her and Emily, but he hadn't realized the full magnitude of what he'd done. His anger must have reminded Deborah of her brother-in-law and how that man's fury had escalated into cruelty toward her sister.

No wonder Deborah no longer wanted to share a house with him. Rob couldn't blame her. His reaction had been extreme. He knew that, just as he knew he needed to apologize and hope she would forgive him. But first he needed to make things right with Emily. He'd hurt her, too.

Less than a minute later, he stood in front of his daughter's bedroom door and knocked. There was no answer. Though it was still relatively early, Emily might be asleep. Not wanting to disturb her but needing to know that everything was all right, he opened the door. The room was empty.

"Bradford," Rob shouted as he descended the stairs, "do you know where my daughter is?"

The butler emerged from his quarters, shaking his head. "No, sir. She did not come down for supper. I've not seen her since Miss Johnson left."

Though he feared it would be useless, Rob began to search the house, moving methodically from one room to another while Bradford checked the garden. With each empty room, Rob's fears increased. There was no question about it. Emily had run away, just as Rachel had done, and it was all his fault.

"What should I do, sir?" Bradford asked when the search was complete and they'd both returned to Rob's study.

"I don't know." Rob sank into his desk chair, wishing he could redo this day. If he had the chance, he would respond far differently to the idea of Noah Chapman courting Emily. But there was no undoing the damage.

When Bradford left the room, Rob buried his head in his hands and began to pray. Moments later, he heard a knock on the front door followed by footsteps. As the footsteps grew louder, he looked up and then rose to his feet.

"Deborah!" he cried, his relief so great it threatened to knock him over. "You came back."

◆ ◆ ◆

He looked different, not at all like the angry man he'd been a few hours ago, not even like the man who'd held her in his arms last night and kissed her so tenderly. This was a new Rob Carmichael. The expression in those dark brown eyes told her something had changed, something vital. For the first time since she'd left her home, Deborah felt hope well up inside her.

"We need to talk," she said, never taking her eyes off the man who'd become such an important part of her life. If he'd changed—truly changed—anything was possible.

"Yes, we do." Though he did not smile, there was no ignoring the warmth in Rob's eyes. "There's so much I want to say, but first we need to find Emily."

Deborah nodded, the bubble of hope growing with the realization that he'd included her in his statement. Rob was acting as if they were once again partners, as if this afternoon had not occurred. Though she could have interrupted, telling him

105

where his daughter was, Deborah wanted to see what else he would say. His attitude would help her find the correct way to approach him on Emily and Noah's behalf.

"She's disappeared," Rob explained. "I know it's my fault, but I have to find her and convince her to come back. The problem is, I don't know where to look."

He was distraught, worried, and willing to do anything for his daughter. Deborah heard all that in his voice. She also heard a humility that hadn't been there before. It seemed that whatever had happened to Rob since he'd stormed out of this room had shown him that he wasn't in control, that he needed help. She offered a silent prayer of thanksgiving.

"You don't need to worry about Emily's safety. She's in my apartment." When Rob's eyes filled with relief, Deborah added, "She's safe, but she's also very unhappy."

"That's my fault."

"Yes, it is." She wouldn't minimize the seriousness of the situation. "Emily wanted your permission to marry Noah, and you refused to even consider that he might be the right man for her. You treated her as if she were a child, incapable of knowing what's best for her. You hadn't even met Noah when you made your decision." Emily hadn't told Deborah whether Rob had confronted Noah or simply approached his employer, demanding that he be fired.

Rob nodded, accepting the litany of criticism she'd leveled on him. "I still haven't met Noah. I only made it as far as Church Corner. I've been home about ten minutes. The rest of the time was spent on my knees."

So much made sense now. He was indeed a new man. "That explains the difference."

Rob blinked, obviously startled by her words. "Is it that obvious? I know I feel different."

"You look different, too. More at peace."

"I still have a long way to go." He stared into the distance for a moment then said, "I've done so many things wrong that I don't know whether I can ever make amends. I hurt my daughter, and I hurt you." Rob's frown deepened, but he met Deborah's gaze as he said, "I realized that the way I acted made you fear me. Believe me, Deborah, I never meant that to happen. I would never hurt you—not knowingly—and yet I did. Can you ever forgive me?"

She nodded slowly then reached out a hand. When he grasped it, she said, "I already have. You're not the only one who spent time in prayer. I realized that I overreacted to your anger. Everything I saw was colored by what had happened to my sister, so I thought the worst of you. That was wrong. I hope you can forgive me for not seeing beyond my fears."

She swallowed, encouraged by the understanding she saw reflected in Rob's eyes. "God helped me realize that anger is part of life. It doesn't always spiral out of control. In my heart, I know that you're not like Adam. You're a good man."

For the first time since she'd entered the room, a smile touched the corners of Rob's mouth. "Thank you. I'm not sure I deserve that praise, but I want to live up to it." He drew Deborah closer, his eyes once again solemn as he asked, "How do I undo the hurt I caused Emily? I love her. You know that."

Deborah looked into his eyes, hoping he'd accept what she was about to say. "Sometimes love means letting go. It's not easy. As Emily's parent, it's only natural you want to protect her, but she's grown up. What she needs now is guidance, not rules and restrictions."

Rob nodded. "How do I start?"

"Give Noah a chance."

Chapter Ten

A chance. Rob looked at the woman whose hand he still held. She was right. If he wanted the chance to win her love—and oh, how he did!—he needed to prove to Deborah that he was worthy of that love. That meant being fair, giving Noah a chance to demonstrate his love for Emily rather than dismissing his suit without so much as having met the man. He had resolved to do whatever he could to make amends to Emily, and treating Noah fairly was high on that list, right after asking for Emily's forgiveness. Deborah had merely confirmed what Rob already knew.

"It's too late tonight, but I'll send for Noah tomorrow morning and let him plead his case."

"That's not what I had in mind." Deborah shook her head ever so slightly.

Surprised by her reaction, Rob tried to defend himself. "But you said I should give him a chance. That's what I was doing."

She shook her head again. "If you meet him here, Noah will be at a disadvantage. This is your home. More than that, it's where he delivers batteries."

Her argument was reasonable. "We can meet at the bank."

"That's not much better." Those lovely blue eyes were solemn as she said, "You're in charge there. Besides, only you and Noah would be part of the meeting."

Why was that a problem? Rob blinked, trying to understand Deborah's concerns. He'd believed he was doing what she wanted, but it appeared he'd been wrong. Women! Would he ever understand how their minds worked?

"I thought that's what you wanted," he said, trying to hide his frustration. "A meeting with Noah would give me a chance to see if he truly loves my daughter."

This time Deborah smiled, a slightly indulgent smile that only increased Rob's confusion. Throughout their marriage, Rachel had told him he didn't understand her. It appeared he didn't understand Deborah either.

"The key word is *see*," she said. "You'd hear what Noah said, but how would you know if his words were empty?"

Rob dropped her hand and raised both of his in the classic gesture of surrender. "I give up. What do you want me to do?" She was the matchmaker. This was her bailiwick. Since it was clear that he had no idea how to proceed, he'd do whatever Deborah suggested.

"I thought the four of us could go to dinner at the InterOcean tomorrow evening. That will give both you and me the opportunity to meet Noah on neutral ground at the same time that we see how he treats Emily."

Though it wasn't a bad idea, Rob could foresee at least one problem. "The InterOcean is the fanciest restaurant in town. The boy will be out of place there."

A shrug was Deborah's response. "Maybe, but maybe not. Besides, if he's going to marry your daughter, Noah needs to be comfortable around wealth."

Rob nodded, realizing once again why Deborah was the most sought after matchmaker in Cheyenne. She had a clear understanding of what was important if a marriage was to be successful. Though he still wasn't convinced Emily should marry a man with as limited a future as Noah's, Deborah's approach was an excellent way to determine whether Noah was the right man.

"That's a good point." Rob smiled at Deborah, wanting to underscore his approval of her plan. "Will you issue the invitation, or should I?"

"Why don't we let Emily do that?"

"Another good idea, assuming she'll even speak to me after the way I treated her."

"She will."

◆　◆　◆

"Do you think this dress is too fancy?"

Deborah beckoned the girl into her room and bade her turn around so she could inspect the gown from every angle. It was a bit of a charade, since Deborah had seen the gown earlier this afternoon when Emily had had her final fitting, but she knew the normally confident girl needed reassurance. Emily had been nervous all day, knowing how much was riding on tonight's dinner.

"Definitely not too fancy," she announced. "Apricot is the perfect color for you, and the pleats around the hem are more flattering than ruffles. Madame Charlotte has outdone herself with this gown."

Her relief evident, Emily scrutinized Deborah's clothing. "Your dress is pretty, too."

Deborah was pleased with the sapphire gown, but that pleasure paled compared to what she'd felt over the way Rob had handled the situation with his daughter the previous evening. When they'd arrived at Deborah's house, there was no doubt of his sincerity as he apologized to Emily. Though the girl had seemed skeptical for a few seconds, when Rob proposed dinner at the InterOcean, she had flung herself into his arms, declaring him the best father in the world.

"We'll be the best-dressed women at the hotel tonight." Though Deborah shared Rob's concern that Noah might feel out of place in the elegant dining room, she did not voice those thoughts.

"If you're ready, let's go downstairs." It was clear Emily was anxious for the evening to begin.

They had reached the bottom of the staircase when they heard a knock on the front door. Her face lighting with pleasure, Emily took a step forward. "It's Noah. I'll go."

Deborah shook her head and laid a restraining hand on Emily's arm. "Why don't you let Bradford usher him in the way he would any other guest?" She emphasized the final word as she added, "We'll wait for him in the parlor."

Emily nodded. "You're right. He is our guest tonight."

As they entered the parlor and found Rob waiting for them, Deborah's pulse began to race. Though she'd seen Rob in formal evening attire before, he looked particularly handsome tonight. He smiled, and while he said nothing, the appreciative gleam in his eye told her he approved of her gown. Her cheeks warmed with pleasure.

The moment was interrupted by Bradford's announcement. "Mr. Chapman has arrived."

Deborah looked at the young man at the butler's side, trying to see him from Rob's perspective. Noah's suit hung loosely on his lanky frame, but his shirt was spotless, and he sported a fresh haircut. She hoped Rob realized that Noah Chapman was doing his best to make a good impression.

Deborah gave Noah a welcoming smile. Though there was wariness in his eyes as he looked from her to Rob, when his gaze landed on Emily, Noah's lips curved into a wide smile.

Rob extended his hand in greeting. "Welcome, Noah. I hope you'll permit Miss Johnson and me to use your Christian name."

"Certainly, sir."

When the introductions were complete, Noah continued to stare at Emily, his expression leaving no doubt that he was smitten. And, though Emily said little, her flushed cheeks and sparkling eyes gave away her feelings.

She took a step toward Noah. "Will you escort me to the carriage?"

He nodded, his Adam's apple bobbing. As they turned toward the door, he said, "You're more beautiful than ever."

Though Noah's words had been little more than a whisper, Emily's reply carried clearly. "It's the gown."

He shook his head. "It's the girl in the gown."

Rob's expression was somber as he extended his arm for Deborah. Waiting until the young couple was out of earshot, he said, "Noah sounds as if he really means it."

"He does. There's no way to fake that gleam we saw in his eyes. He's sincere."

"But will it last?"

Deborah heard the fear in Rob's question and recognized its source. Noah's obvious infatuation with Emily must remind Rob of his feelings for Rachel, making him fear that it would fade when exposed to the reality of marriage.

"There are no guarantees," she told Rob, "but my first impression is that this is not mere infatuation. I believe it's lasting love." Both Noah and Emily had the same glow she'd seen on the faces of her most successful matches. "Let's see how we feel after dinner."

When they reached the hotel, the maître d' seated Emily and Noah across from each other. It was an excellent arrangement, for it gave Deborah the opportunity to observe the glances the young couple shared. Those looks told her a great deal, confirming her initial observations. Though Noah was polite and understandably nervous whenever he spoke to either Rob or Deborah, he became animated when he responded to Emily's questions. For her part, Emily was visibly happy—happier than Deborah had ever seen her. It was a good match.

As Deborah had suggested, Rob kept the conversation light during dinner, but as they enjoyed their desserts, he introduced the subject of Noah's future.

"I don't plan to be a battery boy all my life," Noah said, his voice now filled with confidence. "I've talked to Mr. Sullivan about a position in the plant. That would give me more responsibility and more pay."

Emily laid down her spoon and shook her head. "I don't need money."

"But you deserve a good life." Though it was something Rob might have said, it was Noah who voiced the words.

Rob fixed his gaze on the would-be suitor. "Do you believe you can give Emily that good life?"

Noah nodded. "I love her, and I'll do everything in my power to make her happy. There is nothing more important to me."

It was the perfect response. As Rob looked at Deborah, a question in his eyes, she gave him an almost imperceptible nod.

Rob was silent for a moment as he drained his coffee cup. Then he turned back to Noah. "I like you, Noah. I like the way you treat my daughter." He paused again, this time looking from Noah to Emily and then back to the young man. "You have my permission to court my daughter."

Emily's reaction was instantaneous. "Oh, Papa!" she cried as she leaned to the side and flung her arms around him. "I love you!" Emily pressed a kiss on her father's cheek then whispered something in his ear, something that caused him to grin.

"What did you say to your father when you hugged him?" Deborah asked when Rob took Noah aside to discuss something with him, leaving the two women alone at the table.

"Nothing important." But the impish grin that accompanied Emily's words said otherwise.

"Why don't I believe you?"

"Because you're smart." Emily squeezed Deborah's hand. "If Papa wants you to know what I said, he'll tell you."

Two hours passed before Deborah and Rob were alone. The foursome had returned from dinner and spent the time talking about Noah's plans and Rob's expectations of the courtship. It had been a pleasant time, one that reinforced Deborah's belief that this was a well-matched couple, but throughout it, she had puzzled over whatever it was Emily had told her father.

She wouldn't ask. Not yet, but Deborah was determined that before the evening ended she would learn why Rob had grinned.

"You were right," he said as he settled back into the chair opposite her. "Noah's a good young man. I have to admit I wouldn't have chosen him, but I can't deny that he and Emily seem happy together."

"He'll be a good husband."

Rob's eyes darkened and a frown crossed his face. "A better husband than I was to Rachel. I wish I'd known then what I do now."

The pain in his voice made Deborah's heart ache. "And what is that?"

"That there's a difference between love and infatuation. Love endures. Infatuation does not." He swallowed deeply before continuing. "Seeing Emily and Noah together gives me new hope."

The sight of young love had filled Deborah with happiness and had ignited hope within her heart. Hope that she might know the love of a good man. Hope that she would not remain unmatched for the rest of her life. Hope that Rob was the man God intended for her. The question was, were his hopes the same as hers?

Rob leaned forward, resting his hands on his knees. "It took my daughter to put everything into perspective for me. First she told me I shouldn't spend the rest of my life alone."

Emily had said similar things to Deborah. She had, in fact, gone further, claiming she would play matchmaker for Deborah, that she would find the right man for her. Was that where this was leading? Had God used Emily as part of His plan for Deborah? Was He offering her not only a husband but a daughter, too?

Rob smiled. "That was only the beginning of my daughter's meddling. When I gave Noah permission to court her, she turned the tables on me. She gave me permission to court you."

And he had grinned. Before Deborah could respond, Rob said, "I want you to know that I'm not afraid of living alone. I always assumed I would do that once Emily married, but then I met you and for the first time, I realized I don't want to be alone. I want to share my life with one very special woman—you."

The tiny bud of hope that had lodged inside her began to open into the most beautiful of blossoms as Rob rose and extended his hand, helping Deborah rise. When they were standing only inches apart, he said, "I love you, Deborah. I love you more than I knew it was possible to love."

And then the blossom turned into a full bouquet as Deborah realized that God had indeed answered her prayers. He had turned hopes into reality, for Rob was saying the words she'd longed to hear. Her heart overflowing with happiness, she nodded. "I love you." Smiling at Rob, she repeated his words. "I love you more than I knew it was possible to love."

Rob's smile turned into a grin as he drew Deborah into his arms. "Will you match yourself to me? Will you be my bride?"

"I will."

Amanda Cabot is the bestselling author of more than thirty novels and half a dozen novellas, including Jeremy and Esther's story, *The Christmas Star Bride*, and *Waiting for Spring*, which tells Madame Charlotte's story. Although she grew up in the East, a few years ago Amanda and her high school sweetheart husband fulfilled a life-long dream and are now living in Cheyenne. In addition to writing, Amanda enjoys traveling and sharing parts of her adopted home with readers in her Wednesday in Wyoming blog. One of Amanda's greatest pleasures is hearing from readers, and so she invites you to find her online at www.amandacabot.com.

Playing Possum

by Lisa Carter

Chapter One

Harvest 1895

Me marry you?" Theadosia Holland stared at her brother's best friend. "Are you crazy?"

Hiding behind a haystack, Cage Cooper scowled. "What's so crazy about saving the both of us a heap of trouble?" A muscle ticked in his square-cut jaw. "And what's so crazy about the idea of marrying me?"

Thea planted her hands on her hips. "You? Possum Trot, Wyoming's king of the love 'em and leave 'em wants to get married?"

"I said *pretend* to be engaged. Only till the harvest celebration is over." He grimaced. "I reckon we just have to survive the marriage fever gripping our little town this week."

"That's dumb."

"Not dumb. Brilliant. A surefire way to outfox"—his lips twitched—"outpossum the matronly matchmakers and their matrimonial machinations." He grinned. "How's that for big-city words?"

Thea rolled her eyes. "What have you got against matrimony?"

She flicked her gaze from the top of his sandy blond hair past his sky-blue eyes and scruffy beard to his open-collared chambray shirt and the sleeves rolled to his elbows. "You could probably stand a civilizing influence." There was a hole in his denim work pants. His boots were a disgrace.

He pulled a blade of straw out of the bale. "Which is exactly why I never want to get married. Women hog-tie a man into marriage and then try to change everything about the guy they claimed to love in the first place."

Cage chomped the straw between his teeth and left it dangling from the side of his mouth. "No sirree. No thank you. Not pulling that one on Micajah Stephen Cooper."

He folded his arms. Her eyes were drawn to the fabric pulling tight across his chest.

"I may not be fancy educated like you, but I like my life as it is. I eat when I want to eat. Sleep when I want to sleep. It is a well-known fact women are draining of both time and money, not to mention overly emotional."

"What makes you think any woman in her right mind would want to be hitched to you?" She jerked one of his black suspenders and let it twang against his puffed-out torso.

"Ow, Thea!" Wincing, he rubbed the spot.

"Still think you're God's gift to women, don't you?"

On the other side of the field, voices called for Cage. Female voices. He gave Thea that crooked smile of his. The same smile he'd been giving her since her older brother George began hanging out with this farm-next-door hooligan, and she'd tagged along to keep them out of mayhem.

Her hand itched to smack him like in the old days when they were children. But today the smile—which always set her teeth on edge—also sent a strange flutter in Thea's belly.

Cocking his head, he twirled the straw between his fingers. "I think my popularity with the ladies speaks for itself."

And then Thea did a most unladylike thing—she snorted. Something her long-dead mother would have been aghast to hear. Cage laughed and stuck the straw between his lips.

Why did she let him goad her? Cage Cooper—her childhood nemesis, the most obnoxious human being she'd ever known. Which was saying something, since Thea had become a schoolteacher.

In her brief teaching career, she'd already been pitted against some of the best pranksters childhood could produce. Which was exactly Cage Cooper's problem, of course. He was nothing—despite his twenty-odd years—but a big, overgrown, never serious, seriously annoying child.

This was ridiculous. Laughable. An engagement—even a pretend one—with Cage Cooper? They brought out the worst in each other.

She snatched the straw from his mouth. "You're wrong about every woman wanting to get married. I don't want to marry anyone, much less someone as aggravating as you."

He glared.

"I want to teach school. And I want every woman in the United States of America—not just in Wyoming—to have the right to vote. So we can get rid of idiot men like you in government."

He rolled his eyes heavenward. "Save us from the suffragettes. George told me you'd gone to Cheyenne and gotten a cartload of crazy ideas besides your certificate."

She stomped on his foot with the heel of her shoe.

"Ow, Thea!" He fell into the haystack.

"I wouldn't marry you—even if I was of the mind to marry, which I'm not—if you were the last man on earth."

Straightening, he smirked. "Which is exactly why you and me would make the best pretend couple in Possum Trot, Wyoming. I can trust you. 'Cause you're the only woman I know who doesn't want to get married as much as I don't want to get married."

Cage pretended to polish his knuckle on his suspenders. "It's genius."

She leaned into his face. Despite helping the men erect the new Possum Trot schoolhouse today, he smelled of bay rum, mint and. . .hay.

The pleasing combination only served to irritate her further. At him for smelling so good. And at herself for liking the way Cage Cooper smelled.

"We can stage a public breakup at the dance. I'll take the blame, of course." He gave her that lady-slayer smile of his. "With my reputation, not unbelievable. With their daughters' hearts at stake, the matchmakers will steer clear of me for good."

"How is this little scenario of yours supposed to benefit me?"

"You, my dear Theadosia, with your feigned jilted heart, will be free to pursue your own interests—women's suffrage—amid the town's complete commiseration. Everybody will be happy."

She jabbed her pointy finger into his chest. He flinched. "I wouldn't marry you, Cage Cooper, if I was a prairie on fire and you were the only bucket of water. I wouldn't marry you if—"

"Fine," he growled. "I get the picture. Be that way. Don't help an old friend. Wait till they turn their attention on you. Then we'll see how high and—"

With a swish of her skirt, she whirled and stalked across the recently threshed field toward the schoolhouse at the edge of town. Of all times for George to have taken his new bride on a business trip to Omaha. . .

Thea would have enjoyed telling George about Cage's latest harebrained scheme. This one might top that escapade to build a tunnel to the Chinamen in San Fran. Or Cage's outrageous idea to run away from Possum Trot and become a wild Indian.

Engaged to each other? Her and Cage? Hah. . . Good one.

"Yoo-hoo! Miss Holland? Theadosia. . .!"

Thea ground to a halt. Despite being away from Possum Trot at finishing school, she'd recognize that voice anywhere.

Mrs. Murdock, the church organist and town busybody, waved a lace handkerchief from the work site. At her side stood a hulking brute of a man.

"Theadosia dear, have you met my nephew from Cheyenne?"

◆ ◆ ◆

Cage's cheeks burned. That hadn't gone well. He hadn't exactly expected Thea to jump for joy, but he'd believed her practical enough to see the sense in his plan. A way to resolve his dilemma and what was sure to be hers soon enough. He slumped onto the ground.

Did she really dislike him so much? Sure, he'd pestered her all her lifelong, growing-up years as she tagged along behind him and her brother on every adventure. But the more outlandish escapades had sprung from her imagination, not his.

Neither she nor George had ever acted like they thought less of him—the son of the town drunk. The Coopers' adjacent farm slowly disintegrated until his father passed, and Cage had been able to restore the land back to its potential.

Unlike George and Thea, Cage wasn't educated beyond the basics, but he'd been proud of the life he'd built for himself. He'd worked hard to overcome his father's reputation among the townsfolk. He liked being his own boss and in control of his own destiny.

He'd not anticipated Thea's disdain. Stung, he pinched his nose between his fingers. He wasn't the same reckless kid he'd been. And she apparently wasn't the same sweet, if pesky, girl with the flyaway brown hair and sparkling brown eyes full of life and fun.

Cage sighed. He should've seen it coming when she got off the train last week. Fresh from a teaching post in Council Bluffs, she'd been welcomed like a conquering war hero. Coming home to teach because of Possum Trot's promise to rebuild the schoolhouse, lost to a prairie fire a year ago.

She'd stepped off the train to cheers. In her pink leg-of-mutton sleeves—Cage shook his head again. He so did not get women's fashion. But he remembered the lump that formed in his throat as he'd beheld his childhood playmate for the first time in years.

Theadosia Emmaline Holland had grown up. Seeing her, he went hot and cold at the same time. His heart lurched painfully.

And he'd faded into the crowd, suddenly unsure how this elegant woman in the embroidered shirtwaist and traveling suit would respond to her former compatriot in mischief.

She'd never acted like his standing within Possum Trot society mattered before. It hadn't mattered to the gangly fifteen-year-old girl she'd been. Cage chewed his lower lip. So much for the enlightenment of education.

But he'd have never believed it of Thea—she'd never cared two figs what anyone thought of her. He'd misjudged her. He wasn't good enough and no matter how hard he worked, he never would—

Skirts rustling, Thea plopped beside him behind the hay bale. "About what you said earlier?" She dropped her eyes and smoothed a wrinkle in her yellow plaid skirt.

And something tight in his belly a long time—longer than just this last week—began to loosen a notch.

She lifted her gaze. "I think you were right." Her lips tightened.

He raised his eyebrow into a question mark. "Right about what?"

She fluttered her hand in the direction of Possum Trot. "About everything."

He smiled. "You'll find the longer you stay hereabouts, I'm generally right. About the important stuff at least."

She blew out a breath. "You are the most arrogant—"

"Have I told you how I love it when you sweet-talk me, Thea?" He bit the inside of his cheek. "Was that all you wanted to say? About how brilliant I am?"

She bristled. "You're going to make me say it, aren't you? Make me ask you this time."

He allowed his shoulders to rise and fall, feigning a nonchalance he didn't feel. The look she threw him indicated a burning desire to throttle him. This should be fun. Taking Herself down a peg or two. Or four. . .

"Well," he drawled in his best I'm-just-a-country-boy voice, "you are the one with the advanced education."

"Oh, all right then." She tossed her head with its neatly coiled dark brown locks. "Will you be my fiancé until Harvest Week is over?"

"Your pretend fiancé?" He felt the need to clarify. And rub it in.

"That." She grunted.

"You're asking me to pretend to want to marry you?"

Spots of color peppered her cheeks. "I said that, didn't I?"

Rising, he didn't bother to swallow his smile. "Just wanted to hear you say it so one day I can tell our pretend children how their mama dragged me to the pretend altar of matrimony."

"I'd tell you what I think of you right now Cage Cooper, except my mother taught me not to use words like that."

He laughed. "Think you can put up with me for one week?"

She groaned. "Why does seven days suddenly feel so much longer? Like a life sentence."

"Try thinking of it as our last great adventure." He offered his arm. "Shall we announce our engagement to the world?"

She took his hand. "I'm game if you are."

He plucked a piece of straw from her hair. "Let the games begin."

Chapter Two

Thea watched as Cage wove three long stems of sweetgrass into a braid. He twisted the cord into a ring and took hold of her hand. His touch on her skin set her nerve endings aquiver.

"See if this fits, Thea."

Thea stared at her left hand as he placed the plaited ring on her finger.

"Like you taught me when we were little." He gave her a shy smile. "That summer you wove every dandelion in the meadow into a garland."

Her heart pitter-pattered. Until she reminded herself Cage Cooper didn't have a shy bone in his body. Never had. Like her though, he probably felt the awkwardness of the occasion.

"It's not as grand as the egg-sized garnet your brother put on Mildred's hand." His voice turned gruff.

She'd never liked hearing Cage disparage himself. A bitter legacy from a father too drunk to care and a mother who worked herself into an early grave.

Thea raised her hand to view the ring in the afternoon light. "It's lovely and sweet and just right."

He shrugged in that self-deprecating way of his. "For a pretend engagement, I guess."

She'd take care to keep her hand out of water. So the ring wouldn't disintegrate until its purpose had been served. The thought of next weekend, however, sent a tiny ping into her heart.

He dropped his arms to his side and then as if he didn't know what to do with them, crossed his arms again. "I better get home. Animals to feed."

She turned the ring around on her finger, admiring it on her hand.

"I'll hang the blackboard and help you get the desks in place this week."

She gave him a quick smile, reluctant to let him go. "Will I see you tomorrow?"

He nodded. "Save me a place at lunch." And he strode without a backward glance to the livery where he'd left his horse.

She frowned. What lunch?

At the mercantile, she flashed her hand this way and that while Sue Ellen Oberheimer rolled fabric bundles. The rest of the single ladies in Possum Trot *oohed* and *aahed*. In a far corner, Mrs. Murdock's nephew, a towering man, quietly perused a display of canned goods.

"So romantic," chirped one of the Wendover sisters.

Thea thought so, too.

Nellie Jones smiled. "And spur of the moment creative."

Thea agreed. Cage had been an inventive boy. Now become a man. Her heart thumped. All man.

Sue Ellen didn't say anything. Just kept pinning bolts and stacking the fabric onto the shelf. Thea narrowed her eyes. She and Sue Ellen had been classroom rivals once upon a time. And Sue Ellen, Thea also recalled, had been sweet as a sugarloaf on the young Cage Cooper.

"Quite a catch," Melody Jenkins purred.

Which he was, if Thea did say so herself.

"Kind of sudden." Sue Ellen's lips thinned. "You're not exactly farmwife material. With your New American Woman ideas, I didn't figure you for the marrying kind. Not real sure what a man like Cage sees in you."

Thea arched her eyebrow. "We've known each other since we were children."

Sue Ellen crinkled her big nose. "Getting kind of long in the tooth aren't you, Theadosia Holland?"

Thea's hackles rose. "Funny you should mention that. Seeing as you and I are the same age."

She and Sue Ellen glared at each other.

Lucy Wendover, who never could stand disharmony, broke the tension. "And with Cage Cooper four years older than either of you, none of us figured he'd ever settle down."

Thea laid her hand against her throat where the ring showed to its best advantage. "I only last week returned to town." She fluttered her lashes in a manner she believed both fetching and modest.

"So you'll be needing fabric for a wedding dress." Sue Ellen's lip curled. "Unless you think yourself and your trousseau too good for the likes of Possum Trot's mercantile."

Fabric? Thea swallowed. For a pretend, nonexistent wedding?

Recovering her composure, she gave Sue Ellen a cool look. Round one went to Sue Ellen Oberheimer, who'd backed Theadosia Holland into a proverbial corner. And successfully garnered a sale.

Thea scanned the bolts. The peach fabric? Not her best color.

Nor the mustard one either. She shuddered. Too Sue Ellen for words.

But the plum-colored silk. . .

Cage told her once—when she downed too many plums after a dare—that particular shade of purple looked good next to her face. Of course, her face had been green at the time.

And he held her head when she promptly vomited into the orchard grass. Still. . . She liked purple. Cage, too, apparently.

"I'll take the entire bolt, if you please, Sue Ellen."

Sue Ellen's mouth almost turned inside out. "It will be a busy few days for the women in Possum Trot cooking for the threshing crew. The Murdock farm is tomorrow." She motioned toward the lurking nephew.

Oh. That lunch.

The potluck could be problematic. She'd forgotten about the Possum Trot tradition. Area farmers pooled their monetary resources to hire the steam engine thresher, and took turns as the thresher made a circuit, a ring, of the farms.

All hands from nearby farms brought in the harvest. On their designated threshing day, the farmer's wife was expected to feed the men. As a point of pride, young brides and those-hoping-to-be-brides showed off their womanly arts to the community.

Thea, as a Holland and prominent member of the community, would be expected to contribute. And Sue Ellen knew full well Thea hadn't been gifted with baking skills.

Sue Ellen tallied the receipt. "After all, the way to a man's heart is through his stomach."

Thea handed the money she owed to Sue Ellen.

Nellie squeezed Thea's arm. "You and Cage have always been so sweet together."

Sue Ellen counted out the change. "You're bringing something to the potluck, aren't you, Theadosia?"

Thea squared her shoulders. "Of course, I am."

"And what are you bringing, pray tell?"

Thea fidgeted. "It's a surprise." Which was entirely true. It would be a surprise to Thea most of all.

Sue Ellen sniffed as if she didn't believe her. "My caramel pie is usually the most sought after."

"I like caramel pie," offered the Murdock nephew.

Sue Ellen, Thea, and the rest of the ladies ignored him.

Thea held the bolt of fabric against her chest. "And yet, here you remain, Sue Ellen, unsought yourself."

Sue Ellen's face turned a muddy color. "You've proven you can get a man, Theadosia Holland. Real question is: Are you woman enough to keep him?"

On shaky culinary ground, Thea pivoted and left the store without dignifying Sue Ellen's insults. But making her way outside to the buggy tied to the railing, she racked her brain trying to remember where Mother had stored the recipe books.

◆ ◆ ◆

The next day under a blue Wyoming sky, Cage wiped the sweat off his brow. Setting his hat farther on the crown of his head, he shaded his eyes with his hand and surveyed what the thresher's ring of twenty men had accomplished thus far.

Younger boys had pitched the grain into wagons. Others fed the wheat into the machine. A few men, including him, stacked the straw. Still more would haul the clean grain away.

A good stacker, like Cage, was always in demand. It was a dirty and hot job, but he'd acquired a reputation for quick, thorough work. All day, he stood in the straw stack and arranged the straw in place. Some farmers left the straw in a loose pile where it came off the blower. But not on the threshing crews he worked, a point of pride with Cage.

There was always a bit of prestige involved for a farmer who had a straw stack and not just a pile. He did good work, and when his farm's harvest came round the rotation, his neighbors would do a good job for him. The steam whistle blew, signaling time for the big noon meal at the Murdock farmhouse.

His stomach growled. There was good-natured joshing as the men headed toward the tables spread out in the yard under the pecan trees. Taking his turn at the pump, he worked the handle and stuck his entire head under the gush of water.

Cage scrubbed his handkerchief over his face and took extra care washing up. Stepping out of the way for the next guy, his eyes darted among the neighborhood women. The ladies carried platters of fried chicken, mashed potatoes with big gravy boats, and bowls of garden vegetables. His gaze cut to a long table laden with cakes and pies of every variety.

Then he spotted her. The last one out of the overheated kitchen, Thea carried a tray of biscuits and an assortment of homemade jams. In her blue serge skirt and pale blue shirtwaist with the black, floppy artist tie, it wasn't hard to find her. In spite of the soiled apron pinafore, she stood out like a plumed bird amid the calico and gingham-clad farmwomen. Doubts assailed him once more.

In the dark of night, his brilliant idea hadn't seemed so brilliant. Nobody in their right mind would believe Thea Holland would hitch herself to someone like him. She was nobody's farmwife. And—his heart pricked—never would be.

"Ladies." Jim Murdock, whose farm they threshed today, took his spot at the head of the table. "You've outdone yourself."

There was a general murmur of agreement as the men rushed to find places at the table. Cage caught Thea's eye. She placed her hands on the ladder-back chair in front of her. He slipped into the seat.

She straightened his cockeyed collar. And at her touch, his pulse exploded. The Murdock nephew said a quiet prayer, and the eating commenced.

As the bowls were passed down the table, he helped himself to a cut of beef. "Thea."

"Cage."

She kept her hands positioned on the finials of his chair. Close enough if he leaned back, his shirt could brush her hands. A thought that once again sent his pulse skittering.

He speared a pickle and a slice of tomato. The women would eat after the men returned to the fields. Each farmwife had her specialty and vied for bragging rights. He snagged a chicken thigh from a passing platter.

Behind him, Thea kneaded the wooden finials with her fists. "I butchered that chicken myself this morning."

Mid-bite, he laid his fork on the plate. Despite being country born and bred, Thea had never killed a farm animal—much less fried one—in her life.

He didn't like talking to Thea without being able to see her face. "Are you okay?"

"I—I guess." A slight catch in her voice, she reached past him for his empty glass. "I never realized before how truly useless I am."

He touched her sleeve. "You're not useless. Smartest girl I know. A modern American woman, remember?" Their eyes locked.

"Little good that does me in things that really matter." Her cheeks were rosy with embarrassment. "Nellie and Lucy showed me what to do. They were very patient and understanding."

Her gaze shot over his head toward someone at the far end of the table. "They helped me keep my pride intact."

Cage didn't like seeing her so disheartened. "Thea—"

"I'll get you some tea." Leaning over him, she took hold of his glass, and he let go of her sleeve. "And it's okay to eat the chicken."

She lifted her chin. "Melody says it's as golden a brown as any she's ever seen." She smiled. "I'd forgotten what good friends I have here in Possum Trot."

He nudged her with his elbow. "Like me?"

She patted his arm. "Don't know how this shoulder holds up that big head of yours, Cage Cooper."

He winked at her. "And you've made it your mission to bring it down to size?"

She sniffed as she moved away. "Sounds like a full-time calling for somebody."

He'd tucked into the food by the time she returned with his glass. Throwing his head back, he downed the tea in a single, long swig. The steam whistle on the engine blew, echoing across the field. He set the glass onto the plank table with a dull thud. Hands on the edge of the table, he pushed his chair across the grass.

She scooted the chair out of his way. "Don't you want seconds?"

"Gotta get to work. But I'll be back at the afternoon break." He hooked his thumb between his suspender and his shirt. "I'm looking forward to dessert."

Thea's face clouded. "About that, Cage. . ."

He couldn't resist touching the tendril of hair that had come loose from her bun. He rubbed it between his thumb and forefinger. She closed her eyes for a moment.

With a small sigh, he tucked it behind her ear. "Save me some pie, will you, Thea? You know what I like."

Her eyes dropped to her shoes. But she nodded. And despite the fresh air, he found it increasingly hard to draw a deep breath.

The former little tagalong had a curious effect on his equilibrium. He needed to put space between them. This pretend engagement suddenly felt all too real.

At least to him.

Chapter Three

"You *actually* made pie?" Sue Ellen stuck her nose in the air. "I better warn the neighbors."

Thea wanted to simultaneously smack Sue Ellen and sink into the ground for shame. Her plan had been to slink over to the dessert table, remove her baking fiasco and then chuck the contents into the Murdock pig trough before anyone was the wiser.

But that afternoon, Sue Ellen beat Thea to the dessert table. As usual, the Murdock nephew hovered close by, under the shade of the pecan tree.

"Cage Cooper will take one bite and probably break the engagement." Sue Ellen's gaze flickered over Thea's shoulder. "Oh."

Sue Ellen's mouth flattened. "Hey, Cage."

Cage placed his hand at the small of Thea's back. "Is that the pie you were telling me about yesterday, Sugar Plum?"

Thea blinked at him.

Sue Ellen elbowed the Murdock man out of the way. "Try my caramel pie, Cage."

Murdock's nephew cleared his throat. "I'd like to try your caramel pie, Miss Oberheimer."

Sue Ellen held the pie plate out to Cage.

He ignored Sue Ellen and her plate. "Plum is my favorite." He lifted Thea's pie off the table.

Thea, for the life of her, couldn't speak.

"I hardly got a wink of sleep last night just thinking about your pie, Thea." He held the pie to his nose and inhaled. "Mmm-mm."

Sue Ellen frowned. "You aren't *actually* going to eat that thing?"

He gave Sue Ellen a half-lidded smile. "What else would I do with it, Miss Oberheimer?"

Actually. . .Thea had some ideas. Including pushing it into Sue Ellen's gloating face. But Thea reminded herself she was a Christian woman.

"You're going to take the whole thing?" Sue Ellen's eyes widened. "Glutton for punishment, aren't you?"

Cage stiffened. "I'm not in a sharing mood today. I'm selfish when it comes to Thea."

The Murdock nephew grabbed for Sue Ellen's pie.

"Wait!" Sue Ellen lunged a second too late.

Murdock hugged the plate to his chest. "Sounds like a great idea to me."

Sue Ellen's perplexed consternation was a sight to behold.

Armed with a fork, Cage dug into the crust, and thrust a bite into his mouth. He chewed. Swallowed and brandished the fork in Sue Ellen's direction. "Great stuff."

Sue Ellen huffed.

The Murdock nephew took a careful bite of the caramel pie. His rather forgettable countenance transformed as he rolled the flavors in his mouth. "Why, Miss Oberheimer, tales of your baking have not been exaggerated."

He stabbed the fork in the air. "This is possibly the best pie I've ever had occasion to enjoy. Better than my dear mother's."

Sue Ellen's brow puckered as the man continued to wax eloquent about the flakiness of her piecrust.

Cage nudged Thea. "Would you grab me a lemonade, Sugar Plum?"

Struck dumb, she poured him a glass and followed Cage to the edge of the Murdock yard. Plopping down, he rested his back against a fence post and scooped more pie onto his fork.

Her heart thudded. "Stop!"

Cage paused, fork halfway to his mouth. "What?"

"You've proven your point and saved my honor." She fluttered her hand. "But this is taking things too far."

"It's not that bad."

She hung her head. "Yes. It is."

He inserted the slice into his mouth.

"Greater love hath no man than this. . . ," she whispered. "I'll have it engraved on your headstone, I promise."

He swallowed with effort. "I've got to clean the plate or Sue Ellen will want to know why." He loaded his fork with less enthusiasm this time, though.

"You and your big mouth." Her eyes darted. "Maybe we can dump it under the bush. Or in the creek. Or—"

"And endanger the wildlife?"

She laughed and eased down beside him, careful to set the glass on a level patch of ground.

"Besides"—he eyed the fork with trepidation—"I believe I owe you for a certain dare involving plums a long time ago."

She smoothed her skirt and arranged it around her ankles. He'd saved her from humiliation today. She could at least keep him company while he suffered through the ordeal. "True."

He took another bite. Like taking cod-liver oil, he closed his eyes shut and forcibly swallowed.

Cage took a breath. "With the great cook your dad hired, I've never understood how a smart girl like you could so thoroughly botch cooking."

She pursed her lips. "It's because of that great cook, I don't know how. She never let me into her precious kitchen, especially after Mother died."

"Cooking is nothing but reading and math, Thea."

She rested her chin on her up-drawn knees. She tucked her shoes underneath her skirt. "It's boring following the rules."

Cage snorted. "Spoken like a true suffragette."

He forked a smaller amount this time. And gulped past the apparent boulder lodged in his throat.

She handed him the lemonade. "You may be the bravest man I've ever known, Cage Cooper."

He clapped a quick hand over his mouth. "Don't make me laugh, Thea. I'm having enough trouble trying not to choke as it is."

"Drink something."

He took a long swallow. Against her will, she found herself admiring the corded muscles of his throat. As he lowered the glass, he caught her staring.

She blushed. Fiddled with the grass ring on her finger. "What's the real reason you don't want to get hitched, Cage? Sue Ellen's more than willing."

He scowled. "I don't love Sue Ellen, and she's not in love with me. She thinks I'm her last chance." His eyes flashed. "I don't want to be anyone's last chance. She ought to take a closer look at her admirer."

"Murdock?"

Cage laid aside the fork. "Murdock's nephew. You really don't know who he is? I figured you both being from such high society in Cheyenne—"

Thea shoulder-butted him. "Will you stop trying to make me out to be a snob? Who is he?"

"I'll tell you who he is—he's Frederic Tierney."

At her blank look, Cage cocked his head. "Heir to the Gallagher restaurant fortune."

"The finest eatery in Cheyenne?"

Cage's brows drew together. "In San Fran and Chicago, too. Supposedly Frederic Tierney is a financial genius."

"And he likes Sue Ellen's pie?"

"From his moonstruck look, he likes more than her pie. If her pie is better than his mother's, high praise indeed."

Thea frowned. "Why hasn't someone told Sue Ellen who he is?"

Cage dropped his gaze. "I suspect he prefers to be liked for his own merits rather than his bank account."

"I think he's on to something, though. The way to Sue Ellen's heart may be through her crust." Thea fingered the hem of her skirt. "You still haven't explained why you remain unmarried."

He gave her that lopsided smile of his. "Why would anyone want to marry me and I quote, 'the most aggravating man on earth.' End quote."

She folded her hands in her lap. "I'm not blind. You're not without a certain charm, Cage. I got off the train figuring you'd have a wife and at least three kids in tow."

He grunted.

She tilted her head. "Isn't that what every farmer wants? A wife and a passel of children for exactly this kind of thing?" She motioned toward the fields. "For planting and harvesting."

A muscle ticked in his cheek. "What would any woman in her right mind want with me, son of the town drunk?"

She knotted her fingers. "I think you're wrong about how people in this town see you, Cage. The other men regard you with respect and friendship. The matrons of Possum Trot wouldn't be throwing their daughters at you otherwise."

He hunkered against the post. "What I don't get is why the Hollands ever allowed their children to spend time with the likes of me, the no-good Cooper boy."

She touched his sleeve. "You're not the no-good Cooper boy."

His eyes fell to her hand.

She squeezed his arm. "I don't know which is worst. Poor George trying to live up to our father's reputation. Or you trying to live down your father's. I don't think either of you need to do anything but be yourself."

He wouldn't look at her.

"Are you hearing me, Cage?"

She took hold of his chin with her thumb and forefinger, forcing him to meet her gaze. His eyes were troubled. She hated seeing him doubt himself.

"Cage Cooper is a good man, a good farmer, and a good neighbor. And don't you forget it."

He tried to pull away. She was having none of it. He shrugged off her words.

"You have always been my good friend." She took the pie tin from him and set it on the ground. "And as it turns out, a *very* good fiancé."

His lips twisted. "Not good enough for a Holland."

"Not true. My mother liked you." Thea rested against the post, her shoulder pressing his. "She said only someone as intelligent as you could create such chaos."

"There's a compliment in there, I think. . ." His mouth quirked. "And besides,

131

most of our escapades were your doing, Thea."

She smiled. "But you took the blame so I wouldn't get into trouble."

Thea brushed her cheek against his sleeve. "I think underneath the bravado you're scared. Scared to trust yourself, scared to trust others, and most of all, scared to trust God."

He jabbed the fork into the grass. "I learned early not to trust people. Every time things were good, the other shoe always dropped."

Cage scanned the sky. "Maybe it's an occupational hazard for a farmer to fear the worst. This is the best crop I've harvested in five years. The house and barn are in great shape. Friends—the best of friends like you and George—are home again."

He raked the dirt with the fork. "It's too good to last. Story of my life."

She captured the fork in his hand. "You need to take another look at yourself, Cage Cooper. And see what God sees in you. A person of much value."

"Is that how you see me, Thea?"

Before she could frame a reply, a hint of merriment—and the customary mischief—returned to his eyes. "I thought I was the most conceited, annoying person you knew?"

Trust Cage to deflect when the conversation became too personal.

She blew out a breath. "How do you do it, Cage?"

"Do what?"

She cut her eyes at him. "Be both arrogant and insecure at the same time."

He grinned. "I'm talented, I guess."

"You're something all right."

His eyes darkened. "Something bad? Or something good?"

Only a few inches separated them from each other. Thea became aware of the pounding of her heart. What was happening?

She willed her heartbeat to steady. "You're en-Cage-ing, that's for sure."

If anything, he leaned closer. His breath warmed her cheek. There was an intensity in his eyes. . .

"Were you as glad to see me as I was glad to see you when you stepped off the train last week, Thea?"

"I—I—"

She moistened her lip with her tongue. It was getting harder to breathe. Harder to think of anything besides her brother's best friend. Would Cage kiss her?

Where had that come from? Did she want him to kiss her? Yes—her heart stutter-stepped—she wanted him to kiss her.

But he edged away. "I'm dirty." His face shadowed. "Too dirty for the likes of Theadosia Holland."

He scrambled to his feet. "My part is done for the day. I'll tie my horse to your buggy and make sure you get home."

Disappointment surged. She flushed. And wanted to kick something. Someone, namely Cage Cooper.

For treating her like a fragile porcelain vase. But mainly for not—she sucked in a breath. For not kissing her?

Somehow the boundary between fiction and reality had blurred. They were only supposed to pretend. Suddenly, she didn't feel like pretending.

He put his hand to his stomach. "I'll get the buggy."

◆ ◆ ◆

Headed toward the Holland farm on the dusty road, Cage pulled the buggy reins short. His stomach roiled. *Oh, no.* He wasn't going to make it.

Thea glanced at him. "Why are we stopping?"

He practiced taking deep, even breaths. "I don't feel so good."

Cage willed his gut to settle. *Please, God, not in front of Thea.*

His stomach heaved. Panic rocketed through him. Breaking into a cold sweat, he thrust the reins at Thea. Clutching his abdomen, he leaned over and vomited into the bush. His humiliation was complete.

Laying aside the reins, she rubbed his back. "Oh, Cage, honey."

Could he do nothing involving Thea without making a total idiot of himself?

When he finally straightened, his belly was blessedly serene again. She handed him the reins and fished a handkerchief out of her skirt pocket.

Cage shrank back. "I can't use your fancy—"

She blotted his mouth. "Stop being such a big baby, Micajah Cooper."

He could feel the flush creeping up his neck. "We seem to bring out the worst in each other, don't we, Thea?"

Nobody had taken care of him in a long time. He steeled himself not to get used to it. Good things—at least for him—never lasted long.

She placed the soiled handkerchief on the floorboard. "I wouldn't say that." She brushed a lock of hair off his forehead.

He fought the urge to press into the coolness of her fingers.

"Does your stomach still hurt, darlin'?"

His eyes cut to hers. "A little bit."

She reddened at the realization of what she'd said. "I brought a blue bottle of this milky magnesium stuff with me from Cheyenne. It'll fix you right up."

He made a face.

She twined her arm through the crook in his elbow. "Outside of Jesus, you eating my pie may be the single most wonderful, heroic thing anyone's ever done for me."

With a tiny smile, he slapped the reins. The horses once again set off at a trot. Thea's hero. Someone he'd always aspired to be.

She nestled against his side. "Think we'll win the three-legged footrace tomorrow?"

He could get used to Thea hanging on to his arm. "Sure I do. We make a great team."

She nodded. "A formidable combination. My brains coupled with—"

"My good looks."

She laughed as he meant her to. He enjoyed hearing her laugh.

"You must be feeling better if you've reverted to your overlarge ego." She ran her hand down his arm. "After the dance on Saturday, you can consider yourself forever free of me and from matrimony."

The thought did not give Cage the comfort he'd envisioned earlier in the week.

She sighed. "Then like you said, everybody will be happy."

Would he be happy? Cage wasn't so sure. Not anymore.

Chapter Four

Cage Cooper made Thea laugh. He'd always made her laugh.

He wasn't stuffy or proper. He didn't care a bushel for propriety. And truth to tell, Thea never had either.

"Be still, Thea." Cage crouched close to the ground. "I'm trying to tie the cord around our ankles."

Thea wobbled and laid her hand on his shoulder for support. He looked up, surprised. A muscle in his neck jumped.

She felt the heat of his skin through the ticked striping of his work shirt. She pretended she wasn't bothered by touching him. Or filled with a fierce desire to be kissed by him.

This week, she'd discovered she had a hidden talent for pretending. And this week, she'd also discovered she was getting more practice at pretending than she wanted. While Cage cinched the knot tighter, she surveyed the other Possum Trot couples entering the three-legged race.

Nellie and her longtime beau. There'd be a wedding there before the week was out. Lucy and the young man on the threshing crew. Sue Ellen and—

Thea blinked, not believing her eyes. Sue Ellen and the ubiquitous Frederic. As for the way Frederic Tierney gazed at her arch nemesis, Sue Ellen?

She wished someone, namely Cage Cooper, would look at her that way. She grunted.

"Too tight?" Cage raised his eyes to hers. "I can loosen—"

"No." She bit her lip. "It's fine."

What wasn't fine was that Cage seemed content with pretending. It was a game to him. Mr. Love 'Em and Leave 'Em wasn't interested in anything real. Much less anything from Thea.

Cage rose to his full height. "Did you get up on the wrong side of your feather bed this morning, Sugar Plum?" He wrapped his arm around her waist. "Let's practice moving toward the starting line."

His voice produced pinprick shivers on her arm—her free arm, which wasn't draped around his waist. Cage Cooper was a rogue and a rake. But he was, right now at least, her rogue and her rake. And a most charming one at that.

No doubt how he'd managed to stay alive to this point in his life. Only Cage could so outrageously flirt for his dinner and proceed to waltz out the door without so much as a bye-your-leave, much less a proposal. And do it again and again.

Thea grimaced. With every available female in town. Including her?

She stumbled. Cage counterbalanced. His arm around her was strong, warm, and firm.

"Easy there." He steadied her. "A three-legged race isn't about me or you leading. It's about working together. As one."

Cage leaned close. "Like in marriage."

His breath fanned the tendrils of her hair dangling at her ear. Her heart skipped a beat. Then, he laughed.

She ought. . . Thea tapped her foot on the hard-packed ground. She ought to marry him just to show him she could. That would teach him a lesson. He'd picked the wrong girl to play with her affections—

Thea sucked in a breath. Is that how she felt? Was she fondly affectioned for the likes of Cage Cooper? *Oh, dear Lord.*

Because she had a sneaking suspicion she'd gone far beyond affection. How stupid could she get? Giving her heart to a rogue and a rake.

"This will not end well. Not well at all," she whispered.

"Just try to work with me, Thea. Not against me. It's like math. One. . ." He moved their conjoined legs forward. "Outside leg on two. One. . .two."

He hauled Thea toward the starting point. "It's about synchronization. Like working on the threshing crew. One. . .two. . .one. . .two."

"And the point of this?" she hissed.

"To win, Thea." His arm tightened around her waist. "I always play to win."

She forced herself to swallow against the lump in her throat. "And what is it you aim to win?"

He winked. "Why don't we concentrate on winning first?"

"Ladies and gentlemen, everyone to your places," shouted the reverend. "The course is marked to the oak tree beside the church and back. The race will belong to the swift and the strong."

The couples hopped and inched their way toward the starting point.

"On your mark." The reverend raised his arm high above his head. "Get ready. . . Get set. . ."

Cage strained forward. She held her breath.

"Go!" The reverend dropped his arm.

Cage—with Thea in tow—surged ahead. Cheers and catcalls erupted as the bystanders egged on their favorite couples.

"One. . .two." Cage gritted his teeth. "One. . .two. . ."

She hung on to him for dear life, determined to do her part. Intent on not causing Cage to lose the race. Nor lose the prize on which he'd set his sights, whatever that might be.

At the oak, Lucy and her man fell behind. On the turn, Nellie and her beau collapsed laughing onto the grass. One by one, the other teams dropped by the wayside until there remained only Thea and Cage, Sue Ellen and Frederic.

Figures. . . Thea summoned reserves of oxygen and strength she hadn't known she possessed.

"We can't let Sue Ellen win," she gasped between breaths. "Move faster, Cage. Move faster."

"This fast enough for you?" he growled. "Hold on, tight."

He lifted her off her feet as much as the play of the rope allowed and ran for it. Frederic did the same. The two men jogged toward the finish line.

Laughing, Thea clung to him, both arms around his solid build. She could feel Frederic and Sue Ellen breathing down their necks. Her pulse accelerated. Their lead slowly evaporated as Frederic's longer legs ate up the remaining distance. It would be a race to the finish.

"Put me down, Cage," she whispered. "I'm not as heavy as Sue Ellen. I can help. One. . .two."

"You and this thing with Sue Ellen," he huffed. "One. . .two." But he placed Thea on her feet.

Without missing a beat, she moved in harmonious synchronization with Cage. In a sudden lunge, she and Cage sailed first across the finish line.

Chest heaving, he let go of Thea. He rested both hands on his knees.

"We won!" She gave the red-faced Sue Ellen a triumphant glare. "We won!"

Cage straightened with a wince. "Don't go getting all high and mighty. You ain't the lightest thing I ever lifted, Sugar Plum."

She socked him with her fist.

"Ow, Thea!" He rubbed his shoulder. "Play nice, why don't you?"

"We make a great team." And she hugged him, nearly knocking him off his feet.

Regaining his balance, his hand cupped her elbow, but he didn't allow her to drift far. "'Xactly what I've been telling you all along, darlin'."

"And you were right."

He cocked his ear. "Say that again why don't you? I'm not sure I heard you correctly."

She twisted the grass ring on her finger. "You were right, Cage Cooper."

His arm snaked around her waist again, pulling her closer, staking her place against his side. "And don't you forget it. I'm right about a lot of things, Thea Holland."

Frederic, Nellie, and the others offered their congratulations. Sue Ellen, of course, crossed her arms and sulked.

The reverend presented them with a certificate and a hamper of victuals. "Prepared by the matchmaker matrons of Possum Trot." The reverend smiled. "Not as good, I'm sure, as what your own lovely wife-to-be could fix you, but. . ."

Cage smirked. "If he only knew."

She kept her attention fixed on the reverend. "I'm going to punch you again, if you don't behave, Cage."

"To avoid future injury looks like I'll have to claim my prize when you least expect it."

"What do you mean?" Her eyes flitted to his. "We already won the prize."

"Not the prize I was after, Thea." His blue eyes sharpened. "Not by a long shot." Her pulse fluttered.

◆　◆　◆

The next day, Cage waited on the schoolhouse steps for Thea's buggy to appear on the winding road. But his heart hammered as he recalled the look on her face when he placed the grass ring on her finger a few days ago.

Did she remember how he'd done the same thing one long-ago spring? They'd been children. And Thea's idea—they'd pretended to be homesteaders under attack. As he recalled, George had insisted on being the lone Sioux warrior.

A billowing cloud of dust preceded her arrival. Rounding the bend, she pulled the reins short and brought the horses to a standstill at the front of the little schoolhouse. Rising from the steps, he hurried over to the hitching post.

He helped her step over the side. With both hands at her waist, he swung her to the ground in a flurry of skirts. And he didn't move. Nor did she.

Cage relished the feel of her in his arms. She'd fit so right in the shelter of his embrace during the footrace yesterday. Today as yesterday, she smelled like lavender water. Clean and fresh and lovely. He inhaled without meaning to, and he swallowed against a rush of feeling.

"It's good to have you home in Possum Trot, Thea. It's not Cheyenne, though. Hope you won't be bored teaching school here."

He kept his hands on her waist. And wonder of wonders, she didn't brush him aside or tell him to shove off like in the old days. She looked so pretty in the pink-sprigged ivory-colored dress. Her hair coiled so neatly on the back of her head.

She smiled. "I'm finding home has more going for it than Cheyenne ever could."

Heart thumping, he ducked his head and stepped away. "I put the desks inside the schoolhouse, and hung the blackboard. But I left it for you to arrange."

"Thank you, Cage."

Could she hear the wild drumming of his heart every time he got within two feet of her? "It wasn't a problem."

"No, I mean thank you for everything." She gave him a tremulous smile. "It's been a fun Harvest Week thanks to you."

He raised his eyebrows. "'Cause you finally managed to beat Sue Ellen at something?"

"I'll have you know I've managed to beat Sue Ellen at a number of things over the years."

He grinned. "Like pie making?"

She patted his cheek. "Don't make me hurt you again, Cage."

He laughed and broadened his chest. "You certainly bested her in landing yours truly as your fiancé. The ultimate catch in good ole Possum Trot."

She rolled her eyes. "How you fit a hat on that oversized opinion of yourself, Cage Cooper, I'll never know." She moved toward the steps.

He tied off the horses and followed her into the one-room schoolhouse. For the next hour, she directed and he positioned student desks. He placed the teacher's desk on the raised platform, which ran the width of the front of the classroom.

When he finished, he sank into one of the chairs. Thea scanned the room, turning in a slow circle. Each child would have their own primer. She'd stacked the slates on the edge of her desk. He'd hung the American flag on the wall. Chalk rested in the blackboard tray.

She clasped her hands under her chin. "It's perfect."

He shifted sideways and extended his long legs into the narrow aisle separating the girl and boy sides of the room. "Classes begin soon, right?"

"After harvest till spring planting. Barring a few blizzards here and there."

"You're an answer to many prayers, agreeing to teach in Possum Trot."

"Prayers?" She gave him that coy look, which made him want to kiss her. "Including yours?"

Especially his, hoping against hope she'd answer the town council's call to return. "What can I say?" He tried for a nonchalant shrug. "Being around you keeps me on my toes."

She smiled.

He unfolded from the chair and dusted off his hands. "Best get to the farm. Chores don't end, despite the fun I have with you, Theadosia."

She grabbed her satchel off her desk. "Could I ride out to the farm with you on my way home?"

"To my farm?" He tensed. "Why would you want to go there, Thea?"

"I've got to move my things from home into my new quarters at the boarding-house. I'll be living in town during the school term. Easier when there's bad weather."

"Okay." He nodded. "I'd be glad to help with your trunk."

"It's not that." She glanced down and then up at him. "I want to see the wonderful changes you've told me about at your farm."

She turned the ring around on her finger. "Please, Cage?"

And he found himself agreeing. After all, when had he ever been able to say no to Theadosia Holland?

Chapter Five

Cage jammed his hands in his pockets while Thea got a good look at his restored home.

Did she like it? Her good opinion mattered—had always mattered—far more to Cage than he'd ever let on. And the farmhouse looked nothing like the ramshackle hovel he'd lived in as a boy.

First, George left Possum Trot for law school and then, Thea went away, too. Lonely, Cage spent his spare time rebuilding the house. Every square inch—he realized now—with Thea in mind.

A two-story, white farmhouse with green shutters. Twin rockers sat on a wrap-around porch. He'd trimmed the eaves to resemble gingerbread. Yet despite his hard labor, the farmhouse was nothing like the sprawling Holland mansion down the road.

He flushed and scrubbed the back of his neck with his hand. He was an idiot. Why had he thought. . .hoped that Thea—?

"It's beautiful, Cage. You did this by yourself?"

He concentrated on tying the buggy reins to the porch railing. He couldn't look at her. He couldn't bear to see her pretending for his sake. "It's not grand, but—"

"No buts." She flitted from one end of the porch to the gazebo alcove on the other end. "It's so homey and wonderful and. . . ." She smiled. "How long did it take you to do this?"

He scuffed his boot on the bottom step. "'Bout six years, I reckon. Got some ideas from the Sears & Roebuck catalog at the mercantile."

Cage shrugged. "Just kept working on it little by little once the crop was harvested every year."

"I want to see everything. Top to bottom."

He stared at her. "Really?"

"Really."

Her eyes lit. And warmed Cage.

So he gave her the grand tour. Which took all of ten minutes. But she *oohed* and *aahed* over the hand-carved mantel in the parlor.

Thea slid her hand up the banister of the staircase and marveled at the smoothness. She exclaimed over the richness of the hardwood floors. "It's wonderful, Cage. All you need is some furnishings—"

"It needs a woman's touch."

He propped against the chair railing on the wall. Only one woman he wanted making additions to his house.

She tilted her head. "Which will be problematic as long as you insist on remaining a bachelor."

"Perhaps you could offer a few suggestions on what I might do about the situation."

Her forehead creased. "The situation?"

Cage's mouth went dry.

Her expression cleared. "You mean curtains and such."

That wasn't what he meant at all.

His chest tightened. "I'd be beholden to you, Thea, for any suggestions."

Cage took consolation in the fact he would no longer have to rely on his imagination to picture Thea gracing the rooms he'd created for her. But beyond that was mere wishful thinking.

"The light in the dining room is so magnificent. And with that prairie view?" She tapped her finger to her chin, scoping out the possibilities. "I might have some ideas for you. On ways to dress up the place."

Only way in his opinion to dress up the place would be with Thea herself.

But he couldn't say that to her. This pretend engagement had been his idea. A bad idea. He may have out-possumed himself.

He shoved off from the railing. "Not too female, though. It'll be a man living here, remember."

She gave him that look of hers. "I'm not likely to forget that, Cage Cooper." She cupped his cheek with her palm.

His pulse leaped.

Biting her lip, she dropped her hand. "I want to see everything. The barn. The animals. Everything."

She also insisted on helping Cage feed and water his livestock. In the henhouse, she held up the egg she'd collected.

"Good start." He handed her a basket. "One egg won't feed a hungry man. But we might make a country girl out of you yet, Thea."

"I always liked working with the animals, Cage. Don't you remember?"

Cage remembered a young Thea, almost swallowed by her petticoats, sneaking over to his farm during the summer. She'd loved helping with his chores. And with her by his side, the daily grind hadn't felt as grinding.

His mother, with little joy in her otherwise harsh life, had enjoyed Thea's bright smile and laughter. Most of all, his mother had enjoyed watching him with Thea.

Seeing the fun and boyishness Thea brought out in Cage. In unspoken agreement, however, they'd kept Thea away from Cage's father and his inebriation.

Cage's stomach knotted. No matter how hard he worked or wished, he'd never be anything other than the son of the town drunk.

He turned up the collar of his jacket. The wind had turned brisk, a harbinger of season's change. She shivered in her green traveling suit coat. Tomorrow his neighbors would arrive to harvest his crop. Just in time, if the weather took a bad turn.

Cage claimed the egg basket. "Let's get out of the wind."

She followed him to the porch. But she settled into the rocker and gazed over his fields. "It won't be long before the first snowflakes fall."

Leaving the basket at the door, he eased into the adjacent rocker. "Three more days before the dance."

Her mouth thinned, as if the reminder displeased her. "I guess so."

Would she miss seeing him as much as he—?

He sighed. "Our plan has worked beautifully so far. No one suspects we're playing possum. Everyone believes we're a real couple."

"A real couple." There was a funny note to her voice. As if she, like him, wasn't looking forward to the charade ending.

Which was ridiculous, of course. His imagination at work. Wishful thinking.

He scanned the snow-capped range on the horizon and fought the disquieting dread of how lonely this farm would be—how lonely he would be—with winter's first snowfall and Thea once again out of his life.

And as if Thea, too, didn't want to linger on the uncertainty of the future, she steered the conversation toward the past. Their shared past. He spent a pleasant hour laughing and reminiscing about mischievous exploits from their childhood.

Somehow Thea wormed out of him what he'd been doing the last six years without her. And she gave him a vivid picture of her boarding school in Cheyenne and an insight into her drive to become a teacher. He was surprised at how lonely she painted those years. Almost as if she'd been as eager to come home as he'd been for her to return.

His thoughts drifted on a wave of peaceful contentment. This had been the best week of his life. Today, quite possibly, the best day of his life. But all good things—like their false engagement—were bound to come to an end.

With the sun low and barely above the tree line, he got to his feet. If he wasn't careful, he could get used to this. Too used to this.

"You need to get home before dark. I'll make sure you get there safely."

She rose out of the rocker with some reluctance. Or so it seemed to Cage.

"Not much of a home without George and Mildred." She smoothed her suit jacket. "I've not had a real home since Mother and Father died."

"You have a lot of friends in Possum Trot who are glad to have you back."

Her eyes locked with his. "Friends like you?"

"Like me," he whispered.

She smiled and moved past him toward the buggy. "Old friends are the best friends."

Did old friends make the best sweethearts? Her hand in his, he helped Thea into the buggy. To him, pretend sweethearts or real, they certainly did.

◆　◆　◆

Several days later in the Wendover parlor, Thea scowled across the quilt frame as Sue Ellen harped about her own perfect, tiny stitches.

If Thea had her way, she'd take a stitch in Sue Ellen. And one not so tiny. Stitching shut that mouth of hers.

She and Sue Ellen had been verbally wrangling for *The Best Of* since grade school. Spelling bees, best essay, most As, most friends, you name it.

The other afternoon at Cage's farm had been perfect. Maybe the best afternoon of Thea's life. She could tell by the small smile flitting at the corners of Cage's handsome lips she'd pleased him with her reaction to his farmhouse.

A lovely home. Much more homey than the emptiness of the Holland house after her parents died. And the idea of making a home there with Cage...?

She'd contemplated little else as one hour rolled sleepless into the next. She was tired this morning, especially after working so hard with the other ladies at Cage's farm while the men brought in the last crop of the circuit yesterday.

As Cage's supposed fiancée, she'd been expected to preside over lunch. And thanks to good friends who brought more than their fair share of food, she'd been able to keep her lack of cooking skills under wraps despite Sue Ellen's prying nosiness.

But the proverbial clock ticked toward the end of their pretend engagement come Saturday evening at the dance. A death knell to hopes and dreams she'd hitherto not dared give wings. The noose of pretend was tightening in a stranglehold around her neck. She didn't know what to do to make it stop. Nor how to make this thing between her and Cage real.

Sue Ellen was going on and on about the embroidered linens in her hope chest to anyone and everyone who listened. The other ladies, mostly trying not to listen.

"And long do those linens languish in yonder hopeful chest," Thea murmured under her breath. Maybe not so under her breath.

Nellie pursed her lips. "Shots fired..."

Sue Ellen paused in her running monologue to contemplate Thea's latest not-so-tiny stitch. "Well, isn't that a toe-stubber? You're ruining Nellie's wedding quilt, Thea. Maybe you better go help the Possum Trot matrons in the kitchen. Oh, wait." Sue Ellen cocked her shiny blond head. "That's not exactly your forte either, is it?"

Thea's blood boiled. She'd like to snatch a quilter's knot in Sue Ellen's blond head.

Maud Wendover leaned over her needle. "Volley returned."

Sue Ellen's nose crinkled. "I fear our dear Cage Cooper isn't likely to fare so well under Thea's so-called tender ministrations. Possum Trot ladies may have to put him on an extended food rotation—to make sure he doesn't starve married to Thea."

Thea's fists curled on top of the crazy quilt—all the rage in Cheyenne. Lucy and Nellie exchanged looks.

"I'm sure Cage will be very content with his choice." Nellie jabbed her needle into the fabric, stretched taut. "I, for one, always believed Cage and Thea were meant to be."

Sweet Nellie, her dearest female friend.

"And it takes more than pie to make a marriage." Lucy jutted her chin.

Laughter broke out among the young women.

Nellie arched her brow with a teasing glint in her eyes. "Do tell."

Lucy blushed. "So I've been told. Besides, everyone has different gifts from the Lord. And a good man who truly loves you will appreciate who you are on the inside."

Thea counted herself blessed to have Lucy as one of her friends, too.

Maud—Lucy's younger sister—held her threaded needle between thumb and forefinger aloft. "You wouldn't be speaking of a certain young man who hails from Nebraska on the threshing crew this week, would you now, Lucy Wendover?"

"Hypothetically speaking, of course." Thea winked, coming to Lucy's aid.

More laughter. Lucy reddened again. And Thea resolved to learn to be a better cook. Just in case she ever tied the matrimonial knot for real. Hypothetically speaking, of course.

Sue Ellen pushed back from the quilt frame. Her mouth drooping, she shuffled to her feet. "I brought a variety of spools from the mercantile so we could showcase our stitches."

Thea frowned. Was that a sheen of tears in her nemesis's eye? Old Battle-Axe Sue?

Sue Ellen's chin quivered. "I—I left them in the foyer."

Thea's eyes cut to Nellie. Had she imagined the small catch in Sue Ellen's voice?

When Sue Ellen disappeared into the front hall, Lucy looked at Thea across the wooden frame. "She doesn't mean anything by all that talk. It's her way of trying to fit in."

Thea raised one eyebrow. "By bragging?" Trust tenderhearted Lucy to make excuses.

"She's actually very unsure of herself."

Thea snorted.

"No, really." Lucy's voice got softer. "Sue Ellen's the only one of our crowd without an engagement, and tonight marks the end of Harvest Week."

In the foyer, the front door creaked.

Thea hadn't considered Sue Ellen's situation from that perspective. Getting married had never been as important to Thea as it obviously was to Sue Ellen. Suppose it were Thea, sitting here among the happy brides, and Cage wasn't hers at the end of the week?

She grimaced. At the end of Harvest Week, Cage wasn't hers. And one day, he was bound to decide to get married.

The idea of Cage with someone else sent a shaft of pain through her heart. Suddenly, she was weary of the pretense. She had no reason to feel superior to Sue Ellen.

She stepped away from the frame. She needed to apologize to Sue Ellen. Thea was ashamed of herself. It was high past time that both of them acted like the grown-up women they claimed to be. Time to put aside schoolyard rivalries.

Thea headed toward the foyer. Had Sue Ellen retreated to the porch? Thea needed to do the right thing and reach out in friendship.

Possum Trot was big enough for the both of them. But a feminine giggle halted Thea at the base of the staircase.

Sue Ellen and Cage crouched nose to nose above an overturned willow basket. Spools of shimmering thread lay scattered across the rug. He said something, low and throaty. Sue Ellen swiped away moisture from her cheek. Giggled yet again.

And Thea lost it.

Chapter Six

What part of '*Cage is my fiancé*,' don't you get, Sue Ellen?"

Hunkered over the spilled basket and scattered spools of thread, Cage's head snapped up at the sound of Thea's voice. Sue Ellen blanched. Hands fisted, Thea glared down at them.

Cage bolted upright. "I—I didn't see you there, Thea."

Thea crossed her arms. "Obviously."

He had—obviously and unfortunately—walked into the middle of something at the Wendover house.

Sue Ellen swallowed. "It's not what it looks like."

"You ought to try taking a good look around you, Sue Ellen Oberheimer and claim the man who—daft though he be—seems to think the sun and the moon set with you." Thea's lip curled. "And with the pies you bake."

Cage had the uncomfortable feeling he was in over his head. As if he wasn't always in over his head when it came to Theadosia Holland.

He cleared his throat in an attempt to clear the air. "I came here to ask you, Thea, what time I should take you to the dance."

That met with stony silence.

He moistened his lips. "Sue Ellen needed my help. She—"

"I'm sure Sue Ellen did." The look Thea directed at him could have singed the wings off a butterfly.

Before he could think of a suitable reply, Thea stalked out of the Wendover house and slammed the door behind her. Leaving Cage gaping.

Abandoning Sue Ellen and the spools of thread, Cage went after Thea. She crossed Main and charged down the boardwalk. He had to trot to keep pace with her. She ignored him.

Cage followed her to the schoolhouse. He'd only just put his foot across the threshold when she tried shutting the door in his face. He leaped backward.

"Hey! You almost—"

"Which is just too bad, you womanizing. . ." Gritting her teeth, she whipped around and marched toward the front of the classroom.

Cage edged inside. "If you'd just listen. . ."

She hefted a book off her desk, and then appeared to reconsider. She lay the book down on the desk once more. And instead, seized a piece of chalk.

"Thea, let me—"

She hurled the chalk across the room.

He ducked as the chalk exploded against the wall behind him. He straightened. "If I didn't know better, I'd say you were acting like a jealous, lovesick—"

She stomped toward the woodpile beside the stove.

"Okay. . .okay." He held up his hand as she lifted a chunk of wood. "Simmer down. It was nothing, I tell you."

"Can't stay away from the women can you, Cage?" Her eyebrows rose almost to her hairline. "Flirting is like breathing to you, isn't it? You're going to ruin everything we've done this week."

"I wasn't flirting. The thread rolled out. I was helping her—"

"More like she was helping herself to you."

"I'd never cheat on the woman I love. I'm not that kind of man."

Confusion, doubt, and hurt flickered in her brown eyes. "The woman you love?"

He fought the overwhelming desire to cradle Thea in the circle of his arms. They stared at each other for a long moment. Just once. . . He took a quick intake of breath. Just once he wished. . .

Chin quivering, she knotted her fingers in the folds of her skirt. "I hate you, Cage Cooper." She tore her gaze away.

He exhaled. He knew she did not hate him. "It's wrong to hate anyone, Theadosia."

Cage smirked. "Especially your beloved fiancé."

"Then I strongly dislike you, Cage Cooper," she growled.

He leaned his shoulder against the door frame, ankles crossed. "Have I told you how I love it when you sweet-talk me, Sugar Plum?"

She flung out her hands. "It's all talk with you, isn't it?"

He frowned. "What do you mean?"

She sniffed. "All talk, no action."

He stood up straight. "Plenty of action here, I promise you." He thumped his fist against his chest.

She lifted her chin. "What about that prize you bragged about claiming? What happened to that?"

"Well, I—"

"Don't you think we ought to practice making it seem real?"

His mouth fell open. "What?"

"B–before the dance tomorrow night," she stammered. "To make it look authentic."

"Of all the crazy—" He propped his hands on his hips. "Is this one of those

147

newfangled suffragette notions of yours, Theadosia Holland?" He shook his head. "This is what comes from going to the big city."

He shifted. "Are you asking me. . . ?" He gulped. "Are you asking me to kiss you, Thea?"

"I—I. . ." Panic streaked across her face. "Never mind." She turned to flee.

But she'd not taken two steps before he came after her. And closed the distance between them.

◆ ◆ ◆

Gripping her shoulders, he angled Thea to face him. The flush, which had started beneath her shirtwaist collar, mounted to her cheeks. New American Woman or not, Thea could not imagine what had come over her.

Thea's eyes lifted to meet his.

His Adam's apple bobbed. "You might be right about making it look real." His blue eyes beckoned and went opaque.

She put a hand to the cameo at her starched lace collar. "I—"

Cage crushed her tight against his chest. And as if her arms had taken on a life of their own, she found her hands cupped around the back of his neck. He lowered his head.

Her lips parted, but no sound emerged. His mouth moved closer. His breath brushed across her cheek.

Thea's heart hammered. She couldn't breathe. She thought she might faint. Then he kissed her. Thoroughly. Deliciously.

She decided breathing might be overrated. And she kissed him back. Thoroughly. Deliciously.

After a long moment, he pulled back. "'Course I'm not saying every newfangled suffragette notion is all bad." He raked a hand through his hair.

She fell against the corner of her desk. Glad for its support. Her knees wobbled beneath her skirt.

He grinned that rakish, roguish grin of his. "What kind of modern American man would I be to stand in the way of progress?"

She liked how he looked at her. She ran her gaze over the angular line of his jaw. She liked how the short ends of his hair curled on the nape of his neck—the feel of his hair through her fingers. Her cheeks burned with the remembrance.

"That real enough for you, darlin'?" He traced his finger along the pattern of her features before he stepped away. "And by the way, Thea?"

She held on to the desk for support. "Y–yes, Cage?"

He gave her a crooked grin. "I'll pick you up at seven."

Chapter Seven

C age raised his hand to knock on the boardinghouse door. Then, let it fall to his side. What was he doing calling on Thea?

Him—the no-good Cooper boy.

If his old buddy George had been in Possum Trot instead of Omaha, Cage would've never had the nerve to instigate this farfetched pretend engagement with George's sister.

He glanced down the length of Main. Buggies and wagons from outlying farms were tied to the makeshift railing in the meadow between the church and schoolhouse.

Where, for tonight, a wooden floor had been laid. Hundreds of lanterns lined the perimeter of the dance pavilion. Harnesses jingled as more farmers and ranchers arrived.

Couples thronged the gathering. The women in their swirling skirts danced arm in arm with Harvest Week beaus. Before the night was out, per Possum Trot custom, these same couples would declare their intention to marry.

As for Thea and him?

In the sidelight glass, he checked his appearance. He adjusted his string tie. His hand shook.

Why was he so nervous? There'd been a time when a younger Cage and younger Thea saw each other six days out of seven. But back then, he hadn't felt so...so... He shuffled his shined boots on the porch.

Not exactly true. In those days, he was less bold about acting on his true feelings for Thea. But forced by the kiss yesterday afternoon, he'd come to an inescapable conclusion.

He'd taken a good, long, honest look at his real intentions toward Thea. He grappled with the dilemma of what to do about this pretend engagement into which he'd boxed the both of them. His mouth still burned after the "practice" kiss they'd shared.

Cage bit back a grin. He planned to remind schoolmarm Thea—every chance he got tonight—practice makes perfect. Although, he blew out a pent-up breath, her lips on his seemed pretty perfect to him already.

Smiling, he knocked briskly and squared his shoulders. The door wrenched open. And the breath left him in a whoosh as he beheld the girl—now woman— he'd hopelessly loved for so long.

Lace ruching the neckline, Thea wore a burgundy-colored silk with short puffy sleeves. With her hair coiled in a chignon, a cascade of curls framed her oval face. She was beautiful. And Cage knew he had no business being her fiancé—pretend or not.

She smoothed the sash at her waist. "How do you like my dress, Cage?"

One hand hidden behind his back, he leaned against the door frame. "I—I like it fine."

Her brow puckered.

Cage cleared his throat. "Here." He thrust a bouquet of purple asters into her hands. The last of the prairie wildflowers.

"Thank you, Cage." She smiled. "They're lovely."

"Not as lovely as you," he whispered.

Snow capped the distant mountain range. It'd be a matter of days before snow reached the valleys. The harvest had ended none too soon. As must their engagement.

Tonight, in fact. He'd escape the matrimonial noose just in the nick of time. Only now he wished Thea Holland was truly his to love and cherish forever. A pipe dream for someone like him. Unless he could figure out a way to. . . ?

She disappeared inside the boardinghouse to put the flowers in water and returned with a silky shawl hanging from her shoulders. "Guess what?"

He took her hand and closed the boardinghouse door behind them. "What?"

"My brother and Mildred arrived home today."

Growing dread crystallized in his belly. Time had run out for them. There'd be no more delaying the inevitable. George's homecoming changed everything.

"A storm threatened to close the rail lines. So they decided to return before the blizzard trapped them far from home."

His heart sank. He thought about the grandeur of Thea's childhood home, and his barely-making-ends-meet farm. George with his fancy lawyer degree. And George's wife, Mildred, from one of Wyoming's first families.

Thea deserved much more than Cage could ever give her. Seeing her tonight clarified his resolve and at the same time, made it much harder to do what he knew he needed to do. To carry out what they'd planned from the beginning.

She tilted her head, and a curl danced along her collarbone. He shoved his hands in his pockets, lest he give in to the impulse to coil the tendril around his finger. As he had earlier this week. Which seemed a lifetime ago. All the lifetime he'd ever get to call Thea his.

If he had any sense at all, he'd walk away right now and return to the farm. But he'd never possessed much good sense when it came to Thea Holland. This so-called playing possum engagement, case in point.

Yet he couldn't leave without once... Just once...

This one last time to dream and pretend Thea could be his. Tonight—God help him—needed to last Cage a lifetime.

Because facing a lifetime of aloneness, he wanted to remember Thea as she was tonight. On his arm. In the glow of a hundred lantern lights. His—if only his in pretend.

◆　◆　◆

At the pavilion, Thea greeted fellow Possum Trot residents. The matchmaking matrons sipped from punch glasses. The older men traded fish stories. In their Sunday best, children darted underfoot.

The moon cast a silvery glow, imbuing the meadow with an enchanted, fairy-tale air. Fiddlers sawed from one popular tune to the next. Couples do-si-doed. George and Mildred waved from the dance floor.

Cage's profile hardened. "I hope we'll always be friends, Thea."

Unease sparked along her nerve endings. He'd been quiet all evening. Too quiet. "What's wrong, Cage?"

His mouth thinned. "Nothing's wrong. Merely getting back to reality. To who we are."

Thea's throat constricted. "Who do you think we are, Cage?"

"I'm a farmer. And you?" He took a shaky breath. "You're the beautiful Thea Holland, wealthy heiress, teacher, and suffragette."

She clutched his sleeve. "You're not just a farmer. You're smart and—"

"Face it, Thea." He gave a brittle laugh. "A Cooper and a Holland were never meant to be.

She stamped her foot. "I'm so tired of you selling yourself short. Me being a Holland has nothing to do with anything."

"It has everything to do with us, Thea." His shoulders slumped. "Do you think George wants his sister hitched, pretend or otherwise, with a farmer? I think not."

After the kiss, she'd hoped—

She frowned. "You are George's best friend. I think he'd love having you as a brother for real."

"Not where you're concerned, Thea. He wants better for you." Cage looked away. "And so do I. Someone like Frederic Tierney, who can give you the things in life you deserve. The life you're accustomed to."

Her mouth quivered. "Only one here who is a snob is you, Cage Cooper. How dare you presume to tell me what makes me happy. You—when you're not being pigheaded and stupid—make me happy." Frustration filled her voice.

"We'd only hurt each other." He thrust his jaw out and forward. "You wanting what I can't provide. I'm no good for you."

She threw out her hands. "So you're going to walk away? Leave me on the dance floor? Play out this stupid pretend scenario?"

"It's what we planned. We were playing possum for the duration of the wedding fever. Harvest Week ends at the dance, Thea."

Thea lifted her chin. "Problem is, I don't think I've been playing possum. For your information, I had lots of job offers. I realize now I didn't come back to only teach school in Possum Trot."

She jabbed a finger in his waistcoat vest. "I came back for you. Because you, Micajah Stephen Cooper, are the love of my life."

He sucked in a breath, and fixed his gaze on the snow-topped ridge on the horizon.

She longed with every fiber of her being for him to say something, anything. For him to take her into his arms and kiss her like he'd kissed her yesterday. Yesterday, when the world—her world—seemed bright with promise. A sick feeling welled in her gut.

His posture stiff, Cage faced her. "Dance with me, Thea?"

"Cage. . . Please don't do this. . ."

He clenched his teeth together, his jaw tight. "One dance."

"Just one dance?" she whispered.

"Like we planned, Thea. And then. . ." He hunched his shoulders.

She muffled the tiny sob threatening to explode from her throat. He'd never said he loved her. Everything they'd done was pretend.

But sometime this week, it stopped being pretend. Truth to tell, had it ever really been pretend for her? Pain sliced through Thea. After the kiss yesterday, she'd been so sure Cage felt the same for her as she felt for him.

As the musicians took up the new, lilting tune she'd first heard back in Cheyenne, Cage held out his hand. Conflicting emotions rippled across his face. Sadness and a fierce vulnerability. His gaze traveled to her mouth. And lingered.

Her heart beating faster than the three-four time of the waltz, she took his hand. Her eyes locked on to his. And his eyes smoldered a smoky blue.

With her hand clasped in his and his other arm around her waist, Cage maintained a careful distance between their bodies. She placed her free hand on the broad length of his shoulder.

Elbows up and carriage erect, he never took his eyes off her face. His hold never wavered as he led her in the three-four time of the box waltz. One-two-three. One-two-three. One-two-three.

Casey would waltz with a strawberry blond and the band played on. . .

A muscle ticked in his cheek.

He'd glide cross the floor with the girl he adored and the band played on. . .

One-two-three. One-two-three. One-two-three.

The music and the words flowed over her like gentle rain.

But his brain was so loaded it nearly exploded, the poor girl would shake with alarm.

Cage's chest rose and fell as if he were having difficulty drawing breath.

One-two-three. One-two-three. One-two-three.

He'd never leave the girl with the strawberry curls, and the band played on.

Cage didn't let go. As if he was reluctant as she for this dance to end. For their engagement to end.

Around and around. One-two-three. One-two-three. One-two-three.

He came to a sudden stop and removed his arm from her waist. It took him a moment longer to relinquish her hand.

She closed her eyes as he brushed his lips across her fingers. She wanted to scream. She wanted to moan. This couldn't be happening. Not after everything they'd been to each other over this last week. Not after everything they'd meant to each other all these years.

Dropping her hand, he stepped back. "Thank you, Thea."

Her eyes flew open. Her heart pounded. "Must we stop?" And she wasn't just talking about the dance.

"It's for the best."

She seized hold of his sleeve. "Stop assuming you know what's best for me."

His eyes flicked over her face. "School starts next week. And the rest of your life."

Bleak despair spiraled inside Thea. "A life without you is not the life I want."

Gently, he pried her fingers off his sleeve. "I'm no good for you, Thea."

Hot tears burned the back of her eyelids. She wanted to weep. For herself. For him.

But most of all, for who they could've been together.

❖ ❖ ❖

The love of Thea's life. Cage's chest heaved. As she was the love of his.

But he couldn't tell her that. Not ever. Not and do what he knew he must for her own good. He loved Thea too much to hold her back from the life she was born to live.

Without another word, he left Thea in the middle of the dance floor. It took everything inside him to walk away. To leave her and not look back.

He strode toward the food table where Sue Ellen held court with Frederic Tierney. Grabbing Sue Ellen around the waist, he pulled her close and kissed her full on the mouth.

People gasped. The music jarred to a halt. At the sudden silence, the crowd parted like the Red Sea, leaving an open path between Thea and himself with Sue Ellen in his arms.

Wide-eyed in disbelief, Sue Ellen jerked free. "How dare you? You two-timing scoundrel." She slapped Cage across the face.

Reeling, his face burned from the sting of her hand.

Sue Ellen's eyes darted to Thea. "I'm sorry, Thea. I would've never—"

Frederic Tierney hauled back his fist and punched Cage in the jaw. Cage's head snapped sideways. He staggered and fell to the floor.

"Don't you ever put your hands on my Sue Ellen again, Cooper." Frederic flushed. "I mean, Miss Oberheimer."

Sue Ellen took hold of his arm. "I think maybe you said it right the first time, Freddy." She smiled. Frederic Tierney's face transformed. The band started over with another tune.

Thea stalked off the dance floor and flung aside the well-meaning commiserations from the Possum Trot matchmakers. Mildred went after Thea. Cage hung his head.

George pulled Cage to his feet. "Why are you doing this?"

Cage adjusted his jaw with his hand. Who knew a restauranteur could throw a punch like that? "Figured you'd be pleased to be rid of me."

George sighed. "Which shows how little you understand what's important to Thea or me. You are such an idiot."

"She's better off without me, George, and you know it."

"Thea told me about your pretend engagement to out-possum the Possum Trot matchmakers. I also know how you've pined for my sweet sister all these years."

Cage blinked away the moisture welling in his eyes. "I—I don't know what you mean."

George brushed the dust off Cage's coat. "All these years you used the flirtations to throw the matchmakers off the real scent of your feelings for Thea. Those other romances were the true pretense. You panicked, didn't you, when you saw Thea get off the train? You were afraid she'd pick someone else during Harvest Week."

Cage swallowed. "It doesn't matter what I feel. This is for the best. She can teach and campaign till women get the vote in every state." He made a face. "Which—between you and me—is about as likely as Thea and I getting married for real."

"Thea loves you." His best friend shook his head. "Your pride is misplaced."

Cage wanted to curl up somewhere and die. "I'll never be anything more than the son of the town drunk. And I would never ruin Thea's life."

"You're wrong about my sister. And about yourself. Can't you see that the only thing that will ruin Thea's life is living without you?" George straightened the lapels on Cage's suit coat. "I only hope when you finally admit the truth, it's not too late. Too late for you and Thea to be as happy as Mildred and me."

Chapter Eight

It had been a long, sorrowful weekend. Fraught with violent, booming thunderstorms. During which Cage reminded himself women were nothing but trouble. Thea, most of all.

Sunday passed with Cage trying to convince himself that breaking their engagement was for the best—best for Thea. A Cooper and a Holland? Ridiculous.

Yet early Monday morning when he finally stumbled out of bed after a sleepless night, his heart ached for what could never be. And with Thea teaching school in Possum Trot, he wasn't sure how he was going to handle seeing her so often.

Maybe she'd marry that Tierney fellow and return to Cheyenne. Cage groaned. He shuffled out of the house to the barn to complete his predawn chores. But the farm was filled with memories of Thea.

The animals were especially restless. The chickens squawked. Bellowing, the cow refused to give any milk. Unusually jittery and high-strung, his horse kicked repeatedly at the rails of the corral.

What in the world was wrong with—? It was then he noticed the rosy glow on the horizon of Possum Trot. The sunrise was fiery, beautiful and striking.

The air hung heavy, motionless. Muggy and somehow oppressively ominous. A visceral electric quality charged the atmosphere.

Propping his boot on a fence railing, he stared across the fields toward town. He surveyed the neat stacks of hay, the culmination of a year of hard work. But satisfaction eluded him.

God, what am I going to do about Thea? And though he loved this farm, for the first time he entertained thoughts of selling up and moving out. Somewhere, anywhere, to give his heart time to heal.

He exhaled. Like that was ever going to happen. He'd pined for Thea for six long years. Proving distance had nothing to do with matters of the heart.

A distant clanging from the direction of town caught his attention. He cocked his head to listen. The schoolhouse bell. Thea was probably already there, getting ready for her first big day of teaching.

But the bell—kind of early for the children to arrive. He brushed his hand over his face. Maybe groggy with lack of sleep, he'd laid abed later than usual.

Cage sniffed the air. The pinkish glow stretching across the prairie had deepened to an orange hue. He frowned. That couldn't be right. He stiffened.

Something was burning. Had the lightning storm last night ignited the prairie? His breath hitched. Harvested bales surrounded the town. Tinder to fuel a conflagration.

Cage's heart jolted. The schoolhouse. Possum Trot was on fire. Thea—

He had to get to Thea. Without conscious thought, he shooed the chickens out of the pen. Turned the cow loose outside the barn. Saddled his horse and headed for town. She'd be desolate if anything happened to the schoolhouse. He had to do everything he could to save it for her.

When he arrived, town residents had formed a water-bucket brigade. It was touch and go for a while. Tongues of fire had already engulfed the livery. Sparks from the leaping flames caught hold on the roof of the church.

The threshing crew, the reverend, and the Murdocks shifted their efforts to the church. Nellie Jones, Lucy Wendover, and her family struggled against the encroaching fire threatening homes and businesses along Main.

Sue Ellen, her parents, and Frederic Tierney helped Cage battle the flames in the school meadow. The wind kept shifting, hampering their efforts. Overrunning their success.

Yet no one quit. No one gave up. And thanks to the combined efforts of the community, Possum Trot was saved.

Exhausted, he leaned upon the handle of the shovel. Like him, everyone looked the worse for wear, disheveled and weary. Their faces blackened from the smoke. But together, they'd done it. Cheers erupted.

Frederic clapped Cage on the shoulder and grinned. "Well done, Mr. Cooper. Well done."

Had Thea been right about Cage's standing in the community?

Maybe he wasn't always destined to be the no-good Cooper kid. Perhaps in the town's eyes he never had been. And for the first time, he caught a glimpse of how Possum Trot might see him.

How he ought to see himself—as a hardworking neighbor, a successful farmer, a good friend. The way Thea had always seen him.

Cage suddenly realized who he hadn't seen this morning. "Thea?" His gaze raked over the crowd.

Sue Ellen wiped her sleeve across her mouth and grimaced at the soot. "What's wrong?"

"Has anyone seen Thea?" His heart raced. "In town? At the school? After the fire started?"

Cage dashed from person to person. But no one had seen her. Not since she'd taken one of the horses out of the stable.

Where could she be? A sinking unease roiled his belly. And fear, like none he'd ever known, gripped Cage.

◆　◆　◆

With the thunderstorm, Thea hadn't gotten a wink of sleep the night before the school term was to begin. She hadn't slept well since the Harvest Dance. She was so angry with Cage.

Angry and hurt and confused. Stricken with how little Cage regarded himself. Unworthy of her love. Unworthy of being loved.

She tried to pray. But the loss of him was so great, she found herself at a loss for words. Dragging herself out of bed, she changed into the serviceable brown-striped dress she'd chosen for the first day of school.

Today was supposed to be the best day of her life. Dreams fulfilled that she'd worked hard to attain. Yet without Cage in her life, this day—like the days to come—was without meaning or true purpose.

Slumped in the chair in her boardinghouse bedroom, she gazed dispiritedly out the window. Her eyes wandered over the roof of the schoolhouse at the edge of town. Past the farms and fields. In her mind's eye, beyond the woods to a beautiful, two-story farmhouse. A hip-roofed red barn and to the one man to whom her heart had always belonged.

But he didn't want her. She shook her head. No, he was afraid to allow himself to love her. This never being good enough for Possum Trot or a Holland was rubbish. *If only Cage could see that.*

None of them were good enough, but God loved them anyway. Being good enough didn't matter—not when it came to true love. And God's love for Cage, Thea—even Sue Ellen, though it pained Thea to include her—was the truest love of all.

Thea sat lost in thought until she noticed the orange glow lighting the prairie. A glorious sunrise. She sighed. She really ought to get going.

She had lessons to write on slates. Preparations to make. The glow intensified.

Gripping the chair arms, she tensed. Something was wrong. Then, she was on her feet. The Cheyenne papers had been full of a similar story last summer of a devastating prairie fire in Nebraska.

The town. The school. Everyone's livelihood on the surrounding farms. The harvest would go up in smoke.

Her heart thudded. She flew down the stairs and yanked open the door. Her skirts bundled in her hands, she dashed past a startled Sue Ellen sweeping the boardwalk in front of the mercantile.

Thea gestured at the horizon. "Fire!"

She raced past the church across the meadow and onto the schoolhouse steps. She rang the bell. The clapper clanged against the metal, harsh in the heavy morning air. But there was another sound.

The sound froze Thea to the marrow of her bones. A roaring like a locomotive. Accelerating. The sound of devouring flames.

Possum Trot residents poured out of homes and businesses. Bucket in hand, she ran back and forth a dozen times between the water trough and the school. She thought of her family home—but George and the hands were more than sufficient for that task.

And she envisioned Cage's lovely home. With no one to help him, he'd be fighting the flames alone. Facing the destruction of his dreams.

Thea handed her bucket to one of the threshing crew. Cage wasn't alone. He had her, whether he wanted her or not.

She hurried to the livery. The owner led the horses out of the stalls, setting them free to run to safety. She grabbed the mane of one of the horses. And using the boardwalk as a stepping stool, she swung onto the horse's bare back.

Thea dug her heels into the horse and spurred him forward. On the outskirts of town, the horse reared, almost unseating her. Panicked, she hung on for dear life as the horse fought her. Grappling for control, the heat of the flames warmed her cheeks. Like the horse, she struggled against a growing terror.

But a greater terror for Cage—fighting the prairie fire alone—wouldn't allow Thea to give in to her natural instinct to run in the other direction.

And if the acrid smell set her coughing, what must the overwhelming stench of the fire be doing to the horse's stronger sense of smell? At the fork in the road, the horse halted in its tracks and refused to budge. Its frightened whinnies punctuated the crackle of the licking flames.

God, help me get to Cage. You are the Giver of all good gifts. He was always Your gift to me. Help me to save him and his dream.

With a prayer for courage, she slid off the mare. Thea released her hold. The horse bolted. Holding her pinafore to her nose against the black, billowing smoke, she stumbled down the road to Cage's farm.

A deer darted out of the underbrush. She shrank back. But the sheer horror in the creature's gaze reflected her own. Rabbits, squirrels, antelope. A stream of wildlife followed the deer's frenzied attempt to escape the flames. The wind buffeted her skirts.

She staggered into the farmyard. There'd be no going back. A wall of flame had cut off any escape route into town.

"Cage! Cage?"

Door ajar, the house wore a deserted air. She sprinted into the barn to find the animals gone. Perhaps Cage, too, had already fled. In the hayloft, a spark fanned into flame.

Thea couldn't let him lose everything for which he'd worked so hard. Not while she had breath in her body. She grabbed one of the empty feed sacks and darted for the rain barrel outside the barn.

She plunged the sack into the water, drenched the burlap and angled in time to see one, then two of Cage's carefully piled haystacks burst into flame. Another and another. The entire field.

Pop. Pop. A window on the wraparound porch exploded. A shooting ember kindled the grass at the base of the farmhouse.

Uncertain which blaze to attack first, she spun around. The barn. The fields. The house.

Fire took hold of the curlicue fretwork Cage had carved. Ghastly, crashing sounds as the fire took hold of the barn. Destroying everything in its path.

She rushed toward the fire erupting along the foundation of the house. Hefting the gunnysack over her head, she beat back the flames until the burlap caught fire.

Too late, she dropped the sack. The hem of her skirt ignited—her eyes widened. *Dear Jesus. . .*

She screamed.

Chapter Nine

When Cage barreled into the farmyard on his horse, he reckoned if he lived to be a hundred he'd never see anything as horrible as watching Thea's skirt erupt into flame.

"Don't run, Thea," he shouted above the noise of the fire. "Stand still. Don't move."

Her head snapped up at the sound of his voice. Tears streamed from her eyes—whether from the smoke or fear or both. The tears plowed furrows through the sooty blackness on her face.

The wind shifted, taking the wall of flame toward the field and the surrounding woods. Creating an island, an oasis, free of fire for the moment. And he knew there wasn't a moment to lose.

He leaped off the horse, walloped the horse's hindquarters and set the animal free.

Sobbing, she swatted at the flames. "C–Cage. . ."

He raced toward her. "Don't use your hands. Wait." He beat at the flames with his own hands.

She grabbed his arm. "Stop. You'll hurt yourself."

"Let me go." He jerked free. "It doesn't matter about me. I won't let anything happen to you, Thea."

He ripped off the lower tier of her skirt. He flung the fabric into the yard and stomped out the remaining flames with his boot.

She fell into his arms. "How did you know I was here?"

He wrapped his arms around her. "I started for George's place but then—"

Cage swallowed. He'd felt a still, small voice urging him to turn left at the fork and head for his own farm.

He closed his eyes. If he'd not listened? If he'd made the wrong choice?

Fear of what could've happened—of later finding Thea burned to death among the smoldering ruins of his home—made his knees grow weak. *Thank You, God for saving Thea. For helping me find her in time.*

She buried her face in his shirt. "But your house? The farm? I tried to save it for you, Cage."

His arms tightened around her. "Nothing matters, except you."

Only Thea—not the house or the farm—was the only thing he'd never be able to live without.

She raised her head. "But you've lost everything." Her eyes glistened.

"Have I lost everything?" He fought against the lump in his throat. "Have I lost you because of my stubborn pride and stupidity, Thea?"

Thea cupped his face between her palms. Holding his heart and his future, too.

Something tore inside his chest. "I love you, Thea. Always have. I always will. I should've never said what I did at the dance. Will you forgive me?"

Her mouth curved. "No more fake engagement?"

Cage shook his head. "No more fake anything between you and me."

She ran her thumb across his lips. "Good, because whether you like it or not, I aim to show Possum Trot we're a real couple."

His heart thundered. "I—I like it just fine, Thea." Relief washing through him, he kissed the grass-plaited ring on her finger. "I hear women's suffrage is gaining support in Idaho."

She tucked her head into the curve of his neck. "The only place I want to be is wherever you are."

Cage widened his stance to hip's width. "I might even be willing to carry a few signs myself when you hit the campaign trail."

"National women's suffrage will have to wait, at least for me." She took a long look around the farm. "I think I'll have my hands plenty full in Possum Trot teaching school, being a farmwife, and training you."

"Is this you asking me to marry you? You really are a modern American woman." He gave in to the grin struggling to break free. "But what's this training business about?"

"Get 'em young, train 'em right."

He made sure she saw him roll his eyes. "That civilizing influence you referred to when I proposed last week?"

She elbowed him in the ribs. "Best I recall, you made me propose to you. Your turn this time."

Taking her hand, he dropped to one knee. "Will you marry me now that Harvest Week is over?"

She cocked her head. "You're asking me to marry you for real?" She felt the need to clarify. And rub it in.

He grunted. "I said that, didn't I?"

She gazed down at him. "Just wanted to hear you say it so I can tell our children how their papa dragged me to the Possum Trot altar."

"Whatever you say, dear." He gave her one of his irresistible smiles. "Possum Trot will know the truth. How you hog-tied and hitched me into matrimony."

"Me hog-tie you? This whole thing was your idea. . ." She narrowed her eyes. "You're nothing but a big, overgrown, never serious, seriously annoying—"

161

"Who's seriously in love with you, Thea Holland. As for the farm?" He averted his gaze from the fire leaping from one haystack to the next. His shoulders sagged.

He couldn't bear to watch the destruction of everything for which he'd labored so long. "I've got nothing left. How am I going to start over?"

She pointed to something over his shoulder. "How about with the help of your Possum Trot neighbors?"

◆ ◆ ◆

A buckboard driven by Frederic Tierney emerged out of the smoke. On board, Sue Ellen and the Wendover sisters waved feed sacks above their heads like an army parading its colors. Other wagons followed.

The threshing crew. George, Mildred, and the Holland farmhands. The reverend and the Murdocks. The good townspeople of Possum Trot.

A few hours later, the last spark had been extinguished. Thanks to Cage's neighbors. His harvest was gone, but the house and the barn had been saved.

Mrs. Murdock swiped at a black smudge on Thea's cheek. "I trust now, you and Cage will stop playing pretend and make this wedding a reality."

Thea's mouth fell open. "You knew?"

"Playing Possum Trot, indeed." Mrs. Murdock, the undisputed queen of the Possum Trot matchmakers, fluttered her hand. "You and Cage didn't think you'd invented something new, did you?"

"But your nephew—"

"Just the right nudge you and Cage needed to do what was obvious to the rest of us since you both were children." She pursed her lips. "I knew Freddy and Sue Ellen would make a perfect pair. Though that proved harder than I first believed."

Thea felt like Alice falling through the rabbit hole. Make that a possum hole.

"But all's well that ends well, don't you think?" Mrs. Murdock winked. "You can't kid a kidder, and you can't outplay a player. Murdock and I were out possum-ing Possum Trot before you were a twinkle in your mother's eye."

Thea and Cage had been played. And Thea couldn't be happier about it.

With promises of provisions and seed till he recouped his losses next fall, the townsfolk drifted to their wagons.

"You didn't fool me." Sue Ellen sniffed. "I knew your engagement was a sham all along."

Thea arched a singed eyebrow. "Oh really?"

Sue Ellen hung on to Frederic's arm. "And everything worked out for the best." She and Frederic exchanged smiles. "Pa's going to offer Freddy a job at the mercantile after we're married. We can live in the room at the back of the store."

Frederic squeezed her hand. "Might be kind of cramped, Sue Ellen honey."

"It'll be cozy and wonderful as long as we're together." Sue Ellen's face glowed. Almost making her appear pretty. Almost. . .

Frederic kissed her cheek. "I'm sure I can find something—maybe even better—just so long as we're together." He cut his eyes at Thea and smiled.

She conceded Frederic and Sue Ellen made a sweet couple. She supposed even someone as odious as Sue Ellen deserved a little happiness. Perhaps marriage to a nice man like Frederic would teach Sue Ellen to be nicer.

But Thea would love to be a fly on the wall when Sue Ellen realized she'd been played by the Possum Trot matchmakers, too.

Thea would probably never hear the end of it once Sue Ellen learned the truth about her soon-to-be husband. About how Sue Ellen had snared a Tierney, the most eligible bachelor in Wyoming.

Which was fine by Thea. Because she'd be hitched to Possum Trot's most eligible farmer, Cage Cooper. The only man she'd ever love.

"No more pretending." Sue Ellen's nose wrinkled. "Of course, I'd be glad to give you some cooking lessons, Thea."

Thea stiffened.

"Wouldn't want my dear friend Cage to starve to death."

Her dear friend? As for Sue Ellen becoming nicer? Thea realized that was about as likely as a man walking on the moon. As in probably never going to happen. Frederic threw Thea an apologetic look.

She struggled to remember she was a Christian woman. Jaw jutted, she managed to thank Sue Ellen for her generous offer. Although, begrudgingly.

Through a glint of white, even teeth. . .

She blew out a breath as the last wagon hit the road. "Sue Ellen's finally right about one thing."

Cage waved to their departing neighbors. "What's that?"

She gave Cage her cat-swallowed-the-cream smile. "No more playing possum."

His lips twitched. "You said you wouldn't marry me if I was the last man on—"

"What I said was I wouldn't marry you if I was a prairie on fire." She swept her arm across the charred expanse. "Who can argue with an act of God?"

He moistened his lips. "So does that mean I'm your bucket of water, Thea Holland?"

"That would be a most definite yes, Cage Cooper." She nestled in his arms. "You are my sun, moon, and all the stars in the sky."

"Have I told you how I love it when you sweet-talk me, Sugar Plum?"

Cage made a sound in the back of his throat. "I'll have my work cut out for me with a modern American woman like yourself."

Her insides quivered with a swirl of anticipation.

"It's nothing but talk, talk, talk with you." Smiling, she lifted her face to his. "Are you going to kiss me or what, Cooper?"

And then he did.

Lisa Carter and her family make their home in North Carolina. In addition to *Playing Possum*, she is the author of seven romantic suspense novels and a contemporary Coast Guard romantic series. When she isn't writing, Lisa enjoys traveling to romantic locales, teaching writing workshops, and researching her next exotic adventure. She has strong opinions on barbecue and ACC basketball. She loves to hear from readers and you can connect with Lisa at www.lisacarterauthor.com.

Hog Trough Bride

by Ramona K. Cecil

Dedication

To the memory of my mother and Honeytown gal Frieda Herekamp Jolly, who told me about the custom of dancing in the hog trough and would have loved this story.

Chapter One

Honeytown, Indiana
May 1885

D ance, dance, dance!"
Anger shot through Rose Hamilton at the gleeful chants from the crowd around her. A wedding should be an occasion of joy, not an excuse to engage in humiliation.

"Dance, dance, dance!"

The sound of hand claps now joined with the chants as the jubilant throng moved as one toward the dusty expanse between the Bennetts' farmhouse and barn, pushing Rose along with it. Sadness and disgust curled in her belly when two burly men at the head of the crowd lifted the bride's older sister into a hollowed-out hickory log used to douse hogs in scalding water at butchering time.

"Poor Olive. Too bad she couldn't find a man before her younger sister did." The faux sympathy in the woman's whispered voice near Rose's ear brought the simmering anger inside her to a boil. "Serves her right for bein' so persnickety."

Rose turned and glared at Myrtle Foster. "It's too bad that folks find more enjoyment in embarrassing poor Olive for remaining single than in congratulating her sister, Nora, on her marriage."

"Oh, it's all in good fun." Myrtle gave Rose's arm a chiding tap with her paper fan. "Besides, if Olive don't dance in the hog trough, it'll bring bad luck down on Nora and Sam. You wouldn't want to bring bad luck down on the bride and groom now, would ya?"

Rose looked at a red-faced Olive Bennett lifting her skirts away from her bare feet as she attempted to dance to the tune of "Skip to My Lou" that Dave Kriete sawed out on his fiddle. Nothing in Olive's jerky movements and stiff expression conveyed a sense of someone having fun. To the contrary, her demeanor suggested a person enduring punishment.

Rose's heart twisted again in sympathy for Olive. "It doesn't look to me like she's having fun."

"I doubt she is, but she'll get over it."

At the familiar male voice behind her, Rose glanced over her shoulder. For once, her sweetheart's handsome features with his pale blue eyes and shock of sandy hair failed to make her heart skip. Instead, she experienced a flash of anger. "She shouldn't *have* to get over it, Ty Roberts! She shouldn't have to do it in the first place. We're all Christians here. Why can't we just pray for God to bless Sam and Nora and leave it at that? I can't believe that anyone here actually thinks humiliating Olive will make one bit of difference in Sam and Nora's married life."

Ty's soft chuckle at Rose's ear sent a squiggle of irritation through her. He stepped closer behind her and slipped his arms around her waist. "Aw, don't get huffy, Rose. It's just part of the fun. Besides, Lillie Ann's only ten, so you'll never have to dance in the hog trough. I reckon we'll be wed before the year's out and either of us see our nineteenth birthday."

His light quip sparked another flash of aggravation in Rose. Her promised beau's happy-go-lucky personality, which, along with his good looks, had initially attracted her to him, could also be exasperating.

Swiveling in his arms, she grasped his hand and tugged him away from prying ears, especially Myrtle Foster's, which seemed perked in their direction.

Rose towed Ty to the shade of a big sugar maple tree in the front yard of the bride's parents' home. "It's not me I'm worried about, Ty. It's Violet. I couldn't bear to put Violet through the same humiliation Olive just endured. You know Violet's been like a mother to Lillie Ann and me since Ma died five years ago." Tears stung Rose's eyes at the thought of her selfless older sister publically shamed. "I can't marry you. . .or anyone until Violet is married. Seeing Violet forced to dance in the hog trough would simply ruin my wedding."

Stiffening, he frowned and a hurt look came into his eyes. "Rose Hamilton, are you breaking off our engagement after I stood up and announced it to everyone at the log rollin' in March?"

Rose took her sweetheart's hand. "Of course I'm not breaking our engagement. I made a promise, and Pa taught us to never go back on a promise. Besides, I *do* want to marry you." A renegade tear escaped the corner of her eye. "I just don't want to cause Violet to dance in the hog trough."

Ty reached out and brushed the tear from Rose's cheek with his thumb. "Aw, Sweet, it ain't your fault that Violet's twenty-one and still single. She ain't the beauty you are, but she ain't ugly, either. Her bein' the schoolmarm tends to put fellers off, that's all." He took Rose's hands in his and his tone lifted. "Who knows, maybe she caught somebody's eye today." He grinned. "There's somethin' about seein' a feller take a bride that makes others want to do the same."

Rose looked over the crowd of revelers in search of her older sister. When she finally found her talking with a small group of women—mothers of Violet's pupils—Rose's heart sank. Violet never flirted or put herself in situations designed to catch the eye of any local swain. "She should be out there dancing, not talking to a bunch of women." Left to her own devices, Violet's prospects of marrying seemed dismal.

Ty nodded. "Like I've told Jamie, a feller won't find a wife by keepin' his nose stuck in a book. Reckon it works the same for a gal."

At Ty's wry comment about his older brother, a thought struck Rose like a lightning bolt. "That's it!" She whirled to face him, hope blossoming in her chest. "I can't imagine why it never occurred to me before. Jamie and Violet would make a perfect match!"

Ty's sandy brows shot up and he scratched at his blond head. "Never thought about it either, but I reckon you're right." He gave a half chuckle, half snort. "They're close in age. Jamie's jist a year older than Violet, and both of 'em like book learnin'."

"Yes, yes it's perfect!" Rose's voice lifted, buoyed by her growing infatuation with the idea blooming in her mind. "We must get them together."

Ty frowned. "Get them together? We've all known each other, played together, went to school and church together since we were kids. Seems to me, if they'd wanted to get together, they'd have done it by now."

"You and I didn't become sweethearts until the cornhusking party last fall, and we didn't become promised until the log rolling this March." Rose couldn't help a triumphant smile. "We were just friends and neighbors, too, until we decided we wanted to be more than friends. Jamie and Violet are just shy, slow bloomers. All they need is a little push in the right direction."

"So you think we should sit them down together and say 'It's high time you both were married, so since you both like books, why not marry each other?'" Ty's sarcasm sparked new ire in Rose's chest, tempting an equally sarcastic retort. But arguing with her sweetheart wouldn't put her matchmaking plan into action.

Rose prayed for patience. "Of course not. We have to get them together so they can talk and discover how much they have in common. We need to make them think *they* came up with the idea. Situations like dancing that require them to hold hands could help push them in the right direction." She glanced over at the spot between the house and barn where Olive had earlier done her compulsory dance in the hog trough and, where now, several couples danced a Virginia reel. "If we could figure out a way to get them to dance together—"

Ty shook his head. "I don't know. Jamie ain't much for dancin'. I could ask him, but he'd prob'ly jist tell me to go away and leave him be. But..." He fixed a widening gaze on Rose, a look of inspiration growing on his boyish face. "Now if *you* asked him, he just might do it."

At Ty's suggestion, a plan began to assemble itself in Rose's head quicker than she could speak. "Where is Jamie?"

Ty cocked his head to the left. "Last I saw him, he was sittin' under that catalpa tree with his nose in a book the preacher lent him."

Rose looked at the catalpa tree in the Bennetts' side yard, covered in fragrant white blossoms. "I'll go tell Jamie that we would like to dance but that Dave is short a couple for the next reel. You go find Violet and do the same."

Ty reared back, his jaw dropping in a look of faux horror. "Rose Hamilton tellin' a fib? Never thought I'd see the day!" His eyes twinkled with mischief and the same grin she'd seen on his face when he'd plotted chicanery with his friends crawled across his lips.

Heat infused Rose's face, and she smacked Ty's arm as she mentally swatted away the guilt nibbling at her conscience. "Oh, stop! You know good and well Dave always has trouble getting together enough couples for a reel. Why should today be any different?"

"Aw, I was just joshin', Sweet." With a laugh and a quick peck on her cheek, he loped off in the direction they'd last seen Violet.

Rose strode toward the catalpa tree. Walking with her head down, she mentally rehearsed how she might word her request to Jamie without telling an outright lie. A cluster of fragrant catalpa blossoms smacked into her face and she swerved to sidestep the low-hanging tree branch. Her toe struck something solid, stopping her progress and knocking her off balance. Pitching forward, she emitted a strangled cry before landing face-first in the short-cropped grass.

Burning with embarrassment, she pushed up on all fours, wondering how many onlookers had witnessed her fall. Before she had a chance to see, strong hands lifted her to her feet.

"Oh Rose, I'm so sorry." Jamie Roberts's reddening face held a look of horror while his hands still gripped her waist. "Reckon I had my big feet stuck out. Never meant to trip you. Are you all right? Are you hurt?" Remorse shined in his bright blue eyes framed by a head full of dark auburn curls.

Rose struggled to regain her composure. Thankfully, their somewhat secluded spot beneath the catalpa tree, several yards removed from the milling crowd, seemed to have shielded her mishap from notice. At least none of the other guests had turned gawking eyes her way.

Jamie let go of her waist. With awkward motions, he began to swipe at the grass stains on Rose's yellow cotton skirt then yanked his hand back, his face flushing an even deeper red. "I hope I haven't ruined your skirt."

"Nothing lye soap and some lemon juice and salt won't take out." In the face of Jamie's disconcertment, an odd feeling sprang in Rose's chest and she longed to put him at ease. Her gaze drawn to his thick, dark lashes that fringed his cerulean blue eyes, Rose realized she had never taken this close a look at Ty's older brother. While Jamie's large-boned features lacked Ty's classic handsomeness, she'd always found the combination of Jamie's dark hair and bright blue eyes striking.

"If you're lookin' for Ty, he's prob'ly off somewhere schemin' mischief with Bob Newkirk and Si Thompson."

Rose managed to pry her gaze from his and gave herself a mental shake. "No. I was just talking with Ty. We're trying to get together enough couples for another reel and we'd like for you to join in."

An odd look flitted across his eyes. "I don't know. I'm not much for dancin'."

While the thought of groveling irked Rose, the use of her charms did not. As Ma used to say, "More flies are caught with honey than vinegar."

She batted wide eyes at him. "Would you do it if we found you a partner?"

He glanced down at a book lying in the grass. I hadn't planned on dancin'. I was readin'—"

"Oh my goodness, Jamie, you can read at home!" The same frustration she'd felt moments earlier with Ty, flared again in Rose. She snuffed it with a calming breath and tempered her tone. "Like Ty says, you're too serious. You can read every day, but it's not every day that you get a chance to dance. You should have some fun once in a while."

His look bounced between her and the book. "I don't know, Rose."

"Please. For me?" Affecting her most coquettish smile, she took his hand and experienced an odd tingle when his strong fingers curled around hers.

"All right, I'll do it for you." He grinned. "And to keep Ty from fussing at me all the way home."

As they walked together toward the wide end of the Bennetts' dirt lane where Dave Kriete sat tuning his fiddle, Rose scanned the area for any sight of Ty and Violet. Not finding them, she grappled with how she might stall Jamie until they appeared.

Dave Kriete's booming voice intruded on her racing thoughts. "Don't look like we'll have enough for another reel, so this last tune will be a waltz for any couples that care to dance."

Rose's heart sank, expecting Jamie to bolt back to the catalpa tree at any moment.

Instead, as Dave drew his bow across his fiddle sending out the first haunting strains of "Sweet Evelina," Jamie took Rose's hand in his. "Rose Hamilton, will you do me the honor of this dance?"

Chapter Two

A flash of panic struck Rose along with the urge to flee. "I—I. . ."

Too late. The next moment, she found herself twirling among a half-dozen other dancers, her steps guided by Jamie's strong, confident hands. When her breath returned with her composure, she looked up into his stoic face. "I thought you couldn't dance."

The hint of a smile lifted the corner of his mouth. "Never said I couldn't dance. Just said I wasn't much for dancin'." He raised her arm, allowing her to twirl to the music.

Surprise and admiration mingled in Rose. "For someone who doesn't care for dancing, you do it quite well."

He raised her arm for another twirl. "Ma made sure all us boys learned how to dance." He glanced a few feet away where his twelve-year-old brother Charlie, danced with Lillie Ann and grinned. "Even Charlie can manage a credible waltz."

Somehow, Rose needed to turn the conversation to Violet. Though she'd failed to get Jamie and Violet together for this dance, perhaps she could use the opportunity to act as her sister's advocate. She needed to inject a subject of mutual interest to both Violet and Jamie. "What book were you reading?"

"*The Count of Monte Cristo*. Pastor Tom lent it to me." He raised her arm, initiating another twirl.

"I'll have to ask Violet if she's read it." Rose settled back into his arms. "If she has, maybe the two of you could talk about it together."

"Don't you like to read, Rose?" At his unexpected question, Rose almost missed a step.

"I suppose. Not as much as Violet does, though." The conversation wasn't going as she'd hoped. "Violet has stacks of books. I'm sure she'd be happy to lend you some." Unsure her sister would sanction such an offer, Rose stopped talking. A surge of anger shot through her and she frowned. If Ty had done his job and got Violet here like he was supposed to, Violet could be telling Jamie what books she had and was willing to lend out and Rose wouldn't be in this predicament.

"I'm sorry Ty didn't show up to partner you for this dance." The sorrow in his voice was tinged with another emotion Rose couldn't identify. "I'm afraid he neglects you while he gets up to all sorts of tomfoolery with the likes of Bob and Si and the other rapscallions they run with. If you'd like, I'll give him a talkin' to about it."

"No need." She forced her frown into a smile. Jamie must have interpreted her sour expression as disappointment in not getting to dance with Ty. "I'm used to Ty's mischievous ways. It's part of his charm, I suppose."

Jamie opened his mouth as if to say something but shut it when Dave Kriete drew his bow across his fiddle in a long, final note, signaling the end of the waltz. Relinquishing her hand, Jamie stepped back and gave her a deep bow. "Thank you for the dance. I enjoyed it very much." A grin crawled across his well-shaped lips. "Believe you're right. I should dance more often. And I *will* have that talk with Ty and tell him what he missed." With that, he turned and walked toward the catalpa tree.

Rose gazed after him feeling deflated and a bit forlorn. She'd failed in her first attempt at getting Violet and Jamie together. Renewed determination filled her, sweeping away her sense of defeat. She would need to go at it from the other side and begin to work on Violet.

Her first opportunity to broach the subject came later that evening as she and her two sisters worked together cleaning up the kitchen after supper. Amid a general conversation about the wedding, the newly married couple, and the reception party, Lillie Ann piped up as she handed Rose a washed and dried serving bowl.

"Hey, Rose, why were you dancin' with Jamie when you're promised to Ty? Have you changed your mind about which Roberts brother you like best?"

Stunned by the unexpected question, Rose nearly dropped the serving bowl. Remembering the dance she'd shared with Jamie, her face warmed. "Of course not," she said when her racing pulse slowed. "Ty was just busy, so Jamie stood in for him." While not the exact truth, it was close enough to assuage Rose's conscience.

"I don't blame you." Lillie Ann flipped a sandy-colored pigtail from her shoulder and wrinkled her freckled nose. "Ty is much more fun than Jamie. He's always thinking of funny things to do. Jamie is just a stick-in-the-mud."

"I wouldn't say that." A moment ago Rose had silently blessed her little sister for opening the conversation about Jamie, but now the imp threatened to destroy Rose's entire plan to match Violet and Jamie by putting Jamie in a poor light. She needed to turn the conversation that had taken a dangerous swerve, back on track. "Jamie is just quiet, and he likes to read." Affecting an indifferent tone, she turned to Violet scrubbing a cooking pot at the sink. "I mentioned to Jamie about your collection of books and told him you might be willing to lend him some."

Violet lifted a dripping hand to brush back a straggling lock of chestnut hair from her face. "Oh, I don't know, Rose. Those books cost me dear. I'd hate to lose any of them."

While hesitant, Violet's tone held enough ambivalence to encourage Rose to press the subject. "You'd never have to worry about that with Jamie. He treasures books." The comment scratched at Rose's conscience. While Jamie hadn't shared that sentiment with her in so many words, surely his love of reading made it obvious.

Violet turned an indulgent smile toward Rose. "'Neither a borrower nor a lender be; For loan oft loses both itself and friend, and borrowing dulls the edge of husbandry.' Shakespeare's *Hamlet*."

Violet's teacher voice grated against Rose's nerves, begging a retort and a Bible verse she had committed to memory months ago for a Sunday school contest flew to mind. "'Give to him that asketh thee, and from him that would borrow of thee turn not thou away.' Matthew 5:42." The same exhilaration Rose felt when besting Violet in a game of checkers surged through her, lifting her chin in a triumphant tilt.

To Rose's delight, Violet looked shamefaced. Of course the holy scriptures trumped the English bard. Violet's voice turned humble. "Thank you for reminding me of our Lord's command, Rose." She went back to scrubbing the pot. "Of course Jamie may borrow any of my books he would like."

Later, as they both prepared for bed in the room they shared, Rose decided to build on her earlier victory with Violet. Now that she'd managed to get her sister to agree to loan her books to Jamie, Rose needed to plant the idea of matrimony in Violet's mind. At least she needed to get her spinster sister thinking along those lines.

"Sure was a nice wedding," Rose said as she pulled on her nightgown.

Violet looked up from the open Bible on her lap, yawned, and set the book on the little table beside her bed. "I do hope Ty and his friends didn't ruin Sam and Nora's first night together with their silly shivaree."

Rose ignored the temptation to jump to her sweetheart's defense, which would do nothing to advance her cause. Instead, she decided to go straight to the heart of the subject. Violet wouldn't abide a lengthy discourse at bedtime. "Have you given much thought to marriage?"

Across the room, Violet yawned again and slid under the covers, pulling them to her chin. "I'm a school teacher, Rose, and female teachers are required to be single."

That Violet hadn't ended the conversation outright emboldened Rose to push a bit further. "But you *do* want to marry one day, don't you?"

Violet heaved a deep sigh that almost made Rose sorry she'd continued to prod her on the subject. "If God brings me a good Christian man whom I love and want to marry, then I'll marry. If not, I'll happily remain single and teach school for the rest of my days or until I'm too old to do it any longer. Besides, now that Ma is gone, someone needs to be a mother to Lillie Ann. I expect you will be skipping off to marry Ty Roberts within the next year, so that leaves me to tend to Lillie Ann. Now good night and go to sleep."

"Good night." Guilt-smitten by Violet's words, Rose mumbled the salutation.

Of course Violet would sacrifice her own happiness to take care of Lillie Ann as well as Pa and Rose. Tears of shame slid down Rose's face, wetting her pillow. A surge of anger dried her eyes. No! She would not allow Violet to sacrifice her future happiness and live out her waning years alone and childless and, if Rose could help it, her sister would never be forced to dance in a hog trough. But Violet had brought a new problem to light. Beyond the challenge of matching Violet and Jamie, Rose would need to find a match for Pa as well.

Chapter Three

Trepidation filled Rose's chest as she approached the chicken coop where Lillie Ann and Charlie stood in the dappled shade of the walnut tree feeding table scraps to the chickens. Revealing her matchmaking plans to the youngsters could be dangerous. A slip of the tongue by either of them might unravel Rose's scheme before it ever took shape. On the other hand, making allies of the children could also prove invaluable. Fast friends since they were toddlers, Lillie Ann and Charlie continually traveled between their two farms. Not only could the kids help nudge their older siblings toward romance, they could also provide a liaison between Violet and Jamie. After sleepless hours last night considering the wisdom of taking the two into her confidence, Rose had finally decided that the benefits of doing so outweighed the risks.

Drawing in a fortifying breath, she approached the children. "Lillie Ann. Charlie. I need to talk to you."

The two glanced up at Rose in unison then turned guilty, wide-eyed expressions toward each other.

"It was her idea." Charlie pointed his finger at Lillie Ann.

Lillie Ann dropped the bucket with a plunk, her mouth gaping. Scowling, she pressed her fists against her waist and glared at Charlie. "Charlie, you're such a loudmouth! And that's not fair! You said we should do it, too."

Almost afraid to ask what mischief the youngsters had gotten up to, Rose put a hand on each child's shoulder. "What did you do?"

Charlie shoved his hands in his pockets and clamped his mouth shut.

Lillie Ann looked down at her dust-covered bare toes then glanced toward the chicken coop. "We found some duck eggs down by the pond." She looked back up at Rose, a plea for understanding on her freckled face. "I was afraid the mama duck had left them and I wanted some baby ducks, so we brought the eggs and put them under Henrietta since she's already sitting on her own eggs. She pecked me for it, too, but I got it done." She held out her arm to display several visible red spots. Her sandy brows pinched in worry. "You're not going to tell Violet or Pa, are you?"

Relief rolled through Rose. As transgressions go, this latest one by the pair seemed benign. Stifling a giggle, she schooled her face into a stern expression. "I'll not tell Violet or Pa about the duck eggs if you and Charlie will agree to help me with something, but you have to promise to keep it a secret between us."

Both children's heads bobbed in eager agreement.

Rose glanced around to make sure Violet was nowhere in earshot. "Ty and I would like to get married, but I don't want Violet to have to dance in the hog trough."

"Like Olive did last week?" The grim expression on Lillie Ann's face warmed Rose's heart, glad that her little sister appeared to have also found the custom distasteful.

Rose nodded. "That's right. We need to find Violet a husband, so she can get married before I do. Ty and I have decided that Violet and Jamie would make a perfect match, and we need your help to convince them of it."

Charlie shrugged and cocked his head full of dark curls that reminded Rose of his eldest brother. "That's easy. I'll just tell Jamie that Violet would like to court him, so he should ask her."

At the boy's direct approach, alarm flashed through Rose and she envisioned her matchmaking plans slipping away like water through her fingers. "No! You mustn't do anything of the sort!"

At her shrill tone, Charlie reared back and his dark brows shot up to his tumble of dusky curls.

Charlie's blurted suggestion confirmed Rose's worst fears about sharing her plans with the two youngsters and she began to rue her decision. But, as Violet would say, the Rubicon had been crossed. She must forge onward.

Fighting for calm, Rose lowered her voice and put a hand on Charlie's shoulder. Frightening the youngsters would not engender their help. "That's just it, Charlie. Violet *doesn't* particularly want to court Jamie. Not yet, anyway. Saying anything that direct would just scare Jamie off and make Violet spitting mad." Somehow Rose must make her young confidants understand the delicate nature of their mission and the importance of finesse in carrying it out. "We need to think of ways to get them to spend time together."

Lillie Ann nodded, understanding blooming on her face. "So they will start liking each other like you and Ty like each other."

Rose nodded and turned to Charlie. "Have you heard Jamie say anything particularly nice about Violet?"

Charlie shrugged and his forehead scrunched in thought. "Maybe that she's a good teacher."

Though far from the romantic sentiment Rose had hoped for, at least it was positive.

"Last week at church, Violet said that Jamie had a nice singing voice," Lillie Ann offered.

"Good. That's good." Hope sprung in Rose at the children's willingness to help. "Since they both like to read, I thought maybe we could encourage them to discuss books they both like. What do you think?"

Charlie cocked his head and crossed his arms over his chest. "Last week I heard Jamie tell Ma that he wished he had more books by Shakes...Shakes..."

"Shakespeare?" Excitement sparked in Rose's chest. Violet, too, had a fondness for the English bard's writings. That common interest could be the vehicle to bring the two together.

"Violet has those Shakespeare books." Lillie Ann's face brightened with enthusiasm. "Maybe she could lend them to Jamie."

As much as Rose would like to join in her little sister's childish exuberance, pragmatism dampened her zeal. "Violet might lend out other books, but I doubt she'd ever lend her Shakespeare books."

Lillie Ann shook her head. "But don't you remember, Rose? Violet said she would lend *any* of her books to Jamie."

While Violet *had* said those words, Rose never assumed the offer included her sister's prized three-volume collection of Shakespeare's complete works.

Lillie Ann shrugged. "Wouldn't hurt to ask her. She did say she would lend Jamie *any* of her books, and you know how Violet dislikes it when people go back on their word."

While Rose couldn't dispute Lillie Ann's reasoning, she balked at using her sister's words against her to force Violet to part, even temporarily, with her most valued possessions.

Charlie, who'd stood silent since mentioning his brother's affinity for Shakespeare, turned a thoughtful face to Rose. "Maybe if Jamie asked Violet to lend him the Shakespeare books, she would be more apt to do it, and it would get them talking."

The boy's suggestion struck Rose as pure genius and she couldn't help giving him a hug, from which he quickly wriggled away. "Wonderful idea, Charlie! Do you think if you mentioned to Jamie about Violet's complete volumes of Shakespeare and that she might lend them out, he'd ask her?"

Charlie nodded. "I think he would."

Though thrilled at the kids' enthusiasm to help in her matchmaking efforts, Rose had scant time to enjoy her victory. The thought of sharing her decision to find Pa a match held far more anxiety. How would her baby sister feel about the notion of a new mother? Since Ma's death, Pa hadn't shown any interest in looking for another mate and the subject had simply not come up. But even if they succeeded in sparking a romance between Jamie and Violet, Violet had made it clear that she felt obligated to be a mother figure for Lillie Ann.

Rose licked her drying lips and considered how best to broach the subject.

"Lillie Ann." Rose bent down to look her sister in the eyes. "You know how Violet has taken care of all of us since Ma died?"

Lillie Ann nodded.

"Well." Rose weighed her words. "Even if we manage to get her and Jamie interested in each other, I'm not sure she would marry him or anyone as long as she feels like she still needs to take care of us."

Charlie rammed his hands into his pockets and focused on making a circle in the dirt with his big toe. "If Jamie marries Violet and Ty marries you, you could all come and live at our house and Ma could be Lillie Ann's ma."

At Charlie's solution to the problem, which doubtless seemed quite reasonable to him, Rose grappled for a reply that wouldn't sound both dismissive and unappreciative.

Lillie Ann turned to Charlie. "But then Pa would be lonesome without all of us." She looked at Rose, her eyes widening with inspiration. "We need to think of some nice lady for Pa to marry."

Stunned at her sister's comment, Rose had to suppress a giggle. Reminded of the words of the hymn "God Works in Mysterious Ways, His Wonders to Perform," she sent a prayer of gratitude heavenward. When her voice returned, she gave her little sister a smile and hug. "Why, that is a wonderful idea, Lillie Ann! Who do you think would be a good match for Pa?"

Lillie Ann scrunched up her face and grasped her chin in deliberation. Over the next several minutes the three considered and discarded, for various reasons, a half-dozen local widows and spinsters.

"What about that new lady at church?" Charlie said.

"Nancy Martin?" Rose hadn't even thought of the widow who came last fall from Salem, Indiana, to live with her sister and husband who ran the Honeytown General Store. While Nancy Martin had impressed Rose as both comely and pleasant, Rose hadn't spoken to her beyond a brief introduction and knew little about her except that Nancy was said to be something of a "granny doctor" with an extensive knowledge of herbal medicines.

Lillie Ann gave an approving nod. "I like her. She taught our Sunday school class last Sunday."

Rose could think of no reason not to consider Nancy Martin as a prospective stepmother. "Good. Then we will begin working on matching Violet and Jamie and Pa and Nancy Martin." Rose lowered her voice to a whisper and gave both children her sternest look. "But all this has to be kept between the three of us. If Jamie, Violet, Pa, or Mrs. Martin gets so much as a whiff of what we are about, everything will be ruined."

Chapter Four

Jamie closed the book and put it down on the porch planks beside him with a *plop*. He'd hoped to read another chapter of *The Count of Monte Cristo* before dinner; a well-deserved reward after a morning of planting corn with Pa and Ty. He looked down at the brown cover of the book Pastor Tom had lent him nearly a week ago and heaved a deep sigh. He could recall nothing he'd read since picking up the book ten minutes ago.

Looking across the neat yard of his family's home to the brown dirt of the newly planted fields, his gaze turned eastward toward the neighboring Hamilton farm. He knew what—or more precisely, *who*—had pulled his mind from the novel as well as from nearly everything else on which his thoughts had tried to focus since Sam and Nora's wedding. Try as he might, he couldn't extricate his thoughts from the sweet moments he'd spent dancing in Rose Hamilton's arms.

When he closed his eyes he could see her again, her light brown hair framing her heart-shaped face, her rose-pink lips parted, smiling up at him. The way she felt in his arms. His arms ached with his heart at the memory.

He shook his head in a futile effort to erase the images playing through his mind. He should never have agreed to the dance in the first place, no matter how prettily Rose had batted her cinnamon-brown eyes at him. The familiar mixture of sadness, jealousy, and self-scorn balled in his gut like a tangle of barbed wire. "Fool thing to do. It was a fool thing to do."

Saying it out loud, albeit mumbled under his breath, didn't help. Since the corn-husking party last October when Ty announced that he and Rose had begun courting, the poisonous concoction of emotions now swirling inside Jamie had become his constant companions. As far back as he could remember, he had admired Rose's beauty and spunk. All last summer he had tried to work up the courage to ask her to court him. That his younger brother had beat him to it twisted inside him like a white-hot knife. All winter, he'd expected his mercurial brother to tire of Rose and turn his interest to something, or someone, else. So when the community came together in March to clear a stand of timber from the Hamilton farm and Ty announced that he and Rose were promised, it had hit Jamie like a mule-kick to the chest.

An involuntary snort huffed from Jamie's nostrils. He hated the anger his own brother's name evoked in him these days. Ma called Ty her butterfly; flitting from one interest to another, as changeable as a chameleon and as hard to hold on to as quicksilver.

Jamie's hands clenched at the memory of the disappointment in Rose's pretty face last week at the wedding reception when she'd searched the crowd in vain for Ty. It galled that, with apparent little effort, Ty had won Rose's affection then treated his prize with such a careless, matter-of-fact attitude. As he'd promised Rose after the dance, Jamie did later berate Ty for neglecting his sweetheart. When Ty had responded with a shrug and laugh saying Rose was used to him going his own way, it had taken all Jamie's strength not to pound some sense into his irresponsible brother. Each night, Jamie's prayers included a petition to the Almighty that should Ty tire of Rose and break her heart, Jamie might be there to pick up the broken pieces and that Rose would welcome his attention. Until then, for his own heart's sake, he needed to stay clear of Rose Hamilton.

The sound of laughter pulled him from his reverie and drew his attention to the barn where Charlie emerged with Lillie Ann Hamilton at his heels. As the kids ran toward him, Jamie couldn't help envying their childlike joy. In another eight years or so, he'd probably be attending their wedding.

"I need a chisel." Charlie puffed out the breathless pronouncement as he bounded up to the porch.

"What do you need a chisel for?" Jamie picked up the book and stood. Far easier to show authority to his youngest sibling when he towered over him instead of the other way around.

Lillie Ann climbed up to the porch. "Your pa said I could have one of the new baby pigs—the spotted one—to call my own. But you'll keep her here on your farm until she's old enough to leave her mama." She glanced at Charlie. "Charlie needs the chisel to make a trough for Domino to drink out of when she comes to live at our farm."

How Charlie imagined he might use a chisel to make a trough, Jamie didn't care to guess. "Why didn't you ask Pa for the chisel?"

"Pa's busy in the barn. He said to ask you or Ty, and I couldn't find Ty."

While Charlie had become proficient with most hand tools, Pa didn't allow him to take tools from the shed without his, Jamie's, or Ty's knowledge. Though Pa seemed to have given his permission for Charlie to use a chisel, Jamie wasn't keen on turning his little brother loose with a sharp instrument that could cause him a serious injury.

"I don't know. It'll be a while before that piglet can leave its ma, then Lillie Ann's pa can make it a trough."

Charlie frowned, huffed, and shoved his hands into his pockets.

Lillie Ann lifted watery eyes to Jamie. "Pleeeease? Pa'll just say she can eat with the other hogs, but I want Domino to have her own trough." She reminded Jamie so much of Rose begging him to dance, his heart contracted.

Jamie held up his hand in defeat. "All right, all right." He didn't want an angry little brother and a crying little girl on his hands. "I'll get you a chisel from the tool shed." He poked his finger at his little brother's nose and mimicked Pa's sternest tone. "But, when you're done with it, be sure to get it back where it belongs or I'll tan your hide then turn you over to Pa."

Both children perked up and smiled.

"I will. I promise," Charlie said.

"What is that book?" Lillie Ann looked at the book in Jamie's hand then gave Charlie a sly smile.

"It's just a book the preacher lent me. *The Count of Monte Cristo.*"

"Violet has that book." Lillie Ann grasped a porch post with both hands and began swinging herself around it. "She has lots of books."

"Rose says Violet has Shakespeare books," Charlie chimed in.

"The complete works of Shakespeare. Three whole volumes," Lillie Ann added. Leaning her head around the post, she looked straight at Jamie and her voice turned almost teasing. "She also said she'd be happy to lend them to you."

"She did?" Giving a little chuckle, Jamie struggled to appear unaffected by Lillie Ann's comment, but he couldn't deny his quickening pulse. After reading *Julius Caesar*, he'd longed to read more works by the English bard.

Charlie cocked his head and squinted his eyes, a sure sign he was up to some sort of mischief. "I bet if you go over and ask her, she'd be happy to lend them to you." The telltale sweetness in his voice made Jamie wonder if the two kids were trying to match him and Violet.

The thought at first brought a grin to Jamie's face until another thought wiped it away. If the youngsters were indeed attempting to match him and Violet, could their actions be at Violet's behest? A knot of concern tightened in his chest, and he scoured his memory for any hints of interest the eldest Hamilton sister might have sent his way. Finding none, the knot relaxed. While he liked Violet and admired how she'd stepped into the role of mother after Alice Hamilton's death, she hadn't captured his heart like her vivacious sister Rose had. If Violet Hamilton had set her cap for Jamie, she showed no indication of it at Sam and Nora's wedding reception, a perfect opportunity to catch his attention. Still, Jamie knew little of female wiles and, after condemning Ty for putting Rose's heart in jeopardy, he'd rather not risk doing the same to her sister. Best to keep to his original plan and stay clear of the Hamilton farm.

Jamie managed a weak smile. "Let me put this book in the house, then I'll get your chisel."

A few minutes later as they followed him down the worn dirt path to the tool shed behind the house, Charlie and Lillie Ann kept up a constant banter, continuing to urge Jamie to ask Violet about borrowing her volumes of Shakespeare.

"Tuesday," Lillie Ann said as Jamie emerged from the tool shed with the chisel. "I think Violet will be home all day Tuesday if you'd like to come over and ask to borrow her Shakespeare books."

The temptation to get his hands on the complete works of the bard tugged hard at Jamie, but he'd rather not encourage any romantic notions Violet might have toward him. He gave the little girl an indulgent smile. "I don't know, we're still pretty busy with spring planting. You and Charlie keep a path worn between your place and ours; maybe you can bring the books over sometime."

"No, that won't do!" Lillie Ann turned an anxious face to Charlie, as if for assistance.

"Violet won't allow us to touch 'em. You'll have to come get them from her yourself," Charlie said, looking pleased with himself while earning a relieved, almost adoring look from Lillie Ann.

Warning bells clanged in Jamie's head as he handed the chisel to his little brother. The kids were undoubtedly up to something, but whether or not Violet was privy to their schemes, he couldn't guess. Long ago, he'd determined that the best way to handle a problem was to face it head on. More than likely, Charlie and Lillie Ann would keep pestering him until he asked to borrow the books, and he *would* like to read more of Shakespeare. Violet Hamilton was, if nothing else, the most direct person Jamie knew. From what he'd observed, she possessed little patience for beating about the bush. If she had indeed formed an attachment to him, a face-to-face conversation should confirm it. "All right. Tell her I'll be over Tuesday to talk with her about it."

Charlie and Lillie Ann exchanged a knowing look, giggled, and then scampered off leaving Jamie hoping he wouldn't regret his decision.

Chapter Five

"Mmm." Pa's face scrunched in a painful frown and he rubbed his chest as he looked across the supper table at Violet. "Maybe don't put so much pepper on the pork chops next time, Violet. My dyspepsia is kickin' up like a mule again."

"I'm sorry, Pa." Remorse filled her voice. "I'll be more careful with my seasoning. Just scrape off some of the pepper and after supper I'll fix you some soda water."

Pa shook his head and wrinkled his nose. "Sodee water tastes bad and makes me belch. Just pour me a big glass of milk."

Rose looked up from her plate. Since sharing her matchmaking schemes with Lillie Ann and Charlie, she'd contemplated how best to broach the subject of Nancy Martin to Pa, and this might be the best chance she'd get. Schooling her voice to a nonchalant tone, she speared a green bean on her plate with her fork. "I should ask Nancy Martin about a good remedy for your dyspepsia, Pa. Heard the preacher's wife say she's a wonder with her herbal cures, best granny doctor she's ever seen."

Pa's wide brow wrinkled in thought. "Hmm. Nancy Martin. Is she the woman I've seen at church with the Newkirks?"

Rose nodded. "Bertha Newkirk's widowed sister from over Salem way." That Pa had taken notice of Nancy at all encouraged Rose.

"Yeah, Pa. She's my new Sunday school teacher since Mrs. Ritz is waitin' for the stork to bring her new baby," Lillie Ann chimed in.

Rose strove to keep an indifferent tone to her voice. "Maybe we should ask her over for Sunday dinner tomorrow. Since she's Lillie Ann's Sunday school teacher, I think we should get to know her better."

Her suggestion hung in the air without comment for a few seconds until Violet finally nodded her head. "That's a wonderful idea, Rose. We haven't had company for Sunday dinner in ages."

Pa gave a slow nod and a grunt and went back to cutting his meat. "Suits me. I'll leave it up to you girls to do."

Rose fought the grin tugging at her mouth as excitement bounced around in her chest. Before supper Lillie Ann had whispered that she and Charlie had succeeded in getting Jamie Roberts to promise that he'd come Tuesday to ask Violet about borrowing her Shakespeare books. Rose's matchmaking schemes appeared off to a magnificent start. Unable to suppress her glee, she stuffed a bite of pork chop in her mouth to hide her smug smile. Hopefully Nancy Martin would accept their last-minute invitation while Pa was still in the notion for visitors.

The next morning, in the churchyard, Rose climbed down from the family's wagon, her anxious stomach roiling. What if Pa and Nancy took an immediate dislike of one another, or Nancy declined the invitation outright? Eager to extend the invitation and ease her suspense, she gazed about in search of Nancy Martin.

"You're lookin' pretty today."

At Ty's voice, Rose turned to see the Roberts family advancing toward them. Both the sight of her handsome sweetheart as well as the thought of one day becoming part of his family, made her smile. The friendship between their two families had grown so close over the years that Rose almost felt as if she were already part of the Roberts family. It was Ty's pa, Bill Roberts who, at the news of Lillie Ann's birth, had commented that "With all these sweet girls around, we should call this place Honeytown." The moniker stuck, giving name to the little white clapboard church as well as Newkirk's Honeytown Store. Rose's heart still warmed remembering Bill and Dorothy Roberts's gifts of food and other kindnesses when Ma died. To marry into the Roberts family felt as natural a progression to Rose as graduating from one school grade to the next.

"Thank you." Returning Ty's smile, Rose glanced down at her best yellow calico dress. "It's what I wear most Sundays."

"Reckon it is." A grin moseyed across his lips. "How are you plannin' to decorate your box for the box supper next Friday?" He cocked his head and a freshening breeze tousled his straw-colored hair. "I want to make sure I bid for your box."

His words struck her like a splash of cold water and she gasped. She'd completely forgotten about the coming box supper. "I—I haven't decided yet." Her answer held enough truth to assuage her guilt without admitting the event had skipped her mind. More importantly, the box supper would provide an excellent opportunity to get Violet and Jamie together. "I'll have Lillie Ann tell Charlie how Violet and I plan to decorate our boxes."

"Miss Hamilton." A man whom Rose didn't recognize strode toward them, his arm raised in a hailing gesture. Sporting a grey seersucker coat, white boater hat, and dark tie, he looked to be in his mid-thirties.

Violet turned from her conversation with Dorothy Roberts to greet the man with a wide smile. "Mr. Anderson, how nice to see you here." She proceeded to introduce him as Edmond Anderson, the new singing schoolmaster.

Mr. Anderson doffed his hat, sending a strong whiff of lanolin to Rose's nose and revealing a thick shock of rust-colored hair that matched his well-clipped mustache.

While the man seemed pleasant enough with a quick smile and lively brown eyes, Rose would rather avoid an invitation to his singing school, which she had no interest in attending. Looking to both sidestep the unwanted invitation and find a moment to talk to Ty about her matchmaking plans for the box supper, Rose mumbled a greeting then excused herself in the same breath.

She slipped her arm around Ty's and tugged him to a secluded spot near the back of the wagon. When they were out of earshot, she lowered her voice to a whisper. "Ty, you need to make sure that Jamie bids on Violet's box next Friday." Though tempted to remind him of his failure to deliver Violet for the dance with Jamie at the wedding reception, Rose decided that scolding him wouldn't enhance her chances of getting his help Friday.

"I'll have Violet tie a sprig of violets to the ribbon decorating her box. That's how you'll know it's hers." She gave him a conspiratorial smile. "Lillie Ann says Jamie has already agreed to call on Violet this week and ask to borrow some of her books."

Ty's eyes sparkled. "You're a wonder." Grinning, he shook his head. "The way you're goin', we could have a double weddin' by this fall." Planting a quick kiss on her cheek, he turned and loped off to talk to Bob Newkirk and Si Thompson.

Rose resumed her search for Nancy Martin and her gaze locked for a moment with Jamie's. The intense look in his blue eyes caused her heart to make a funny hop. Had he overheard her conversation with Ty? Or had Charlie spilled the beans about Rose's matchmaking plans to his eldest brother? No time to worry about that now. Giving him a weak smile, she glanced around the churchyard until her gaze lit on Nancy Martin, who stood talking with Selma Ritz. Rose started toward them as fast as good manners allowed.

"Mrs. Martin," she called, hoping to stop the two ladies now headed toward the open church door.

"Rose Hamilton, isn't it?" Turning a pleasant smile to Rose, Nancy offered her hand while Selma murmured a greeting and headed into the church. "I'm looking forward to visiting your family today." Nancy glanced across the churchyard where Violet and Pa stood talking with Bill and Dorothy Roberts.

Rose's cheeks warmed. Violet must have already offered the invitation. A nervous giggle popped from her lips and her face turned even hotter. "I'd come to invite you, but I reckon Violet beat me to it."

"Actually she didn't." Nancy's green eyes sparkled and, for the first time, Rose took a close look at the woman she hoped would become her stepmother. Trim, with neat brown hair peeking from beneath her crisp gray bonnet, Nancy Martin exuded a quiet charm that put Rose at ease. Nothing she saw made her want to abandon her matchmaking plans between Nancy and Pa.

"Oh, then Lillie Ann must have."

"No, your father asked me." Nancy's smile widened and, unless it was a shadow cast by the woman's bonnet, Rose thought she saw Nancy's cheeks pink.

Dumfounded, Rose groped for an intelligent reply. "P–Pa asked you?"

"Yes." A troubled look flashed across her eyes. "But if my visit today will cause you and your sisters extra work—"

"No. Not at all." Keen to allay Nancy's concerns, Rose's words popped out quicker than she would have liked. She tempered her tone. Best not to look too eager. "We're all very much looking forward to your visit."

The lines between Nancy's eyes relaxed and her smile returned. "I'm looking forward to it, too."

As she walked into the church with Nancy, Rose could scarcely contain her delight. Perhaps matching Nancy and Pa would prove a far easier task than she'd imagined. *Thank You, Lord!* Forcing a restrained smile, she sent the silent prayer heavenward, chased by a petition that God would continue to smile on her match-making efforts.

Later, at the Sunday dinner table, Rose fought to tether her rampant joy as the answer to her earlier prayers played out before her eyes. Pa and Nancy sat across the table from each other laughing and talking like old friends, already calling one another by their first names.

"I know just the thing to fix your dyspepsia, John." Nancy smiled up from cutting a piece of roast chicken. "Rhubarb, goldenseal, Peruvian Bark, cloves, and ginger, all pulverized and taken with milk after a meal should do the trick," she said with an emphatic bob of her head. "I've never seen it fail." She sent Pa a bright smile. "I'll put the concoction together and bring it to church next Sunday, if you'd like."

"Or maybe you could bring it to the box supper, Friday," Rose said. "That is, if you're planning on attending the box supper."

Nancy's eyes widened. "I must say, I hadn't given it much thought. But yes, yes I think I will take a box. I understand the money raised will go to missions, and I'm all for that." She gave Pa a smile and forked a piece of chicken into her mouth.

"Any idea how you will decorate your box?" Rose kept her gaze fixed on her plate.

"Hmm. I do have some bright blue ribbons in my sewing box."

At Nancy's muse, Pa perked up.

Nancy lowered her voice and her lips tipped up in a sly smile. "Or perhaps I shouldn't have mentioned that," she murmured, sending Pa a shy glance before returning her focus to her dinner plate.

By the time they bid Nancy farewell, Rose had begun mentally planning Pa and Nancy's wedding. Lillie Ann seemed enthralled with the woman, and Violet remarked on Nancy's sweet personality and nice manners. As for Pa, his distracted demeanor and almost giddy mood mimicked a young swain in love—at least to the extent that a middle-aged man with graying hair and expanding girth could resemble a young swain.

By the middle of the week, Pa's several trips to the Honeytown store convinced Rose that Nancy Martin would soon become her stepmother. The thought made her smile as she lugged the front room carpet out the front door for a much-needed beating. Pa had smiled and laughed more since last Sunday than he had in the five years since Ma's death. And, true to her word, Nancy had gifted him with a concoction that seemed to have cured his dyspepsia, gaining both his appreciation and affection.

While more than pleased with her matchmaking progress concerning Pa and Nancy, Rose's efforts with Violet and Jamie had yet to yield success. Despite Lillie Ann's insistence that Jamie had promised to come on Tuesday to ask Violet about borrowing her Shakespeare books, yesterday came and went without any sign of him.

Disappointment slithered through Rose as she yanked the rolled-up carpet down the porch steps with an exasperated huff. Unlike Ty, She'd never known Jamie to renege on his word. That, coupled with his penchant for books, suggested that he was avoiding their farm. When pressed, Lillie Ann had insisted that Charlie hadn't revealed Rose's matchmaking plans to Jamie, but Jamie's failure to appear made Rose wonder.

Rose's arms ached with her attempt to load the heavy carpet onto the wheelbarrow in order to roll it to the clothesline. "Ugh!" She let the furled rug drop back to the ground, sending up a plume of dust. With the back of her hand, she swiped at her hair that had pulled loose from the knot at the back of her head and straggled into her sweaty face. Maybe she should wait until Pa returned from the store, or at least until Violet returned from the schoolhouse, where she'd gone to attend a meeting about the summer singing school.

"Looks like you need some help."

At the male voice behind her, Rose whirled around to face Jamie Roberts.

Chapter Six

At the sight of Rose Hamilton, Jamie's pulse quickened. Something about her disheveled look, brown tendrils of hair falling down to frame her flushed face, sent his heart galloping. Still, he couldn't help grinning at her disconcertion.

"I—I. . ." Her brown eyes grew wide, reminding Jamie of a cornered calf. She glanced down at the rolled-up rug. "I reckon I do."

"Where do you want it?" Jamie needed to get his arms around the rug to relieve the temptation to slip them around Rose's trim waist.

"The clothesline." In an unnecessary motion, she pointed westward. Jamie knew the Hamilton farm as well as his own. "Why are you here?" she asked as he shouldered the carpet like a sack of grain and started toward the clothesline. "You were supposed to come yesterday."

The shame and guilt he had felt all day yesterday, sizzled again inside Jamie. Of course Lillie Ann would have told Rose as well as Violet about his promised visit. "I know. I'm sorry if I inconvenienced Violet by not coming yesterday. Pa, Ty, and I had to clean some brush from a fence line." While true, Jamie knew that cowardice, not the chore had prevented his promised visit. The thought of encouraging Violet's affections when he had no intention of reciprocating them twisted in his belly like a hot poker. At the same time he had given his word, and, in the end, he knew he had to come.

Jamie slung the rug over the clothesline, glad for a reason to keep his face averted from Rose. "Is Violet about? Lillie Ann tells me she would be willing to loan me her complete works of Shakespeare."

"Yes, Violet said she'd be happy to loan you any books you'd like to read, but. . ." Disappointment dragged down Rose's voice. "No, I'm afraid she's not here right now. She's down at the schoolhouse attending a school board meeting." Her voice rose with a hopeful lilt. "She should be back soon though, I would think." Her last three words held little conviction.

Jamie hated the gush of relief swooshing through him. At some point, he would need to face Violet and squelch any hopes she might have of a romantic relationship between them. Freed for the moment from that disagreeable chore, the temptation to linger a while and spend some time alone with Rose tugged hard.

"Since Violet has given her permission for me to borrow the books, maybe you could get them for me." Jamie could almost hear the soft hissings of a horned, devil-like tempter on his shoulder whispering suggestions Jamie knew he should eschew. "I did walk all the way over here." He deserved a beating worse than the Hamiltons' dusty carpet did for preying on Rose's kind heart and sympathy.

She caught her plump bottom lip between her ivory teeth and glanced westward as if hoping to see her sister returning home. "Well, I suppose I could loan you one volume." Her demeanor brightened with her voice. "When you return it, you and Violet can discuss what you read."

Before Jamie could think of a reply that wouldn't sound like either an agreement to her suggestion or an outright insult to Violet, Rose turned and headed toward the house.

"I'll be right back with the book," she said over her shoulder as she jogged across the yard. "If you like, you can wait on the porch swing." Lifting the hem of her faded blue skirt above her trim bare ankles, she ran up the porch steps and disappeared into the house.

Egged on by the devilish tempter on his shoulder, Jamie plodded across the yard and up the steps then plopped himself down on the white-painted swing that creaked with his weight. He gazed eastward across the Hamiltons' neat yard to the graveled lane lined with lilac and scarlet quince bushes. When Rose returned he should simply thank her for the book then head down the lane toward home. That's what he *should* do. The tempter's fiendish laughter in his ear faded at the sound of the front door opening.

Rose stepped out onto the porch, pulled the door shut behind her, and held out a blue cloth-bound book with gold and crimson markings that read *Shakspere, edited by Charles Knight, volume II.*

Jamie stood and took the book. "Thank you." He glanced at the porch swing. *Don't do this. Don't. . .* "Would you sit with me and help me decide which story to read first? Looks like you could use a rest."

A charming giggle bubbled from Rose's pink lips as she glanced down at her well-worn blue skirt. "I must look a mess."

You look like an angel. "Not at all." Somehow Jamie managed to push the three words past his drying throat.

To his amazement, she sat down on the porch swing. To his horror, he joined her. *She is Ty's intended.*

Rose took the book from his hands and their fingers touched, sending an electrical charge up his arm to his shoulder. "I brought this volume because Violet has marked a page with a scrap of paper." She opened the book to a page with the heading *Romeo and Juliet.*

Jamie's chest constricted until he feared for his next breath. Was Violet trying to send him a message? His heart felt as if it turned inside out and he struggled to repress a sardonic laugh. Could even the Bard invent a more tragic situation than his own, a villain more vile than himself? His brother's intended owned his heart while he owned the heart of her sister. He should thank Rose, take the book, and go home before another moment passed.

Rose's soft voice as she read from the page kept him on the porch swing.

> "Two households, both alike in dignity,
> In fair Verona, where we lay our scene,
> From ancient grudge break to new mutiny,
> Where civil blood makes civil hands unclean.
> From forth the fatal loins of these two foes
> A pair of star-cross'd lovers take their life."

They took turns reading, laughing together over their certain mispronunciations of the old English. With his head leaned close to Rose's, Jamie rested his left arm across the back of the porch swing, allowing his fingers to brush against her shoulder with the swing's motion. By the last act of Scene I, Jamie could no more deny his feelings for Rose than Romeo could deny his for Juliet. When he read Romeo's description of Juliet to a servant, the words were no longer Romeo's, but Jamie's own, describing his feelings for the girl sitting beside him. His heart throbbed as he read.

> "O, she doth teach the torches to burn bright!
> It seems she hangs upon the cheek of night
> Like a rich jewel in an Ethiop's ear;
> Beauty too rich for use, for earth too dear!
> So shows a snowy dove trooping with crows,
> As yonder lady o'er her fellows shows.
> The measure done, I'll watch her place of stand,
> And, touching hers, make blessed my rude hand.
> Did my heart love till now? forswear it, sight!
> For I ne'er saw true beauty till this night."

He didn't dare look at Rose as he waited for her to read the next line. Could she hear his heart pounding? Did his voice betray his feelings?

"Are you going to the box supper Friday night?"

At her unexpected question, Jamie's heart jolted and heat infused his face. Awkward seconds passed as he fought for breath and control of his voice. "Yes." The tumult inside him ebbed as the reason for her question dawned. He forced a weak grin. "I'd be happy to pass on to Ty any hints about how you plan to decorate your box."

She gave a dismissive shrug. "Lillie Ann has told Ty how my box will be decorated." She looked down at the page and her tone turned quiet. "But, for anyone who's interested, Violet's box will be decorated with a bouquet of violets."

Jamie's heart dropped to his stomach like a chunk of lead. Violet *was* interested in him romantically. "I'll keep that in mind." His face hurt with his forced smile as he glanced down the empty road in front of him. Friday he would bid on Violet's box, and while they shared its contents for supper, he'd use the opportunity to disillusion her of any romantic notions toward him. "Reckon I'd best get back home."

Somehow he managed to stand. The desire to find a reason to spend more time with Rose once again summoned the invisible devil on his shoulder. "Since we didn't get to finish the story today, I'll bring the book back next Wednesday and we can pick up with it where we left off, if you'd like."

Rose started to stand and he took her hand to help her up. "I'd like that." Her sweet smile set his pulse galloping.

Their eyes met and, for an exquisite instant, Jamie could have sworn an understanding passed between them. A soft gasp escaped her lips, and she blinked eyes wide with surprise.

"What are you two up to?" Ty's voice behind them broke the spell.

Chapter Seven

At the sight of her intended, Rose's heart vaulted to her throat. She dropped his brother's hand and jumped back from Jamie as if he'd turned into a giant serpent. The confusing emotions swirling inside her like a raging tempest sucked away her voice. Jamie saved her.

"I came to borrow one of Violet's books." Nothing in Jamie's placid demeanor reflected the bolt of emotional lightening that had fused their gazes a moment earlier. He held up the book.

Rose fixed Ty with a knowing look. "Don't you remember I told you that Violet offered to lend Jamie her books by Shakespeare?"

"Oh, yeah." Ty's head bobbed with an understanding nod, and then he turned to his brother. "Pa's decided to put another acre in corn and wants you to disc it up while me and him plant the ground we worked up yesterday." He sent Rose a wink as he tugged Jamie down the porch steps. "See you Friday at the box supper, Sweet. Be sure to put some good corn bread in with your box of fried chicken."

Halfway to the road Jamie stopped, turned back, and lifted the book in his hands. "Thank Violet for lending me the book, Rose." His tone softened with his gaze. "Tell her I'll take good care of it and I'll be back with it next week."

Joy bounced in Rose's chest like a bunch of rubber balls. She told herself that her happiness sprang from the progress, albeit meager, she'd made nudging Jamie in the direction of romantic thought toward Violet.

Her joy ebbed as she watched the brothers walk westward down the road toward their farm. Feeling oddly deflated, she trudged to the clothesline while an unease she couldn't identify churned inside her.

At the clothesline, she picked up the cane rug beater she'd left there earlier and took a whack at the hapless living room carpet. Over and over, she beat the rug as if trying to beat out her discontent, sending clouds of dust into the air until her arms ached and the carpet had no more dirt to give. Still she couldn't exorcise the vexing feeling that had taken hold of her.

Two days later the disconcertion that had gripped Rose after Jamie's visit still persisted when she and her sisters, with boxes in hand, walked into the annex room of the church where the box supper would be held. Rose scanned the milling crowd for Ty and his brothers. She didn't find them, but she did notice Nancy Martin with her own decorated box waving to them from across the room; an obvious invitation for Pa to take a peek at her blue-ribbon-decorated box before the auction began.

"You girls go along. I'll take these to the auction table." Violet gathered the three boxes into her arms.

"Thanks, Violet." Glad for the opportunity to search for Ty before the auction, Rose relinquished her box and headed out to the churchyard.

"Looking for Ty?"

Rose turned at the familiar male voice behind her shoulder. "Yes." For an inexplicable reason, the sight of Jamie Roberts took Rose's breath away. *It's just because he startled you. That's all it is.* She didn't entirely believe the voice in her head.

A freshening breeze played through the dark curls falling over his broad forehead. His cerulean blue eyes looked intense beneath his dark brows. Why hadn't she noticed Jamie Roberts's handsomeness before? Perhaps Ty's outgoing personality had overshadowed his more sedate older brother. One day Violet would thank Rose for matching her with such a handsome, kind, and intelligent man. The odd squiggle in Rose's midsection squirmed again.

"Last I saw him, he was over by the church steps talking to Si Thompson." Jamie's gaze seemed to burn into hers like a blue flame. "It's not right that he always makes you go searching for him, Rose." Something about the way his dark brows pinched together in deliberation set Rose's pulse pounding. "If you were my girl—"

"I need to let you know that Violet's box has a lace ribbon with a bunch of violets on top." Rose ignored his comment that threatened to take their conversation down a path she didn't care to travel, but she wished her voice didn't sound so breathless.

Jamie glanced down at the ground for a moment. When he looked back up, his smile didn't reach his eyes. "I'll remember that." His smile brightened. "I'm enjoying the Shakespeare volume. I'm almost through *Richard II.*"

"So you finished *Romeo and Juliet?*" Why that thought saddened Rose, she couldn't explain.

"No. I'm still planning to come to your place Wednesday and pick up with the story where we left off."

Rose's pulse quickened again. She shook her head in an effort to clear the gathering cobwebs of confusion. "Wednesday won't do. I'm sure you'd rather finish reading the story with Violet. She's read all the stories several times." Rose attempted a light giggle that sounded nervous. "She can even pronounce all the words right. But she'll be gone much of the day Wednesday helping to organize the new singing school. Could you come another day?" She'd failed to get Jamie and Violet together last week. She couldn't allow the same thing to happen at his next visit. Hopefully Jamie and Violet would begin their discussion of the Shakespeare stories this evening over a shared box supper and want to continue their discussion when Jamie visited their home this coming week.

"Wednesday is the only day I have free. And, as you said, Violet has already read the story. Don't you want to know how it comes out, Rose?"

Rose wanted to say no, but that would be a lie. She couldn't deny that she enjoyed the time they'd spent together on the porch swing reading *Romeo and Juliet*. But as much as she might enjoy finishing the story with Jamie, it wouldn't help in getting him and Violet together. "Well—"

"Hey, Sweet." At Ty's voice, Rose's heart shot to her throat. Her face flaming, she jerked around. She shouldn't feel uncomfortable for Ty to find her talking to his brother, but she did. He held out a bouquet of pale pink roses she suspected he'd cut from the bush beside the church steps.

"Wednesday," Jamie murmured before he turned and headed toward the church annex.

Rose cast a parting glance at Jamie's retreating back before turning to Ty. For the moment, she'd have to cede the battle in changing Jamie's mind about Wednesday's visit. Hopefully he and Violet would share a supper this evening talking about books, and he'd want to spend more time with her.

"I shaved off most of the thorns," Ty said as she took the flowers.

"Thank you." The sweet, uncharacteristic gesture warmed Rose's heart as she inhaled the blossom's fragrance.

"Roses for a Rose." He grinned and placed a quick kiss on her cheek. "Your box has a lace ribbon with a rose on top, right?" His tongue peeked out to lick his lips. "Got my mouth all set for that fried chicken and corn bread."

Rose nodded then glanced toward the church to make sure Jamie was nowhere in sight and lowered her voice to a whisper. "I think I've talked Jamie into bidding on Violet's box. Has he said anything about her at home?"

Ty's face puckered in thought. "He said he's likin' that Shakespeare book she lent him. Said he wanted to make sure he thanked her again for loaning it to him."

"That's good." Oddly, Ty's report didn't generate the excitement in Rose she might have expected. "I'm thinking that if Jamie wins Violet's box and they spend supper together talking about Shakespeare, they could be promised by the time we all head home this evening." Though overly optimistic, Rose felt the need to bolster not only Ty's but her own fervor for the matchmaking project. "Maybe the four of us could have a double wedding or triple wedding if Pa asks Nancy Martin to marry him as well."

Ty's sandy brows shot up and his voice rose a decibel. "Your pa's marrying Mrs. Martin?"

"Shhh!" Rose glanced about, hoping no one had heard his blurted question and kept her voice to a whisper. "Pa hasn't ask her yet, but since I got them together, they've become good friends. I expect it's just a matter of time before they're wed." Rose couldn't help the pride that crept into her voice as she recounted her one successful effort at matchmaking.

Ty's expression turned bewildered. "I thought you were trying to match Jamie and Violet. What do your pa and Nancy Martin have to do with it?"

Rose gave an exasperated huff, wishing Ty had inherited a bit more of his older brother's intelligence. "Don't you see? If Pa is married, Violet won't feel obligated to stay home and take care of him and Lillie Ann. She'll be free to marry Jamie when he asks her, and then we can get married and Violet won't have to dance in the hog trough."

"Hmm." Ty's tepid response and the way his gaze skittered away kindled a flash of irritation in Rose.

She opened her mouth to chide him for his apathetic attitude, but the sight of Lillie Ann running across the churchyard toward them stopped her.

Lillie Ann bounced on the balls of her feet. "You need to hurry up and get inside! Mr. Isaacs is about to start the auction." She grinned at Ty. "Your pa gave Charlie fifteen cents to bid on my box."

Ty chuckled. "Charlie hasn't done fifteen cents' worth of work this whole week." Grinning, he gave one of Lillie Ann's pigtails a playful yank as he and Rose followed her into the building.

Inside, the room buzzed like a happy beehive with a cacophony of cheerful voices. At the front of the room, Will Isaacs stood behind a long trestle table filled with an assortment of decorated baskets and wooden and pasteboard boxes. The scent of fried chicken permeated the space, making Rose's mouth water.

Will Isaacs raised a muscular arm, silencing the crowd. He regarded the gathering with as stern a look as his round, congenial features allowed. "Now fellers, you'll be biddin' on these boxes for, I've been told, some of the best fried chicken in southern Indiana. Not that I would know." He laughed and patted his rotund middle. "Now, all proceeds go to the missionary fields, so be generous with your bids." Growing serious again, he folded his arms over his broad chest, his gaze taking in the entire group. "Once you've bought a box or basket, you are obligated to share the contents with the lady whose name is attached to the box." He wagged his beefy finger at the crowd. "There will be no exchangin' or swappin'. You gotta keep the box you bought and share the contents with the lady who made it."

Over the next several minutes, Will made his way down the length of the table, auctioning off the various containers of food. Rose had to suppress a smug smile when Pa bid and won Nancy Martin's box. He might as well have announced his matrimonial intentions toward her. When Charlie Roberts bid and won Lillie Ann's box, Rose smiled again. Her smile faded and her pulse quickened when Will held up Violet's box. She sent up a prayer that Jamie would offer a bid. When he offered twenty cents, Rose's tense nerves relaxed until Oscar Bennett bid twenty-five cents and Rose held her breath.

"Fifty cents." Jamie's voice boomed from the back of the room followed by the sound of soft gasps and hushed twitters.

When Will called for a higher bid with no responses, he clapped his hands to signal the end of bidding on the box. Lifting the box, he peered at the bottom to read the name on it. "Jamie Roberts has won the box belonging to Rose Hamilton!"

Chapter Eight

Rose felt as if someone had punched her in the stomach. Her legs turned to jelly and she might have collapsed to the floor in a heap if a strong arm hadn't encircled her waist, supporting her.

"Come on, Rose. Let's go get our supper." Only a hint of surprise tinged Jamie's voice.

"But—but, he has it wrong. That's not my box." Rose's stammered objection went ignored as Jamie half-carried her to the front table. There, she shook her head at Will. "That's not my box. It's Violet's box."

Will frowned and pursed his lips like he'd just bit into a green persimmon. Lifting the box, he peered at its bottom and read her name again then tipped it toward her, inviting her to read it for herself. "See, it says clear as day, 'Rose Hamilton.' Reckon I can read well as you." His usual jovial voice took on a perturbed tone.

Smiling, Jamie took the box from Will's hands. "Thanks, Will." His smile widening, he glanced at Rose. "Money well spent."

As Jamie shepherded Rose to a waiting row of tables and chairs set up along the wall, Rose scoured her mind for an answer to how she could have made such a mistake. Remembering that she and Violet had allowed Lillie Ann to decorate the boxes she groaned, knowing she'd found her answer.

Ty stepped in front of them, hurt and anger sketching deep furrows in his brow. With his thumbs hooked around his suspenders, he glared at Rose. "Hey, you said your box would have a rose on it!"

"That's what I'd planned." Rose hated the tears stinging her eyes. "Lillie Ann must have put the flowers on the wrong boxes."

Ty gave her a withering look. "You should have done it yourself." His glare shifted from Rose to Jamie then back to Rose. "Everybody knows we're promised. Just don't like to be made a fool of, that's all."

Jamie put a calming hand on his brother's shoulder. "Just bid on Violet's box and we'll all sit together. "I'm sure all three boxes have the same supper in them. Am I right, Rose?"

Rose managed to nod, unsure if she would be able to get even one bite past her drying throat. If they all sat together as Jamie suggested, Violet and Jamie would have no time to themselves to foster a special relationship.

Jamie cocked his head toward the front table. "Better be ready to bid, brother. Will has Violet's box in his hand."

Grumbling something Rose couldn't make out, Ty pushed past his brother, his shoulder bumping Jamie's harder than Rose thought necessary.

Seeming unfazed by Ty's petulant attitude, Jamie chuckled and pulled out a chair for Rose. "Don't worry, Rose. He'll get over it."

A few minutes later, Jamie's words proved prophetic when a smiling Ty and Violet joined them at the table. After Jamie offered a short prayer, Ty, sitting beside Violet, dug into their shared box of fried chicken, corn bread, fruit jar filled with potato salad, and apple pie.

"I'm afraid the confusion is my fault." Violet forked some of the potato salad onto her plate. "I should have checked the boxes after Lillie Ann decorated them."

"No harm done, I reckon," Ty said around a big bite of chicken leg. He grinned. "Kinda funny, really. Makes me wonder if the little scamp did it on purpose." He glanced at the adjacent table where Lillie Ann sat with Charlie sharing their own chicken dinner. "Now there's a gal after my own heart."

"That reminds me." Jamie lifted a chicken thigh from his and Rose's box and cast a quizzical glance at Ty. "Herman Frische said that somehow his brand-new spring wagon got up on top of his barn the other night. Said unless it sprouted wings and flew up there, he reckoned somebody, or somebodies, took the whole thing apart during the night and put it back together on top of the barn. You wouldn't know anything about that, would you?"

Ty laughed, almost choking on the piece of chicken in his mouth, making Rose fear she'd need to pound him on the back. "Can't say," he finally said when he'd recovered and swallowed. "Did hear that old man Frische and his boys had the devil of a time gettin' the thing down." He stifled his chuckle with a big bite of corn bread.

The look of dismay on Jamie's face reflected Rose's feelings. "Pa's right. It's high time you quit these stunts and grew up." He glanced at Rose. "Especially if you're lookin' to take on grown-up responsibilities soon."

Rose felt her cheeks warm, but she had to agree with Jamie. Ty's antics were wearing thin on her. If he put half as much energy into helping her match Violet and Jamie as he did with tomfoolery like the wagon stunt, her sister and Jamie might already be promised.

Ty snorted and waved a dismissive hand in front of Jamie's face. "Aw, you're too serious. Nothing interestin' ever happens around here. If a body wants any excitement, he has to make it himself or find it somewhere else." He looked over at their younger brother. "Even Charlie craves excitement, says he wants to leave Honeytown and be a missionary to Africa when he grows up."

Jamie's voice turned dry. "At least Charlie's idea for generating excitement is laudable. Yours, on the other hand, are usually not."

Bristling, Ty glared at his brother and Rose feared the two might come to blows. Her heart sank. She needed to salvage—albeit tattered—the remnants of this opportunity to engage Violet and Jamie in meaningful conversation. She turned to Violet. "Jamie tells me he's been enjoying the volume of Shakespeare you lent him, Violet."

Jamie's sullen expression brightened and he shifted his attention from Ty to Violet. "Yes, I am. Thank you very much for loaning me the book."

Soon, Jamie and Violet were engaged in an animated conversation about King Lear. Looking bored, Ty polished off his piece of apple pie then excused himself and headed outside.

As Jamie and Violet talked, Rose packed the remnants of their suppers back into the boxes, confused about her own feelings. She should be thrilled. For weeks she'd worked toward this moment: Violet and Jamie together, laughing and talking about their mutual love of books. But instead of joy, an emotion more akin to sadness gripped Rose.

"You have such a nice singing voice, Jamie, I do hope you'll attend the new singing school this summer. We'll be having our first class this Wednesday afternoon, and Master Anderson is hoping for a good turnout." Violet handed Rose their plates and flatware to pack away.

"I'm afraid not." Jamie looked at Rose. His voice softened and his gaze turned so tender it snatched her breath away. "I have something important I need to do Wednesday."

◆　◆　◆

"For never was a story of more woe
Than this of Juliet and her Romeo."

The sorrow in Rose's voice as she read the last lines of the play reflected Jamie's own feelings. How he wished the story could go on and on forever. With its end, Jamie had no further excuse to spend time alone with Rose.

Watching the afternoon breeze playing through the wispy tendrils of brown hair that had pulled loose from the bun at the back of her head, Jamie's heart throbbed and he felt an affinity with Romeo and his doomed love. Worse, unlike Romeo's, Jamie's love for Rose went unrequited. Or was it? More than once, he'd glimpsed in her eyes a look that made him wonder—or perhaps hope—that her feelings for him were more than those for a future brother-in-law. But if she did have feelings for him, wouldn't she have given Ty the mitten by now?

"It's so sad." Rose's soft words jerked him from his reverie.

"Yes. Yes, it is." While he knew her words referenced Shakespeare's tragedy, they could also describe Jamie's situation. "Reckon it shows that things don't end well when we fail to trust God and look to Him for guidance." Again, he searched her eyes for a hint that she reciprocated his feelings. For an instant he caught a glimpse of the look he sought, and his heart rejoiced before she lowered her gaze to her hands in her lap.

"Of course we know that God doesn't want us to harm ourselves like Romeo and Juliet did, but how can we always know if our plans fit with God's will?" Her fingers played with the stained white apron covering her faded blue and brown calico skirt.

Was she struggling with deciding between him and Ty? Beads of sweat broke out on Jamie's forehead, and he had to clear his tightening throat. She was right. Whatever her decision, it needed the Lord's approval. Swallowing down the painful knot in his throat, he scoured his mind for scripture that spoke to her question. "Proverbs has a good bit to say about that, as I remember. Proverbs 3:5–6 says 'Trust in the Lord with all thine heart; and lean not unto thine own understanding. In all thy ways acknowledge him, and he shall direct thy paths.' And Proverbs 16:9 says, 'A man's heart deviseth his way: but the Lord directeth his steps.'" He ran his thumb over the scarlet lettering on the book's blue cover. "Accordin' to the scriptures, if we pray and ask God to guide us in makin' all our decisions in life, He will."

A tiny frown knit her brows together. "What if we just do something and forget to ask for God's direction?"

The need to touch her, to comfort her in her mental struggle grew too strong and he covered her hand with his. "Rose, is there something you're needin' to make a decision about?"

Nodding, she looked up, and her cinnamon eyes swimming with tears shredded his heart. "It's just that I need to know if. . .if something I'm doing is what God wants me to do."

Please God, if I'm the man who can love Rose best, turn her heart away from Ty and toward me. Jamie didn't want to think about the ramifications that an affirmative answer to his impulsive prayer might bring: heartbreak for Ty and anger and enmity between him and his brother. He tried to swat away the troubling thoughts without success. While he couldn't bring himself to rescind his petition, he assuaged his conscience by adding *But Thy will be done, Lord.*

Inside the house, the Hamiltons' living room clock struck three, and Jamie could hear John Hamilton moving about. Soon Violet and Lillie Ann would return home from the singing school. He gave Rose's hand a gentle squeeze then relinquished it as he relinquished their futures into God's hands. He needed to go. The swing creaked as he stood, and he forced his mouth into a smile. "I'm sorry the story had such a sad ending, but I enjoyed reading it with you all the same." Taking her hands he helped her up but kept her hands enclosed in his. "I'll be praying for God to help you make whatever decision it is that's weighing on your mind."

He gazed down into her eyes and what he found set off a barrage of fireworks in his chest. Casting all caution and reason aside, he let go of her hands and slipped his arms around her waist. *You can't do this. She's Ty's intended.* Ignoring the voice in his head, he leaned his face toward hers.

At the sound of a horse and buggy coming down the lane he sprang away from her, his heart pounding and his face flaming. With a muttered good-bye, he headed down the steps and toward home, berating himself for a coward and a cur.

◆ ◆ ◆

Rose watched Jamie's back until he disappeared behind the honeysuckle vines that grew along the lane. Remembering to breathe, she sucked in a shaky breath, inhaling a lungful of honeysuckle and rose-scented air, then sank again to the porch swing. What had just happened? She strove to make sense of the feelings swirling inside her. *Had Jamie almost kissed—*

The front door creaked open, and Pa stepped out onto the porch. "Hey, Rose, was that the horse and buggy I heard?"

The sound of old Bluebell pulling the buggy down the lane filtered weakly into Rose's consciousness.

"Why didn't you tell me your sisters are back from the singing school?" When Rose didn't answer, Pa headed down the porch steps toward the barn.

Still shaken, Rose scarcely noticed Lillie Ann race past Pa in the yard and bound up the porch steps.

"Rose, Rose!" Lillie Ann grasped Rose's arm, her breathless voice full of urgency. "We can't let Pa marry Nancy Martin!"

Chapter Nine

R ose, did you hear me?" Lillie Ann's voice strained with her desperate whisper and she shook Rose's shoulder. "We mustn't let Pa marry Nancy Martin!"

Rose stared at Lillie Ann's frantic face and struggled to make sense of her little sister's astounding words. "What are you talking about?"

Lillie Ann glanced across the porch toward the barn as if to assure herself that Pa wasn't in earshot. "Charlie and his ma were at the singing school this afternoon, and Charlie told me he overheard Myrtle Foster and Lizzie Salter talking outside the schoolhouse. Lizzie said that Mrs. Martin killed her husband."

"What?" Fully alert, Rose pulled Lillie Ann down beside her on the porch swing.

Lillie Ann nodded, tears filling her wide eyes. "Charlie heard Lizzie say that Nancy poisoned her husband with herbal concoctions."

At the names of the two most notorious gossips in the area, a large measure of the concern building in Rose's chest ebbed. Rose took hold of Lillie Ann's shoulders and looked into her little sister's face, which was threatening to crumple. "Charlie should know better than to listen to anything Myrtle Foster or Lizzie Salter say. The preacher's wife told me that Nancy's husband died of a wasting cancer." She brushed the tears from Lillie Ann's wet cheeks with her thumbs, angered that careless talk by the local gossips had upset her little sister. She drew Lillie Ann into a warm hug. "Don't you worry a minute about what those silly old biddies said, do you hear me? There's nothing to it." She pushed her away to look in her face again. "Now don't you go repeating that gossip, and tell Charlie not to either."

Lillie Ann frowned and brushed the remnants of tears from her eyes. "Lizzie and Myrtle shouldn't have said those awful things about Nancy, but I'm glad they're not true. I won't repeat what they said, and I'll tell Charlie not to when he comes tomorrow." Her now relaxed features brightened. "Charlie's making a water trough for Domino."

"A water trough?" Rose smiled, eager to change the subject. Since Bill Roberts gifted Lillie Ann with the piglet, the child spent hours each day at the Robertses' farm visiting her new pet.

"You know that three-cornered brown rock beside the chicken house?"

Rose nodded.

"Charlie's pa didn't have any wood to give him, so Charlie's chiseling out the rock to make Domino a trough."

Rose couldn't help a chuckle. "That won't make much of a trough, will it?"

Lillie Ann gave an unconcerned shrug and headed into the house.

Left alone again, Rose's thoughts returned to the incredible last moments with Jamie. Surely she had misinterpreted his actions. The jolt near her heart at the memory belied that conclusion.

◆ ◆ ◆

The following week, Jamie began attending the singing school and invited Violet and Lillie Ann to ride along with him, his mother, and Charlie—an arrangement Violet seemed overjoyed to accept. By the end of June, Violet's eagerness for her Wednesday afternoon buggy rides with Jamie convinced Rose that Violet had, indeed, set her cap for him. Inexplicably, that thought brought Rose no joy.

"Are you sure you don't want to come to the singing school with Lillie Ann and me?" Violet asked Rose the first Wednesday in July as she finished pinning up her hair in front of the chifforobe mirror. "There is plenty of room in the buggy, and I'm sure Jamie wouldn't mind."

Rose's heart felt the now familiar sting at Violet's mention of Jamie's name. She shook her head. "Nancy may stop by this afternoon with some yellow tomatoes and her recipe for tomato preserves." Though unsure if Nancy, who had become a frequent visitor would choose today to stop by, Rose grasped at the excuse to stay home.

Violet poked another pin into the bun at the back of her head and smiled at Rose. "Tomato preserves would be nice. We should take a jar or two to the Robertses' threshing party next week. Oh!" Violet's eyes flew open wide. "I almost forgot. I promised Jamie I'd lend him my copy of *Moby Dick*."

Rose experienced another heart-prick as Violet hurried to the bookcase that filled half a wall in their shared bedroom. Rose gave herself a mental shake. She should be happy. Her efforts to match Violet and Jamie and Pa and Nancy were finally bearing fruit. Pa seemed happier than he'd been since Ma's death, and Rose couldn't remember when Violet had been more joyful.

Weeks ago when her matchmaking efforts had seemed a failure, Jamie suggested that Rose pray and ask for God's guidance. She'd taken his advice and now everything appeared to be working out, surely a sign that her efforts had earned God's nod of approval. So why did she feel so miserable?

"Ah, here it is." Book in hand, Violet turned from the bookcase. "If Nancy does come by, ask her if she's changed Pa's stomach tonic. Last night he complained that the concoction she gave him Sunday tastes bitter."

At Violet's comment, an uncomfortable feeling stirred in Rose's midsection. While she thought she'd dismissed the ugly gossip Charlie Roberts had heard about

Nancy, a tiny grain of it had taken root in her mind. Rose later realized that what the preacher's wife had told her concerning the death of Nancy's husband had come from Nancy herself. Could Myrtle and Lizzie have had it right? The uneasy feeling in her stomach churned harder. Rose had brought Nancy into Pa's life. She mustn't allow her growing affection for Nancy to blind her to the possibility that the woman might, indeed, intend Pa harm.

◆　◆　◆

A week later, as Rose and her family arrived at the Robertses' farm for the threshing party, Rose's concern about Nancy Martin continued to ferment in her mind. When she'd questioned Nancy about the stomach tonic's bitterness, Nancy had seemed both puzzled and dismissive, elevating Rose's suspicions. While the tonic's odd taste didn't seem sufficient reason to worry Pa with her concerns, Rose resolved to stay alert to any further signs that Nancy might have less than pure intentions toward Pa.

Pa finished helping Violet and Lillie Ann down from the wagon. "If you gals can get the food to the house, I'll say a word or two to Nancy then head on to the barn with the fellers."

"You go on, Pa. We'll take care of the food." Violet grinned after Pa as he loped off toward Nancy, who stood talking with her sister and some other women in the Robertses' side yard. Violet lifted a basket of food from the back of the wagon. "I'm guessing our household will increase by one before this winter."

"Then when Rose marries Ty, we'll be back to the same number of people." Lillie Ann smiled up at Rose as she accepted a linen-swathed plate of sugar cookies from Violet.

At Lillie Ann's comment, Rose experienced a tiny cringe. Attributing the uncomfortable feeling to her desire to not marry before Violet did, Rose made no reply as the three headed toward the house with baskets of food in hand.

The busy morning proved a blessing, allowing Rose little time for musing amid the chaos of a dozen women crowded into Dorothy Roberts's small kitchen working to prepare the noon meal for the threshing crew. As midday neared, Rose helped to carry the huge platters and bowls of food to the long trestle tables set up in the yard. On one such trip, she overheard Nancy Martin talking with Dorothy Roberts.

"What a lovely shade of morning glory, Dorothy." Nancy fingered a bluish-pink blossom on the vine climbing up the side of the Robertses' milk house. "I was wondering if I might have a start of it?"

At the table, Rose stifled a gasp and set down the bowl of corn and tomatoes before she dropped it. While she might not have Nancy's extensive herbal knowledge, she was aware that morning glory plants were poisonous when ingested.

Her chest tightened and her stomach turned queasy. She had to warn Pa. Now! Any moment, the men should be coming in from the fields. Willing her shaking legs to move, she headed toward the barn and met Bill Roberts walking toward her, mopping the sweat from his brow with his red handkerchief.

"Bill, have you seen Pa?"

Bill glanced back at the barn and cocked his head. "Should be bringin' one of the teams into the barn soon." Concern furrowed his broad brow that reminded her of Jamie. "Ever'thing all right, Rose?"

"Y–yes." Rose mumbled as she hurried toward the barn. She needed to get Pa alone, away from prying eyes and ears.

Inside the barn she stopped, waiting for her eyes to adjust to the dim light. The scents of hay, manure, and animals filled her nostrils. The sounds of jangling harness, plodding hooves, and huffing horses drew her attention to the barn's open end.

"Pa?" She headed toward the two harnessed black Percherons advancing into the barn.

"Whoa!" The horses stopped, but the voice didn't sound like Pa's.

"Pa?" Rose started to walk around one of the horses when it jerked and took another step, almost knocking her down. "Ahhh!" Scrambling to get out of the horse's way she slammed against a stall door, tripped, and pitched forward toward the animal's massive rump. An instant before her face smacked against the Percheron's sweaty flank, strong arms caught her and pulled her upright.

"Rose, are you all right?" Jamie's voice sounded breathless and fear flashed like blue lightning across his eyes.

"Y–yes." Her stammered reply held no more truth than it did moments before with his father.

Despite her claim, Jamie kept his arms around her waist. His gaze softened, melting into hers like azure pools of water. "Rose." As he breathed her name, he pulled her against him. His dark lashes swept down and she closed her own eyes. The next moment might have spanned an instant or a millennia. Time stood still as his lips caressed hers.

At the sound of another team of workhorses nearing the barn, he let her go. Shaken, Rose ran from the barn, all thoughts of finding Pa carried away with the cyclone swirling inside her. Outside the barn, she pressed her back against the building's sun-warmed walls in an effort to calm her racing heart and trembling limbs. She needed solitude to make sense of what had just happened and to let her rampant emotions settle. Feelings she'd repressed for months came washing over her like a deluge. The revelation hit her as hard as if the Robertses' entire barn had fallen on her. She loved Jamie Roberts! And *he* loved *her*!

Another realization hit her equally as hard. She couldn't marry Ty. Remembering her promise to him last May that she wouldn't break their engagement, she felt sick. Also, if she were to end her relationship with Ty and begin a new one with Jamie, it would almost certainly cause a rift between the brothers that might never heal, something she couldn't live with.

"Rose." Strong but gentle fingers gripped her upper arm.

Rose turned to face Ty and a new flash of panic leaped in her chest. Had he witnessed his brother kissing her in the barn?

Instead of the anger she expected to see in his face, she found regret tinged with shame. He glanced down at the bare dirt beneath their feet, worked soft by the horses' hooves. "I know I ain't paid you much attention lately." His pinched gaze lifted back to her face. "But I've been thinkin' on it hard, and I think it's time we talked."

Rose's panic turned to terror that threatened to send her heart lurching out of her chest. *Oh dear Lord, no! He wants to set a wedding date!* She pulled away from his grasp. "I—I have to get back to the kitchen." Lifting the hem of her skirts away from her feet, she fled to the house as fast as her wobbly legs would carry her.

The rest of the day she managed to avoid both Ty and Jamie by staying in the kitchen to help with the meal cleanup. Then, complaining of a pounding headache, which wasn't a fabrication, she headed home alone on foot. By the time Pa and her sisters returned home, Rose's headache had eased, but her heart felt as bruised as if it had been trampled by a team of draft horses. Knowing that her feelings for Jamie were reciprocated but, if acted on, would tear both their families apart, shredded her heart. She'd turned the problem every which way in her mind and the only way she could see to untangle the mess she'd made between her, Violet, and the Roberts brothers was for her to reject both Ty and Jamie. As for her concerns about Nancy Martin, she needed to share them with Pa as soon as possible but away from Violet and Lillie Ann.

"Hope your head feels better, honey." Pa looked up at Rose sitting on the porch swing as he walked toward the house with Violet and Lillie Ann. "Nancy said you prob'ly got overheated in the kitchen. Said to tell you to drink some ginger tea then wring out a vinegar-soaked cloth and tie it around your head."

"Thanks, Pa. I do feel much better." She managed a weak smile. "I'm sure Nancy is right, I just got overheated."

Pa turned to Violet and Lillie Ann, both carrying baskets. "You girls go on in. Reckon I best wash off some of this sweat and hay dust at the pump by the barn, 'fore I come in the house."

"I'll pump for you." Snatching at the opportunity to get Pa alone, Rose jumped up from the porch swing and followed him toward the barn. Halfway there, she stopped beneath a walnut tree. "Pa, there is something I need to talk to you about." She licked her drying lips. She mustn't lose her courage now. Pa's life might depend upon it. "It's about Nancy."

"What about Nancy?" Pa smiled, as he always did when mentioning Nancy's name.

Unsure what emotion to expect from him, Rose blurted what Charlie Roberts had heard about Nancy. "You said the last stomach concoction she gave you didn't taste right. Then today, I heard her asking Dorothy for a start from her morning glory vine, and you know that morning glory is poisonous."

An array of emotions played across Pa's face, settling on an angry scowl. "That's ridiculous! You know good and well that Nancy's husband died of a wasting cancer."

"That's what Nancy told everyone. We have no way of knowing if she's telling the truth." Rose had feared Pa would reject her concerns outright.

Pa's glare darkened. "Well I'd believe Nancy a sight quicker than I would Myrtle Foster or Lizzie Salter, I'll tell ya that!" He shook his head and snorted. "I'm surprised at you, Rose. You should know better than to believe those old gossips." He gave another dismissive snort. "And why on earth would Nancy want to poison me, anyway?"

"This farm, Pa." Rose flung out her arm. "I doubt Nancy wants to live with her sister and husband forever. Don't you think that a woman in her position would jump at the chance to get her hands on a farm as prosperous as ours?"

The frown lines on Pa's forehead deepened. "That's enough, Rose! Nancy is a fine woman. She means none of us any harm, and I won't hear another bad word against her, you hear me?"

"But Pa, at least consider—"

"There's nothin' to consider." Pa held up his hand and glanced down. When he looked back up, his expression and voice softened. "I know it's hard for you to accept the notion of another woman comin' in and takin' your ma's place." His tone gentled. "You know that your ma will always have a special place in my heart. Nancy just has a new place, that's all." He blew out a deep breath and glanced away for a moment. When he looked back at Rose, his face turned serious. Resolute. "I was going to wait till I had all three of you girls together before I said anything, but I'll tell you now: Nancy has agreed to marry me, and we'll be doin' that sometime before Christmas."

Chapter Ten

For Rose, the rest of the summer passed in a miserable mixture of regret, heartache, and dread. While Violet reveled in the singing school, planning Pa and Nancy's coming wedding, and preparations for the winter school season, Rose stayed close to home, caring for the house and canning the vegetable garden's bounty. She came to dread Sundays most of all, becoming adept at avoiding interaction with either of the eldest Roberts brothers. Ty had said no more about their brief interaction at the threshing party or what he'd wanted to talk with her about that day. Several times she'd considered breaking off their relationship, but each time he would say something sweet or hand her a flower and she'd lose her nerve. For the most part, keeping her distance from him hadn't been a problem. Between farm work and mischief-making, he'd made little effort to spend time with her. Jamie simply avoided her as if she were contagious.

Violet, on the other hand, fairly glowed with happiness, especially on Wednesdays following singing school. Each Wednesday she'd wait with bated breath for Jamie's arrival. While she never said in so many words that she'd fallen in love with him, Rose couldn't deny that her sister showed all the signs of a woman in love.

As summer gave way to autumn and the many fall social parties neared, Ty began pressing Rose to attend them. She faced each event dreading the very things she'd hoped for last spring at Nora Bennett's wedding reception: a set wedding date for her and Ty, plus an engagement announcement from Jamie and Violet.

So when neither of those things occurred during a log rolling at the Bennett place and an apple paring at Will Isaacs's, Rose faced the cornhusking party at their own farm in early October with building trepidation.

As for Rose's worries about Nancy Martin, the woman had done nothing to further Rose's suspicions, and Pa's stomach and heart both appeared to thrive under Nancy's care. Still, Rose couldn't shake her lingering concerns.

By the night before the husking, Rose could no longer bear the weight of worry pressing down on her. Her pillow wet with tears, she crawled to the Lord and unburdened her heart. Whatever plans God had for her life and the lives of her loved ones, she relinquished it all into His hands. Tomorrow, with God's help, she would finally tell Ty that her heart had changed and that she could no longer keep their engagement, and she'd ask him to release her from her promise. If Jamie and Violet announced their engagement, Rose would rejoice with them and wish them well.

So the next day, with her heart at peace, she walked into the barn already alive with the happy voices of her neighbors, most of whom were milling about or seated on trestle benches shucking baskets of corn. Rose lifted one of the bushel baskets that lined the barn wall and searched for an empty spot at one of the benches.

"Rose, come sit here." Bertha Newkirk beckoned from her seat at the east side of the barn. "Looks like we're gonna be kin soon."

Smiling, Rose set her basket down beside Bertha's. "Yes, Pa and Nancy are planning a December wedding."

Beside Bertha, a plump woman Rose didn't recognize, gave her a cheerful smile. "I was so happy to hear about Nancy's good news. Bertha speaks so well of your pa."

Bertha blinked. "Oh, Rose, I expect you haven't met Lydia Engle. She's from over Salem way."

Lydia shook her head, her expression turning sad. "So awful about Nancy's husband, Paul. A wasting cancer took him, ya know." She sniffed and picked an ear of corn from her basket and began to shuck it. "My own brother attended him the last months of his life." She smiled. "He's the doctor in Salem, don't ya know?" A tinge of pride crept into her voice.

"No. No, I didn't know." Nancy had told the truth. A mixture of relief and shame swooshed through Rose. She held out her hand to the woman. "It's so nice to meet you, Lydia. We've all come to love Nancy very much." And she meant it.

Pa, with Nancy at his side, beamed as he stepped to the center of the barn. "Thank you all for coming, and be sure to holler out if you come across a red ear of corn." He glanced at Nancy and his grin widened. "It'll earn a gal a kiss from each gent, and a gent a kiss from each gal."

Glancing about, Rose noticed Violet sitting with Jamie and the singing school master, Edmond Anderson, all three in laughing conversation as they worked. At that moment, Jamie looked at Rose, catching her gaze and sending her heart into pounding contortions.

Willing her hands to stop shaking and her lungs to breathe, Rose managed to tear her gaze from his and shift it back to the ear of corn in her hand. *Dear Lord, help me think of him as a brother. I must learn to think of him as a brother.*

"Red ear!" Violet's triumphant announcement stilled the crowd an instant before a collective cheer filled the barn. Standing, she waved her red-kerneled prize over her head.

To Rose's surprise, the singing school master claimed the first kiss, and Rose wondered at Jamie's thoughts when the man kissed Violet directly on the mouth. Jamie then placed a chaste kiss on Violet's cheek igniting a flash of jealousy in Rose. When Ty's turn came to claim his kiss, Rose felt nothing as her intended embraced

Violet and kissed her cheek, erasing any lingering doubt that Rose needed to break her engagement to Ty before the evening ended.

Sending up a silent prayer for courage and peace, Rose picked another ear of corn from her basket and began pulling the dry, brittle husk and brown silks from the ear. For months, she'd tried and failed to think of a painless way to break her engagement to Ty. She ran her fingers down a rough row of hardened golden kernels, trying again to gather the right words that would end her relationship with Ty while inflicting minimal pain.

The sensation of a hand on her shoulder pulled Rose from her musings. She looked up into Ty's face and her stomach tightened. *All right, Lord, I hear You. Now is the time.*

His expression somber, Ty shifted from one foot to another, while not quite meeting Rose's gaze. "Rose, I need to talk to you." Offering a nod of acknowledgement, he gave the older women beside her a weak smile. "Bertha. Mrs. Engle."

Ignoring the women's soft twitters, Rose stood on shaky legs and struggled for breath. She followed Ty to a spot near the horse stalls, away from the crowd.

Ty took Rose's hand, cleared his throat, and finally met her gaze. "I've been thinkin' and prayin' on this real hard for a long time." He cleared his throat again and glanced down before lifting his gaze back to her face. "I don't think I'm ready for marriage." His throat moved with what seemed a hard swallow and he winced. "I need to ask you to release me from my promise to marry you. You deserve a man who loves you better than I can. Besides, farmin' ain't for me. I plan to leave Honeytown and even Indiana."

Stunned at Ty's news, Rose felt her jaw go slack while a mixture of relief and concern swirled inside her. "Leave? B–but where would you go?"

His eyes lit with excitement. "The Great Lakes, to be a merchant marine." He shook his head. "There's too much world out there to see for me to stay stuck here in Jackson County, Indiana." The exuberance in his eyes dimmed and they turned anxious, begging for understanding. "So, will you release me from my promise?"

Rose couldn't rein in the smile stretching her mouth wide. "If that is what you want, of course I will. With a full heart." The tears stinging her eyes surprised her. "But you must promise to write often and let us know of your great adventures."

"Thank you, Rose. I will." Smiling, Ty hugged her then wiped away the tear that had slipped down her cheek. "You'll always have a special place in my heart, Rose." He glanced across the barn. "But I reckon a girl as pretty as you won't be without a feller very long." Giving her a parting wink, he took off across the barn at a jaunty pace.

For a long moment Rose stood still, trying to process what had happened. When she finally made her way back to her seat beside Bertha and Lydia, she couldn't help humming the hymn "God Moves in a Mysterious Way."

Bertha and Lydia exchanged a knowing grin, and then Bertha turned a smug smile toward Rose. "So, have you and Ty Roberts set a wedding date?"

Rose bent down and picked an ear of corn from the basket. "There's not going to be a wedding. At least not between me and Ty." She smiled at the women's puzzled frowns, deciding to let them draw their own conclusions.

As she began to pull the husk from the ear of corn in her hands she glimpsed a deep reddish color.

"Red ear! Red ear!" Bertha stood up and pointed at Rose then bent and whispered, "Bet you'll be gettin' yourself a new feller quick."

Jamie Roberts stood up and began to stride toward Rose, and her heart seized in her chest. Her breaths came in soft gasps as he reached her and helped her finish shucking the red ear of corn. The barn turned silent except for the chirping of the crickets.

"I've come to claim my kiss," Jamie announced in a voice that carried across the barn. "And more," he whispered to Rose before he took her in his arms and pressed his lips down on hers.

Everyone else in the barn disappeared as Rose floated in a sphere that held only her and the man she loved. When Jamie released her, dropping her back to earth, the sound of hushed murmers filtered into her consciousness.

Jamie took her hand and gazed into her eyes, his October blue ones filled with love and hope. The next moment, he dropped to one knee. "Rose Hamilton, I ask you in the presence of God, our families, and neighbors, will you do me the honor of becoming my wife? Will you marry me?"

For a long moment, Rose stood frozen, wondering if she'd been caught up in a wonderful dream. When Jamie didn't evaporate into a mist, her heart began to beat again and she managed to make her head nod amid a flood of tears gushing down her face. "Yes. Yes, I'll marry you."

She'd scarcely choked out the words when he stood and kissed her again. When he finally let her go, she blurted the question blaring in her mind. "B–but what about Violet?"

Violet, who had come to stand near them along with both their families, hugged Rose. "I am thrilled for both of you, and so is Edmond."

"Edmond?" Rose blinked as the singing school master stepped to Violet's side and slipped an arm around her waist. Since their first meeting in the churchyard back in May, Rose had paid the man scant attention.

Edmond reached his hand out to Rose and she accepted it, impressed by his firm but gentle grip. "Congratulations, my dear." He angled a smile at Violet. "Soon to be dear *sister*."

Rose gaped as Edmond and Violet disclosed their own engagement, kept secret until tonight.

Violet beamed. "Edmond and I are planning a May wedding."

Jamie put his arm around Rose and smiled at Edmond. "Then I hope to beat you to it." Giving Rose a hug, he shifted his smile to her. "If you're in agreement, love, I'd like for us to get married as soon as possible."

Rose experienced a flash of panic. "No!" she blurted, extinguishing Jamie's smile and sending him back a step. At his surprised look, she took his hand and tempered her voice. "But darling, if we get married before Violet and Edmond do, Violet would have to dance in the hog trough, and I won't have it!"

At the back of their small group, Ty chuckled and said, "I told you, brother."

Smiling, Jamie slipped his arms around Rose's waist, his azure gaze melting into hers. "Then I propose a double wedding with no hog trough dancing involved."

"I think that's a wonderful idea, darling," Rose murmured through her irrepressible smile. As she snuggled into her intended's embrace, the words from Isaiah drifted into her mind: "For my thoughts are not your thoughts, neither are your ways my ways, saith the Lord." Rose sent up a silent prayer of thanks for God's perfect ways and impeccable matchmaking.

Ramona K. Cecil is a wife, mother, grandmother, freelance poet, and award-winning inspirational romance writer. Now empty nesters, she and her husband make their home in Indiana. A member of American Christian Fiction Writers and American Christian Fiction Writers Indiana Chapter, her work has won awards in a number of inspirational writing contests. Over eighty of her inspirational verses have been published on a wide array of items for the Christian gift market. She enjoys a speaking ministry, sharing her journey to publication while encouraging aspiring writers. When not writing, her hobbies include reading, gardening, and visiting places of historical interest.

The Tinman's Match

by Lynn A. Coleman

Chapter One

D o you believe him to be the man of your dreams, Miss Wooley?" Xander leaned forward placing his elbows on his knees. He'd worked hard on this match. John Sprouse was a good man but ten years older than Miss Wooley. Age difference was the one concern he had.

Sarah Wooley looked up at him with moistened blue eyes. "Yes," she whispered. "I believe he is. Have you consulted with Father?"

Xander nodded. It was difficult matching women with men when parents paid for the service. Xander believed he had a responsibility to the future spouses. Ultimately, they were the only two people who mattered with regard to the decision. In Miss Wooley's case he felt the need to be certain that she wasn't being pressured into a relationship she wasn't ready for. He would not bring her to Tennessee unless she showed genuine desire and interest for John. "Yes. However, Mr. Sprouse would not be interested in you if you personally did not desire to come and meet him."

Sarah nodded. Her golden-blond hair stayed in place. He often wondered how long it took a woman to pile her hair upon her head in such a manner.

"Excellent. I will wire Mr. Sprouse and let him know you are coming." Xander stood up. "We will leave in seven days. I will pick you up." He pulled a folded paper from his pocket. "This is a list of the items you should bring. Additional items can be shipped after you are settled in Tennessee."

"Thank you, Mr. Russell. I appreciate your care in this matter."

Xander gave a slight bow. "I'm glad I could help."

Another woman entered the room; she was about the same age as Miss Wooley. Her features were more delicate, but the similarities with Miss Wooley spoke volumes. He gave a nod of his hat to her and continued out the door. The Wooleys' home was of moderate income, perhaps on the border of being wealthier than most. However, they were frugal with their finances, and the livestock they raised added to their income. Mrs. Wooley had purchased many of his tin wares over the years.

Xander's wagon of wares stood in the front of the house on the edge of the street where there would be a curbstone if this were a larger town. Pearisburg was one of the oldest farming communities in this part of Virginia. The brick courthouse in the center of the town had been built in 1836. Mentally, he calculated the rest of his stops. He still found it hard to believe his business of making and selling tinware had produced a side business of matchmaking. The Wooleys were a prime example of how he helped folks. Xander's talent with tin design had given him a fair hand at sketching, and he was able to sketch the faces of his clients. His smile broadened as he remembered Sarah looking at the sketch he'd drawn of John. Sarah Wooley was not unpleasant to the eye but she was rather plain, and the men of Pearisburg, Virginia, hadn't taken the time to get to know Miss Sarah. It was their loss and now John Sprouse's gain.

"Mr. Russell, may I have a word with you." Mr. Wooley came out the front door.

Xander paused and turned back to meet his client. "Yes, sir."

"I wish to send a dowry with Sarah, and I understand your wagon doesn't have enough room. Would it be appropriate to hire another wagon and driver to accompany you?"

Xander shrugged. "Most of the roads are in good repair. But let me show you what I've done to my wagon to prevent a broken axle on route. Why not send the freight by train?" After all, the Pearisburg station was a mere six miles from here.

Mr. Wooley came up beside him, a robust man with a balding pate. "I'd feel better having the wagon come with her so that Mr. Sprouse will find her not a burden but an asset."

"If you wish." Xander knelt down and pointed to the axles. "Note they are more rugged than an axle for driving in a city or around town. Of course, my equipment is heavier than clothing your daughter might bring with her."

"She'll be bringing a full set of china, a few baking pans and other items my wife has put together for her from our kitchen, as well as some herbs, spices, and some seeds for spring planting. Sarah is a very good cook. You might want to take advantage of her culinary skills on the road."

"I'd be happy to. However, most nights we shall be staying in various inns along the route." Admittedly, most were farmhouses, like the Wooleys' home. The owners would rent a room for a night or two to those passing by, travelers heading west or, in his case, merchants running back and forth selling their wares.

Mr. Wooley's smile broadened as Xander went over a few of the other adjustments he'd made. He didn't know whether Mr. Wooley would be able to procure another vehicle for the trip in seven days, but that was not his concern.

Xander climbed aboard his wagon and headed a couple of miles out of town to the home of the Reddings. They had placed a small order of new tinware, and he had finished the items earlier that day.

He liked his life. Even though he spent a lot of time on his own, he enjoyed the interaction with his customers. He even scheduled extra time for some of his older customers who loved to tell tales. He'd be on the road for two days, spend a few with his family, then return to Pearisburg and pick up Miss Sarah Wooley. A caravan was a slower way to travel. Xander sighed. He'd have to rethink his travel plans and allow for the additional wagon. He only hoped and prayed Mr. Wooley would rent a suitable one for the cross-country trip.

◆ ◆ ◆

Seven days later, Jo still could not convince her cousin to stay in Pearisburg. She had to admit the sketch of John Sprouse was not an unpleasant one to look at. He wasn't the kind to make her heart swoon, but Sarah wouldn't be stuck with a man she would not want to be seen in public with. And he seemed decent in his letters. Still. . .it just didn't seem right. Jo couldn't help but wonder if Sarah's parents were simply getting rid of Sarah, marrying her off so Abigail could marry.

Jo went to the armoire and started to pack. Aunt Margaret and Uncle Felix didn't care if she married or not. They'd housed her since her parents went to Europe and hadn't returned in two years. Jo often wondered if something had happened to them. But occasionally she would receive a letter telling her of the wonderful places they were seeing in Europe. Why they hadn't taken her she couldn't fathom.

She pulled open the door to the left side of the armoire and took one of her dresses off the hanger, folded it, and placed it in her carpetbag. She selected another casual dress more suited for travel and put that in the bag as well. Then she selected the unmentionables she would need for a week of travel and placed them in the carpetbag. She removed her housedress and put on a traveling costume and changed into more durable, small-heeled shoes for travel. *Sarah doesn't know it, but I'm coming with her.* She didn't trust this Xander Russell. It seemed odd to her that a man would hitch up men and women from different parts of the country. He was a tinsmith, not a matchmaker.

Uncle Felix had hired a man to drive a second wagon with all of Sarah's belongings out to Tennessee. There was bound to be enough room for her.

Once changed, Jo burst into her cousin's room. "I'm going with you, Sarah."

"What?" Sarah held the dress up in front of her.

"I'm going with you. I've packed my bag and I'm ready. It isn't right for you to go by yourself with this stranger."

"Jo, I'm going. You can't stop me."

"I'm not stopping you. I'm going with you. Together we'll meet this Mr. John Sprouse and see if he's worthy of you." Josephine closed the bedroom door and lowered her voice. "You said it to me before. Abigail can't marry until you are married. I know this is why you're settling for this man."

Sarah rolled her eyes. "Did you not read his letters? He's a kind man."

"Yes, I read them. You know that. He may be a kind man. Or it might simply be a ruse. I've packed my father's six-shooters."

Sarah's blue eyes widened. "Do you know how to use them?"

Jo shrugged. "Of course I do. You simply aim and pull the trigger. What can be so hard with that?"

Sarah slipped into her dress. Jo came up beside her and helped fasten some of the buttons. "It would be nice to have someone with me."

"Thank you."

"But you haven't packed the items on Mr. Russell's list."

"We have an hour for me to run to the general store. What do I need?"

Sarah went over the list.

"I can purchase the mosquito netting and food items. I have just about everything else." Jo took the list and headed for the door. "I love you, Sarah. I only want what is best for you."

"I know you do, Jo. But Father and Mother were quite careful before choosing Mr. Russell."

Jo sighed. "I know. I'll be right back. Don't let Mr. Russell leave without me."

Sarah waved her off. Jo hurried toward the stairs as Aunt Margaret was coming up. "Where are you rushing off to?" she asked.

"I'm going to the general store and..." Jo hedged for a moment. "I've decided to accompany Sarah out to Tennessee."

Aunt Margaret leaned back and grasped the railing. "You're what?"

Jo repeated her intentions.

"I realize you don't believe your uncle and I are responsible for you, but we are. Did you think for one moment we would let you go without our permission?"

Jo paled. She knew she had a tendency to jump in when others would think and ponder. "I'm sorry. But don't you think it would be wise if I were to accompany Sarah?"

"Josephine Wooley! I don't know what your parents will do with me if I were to let you go..."

"But you're subjecting your own daughter to the same travel."

Margaret closed her eyes. "You're right. Fine, go. Not that I could have stopped you."

Jo leaned over and gave her aunt a kiss on the cheek. "Thank you, Aunt Maggie."

"Your uncle will not be pleased."

"You can convince him, I'm certain of it. Forgive me, I must go and get the items on Mr. Russell's list."

Aunt Margaret moved over to the right. Jo flew down the stairs and out the door to the store. In a way she understood her parents and their love for travel. Half of Jo's life had been spent living with her aunt and uncle as her parents roamed the world. There was no doubt in Jo's mind that she'd picked up the same wanderlust that her parents had.

She scanned the shelves of the general store, picked up the mosquito netting, and noticed some galoshes. They weren't on the list, but she picked up a pair for her cousin as well. The parasols she had at home were for fashion so she picked out one that would shed water, another item not on Mr. Russell's list. A few other necessities not on the list she purchased as well: a jackknife, oilcloth, strikables, some thin leather straps for ties, a roll of bandage cloth and dried beef. She debated about a small tent, but according to Mr. Russell they would be staying overnight in some inns along the way. She brought everything to the counter. As the storeowner was tallying up the order Jo spotted some candles. "Add a dozen of these as well."

Mr. Gaven smiled. "As you wish. I take it you are heading out to Tennessee with your cousin."

"Yes, sir. We'll be leaving later today."

"Would you pass a message on to Mr. Russell for me?"

"Sure."

Mr. Gaven leaned over and scratched out a note, then folded it and sealed it with some sealing wax. He handed it to her. "Thank you."

Jo stuffed the note in her pocket. "You're welcome."

The order packaged, she hustled back to the house. Outside the front of the house stood Mr. Russell's wagon, along with the other one Uncle Felix had hired. A man was leaning under it, Mr. Russell she presumed. Sarah came out of the house with her father carrying a couple of her bags. Jo hustled up to the wagons. "I'll be ready in a few minutes."

"Josephine Wooley," her uncle said sharply. She stopped in midstride. "Your aunt spoke with me, and it is not necessary for you to accompany Sarah. I have it on great authority that Mr. Russell is a man of honor."

Mr. Russell raised his head up and bumped it on the underside of the carriage. "Who's accompanying who?" he said as he rubbed the black curls on the back of his head.

Jo squared her shoulders. "I've decided to come with Sarah and make certain she is being well cared for."

He scanned her from head to toe then turned toward her Uncle. "I promised to care for your daughter, not a wagon train of others."

◆ ◆ ◆

"Josephine!" Felix Wooley bellowed. "You will not ruin Sarah's chance at happiness."

"Of course I won't, Uncle. I merely want to be certain she is well cared for on the trip and that Mr. Sprouse is as honorable as Mr. Russell claims him to be. Don't you agree it would be wise to have another there in order to make certain Sarah is in the best hands?"

"Since you've come of legal age you've been insufferable, just like your father." He waved his hands at her. "Go, go if you must."

She ran to her uncle and embraced him. "Thank you."

Xander turned away. *Great. . .a strong-willed woman who can manipulate a man with a simple phrase or the bat of an eye.* Xander groaned and made certain the line was taut. He wanted to say he would not be responsible for the young woman's care, but he knew better. He would do everything in his power to keep her safe, just as he would with Sarah Wooley, his charge.

"Let me get the rest of my things." Josephine Wooley ran into the house.

Miss Sarah came up beside him. "She's a good traveling companion. You don't have to worry about Jo."

Jo. . .she even has a man's name. "I'm certain it will give you great comfort to have your sister."

"Cousin," Sarah supplied.

Xander helped load the rest of the women's belongings into the hired wagon. Mike Ellsworth seemed a competent driver. He'd been hired to bring the wagon to and from Tennessee. He was a young man, perhaps seventeen years old. He would sleep in the wagon each night and protect the women's freight.

Xander pulled out his pocket watch. "We need to leave or we won't make it to our first stop before dark."

Mike hustled up on top of his wagon. Sarah Wooley joined him. Josephine glanced at the full seat then at Xander's wagon. "You may join me, Miss Josephine."

Mrs. Wooley came out with a basket. "Here's a little something for your trip. It isn't much but it will at least give you a nice lunch today."

"Thank you, Mother." Sarah embraced her. Tears flowed from both women's eyes. This was perhaps the hardest part. There was a good possibility the two would never see one another again, and each knew it. He hoped the parents would travel at least once to see their daughter and her family but it wasn't always possible. Perhaps, with the expanding railways people would find it easier to travel.

Xander checked his emotions and sat down on the bench. Josephine hugged her aunt and uncle and said, "I'll be back as soon as I can. And I'll make certain he's a good man."

Felix Wooley chuckled. "He is, darling, or I wouldn't send such precious cargo."

Josephine Wooley smiled and shrugged her shoulders. "You know me."

"All too well, dear. All too well," her aunt said as she hugged her.

Josephine was a rather stunning woman. She had petite features and was much prettier than her cousin Sarah. *Why hasn't she married?* he wondered, then thought back on the interchange with her uncle.

Josephine climbed up without the assistance of a man. *That's a good sign.* Her attire was casual, a bit fancy for his tastes, but not as fancy as some of the ladies. The skirt of her dress was not overwhelming but appropriate for travel. Her shoes were sensible for travel as well. Perhaps this woman would not be a huge burden.

Xander jiggled the reins. . .the horses stepped forward in unison. Miss Josephine Wooley moved with the rhythm of the wagon. She placed a hand on the cushion he had on the bench seat. "This is nice."

"Thank you. My mother made them for me."

"Does your mother know that you sell women?"

Xander tamped down his anger. "I do not sell women, Miss Wooley. I merely provide a suitable match for them."

He couldn't believe she was so antagonistic about his role in bringing Sarah to her future husband. Why was she coming? Was she planning on ruining Sarah and John's potential happiness?

She nodded and held her tongue. Which was advisable. He didn't need to bring this woman. He could dump her out on the streets here. They were not even five blocks away from the Wooleys' home. "If your intention is to sabotage Sarah and John's marriage before they are acquainted I'd be more than happy to stop right now and let you walk back home."

"I will not stop Sarah from making this choice, unless Mr. Sprouse is not the man he purports himself to be."

"I hope I have your word on that, Miss Wooley, because I know John Sprouse. He is an honorable man and will make a fine husband for your cousin."

"So you say," she whispered. She may have thought he didn't hear her, but he did. He'd have to watch this woman. She might be pretty on the eyes, but she definitely challenged a man's stability.

They continued the rest of the morning without speaking to one another. They stopped for lunch where the horses could be refreshed. Mrs. Wooley had been correct—the food was very tasty.

"Mr. Russell?" Sarah Wooley came up to him. "Jo tells me your seat is cushioned. Would it be an inconvenience for me to sit with you?"

"I'd be honored, Miss Sarah."

Sarah Wooley's blue eyes brightened. "Oh, thank you. I don't think my backside would have made it the rest of the way."

"I understand completely. Which is why my mother has made those cushions for me." Perhaps a hard seat would help soften Josephine Wooley's hard heart, tenderize her a bit.

Sarah walked over to her cousin. They exchanged a few words then a hug. He watched as Josephine climbed up on the other wagon. Perhaps her heart wasn't that hard.

Chapter Two

Jo wished she could rub her backside and work off the pounding it received for the entire afternoon. Being a lady, it was out of the question. Something needed to be done to make the rest of this trip more endurable. Mike Ellsworth didn't have a lot to say. Most answers were a grunt, a nod, and an occasional grin. He drove a team well for such a young man. Having grown up on a farm, he'd probably been driving teams through the fields since he was six.

The first inn they stopped at was a farmer's house with spare rooms. Dinner was a delicious hardy beef stew with wonderful brown gravy, heavy on the vegetables and meat. The dinner rolls were light and fluffy.

Sarah was in good spirits. Mr. Russell ate and carried on a conversation with the Wilsons as if they were old friends, and perhaps they were, since he was so familiar with this route. Jo wanted to ask for a warm bath to soak her weary body. Instead, she kept her tongue. She didn't want Sarah feeling like she'd put her cousin out.

"Mrs. Wilson, thank you for this fabulous dinner. I wonder if you might have some extra material and batting that I might be able to purchase from you?" Jo asked.

"Quite possibly. What are you in need of?"

"Mr. Ellsworth's wagon does not have any padding on its bench seat, and I was hoping I could make something for the rest of our journey."

"Ah, I understand. I'll take a look and see what I might have." Mrs. Wilson pushed away from the table and scrambled off.

"I'm fairly used to that bench," Mike said as he shoveled a spoonful of stew into his mouth. "But," he said with his mouthful, "a cushion would be nice."

Xander smirked and focused back on his meal. *If he wants to think I'm too soft for travel, let him.* Jo sopped up the rest of the gravy with the buttered roll.

"I daresay that bench is frightful," Sarah added. "If you can't make a cushion, cousin, perhaps we can alternate wagons."

"I'll be fine, Sarah. I'll sit on my carpetbag if I have to." Everyone chuckled.

Mrs. Wilson returned with a fleece of wool. "This should help."

"Thank you. What is the price?" Jo asked. They worked out a fair deal and Jo took the fleece up to their room.

"I'm sorry you're so sore," Sarah said as she changed into her nightdress. "Mr. Russell's wagon was a welcome relief. I'm still bruised from the morning's ride."

"I'll be fine. I might have a black-and-blue buttocks, but I'll be fine." Jo laughed to ease her cousin's worry.

"Mr. Russell said we're doing well, a bit slower with the second wagon but still keeping our schedule."

"Did he have anything more to say about John Sprouse?"

"Not too much, except that he's known him for five years and he's a good farmer. He's seen people come and go and not make it on their moves out west. But Mr. Sprouse isn't that way. He said he's stayed through good weather and bad and kept working on his farm. He's older than me, but he's strong and healthy."

"Ten years, right?"

"Yes."

Jo sighed.

"What?"

"Nothing, I'm sorry. I hope Mr. Russell is correct and he's found a good match for you. It's just hard to believe a man could make such decisions. I mean, I've heard of women matchmakers. . .but a man?"

"He says he didn't set out to be one. He simply made mention to a friend along the way that he knew a gal back east that might make a good spouse and, boom, his matchmaking service started." Fully changed, Sarah came out from behind the privacy screen. "At first he didn't charge people. But as time went on and it took time away from his tin business he started charging his hourly rate."

"Interesting." Jo took her nightgown behind the divide and started to undress.

"It really is." Sarah took out her hairbrush and began counting out a hundred strokes. It was a nightly ritual, something they both enjoyed doing. "I am so excited. Can you believe I might be married in a couple of weeks?"

Jo paused. She'd promised her Uncle that she wouldn't talk Sarah out of this marriage. Jo closed her eyes and fired off a prayer. "It is hard to believe. But we'll trust the Lord."

"I have been. I can almost see John when I pray for him each night."

"Mr. Russell's sketch is helpful." Jo finished changing.

"Yes, but it's more than that. It's. . .oh, I don't know. I'm just sounding foolish, like a young schoolgirl with her first crush."

"If Mr. Sprouse is the man of your dreams then what is not to be giddy about?"

Sarah giggled. "I suppose you are right."

Jo joined her cousin on the bed. When they were younger Jo, Sarah, and Abigail used to share a room, even a bed. Now they each had their own rooms. "Feels like we are kids again, doesn't it?"

Sarah wiggled under the covers. "Yes." Sarah paused. "I'm so glad you came, Jo."

"I'm glad I came, too. Just not my backside."

The girls laughed and turned off the light. Tomorrow would come soon and Jo was certain her backside would not be ready for it.

◆　◆　◆

Xander actually felt sorry for Miss Josephine Wooley, and Mike. He was glad that she'd spoken up and purchased the fleece from the Wilsons. But he was equally glad to have Sarah as his traveling companion over her cousin.

He rose early and hooked up the wagons. Mike joined him about fifteen minutes later and finished hooking up his team. The ladies arrived on time. Jo carrying the fleece over her carpetbag and Sarah carrying nothing more than her purse. *Interesting*. He noted that Jo was taking her role of watching over her cousin a bit further than he expected. "Good morning, ladies. Did you sleep well?"

"Like schoolgirls," Jo answered. Sarah giggled.

Xander rolled his eyes. He tried not to have more than one woman at a time on his journeys. He never quite got used to their giggling ways. It always seemed to him that two or more women together could be like a flock of chirping and giggling hens. He snapped his hat against his thigh. "Glad to hear it. Time to go." He hoped he didn't sound as brisk in his tone as he felt in his heart. There was something about Josephine Wooley that seemed to set him on edge.

"Did you sleep well, Mr. Russell?" Sarah asked as she settled beside him on the wagon's bench.

"Yes, thank you."

She knitted her fingers together and set her hands on her lap. "Good. How far are we going today?"

"If good weather prevails we'll get in a full day's traveling and should reach the outskirts of Dublin." Xander snapped the reigns and urged the team forward. The wagon jangled. The creak of the wheels brought a welcome sound to his ears. He supposed he loved traveling as much as he loved his occupation of making items from tin. He'd converted his wagon for long distance. He had put in a small desk, and both wagon sides could come down to form a sleeping area for himself and another traveler. The canvas flap would shed the rain and weather. But most of the time when he brought a bride out west, he didn't have need. He'd made several arrangements with farmers, such as the Wilsons, to provide his female passengers the comfort of a soft warm bed. He learned early on that women didn't have the same fortitude as men with regard to travel. After the first grumpy bride delivery, he'd made the change.

It was a satisfying business. He enjoyed providing good men with good women. In a way he felt he was helping the Lord by bringing a wife to a man who needed one and would appreciate her. He couldn't count how many men he'd turned down over the years because they didn't want a life partner, just someone they. . .well, he didn't like to think about it. He was just happy he had the forethought to know when a man wasn't really ready to sacrifice and treat his wife as a gift as well as a partner.

The rest of the morning went on without a hitch. They stopped for lunch and then made it to the next farm without delay. The ladies departed into the Shelbys' house while Mike and Xander unhitched the horses and brought them to the barn. Once inside, they fed and started to brush down the animals. "Check their shoes," Xander encouraged.

"Yes, sir." Mike continued to brush down his horses.

"Did the fleece help?" Xander asked.

"Yes, some, although I'd love to have the padded seat you have."

"My mom took pity on me."

"Do you make tinware in your wagon?"

"I have the equipment to make small pieces, and I do some mending on items in the wagon. I use my father's shop back in West Virginia. How do you plan on making your living, Mike?"

"Farming, like my dad. I'm the oldest son, so I'll inherit the greater portion of the land. Dad's a good farmer and I'm learning a lot from him. Was your father a tinsmith?"

"No, he is a blacksmith. I took on tinwork when I was a young man. Then I read an old article about the Yankee tinsmiths coming south to sell their wares, and I thought I could do that. And how much better for a southerner to purchase from another southerner."

Mike nodded and bent down to check the shoes of his horse. Xander did the same. He cared for his horse's hooves then washed his hands at the old pump outside the barn. "You're in luck tonight, Mr. Ellsworth. The Shelbys have an additional bed for a dollar a night."

Mike nodded as he rinsed his hands. "I'll save the dollar and sleep with the wagon again."

"Fair enough. Come on, dinner should be ready."

They headed to the house. The ladies were seated at the table, along with three of the Shelby children. Mr. and Mrs. Shelby brought the meal from the kitchen. "Evening Xander, and who are your traveling companions?" Mr. Shelby asked.

Xander gave the introductions and sat down for the meal.

The next day progressed in a similar manner. There were no problems on the trail, and for the most part he'd been able to avoid Josephine Wooley. Their fortunes changed the next day as rain began to fall. They made it to Fort Chiswell. The American Revolutionary fort was gone now, but a small town had developed in the area and kept the name. Xander set up his forge and equipment at the blacksmith's shop, but due to the weather not too many people came out for repairs. His other business also required staying in town for a bit longer. He had some correspondence to pass out.

Out the corner of his eye he saw Josephine Wooley pass an oilcloth to Sarah as well as a strong umbrella—not a fashionable parasol but an instrument that would provide shelter from the elements. Josephine Wooley seemed more competent of a traveling companion than he'd given her credit for. The ladies went on to explore the town and he went to work.

After an hour, Josh Wheaton came in to the blacksmith's shop. "Morning, Xander, any news?" Josh had been waiting to hear from Rachel Adams, a young widow with a child. They both had lost their spouses and had similar family values. "If not, I'll move on."

"As a matter of fact, Josh, I have a letter right here where she states her arrival date. She has a few more legal matters to clear up with her husband's estate, but she's willing to come and work for you for the next six months. If during that time the two of you wish to take the relationship further, you'll decide then."

Josh gave a firm nod.

Xander climbed into his wagon and pulled out Rachel Adams's letter. "Here you go."

Josh caressed the note in his hand. "I think it is wise that we wait. I still miss Haddie so much. But the children need a mother."

"I understand. And I've watched Rachel with her son. She is a good mother. I even checked with some of her neighbors. I believe she is a good woman and will work well with your three children. Will you have the room built in time for her arrival?"

"It's near completion." He opened the letter. His eyebrows rose. "I'll get some men to help me."

"She doesn't need it fancy. Her home in the city is quite functional, not overtly fashioned."

Josh nodded. "Thank you, Xander. I appreciate your help in this matter." He pulled out two gold coins and handed them to Xander.

"Mr. Russell," Josephine called out as she marched into the blacksmith's store then halted. "Pardon me, I didn't know you were busy."

Josh put his hat back on his head and shook Xander's hand. "Thank you, again." Then Josh turned toward Jo. "We're finished."

◆　◆　◆

Jo couldn't believe she had stormed into the barn without any thought of Xander Russell working, even though she knew they had stopped in this small town for that very purpose. "I'm so sorry. I was wondering how soon before we got on the road?"

"Another couple of hours," Xander mumbled, and went back to his work.

"If you don't mind, we'll go to the hotel and order a bath. It's been days without a good. . ." *soaking*, she wanted to say but decided she didn't need to give the man any mental images.

"Fine," he mumbled again and continued his work.

Jo shrugged and went to gather her cousin. She couldn't believe her eyes when she saw the sign in the hotel's window offering such a good price on the baths. Her concern would be the cleanliness of the water. It was early enough in the day that hopefully they'd be the first to use the tub.

Thirty minutes later Sarah and Jo were sitting in warm, sudsy water. "This is wonderful. Thank you, Jo."

"You're welcome." Jo leaned back and closed her eyes.

A quiet knock at the door followed by a squeak of the hinges made Jo open her eyes to see another bucket of hot water coming in. A chambermaid clothed in a light gray dress and white apron carried the water over and poured it into Sarah's tub.

"Thank you."

The chambermaid smiled and shuffled back over to the doorway where she kept guard. The chambermaids would help the ladies, and male stewards assisted the men. Whoever wasn't needed on the inside would be the one to run the buckets from the stove to the bathing room. It was a good system as long as they only had two customers at a time. In any case, Jo felt the dollar spent was well worth it after the beating her body had received from the wagon.

"Jo?"

Jo opened her eyes to find her cousin tracing the water with one finger as if she were drawing on its surface. "What's the matter?"

"Nothing."

"Something. I've seen that look before."

Sarah rolled on to her hip and placed her forearms on the edge of the tub. "Do you really think I'm doing the wrong thing here? I mean. . .I'm marrying a man I don't know. You're right, it sounds so foolish."

Jo held back from voicing her concerns. "I think that because I'm coming with you, you have more freedom to say no when you meet him than if I weren't."

"We could probably catch a carriage back home."

"We probably could. But why the change of heart?" She'd promised her aunt and uncle not to talk Sarah out of marrying John Sprouse before she met him. But did that mean she was supposed to encourage her to continue the journey to at least meet him?

Sarah turned back and sighed. "I don't know. It's so far away. I'm tired. I'm sore, and I guess I'm getting cranky."

"Are you afraid?"

"That, too. Mr. Russell doesn't talk all that much. He makes me nervous."

"Would you like me to sit with him for the rest of the trip today?"

"Would you? I don't want to sit on that horrible wagon bench, but I don't think I can sit and be quiet for another day. I need to talk."

If anything were true about her cousin when she was nervous, she had to talk—not necessarily what she was nervous about; she just needed someone to speak with from time to time. Mr. Russell wasn't the communicative sort. "I'd be happy to."

"Thank you. Perhaps young Mr. Mike will make better company."

"He hasn't spoken with me all that much either. I guess not all men like to talk. At least not like our fathers."

"I wonder about Mr. Sprouse," Sarah said.

"Would you ladies like me to wash your hair?" the chambermaid asked.

"Oh, Jo, that would be delightful."

"Yes it would, except that our hair will be wet and down for the rest of our travel time today."

"Thankfully, it's stopped raining and our hair will dry." Sarah gave Jo her best puppy dog eyes. Something she'd been doing since she was a baby, no doubt. It not only worked on her parents but apparently on Jo. "Fine. I wonder if Mr. Sprouse will be able to say no to those eyes."

Sarah giggled. "I hope not."

Chapter Three

What are you doing?" he asked as Jo climbed up to join him on the bench seat of the wagon. Xander was not in a good mood. Not only had the ladies delayed them by forty-five minutes, they'd come back with wet hair. He prayed they wouldn't catch a cold, as the temperature would be going down soon, not to mention gray clouds were building again. They were heading toward Wytheville. He glanced up at the sky; hopefully they would get to their evening destination in time.

"What's it look like I'm doing?" Jo huffed, "I'm riding with you this afternoon."

"Fine," he mumbled.

He lifted the reins and snapped them. The jolt of the wagon sent her flying. He halted the horses and she fell back the other way. Horror washed over him. "I'm so sorry. I thought you. . ."

The other wagon came up beside them. "Problem?" Mike asked.

"No. Miss Wooley wasn't ready, and the jolt caused her to lose her balance."

Jo glared at him. He cleared his throat. He wanted to pull on the collar of his shirt but didn't. He could feel the crimson heat rising on the back of his neck.

"Jo, are you all right?" Sarah Wooley asked.

"I'll be fine."

"You go on ahead. I'll follow," Mike said.

Xander turned and looked at his passenger. "I'm sorry. Are you ready?"

Jo nodded. His jaw clamped shut. Her blue eyes focused on the road ahead.

Xander called out to his team and snapped the reins. *Oh yes, this is going to be a delightful trip.* Not that he didn't blame her for being upset with him.

"I'm sorry we were late," Jo apologized.

"And I didn't mean for you to lose your footing. Those forty-five minutes will cost us. We won't reach Wytheville before the sun goes down."

She took in a deep pull of air and released it. Keeping her eyes focused on the road she said, "Wytheville was named after George Wythe, wasn't it? He's one of the original signers of the Declaration of Independence. Where will we stay?" she asked.

"We will have to camp by the side of the road. And yes, Wytheville is named after George Wythe."

"Oh." She folded her hands in her lap and didn't say another word. Her cousin had tried to engage him in conversation, but he responded with the briefest of replies. He wasn't exactly sure why he wasn't more conversational with Sarah. Although having the extra wagon and her cousin along added to the pressure he always felt in matching people with one another. Or perhaps it was just her cousin Jo. Xander caught a glimpse of her from the corner of his eye. The gentle swoop of her nose fascinated him. The point of her chin wasn't too sharp; neither was it squared. It was perfect for her face. She was incredibly beautiful. And her knowledge of the area and its history surprised him. He could try speaking about the Wilderness Road they were connecting with and Daniel Boone but. . .

Xander shook off his wayward thoughts and focused on the road ahead. They had mountains to the north and south of them. It seemed the good Lord when He created this area saw fit to put in a natural pass between the mountains. At fifteen miles a day they could reach Knoxville in fifteen days. At this rate he'd be lucky to reach it in twenty. Which of course wasn't fair to blame strictly on the ladies, since he would need to stop and work at various towns.

As they reached the crest of the mountain Jo commented, "The fields look like they've yielded a good harvest."

His focus joined hers. He scanned the multicolored hills. Some were still covered with grass and grazing livestock, others were brown and thick with the rich soil of freshly turned earth. And still other patches of winter wheat were ready to be planted or recently had been. Not to mention the remains of cornstalks that would be rooted by the pigs. "Yes, the Good Lord seemed fit to bless Virginia with good land."

He could feel the wagon's wheels digging deeper into the soil, slowing their progress even more. It must have rained heavier in this area than he'd thought. "I'm sorry," he apologized again.

"I understand we delayed you. But more than that, I understand that you are not pleased with my presence, which is fine."

Xander sighed. "I'm sorry about that, too."

"Forgive me for saying so, but, Mr. Russell, you do not have to be my friend nor I yours. I am here to help my cousin. I understand that others find you respectful but. . ."

"But you do not," Xander finished for her.

"It isn't you, exactly. It is this entire idea of Sarah's parents arranging such a thing. I know my other cousin, Abigail, is interested in marriage, and her father wants Sarah married first, which makes no particular sense to me. Of course, I'm an only child and have no apparent need to marry young. In fact, my parents are quite content to leave me for years at a time, now that I've come of age."

"Your parents leave you?" Xander couldn't imagine. He'd been on the road for years, but he always returned home. And his parents took an active interest in him and his business.

"I've lived half of my life with Uncle Felix and Aunt Margaret. But I am thinking it is high time I move out and find my own home."

"Why?"

"Because I have a healthy stipend that my parents send to me. I give my uncle and aunt about half to cover expenses for living under their roof. Most of the rest I put away in savings. Truthfully, I love to travel. Perhaps I should travel to Europe and meet up with my parents."

Xander sat back. He also loved to travel but certainly didn't have the funds to travel abroad, not without working. "What do your parents do in Europe?"

"Mostly travel, but Father speaks on various topics. He and Mother are quite educated, and I guess his proper title is Distinguished Full Professor of American History, which keeps him in demand in Europe. It seems they are rather interested in our unique country. Of course, we as a country have strong European roots."

Xander smiled. He knew his American ancestry only dated back a couple generations on his mother's side. Grandpa Heinz came from Germany seeking work as a stonecutter. "True."

Why was he opening up to this woman? He focused back on the road. "I hope you don't mind, but I'm going to leave you and the others at an appropriate place to set up camp for the evening. I'll ride into Wytheville to take care of some business. I'll return late. Do you think you can handle yourselves once I get all of you set up?"

"I see no reason why we shouldn't be able to." Jo knit her eyebrows then looked away.

For the next two hours she didn't say a word, nor did he. He found a smooth area off the road and pulled in. "Let's set up camp here."

"I purchased material for a tent."

"There's no need. You and your cousin will camp in my wagon. I've set it up so that two cots come off the sides."

She looked at him as if he had two heads.

"You'll see."

◆　◆　◆

Jo was surprised by Xander Russell's creative genius. He truly had designed an interesting wagon. Most of the sidewall came down and leveled out, supported by poles that affixed them between its underside and wagon frame. A smaller set held up canvas tents he'd made that extended out from the top of the sidewall, forming a roof over the foldout bed. A thin straw mattress rolled out to complete the bed. They wouldn't be much more comfortable than sleeping on the ground but they would be off the ground.

"That's remarkable," Mike said.

"Thank you. Now I must leave if I'm going to arrive in Wytheville before dark." Xander buckled the flaps of his saddlebags. "You're certain you'll be all right? I should be back by ten at the latest."

"I'll take care of the ladies." Mike looped his thumbs around his belt and squared his shoulders.

"We'll be fine," Jo said, knowing she had packed her father's pistols.

"Very well." Xander swooped up on his horse with the ease of a man quite familiar with the process.

"Shall we make our supper?" Jo rubbed her hands together.

"Already started," Sarah answered. "Mike, if you can get the fire going I'll have a pot ready in ten minutes."

"On it," Mike answered and scurried off.

"What can I do?" Jo asked.

"Make up our beds. I'm exhausted." Sarah pointed to Mr. Russell's wagon. "Have you ever seen such a thing? Do you think it will hold us?"

"No, I think it's ingenious. And yes, I believe it will hold us. Mr. Russell knelt on both of them snapping down the canvas, and he's heavier than either one of us."

"True." Sarah continued to chop an onion.

"What are you making?"

"Mr. Russell had some canned beef and vegetables. I'm adding some fresh onion, a bit of suet and some spice to the pot."

"Sounds good. I'll go take care of our beds."

Jo walked over to Mr. Russell's wagon and climbed the step he had fashioned on the rear. It was the first time she'd been inside. He had a small desk. There were ledgers and letters—lots of letters—and a sketchbook. She reached over to touch them then pulled her hand away. It wasn't her business to read his letters or see his sketches. She shifted her attention to the beds and worked some magic with the woolen blankets and cotton sheets.

She took a couple of moments to scan the rest of the wagon. There was a chest on either side that provided a seat or step up to the beds. She could only assume it held his clothing, tools, and perhaps a few other items Mr. Russell felt he needed after years on the road. An oil lamp hung on an iron bracket. It wasn't a heavy iron but a well-crafted bracket strong enough for the task yet decorative enough to be placed in a home. Obviously the lamp was made from tin, matched by another tin lamp on the desk. How did it travel without breaking the glass chimney? she wondered. Narrow shelves lined the walls on either side of the lowered beds. Canvas and leather straps held in some books, a Bible, and what appeared to be some glass bottles of men's cologne and shaving equipment.

Jo placed her hands on her hips. Xander Russell certainly knew how to prepare for travel. . .and the unexpected, she hoped. Jo reached into her satchel and strapped on her father's six-shooters. There was no sense being unprepared in the open wilderness.

Sarah clanged the cast iron pan and called out, "Come and get it!"

Jo chuckled as she exited the wagon and headed toward the campfire.

Mike Ellsworth had fixed a bedroll for himself near the fire. "Smells fine, Miss Sarah."

"It really does," Jo added.

"Thank you." Sarah grinned and scooped out a healthy serving of the impromptu beef stew.

Light conversation about the day's ride and curiosity about the day ahead salt-and-peppered their discussion while they ate their dinner. "I wonder if we'll have to travel twenty miles tomorrow to make our next scheduled stop," Mike questioned as he finished off his stew. "It might be wise for us to get our shut-eye early and be ready to start with the sunrise."

"It would probably be best," Sarah said, and placed her empty bowl in the pot of boiling water.

"I'll take care of the dishes and cleanup. After all, you cooked," Jo offered.

"Thank you. I made up some corn biscuits. We can heat them up in the morning."

Jo nodded toward the wagon. "Go get yourself ready for bed. I'll be in shortly."

Sarah scurried off.

Mike grabbed some logs and set them by the fire. "These will be ready for the morning. I don't mind saying I'm looking forward to some good old corn bread."

Jo chuckled. "You ate a ton of it two days ago."

"True, but there's nothing like corn bread. A man could live off of it."

Jo chuckled again and continued to wash the dishes. Next she cleaned out the pot they had boiled the water in. While putting things away, she heard a twig snap in the woods. She reached for her gun and listened.

◆ ◆ ◆

Xander was on his way back from Wytheville. He'd managed to settle his business in mere minutes. Passing on a letter could sometimes take hours. But not this time. Evan Brewer was not pleased with the letter he'd received from Karen Scott. As much as Xander had tried to match the man with the right woman, Evan seemed to always find fault. At least this time he had warned Miss Scott not to get her hopes up, unlike the heartbreak he'd delivered to Maggie Chilson two months ago. Xander agreed to try and find one more match for Evan but assured him it would be his last attempt. He hoped to reach the wagons before the ladies went down for the night. He had some paperwork to go over and wouldn't have any time in the morning.

A shot rang through the air. Xander leaned forward and spurred his horse into a gallop.

What seemed to have taken hours probably only took two or three minutes. He arrived to see Jo with a six-shooter in her hand still aimed toward the woods. Mike was standing beside her trying to see whatever Jo was aiming at. Sarah peered out the back door of the wagon.

"What happened?" Xander asked as he slid off his horse.

"Someone moved out there," Jo said, keeping her gun aimed. "You better come out now," she demanded, "or I might just kill you."

Xander placed his hand on his gun and scanned the shadows. Nothing moved. Nothing even stirred. "Are you certain you saw someone?"

"No. I just heard him."

"Sarah, please give me my lantern hanging on the hook inside," Xander ordered. "Mike, you stay with the women." He narrowed his gaze toward Jo. "And put that away before you shoot me."

Jo hesitated for a moment but slipped the gun back into its holster. When had she picked up those? he wondered.

Sarah handed him the lit lantern and he stepped toward the woods. He could hear Jo walking behind him. "Please stay back, Miss Wooley."

He didn't turn around but he heard her stop. Xander continued on. He placed the lantern low. The ground looked undisturbed. More than likely it had been an animal, and the gunshot had scared the critter away. He held the light up and scanned the area one more time before returning back to the campsite. Jo would probably be upset with him not doing an extensive search but. . .

He stepped out of the bushes. The three of them stood there, waiting on him. "Well?" Jo asked, her arms crossed.

"It's too dark, I couldn't find anything. It was probably an animal." He prayed she didn't challenge him.

"It is always possible," Jo admitted.

Xander relaxed. "We should buckle down for the night. We have a long day ahead of us."

Everyone said good night and went to their respective corners. Xander had no problem giving the ladies the comfort of his wagon, though after the day he'd had, a nice bed sounded wonderful. Instead, he rolled out his sleeping mat next to the fire. Mike leaned over. "Do you think it really was an animal?" he whispered.

"I hope so."

"So. . .you're afraid of highwaymen?"

"Always a concern. I'll take the first watch."

Mike nodded. "Wake me when you need to."

Xander traveled these roads on a regular basis and had never been robbed. He'd met more than one unsavory person along the way but he'd always been spared. He spent the first hour of the watch in prayer. Around midnight, and nothing stirring, he woke up Mike and asked him to watch for an hour then go to sleep if everything remained quiet. Mentally, he decided to wake at four. It was a gift to be able to set his internal alarm clock. So far it had never failed him.

If there were men out there, he would be prepared if they tried something in the morning.

Xander rose at four and readied the wagons for departure. When everyone else woke at five thirty, they dressed, ate, and were on the road by six. Not bad for folks who never traveled. Thankfully, there'd been no real threat. He had searched the woods and found no evidence of a human predator, only some raccoon, black panther, and deer tracks.

Sarah sat next to him this morning. He'd been hoping for Jo so he could have some private conversation about the gun she was carrying.

"Did you sleep well?" Sarah asked.

He smiled. "Well enough."

"Mike suggested we might try to go twenty miles today to make up for the lost miles yesterday."

Xander knew Sarah was trying to make conversation and closed his eyes for a brief moment and prayed for guidance. He'd never been so tight-lipped and protective of his business with the other brides. "It's a good idea, but we'll have to see how the roads are. Some of them were fairly wet yesterday." He paused. "I didn't realize your cousin was carrying six-shooters."

Sarah nodded. "They are her father's, or rather *were* his. He'd given them to her for safekeeping. Bringing them to Europe didn't seem a proper thing to do. Uncle Joe picked them up on one of his trips out west. He was working on a paper for the college back east about the expansion into the West. He really is quite a learned man."

"Jo is named after her father?"

"Sort of. His name is Josephus and hers is Josephine. Uncle Joe is spelled with an *e* and Jo's is not."

He didn't want to appear too interested so he switched the conversation back to the guns. "Does she know how to shoot?"

"She's used them for target practice." Sarah shrugged. "I've shot them once. Personally, I don't care for the noise they make, so I wasn't very interested in learning more."

"They are loud." Which he was grateful for. It had pushed him to ride faster to the campsite. He supposed he should test her skills when they stopped for lunch today.

"Are you upset?"

"Let's just say I'm not pleased to learn she has six-shooters. There's no question a little extra security when traveling is helpful. I'm just not certain a woman should be wielding a weapon."

"Don't let Jo hear you say that." Sarah laughed. "Are you telling me your mother never used a rifle or a gun? Don't most farmers, male and female, know how to use a weapon?"

"As a matter of fact, my mother, to the best of my knowledge never shot a gun or rifle in her life. Father is the local blacksmith. We didn't live on a farm."

"And during the War of Aggression she didn't know how to protect her family? I find that odd."

Horror swept through him. He never thought much about his mother being at home when the War was going on. She would have fed the troops if they needed food but. . . "I don't know. I suppose she did."

Sarah nodded.

Xander thought back over the past few years. He'd left for the War and fought for the South. He never asked his parents how they fared or if the War had taken its toll on them, as it had on so many others. Did his mother know how to handle a firearm? Was she perhaps more self-reliant than he realized? Did he really understand women at all?

Chapter Four

Two days later Jo found herself a bit weary and wishing they could take a day off from travel. They entered a small town referred to as Greever's Switch, named after the man who operated the switch for the trains. Jo couldn't help but think of how much time they would have saved if they'd traveled by train from Pearisburg to Greever's Switch. The thought gnawed at her most of the afternoon. They were staying in a small farmhouse, which also seemed a bit odd, rather than staying in the larger, almost hotel-like structure.

Xander exited his wagon, stuffing some letters into his inside suit coat pocket. He carried the leather satchel she'd noticed in his wagon the night she and Sarah had slept in it. "Mr. Russell, may I ask you a question?"

"Certainly, Miss Wooley."

He paused. She pondered his strong shoulders, his dark, short-cropped beard, and dark curled hair. He certainly filled the "handsome" slot. Jo swallowed and cast her eyes toward the ground. "I'm curious why we didn't take the railroad. We could have arrived here in a day, possibly hours. Surely Knoxville has a railroad station as well."

He fixed his gaze on her. His shoulders tightened then he relaxed his stance. "Because I have a business to run and stopping every few miles to load and unload a wagon on a train is neither wise nor economical."

"Wouldn't it have been easier on Sarah to arrive in Knoxville and meet Mr. Sprouse there?"

"Perhaps. But your uncle felt it best for Sarah to travel with me."

Jo couldn't fight the fact that her uncle had made the decision. But she couldn't wait to speak with him and suggest the trains would be a far more efficient means of travel in the future than the many days seated on a wagon with your backside aching.

"I see. Thank you," she replied and turned toward the farmhouse, lifted her skirt, and headed inside. Tonight they would be able to bathe. It had been four days and she could hardly stand the dirt and grit on her clothes and body. She turned back with a glance at Xander as he walked over to a young lady and handed her one of the envelopes he'd put in his pocket a few moments before. The girl's hands trembled. Jo couldn't take her eyes off of the exchange.

He reached into his satchel and pulled out a sheet of paper. Curious, Jo caught herself taking a step toward them but then stepped back. It wasn't her place.

The young woman examined the sheet of paper and smiled. Then she ripped open the letter and began to read. She squealed in delight as she hopped in place. Xander grinned.

The girl ran off toward a neighboring farm, stopped, turned around, and ran back to Xander and gave him a bear hug then scurried off again.

Xander shook his head back and forth then headed in the opposite direction.

Jo thought back on what it must have been like for Sarah to receive her letter from John Sprouse. She doubted it was as enthusiastic as what she'd just witnessed. No doubt Sarah had been excited about the prospect of marrying Mr. Sprouse. Were Sarah's increasing doubts her fault? Jo fired off a prayer, hoping she hadn't stolen her cousin's joy.

Later that night as they lay in their separate beds, Sarah confessed she was thinking of returning home. "We could secure a ticket for the train and be home tomorrow. Father wouldn't mind, I'm sure of it."

"I'm not." She remembered her aunt and uncle's warnings about ruining Sarah's chance at happiness. "Your father will have my hide. Come on, we're halfway there." Perhaps not halfway exactly but close.

"How can I marry a stranger? What was I thinking?"

"Sarah, let's continue to Knoxville, meet Mr. Sprouse, and then decide."

"But the train switching station is right here," Sarah whined.

"You're just nervous. . .and who wouldn't be?" Jo rolled over and lifted herself up on her elbow. "I witnessed a young lady receiving a letter from one of Mr. Russell's customers today. She was so excited. Nervous at first but genuinely excited. Were you excited when you read John's letters?"

Sarah smiled.

"Think on those moments. You don't have to marry him if you don't feel right at the time. I'll be there by your side either way."

Sarah shook her head back and forth. "I can't believe you're encouraging me after everything you said before we left."

"I promised your parents I wouldn't talk you out of marrying John Sprouse, but I don't want to see you making a hasty decision. We've come this far, we should keep going and find out who this man really is."

Sarah took in a deep breath. "You're right. Thanks for coming with me."

"You're welcome."

"What did you think of those baths tonight?" Jo asked, changing the subject. "That was an incredible way of heating up the water."

"Mrs. Knight said her husband got the idea from the Saltville salt factory. Apparently they pump the salt water up from the ground then boil it down to produce the salt in metal bowls similar to the ones Mr. Knight used to heat the water for our tubs."

"I daresay I wouldn't mind having something like that in my home, if I should ever have my own home."

Sarah chuckled. "You will. Do you fancy Mr. Russell?"

Jo huffed. "You better wear a hat tomorrow. The sun's baking your common sense right out of you."

Sarah continued laughing and rolled over. "Good night, Jo, and thank you."

"Good night, Sarah, and you're welcome." Jo lay down and closed her eyes. Sarah's question about Mr. Russell rattled around for a long time before she succumbed to sleep.

◆　◆　◆

Xander had the wagons loaded and ready for travel before the ladies were up. He had to admit it would have been easier on the women to travel most of the distance by train. But Mr. Wooley felt the travel time would be good for his daughter to realize just how far away she and her family would be from them. Xander appreciated her father's intent. With all the traveling he did he still managed to get to his parents' at least two to four times a year. Most of these women would not be able to return home after they married these hardworking, good men. Most of them were farmers who could support their wives and children but couldn't afford trips that would take a month or more on the road. Perhaps it would have been easier on him personally to send Miss Sarah Wooley by train— at least then he wouldn't have to deal with her cousin. Although he was finding her to be less irritating than the first couple of days. She also proved to be resourceful. He still couldn't imagine her bringing along her father's six-shooters, not to mention wearing them.

Jo exited the house first. "Good morning, Miss Wooley. How are you today?"

"I'm well, Mr. Russell, although I wouldn't mind taking a day off from travel."

Xander grinned. "I understand."

She climbed up on his wagon then wrung her hands together. "I asked Sarah if I could begin today's journey in your wagon."

Xander nodded and braced himself for another issue she had with him or the way he was bringing her cousin to Knoxville.

She hesitated for a moment. Sarah came out of the farmhouse waving at Jane Flinch, their evening hostess. "Thank you, again," Sarah said as she hurried toward the second wagon.

Once all were settled, he grabbed the reins and flicked his wrists. "Yah!"

The wagon bucked forward. He circled around the front of the Flinch's entry and headed out toward the old Wilderness Road. It never ceased to amaze him that Daniel Boone once came this way looking for a shorter route to the West. Soon they would be approaching the turn where Boone's route headed north toward Kentucky and theirs would continue south toward Tennessee.

"I'm concerned about Sarah," Jo confided after a while.

Xander stiffened. What had Josephine said to her now?

"She was talking about going back home to Pearisburg."

"What did you say?" His grasp tightened on the reins.

As if sensing his temper rising, she placed her hand on his right one. "Do not worry. I encouraged her to go on to Knoxville. Do the women you bring west often change their minds along the route?"

He relaxed. "It hasn't happened yet. However, on occasion they have expressed their doubts. That is normal."

Jo sighed. "Good. I was hoping it was that and not my presence."

"I thought you weren't. . ." He changed his mind and continued. "What changed your mind?"

"Oh I still hold the same opinion and that will be and always has been what is best for Sarah. I have to admit I have observed you with some of these women and their reactions. Like the young girl yesterday. . . She is young, isn't she?"

"Sixteen, and her father has given her permission to marry. However, by the time I bring letters back and forth she'll be seventeen. In their case, they knew each other before he went west, though she was only thirteen at the time."

"That's too young."

Xander chuckled. "I would agree, except that some of the mountain folk in this area view seventeen almost an old maid."

Jo shook her head no. "I'm twenty-one and I'm not ready."

Xander chuckled. "I'm twenty-eight and I'm not ready. Of course, my lifestyle isn't good for a wife and children. Until I'm ready to settle down in one location I'm not considering a wife."

Jo stared at him for a bit. "That is probably a wise decision."

He smiled. "I thought so. My parents feel differently. And I'll admit from time to time I've wondered, after helping unite so many couples, what it would be like to get married myself."

"I haven't given marriage much thought with my parents in Europe for the past two years. Any possible suitor knew my father wasn't around to ask permission to court me. Not that Uncle Felix couldn't have given the go ahead on the matter. Besides, I wasn't ready. I mean. . ." She paused. "It's hard to explain, but having my parents out of my life for nearly half of it, I am in no rush to settle down. I guess I have a bit of the wanderlust like my parents."

"Why didn't they take you?"

"I've asked that question myself many times. Father said he wanted me to finish my education in the States. Personally, I wonder if it has more to do with my strong personality. Truthfully, I don't know. And I guess that makes me insecure about agreeing to marry anyone. Not to mention I've never met a man I'd be interested in making a life with. Don't get me wrong, I love my parents, and they truly love one another. I just don't believe parenting was their top priority."

"I'm sorry."

She shrugged.

"My folks are good, hardworking people. In a way, it is part of why I started to agree to this matchmaking business. I saw a lot of men like my dad who worked hard and made an honest living for themselves. However, they didn't have the means to find a wife. In several areas women are scarce or too young for marriage. I try to find women who have had similar backgrounds to the life they'll be marrying into. At least they'll know in part what it is like to live on the farm, like your cousin. John is definitely older, but his first wife came out west with him and had trouble adjusting to the primitive conditions."

"Primitive?"

Xander chuckled. "You would not be one I would set up with a farmer who was still building his home. However, John's house is finished. He has a nice home for Sarah."

"What happened to his wife?"

"She died the first year they were in Tennessee. It's been ten years, and John is ready."

"But what about love?"

"Love." Xander swallowed. "I use the scriptural mandate in First Corinthians about charity being patient, kind, not puffed up or rude. I try to find people with these characteristics."

"But some men are not kind to women. I've seen it over and over again where the wife is treated as a tool to clean the house, feed him, and raise his children. How do you. . ."

"I will not find a match for a man who I think will treat a wife poorly. I have refused many a man for such reasons."

"Really?"

"Yes, of course. Who do you think I am? Oh, I forget—you judged me before you ever spoke with me. I understand why your parents might not have taken you to Europe because of your strong personality, as you put it." Xander stopped himself from speaking another word. He didn't want to inflame her, especially if Sarah was already concerned if she was making the right choice by agreeing to come west to marry John.

Jo's cheeks flamed. She broke her gaze and fixed it on the hills in front of them. She said nothing the rest of the morning. When they broke for lunch, she busied herself preparing the meal.

Xander noticed how Sarah walked around the area with her shoulders slumped. He should share some personal stories regarding John. He walked over and asked, "Are you riding with me this afternoon, Miss Wooley? I'd be happy to talk about John and his farm."

Sarah smiled. "I would like that, Mr. Russell, thank you."

◆ ◆ ◆

Jo was grateful that Sarah was riding with Xander Russell this afternoon. She didn't know what it was with him that he would take offense to the littlest thing. But he had, and she didn't need his tension in her life. She had enough of her own. This trip had certainly been an eye-opening one. She'd been thinking about her parents a lot, about their leaving her with her aunt and uncle. She understood how, when she was younger, they would need to bring a nanny if they brought her along. It was easier to have her stay with her aunt and uncle. But she was a grown woman and still they left her behind. She thought about her future more and more. What kind of a future did she have? What did she want?

She made a point of staying out of Xander Russell's way. Obviously he didn't find her pleasant company. Not that she could totally blame him. She had started this trip with an attitude.

After long, jostling hours they came at last to a halt. Tonight they were camping on the road. Xander offered his wagon for the ladies to sleep in. Jo didn't want to accept, but she couldn't have her cousin sleeping on the ground.

As Xander took out his tools and started to work on some tin, Jo couldn't help but marvel at Xander's preparation and traveling conveniences. She helped Sarah with the cooking for dinner. Mike took charge of the fire and setting up the spit. Jo cut the meat into small cubes to cook faster. Sarah cut the fresh vegetables.

"There's a stream five hundred yards in that direction"—Xander pointed off to their northeast—"where you can get fresh water."

"I'll be happy to fetch the water, ladies," Mike offered.

"Thank you, Mike," Sarah said and handed him the large stew pot and coffeepot.

Jo watched as Xander placed two triangular pieces of metal across the spit. He turned and saw her staring. "Use these to put the skewers on. That way they can all cook at once."

"Did you make those?" Jo asked.

He nodded.

"Ingenious."

He smiled and went back to where he was setting up his tinwork.

Jo glanced up at the sky. Mike was on his way back from fetching the water. Jo finished putting the meat on the skewers. She thought back on the container she had retrieved the meat from. It was a wooden box lined with tin that contained ice and water. It must be another of Xander Russell's inventions. She thought back on the beds he'd made from the sides of the wagon. He really was a marvel. And she couldn't fault him for being upset with her because of her questioning his ability to match men and women together. Perhaps there was a lot more to this man? And a lot less of herself? Jo gnawed on her lower lip. Tonight she would slip over to that river and have a little private time before she turned in for the night.

"Jo?" Sarah called her back to reality.

"Yes?"

"Did you and Mr. Russell have a disagreement?"

Jo sighed. "You might say that."

"What did you say now?"

"Why do you think it was me and not him?" Jo placed her hands on her hips then thought better of it and relaxed her stance.

Sarah shrugged. "I love you, Jo, you know that. However, you have a way. . ."

"Of speaking my mind before I think? I know. I'm sorry."

"Are you all right?"

Jo feigned a smile. "I will be."

"You wouldn't believe the stories Mr. Russell was telling me about John Sprouse. He seems to be quite an honorable man."

Jo smiled for real this time. "I'm glad, Sarah. I truly am."

"I know, and thank you. I'm certain you suggested to Mr. Russell that he share a bit more about Mr. Sprouse with me."

Jo nodded and took the skewers over to the fire. She turned them as often as needed and called everyone to dinner when they were ready. Tensions eased with everyone, except Jo. The pressing need to get away and think on her own increased with each passing moment. As soon as it was possible, she headed out to the river and faced her fears and growing doubts. Did her parents not want to be around her? Was she not desirable enough as a person to find someone who would want to live with her the rest of his life? "Dear God, am I that horrible?" she cried into her hands.

Chapter Five

Xander heard Josephine's cries. He felt like an intruder as well as the person responsible for her recriminations. She was an incredible woman. Her fortitude, her assistance with her cousin had been invaluable. Even the various items she'd purchased before and during the trip had been helpful not frivolous. Unwilling to interrupt, he made his way back to the wagons and settled down for the night. He heard her slip into the wagon late and could hear whispers coming from within but could not distinguish the words. *Perhaps her cousin will be of help to her.*

The next two days were uneventful. They stayed in farmhouses along the way on their trek west until they split off from Boone's Wilderness Road then headed farther south toward Tennessee. After a day and a half journey on the southern route, they'd head west toward Knoxville. He still hadn't spoken with Josephine, though the tension between them had lessened. He tried not to provoke her. And he couldn't get over the feeling that she looked like a wounded bird with a broken wing.

Tonight they would make camp out in the wilderness again. Unfortunately it was looking like rain. During dinner, Jo asked, "Where will you sleep if it rains?"

"Under the wagons," Xander admitted. He wasn't looking forward to a wet night's sleep but would be glad to stop at the Smith farm and have a warm bath tomorrow night.

"I have some oilcloth if you think it will help keep you dry."

"I was wondering about hanging a hammock inside your wagon," Mike suggested.

"It would work. But it wouldn't be proper for the ladies to have men sleeping in the same quarters."

"Ah." Mike took a fork full of food and nodded. "I'd like to try some of that oilcloth, Miss Jo."

"Be happy to." Jo jumped up and ran to Mike's wagon where she pulled out a carpetbag and a huge amount of oilcloth.

"How much did you purchase?" Xander asked.

"Eight yards," Jo answered and sat back down with the others.

"We could roll ourselves around two or three times with that much." Xander chuckled.

Everyone joined the gaiety. Then Jo suggested, "What if we sewed it together and made a lean-to off the side of the other wagon?"

"Or I could rivet it together," Xander added. "It might be faster, and night is approaching."

"Do you have large rivets to secure it to the side of the wagon?" Mike asked.

"Sure." Xander placed his unfinished meal to the side and ran into his wagon. Within minutes he had the rivet pliers and rivets in hand. He found the ladies cutting the cloth in half. "To seam it, fold the ends together and lay them flat on one side of the cloth."

Slowly, they worked their way down the cloth and had it riveted together in one sheet. Mike had hammered in some nails on the wagon. Xander placed the larger rivets on the top and lined them up with the nails. Within an hour they had an oilcloth lean-to hanging off the side of the wagon. Jo and Sarah tied and pulled a line taught from the wagon to the ground then staked the line into the ground.

Jo stood with her hands on her hips. "What if the wind blows? Did you bring some clothespins, Sarah?"

"Yes. I'll get them." Sarah climbed into Mike's wagon.

Xander slapped Mike on the back. "It appears that we shall not be getting wet this evening."

"I'm happy about that." Mike smiled.

"Thank you, ladies." Xander turned toward Jo. Sarah hadn't returned yet. "Do we need to give her a hand?"

Jo glanced at the wagon. Xander's gut cinched. He still hadn't apologized. He gave her a weak smile. "She'll find them." Jo glanced around as if uncomfortable. "I better clean up our dinner."

"Would you heat up mine? I wasn't finished." Xander stuffed his hands in his pockets. "If it isn't too much trouble."

"I'd be happy to," Jo said.

"Mine, too, please?" Mike gave her a cheesy smile.

"Round two for dinner coming right up," Jo said with a smile and went back to the fire. She took the metal plates and put them on some of the cooler coals and set the pot over the hotter coals.

"She's remarkable," he whispered to Mike but not quietly enough.

"You might want to encourage her. She's seemed pretty low the past few days. What happened between the two of you?" Mike asked.

"Nothing."

"And if you think I believe that. . ."

"A difference of opinion," Xander offered.

"That's not it," Sarah said coming up behind them. "She is. . .never mind. It isn't my place to say."

Xander knew all too well what the real problem was and that he in part was the cause of it. "It is none of our concerns. Now let's finish fixing our lean-to."

An hour later they were done eating their second course and ready for bed, just as the rain began to fall. It fell all night and throughout the morning. By lunch the sun came out. Everyone took advantage of the dry air and changed their clothing. They stretched out the oilcloth to let it dry then folded it up.

Jo walked away toward the river, and Xander knew he had to apologize. He followed behind her and held his breath as he caught her crying out to God again. The knife in his gut twisted. "Miss Wooley, I'm so sorry."

◆　◆　◆

Jo turned at Xander's voice. Humiliated, she turned away. "Please, leave me alone."

"I'm sorry. I came to apologize. I spoke harshly with you, and you didn't deserve it." She couldn't turn around. She wanted to, but it was too embarrassing.

A twig snapped between them. He grasped her shoulders. The comfort she felt from his hands made her spine crumble. He turned her into his arms and held on to her. He smoothed her hair. "I am sorry. I didn't mean to be hurtful. You are an incredible woman."

She sniffed and shook her head no, pushing away. "No, I'm not. My strong will and inability to keep my opinions to myself push people away."

"Perhaps." Xander released her, leaned against a tree, and crossed his arms. "But isn't it possible God equipped you with a strong will for a greater purpose? You're an intelligent woman; you think quick on your feet; you can see problems and come up with solutions faster than anyone I've ever known before. Like the lean-to."

She didn't want to whine. . . "I'm sorry for judging you and your business. It is hard to accept a man would be a matchmaker."

Xander chuckled. "You have no idea. It took me several years to admit that I was a matchmaker. Those words, even today, are difficult to say. I simply was in the right place at the right time. God used. . .*uses* me to help bring people together."

Jo sat down on a log.

"Believe it or not, it is a hard job. I pray over every man and woman and pray for the Lord's guidance. It isn't easy. There is this one man who I doubt I will find an acceptable spouse for. He's turned down two brides-to-be so far, and I told him that if this last one doesn't suit him that I can no longer look for him. I hate that women get hopeful and he turns them down for something minor."

"No, I imagine it isn't easy if you are. . .I mean, because you are so careful. I'll admit I didn't believe a man could do this occupation, but I've seen how thorough you are and you have a devotion to the Lord that runs deep. Deeper than mine, I daresay."

He leaned forward and started to reach out his hand but pulled it back. Jo wished for the contact. The few moments in his arms were so calming.

"We all have moments. . ." His words trailed off.

Jo nodded. Of course she wasn't the only one to have a crisis of faith. Or was it not really a crisis so much as it was a time of conviction? Either way, she knew she'd pull through this. "I do not wish to be a burden," she admitted then glanced at the sun. "We need to get going."

Xander held her gaze for a moment then checked out the sun's location. "Yes, you are right." He stood and offered her a hand up.

She placed her hand in his. Warmth spread through her body. She felt. . .what? It couldn't be love. More like acceptance. Yeah, that was it. Accepted by Xander Russell. Her mind flickered. Whom would he pair her up with, if she asked?

As the day wore on, a peace filled Jo. Had God made her with a strong personality for a reason? And if so, why? What was she supposed to do?

That evening those questions continued to rattle around in her brain. The next morning she and Sarah worked on breakfast as the men hitched up the wagons. They had developed a pattern, and oddly enough Jo was comfortable with it. She took her place on Xander's wagon, and after they'd been on the road for an hour he asked, "You look well. Have you forgiven yourself?"

She gave a quirky smile. "Yes. I must say I'm still at a loss for my future, but I'm at peace with who I am."

"Good. God doesn't make mistakes."

She played with the fabric of her dress in her lap. "I was wondering. Do you think you might know someone who would want to marry a woman like me?"

Xander leaned back, unfortunately pulling the reins a bit with him. He released his grip and gave the lead back to the horses. "You want to get married?"

"I think so. But it would have to be a man who understood me. Who wasn't afraid to speak his mind if it were contrary to mine. As you pointed out, I'm strong-willed, and I believe it would take a man of equal strength of will to help me navigate through the decisions we would need to make together."

"I suppose so." Xander paused for a moment. "I'll have to think on that a bit. There are a lot of strong and bull-headed men, but you would need someone who would be sensitive to you as well. He'd have to cherish you and see the gift you are from the Lord. A rare and precious jewel."

Heat infused her cheeks. All of a sudden she knew that the man who equaled her in strength and determination, who was patient and would cherish her was sitting inches away. Unfortunately, he wasn't interested in finding a wife for himself. "Thank you," she said so quietly he almost missed it.

"Give me time, Josephine, and I'll find just the right man for you."

Jo smiled and turned her head away. The question was could he find it in himself?

◆　◆　◆

Xander's throat thickened from Jo's request. The strong-willed men he knew were not gentle with their words. Although someone like John Sprouse might be able to keep up with Josephine. She was easy on the eyes. No man, at first sight, would want to turn her down. But he couldn't put her in a situation where she'd try to bully the guy into doing her will or she'd be verbally beaten into submission—if not worse. She would probably be his hardest client to find a mate for. She could cook, clean, and sew, and she was creative, with an inventive mind. Not to mention how thoroughly she thought through things, he recalled, having prepared for this trip in less than an hour. That kind of quick thinking could put a man into a tailspin. She was incredibly practical. His mind flashed to Don Bishop over in Spencer, Tennessee. He was a pig and tobacco farmer. Xander shook his head. No, he couldn't see Jo as a pig farmer.

He took in a deep pull of air and released it slowly. How could he find Josephine a husband when he was beginning to have feelings for her himself? "I'll work on it, Miss Wooley."

He should have her write the letter of introduction, as he required of all the others. But he'd wait a few days. *Perhaps she'll change her mind.*

Xander glimpsed her from the side and marveled at the change in her demeanor. If it were possible, she was even prettier than the first time he'd met her.

For the next five days they continued on without speaking any further about Xander finding a spouse for her. At the same time, he found her more and more engaging. Sarah, on the other hand, was about ready to jump out of her own skin. The closer they got to Knoxville the more she seemed agitated. "How's your cousin?" he asked Jo as she stepped up to his bench seat.

"She's really nervous. You're certain John Sprouse is the right man for her?"

"I was. But I'm not sure how he'll handle her nerves. He's been through the mill with his first wife dying. He won't want to. . . Let's just pray." He took her hand in his and prayed. "Father, calm Sarah and give her a peace about John. He's a good man and he will love her. Amen."

Jo rubbed the top of his hand with her fingers. "Father," she prayed, "we know the strain this long trip has been on Sarah. Please calm her. I'm trusting Mr. Russell has heard from You on this match. We pray for John and Sarah and trust You to give them the future together that has You at the center of it. Amen."

"Amen." He squeezed her hand and slipped his own out from her grasp. His heart had warmed to her touch. His pulse quickened. *Dear Lord, I don't think I can help Josephine Wooley find a husband.*

"*Look inside,*" a voice whispered inside his mind.

God?

No response.

Xander got up and went through the contents of his wagon. For the life of him, he couldn't figure out what he had in there that God would want him to see with regard to finding Jo a husband.

Chapter Six

Jo licked her lips and closed her eyes. She couldn't believe how much she was beginning to care for Xander Russell. Even in this dusty town where they had stopped for Xander to sell his wares, his dark brown eyes showed a soft compassion. How had she not noticed them before? She wanted to be wrapped in his strong arms and comb her fingers through the gentle curls of his silky hair. She knew his hair, if straightened, would be twice as long. But the way the waves tumbled over each other made his hair appear rich, thick, and full. He kept his beard trim, and while she didn't see him groom himself each morning, she knew he was very careful with his appearance. Not like some men she'd known back home in Pearisburg. Of course, a well-groomed man would sell more products. She glanced over at Xander as he was making his sales. She admired how he listened and took a personal interest in each of his customers.

Her cousin lifted her dress and stepped up onto the wooden sidewalk. "Sarah," Jo called and waved her over.

Sarah approached. She seemed in better spirits today after yesterday's prayers. "Watch," Jo said as she pointed to Xander. "Listen to his conversation with each of the customers."

Without saying a word, Sarah did.

"Mrs. Favour," they heard him say. "How are you today? How's the family?"

The woman, perhaps in her early thirties, swatted him on the upper arm. "Don't you be callin' me Mrs. now. You know me too well."

Xander chuckled. "Ah, that be true. So how are you?"

Her face lit up. "Wonderful. You were right. Charles and I are a good match, and he's been tremendous in getting my Daniel to settle down. His Kayley. . .she was a handful. However, I've been teaching her how to sew, and she has a fine hand. She's confiding in me as if I were her own mom. Thank you."

"You're so welcome. And what about little Charlie."

Mrs. Favour laughed. "He's prattling around the house at two years of age like he's in charge. You wouldn't think such a thing were possible. Young Charlie will be running his papa's store by the time he's fifteen," Mrs. Favour leaned in and whispered.

Xander smiled and hugged her. "Congratulations. March?"

The smile on Mrs. Favour's face broadened. "Yes." She reached in her purse. "Here's your payment for our last order. There's a list in the envelope for Charles's next order. He's wondering if you can ship them sooner if it will be more than a month before you can fulfill it."

Xander pulled out a piece of paper from the envelope.

Jo grabbed her cousin's elbow and led them away from Xander. "The reason I asked you to listen was to show you how much Mr. Russell cares for each of his customers. I'm sure he showed at least as much if not more care in selecting John Sprouse for you."

Sarah nodded. "She seemed quite happy with the match Mr. Russell made for her."

"Yes, she did. I didn't expect to hear that. But making a match between two widows with children, that had to be a difficult one."

Sarah shrugged. The heels of their boots tapped on the weathered boards as they walked in silence. "Do you really think he is that careful all the time?"

"From what I've seen of him, yes. In fact, I asked him to find me a match."

Sarah stopped. Jo stopped and turned around. "What?"

"You're not joking?"

"No, I'm not joking. Who would joke about something as serious as marriage? I'm getting older, and men aren't exactly pounding at my door. My personality is. . . well. . .you know. It would take a special man to see my full potential as a wife and not wither under my bristling tongue."

Sarah took the step between them and hooked her arm around Jo. "Jo you're a wonderful, strong woman. Any man would be honored to have you for a wife."

Jo laughed. "Have you seen Harvey Denton walk away when I enter the fellowship hall at the church?"

Sarah joined in the gaiety. "Well he doesn't know what he's missing. Besides, you were right to tell him that his momma shouldn't be telling him what to wear, what to eat, and what to do with his day. The man is nearly thirty years old!"

Jo had to admit that had been a real shocker for her and the reason she decided she couldn't even entertain a date with him.

"Do you really believe Mr. Russell took such care in matching me with John Sprouse?"

"Yes, I do. I'm sorry I opened my big mouth and voiced my objection. It wasn't my place, and I terribly misjudged Mr. Russell."

Sarah sighed. "I'd like to know even more about John."

"Ask him when you ride with him next. I'm certain he'll be happy to tell you what you want to know about Mr. Sprouse."

Sarah nodded. "I suppose it's better than worrying that I'm making the wrong decision."

Jo hugged her. "I'm so sorry I've made you doubt. I was just so shocked that Uncle would arrange such a thing."

"I know you were worried about me. Now I'm worried."

"I know, and I'm sorry."

"You're forgiven. Come on, let's go to the mercantile and purchase some candy. I've been hankering for some sweets for a few days now."

Jo laughed. Her cousin always had a sweet tooth. "I could use some lemon drops. I hope they have some."

"Me, too."

As they strolled over to the mercantile Jo sensed a new lightness in Sarah's step. *Lord, please fill her with Your peace.*

The mercantile was limited compared to most, in Jo's experience. Nonetheless, the variety caught one's eye. She surveyed the shelves, counters, and every nook and cranny of the store and came across a section of fabrics. Jo sorted among them to find material for a new skirt, one that had a seam up the center for separate legs so she could more easily climb the wagons. She'd made one for herself years ago and thoroughly enjoyed it. It had turned a head or two. But in the end, with all the traveling they were doing, and as the air was beginning to get cooler, the pant-like skirt would serve her well. She purchased enough brown wool, plus some sultan satin for a lining. Wool would keep her warm, even if it did tend to itch. She fingered some fine white silk and lace and imagined wearing a dress of white for her wedding one day.

Jo dropped the fabric like a hot coal. She had to stop thinking. Granted, she had asked Xander to find her a husband, but she didn't really believe he'd be able to. Not with her charming personality.

"You are who I intended you to be."

She spun around looking for the voice. Seeing no one near, she paused and closed her eyes.

"You do that, too?"

Jo's eyes popped open. The woman who had spoken to Xander earlier stood beside her. "What?"

"I imagine what I can make with the fabric. Can I help you with anything?"

"I'm—" Jo's voice caught. "I'm going to purchase this wool and sultan satin for a skirt."

"Excellent choice. The air is about to turn cool soon. Do you have enough thread?"

"Thread would be good. Both colors."

The woman pulled a drawer open and fished out a couple of wooden spools. "These should work. Do you need any straight pins?"

Jo nodded. She had brought a sewing kit for travel. She included some needles and small amounts of thread, even a small pair of scissors but few straight pins.

Tonight she'd draw out the skirt and cut the fabric. "Do you have some chalk?"

"Certainly." She pulled the same drawer out farther and retrieved a thin piece of rectangular chalk. "Anything else?"

"No thank you, this will be plenty."

Jo turned to bring her items to the counter and there in front of her was Xander with a puzzled look on his face. Instead of waiting for a question she said, "I'm making myself a skirt more appropriate for travel."

The woman lit up. "Oh my, are you a new bride?"

Jo's cheeks flamed. "No, my cousin Sarah is."

Xander crossed his arms over his chest. "Well now, I thought you asked me to find you a husband, Miss Wooley."

Whatever shade of pink had filled her cheeks a few moments earlier intensified now. She needed a cool compress. "Yes, I did. But you have not found me a husband yet, so I could not say that I am a bride, could I?" she challenged.

"Touché. Are you and Sarah about done?"

"Yes, sir. Give us a moment to pay for my purchases."

He nodded and stepped out of the store. At the counter, she asked if they had some lemon drops. The woman smiled. "I'm sorry, dear. The lady who was here a moment ago purchased the last of them. I do have some molasses candy I made. It's soft and chewy." She reached into a glass jar and pulled out a piece. "Here, try it and see if you like it."

Jo took the piece and popped it in her mouth. "I'd love some. You said you made these?"

"Yes 'm. It's a simple recipe—a cup of molasses, a cup of sugar, a tablespoon of vinegar, and a walnut-size piece of butter. Once that starts boiling, test it until it starts to harden in a glass of water. Then add a teaspoon of soda and stir, and pour it onto a buttered pan. As it starts to cool, pull it a bit and cut it up into bite-size pieces." She turned and scooped about a quarter of a pound of the candy out of the jar. The pieces were individually wrapped in wax paper.

"Sounds easy enough. Thank you." They finished up Jo's order and the woman leaned over the counter. "Xander Russell is a wonderful matchmaker. Charles and I have been together for four years and I haven't regretted a day in making the decision." She patted Jo's hand. "Trust the Lord and listen to Xander. He's a good man."

Jo's throat thickened. She did trust Xander. Unfortunately, she'd like nothing better than for him to pick himself to be her husband. "Thank you, I will." Which was true. She would trust the Lord and Xander Russell. But oh how her heart hoped for something more.

◆　◆　◆

Xander was pleased by the questions Sarah was asking about John. It made him relax some. He knew she'd doubted her decision to marry him. In part, that was her cousin Jo's fault. He had to admit she had convinced Sarah to trust him and the choice he'd made. Of course, the ladies didn't know he'd been walking behind them when they were discussing it. A smile curled his lips remembering Sarah's reaction that Jo had asked him to find her a spouse. She was right; it would take a special man, one who would not wither under her sharp tongue. Oddly enough, he'd grown to appreciate her love and care for others. Teaching Jo to curb her reactions in a public setting would be all it would take to help her secure a good husband. He'd need to be strong but patient. Xander went through a list of the men he thought might be able to handle her. He then narrowed it down to men who would be patient, men who would allow a wife to have a voice, an opinion in their decision-making process.

Xander chuckled.

"What?" Sarah asked.

"Forgive me, I was thinking about a possible mate for your cousin."

Sarah crossed her arms and scrunched her face up a bit. "She's the most loving person I know. And she'll fight tooth and nail for you. She can't tolerate injustice." Sarah chuckled. "If she were male, I think she would be a lawman in the Wild West."

Xander roared. "I can see that. We better find her a man in the East, before she becomes this town's next sheriff."

Sarah laughed. "Oh she would, wouldn't she?"

They laughed and carried on for a while. Then Sarah turned toward him. "He would need to be strong but gentle."

"Yes, I agree."

"Do you have a man in mind who you think would meet that criteria?"

"Not at the moment. I'll keep looking. She needs to write the letter of introduction about herself and specify what she's looking for in a husband before I can really begin."

Sarah nodded. "You might want to think about yourself."

Xander nearly choked and vigorously shook his head no.

"Why not? She thinks the world of you now and how you've developed your business. She hasn't complained once about this trip. She's rugged and well prepared for whatever happens on the trail." Sarah paused, tilting her head to the right. "It's just a thought."

Xander gave her one curt nod. "I'm not planning on getting married until after I settle down. My life is not compatible for marriage. I wouldn't put a woman through that."

As if understanding his discomfort in discussing his own marriageability, or rather in not considering her cousin as a potential wife, Sarah gave him a single nod and focused on the road ahead of them.

Sarah's words rang over and over in his mind. Jo was a fascinating woman. She was a true beauty, yet not vain like some of the women he'd met, most of whom lived financially above the norm of most of the farmers he knew. He didn't know how much money the woman had but she seemed to have plenty, judging from the stock she'd purchased before the trip and the items she'd purchased on the road. She was not foolish with her finances and understood the value of a dollar. . . *Could she be the one for me?* He shook his head no and tossed the silly thought out as fast as it entered. Josephine Wooley definitely needed just the right man. Who was he? And how was Xander supposed to find him?

◆　◆　◆

For the next few days Sarah's comments about Jo tumbled around in his head. He watched and observed. Jo was certainly everything her cousin described and so much more. She moved with grace, and yet she could lug a log through the forest and chop wood with the best of them. Her new self-made skirt was practical—a split skirt that allowed the lady's legs more freedom and yet concealed with modesty.

He wagged his head as if trying to shake off the flow of images. They were a couple of days out from Knoxville. He'd send her home on the train.

"Mr. Russell?" Jo's voice broke through his ramblings.

"Forgive me. What can I do for you, Miss Wooley?" He smiled.

She reached out and took his hand. "Are you all right?"

A slow glow of warmth radiated up his arm and through his chest to his heart. He closed his eyes then opened them and focused his gaze on her. Her eyes, blue like her cousin's, possessed a cooler shade, like blue steel. Xander swallowed. His heart started to pound. He felt like his hammer had ricocheted off the anvil and hit him in the chest.

As if sensing his emotions, she pulled back and released her grasp. "I'm sorry. I didn't mean to be so forward."

"No offense taken. Now, what can I do for you?"

"I've been thinking about the letter you suggested I write, and I'm puzzled by it."

"How so?" He kept his eyes forward and on the road. He couldn't trust his own emotions at the moment.

"Well, I'm not certain what man would want a woman like me."

He turned and faced her at that moment. "You're an astonishing woman, Miss Wooley. I'll admit most men would find you a challenge, but I daresay you'd be good for every one of them. Unfortunately, not every man could accept a woman with as much— or possibly even more—intelligence than they themselves might have."

"Isn't it really just different, smarter only about some things?"

Xander smiled. "You are correct, again. And that is exactly what would frighten most men. They would feel threatened and not take the time to get to know you."

"Such as yourself."

Xander chuckled. "Yes, such as myself."

She smiled. He loved how her countenance shined. "Good," she said. "You're rather incredible yourself."

◆ ◆ ◆

Jo couldn't believe the words coming out of her mouth and clamped it shut. This was exactly why she probably would never find a husband.

"We should stop this line of discussion before we say something we can't take back."

Jo agreed with the nod of her head. At that very moment she knew she was falling in love with Mr. Russell. "You said you don't feel it is right for a man of your position to take on a wife."

"Your cousin has been talking." His Adam's apple bobbed up and down. "Yes, it would be unfair to leave a wife for months at a time."

"Why couldn't she travel with you?"

"Traveling with a bride would be a bit difficult, wouldn't you say?"

"Possibly."

They rode on for another mile before she spoke aloud what rumbled through her head. "But you've made your wagon quite comfortable for travel. Why wouldn't a woman find it acceptable?"

"She would have to be the right one. Most women I've met, and I have met quite a few, seem to prefer the comforts of home, preparing meals for their family. Some of the more industrious ladies even find ways to earn some money from their homes. I'm a tinsmith. I travel. I rarely manage to visit my folks more than two to four times a year. If I were to marry, I would hate to only be able to see my wife and family that seldom. That, Miss Wooley, would be unacceptable."

"I agree. Which begs the question, why not develop a mail-order business? I heard what the storekeeper's wife, Mrs. Favour, said to you. They would like to get their items faster than you can provide on your own. Shipping by train must be faster than you personally delivering your products from town to town."

Xander let out a nervous chuckle. "You do get to the point of the matter, don't you?"

"I suppose I do." She shrugged. Was she trying to convince him to think about marrying someone who would love to travel with him, who would love to help develop his business? Herself, perhaps?

He reached over and placed his hand on hers. "You've given me something to think about. My mother has been harping on something similar. She wants grand-children." A strained, single laugh squeaked out. "But I do not know a woman who would be willing to live such a life."

"Perhaps you aren't looking."

He narrowed his gaze on her and held it. The heat of his honesty and intensity of his gaze blazed down her spine. She closed her eyes.

His leather-gloved finger lifted her chin. "Are you suggesting. . ." His words trailed off.

Neither one of them wanted to address the emotions they were feeling at the moment. She opened her eyes. His rich brown eyes the color of mahogany ignited her soul. Her lips parted, attracting his gaze. Jo raised her face into the breeze, tossed her head back and forth and looked away.

Xander cleared his throat and slapped the reins. The horses jolted forward, along with her heart. Jo clasped her hands and held them tight. Never in her entire life had she ever felt such a connection with another person. Was this love? She had read enough love stories over the years to know that women could swoon, their hearts all aflutter but. . . She didn't dare put into words the sudden, drawing energy she felt toward Xander Russell. It seemed more powerful, more unstoppable than the largest locomotive barreling down the track.

"We'll be arriving in Knoxville in two days," Xander said.

Jo couldn't speak. Would Mr. Russell see himself as the best husband for her? Because deep down, she knew he would be.

The wagon bounced. Jo grabbed on to the bench. Then it jerked wildly and tipped down to the left at a crazy angle. The horses cried out. Xander took control. Jo held on to the wagon and prayed they wouldn't tumble down the side of the hill.

Chapter Seven

Xander held on with all his might as the horses and wagon started to slide down the side of the mountain. The left rear wheel had broken loose, of that he was certain. He stayed focused on what was in front of them. The horses strained. Their hooves dug into the dirt. "Jump, Jo."

He held on. Jo didn't move.

"Jo, jump. Now!" If he was going down the side of the mountain, he didn't want her crushed by the wagon.

She released her grip and lunged from the bench. The wagon swerved, the horses held. He yanked hard on the reins and everything came to an abrupt stop. He surveyed the damage. The wagon's left corner dangled over the cliff's edge. He encouraged the horses to move forward a couple of steps. Jo, he saw, seemed unhurt, heading toward him. Once the wagon was safely secured, he jumped down and brushed down his horses, making certain they weren't lame.

Sarah ran up to her cousin. Mike ran up to him. "That was some fancy driving."

"God was with us."

"Amen. How are your horses?"

"Good." He patted down their legs. "They did well. Time to fix that wheel. Did you see where it went off to?"

Mike turned behind and pointed to the left. "Rolled on down that way."

Xander nodded and grabbed the jack from beneath the bench seat to lift the wagon up from the ground. "I've got a spare under here." He leaned under the wagon. "I do too much traveling not to carry one. Let's replace it then we'll go find the other."

Jo came around the side of the downed corner of the wagon. "Are you all right?" he asked.

She rubbed her elbows. "I'm fine. I thought we were goners."

"Thankfully, it wasn't our time." Xander grinned.

"Amen," Sarah and Jo said in unison.

He and Mike worked for thirty minutes putting the new wheel on. Mike took care of the horses, unhitching and grazing them while Xander followed the trail of the broken wheel. The side of the mountain was steep enough in some spots that he had to be careful with his footing. Once he located the broken wheel, he realized there wasn't anything worth saving. He supposed he could save the boxing for the axle for the new one he'd have to have built. Xander knelt down and examined the boxing for the axle and saw it was worn. He stood up, brushing his hands on his pants. It wasn't worth lugging. He would have to replace it anyway.

He pulled out his pocket watch and looked up at the sun. They could get another five to six miles up the road, but that would be it. They were going to be a half a day late of their arrival time in Knoxville. He set his foot and began the climb.

Gravel and rubble started to slide down in front of him. He glanced up. "What are you doing?"

Jo slid to a stop. "I came to see if I could help."

Xander closed the distance between them. "You do realize that most sensible women would wait up there where it was safe."

"Since when have you known me to be sensible?" Jo snickered.

"Prior to this moment, you've been very sensible." Xander came up beside her. He wrapped her in his arms. "How am I to find a husband for you?" he mumbled. "You're so beautiful." He froze, stunned by his own words.

She smiled. "I think you're rather fine yourself."

"Would a simple man like myself make a suitable husband, Miss Wooley?" He released his hold and stepped back. They were still on the side of the mountain and at an awkward angle.

"Yes, Mr. Russell, I believe you would."

Xander shook his head back and forth. "I can't believe this is happening to me. You do not fit my timetable. I had a plan. . ."

"Kiss me, Xander," Jo whispered.

He stepped back into her embrace. The war of logic and practicality waged heavy against the growing desire to make a match with this woman, for her to be *his* woman, his bride, his wife. He leaned down and brushed her lips with a delicate kiss. His mind raced. His heart drummed so loudly in his chest that he trembled. The kiss deepened. He couldn't tell if it was Jo or himself who breathed new life into the kiss. But one thing was certain, she would be his wife, of that he had no doubt.

◆ ◆ ◆

Jo pushed gently away. She touched her lips then wrapped her body in her own embrace. Her heart raced. She opened her eyes.

Xander's brown eyes sparkled back at her. "You're an amazing woman, Josephine. A man would be honored to have you at his side."

Jo smiled. She slid her hand in the fold of his elbow. "We should get back."

His eyebrows furrowed.

"You are the only man who has struck my fancy, Xander. I am both proud and ashamed. . .ashamed because I did not see your integrity straightaway."

Xander took the lead. "Do you require a long engagement, Jo?"

"Engagement? I haven't been asked."

Xander chuckled. "And I haven't asked yet. I am curious. Would I have to wait for a year?"

Jo thought about the possibility. It would give them time to get to know one another better. And it would give her time to get in touch with her parents and have them return from Europe for her wedding. But what kind of a wedding did she want? She knew her mother would want it to be the social event for everyone to speak of for years to come. "There are several matters to consider. First, my parents. . .with them being in Europe, it would require quite a bit of notice. On the other hand, my uncle could give his permission. Not that it is required. I am old enough to make my own decision on the matter."

He helped her over the final rise, where Mike and Sarah waited for them by the wagons.

She whispered. "May I think on the matter?"

"Certainly." Xander stepped away, caught her gaze, and winked. His trim beard exposed a wonderful wrinkle in the form of a dimple. "I have fallen in love with you, Josephine."

The heat of blush infused her cheeks. "As have I, Xander."

He squeezed her hand then ran toward Mike. "All set?"

"Yes, sir," Mike replied.

Xander gave out orders. He wanted to get at least a couple hours down the road.

◆ ◆ ◆

The next two days Jo found herself spending more and more time with Xander. They were entering Knoxville, and she still hadn't decided if she wanted a long or short engagement. They strolled each evening and talked. He had been the perfect gentleman, only offering his elbow when appropriate. She wished and prayed for another kiss. He had come close last night but whispered in her ear that it would be improper for them to be so intimate when they were out in the wilderness alone.

On the third day they pulled into the inn where John Sprouse sat on the front porch. He stood up as they approached. "I was beginning to wonder." John hugged Xander and slapped him on the back.

"We are only a half a day off schedule," Xander defended.

"I know." John turned to Jo. "Xander must be slipping. You are more beautiful than his sketch."

"This is Josephine Wooley, Sarah's cousin." Xander turned toward Mike's wagon. Sarah stood, preparing to get down.

John reached out and grasped her waist, setting her on the ground. "You're even prettier than your cousin. I'm honored to meet you, Miss Wooley."

Sarah smiled. "Pleasure to meet you, too, Mr. Sprouse."

"John, why don't you escort Miss Wooley to the general store and get to know one another."

John offered his arm. Sarah slipped her hand in the crook and joined him. The two began speaking comfortably with one another.

Jo smiled as she and Xander watched from the wagon. "That looks promising."

Xander turned toward Jo. "Yes, it does. So, do you have an answer for me?"

"In truth, I haven't been asked the proper question," she teased. She knew she was going to say yes, and she wanted to make it a double ceremony with Sarah and John. But before she could speak Xander ran off.

The wagon jostled as Xander climbed into the rear of the cabin. It wiggled some more then bounced. He must have jumped off the rear. He came back to the front and offered her his hand to get down from the wagon. Jo placed her hand in his. It belonged there. For the first time in her life, she belonged. After she found her footing, he went down on one knee and held her hand. "Josephine, will you do me the honor of becoming my bride?"

Joy unstoppable washed over her soul. "Yes, Xander, yes, yes!"

He opened his other hand. "This ring was my grandmother's. I made a mate to go with it for myself, if I were to ever find a wife. Will you accept it as a token of my love, a seal of our engagement?"

She nodded. Tears filled her eyes. He slid on the gold band with tiny diamonds swirling toward a center filled with a round ruby. It slipped on her finger as if it had been made for her.

He stood and took her into his embrace. He captured her lips with a tender kiss. "How long will I have to wait, my love?"

"Can we get married with John and Sarah?"

Xander blessed her with the biggest smile she'd ever seen. "Your wish is my command."

"And don't you ever forget it," she teased.

Xander laughed.

Mike cleared his throat. Jo turned and saw him leaning against the other wagon, staring at them with a wide grin. "So the matchmaker met his match."

Jo and Xander gazed into one another's eyes and nodded. "Yes," they said in unison.

"Best dollar I ever lost."

"What?" Jo asked.

"I bet your uncle before we left. He thought you might fall in love with this guy. He said that Xander would have his hands full but that the trip would be long enough for the two of you to fall in love. I took one look at the steam floating out of Jo's ears and said, 'Not possible.' I guess he knows Jo a whole lot better."

Jo giggled. "I guess he does, even more than I know myself."

Epilogue

"Jo, come look at these designs. What do you think?"

Jo leaned over her husband's desk. They'd been married for a little over two months now. Sarah and John were settled in at John's homestead. Mike sold the wagon and took the train back to Pearisburg. Jo and Xander had spent the past month finishing Xander's circuit, selling his wares.

The drawing was perfect and detailed. "This is incredible. Do you think it would work?"

"Yes, I believe it will." He pointed out the designs for a new wagon that would accommodate the two of them, having a full-size bed for their travels. Camping along the roadside would save them enough money after a year that they would be able to invest in a single shop and send the tinware via the trains. He wouldn't be playing matchmaker after they settled down, but with any luck his time would be full playing with his son or daughter.

"I love it." She kissed the top of his head.

"Are you feeling better?" He wrapped her in his arms.

"Yes, much, thank you."

"Do you think?" He glanced down at her tummy.

"Too soon to know, but I hope so." She stepped from his embrace and reached for the board she'd been working on and held it up to him. "What do you think?" she asked.

His eyes lit up. "Oh, honey, this is splendid. Thank you. You did this? All of this?"

She smiled and nodded.

"I'll make a tinsmith out of you, yet. This is very good."

"Thank you. What do you think of the name?"

"Russell's Tin Shop," he read aloud.

"I like it, Mrs. Russell. I can't believe we're opening our own place in a year. You're a wonder, Jo. I never would have done it in less than five years without your help. I love you."

"I love you, too," she whispered.

He reached for her again and kissed her with the love and determination of a master craftsman working a sheet of metal into something beautiful.

Lynn A. Coleman is an award-winning and bestselling author of *Key West* and other books. She began her writing and speaking career with how to utilize the Internet. Since October 1998 when her first fiction novel sold, she's sold thirty-eight books and novellas. Lynn is also the founder of American Christian Fiction Writers Inc. and served as the group's first president for as a member on the Advisory Board for two years. One of her primary reasons for starting ACFW was to help writers to develop their writing skills and to encourage others to go deeper in their relationship with God. "God has given me a gift, but it is my responsibility to develop that gift."

Some of her other interests are photography, camping, cooking, and boating. Having grown up on Martha's Vineyard, she finds water to be very exciting and soothing. She can sit and watch the waves for hours. If time permitted she would like to travel.

She makes her home in Keystone Heights, Florida, where her husband of 42 years serves as pastor of Friendship Bible Church. Together they are blessed with three children, two living and one in glory, and eight grandchildren.

Miss Matched

by Susanne Dietze

Dedication

*To the Lord, who makes the best matches: He made us for Himself,
places us in families, blesses us with friends, and has a loving plan for each of us.*

Acknowledgements

*A thousand thanks to two writing sisters with whom God matched me
and who helped me with this manuscript: Debra E. Marvin and Jennifer Uhlarik.*

*Trust in the LORD with all thine heart; and lean not unto thine own understanding.
In all thy ways acknowledge him, and he shall direct thy paths.*
PROVERBS 3:5–6

Chapter One

Colorado
Spring, 1879

Everything was perfect.

Grace Perkins stepped back from the dessert table with a satisfied sigh. A frosted, two-layer cake on a porcelain stand awaited cutting, alongside vibrant-pink strawberry punch mixed in Ma's crystal bowl. Ma's finest linens covered the rough-hewn tables in the parish hall, and vases of wildflowers added color to the rustic space. Preparations for the party took some effort, true, but Grace didn't mind. This party was for Bess, and she deserved the best. After all, she was the bride-to-be, and she should have a faultless, memorable party—

A soft *swoosh* sounded behind her.

Grace's shoulders fell. "Not again."

But it had. The grommet-perforated sign she'd tied to a ribbon streamer slipped for what must be the fourth time. The banner folded in on itself so the outer letters were legible, but the middle crinkled into a mess.

Instead of reading *Congratulations Bess and Elmer*, it said *Congralmer*.

Upending the wood crate she'd used to transport the cake to the parish hall, she eyed the asymmetrical sign. She set the crate on its side and clambered atop. It wobbled with her weight, but this would only take a moment. She stretched to push the ends of the sign taut.

The parish door opened. She'd best hurry, since guests were arriving—

The box leaned with her. Gave way, spilling her sideways.

Strong arms caught her around the waist and shoulders, preventing her from landing on her backside. Being caught didn't hurt as much as falling on the floor would have, nor was it quite as embarrassing, but it still jolted her bones and stung her pride. Why did people think a man catching a falling woman was romantic?

Besides, it was just Mitchell Shaw. Nothing romantic about her father's medical partner, whom she recognized by his soapy bay smell a half second before she looked up to his face. Such a nice face, square-jawed and framed by a thick shock of unruly, dark-blond curls. A nice face to see every day.

"You hurt, Grace?" Mitch set her on a chair at one of the tables then dropped to his haunches to look her in the eye.

"Fine, thank you. My, you were quick." Were his green eyes always flecked with gold? She'd never noticed before. Then again, he'd never looked at her like this, as if he were checking her pupils for signs of trauma.

"You know how we doctors are about prevention. We'd prefer no one get injured or sick in the first place." He peered down at her black half-boots. "That ankle twist?"

She rotated her foot. "It doesn't hurt."

"Shock can forestall pain, you know. And your eyes are kind of bright."

"That's because this party must be perfect for Bess, and I need to fix that sign." That explained the jittery feeling in her abdomen, too. Too much to do, and Mitch prevented her, gently squeezing her ankle through her boots to see if she'd wince. She didn't.

"Bess will love the party, sign or no sign." With his usual gentleness, Mitch lowered her foot to the floor. For such a big man, he was mild as a lamb, except when it came to that punching bag he kept in his basement. Unlike Pa, Mitch believed exercise played a role in good health. She should be glad of his habits today, since he'd been strong enough to catch her. Mitch rose to his full height. "You don't have to impress her, you know."

"Honor her," Grace corrected. "I almost lost her, you know."

"To a teaching job in Denver. That's a dozen miles, Grace. You could've visited plenty."

"It's not the same. I know it's selfish, but I wanted her to stay in Emerald. For her pupils, and for me. And now that I've found her a husband, she will."

"You found Elmer? I didn't know he was lost. The man sits two pews behind you in church." Mitch helped her to stand.

Her eyes rolled. "You know what I mean. I played matchmaker."

"I didn't know that." Mitch still eyed her feet. "Does it hurt now?"

"No, but if my ankle swells, I'll wrap it." It wasn't like she didn't know how. Since Ma died eight years ago, Pa had allowed Grace to help the sick folks of their town of Emerald. Mitch joined Pa's practice five years ago, fresh out of medical school, and had never treated Grace as anything less than an essential part of the practice. She may not be a doctor, but she made a fair nurse, and like Pa, Mitch respected her opinions and appreciated her assistance. He'd also come to be one of her two best friends.

Now that Bess was staying in Emerald to marry Elmer, everything would stay just as it should. She patted Mitch's arm.

Mitch scooped up the crate then glanced at her saggy sign. He perched on the toes of his long shoes and pushed the grommets apart until the sign was taut again.

Grace fisted a hand on her hip. "Must be nice to be tall."

He grinned and handed her the crate. "Don't use it as a stepladder again. I'll be right back."

Where was he going? To find her a stepstool? "Mitch, we don't need one now—"

He was out the door. Then Bess and Elmer arrived, along with their families, Bess's students, and half the congregation of Emerald Church. Not Mitch's mother, Mrs. Shaw, though. The damp weather must be troubling the widow's joints.

Grace stowed the crate under the dessert table. Mitch or no Mitch, she had punch to serve.

"Everything's beautiful." Dark-haired Bess Ellis, pretty in a simple gown of blue calico, left her fiancé Elmer's side to hug Grace. "And strawberry punch? My favorite."

"I used the final bottle of last year's strawberry syrup."

Bess smiled. "Elmer planted strawberries at the farm for me. We'll have plenty to share with you this summer."

"He's a thoughtful fellow." That was part of why Grace chose him for Bess.

"Speaking of considerate men, is your father coming?" Bess asked.

"He's at the clinic keeping an eye on Mrs. Dooley." No need to add that Pa, who hadn't stepped on church property since Ma died, wouldn't even enter the parish hall. Not even for Bess's party.

"Poor Mrs. Dooley." Bess sighed, but before she could comment further on the widow with a mysterious malady, she was swallowed up by a crowd of well-wishers. Grace turned back to the punch bowl.

All the hard work had been worth it. The smiles in the room, the laughs and teasing. Bess and Elmer looked so happy.

She'd ladled a dozen cups of punch when Mitch returned, her pearl-inlaid sewing box in his hand. She kept it at the clinic so she could mend during slow times, as Mitch well knew. Earlier today, she'd repaired a rip at the hem of the yellow dress she now wore. With its sunny hue, pleated layers, and silk draping, it seemed the most fitting dress to wear on such a happy occasion, and Pa said it didn't clash with her reddish-brown hair. That was Pa's way of offering a compliment.

Mitch plopped the sewing box on the table and she cast him a quick grin. "Why didn't I think of sewing the sign in place?"

"Because you're busy with other things." He pulled needle, thread, and scissors from the box and got to work. A few precise stitches, and the bows tying the grommets to the ribbon were stitched in place.

"I always said you were handy with a needle." Elmer Kohl, the future groom, pointed at the thin white scar bisecting his left eyebrow.

Mitch had sutured that particular laceration a year ago. Deep and ugly, the wound was a challenge to close neatly. That experience showed Grace yet again how talented a physician Mitch was, and exemplified Elmer's long-suffering character. The trait was a good complement to Bess's impatience. "Punch, Mitch?"

He took the cup with a nod of thanks. "Anyone can learn to stitch, Elmer."

Elmer laughed. "Buttons, maybe, but I couldn't put a person back together if I tried."

"You did me." Bess pinked.

"Aw, sweetheart, we helped each other. Now neither of us is lonely."

Grace lowered her head to hide her grin. Bess and Elmer made a perfect match. And it had all been her doing. It was difficult to snuff out a sense of pride at her accomplishment.

"To the bride and groom!" Elmer's younger brother Lou lifted his cup in toast. Grace ladled a cup so she could join in.

"And to Grace, who played matchmaker." Bess raised her cup in Grace's direction.

"Really?" One of the young ladies present, blond Flossie Hawkins, popped to her tippy-toes. "You did that, Grace?"

Grace nodded. "I saw potential for a good match."

The conversation carried on, away from Grace, but she didn't mind being left to observe the others enjoy themselves. The room's volume dipped when the children dashed out to the churchyard, led by Mitch. A rousing game of tag began, and the children's happy shrieks carried through the open windows. Mitch was good with little ones, which had served him well as a doctor.

Smiling, Grace sliced the remainder of the cake.

She looked up from her task. Mitch ambled back into the parish hall, his ascot tie rumpled and his cheeks flush from exertion. As he joined her at the dessert table, he brushed back a shock of hair that had fallen over his brow.

"I liked it how it was." She poured him another cup of punch.

"All right." He mussed his hair, making her laugh. But she did like it, curly like that. She'd told him a time or two 'twould be a shame to slick away those curls with Macassar oil.

Mitch took a long draught of the punch. "So you played matchmaker for Bess and Elmer? Because you're a marriage expert?"

Saucy man. "I may be twenty-five and never courted, but I know a thing or two."

"Do you, now?" His brow quirked. "How'd you figure it out, then?

She spun to him, too excited not to share. She'd been sitting on this for weeks, and Mitch would be sure to approve. "Using something I'm good at."

"You're good at blueberry pie," he teased. "Singing. Pulling splinters. Strawberry punch, too. You're good at a lot of things."

"You forgot something, silly." She stood on tiptoe so he wouldn't miss it. "Science."

◆ ◆ ◆

Mitch leaned against the wall so he could better look Grace in her lovely hazel eyes. "Scientific matchmaking?"

"Remember that journal article we read a few months back appealing to the procedure of scientific experimentation? The author said it should be done systematically, concerned with the process of fact gathering over instinct or imagination."

"The author called the process the scientific method, although the practice has been in place a long while." For centuries, in one form or another.

"Well, I used the scientific method described by the author. The first step is identifying a problem, which I had: Bess wanted to be married, hadn't been courted in Emerald, and intended to take the job in Denver in hopes of finding a husband."

Oh boy. "So you conducted an experiment to find her a husband here?"

Bess dashed around the table, preventing Grace's answer. "Thank you, Grace. What a wonderful party."

Elmer shook Mitch's hand, and after the usual talk about the party and wedding, folks started leaving. Mitch pulled down the sign, eager to have enough privacy to ask Grace about her science experiment.

Love didn't work according to formula. At least, not in Mitch's experience. He'd only loved one woman, but marriage wasn't in their future, so he'd determined to be a good friend and appreciate every day he spent with her at the clinic. He grinned at her now.

His Grace.

When everyone had gone, they finished cleaning. Then Grace took up her baskets. "Ready?"

Nodding, he hoisted two of her crates and dipped his knees so she could plop the soiled linens on top. That was one of the things Mitch liked best about his relationship with Grace. They didn't always have to talk to know one another's minds—but he'd sure like to know what she was thinking now. "So tell me how you created a science experiment to find Bess a husband."

Grace passed him out the door. "Not just for Bess. The results can be applied to anyone."

He moved to her far side, protecting her from the street traffic as they made the short walk to her house. The sun was beginning to dip behind the Front Range of the Rocky Mountains, casting Grace in a pinkish light that made in her auburn hair shine. Why hadn't anyone else in Emerald noticed how pretty Grace was?

Then again, Mitch was glad they hadn't. He wanted her all to himself. "Go on."

"Once I identified the problem, I asked the question, what traits comprise a successful match? To find answers, I conducted research by observing happy couples—adults, mind you, not addlepated youngsters—and came up with four criteria they share. Next I hypothesized that I could apply those four principles to create matches. I tested the hypothesis through experimentation."

"How?" This was fascinating. Mad, maybe, but fascinating.

"I observed Bess's reactions whenever she encountered an eligible male. Church. Saturday night group. The general store, even."

"And you took notes, I assume."

"In that green leather journal you gave me for Christmas." She grinned. "Then I assessed the data, drew a conclusion, and informed Bess of my findings."

"That Elmer was the one for her."

She nodded. "My hypothesis was proven correct. Matchmaking can be achieved scientifically using my four principles."

"Sir Francis Bacon and Sir Isaac Newton would be pleased by your methods." They turned the corner to her street. Her brick, Italianate-style house was first on the left, flanked by the small, two-story former house on the northeast edge of the lot that now served as the town's medical clinic. As they'd done countless times before, he and Grace took the narrow walkway between the two buildings around the back of her house to the kitchen. Balancing the crates, he opened the kitchen door for her. "So what are those four principles you mentioned?"

She lowered her parcels to the oak table and nodded that he should do the same with the crates. "First, the man and woman should be similar minded, spiritually and in willingness to commit to a marriage."

"Sounds right." He dumped the soiled linens by the back door. That way he'd remember to put them with the clinic's outgoing laundry for Nell Vaughn, Emerald's laundress. "And the second principle?"

"They are attuned to one another. They show interest or sympathy." She reached around him to grab a clean dish towel off the shelf.

"Some might call that attraction." Like what he felt right now, when she brushed his sleeve.

"No, it's more compassionate, intellectual, and lasting than physical signs of attraction. Those are important, however, so I included attraction as the third observable trait I looked for—as far as can be measured by science, that is. When the potential beloved is near, one feels giddy, nervous, or excited. He or she might experience flushed cheeks, a racing pulse, the propensity to babble or, its opposite, be tongue-tied."

He'd never distilled the craziness of falling in love to a checklist of indicators. Took all the fun out of it. "Let me guess. Bess babbled. Elmer's lips were clamped like he had lockjaw."

"It was funny to watch." She laughed and wrapped the dish towel over a pie plate of cake, dessert for him and Ma, probably. Ma had hated to miss the party.

"And the fourth principle?" He held up the kettle to heat wash water in a silent question.

"Complementary personalities." She nodded at the kettle. Funny how they could have two conversations at once.

"Opposites attract, then?" He pumped water into the kettle while she unpacked the dirty dishes into the dry sink.

"Not quite. The partners in the successful marriages I observed were different from one another in key, defining traits. For instance, one is shy, the other outgoing.

Elmer is patient, Bess is not. In this manner, they strengthen one another's weaknesses, care rather than compete." She flaked dish soap over the stack.

"Like a team. They fit one another." Seemed like a good way to describe a husband and wife. At least, that's what he'd always thought it should be. His parents hadn't been like that at all, though.

She hummed a response. "Based on my findings, I think Elmer and Bess will be happy."

Mitch lit the stove. "Marriage is about more than happiness, though. It takes work."

"Of course. I wanted to create a system of matchmaking with the strongest hope of match*keeping*, if that's a word. Building a foundation on which to withstand the storms of life. Remember my first principle?"

"Mutual commitment in faith and life."

"Every marriage has its share of trials and troubles. And even then, there are no guarantees. Your father passed on. My ma, too." A shadow crossed her features. Grace missed her mother, but she also grieved how her pa's heart hardened after her ma died.

"Your mother would have loved you using her dishes and punch bowl for the party, I'm sure." Mitch squeezed her arm, a friendly gesture. Just like catching her when she fell off that rattletrap box, although he'd been tempted to hold her to his chest and run away with her. It wasn't always easy to keep things friendly when he wanted so much more. Even if it could never be.

She smiled. "She'd be glad Bess is staying in town, too. Almost as glad as I am. Nothing's going to change."

"Bess is marrying. I'd say that's a change."

"But she'll be *here*. Everything will stay just as it is. Perfect."

Mitch exhaled. Maybe this was the time to tell her. He'd planned to wait until things were definite, but—

"Mitchell Shaw!" A familiar male voice carried through the open window. "That you in the kitchen?"

So much for telling her anything. Mitch turned and stuck his head out the window to greet his mentor, friend, and boss, Dr. Sidney Perkins, who, likewise, leaned out the window of the clinic's former kitchen. The form of communication had served them fairly well the past five years. "Hello, sir. Do you need me?"

Sidney's balding head shook. "No. Mrs. Dooley just left. She won't stay for observation, despite her pain. Just wondering if you're staying for supper."

Grace leaned over Mitch's shoulder, smelling of strawberries and dish soap. "Haven't asked him yet."

"Since when does he need an invitation?"

"I should get back to Ma." Mitch knew she was waiting for details of the party.

And he had some praying to do. "I'll check in with you, Sidney, once I finish helping Grace."

"Suits me fine." Sidney disappeared and shut the window.

"I wonder why Mrs. Dooley won't stay." Grace chewed her lip.

"Maybe she'll tell you her reasons, since she won't enlighten me or your father." Steam swirled from the hot kettle. Mitch shed his coat, wrapped the kettle's handle in a towel, and poured the hot water over the dishes.

"It's always the same, isn't it?" Grace grinned. "I wash, you dry."

He smiled, except she was wrong.

Things wouldn't—couldn't—stay the same. Everything was about to change.

Chapter Two

Well, this was new. Grace almost felt popular.

In the week since Bess and Elmer's engagement party, word of Grace's matchmaking had spread from Flossie Hawkins to two others, Myra Olson and Emerald's laundress, Nell Vaughn. Now, the trio cornered her in the Hawkinses' richly decorated parlor, where the church's unmarried folks gathered for games and a devotional, as they did every other Saturday night. Flossie's father ran the mercantile, and the family boasted the only parlor in Emerald large enough to accommodate them all. Besides, the joke went, if they didn't meet at Flossie's, the girl wouldn't arrive until the gathering was half over. Maybe styling her elaborate curls was what made her tardy.

Grace couldn't remember a time when females her age clustered around her, hanging on her every word. Nor had they ever clutched her arms as if she were in danger of floating away, but dark-haired Myra Olson's grip could serve as a tourniquet.

"So you'll help us?" Myra squeezed.

"I'm happy to find matches for you."

"And it'll work?" Flossie twisted one of those strawberry-blond curls around her index finger.

"It did for Bess and Elmer. It's based on scientific theory that should apply to everyone." Grace shrugged, but the gesture didn't dislodge Myra's clasp.

"I don't know about this." Fair-haired Nell chewed her lip.

Myra released Grace to clutch Nell's arm. "You want to be married, you said so."

Nell's pale cheeks flushed pink as the berry-red accents on the lamps and chandelier crystals in the rococo-style parlor. "Yes, but that doesn't mean I want the town hearing of it."

Grace rubbed her arm, right where Myra's grip almost cut off her circulation. "You'd have to want marriage. That's the first criterion for a successful match. I can't make matches for you if there aren't any churchgoing, marriage-minded gentlemen in town to pair you with."

Myra hopped, making her bustle bounce. "I know of a few, and they're here tonight. My brother said Elmer was at Irvin's flour mill Thursday, talking up being engaged, and some of the other fellows there said they'd like to be married, too."

"Who?" Pity Grace hadn't brought her notebook.

"Silas and Irvin."

Grace nodded. Silas Lee was the barber who cut Pa's hair, and mustachioed Irvin Brown owned the flour mill.

"Lou was there, too." Elmer Kohl's brother.

"Anyone else you know of? From church who has expressed interest in marriage?"

"What about Dr. Mitch?" Flossie giggled.

"He hasn't indicated an interest in wedlock." Grace suppressed the sudden rise of irritation souring her words.

"Could you ask? You're with him all the time."

"I don't need to ask. Mitch is a stalwart bachelor." She couldn't explain why to these ladies, though. "Anyone else?"

Myra peeked at the gentlemen gathered around the punch bowl. Mitch stood a few inches taller than the rest. "Now we know Flossie's sweet on Mitch."

"I am not." Flossie scowled.

Good. Mitch would not make a good match for Flossie. The idea set Grace's teeth grinding together.

Nell hid her eyes behind her hand. "This is mortifying."

"But you'll let Grace do it, won't you?" Flossie's brows lowered.

Nell nodded. "I'd like a—you know. Family of my own."

Poor, shy Nell. Grace relaxed, now that they were no longer speaking about Mitch. "There is nothing of which to be ashamed. It's right there in Genesis: marriage is a good thing. I'll make some observations and analyze my findings. I'll let you know who I determine to be the best suitor for each of you."

"What if the fellas don't like us?"

"Never have I seen any indication of dislike from a single member of our Saturday night group toward another. But I'll ask the gentlemen if they're interested in my matchmaking first."

All three girls nodded, Myra and Flossie with enthusiasm, and Nell with her hands pressed to her cheeks.

Bess beckoned the group to the open space between the Hawkinses' parlor furniture and the grand dining room table. "Ready for a game?"

"What does your book have for us tonight?" Mitch leaned against the mantelpiece. Grace liked the grin he wore. Despite being thirty, he was the first to jump into a game. It was hard not to find his playfulness contagious.

Her eyes twinkling in amusement, Bess held a tiny down feather aloft. "We keep this feather in the air as long as we can without using hands. Just our breath. And no one can blow it twice in a row."

The group gathered on the plush rug, murmuring and giggling. Grace used the opportunity to eye up the three prospective suitors for her matchmaking experiment. Perhaps she should be taking deep breaths in preparation for the game, but—oh! Bess blew the feather. Nell ran under it and puffed out a huge breath, sending it drifting past Grace. She followed its progress to Mitch—

"Nell?" Lou Kohl dodged around Grace. "Nell!"

Grace spun. Lou's arms caught Nell just as she slumped, unconscious.

◆　◆　◆

Mitch lunged to capture Nell's shoulders and neck. "The sofa."

They laid her atop the cushions. Mitch knelt over her. A quick shove of her lace cuff up her arm, and his fingers pressed into her wrist. "Pulse strong but fast."

Grace bent over his shoulder. "Her color's off."

Nell's breaths were shallow but even. Skin cool to his touch. His thumbs brushed her eyelids to check her pupils, but before he could lift her eyelids, they fluttered. "Oh," Nell moaned.

"Syncope?" Grace asked.

He nodded, sighing at the dark rings under Nell's eyes. "You fainted, Nell. Has it happened before?"

She blinked. "Not in a long time."

Lou pressed in, Irvin peering over his shoulder. "Is she fine now?"

Mitch smiled down at Nell. "I believe so, but I'd like to take you to the clinic for a quick exam just to be sure, Nell."

She nodded.

Lou, his arms strong from working a plow, hoisted Nell as if she were light as cotton batting. "Lead the way, Doc."

Mitch waved at the others on his way out, Grace at his heels with their coats. "We'll send word, but I think she's fine. Thanks for the nice evening."

Half the ladies had their hands to their mouths.

Grace kept pace all the way to the clinic. "I could've fetched your bag, but you want to speak to her in private, don't you?"

How well she understood him. "I think it best."

She dashed ahead, opening the clinic with her key and setting the little bell above the door to jangling. The little edifice boasted three upstairs chambers with two beds each for overnight patients, while the first floor's kitchen allowed a workspace and the old parlor served as an office, leaving two rooms off the tiny foyer for examinations and surgery. With a whiff of sulfur, Grace struck a match and lit the lamps in the examination room on the right. Mitch passed her to wash his hands in the corner basin. When he finished, Lou had set Nell on the examination table. "I'll fetch her mother."

"Thank you." Mitch opened his leather bag wide and pulled out his binaural stethoscope.

"Am I sick, Doctor Mitch?" Nell teared up. Grace took her hand.

"Fainting is caused by a lot of different things. Let's rule a few out."

Mitch pressed the stethoscope's chest piece below Nell's clavicle and listened. At his elbow, Grace took a pencil and paper and wrote *auscultation*. "Heart's strong, Nell."

Grace scribbled the results on the sheet.

He moved the chest piece. Nell's lungs sounded clean, quiet. Not at all like her stomach.

"Have you eaten today?"

"Some mush. This morning."

Grace met his gaze. When Nell's father died last year, Nell and her mother supported themselves by taking in laundry. Mitch was relieved to pay them for the chore, what with Ma's rheumatism and all. Likewise, the clinic hired Nell to boil and wash its soiled linens. Nell must not have found many more clients, however, for her cheeks had grown hollower as the months passed.

His hand patted her bony shoulder. "You need proper meals. Meat. Vegetables."

With a rustle of fabric, Grace slipped out of the room. Probably to get some leftover soup from the house.

A thin tear snaked down Nell's cheek. "I'll try."

"You can't build a strong fire under your wash kettle without good wood, can you? Your body's the same. It won't work if you don't give it substantial food."

She sat up and swung her feet over the edge of the table. "At least I'm not sick. I can work."

"Yes, but—"

Mrs. Vaughn, Nell's mother, burst in the clinic door, her face etched with dread. Behind her, the concerned faces of their friends appeared in the foyer—Silas, Lou, the ladies. Good folks in Emerald. Mitch pushed the thought aside and beckoned Mrs. Vaughn into the exam room, closing the door behind her.

When he finished, he smiled. "No need to stay here overnight, but remember, food and drink on a regular schedule."

"Yessir, Doc." Mrs. Vaughn took Nell's hand.

"But Ma, we can't—"

"How much do we owe?" Mrs. Vaughn's chin tilted with determination. She wouldn't accept charity.

"Could we barter? We've got a sack of sheeting that needs laundering." A small sack, but at least the Vaughns wouldn't perceive Nell's care as a handout.

A soft knock, and then Grace slipped inside the door, carrying an old lard pail. "I'm glad I caught you before you left. Could you take this soup, please? I put too much barley in it, so then I had to add more broth. Now there's too much for us to eat before it spoils, and Pa doesn't like barley anyway."

Neither woman seemed to believe Grace, but they took the offering. "Thank you, kindly."

"You're doing me the favor, truly. I already sent some with Mitch."

"Good meal." He patted his stomach, smiling. The smile fell when Nell, her mother, and their friends left the clinic and he and Grace were alone. "Thanks for sending the soup. That was amazingly done."

"Who's amazing?" Sidney Perkins, Grace's Pa, ambled into the exam room, quiet in his stocking feet. A grin creased his stout features. "You aren't talking about me, are you?"

Grace kissed the thick gray whiskers curving down his cheek. "You know what we're talking about. You watched me ladle the soup."

Sidney gestured at the exam table. "That's why I didn't rush in. Figured they didn't need all of us badgering them to eat."

Mitch nodded, adding a few notes to the page Grace started for Nell's file. "The only patients we've had today are stubborn women. Mrs. Dooley's pain was worse, but she still won't stay overnight."

Sidney grunted. "No, more's the pity. Can't watch how the pain spreads at night, as she says, if she won't stay here. If we understood her problem, we could better treat it, even if we never discover a diagnosis."

Mitch filed his report in the cabinet. "I've prayed for Mrs. Dooley's healing, and if that's not God's will, then at least His help making her more comfortable."

Then Mitch realized what he'd said aloud. Grace did, too, for her hazel eyes were round as half-dollars.

Mitch squared his shoulders. He'd done nothing of which to be ashamed. The opposite, in fact.

Nevertheless, Sidney glared. "You want to pray, fine. But not here. No God allowed in my clinic."

"Pa," Grace pled, but Sidney had already thumped out the back door.

"I'm sorry." Grace's hands clasped under her chin. "I don't like when he does that."

"I'm sorry, too. He's angry and suffering. The only thing the man trusts is science." Mitch straightened his cuffs. He didn't want to talk about it right now, though. Nell's empty belly, Mrs. Dooley's pain, Sidney's grief—all weighed on Mitch, and he needed to give them to the Lord. But he also yearned for rest. A light conversation. Time with Grace. "Speaking of science, I hear word's spread about your matchmaking scheme."

"It's not a scheme, and we can talk about Pa, Mitch. If you want."

"I don't need to talk about it. I know where I stand, with your pa and with God. So tell me about your evening, before Nell, that is. With the ladies. Looked like Myra was cutting off the circulation in that arm."

She laughed and shook out her arm. "Nell, Myra, and Flossie asked me to play matchmaker for them, using my theory."

"Maybe you should patent your findings. You'll be famous." He leaned against the exam table.

She curtsied as if she were on stage. "They'll call me Miss Matched."

His brow quirked. "You know 'mismatched' means two things that don't go together, don't you?"

"You know what I mean." She rose and spelled it out. "I'm the *miss* who makes *matches*. If you had come up with the idea, you could be Dr. Matched."

"Then we'd have to change the sign over the door from Doctors Perkins and Shaw to Perkins and Matched," he teased.

Then his smile fell. The sign on the door. . .

She looked so pretty in her pink party dress, smiling at him like that. He hated to ruin the moment, but the time had come.

"Grace, I have something to tell you."

Chapter Three

The last time someone had looked at Grace with that grim set to his lips and announced he had something to tell her, it was bad news. Pa had told her Ma wouldn't live out the week. Grace clutched her arms to her chest. "What is it? Your mother's worse?"

"I don't mean to scare you. No one is ill. I—I have to leave town."

She expelled a shaky breath. "On a trip?"

"I mean, I need to find a new job."

Her stomach clenched tight. "Why?"

But she knew already. Pa.

She sank to the bentwood chair in the corner, wrapping her arms around her torso.

"Your father is a skilled doctor, Grace. Learned, good with patients, my mentor and friend. But he wants God kept out of the clinic, and I won't stop praying for our patients. *Can't* stop. It's who I am. God's the Master Healer; I can't be a physician without His help."

"Pa's a doctor, he knows people get sick and d–die." Grace fought the panic rising in her throat. "He just couldn't accept it in his own family. Give him time."

Mitch sat on the floor at her feet. "For a while, I've felt God calling me to head my own clinic. I've prayed for discernment, but the instruction hasn't changed."

She couldn't argue against God's call on Mitch's life, but she didn't like it a lick. Working alongside the two men she admired most was what made her happy. Losing that would be harder than anything since losing Ma. Even now her insides trembled, her mouth dried, her fingers shook.

Maybe—maybe she couldn't argue against Mitch opening his own clinic. But she could still keep him close.

"Is there more to it? You want to leave Emerald to find a s–spouse, like Bess?" The words blurted out before she could stop them, and they tasted bitter on her tongue. "I could play matchmaker for you, just like I am for Myra and Nell and Flossie—"

"My parents' marriage was terrible, you know that." His words were as gentle as his touch on her arm. "The fighting over my father working late at the law firm, my mother's resentment at his choosing his clients and partners over her. I don't want a marriage like that, Grace. And I would. I keep odd hours. My wife would come to resent me, too."

She nodded. The information wasn't new, but it still hurt that Mitch was wounded this way. She'd tried arguing that her mother never minded Pa attending births or deaths, no more than the pastor's wife objected to her husband's odd-hour calls. But Mitch was resolute, and it saddened her that he'd closed himself off to love.

To her shame, however, relief spiraled through her body like warm, soothing steam. The idea of him wedding some faceless woman didn't sit well on her stomach.

Mitch rose from the floor, extending his hand to her. "Besides, I can't stay in town to rival your father, Grace. I respect and care for him too much. That means I have to leave Emerald."

She took his fingers in hers. "Emerald needs you." *I need you.*

"Change is hard, Grace, but you fight it like no one I've ever seen. Look what you've done to keep Bess in town. Things are still going to change, though. Once she marries Elmer, she won't be in our Saturday group anymore. She'll live on the farm, and you won't see her as much, especially since her superintendent will make her stop teaching once she gets in the family way. She'll still love you, but it won't be the same."

The truth of his words sunk into her bones. She'd known it, but everything was so good right now. Couldn't it stay like this forever? Or at least a little while longer?

She stood, facing him, but couldn't quite meet his gaze. "You and Bess are my best friends, Mitch. I can't say good-bye to either of you."

"I'd never say good-bye to you, Grace." He pulled her arm so her hand rested on his shoulder, and then he wrapped her in a gentle hug. "You're my best friend, too."

Then why are you doing this to me?

"I'd like to be the one to tell your father, when the time is right."

She nodded into his chest. The hard bone of his jaw rested atop her head. It was easy to enjoy this, his bay smell and closeness, so comforting and at the same time, singularly unsettling in the unfamiliarity of it. She'd wanted things to stay the same. But there was nothing the same about this hug of his, so unlike his other quick squeezes. This made her stomach flip. No, her nerves caused that sensation because she was sad.

"I won't fight you, Mitch. I understand. Forgive me for pressing."

"I'm glad to know you'll miss me." He released her but stood there, as if waiting for something, but she couldn't meet his gaze. Then he sighed. "I'll close up. See you at church tomorrow?"

She nodded, turned on her heel, and hurried out the back door. She'd missed people before. Grieved. This didn't feel like those had at all. This was panic twisted with something she couldn't name.

If only there was a scientific explanation for how she felt, she could treat it. Until then, all she could do was pray for peace.

◆　◆　◆

Peace settled over Mitch's shoulders Sunday morning as the final chords of the hymn trilled from the organ. Another worship service concluded. How many more would there be for him, here in Emerald? A sad thought, but God had the situation in hand.

Before Mitch could slip the hymnal back into its pocket in the pew, a figure appeared at his elbow. Grace in her spring-green Sunday dress, which was prettier than a May day with her reddish hair and freckled complexion. "Morning."

"Good morning." Her mouth was set in a grim line.

He stifled a laugh. He should've guessed she'd continue last night's argument. She was predictable, his sweet Grace. And stubborn as the proverbial mule about change. He escorted her to greet the pastor on the way out.

"I have a basket lunch waiting at the house for you and your mother."

So that was her plan, to get his mother on her side. Well, it was time he told Ma his plans, anyway. "She'll be glad to see you. Will your father join us?"

Her head shook. "He's researching possible diagnoses for Mrs. Dooley, but he sends his regards. Which reminds me, I stopped by Mrs. Dooley's house before church. I know why she won't stay overnight at the clinic. Bertie."

Bertie? But Mrs. Dooley had no family. No husband. Unless—

Grace brushed something off her sleeve that looked suspiciously like cat hair.

Mitch laughed. "Bertie is a feline companion?"

"Orange as a pumpkin and almost as round." Her hands spread as if she described a Thanksgiving turkey. "I told her Bertie could stay at the clinic with her, and she agreed to come next time the pains overtake her."

Surely the cat couldn't be *that* big. "If it brings her comfort, it's a wonderful idea."

They passed Lou, Silas, Irvin, Flossie, and Myra, clustered around Nell. It was good to see how they cared for their friend. Hopefully Nell and her mother found something to eat today. Then the ladies looked up and waved at Grace, giggling. Myra batted her eyes at one of the fellows. No doubt Grace took mental notes as data for her matchmaking hypothesis.

After thanking the pastor for his message—and accepting the pastor's request to call on Ma, who'd been unable to make it to church today—Mitch and Grace retraced the steps they'd taken after the party for Elmer and Bess. It was hard not to think of Grace's distasteful offer to make him a match. If she only knew how he'd struggled with his determination not to get married since falling in love with her. One look at her freckled cheeks and sparkling eyes, and he'd been a goner.

When they reached her house, he realized neither had spoken a word. "You're still mad at me."

"I'm not mad. Just a minute." Grace left him on the street to stomp around the house to the kitchen door. Within seconds she returned with a basket.

He took it in one arm and offered her the other. "If you say so."

She rolled her eyes, but at least she took his arm as they strolled the two short blocks to his whitewashed house. "I'm not angry. I'm upset. I think it's a fair response."

"So you're enlisting Ma's help in your cause?"

She craned her neck to look up at him. "Is that what you—I figured you hadn't told her yet. I just thought I'd like to spend time with both of you if you're leaving Emerald soon."

If his heart could grow from love for her, then it swelled against the confines of his rib cage. "I'm glad. But you're right, I haven't told her yet. Maybe today."

Ma was propped on the horsehair sofa in the gold-papered parlor, a quilt in hues of green over her lap. She'd dressed and combed her fading blond hair into a neat bun at her nape. Setting aside her Bible, she grinned at them. "Grace, land sakes, you look pretty today. Doesn't she, son?"

Clearly, Ma felt well enough to jab at him. He smiled, but glared at Ma. "She does."

Grace bent to kiss Ma's cheek. "It's good to see you smile. Sorry you weren't up to church today."

"I'm better now. The salve helps my joints. Not so bad, having a doctor for a son, eh?"

Ma's extreme swelling and joint pain concerned Mitch, especially considering Ma wasn't much over fifty, but he'd seen young suffer from rheumatoid arthritis as well as old. "Grace brought lunch."

"Pa sends his regards." Making herself at home, as she always did here, Grace ambled to the kitchen. Mitch followed her, pulling plates from the cupboard while Grace emptied her basket onto the table.

The savory smells of ham and dill wafted through the air. Mitch's stomach rumbled. "Mustard-dilled green beans?"

"Of course." She grinned, as if she'd made them just for him. Then she sauntered out to poke her head into the parlor. "Would you like to sit at the table, ma'am, or may I bring you a plate?"

"Let's picnic in the parlor." Ma's voice was stronger than it had been in a week.

Within minutes, he and Grace found spots on the matching green velvet embroidered parlor chairs near Ma. They gave thanks, set their plates on their knees, and tucked into the cold food, telling Ma about the sermon and Nell's attendance.

"After last night's fainting spell, I wasn't sure she'd be there," Grace said.

"Have you picked a match for her yet?" Ma's eyes twinkled. "Mitchell told me about your hypothesis."

Grace patted her lips with her napkin. "I think I have."

"Already?" Mitch's question was for Grace, but his gaze fixed on Ma's plate. She'd barely touched her ham. Was she too sore, or too excited? Either way, her eyes shone bright, and Mitch couldn't help but give thanks she was happy.

Ma leaned forward. "Who's the unsuspecting fellow?"

Mitch finished his beans. What was with women and matchmaking?

"Not a one is unsuspecting. I spoke to them this past week." Grace smiled. "I believe they thought it a lark, but they are all interested in marriage, so they agreed."

Mitch stretched his legs. "So, Irvin Brown, Silas Lee, and Lou Kohl are the gents, and Flossie Hawkins, Myra Olson, and Nell Vaughn are the gals."

Ma rubbed her hands together. "Who with whom? Don't keep me in suspense."

"After watching them interact this past week, as well as drawing upon my experiences during our years-long acquaintanceships, I don't think I require more research. I've matched Nell with Lou Kohl."

"Lou?" Ma clapped.

"He was the first to see Nell faint. He carried her to the clinic. I believe that means he is attuned to her, which is one of the criteria I use to make matches."

"He's sweet on her, then?" Ma grinned.

"I couldn't tell for sure. I wasn't able to feel his pulse," Grace said with all seriousness.

Mitch swallowed. "Pulses don't tell you everything." For instance, his was steady right now, despite wanting to kiss Grace on her freckled nose.

"Well, Nell blushed when Lou spoke to her after church today. That counts as a measurable sign of attraction." Grace shrugged.

"I always thought Irvin might be sweet on Nell." Mitch set down his fork.

"Why?"

Something seemed to change in the air when he was in their midst. "Intuition, I suppose."

Grace shook her head. "I don't know Irvin well, true, in part because his hard work at the flour mill has prevented him from socializing much. In part because he's the shyest fellow in the bunch. I think Myra Olson's exuberance is a good foil to Irvin's bashfulness. That's another of my principles, complementary traits."

"So Irvin and Myra. Nell and Lou." Ma's face hadn't shown this much color in a week.

"Have a bite, Ma. You love Grace's green beans." Mitch pointed with his fork.

"*You* love them." Ma speared a cube of ham. "Did you pair Flossie and Silas because they're the only two left?"

"Not at all. Again, it was the principle of complementary traits. Flossie is chronically tardy. Silas is punctual, maybe because he runs his own business as the barber. And she batted her lashes at him. That settled it. I'll tell them all of my findings, and then it's up to them. Just as it was with Bess and Elmer. I imagine our Saturday night group will provide opportunity for each to pair up and talk."

"How romantic." Ma sighed.

Mitch snorted. "It's not romantic at all."

"It's science." Grace nodded. "Courting and weddings are romantic. But marriage is hard work, faith, and sacrifice."

"That we can agree on." Mitch gathered their plates. At least Ma had eaten part of her lunch.

"This town is romantic." Ma pulled the quilt to her lap. "Folks think it was named because a miner found an emerald here during the gold rush, but in truth, one of the first settlers named it for his wife. Now that's sweet."

"Sweet as Grace's blueberry pie." Mitch grinned.

"Grace?" The way Ma said it took three syllables, and her eyes held a wicked, gleeful glint. "Why don't you find Mitchell a match?"

Grace stood. "He's not, that is—I should go. Keep the leftovers. You can bring the tins with you to the clinic tomorrow, Mitch."

The sofa groaned as Ma pushed up to stand. "Why won't you match Mitchell? Is it because someone has already caught his eye?"

He almost told his mother not to be ridiculous, but that would be lying. Grace spun to face him in a swirl of green fabric, her eyes wide. Not with curiosity. More like a deer caught munching lettuce in the garden.

He didn't know why she'd look panicked, but he understood his alarm well enough. He'd hid his feelings for Grace for so long, he couldn't reveal them now. He took a deep breath.

"Because I feel called to open my own clinic, Ma. And since I don't intend to compete with Sidney, I need to leave Emerald. *We* need to leave."

Ma unbent to her full height, the top of her head at Mitch's chin. She tossed the quilt to the sofa with a thump.

"Over my dead body, Mitchell Aloysius Shaw. Unless that's your plan, to kill me with this news. *First, do no harm*, Mitchell. Remember your physician's oath?"

That was the tone he remembered from his youth. This was why he could never marry. Never.

Chapter Four

"M itchell? Have a moment?"

Mitch turned from cleaning an ivory tongue depressor with carbolic acid to see Sidney in the threshold of the exam room, his plump hand on the doorjamb. "Sir?"

"Busy for a Saturday."

Mitch nodded. It had been almost two weeks since he'd told his mother of his plan to leave Emerald, but he hadn't yet found the proper time to inform Sidney. Mitch had thought today might offer the opportunity for a long talk, since the clinic wasn't usually open on Saturdays and he and Sidney planned to catch up on paperwork.

Instead, they'd been bombarded with patients today, folks suffering carbuncles, cankers, and catarrh—and a screaming infant who waited in the office.

At this rate, he wouldn't make Saturday night group, but this was his job, and he was thankful to be of use. "Glad we happened to be in the office to take them all."

Sidney grunted. Mitch looked at him, really looked at him. Sidney's jowls seemed puffier, as if he'd put on weight, and dark circles smudged under his eyes.

"How are you feeling?"

"Middling after a long day, nothing a nap can't cure. My intention is for you to attend your group with Grace tonight, but if you could examine the infant, I can dash to the house for supper. No chance to go later, now that Mrs. Dooley is settled upstairs with that *cat*." The way he said it was akin to the noise said feline made when coughing up a hairball.

Sidney may not be thrilled about Bertie's presence, but a pan of sand, a bowl of water, and the promise to sweep the shed cat hair seemed a fair price to pay for keeping a closer eye on Mrs. Dooley, who'd come in an hour ago in such agony she could hardly walk, but her grip on Bertie had been strong. Sidney hadn't uttered a word, but he grimaced when he brushed cat hair off his shirtfront.

"Go on, sir. I'll stay until you get back." Mitch wiped the final depressor dry while Sidney left. Sidney had made a kind offer, but Mitch wasn't sure he'd attend group. He wasn't dressed for it, in his plain frock coat, string tie and work-wrinkled shirt, and he hadn't eaten supper. A quick glance out the window at the setting sun assured him time was too short to run home. A familiar blurred figure passed the window and turned onto the path up to the clinic.

He hurried to meet her at the door. "Ma? What are you doing here?"

"Visiting. You're my son, aren't you?"

"For the past thirty years, but you don't make a habit of checking up on me at work." He led her to the empty exam room. "You must be feeling better tonight, to walk here."

"You're always nagging me about exercise, saying it'll give me stamina, so here I am. You're wrong, though. I'm plumb worn out."

"It takes time, Ma."

She dropped the bundle on the table and collapsed onto one of the bentwood chairs. "Who's that crying baby?"

"Little Melissa Hubert, my next patient." A subtle hint that he had work to do.

"You used to cry like that when you had growing pains. I was so glad when you could reach down and pat your leg, so I knew what troubled you." She showed no sign of moving. Meanwhile Melissa's screeches hurt his ears and stirred his sympathies.

Mitch inched toward the door. "Why don't you rest while I tend the baby—"

"Oh, I'm not staying to listen to that poor thing cry. Want to get home before it's dark as pitch, anyway. I brought you a sandwich and your good clothes for tonight. Figured you didn't have time to come home first." She stood and squinted at his appearance. "Too bad I didn't think to bring a clean shirt and some Macassar."

"I never use Macassar."

"Your curls are uncontrollable."

But Grace liked them, so that was good enough for him.

"Change now, so I can take your dirty coat home." She unwrapped the bundle and handed him a fresh tie, blue waistcoat, and coat. He'd rather wait until he was finished with patients, but no matter. He shrugged out of his dirty clothes and into the clean ones.

"I'm glad you came by." He was grateful for the food and clothes. Even more grateful to see Ma dressed and out of the house.

"I have to prove I'm no invalid. You can leave Emerald, but I'm not going anywhere."

Mitch sighed. He didn't want to leave any more than she did. God's call hadn't changed, although he'd been too busy at the clinic the past two weeks to send queries. Each day had been like today, full of sick folks and late evenings.

"Don't overdo." He kissed her cheek and sent her out the door. Then he brought Mrs. Hubert and her unhappy infant into the examination room.

"Come here, sweetheart." He took the squalling baby in his arms. His inspection verified what he'd found yesterday: low-grade fever and swollen, sensitive gums. Accompanied by little appetite, the symptoms indicated Melissa was teething, just as he'd told Mrs. Hubert yesterday. "Did you try the icy washrag?"

Mrs. Hubert's chin quivered. "My granny swears by a diff'rent remedy. She told me to rub it on her gums."

"What was that?" *Please, not whiskey.*

"Fresh mashed rabbit brains."

Mitch's stomach lurched. "You—tried that?"

She nodded so hard her calico bonnet flopped backwards. "But she jus' keeps cryin'."

"I hate to disagree with Granny, but I believe her remedy could harm Melissa. Milk is all she needs right now, anyway."

"She ain't eatin' much." Mrs. Hubert swiped her watery eyes with a handkerchief.

"It's a rough time for both of you, but it'll pass once the tooth breaks through. Let her chew on an icy, wet rag, like I told you. It'll numb her gums. She'll catch up nursing when she feels better."

Mrs. Hubert nodded then sneezed.

"But you've developed symptoms since yesterday. Sit down and let me look at you."

"Just catarrh." She shrugged, but at least she perched on the examination table.

"I've seen seven cases today." Still holding the baby, he checked Mrs. Hubert's ears, mouth, and nose. His exam yielded no surprises. Congestion, mild fever, and aches. The common cold, accompanied by the challenge of caring for an unhappy five-month-old. "The usual tonic can help. Try to rest as best you can, with the baby as fussy as she is."

At the moment, however, Melissa was anything but fussy. Her tiny fist gripped the top button of his waistcoat while she gnawed the surrounding fabric into a slobbery, crumpled mess. But he didn't mind. She felt good snuggled against him.

He'd never thought he'd be a father, but right now, the desire for a family tugged at him. *God, did I make the right decision to never marry?*

Once Mrs. Hubert and Melissa left, he mounted the stairs to the clinic's overnight rooms and paused at the first one on the right.

Grace, dressed for their Saturday night group in her flattering yellow dress, occupied the chair beside Mrs. Dooley's bed. She turned up the wick of a lamp as fancy as those in her house, etched glass on an enamel base. Likewise, a landscape painting of the nearby Rocky Mountains hung on the wall opposite the lace-curtained window. By making the rooms homey, Grace reasoned folks might heal faster.

That was the hope in having Bertie here, too. The overfed cat dozed atop Mrs. Dooley's bone-thin legs. Mitch ambled into the room. "How do you feel, ma'am?"

"Better now, with that powder Doc Perkins gave me."

While Mitch checked Mrs. Dooley's pulse, Grace brushed a lock of the woman's white hair from her brow. "Is there anything you or Bertie need?"

"Just each other. He's all I've got, since Horace passed. My best friend in the world until I meet my Horace again." Mrs. Dooley sighed. "I heard a baby crying."

Mitch lowered Mrs. Dooley's arm to the blanket. "Melissa Hubert is teething. She'll be fine."

"Did she teethe on you, Mitch?" Grace eyed his wrinkled waistcoat, reached to smooth it, and then grimaced at its soggy state. "Feels like it."

Mrs. Dooley cleared her throat. "The thing is, Doc, my Bertie's scared."

The cat looked apathetic, at best. Mitch exchanged a look with Grace. "Of staying here? How can we help?"

"I think I'm dyin', Doc. I've got no quarrel with God, and I've lived a long time. But I don't know what'll happen to Bertie. And this hurts somethin' awful. Pray for me?"

"I'd be honored." He squeezed her cold fingers and Grace's warm ones, too. How he'd miss this—praying with her, helping patients together, dressing up with her on Saturday nights.

He fixed his attention on the Lord. Praying aloud, he thanked God for Mrs. Dooley and Bertie and asked for fear and pain to ease. He also prayed for a diagnosis, if it was God's will.

He hadn't heard Sidney return to the clinic, but when Mitch opened his eyes, his partner leaned in the threshold. Sidney's bushy brows pulled low over his eyes.

Mitch braced for the lecture, but Sidney waved them out, instead. "Don't you two young folks need to be going?"

"Are you certain?"

"We're fine here. Mrs. Dooley, me. And. . .Bertie."

But Mitch was certain things weren't fine with Sidney, not in the least.

◆　◆　◆

From their perches on the two red velvet ottomans in Flossie Hawkins's parlor, Grace and Mitch touched knees, the better to balance the book they used as a lap table on which to scribble their quiz answers.

Mitch didn't seem to notice they touched, but Grace couldn't think of much else. Her knees sizzled and weakened, like something melted beneath the patella bones.

Maybe her sitting position pinched a nerve. She could shift her legs, but the book on their laps would wobble, messing up their answer page. Or Mitch might wonder why she moved, and what would she say? That her knees were on fire?

She'd stay put.

With the catarrh going around, their Saturday night group had just ten in attendance: five men, five women. Grace's matches were here, as well as Bess and Elmer, leaving Mitch and Grace as a team for the Bible quiz.

Except Mitch was writing the wrong answer.

"Mount Horeb, not Hermon." She nudged him. The odd melting sensation of liquefaction traversed from her knees to the direct spot on her shoulder where she'd bumped him.

"It says Horeb," he whispered, nudging back. The sensation spread.

"That doesn't look like a *B*." She rubbed at the spot. "Your handwriting is sloppy when you write fast."

With a mock look of exasperation, Mitch rewrote Horeb, curling the *b* with deliberate slowness. "Better?"

A giggle escaped her lips, loud and girlish. What on earth!

Flossie bent at the waist to peer at them. "What's so funny?"

Grace hadn't meant to distract anyone. "Sorry."

Mitch tapped the pencil against the next question. *What is the name of King David's daughter?*

"Tamar, I think." Mitch's whisper fluttered the hair by her ears.

A shiver slithered down her spine.

This wasn't right. Her knees and shoulder. Now shivers. Was she coming down with catarrh? Her hand flapped to her forehead.

Mitch's brows lowered. "Am I wrong?"

She couldn't think. The shiver had subsided, but she still felt cold. Or hot, 'twas hard to tell. But she didn't present with any congestion, aches, or other symptoms. Her hand fell.

"Something's wrong." Mitch's eyes bore into hers. But not with the "doctor look" he wore when he checked someone's pupils. His brow scrunched. His head tipped, so close his breath warmed her cheek, and more shivers prickled her skin.

Something *was* wrong. Had been wrong for a while, if she was honest. Since Mitch announced his intention to leave Emerald, she couldn't eat or sleep. He filled her thoughts every spare moment, distracting her from her tasks. And now this.

Hypersensitivity to touch, emotions close to the surface. She must be suffering from a malady of the nervous system.

Oh dear.

She'd always felt free to tell Mitch anything. He was a doctor as well as a friend. He could help her. But not with this.

If she were sick, he might stay in Emerald, and she couldn't bear the burden of knowing she'd prevented him from answering God's call.

"Grace?"

She blinked. *Say something.* "I can't remember the answer, is all."

"I'll write Tamar, then. Are you sure you're well?" He shifted on the ottoman, brushing her legs with his. More chills and melting wax under her skin.

291

"Just confused." But not by the quiz. She turned, looking at everything but Mitch.

Bess and Elmer giggled from their corner of the floor. But by the fireplace, Nell refused the pencil Lou held out to her. While everyone was supposed to whisper so as not to reveal their answers, Nell's "you first" and Lou's "no, after you" were audible.

A hasty glance revealed Myra scribbled answers while her partner, Irvin, threw his hands heavenward. "I'm not sure—"

"Well, I am." Myra cut him off.

At least Flossie and Silas were both flushing, exhibiting signs of attraction.

"Last question." Mitch bent forward. "What does manna taste like? Milk and honey." Mitch's whisper tickled her ear.

This was madness. The worst of it was, it wasn't entirely unpleasant when his words sent shivers over her skin.

In the end, Mitch and Grace tied with Bess and Elmer with perfect marks. Myra, Nell, and Flossie were quick to leave their partners to gather the refreshments from the kitchen.

Grace hopped to her feet before Mitch could offer her a hand up. "I'm going to help with dessert." The words came out in a blur.

Mitch's brows knit, but she spun away. In the kitchen, she picked up the plate of sliced cheese she'd brought tonight and sidled to Nell, who prepared a tray of coffee cups. "Want a piece before I take it out? You know the men will make quick work of it."

Nell's cheeks were fuller than the night she'd fainted, but not much. It was gratifying when she took a slice of the nutritious snack. "How about you?"

Grace's throat closed. "I'm not hungry."

"Come on." Flossie carried a platter of cookies. Nell and Grace followed suit with their offerings. As predicted, the fellows swarmed the table.

Grace stood back. She should be observing her matches, but that was impossible when the men and women socialized in separate groups. Besides, she couldn't concentrate, the way her heart pounded in her chest like a caged bird, beating to get out.

She couldn't bear it anymore. Her symptoms listed in her head like a checklist. "I'll be right back," she whispered to Bess. Then she dashed out the door.

Chapter Five

Grace ran the half-block to the clinic but stopped on the porch. She didn't need to give Pa apoplexy by bursting in and frightening him. Still, the bell over the door jangled at her entrance, which would alert him to her presence.

"Just me." She spoke loud enough for him to hear without awakening Mrs. Dooley, if the poor lady dozed.

Pa poked his head over the landing. "Grace?"

"Just wanted to look up. . .something."

He nodded and disappeared. Grace picked up the single kerosene lamp burning in the entry and carried it to the office, where Pa's books lined the shelves. From upstairs, Pa and Mrs. Dooley's voices carried down.

She ruffled through one book. Then another.

Loss of appetite. Difficulty sleeping. Trembling limbs. Nervous disorders. Maybe heart, too, but her symptoms didn't match anything she found. Her hand flew to her lips. "Am I dying?"

"Grace?"

She spun. A shadowy figure stood in the threshold. Mitch.

The book fell to the floor with a resounding thump. "I didn't hear the bell."

"I came in the back." He scooped up the book and handed it to her. He didn't touch her, but he might as well have. Her skin shivered and her lungs tightened.

She turned away to replace Pa's medical books. "Checking on Mrs. Dooley?"

"Checking on you. You left in a hurry, without your cloak or bonnet."

"I'm coming back." She brushed past him without touching him, but he caught her elbow. His light grip anchored her to the spot.

"What are you looking up?"

"I'm not sure, actually." It wasn't a lie.

"Maybe I can help."

"I don't think you can." Her teeth caught her lower lip, and his hand fell.

"Of course. You prefer your pa as your physician." Did a look of hurt flash across his features? It was hard to tell in this dim light.

"That's not it. I think I'm just tired." Her hands met over her empty belly and clenched together.

His palm covered her forehead. Must have found it cool, for it fell away, leaving an imprint of fire. "You look tired."

The usual Grace would laugh. But tonight, her insides twisted along with her fingers. "I'll get to bed earlier tonight."

"Try some warm milk first. I'll go fetch your cloak and bonnet. And that tray you brought the cheese on. I can leave them here for you—"

"No, I'll go back. I don't wish to be rude." Yet she'd bolted from the gathering like her hem was on fire.

Mitch's expression was disbelieving, too. But then he sighed and gestured that she should precede him into the foyer.

Grace craned her neck to call up the stairs. "Leaving again, Pa." He wouldn't answer back. She returned the lamp to its correct spot and folded her arms to signal she wouldn't take Mitch's arm. He frowned and opened the front door. The cool night air stung her cheeks and sent her already shivering skin into gooseflesh.

He shrugged out of his coat. "Put this on."

It landed on her shoulders, heavy and warm and smelling of bay. Part of her wanted to refuse. The other—stronger—part wanted to wrap in the coat and not give it back. She gripped the lapels. "Won't you be cold?"

"I'm never cold."

It was a typical Mitch thing to say, so silly yet spoken so seriously. She didn't need to look at him to know his mouth twisted in a grin.

Despite her anxiety, she grinned, too. "I'll remind you that you said that in January, when icicles dangle from your hat."

But then her smile fell. Mitch wouldn't be here in January.

He didn't answer, either. In fact, they didn't speak the rest of the walk. On the Hawkinses' porch, she divested his coat and handed it back with a quick "thank you" and hurried inside.

Myra peeled from the group. "There you two are."

"Sorry. I needed something." Grace tried to smile.

Mitch moved past her, donning his coat—oh dear, now everyone knew she wore his coat. What must they think?

Myra eyed them askance but then shrugged. "We've just planned a picnic by the river tomorrow after church. Join us?"

"Depends on my mother." Mitch took the cup of coffee she offered. "She had a good day, though."

Bess sat alone on the maroon plush sofa in the corner, wide-eyed and patting the empty spot beside her in a none-too-subtle invitation. Grace took the seat.

"What happened?" Impatient Bess wasted no time with her interrogation. "You were wearing Mitch's coat?"

"He thought I was cold."

"Where were you? You slipped out the door and Mitch got agitated as a wet cat. Then he rushed after you. I thought he followed you to the *necessary*," Bess whispered.

"He wouldn't have followed me *there*. Besides, the necessary's out back not out front."

"You're right. I wasn't thinking. Just marveling at you two."

There was no *two* about it. She glanced at the others, who engaged in a hearty conversation about tomorrow's picnic. Maybe she should confide in Bess.

She took a deep breath. "Please don't say anything yet, not even to Elmer, but Mitch is leaving Emerald. He feels called to start his own clinic, and he won't compete with Pa by setting up a rival clinic."

Bess gaped. "What a shock."

"I can't blame Mitch, because Pa gets so angry when Mitch prays in the clinic. Even tonight, Pa found us praying for Mrs. Dooley, and I know poor Mitch will hear about it later."

"That's a conundrum, for certain. Faith isn't something you put in a box and take out when you feel like it, like a hat. It's part of you. Your whole self."

"I know. This insistence of Pa's is the only thing in my life I wish were different. Everything else is perfect. Working with Pa and Mitch at the clinic. You in town. Our group."

"Until some of us have children, or—oh, Grace, don't cry."

"I'm not." She blinked back the traitorous tears. "You sound like Mitch. He reminded me you'll move out to the farm, and I won't see you as often."

"It's not just me who's changing, Grace." Bess took Grace's hand. "You are, too."

"No, I'm not. I'm still me."

"Of course you're you, but you're not the carefree girl you were when we met. We all change, inside and out."

"I think something's wrong with me, Bess."

Bess's dark brows met in a concerned line. "What's the matter?"

"Since Mitch told me he was leaving, I've been miserable. That's understandable, of course. Yet when he's around, I'm less miserable. Almost giddy, because I want to spend time with him before he goes away. All of that makes sense, but it's so extreme, I think I have a nervous malady. That's why I went to the clinic now, to find a condition in Pa's books that might explain my other symptoms."

"What are they? I don't have your experience, but maybe I can help."

What would it hurt? "I can't sleep or eat. I'm anxious. My heart beats hard when I'm not exercising or frightened. And when Mitch touched me tonight—nothing improper at all—my bones felt like butter, and my skin—I have chills but not the kind that accompany fever."

"Does it happen when I touch you?" Bess lifted their clasped hands.

"No. It comes and goes, I suppose. I should write that down."

"Darling." Bess leaned forward. "You are the smartest woman I know, but you are a slow-top with this. You're in love with Mitch."

"No, I'm not." The words blurted out.

"Bones to butter? Chills at his touch?"

Grace's head shook. Hard. "Those aren't measurable signs of attraction, not like flushed cheeks and racing pulse. Which I don't have."

"I didn't tell you about the shivers." Bess pinked. "Or the nights I spent awake thinking of Elmer."

"No. If this isn't a malady, it's a reaction to losing his friendship—"

"Oh, honey. You've always loved Mitch. Think of your hypothesis. You're attuned to him. You make his favorite foods to please him. You can't stop watching him, oh yes, I caught you just now."

Grace's jaw clenched.

Bess smiled. "You and he make each other better, in the clinic and out of it. But his intention to leave has accelerated things."

Love Mitch? Grace shook her head. "It doesn't matter. The first principle of my theory is the couple must both wish to marry. He's an unwavering bachelor, due to his parents' difficult marriage. He and I are not compatible in that way."

Bess's eyes crinkled in sympathy. "Let the idea simmer a while."

"Simmer?" Elmer broke from the group and fell at Bess's feet. "You gals talking 'bout what you're bringing to the picnic tomorrow?"

"I was thinking pork pasties because you like them, dear." Bess tapped the top of her fiancé's head but glanced at Grace as if to say they'd talk later. Then she looked up at Mitch, who'd followed Elmer. "What do you want for the picnic?"

"Blueberry pie," Grace answered for him. "Always."

Mitch laughed. "Can you blame me? It's the secret ingredients in Grace's filling. Any jars left in the cellar?"

"One or two." Grace's cheeks warmed. Was Bess right? She'd prepared extra jars last summer because she knew how much Mitch liked the recipe. And she liked baking for him.

She did love him. His messy curls. His big heart. The way he smiled at her now.

Bess nudged her. "Secret ingredients?"

"That's between us." Mitch wagged a finger. Then he spun around, in answer to a call from Silas. "Sure, I'll play battledore tomorrow."

"Should be an enjoyable picnic." Bess peered at Grace with raised brows and a saucy smile.

Or the worst picnic ever. She stood. "I'd better go home and start that pie."

And figure out what she would do with the knowledge that she loved Mitch, just in time to lose him altogether.

◆ ◆ ◆

Mitch loved these picnic days after worship services. Perfect weather, good company, fine food, and exercise. He lunged for the cork-and-feather shuttlecock, swinging his wooden racket. He landed on his side on the grass as the racket connected, hitting the birdie back to Silas and Irvin's side of the court they'd marked with rocks on the grassy bank of the Platte River.

Good thing he wore his dark trousers, the way he slid on the morning-wet grass. Still, they were church-quality trousers, too fine for sport, but he hadn't had time to change considering their group had left directly after Sunday services for the river. They'd picnicked on the ladies' fine cooking and now relaxed at various pursuits. Other parishioners had come to enjoy the fine spring weather, too, but not Ma, who'd stayed home from church after a bad night. He'd offered to stay home with her, but she sent him off with a laugh, declaring picnics a thing for the young. He didn't agree, but everyone here was shorter on years, including a gaggle of screeching children, dipping their toes in the frigid waters of the Platte.

He'd helped usher a few of those little ones into the world. Watched them grow. *God, I will start my own practice because You've told me it's time, but I can't say I'm totally happy about it. Still, I trust You.*

Mitch scrambled upright, ready for the return.

"Excellent hit." Lou, his teammate, swung at the birdie. He missed.

"Aw, nice effort, Lou." Flossie, who perched at the side of the so-called court, shook her head in sympathy.

"Shouldn't you cheer for my side? We earned the point." Silas, Flossie's match according to Grace, shook his head.

Flossie rolled her eyes. "Hey, ho, for everyone."

"Replace me?" Mitch extended the racket to her. "I could use another slice of pie."

Grinning, she took the racket. "That fine by you, Lou?"

Lou's cheeks flushed, and not from exertion. "Just fine."

"Fine by us, too." Silas thumped Irvin's bicep. "I doubt Flossie will follow Mitch's example and dirty her Sunday dress to beat us."

"Watch me." Flossie hoisted the racket over her head, tossed the birdie into the air, and smacked it.

"Well done, Floss." Lou's besotted smile told Mitch where things stood.

Grace wouldn't like it, though. She sat alone on the red-checked cloth they'd shared with Bess and Elmer, who now strolled along the river. Grace watched Mitch approach, her lips pressed into a straight line.

She should be happier, with love blossoming among their friends and on such a fine day. The pine-and-grass scented air filled his lungs, cool and clear. Above, a blue sky dotted with lamb's wool clouds formed a canopy over the mountains, and below, mint and wildflowers poked through the grass. Blue columbine, white flowers he couldn't name, and purple bee balm—*monarda*. He'd have to come back to collect it for poultices. He and Grace could gather the herbs together, like they'd done countless times.

Except that something had changed. Grace didn't want to talk to him about what bothered her. Mayhap she suffered a female malady and was embarrassed to share with him. He could understand that.

But her distant behavior made it all sting. Today, her gaze darted to him then fled, as if looking at him hurt her eyes.

That, more than anything, wrenched his heart like a wet rag. They had so little time left together. He set aside his pain and determined to enjoy being with Grace while he could.

He lay beside her, propping his head on his fist. "Plenty of bee balm thataway."

"Plenty of other stuff thataway, too." Without being asked, Grace cut him a second slice of blueberry pie and slid it onto his plate. "Silas doesn't like Flossie playing against him."

"If he loved her, I don't think he'd care if she was his opponent or his teammate. He'd be happy just to be near her." Mitch felt that way about Grace. It was fun when they were on the same side, like the Bible quiz, but when they weren't, he couldn't get enough of watching her. Cheering for her.

"They're a scientific match, though." Grace's cheeks pinked as she dunked the silver dipper into the water jug and refilled his cup. "She batted her eyes at him in church, remember?"

The cold liquid refreshed him, inside and out. "Maybe she was flirting. Maybe she had a speck in her eye."

"You're an incorrigible tease. Don't forget, she's always late. He's early. Complementary traits."

"Her tardiness hasn't improved a lick since you paired her with punctual Silas." Even from here, it was clear Silas harangued Irvin for failing to connect with the birdie. "I think he wants to win. That's more competitive than complementary."

She sat straighter. "Males of several species show off for potential mates. Silas could be acting out because he wants to look good in front of Flossie."

Silas threw the racket to the ground. "He's not doing well, if that's the case."

Irvin, bashful, nonconfrontational fellow that he was, didn't respond but handed the racket off to a watching Myra.

"Why didn't Myra defend Irvin? She's supposed to be the bold one in their relationship. I'd have expected her to stand up for him." Grace frowned.

"She'd rather play battledore, I s'pose."

Irvin ambled over to Nell's blanket and plopped beside her with a laugh. Nell laughed, too. Loudly. Mitch hid his smile by bending over his plate to scrape the last vestiges of blueberry sauce onto his fork.

"I don't understand. They're both so shy."

"Not with one another, I guess." Mitch sat up. "Grace—"

"I know that tone. You have something to tell me." She blanched. "If it's about last night—"

"It wasn't, but now that you mention it, if you want to—"

"I can't." Her head shook, wobbling the curly tendrils on her shoulders. "I'm sorry."

"Grace, you're scaring me." More than usual. The woman was the most frightening thing that had ever happened to him. Most beautiful, too.

"Don't tease me, Mitch."

"I'm not teasing." This was going all wrong. Just like her matchmaking.

"What did you want to talk about? Is it Pa? He didn't say anything about us praying with Mrs. Dooley, by the way."

He stilled her with his hand. "I can handle your father. We differ on some important matters, but we respect one another."

"Of course you do. He'll understand there's work enough for two clinics in Emerald. You'll stay in town, then?" Her face lightened, as if twin candles flickered behind her eyes.

His hand pulled back. "I won't compete with him, sweetheart."

He'd never called her that. Shouldn't have done it now. She twisted away, and the brim of her straw bonnet hid her face. Was she that offended?

"Then what?" She still wouldn't look up at him. "You've got a job already?"

"I haven't sent queries yet." He took a deep breath. "I wanted to talk about your hypothesis."

Chapter Six

Grace clambered to her knees and gathered the dishes. She didn't want to talk anymore, now that she utterly embarrassed herself by revealing how much she wanted Mitch to stay. She dropped the used forks into a mason jar with a clatter.

"You're upset about the hypothesis." Mitch wrapped their cups in their soiled napkins and placed them on top of the dishes in the hamper—just the way she liked them packed. He knew her habits so well.

Why had she taken him for granted for five years?

"No, I'm not." She was a sturdy, sensible, scientifically minded woman. She didn't boo-hoo over a faulty hypothesis any more than she did spilled buttermilk. "But I am upset the matches didn't work. These are people I've trifled with."

"No one seems to mind. Look. Love is in the air." He stood and helped her do the same.

Irvin—shy, uptight Irvin—sprawled supine on Nell's picnic blanket, the picture of ease as he gazed up at the sky. Nell—usually timid—wore a sly smile as she sat beside him, plucking clumps of grass and showering them over Irvin's face. He took her hands and set them back on her lap. Not a second passed before she ripped more grass and rained it over him again. Irvin took her hands again and set them on her lap. Again. She reached for more grass.

They were enjoying this.

Over on the makeshift battledore court, Lou cheered Flossie. If he minded that his scientifically made match, Nell, drizzled grass over another man, he didn't show it, for his gaze didn't leave Flossie. The game seemed to have stalled while the couples chatted. Irvin's scientific match, Myra, folded her arms at Silas, who bounced the birdie on his racket and counted how many times he'd done so without dropping the birdie. He was on thirty-five when Myra mussed his neat, Macassar-slick hair.

Grace gasped. As town barber, Silas was proud of his tidy coiffure. But he didn't protest the indignity at all. Instead, he yanked Myra's dark curls.

Silas's scientific match, Flossie, didn't notice any of it, considering she doubled over laughing at whatever Lou just said.

Just because Lou had been watching Nell when she fainted didn't mean he was attuned to her. Irvin and Nell might be shy with everyone else, but not with each other. Flossie's tardiness didn't bother Lou at all, and Silas's promptness seemed his least-interesting trait where Myra was concerned.

The flushes Grace had observed and recorded in her journal...they didn't signify attraction. They could as easily have been the results of frustration or embarrassment or even being overwarm.

The snap of fabric drew her back to Mitch. He shook grass from the picnic blanket and folded it in an untidy lump. "See what I mean?"

"Each lady I matched is now frolicking with a different gentleman, and no one seems the least bit unhappy about it."

"Don't take it personally."

"I missed something." It was easier to talk science than mull over her breaking heart. "Biological reactions?"

"Or another scientific field altogether, perhaps. Chemistry."

"This has nothing to do with elements." She took the blanket and handed him his coat, which she'd folded when he removed it for his game of battledore. His sleeves were still rolled up to his elbows, revealing the corded veins and muscles of his forearms—

Oh dear. Now she understood what Mitch meant.

That sort of chemistry.

"Sparks fly, or they don't. It's a reminder, I suppose. God is the best matchmaker."

Well, sparks were certainly flying now that Mitch took her elbow to escort her home. His light touch ignited her nerves like a match to a Roman candle.

It didn't help that Bess waved good-bye with a cheeky grin. Grace steered her thoughts back toward science, where things were safe. "Does that mean God didn't give us the wisdom to recognize indicators of a strong match?"

"That's not what I said. Just that He knows what's inside a person. The secret hurts and struggles and strengths. Things no one else sees. Things we don't always see about ourselves."

Grace certainly hadn't known what was inside her where Mitch was concerned. "You're right."

"That doesn't mean all is lost with your matchmaking. There's no such thing as a failed experiment, remember? If the results don't align with your hypothesis, the data isn't wasted. It becomes research for a new hypothesis. You can test different criteria now."

Grace laughed. "I won't be matchmaking again."

"Why not?"

"Folks are pairing up fine without me. Besides, a twenty-five percent success rate is abysmal. I'll let things take their natural courses."

"Don't forget, Myra and Flossie and Nell asked for your help. You didn't promise true love, just your interpretation of evidence. No one can blame you, and I don't think they do. You started them on the right paths."

That was something she'd always appreciated about Mitch. His kind tone, straightforward facts, and unconditional friendship comforted her like nothing else.

"I'm sorry your mother couldn't make it to church today."

"I loved her visit last night, but she overdid it. She's sore today but not so fatigued she can't nag me about how she won't leave Emerald. And if she won't leave, I can't leave. She can't be alone when she suffers from her pain spells."

Grace sighed. Poor Mrs. Shaw. And poor Mitch. "I don't know how, but it'll work out."

It had to. Even if she and Mrs. Shaw didn't get what they wanted. Grace had to trust God with all of this.

They passed the church and turned toward her house. "Will you come inside?" She could fix a plate for his mother. Or he'd help her with the dishes. Either way, he'd be with her.

He nodded. "I want to check on Mrs. Dooley."

Of course. She admired his dedication to his patients even as she wished, selfishly, that he wanted to come in for her.

Again, science—or at least doctoring—was the safer subject. "What do you think ails her? I know you can't find a diagnosis. You've telegraphed more colleagues and devoured more journal articles than I can count. But what does your instinct tell you?"

Mitch hoisted his coat over his shoulder. "That she's dying. But I don't know why or when. This is one of those mysteries I may not be able to solve. It's frustrating, because if we only knew what ailed her, maybe we could treat her."

"You're doing all you can. Treating her suffering, caring for her, working on her behalf. Praying for her healing, either on earth or by being taken to God's side."

Mitch's smile warmed her to her toes. "Thanks, Grace. I needed to hear that."

They'd reached her house and walked the narrow path between the house and the clinic. "I'll go with you to visit with Mrs. Dooley. Come with me to drop off the hamper, first?"

"Of course." Mitch opened the kitchen door for her. "Maybe if there's any pie left—"

"Had fun today, you two?" Pa's voice met them when they crossed the threshold, but his tone was hard. Cold, even. Grace couldn't make out his expression after being out in the bright sunlight, but surely she'd misheard the harshness in his tenor.

"Pa?" She stepped forward. "I thought you'd be at the clinic. We were just heading there now."

"Were you." It wasn't a question the way Pa said it. Now that Grace's eyes adjusted, it was evident Pa's hands shook and his mouth set in a grim line.

Mitch set the hamper on the table. "How's Mrs. Dooley?"

"Dead."

Grace gasped at Pa's blunt response. "Oh! I'm so sorry."

Mitch shook his head. "What a shame."

Grace's mind whirled with questions. What would they do? Who would take care of Mrs. Dooley's cat? Was there any family to come? She settled on one. "When, Pa?"

"While you two were frolicking on the riverbank."

Grace's head hung like a scolded dog's. Her father might be upset and frustrated over Mrs. Dooley's loss, but he never spoke to her like this. Never shamed her.

Mitch stepped between her and Pa. "I'm sorry I wasn't here."

"It wouldn't have helped. Nothing you've done for her helped. Not bringing in that cat, and certainly not your worthless prayers." He snorted.

"The cat made her calm. Our prayers gave her fellowship. God gave her comfort through them. He heard, even if He didn't answer how we wanted Him to."

"No God talk in this clinic. Or this house."

That was enough. Grace pushed around Mitch. "I live here, too, Pa. I won't stop praying or talking about God, and you know it."

But his furious gaze hadn't torn from Mitch's. "No more in the clinic, hear?"

"I understand."

"Good."

"That's why I'm going to start my own practice." Mitch's tone and expression remained calm, kind. Grace's heart swelled with admiration for him, even as it broke for losing him.

Pa blinked. "That's pride talking, Mitch."

"For a while now, I've felt God's call to head my own practice. I've appreciated every moment of our time together. Your training and encouragement made me the doctor I am."

Pa spun to Grace. "You knew this?"

She nodded. "I don't like it, but I can't argue with God."

"Well, I can." Pa threw up his hands.

Then his arms drooped, like he was a marionette whose strings had been cut. Grace dove forward, gripping his shoulders. "Pa?"

She couldn't bear his weight. He dropped to the kitchen floor, taking her down with him.

◆   ◆   ◆

Mitch sprang behind Grace, seizing Sidney. "Open the clinic, Grace."

Wide-eyed with fear, Grace nodded and dashed ahead, flinging wide the kitchen door for him. Mitch hoisted Sidney in his arms, no easy task considering his mentor's bulk. Mitch kicked the door shut behind him and hurried to the clinic, following the path of light to the first examination room as Grace flung wide the curtains.

"Sidney? Can you hear me?" Mitch lowered him to the table. No response, no noise but a *scritch* accompanied by a whiff of sulfur as Grace struck a match for the lamps.

Some family members panicked when their loved ones were in medical crisis. Not Grace. She must be frightened, but the moment the lamps were lit, she busied herself with unbuttoning Sidney's shirt and loosening his shoelaces.

Mitch would have to acknowledge her bravery later. Now, every second mattered.

Sidney's pulse was irregular and weak. His breath came in short, wheezing gasps. "Prop him up. He isn't getting enough air."

Grace jostled pillows under her father's head. "Is it his heart? It is, isn't it? Oh, Mitch."

If he could take the time to comfort her, he would, but all he could spare at the moment was a quick squeeze of her arm before he pushed Sidney's shirt aside, revealing dark, purpling skin stretched taut and shiny over his chest and arms.

Mitch reached for his stethoscope. "Has he complained of chest pain? Breathlessness?"

Her head shook.

"Has he been drinking more than usual?"

"He said I used too much salt the past few days, for he couldn't slake his thirst." She stepped back and swiped her eyes with the heel of her hand. "What can I do?"

"Pray."

And she did, folding her father's clothes while Mitch listened through the stethoscope and palpated Sidney's swollen abdomen. When he stepped back, she draped a sheet over her father. "He looks cold, with his toes blue like that."

"Stay with him. I'll be right back."

He dashed to the office and yanked open the medicine cabinet. Aloe, alum, ammonium carbonate—his gaze skittered down, past camphor. There it was. He grabbed the correct bottle.

"Mitch! He's coming to."

His chest expelled a mighty breath. "Thank You, God." He jogged back to the exam room.

Sidney blinked. "What's all this fuss?"

Mitch checked his pupils. "Dropsy, sir. Your heart is enlarged. It's not effectively pumping blood, and fluid has built up in your tissues. I'll run tests—you know the procedure. But I'd like to start digitalis now."

Sidney rolled his eyes. "Sounds about right."

"Dropsy?" Grace took her father's fingers. "Didn't you notice the symptoms, Pa? Retaining liquid, shortness of breath?"

"Of course I noticed." Sidney grunted. "Didn't want to think about it."

"You know doctors, Grace. We often make the worst patients, and we consider others' health before our own." Mitch measured out the dose.

"I should have noticed." Grace laid her forehead against her father's. "I've been so focused on my—matchmaking. I'm sorry."

"Don't be ridiculous, Gracie. Now, help me with the medicine cup." Sidney obediently took the dose. A grimace rippled his features. "Foul stuff."

"I'll add cinnamon to your next dose." Grace smiled and lowered his head back to the goose down pillows.

Cinnamon—one of her two secret ingredients for blueberry pie. Mitch smiled and jotted down the dosage and time of administration. "I'll stay tonight to monitor you, Sidney."

"Are you sure?" Grace's brows knit. "What about your mother?"

"She'll understand. I'll send a note 'round." Although Mitch didn't like leaving her alone tonight. He'd have to trust God to care for her.

"Wait to write the note until we've seen how Pa does with the digitalis. If things improve—"

"I know you're capable of nursing him, Grace. But whether or not he rallies, Ma or no Ma, I'm staying here tonight." He owed it to Sidney, his patient and friend, to watch over him. And talk things out, if God willed it.

Her hands fisted on her hips. "That's not what I was going to say at all, Mitchell Shaw. I wanted you to tell your mother I'll stay with her tonight, if it's safe for me to leave Pa's side. But you, Pa, will comply with Mitch's orders, do you hear me?"

"I've got edema, not hearing loss." Sidney shut his eyes.

Warmth suffused Mitch's chest—like his own form of dropsy, where his heart swelled with affection and gratitude. "Ma will love that, you know."

"A ladies' night, just the two of us." Grace smiled. "Well, that's not entirely true."

"What balderdash is this?" Sidney's eyelids opened.

"You're planning on inviting someone to my house?" And who? Despite his best intentions, Mitch's innards clenched with jealousy.

Grace fussed with the sheeting over her father. "Someone handsome, if I may say so."

This sort of flirtation wasn't like Grace, and Ma didn't need menfolk parading through her house when she was rheumatic. Mitch dunked the pen in the inkwell stand with more force than necessary.

"Oh, Mitch." Grace laughed and squeezed his arm. "Don't worry. She'll love it."

Ma might. Grace might, too, and he wanted to see her happy.

But Lord help him, he didn't love the sound of this a lick.

Chapter Seven

Despite Grace's efforts to hurry, it was dark before she let herself into Mitch's house. "Mrs. Shaw? It's Grace."

"In the parlor."

Grace latched the bolt behind her and carried her bags to the gold-papered room where Mrs. Shaw snuggled in her usual chair. Her favorite green quilt spread over her knees.

"What a day you've had." Mrs. Shaw pushed herself up. The effort made her wince.

Grace deposited her bags on the sofa and rushed to assist Mitch's mother. "Are you uncomfortable? What can I do?"

"Nothing just now. So nice of you to come, Grace. I'm sorry about Mrs. Dooley and your pa." Her tongue clicked. "Mitch's note said he's already showing signs of improvement."

"Digitalis works fast. Some of Pa's habits must change, but—thank you." She mustn't spill her worries onto Mrs. Shaw. "You had a rough night, I heard."

"Just tired after my walk to your house last night. Maybe Mitchell's right and I should exercise more."

"Let's take a brief constitutional in the morning, then."

Mrs. Shaw sighed then nodded. "Enough of that. Mitch's note said you had something intriguing in store for tonight."

"Ah, yes." Grace dropped to her haunches and pointed to the first hamper. "Supper of pork roast with dried apples."

"Tasty but not intriguing."

"You'll like this one better." Grace opened the second hamper, a worn, splintery thing which her mother had used decades ago. To Grace's pleasure, Mrs. Shaw bent forward, eyes wide, no trace of pain etching her features.

"Well?" Mrs. Shaw squinted.

Grace had thought when she opened the lid, he'd come right out. Instead he licked his paw. This cat was the laziest creature in Colorado. She scooped her hands underneath Bertie's warm girth and lifted. More like heaved. What did he weigh, anyway?

Mrs. Shaw gasped. "Who is this ginger-winger pumpkin-bumpkin?"

Grace lowered the hefty cat to Mrs. Shaw's lap, where it snuggled into the soft folds of the quilt. "This is Bertie, Mrs. Dooley's cat. I didn't want him to be lonesome tonight. I hope you don't mind."

"Missing his mama, poor baby-waby." Mrs. Shaw's gnarled hands rubbed his broad back. "Aren't you the sweetest widdle baby?"

Little? Ha. "Do you want to eat supper in here again?"

"That'd be fine, Grace. Bertie-wertie needs supper, too, I reckon. Don't you, hungwy-widdle baby?" She glanced up. "What does he like to eat?"

From the looks of him, everything.

"I don't know. I suspect he's not much of a mouser, though." Grace managed not to snicker.

"We'll see about that, widdle Bertie-wertie." Mrs. Shaw continued to coo while Grace fixed two plates. She'd hoped to solve two problems tonight: Bertie needed a home, and Mrs. Shaw could use cheering.

They spoke of Pa's dropsy and Mrs. Dooley's funeral arrangements while they finished their meals and Bertie nibbled from Mrs. Shaw's fingers. Then Mrs. Shaw shifted in her seat, adjusting Bertie to a different position. "How are your matches, dear? Will wedding bells ring?"

"I'm certain they will, just not for the matches I made, aside from Bess and Elmer." Grace tidied up while she explained the day's pairings at the picnic. "Nell and Irvin. Flossie and Lou. Silas and Myra, all after I matched them to other partners. It's like they all woke up today and noticed one another."

"It's possible. Sometimes love appears sudden-like and without warning. Other times, though, it lies dormant, a seed in a field. Then, with the sun's warmth and spring rain, something sprouts and pushes its way to the surface." Her eyes held a curious gleam, much like Bertie's had when he licked pork from her fingers.

Grace's hand pressed over her thumping heart. That was how it was with Mitch; Grace could see that now. The seed of her feelings for him had planted in the soil of her heart a long time ago. Had Mrs. Shaw understood it all along?

She hesitated, still holding the plates. She could hide in the kitchen and scrub dishes. Or she could sit back down again and seek a mother's advice.

Grace set the plates on the coffee table and curled at Mrs. Shaw's feet, leaning back on her palms. "Did Mitch tell you I offered to make him a match?"

Mrs. Shaw's fingers stroked the plane between Bertie's eyes. "He didn't tell me, but I reckon he declined."

"It was a desperate, selfish ploy to keep him in town. But you're right, he passed. He's a resolute bachelor." Did the words sound tart? She hadn't intended it, but the tone slipped out.

"I thought he'd change his mind when the right young lady came along. But that's not why he turned you down flat as a flapjack. He doesn't want *any* match. Not when he's in love."

"He is?" The pork and apples in her stomach mutinied. Grace covered her mouth.

"Don't play coy—oh, you're never coy, are you, dear? You truly don't know he's besotted with you." Mrs. Shaw's eyes crinkled with pity.

When Grace was able to breathe again, air came in gasps. "He's not." Was he?

Mrs. Shaw cackled. "He's never spoken a word of it, but a mother can tell. Just like I know Bertie is comfy-womfy on my lap. Yes, you are, widdle pumpkin."

Bertie blinked at Grace, as if judging her for her lack of understanding, too. But Mitch had never indicated…had he? Grace's insides twisted with disbelief and hope and happiness—and then she realized that even if Mrs. Shaw was right, it didn't matter.

"He's leaving Emerald."

"So stop him. You love him, too. It's as plain on your face as your freckles."

Did everyone know her feelings before she did? "I can't argue with God's plan, and frankly, I think it's time for Mitch to head his own clinic. He's an excellent doctor, but that's not the biggest obstacle. Mitch holds a high regard for marriage, but he's made it quite clear he won't marry, himself."

"I'm responsible for that, I fear. I shouldn't have put Mitch in the middle like I did. His pa was always working, and on those few occasions he was home, he couldn't read my mind about how much I wanted him around." Mrs. Shaw cringed. "I'm not proud of how I treated him, berating him instead of telling him how I felt. He's the one who chose to *wander elsewhere* after one too many arguments, but I didn't help matters. Neither of us sought the Lord to help repair things. And Mitch paid the highest price of all."

Grace had never heard of Mitch's father's adultery. Just allusions here and there to arguments and standoffs.

"Love is a lot more complicated than I want it to be." Her mismatches were proof of that. She almost laughed. She was Miss Matched—mismatched—after all. She'd paired things that didn't fit together.

"No one ever said love—of any kind—is easy. I said things to Mitch I shouldn't have, to keep him from uprooting us from Emerald. Love that boy to pieces, yet I'm still capable of stabbing him through the heart with my words. How is that loving?"

Grace's finger plucked the rug. "The two men I love most in the world are in the clinic, one's ill and the other leaving town, and they're probably fighting."

Mrs. Shaw's hands left Bertie for the first time since Grace arrived with the cat. "Oh, Gracie. Love is tomfool crazy, whether it's for your man or your kin or a cat. But it gives you the strength to work for your beloved's best. You keep on loving them, you hear? Even if neither comes around. Mitch may cut off his nose to spite his face and miss out on a loving life with you. Your pa may doom himself to a life of anger at God and reject His blessings. But you keep loving them and praying for them and working for their best, and I'll seek His help so I can do the same."

Bertie nodded. Maybe he was falling asleep, but Grace preferred to think he agreed with Mrs. Shaw. A laugh bubbled to her lips—happy. Restful. She couldn't change the minds of either Mitch or Pa—or God, calling Mitch to head a clinic—but she could trust God to accomplish His purposes.

She stood and kissed Mrs. Shaw's forehead. "I love you, too, you know."

"Of course I know that. You're sweet as taffy, sharp as a pin, and the best fit for my Mitch. Why else have I been playing matchmaker, praying for five years for you to be my daughter-in-law?"

◆　◆　◆

Mitch stood over Sidney's bed and tugged the stethoscope's earpieces from his ears. "Swelling's going down already and your heart sounds much better. Want to listen for yourself, Doctor?"

"No need. You're more than competent." Another heartfelt compliment of Sidney's.

Mitch chuckled and returned the stethoscope to his bag. "I'll check on you in a few hours. Unless you need something else?"

"One thing. I want to talk to you about what you said before I—you know." He gestured toward his heart. "You're leaving the practice?"

Mitch hoisted a bentwood chair bedside the bed and sat down. "You've taught me so much, Sidney. I'm not ungrateful, but it's time I head my own clinic."

"Can't say I'm surprised, the way I've pushed you away."

"It's true that I can't leave my faith at the clinic door. God works miracles and healing, and I can't do my job without Him. But I don't want to leave. Not Emerald or you or—Grace." Had Sidney heard the catch in his voice? Mitch rubbed the back of his neck. "I hope you understand."

Sidney nodded. "Not easy to say this, but you'll be missed."

"You have an asset in Grace." An understatement if he'd ever uttered one.

"She'd have made a fine doctor. Don't know why she wouldn't try medical school."

"Because she never felt called to it. She likes how things are."

"You're not going to try to take her with you, then?"

So Sidney had noticed Mitch's affections. Well, it didn't matter. "She wouldn't go if I asked. Grace thinks of me as a friend."

"Grace thinks of you as a resolute bachelor. You've made that point quite clear over the years."

That. Mitch propped his elbows on his knees. "I'm not sure that was God's will as much as my fear. But she's not interested in me that way."

"How do you know, eh? You two are the biggest fools in Emerald. After me, o' course, for punishing the Almighty for taking my wife, fighting Him. I know what it's like to lose the woman you love, Mitchell. Broke my faith."

Mitch sat up. "But God didn't break with you."

Sidney sighed. "I know. Got some thinking to do. But so do you. You love Grace, and don't you deny it. Try imagining life without her for a minute. Go on, do it. If you can tell me you're fine living without Grace, I'll drop the subject."

The thought induced panic. Pain.

He didn't even have to speak. Sidney chuckled. "You'd best have a heart-to-heart with my girl. Find out if she'll marry you."

"Hold on there, Sidney. Are you saying what I think you're saying?"

"About you having my blessing to marry Grace? Thought you were quicker witted than that."

Mitch laughed, but pain still sluiced his insides. "Thank you, sir. I mean it. But I couldn't pull her from Emerald. Or you." Especially now that Sidney was ill.

"You're a fool, Mitchell." Sidney patted his shoulder, as if he pitied him.

"A sorry one." Mitch rubbed his forehead, as if the answer lay in his brain somewhere.

He couldn't live without Grace.

Nor could he live with her, away from her father, even if she loved him back.

But he couldn't help hoping that she did.

Chapter Eight

Monday morning, Grace unlocked the clinic and opened it wide for Mrs. Shaw. "Take a seat. You must be winded after the walk over."

Unlike Grace, whose tumbling thoughts kept her awake most of the night. She'd given up, gotten dressed, cleaned house, started oatmeal for breakfast, and soaked beans for supper. She'd prayed while she worked but had no answers. Only the unquenchable desire to hurry home.

Was it Pa? Mitch? The way her heart cleaved in two, Grace was certain it was both.

"As I keep reminding Mitchell, I am not an invalid." Mrs. Shaw settled in one of the plush foyer chairs. "Hand me the hamper. Bertie wants to see."

Grace opened the basket instead, her gaze on the staircase. The menfolk should be awake by now. Unless something was wrong—

The back door slammed shut. "You're a good doctor but not the best cook," Pa said from the direction of the kitchen.

"Pa!" Grace dropped the cat atop Mrs. Shaw's lap as her father and Mitchell ambled into the foyer. "You're out of bed."

Pa's thick brows met. "Mitchell's orders. He said I need to move about."

"He tells me the same thing all the time." Mrs. Shaw rolled her eyes.

Grace patted Pa's whiskered cheek. "I've been worried about you."

Pa patted her cheek back. "I know, poppet. But I'll be fine."

"With rest, treatment, and a few changes of habit." Mitch hugged his mother.

Grace allowed herself to look at him for the first time this morning, really look at him, now that she was assured Pa was fine. If she'd looked at Mitch first, she might never have turned her gaze on anything else.

How could she not have guessed she loved him, all this time? The way his smile crinkled his eyes and coaxed her smiles in return. The way he loved his mother and played with children. The way his strong hands worked to heal. How he looked, even unshaven and wearing yesterday's rumpled clothes—all the more appealing because he'd forsaken a razor and clean shirt to tend to her father. The way he served God, with his body, mind, and spirit. The way he looked at her right now, which weakened her knees and robbed her of breath.

Pa walked between Grace and Mitch, breaking their held gazes. "Got some news for you all—what's this?" He sat beside Mrs. Shaw. "That cat's back?"

Mrs. Shaw covered Bertie's ears with her fingers. "Just to visit. He wants to live with me, don't you, widdle pumpkin?"

Mitch hid his laugh behind his hand.

Grace patted Bertie's head. "If that's well with you, Mitch?"

"Who cares what he thinks?" Mrs. Shaw interrupted. "I'll be alone in that house. If I want Bertie, he stays."

"Calm down, Enid. Mitch isn't going anywhere."

Even Bertie's head turned to Pa.

"What do you mean?" Grace's gaze flitted from Pa to Mitch and back.

"Had long talks with God and Mitch last night. I've decided to make some changes. The first is escorting you to Mrs. Dooley's funeral Saturday, Grace."

"But it's at the church." He hadn't set a toe on the property since Ma died.

"I know. Can't promise I'm not still angry at God, but I'd like to get reacquainted with Him. I'll take you to church Sunday, too."

She wanted to leap for joy but that would embarrass Pa. Instead she nodded. "I'd love your escort."

"Next bit of news—I'm scaling back my hours. To almost zero."

Grace's breath hitched. "You're sicker than you let on."

"On the contrary, I'm keen to try new things. Like see the ocean. So I need to leave the clinic in capable hands. Maybe I can consult once in a while, when I'm in town. And no one's hands are more capable than Mitchell's."

Mitch grinned, unsurprised. They must have discussed it already. "I discerned the call to head a clinic. Turned out this was the clinic God meant, all along."

"Suits me fine," Mrs. Shaw said, as if they were deliberating dinner plans.

"And you, Grace?" Mitch stepped forward. "Does it suit you?"

Her pulse thrummed in her veins. *He wasn't leaving.* "You don't mind staying?"

"I never wanted to leave. Not just Emerald, but—"

The clinic door swung wide on its hinges and a crowd of young people spilled into the foyer. Bess and Elmer, Silas and Myra, Lou and Flossie, Irvin and Nell, all talking one over the other.

"Doc Perkins!" Bess kissed Pa's cheek. "So good to see you up and about."

Pa harrumphed. "Word travels fast."

Elmer shook Mitch's hand. "Lou and I stopped at the flour mill this morning. Heard about Mrs. Dooley. Anything we can do?"

The menfolk spoke of Mrs. Dooley's lack of family, Saturday's service, and the lack of a diagnosis while the women gathered around Mrs. Shaw, exclaiming over Bertie.

"We heard about you, too, Doc Perkins."

"Touch of dropsy. I'll be fine."

"Good, because we want you at the weddings."

More than one?

"Mine and Elmer's in two weeks." Bess pushed a vermillion-flushed Nell forward. "And Nell?"

Irvin took Nell's hand. His other hand held envelopes. "Invitations. Nell and I made it official last night. We're gettin' hitched in three weeks."

"And we owe it all to you, Grace."

Grace gaped. "But I matched you all with the wrong people."

"And started us on the path toward the right ones." Silas winked at Myra. Flossie giggled at Lou.

After handshakes and hugs, the group departed to deliver the rest of their invitations.

"You're going to deliver a few babies this time next year, Mitchell." Pa chortled.

"Back to doing our own laundry, if Nell's marrying the richest man in Emerald." Mrs. Shaw sighed. "But she'll eat well now."

Grace hadn't stopped looking at Mitch. "Can you believe it? The two shyest of the group were the quickest. I guess you're right. With each other, they weren't shy at all."

"Neither am I. Shy, I mean." He gripped her hand. "I have a hypothesis I need your help testing."

Now? She stumbled after him to the office.

He shut the door behind them and pulled her into the room. "Before one creates a hypothesis, one has to encounter a problem to solve, right?"

"Of course." He didn't need her to tell him that, but he smelled of bay and soap and oh, he was still holding her hand.

"So here's my problem." A small smile broke his serious expression. "I love Grace Perkins and want her to be my wife. Want it more than I've ever wanted anything."

She couldn't speak. Couldn't breathe. *He loved her.*

His fingers tightened on hers. "How best to discern if Grace will have me? Research reveals that her theory is sound, so if I use it, I'll be able to tell if we'll be a good match."

"My hypothesis was hooey." There, she found her voice. And it was as husky as if she had catarrh.

"First criteria," he continued as if she hadn't spoken, "are we compatible in our faith and view of marriage?"

She shook her head. "I thought you were happy being a bachelor."

"That choice wasn't God's plan, it was mine. I feared my odd hours and late nights would strain a marriage like it had my parents'. But you don't just understand my work, you're my partner in it. Besides, I realized my mistake the moment I contemplated a life without you. So shall we consider the first criteria satisfied?"

A tiny smile pulled at her lips. "Yes."

"Second criteria: Are we attuned to one another? I say yes. We have two conversations at once sometimes, because we know one another so well. You care about my mother and you make me blueberry pie just to make me happy. Am I right?"

"I never recognized it for what it was, but I do like making you happy. And you support me and catch me when I fall—figuratively and literally, like in the church hall."

"Third criteria. Are there measurable signs of attraction? You tell me." He lifted their joined hands and pressed hers against his chest. His heart pounded hard and fast, like he'd run miles.

"Oh." Heat flooded from her chest all the way to her scalp.

"You're blushing something awful right now and I can see your pulse, quick as a rabbit's, right here." He moved his hand to rest his thumb on her jugular. Bent down a fraction.

"What about—" She swallowed hard against the gentle pressure of his fingers. "Number four?"

"What's number four again?" His breath warmed her cheek as his fingers caressed the back of her neck, under her ears, sending shivers down her arms.

"Comple—mentary traits."

His lips hovered over hers. "You help me be a better doctor. And a better man."

"You—challenge me, too." It was hard to think straight.

"So my hypothesis is that we're a good match." He moved so his lips grazed her ear.

Her breath hitched. "How do you propose testing it?"

"Never mind. Let's skip the testing and just get married."

Grace gasped. Then grinned. "Skip testing? Your conclusion is not according to the scientific method, Doctor—"

"I've wanted to kiss you for five years, Grace. I don't want to wait a minute more." So she lifted her lips.

His kiss was soft at first then more demanding, and she didn't think about science at all.

Then he pulled away, leaving her woozy. His hands skimmed her arms to take her fingers, never breaking contact with her. He lowered to his knees.

Grace's wooziness vanished. "Mitchell!"

"This is no science experiment. It's just me, promising to love you all my days. I know I should court you properly—"

"No."

"No?" He looked stricken.

"No courting. I don't need to get to know you better. You're my best friend. My love. I want to marry you."

Her favorite grin returned. "Then I s'pose I should ask. Will you marry me?"

"Oh, yes, Mitch. Yes. Now will you stand up and kiss me again, please?"

Epilogue

Three months later

Everything in the parish hall was perfect.

"It's beautiful, Bess." Grace Perkins—mere minutes from becoming Grace Shaw—admired the frosted four-layer cake atop the dessert table, waiting alongside Ma's crystal bowl full of strawberry punch, for the wedding reception. Bess, now Mrs. Kohl, had decorated the rustic hall with fresh linens and pink wildflowers, as exquisite as the fragrant white roses Pa ordered from Denver for Grace's bouquet.

Bess fussed with the lace at Grace's throat. "You deserve the best, my dear."

Behind them, a soft swooshing sound announced the banner, hung on grommets with bows, had slipped. Again. The ladies turned.

The banner's middle was an illegible mess of letters. Instead of reading *Congratulations Grace and Mitch*, it said—

"Never mind." Grace took her matron of honor's hand. "Everyone knows what it's supposed to say, and I love it."

Pa bustled into the parish hall, resplendent in his best suit. "Ready, Gracie? Let's show that man of yours how pretty you look."

Grace crooked her arm through Pa's and kissed his cheek. "Thank you, Pa. You look handsome, too."

The trio made their way to the church, watching their steps so as not to stir dust around the lacy hem of Grace's new gown. She was rather fond of the ivory satin trimmed with silk flowers. Would Mitch like it, too?

Silly question. Mitch didn't look at her dress at all. His gaze stayed fixed on hers throughout her short walk down the aisle.

Passing her bouquet to Bess, she glanced at the assembled guests. Pa, gaining strength as he made peace with God. Nell, who, with her mother, had grown more robust since Nell's marriage to Irvin. Silas and Myra, engaged and giddy. Lou and Flossie, not yet betrothed, but inseparable. Bess and best man Elmer, both glowing with the as-yet-secret news that a baby would arrive in the winter, confirmed by Mitch a few days ago.

And Mrs. Shaw in the front pew, pink-cheeked and content, despite having left her companion Bertie home during the service—her new home, an empty room in the clinic. For now, at least. Grace and Mitch had expected her to stay in the white house with them, but she'd moved to give the newlyweds what she called "private time."

She and Mitch wouldn't live with either parent but would see them every day at the clinic.

God was so good, providing for their families' needs. Why had she doubted He would care for them? Grace couldn't stop smiling, not through Mitch's tender vows, not when he took a gold band from Elmer and slipped it onto the fourth finger of her left hand. Especially not when the preacher pronounced them husband and wife.

"You may now kiss your bride."

Mitch's fingers brushed the lace edging of her veil from her cheeks and lowered his lips to hers. It was the smiliest wedding kiss ever, maybe. But how could it not be?

God had Mitch in mind for her all along, her perfect match.

No science experiment required.

Susanne Dietze began writing love stories in high school, casting her friends in the starring roles. Today she's blessed to be the author of over a half-dozen historical romances. Married to a pastor and the mom of two, Susanne loves fancy-schmancy tea parties, genealogy, and curling up on the couch with a costume drama and a plate of nachos. She loves to hear from readers! Come say hi on her website, www.susannedietze.com.

The Backfired Bride

by Kim Vogel Sawyer

Dedication

For Aunt Linda,
whose matchmaking brought The Hubs and me together

*A man's heart deviseth his way: but the L*ORD *directeth his steps.*
PROVERBS 16:9 KJV

Chapter One

Lyla Emerson peeked into her family's post office box, and her heart leaped into hopeful double beats. A large brown envelope, rolled into a tube, awaited removal. Could it be? With trembling fingers, she slid the envelope from the narrow box. The tube unrolled against her palms, and she spotted the stamped return address. She couldn't stifle a little cry of elation.

Her childhood friend, Jared Hardwick, turned from the painted board holding WANTED posters and other bulletins. Curiosity lit his narrow face. "What is it? Good news?"

She nodded so hard her bonnet's strings bounced against her chin. "I haven't opened it yet, but I'm certain it's good news." A denial would come in a letter-sized envelope. Only certificates were mailed in large envelopes. So this surely held her longed-for teaching certificate.

Jared ambled over, his worn heels scuffing up dust from the warped plank floorboards. The postmaster needed to take a broom to these floors more often. "Are you gonna open it and see for sure?"

She clutched the envelope to the bodice of her green calico dress, the same dress she'd worn when she took the test almost three months ago under the county superintendent's watchful gaze. A giggle, high-pitched and breathy, escaped her throat. "I'm half afraid to."

Dreams were wondrous things to ponder in the peacefulness of night, but they were easily shattered in the harsh light of day. What if she hadn't passed the examination? What if she'd have to wait another year and take the test again? What if—

Jared bopped her lightly on the arm. "Stop being a silly girl and open the envelope."

Stop being a silly girl . . . For years he'd used the familiar taunt to coerce her into climbing higher in the tree, wading across an ice-cold creek, weaving a wiggly worm onto a fishhook, or sneaking out her bedroom window at night to catch frogs. Automatically she slipped her thumb beneath the flap and slid the thick yellow paper from its envelope.

She shrieked and turned the certificate to face Jared. "I passed!"

He squinted at the page and began to read aloud. "'This certifies, that Miss

Lyla Emerson, who is a person of proper learning, ability, and experience, and of good moral character, and Specially Meritorious, has been granted this Certificate of Qualification, with authority to be employed and to teach in any public school in Kansas for the period of Five Years from and after the date thereof. Given under my hand and the seal of this office this ninth day of February 1889.'" He bent closer to the page, scowling, then straightened and scratched his head. "I can't make out the signature."

Lyla whipped the certificate around and examined the scrawled, slanted name written above the printed title *State Superintendent of Public Instruction*. She giggled again. "Neither can I. He would never receive a passing grade for penmanship in my class. But it doesn't matter if we can't read it. The certificate bears the state seal so it's official." She gently fingered the raised circle with KANSAS DEPARTMENT OF EDUCATION stamped around the circumference and sighed. "Can you believe it, Jared? I'm a teacher. I'm really a teacher."

"Good for you." He grinned and flicked the brim of her bonnet with his fingers, making it fold back.

Oh, such a pest he could be! And how had he learned to so adeptly flip her brim? He had no sisters on whom to practice, yet he was as skilled at brim-flipping as she was at frog-catching. Of course, frog-catching wasn't a skill Aunt Marion appreciated, but Lyla's ability to match a frog's leap and catch the amphibian midair had certainly impressed Jared over the years and earned her a nickname she hoped to leave behind when she moved out of Friendly.

She huffed and smacked the brim back into place. "Now that I have my teaching certificate, Aunt Marion will grant permission for me to travel to Oklahoma Territory, and—"

He waved his hands. "Wait...Oklahoma?"

She grinned smugly. "That's right."

"But the certificate's for Kansas."

Lyla shrugged, smiling at the certificate. "Yes, it is, but truthfully I don't need a certificate at all to teach at one of the Indian reservations in Oklahoma Territory. I earned it to prove to my aunt that I have the knowledge to be a teacher. She wouldn't let me go otherwise."

He gaped at her.

She chucked him under the chin. "Close your mouth, Jared. You look as though you've lost all sense."

He clamped his mouth closed and shook his head. "I can't believe it. Little Lithe-Legs Lyla is gonna teach at an Injun Reservation."

She scowled. "In-di-an, not Injun. And no more of that 'Lithe-Legs Lyla' either." When they were ten years old, the nickname flattered her. At thirteen, it irritated her. Now, at nineteen, it made her blush.

Jared snickered. "Sounds like a pretty good In-di-an name to me."

Despite herself, she laughed. How he loved to tease, and he could always make her laugh. She would miss her friend—the very first friend she'd made after Mama and Papa died and she came to live with Uncle Owen and Aunt Marion—when she moved from this little town.

He folded his arms over his chest and grinned at her. "When do you think you'll go? Summer?"

She slid the certificate back into its envelope and held it snug against her rib cage. "I hope sooner than that. If the children on the reservations are to have any kind of future at all in the United States, they will need an education." But she wouldn't only teach the children. She would teach any adults who were interested in learning, too.

Many held the opinion that "the heathen savages" were incapable of learning, but her school-teacher papa had taught former slaves—another group of people sometimes viewed as ignorant—to read and write, disproving the theory that they were "unteachable." Papa had believed education was the only path to betterment and that everyone regardless of social status, wealth, or skin color deserved a chance for betterment. A lump formed in her throat. She missed her parents so much. Not even eleven years had erased the deep ache of loneliness. But wouldn't they be proud to see her following in Papa's footsteps?

"Hmm. . ." Jared tapped his chin, his eyebrows high. "Kinda odd that you plan to go to Oklahoma, all things considered."

She sent him a sharp look. His tone had changed. No longer lighthearted or teasing but contemplative and perhaps even a little morose. "Why is that?"

He cupped her elbow and guided her to the east wall of the small post office where a dozen posters cluttered the bulletin board. He tapped one wrinkled poster partially hidden by an advertisement for an implement called a Chilled Plow. "Look at this."

The dirty windows prevented sunlight from fully penetrating the office, but if she squinted she could make out the print. She read silently then gawked up at Jared. "Are you interested in doing this?"

Jared's forehead pinched into furrows. He fingered the edge of the paper offering the chance to claim free land in Oklahoma Territory. "I've been thinking on it and praying about it for more than a month already. I keep coming in here and looking at the date, reminding myself that time's gonna run out for me to get to Arkansas City in time to be part of the land run."

"But. . .but why would you want to claim land in Oklahoma? You have a good job at Hardwick & Sons." Jared's father, Grover Hardwick, operated the biggest general store in all of Wilson County. Both of Jared's older brothers also worked there, giving the entire family secure jobs.

He hung his head and toed the floor with his scuffed boot. "If you wanna know the truth, Lithe Legs, I'm not much for store-keeping. Ma always said I had too much Lister blood in me to be content closed up indoors all day. Her pa was a farmer, you know."

Lyla nodded. She remembered Jared's Grandpa Lister, and she recalled some lonely summer weeks when Jared stayed out at the Lister farm with his grandpa and grandma. "Why not take over the Lister farmstead then?"

"Ma's brother inherited it, and he's got two boys of his own to help out. They don't need me." He heaved a sigh and gazed at the poster again. "Pa doesn't need me at the store, either. Not with Ned and Dan already there. The only reason I've stayed in Friendly is 'cause Pa depends on me to do the cooking and so forth at the house." Pink stole across his cheeks. "Guess it's not too manly, is it, to cook and clean?"

She touched his arm. "There's nothing unmanly, or even unseemly, about you helping your pa now that your ma's gone on to her reward. You couldn't let him starve, live in a filthy house, or wear dirty clothes to work, could you?"

"No." He puffed his cheeks and blew out a breath. "And if I leave for Oklahoma, that's what'll happen to him. He'll have to wear dirty clothes and eat canned beans every day of the week." A small, sad grin lifted the corner of his lips. "All that taking care of things in Pa's house makes me know that I can handle a farmstead on my own. But Pa..."

Lyla cringed. She understood Jared's uncertainty. Uncle Owen died the same winter as Mrs. Hardwick, both from the fever that came through the town. Now Aunt Marion depended on Lyla for companionship. Sometimes Lyla thought the reason her aunt fussed about her wanting to teach at a reservation was fear of being left alone.

She shook her head, regret releasing on an airy sigh. "It's too bad your pa and my aunt didn't marry up with each other. Then she wouldn't be lonely when I go away, and your pa would have someone to look after him."

Jared's mouth dropped open, his eyes flew wide, and he grabbed her arm. "Yes!"

Chapter Two

J ared nearly bounced in place. Excitement roared through him. Why hadn't he thought of it himself? If Pa was married, then he wouldn't need Jared at all. He could pack his trunk, withdraw his money from the bank, and buy a train ticket for Arkansas City. He could claim a parcel of land for himself and work it the same way Grandpa Lister had done.

Lyla wriggled and glared at him. "Let go, Jared. You're about to pinch me clear through."

He gave a jolt and released her. "Oh. . . Didn't realize I was holding so hard."

She laughed and rubbed her arm. "Little wonder you never lost your grip on a slippery frog. I thought I was caught in a beaver trap."

He grinned and flicked her bonnet brim, self-consciousness striking. "Sorry about that. But you got me all worked up."

"I did? How?"

He sent a glance around the post office. No other townsfolk had come in, but the postmaster was lurking somewhere. He had big ears. And a bigger mouth. They'd already risked being the topic of gossip at the barbershop by talking about their plans in Oklahoma. He wouldn't let that gossip include the idea Lyla had just given him.

He caught her arm again, gently this time, and herded her to the door. "I wanna tell you how, 'cause I'll need your help. But we can't talk here. Let's go. . ." He searched his mind for a likely spot. Then he grinned. "To the tree house."

She came to a halt at the doorjamb and put one fist on her hip. "Jared Hardwick, I am not climbing up into that rickety tree house in my best dress."

He glanced at her full skirt. She did look fetching in the bright green dress that brought out the emerald flecks in her blue-green eyes. He grinned, memories flooding his mind. If his pa and her aunt ended up hitched together, his best childhood pal would be his. . .what? He didn't know. But wouldn't it be fine to see her aunt and his pa happy together so he and Lithe Legs could pursue their dreams?

He planted his palm on the small of her back and propelled her onto the boardwalk. "We won't climb up in it. Wouldn't want you to tear your pretty dress an' get a lickin'." Her cheeks flamed red, and he laughed. "C'mon."

A gust of wind whirled around the last building and lifted the tail of her shawl as they left Main Street and hurried toward the stand of cottonwoods at the edge of town. More than half a dozen years ago he, Lyla, and a couple of boys from school had built a tree house out of boards scavenged from the lumberyard's discard pile. Younger school kids had claimed the warped platform for their own, but school wouldn't let out for another hour or so, so they'd have privacy out there.

They cut through a patch of thick brush, him pushing aside the bare, scraggly limbs to allow Lyla's passage. They moved close to the large, rough trunk of the tree house tree and stopped, facing each other.

She hugged the envelope against her middle and peeked up at him. "All right, what was so important we had to c–come out here to d–discuss it?"

Her teeth were chattering. Last week's snow had melted, but it was colder than he'd realized. He shrugged out of his jacket and draped it over her shoulders. Then he jammed his hands into his pockets and hunched his shoulders, fighting the urge to shiver. "Your aunt and my pa, that's what."

She wrinkled her nose. "You aren't making sense."

"Gimme a minute and I will be." He leaned close and lowered his voice, even though there wasn't a soul around. "Is your aunt gonna be lonely when you go to Oklahoma?"

Remorse tinged her expression. She nodded.

"And my pa's gonna be hungry and helpless. But like you said, if your aunt and my pa got married, then she'd have my pa's company and my pa would have someone to cook and clean for him. They'd both be happy, and we wouldn't have to worry about them, so we'd be happy, too."

She huffed, her warm breath forming a little cloud that brushed his chin. "I was only musing, Jared. Aunt Marion has never expressed any desire to remarry." She bit down on her lower lip for a moment, frowning. "Is. . .is your pa interested in her?"

"I dunno. He's never said so. But then, he's had me taking care of everything so he probably hasn't thought about it."

"Well, if neither of them are interested in the other, then—"

"Then we have to make them interested."

She scrunched her face. "What?"

He laughed. He couldn't help it. For a smart girl, she was sure slow to catch on. "We have to make them interested. You have to convince your aunt she'd be a lot happier if she was married, and I have to convince my pa he needs a wife again."

She shook her head. "Even if I could convince Aunt Marion she'd be less lonely if she got married again, there's no guarantee she'd be interested in your pa. Or that he'd want to court her. It isn't as if they haven't had the chance to, er, connect. They've gone to the same church and lived next door to each other for years."

Jared nodded, eagerness filling him. "Which makes them the perfect match.

They already have things in common. All they need is some encouragement."

"And you think we should encourage them."

Not a question, a statement. Now she was catching on. He grinned. "Yes. That's exactly it. We can be their. . .matchmakers."

"I don't know, Jared." She pursed her lips. "It would be nice to not worry about leaving Aunt Marion all alone, but isn't it manipulative—even selfish of us—to push them at each other?"

"How is it selfish to want to keep Pa from starving to death? Or keep your aunt from withering away from loneliness? It isn't selfish. It's. . ." He snapped his fingers. "Benevolent."

She gazed up at him, her brow wrinkled and her cheeks red. But she wasn't arguing anymore.

He stuck out his hand, palm up. "C'mon. Pact?"

She chewed her lip, staring at his waiting hand with apprehension and hope warring on her face. Finally she blew out a breath and placed her hand over his, palm to palm. They bounced their hands twice and chanted, "Pact," then quickly jerked their arms back so their hands slid free, as they'd done when they were children making a promise.

She slipped off his jacket and held it out to him. "I've got to get home, Jared. Aunt Marion is probably wondering why my trip to the post office is taking so long, and I want to show her my teaching certificate."

He eagerly donned the jacket. "You better go then. But let's meet tomorrow sometime—maybe noon at the café?—and plan our strategy."

"Strategy?" She giggled as she stepped past him. "You make it seem like we're going to war."

He followed her on the narrow path, grimacing. Budging Pa from his comfortable practice of relying on his youngest son would be a battle. But it was a battle he intended to win. His future depended on it. And so did Lithe Legs'.

◆　◆　◆

"Aunt Marion, I'm home!" Lyla hung her shawl on the graceful hall tree next to the front door then hurried through the parlor to the kitchen with the envelope gripped tightly in her hand.

Aunt Marion turned from the stove, wooden spoon in her hand and a frown on her face. "Gracious, child, I was beginning to think you'd run away from home."

Guilt attacked. She'd been gone less than an hour and Aunt Marion had missed her. What would her aunt do when Lyla was a whole state away? "I'm sorry I worried you."

The frown melted and a warm smile replaced it. Aunt Marion slipped the spoon into the kettle and gently stirred, raising the wonderful aroma of vegetable stew. "No harm done." She glanced at the envelope. "What did you find in the mailbox?"

Lyla bustled forward. "It's my teaching certificate. With the state seal and everything. It even says 'Specially Meritorious,' which means I scored at least ninety percent in every category." She held her breath, hoping her aunt would offer words of praise. Papa and Mama would have shouted with glee if given such wonderful news about their daughter's academic ability.

A weak smile tipped up the corners of Aunt Marion's mouth. "That's. . . commendable."

The words were kind, even complimentary, but the delivery held such apprehension not an ounce of congratulations remained. Lyla hung her head.

Aunt Marion released a heavy sigh. She stepped away from the stove and wrapped Lyla in an embrace. "Forgive me, dear one. It's selfish of me to steal your joy. I am proud of your accomplishment, and I will. . .will wish you well as you set out for Oklahoma Territory. But, oh, how I shall miss you."

Lyla clung to her aunt, tears pricking her eyes. During her walk home, away from Jared's convincing words and fervent expression—tactics he'd always utilized to entice her to follow his lead—she'd told herself it would be underhanded to plot a courtship between his father and her aunt, and she'd intended to tell him so when they met for lunch tomorrow.

But in that moment, with her aunt's ragged confession hanging in the air, uncertainty crept in. Aunt Marion needed companionship. Grover Hardwick needed tending. As Jared had said, their union would benefit them both. Should she leave without at least making an effort to ease her aunt's loneliness?

Chapter Three

Lyla slid into the booth across from Jared and laid her folded shawl on the edge of the table. The aromas of coffee, fresh bread, and fried chicken hung heavily in the small dining room of Sally's Café. Her mouth watered, hunger striking harder than she'd expected given the turmoil rolling through her belly, and she raised her hand to summon the café's owner.

Jared caught her hand and pressed it downward. "I already ordered two specials."

Sally's Friday special was always two pieces of pan-fried chicken, mashed potatoes with gravy, buttery corn, and biscuits. She licked her lips. "Perfect."

He stacked his arms on the edge of the table and leaned in. "Did you think at all last night about how you can get your aunt to look at my pa as a potential beau?"

Lyla glanced around. At least a dozen other townsfolk were enjoying one of Sally's specials, but the tall backs on the booth's benches offered a bit of privacy, and no one seemed to be paying them any attention. She cringed and fiddled with the cloth napkin lying in front of her. "I thought about it quite a lot. But I didn't come up with anything worthwhile. Mostly what I kept thinking was Aunt Marion's known Grover Hardwick most of her life. If she hasn't already considered being courted by him, how can I make her see him differently?"

Jared rolled his eyes. "Lithe Legs, I've never known you to back down from a challenge."

"Who says I'm backing down?"

"For someone who isn't backing down, you sure look like you're waving a white flag."

As usual, his mild taunts rallied her determination. She skewered him with a glare. "I'm not waving a white flag. But I do think this task is going to be harder than you make it sound. Convince two people who are set in their ways to fall in love with each other? This isn't a fairy tale story—this is life. And life isn't so easily manipulated."

Sally bustled to their table, balancing a large tray on her thick hand. She transferred two mugs of steaming coffee and two earthenware, chipped plates overflowing with food to the table. She tucked the empty tray under her arm, shot them a smile, and hurried off.

Lyla folded her hands in her lap. "Do you want to say grace?"

He nodded and bowed his head. "Dear God, thank You for this food, and thank You for giving me the idea to bring Pa and Mrs. Tuttle together in holy matrimony, a worthy estate You planned from the beginning."

Was he praying to God or preaching at her? Lyla opened one eye and peeked at him. His clasped hands and reverent expression snapped her eyelid closed.

"If it's Your will for these two folks to be joined, then give Lyla and me ideas to help them realize they need each other. If it's not Your will, help us. . .well, help me. . . to accept it. Amen."

His request to honor God's will shooed away the remaining wisps of Lyla's apprehension. She picked up her fork and slid it into the mound of potatoes. "Did you come up with any good ideas?"

He broke off a piece of meat from the crispy chicken leg on his plate, jammed it in his mouth, and spoke around the bite. "Yep. Started thinking about all the things my brothers did when they were courting—taking their girls on picnics, escorting them to barn dances and church socials, asking them to supper at the café, giving them flowers or little presents. . ."

Lyla would enjoy all of those things, and Aunt Marion likely would, too. "I can't see them going on a picnic in February, but I did hear there'll be a barn dance tomorrow night at the Swensen place. Aunt Marion hasn't gone to a barn dance since Uncle Owen died, but I could ask her. And you could ask your pa."

He swiped his lips with his napkin and grinned at her. "Good thinking, Lithe Legs. Soon as you get there, cozy your aunt up to the food table—that'll be the first place Pa will want to head. We'll spend a little time all talking together, just so they don't suspect any shenanigans, then you and me'll sneak off and leave 'em to talk on their own."

The plan held merit. Except for one thing. "What if they don't want to go to the dance?"

Jared snapped his napkin into his lap and picked up the chicken leg. He used the half-eaten leg like a pointer to punctuate his words. "Then we'll convince 'em otherwise. Tell 'em they've been cooped up all winter, it's time to get out. Tell 'em half the town'll be there and it'd be plain snobbish to stay away. Tell 'em—"

"Jared Hardwick, stop playing with your food, for mercy's sake!" The café owner grabbed Jared's wrist and pushed it above his plate. "You're sending pieces of breading all over my clean floor."

Jared ducked his head, pink stealing across his cheeks. "Sorry, Sally. I forgot I had it in my hand."

"*Hmph.* Don't reckon that says much about my cooking if you can forget to carry a piece of my fried chicken to your mouth." The woman shook her head, her rosy lips forming a pout. "But now that you've been reminded, eat your food instead of waving it around." She departed, muttering under breath.

Lyla giggled. "You better leave her a good tip. Or better yet, offer to mop the floor for her."

Jared smirked. "I do enough mopping at home. I'll just slip an extra dime under my plate. Now. . ." His blue eyes lost the teasing sparkle and a steely determination replaced it. "Are we ready to put our plan into action?"

Nervous tremors wiggled through Lyla's stomach. She pressed her palms to her midsection and tamped down the uncomfortable feeling. This plan was for Aunt Marion's good. She gave a staunch nod. "I'm ready."

◆　◆　◆

Jared strode up the center aisle of his father's general store, sidestepping around customers. He held a wax-paper wrapped sandwich which, admittedly, he'd purchased from Sally as a bribe. His brother Ned was at the counter and Dan, the oldest of the Hardwick boys, was stocking shelves, so Jared headed straight for the storeroom. He found Pa scooping tenpenny nails into paper bags.

"Hey, Pa, I brought you a sandwich. Ham on rye with that white cheese you like so much."

Pa turned from the barrel, pleasure igniting his lined face. "That sounds real good. Set it there on the shelf, wouldja? Need to finish filling these bags."

Jared took the scoop from his father's hand and plopped the sandwich onto his wide palm. "You eat. I'll scoop. Five pounds per bag, right?"

Pa plopped onto a barrel and peeled back the waxed paper. "Yep. Want a dozen of 'em ready to go."

Already seven bags formed a neat row on a low shelf. Jared set to work, watching Pa out of the corner of his eye. When he'd made it halfway through the sandwich and looked as relaxed as a cat in a ray of sunshine, Jared cleared his throat.

"While I was at Sally's, I heard there's gonna be a barn dance out at the Swensen place tomorrow evening. I plan to go." He rolled the top on a bag and set it next to the others, as nonchalant as he could be. "Wanna come with me?"

Pa made a face. "Aw, Jared, I don't know. . ."

He'd expected resistance, so he was ready. "Oughtta be fun. 'Specially after being cooped up all winter." He scooped nails into another bag, weighed it, and added a few more nails. "Old man Tanner'll have his fiddle, so there'll be dancing."

"I haven't danced since—"

"Since Ma died, I know." Sadness struck. He still missed his ma, and Pa had to be lonely. He paused and turned to fully face his father. "Ma would be the first one to tell you to get out, enjoy yourself some. Besides, it's good business sense to rub elbows with the ones who buy your goods, isn't that what you always tell us boys?"

Pa pushed the last bite of the sandwich into his mouth and chewed, uncertainty creating furrows across his forehead.

Jared fired his final argument. "And there's always good food at the barn dances—sandwiches and cakes and pies. Bet Mrs. Swensen'll set out some of her brown sugar pies. How long's it been since you had a piece of brown sugar pie?"

Pa swiped his mouth with the back of his hand and rose. "Too long. Hard to pass up the chance for a piece or two of brown sugar pie."

Jared reached for the last bag, hope quivering through his chest. "So. . .you'll go with me?"

Pa shrugged. "Sure. Why not?"

Chapter Four

J ared turned another furtive glance toward the barn doors. When would Lyla get here with Mrs. Tuttle? He and his father had already listened to three lively tunes from Mr. Tanner's fiddle, and Pa was on his second slice of brown sugar pie. He was also fussing about the amount of dust being stirred up by the dancers—"It makes my throat go tight," he said. If Lyla didn't hurry, Pa might decide he'd had enough fun for one evening and head home before he and Mrs. Tuttle even laid eyes on each other.

The barn door squeaked open, and Jared leaned sideways to peer past the couples whirling around the dance floor. Lyla slipped through the opening. Finally! He held his breath, watching, hoping. Relief exploded through him when her aunt followed.

Lyla took hold of her aunt's elbow and guided her, just as he'd instructed, to the food table. "Good evening, Jared and Mr. Hardwick."

"Hey, Li—" He bit down on the tip of his tongue. Mrs. Tuttle would not approve of his nickname for her niece. "—Lyla." Smiling big, Jared nudged Pa with his elbow. "Look who's here. Our neighbors."

Pa bobbed his head above the forkful of pie. "Good evening, Mrs. Tuttle, Miss Emerson."

"Good evening, Mr. Hardwick." Mrs. Tuttle sent a slow look across the dance floor. "I felt certain Lyla was exaggerating when she said everyone would be at the barn dance, but it seems she spoke truthfully. Why, even Reverend Bent is leading his wife in the do-si-dos."

Jared's pulse leaped at the perfect lead in. "And why should he and Mrs. Bent have all the fun? Wanna dance, Lyla?"

Her blue-green eyes went wide. She glanced at the dancers, longing in her expression, then turned to her aunt. "Do you mind?"

Jared caught hold of her right hand and gave a not-so-gentle tug. "Pa will keep your aunt company, won't you, Pa?"

"Well—"

He led Lyla into the midst of the dancers as the fiddle player transitioned into a slower tune. A few couples left the circle, and others moved in. Jared placed his right hand slightly below her shoulder blade and held her hand aloft. She settled her free hand on his shoulder, and they slipped into movement as easily as if they danced together every day.

He grinned at her. "That went pretty good, don't you think?"

A cloud of dust billowed around their feet, a few puffs rising high. She wrinkled her nose. "I think it went pretty fast. I hope Aunt Marion doesn't feel as though I abandoned her."

"If you stick close to her, she won't have a reason to talk to anyone else." He guided her into a turn that put them at the outer edge of the couples. "It's good that we left them alone over there together." She angled her gaze toward the food tables, giving him a view of her profile. She'd done something different with her hair, swept it up into a pouf that sat high on the crown of her head. A gold barrette was nestled at the bottom of the pouf, reminding him of a little crown. He liked the way her hair looked, and he said so.

"Aunt Marion fashioned it for me. That's why we didn't get here right when the dance started. It took longer than she expected."

The style gave her a sophisticated, ladylike appearance, so different from the tomboyish braids he remembered from their childhood. "Well worth the delay, Lithe Legs."

A rosy blush stole across her cheeks. "Thank you."

Their steps flowed with the music, her fingers on his shoulder tightening with the turns. He pulled her closer as other dancers pressed in, and the color in her cheeks deepened. Heat flooded his face—from the exertion of dancing or something else? While he guided her into another gentle turn, he examined the sweet dimple in her chin and the single beauty mark on her left cheekbone. Up close, she resembled a porcelain doll with creamy skin, rose-tinged cheeks, and full sweeping eyelashes.

He cleared his throat. "Fact is, you're downright beautiful." His voice cracked on the last words, unexpected emotion rising up to choke him. Why hadn't he noticed before just how pretty she was?

She turned her face to the side again, and then she stopped so abruptly he nearly stumbled.

"Lyla, what—?"

She pulled loose from his hold. "Your pa's still at the food table, but Aunt Marion. . ." She huffed. "She's gone!"

◆ ◆ ◆

Lyla fanned herself with her hand as she moved away from the dancers. Away from Jared. What had compelled him to tell her she was beautiful? The comment echoed through her mind and left her dizzy and weak.

He moved up behind her, his breath warm on the back of her neck. "Where did she go?"

"I don't know. I hope she didn't go home already." If Aunt Marion had taken their wagon home, Lyla would be stranded. She moved along the periphery of the large wooden structure, scanning faces. She nearly collapsed when she spotted Aunt Marion with a few folks from church. "There she is." She lifted the hem of her skirt and hurried across the dirt floor, torn between wanting Jared to follow and hoping he would go to his father.

Lyla reached her aunt's side. "Aunt Marion, why are you over here?"

Her aunt raised her eyebrows. "I'm talking with my friends. You know Mr. and Mrs. Kinney from church. Before your uncle passed away, we visited each other on Sunday afternoons. Don't you remember?"

Lyla remembered. But Mr. Kinney already had a wife. Aunt Marion was only wasting her time talking with the couple. She offered the pair a polite smile and then chewed her lip for a moment.

The three began chatting again.

Lyla leaned in. "Aunt Marion, did you get something to eat?"

Aunt Marion sent Lyla an impatient look. "No, dear, but I'm not hungry."

Lyla glanced over her shoulder. Jared and his father were near the food tables. How could she get Aunt Marion to join them? She blurted, "I am. Hungry, I mean." Oh, what a blatant fib. How could she eat a bite when her stomach was full of rocks? She risked another peek at Jared and found him staring at her woefully. She jerked to face her aunt again. "I want some...pie. Would you come with me?"

Her aunt chuckled. "Now, Lyla, I'm certain you don't need my help to choose a piece of pie. You go ahead."

"But—"

"Mr. and Mrs. Kinney are heading back to town now. The dust bothers Adolyn. They've offered to give me a ride, so I think I'll go on home. But you stay as long as you like. Enjoy some pie, and dance some more."

"But, Aunt Marion, I—"

The fiddler struck up a new song, this one lively and cheerful. Mrs. Kinney chortled and patted Lyla's cheek. "Before you step onto the dance floor, you might want to sip a cup of cold cider. Your cheeks are flushed and your forehead is sweaty. One would think you'd been dancing a jig rather than waltzing."

Lyla moved backward a few inches, forcing a light laugh. "It's a little warm and... and close on the dance floor. That's all." Another fib. Her closeness to Jared and his warm words—". . .*you're downright beautiful*"—were the cause of the fire blazing beneath her skin.

The older woman's eyes held a knowing twinkle. "Well, whatever the cause, a cup of cider, a slice of pie, and a few more circles around the dance floor with a handsome young man should cure your ills." She slipped her hand through her husband's elbow. "Are you ready, Marion?"

Aunt Marion planted a quick kiss on Lyla's cheek and accompanied the Kinneys to the door. Lyla gazed after them, defeated.

"She's leaving already?"

She released a squawk of surprise. She whirled on Jared, who stood directly behind her. "Don't sneak up on me."

"I wasn't sneaking." He held his hand toward the fiddler. "The music hid my footsteps."

He was probably right, but she continued to scowl at him even though she was more upset with Aunt Marion than with him. "Yes, she left. Now what are we supposed to do?"

A slow grin crept up his cheek. "I guess. . .dance?"

Shivers attacked. She hugged herself. "What will that do for Aunt Marion and your pa?"

"Not a thing. But just because they're being stubborn and not talking to each other doesn't mean we shouldn't have some fun." He waggled his eyebrows. "Besides, while we're out there dancing we can plan our next move."

Lyla groaned. "Jared, are you sure this idea is going to work?"

He slid his hand around her shoulders and steered her toward the dancers. "Consider it a game of chess, Lithe Legs."

She angled a wry grin at him. "I've never played chess."

He caught her hands. "I have, lots of times with my brothers. So I can tell you, you never win chess with a single move. It takes several moves and eliminating lots of barriers before you can put the opponent in checkmate. So we need to think of tonight's attempt as just one failed move, not a total defeat."

"But—"

He gave her hands a tug. "C'mon, Lithe Legs. Let's dance."

Chapter Five

Jared pulled his skin taut and scraped the razor along his jaw. Both of his brothers and his pa grew beards in the wintertime. They said he should, too, because it saved time, shaving soap, and the razor blade. But he'd never cared for the itchy feeling that came with facial hair. He set the razor aside and examined his reflection to be certain he hadn't missed any stubborn whiskers. He drew back, surprised to find a smile beaming at him from the mirror. And it was plastered to his face.

But then, maybe the smile wasn't such a surprise after all. He'd fallen asleep with it thanks to the happiness filling his chest, and he'd wakened with the same happiness. All because of Lyla. They'd danced until ten o'clock, until the food tables were emptied, the fiddler sagged from exhaustion, and Mr. Swensen said everyone had to go. Then he'd fallen in line behind her wagon for the drive back to town and spent the ride admiring the glow of moonlight on her upswept hair. What a wonderful night. And it promised to be a wonderful day.

Whistling, he hurried to his wardrobe and changed into his best suit for church. They'd made arrangements to sit with each other during service. Her aunt always sat with her, and Pa always sat with him, so if the two of them sat together they'd put Mrs. Tuttle and Pa in close proximity. After the service Lyla intended to invite him to lunch. And of course Mrs. Tuttle would suggest Pa come, too. Anything else would be impolite, and Mrs. Tuttle was always polite.

His fingers trembled as he adjusted his tie. So far Pa didn't suspect anything. He'd joshed Jared a bit on the way home about the number of times he danced with Lyla, but he didn't say a word about being left at the table with Mrs. Tuttle. Maybe it was best Pa thought all this coming together was meant for the two young people. Then maybe he'd get a little jealous thinking about Jared joining up with somebody and would start thinking about matrimony for himself. But pretending to fall in love with Lyla wasn't part of their plan. He'd better have a frank talk with Lyla about his pa's suppositions. As much fun as he'd had last night, she'd stayed a mite skittish. Probably because she noticed the teasing glint in Pa's eyes. He didn't want her to run scared and spoil the whole plot.

He didn't want her to run scared at all.

And why was he spending all this time thinking about Lyla when he should be thinking about Pa and Mrs. Tuttle? He marched to the small mirror above the washstand and aimed a stern look at himself. "Lyla's got her plans in Oklahoma Territory and I've got mine. The only two people who are s'posed to come together are Pa and Mrs. Tuttle. Try to remember what you're doing."

But when he got to church and spotted Lyla in her springtime green dress, her hair all fixed pretty like she'd worn it at the dance, his intention to focus on Pa and Mrs. Tuttle flew right out the church's belfry.

He hurried across the floor and touched her shoulder. "Good morning."

She looked up and offered a timid smile. "Good morning."

"Do you still want to. . .sit with me?" He held his breath. Had she changed her mind? She nodded, and his breath escaped in a relieved whoosh. "Good. Where would you like to go?"

Most folks who attended Friendly Bible Chapel sat in the same place every week—almost like staking a claim. Lyla led him straight to the fourth bench on the left side of the church where she sat every Sunday with her aunt. Mrs. Tuttle was already settled with two other maiden ladies, but there was enough room for him and Pa if they scrunched together. He wouldn't mind scrunching close to Lyla.

Stop that!

He waved Pa over. Pa ambled up the aisle, a sly grin creasing his face. Jared knew what Pa was thinking, but he acted like he didn't notice. The men slid in next to Lyla, and Lyla leaned forward a bit to address both of them at the same time.

"Good morning, Jared and Mr. Hardwick. I hope you're both well this morning."

"Very well," Pa said, giving Jared's arm a little bump.

Jared bumped him back. "We're just fine, Lyla. How 'bout you?"

"Fine, thank you." Her sweet smile shifted past Jared to Pa. "Will you join my aunt and me for lunch after service? Aunt Marion baked a ham, and it's too much for the two of us. We'd be honored if you would help us eat it."

Jared already knew what she planned to say thanks to last night's plotting, but it still thrilled him to hear her offer the invitation. He aimed a hopeful look at Pa. "I'd like to eat with Lyla and Mrs. Tuttle. What about you, Pa?"

That ornery glint still twinkled in Pa's eyes. He bumped Jared again, and Jared folded his arms over his chest. Pa chuckled. "Seems to me the two of you already have a chaperone with your aunt there, but if you're bent on inviting both of us, I reckon I'll come."

Lyla's face had blazed pink, but her smile remained in place. "Wonderful. Just follow us home after service then."

The preacher stepped onto the dais at the front of the small sanctuary, and they aimed their attention forward, but Jared heard little of the sermon. Lyla's perfume—something flowery and light—filled his nostrils. When she turned the pages of her Bible, her elbow connected with his arm. Only a soft brush, but the contact sent tremors of reaction through his chest. He'd grown up with her. Had chased her and teased her and considered her one of his pals. Why, in the past few days, had she suddenly changed? Or, perhaps more accurately, why had his view of her changed? He needed to put the plan for starting his new farm into action, not become so besotted that all ability to plan was stolen from him.

He tried once more to pay attention to the reverend's deep voice, but after a few minutes his thoughts drifted to the woman sitting attentively beside him. He gave himself a mental kick. He and Lyla better get Pa and Mrs. Tuttle hitched fast. The quicker the widow and widower married up, the quicker he and Lyla could head for Oklahoma and their separate dreams. And he could put this schoolboy silliness behind him.

◆ ◆ ◆

Lyla considered kicking her aunt in the shin. Not a hard kick. Just a tap to bring her to life. Why was she so taciturn? Granted, they hadn't invited guests to dinner since Uncle Owen's passing, but when he was alive, guests and chatter often surrounded their table. Aunt Marion knew how to entertain. She'd taught Lyla to be a gracious hostess. Other than asking the men if they'd like a second helping of potatoes or another slice of ham, she allowed Lyla to do the talking. How would Mr. Hardwick get to know Aunt Marion if she refused to release a conversational sentence?

She tucked her crossed ankles under her chair, lest one foot sneak out and bop her aunt under the table, and forced a smile. "Leave room for dessert, Mr. Hardwick. Aunt Marion put a peach cobbler in the oven before we sat down to eat, and it will be ready soon."

"Peach cobbler, hm?" The older man clacked another spoonful of green beans onto his plate, chuckling. "Seein' as how peach cobbler is my favorite dessert, I'll not turn it down, but I can't resist havin' some more of these beans. Jared, you need to find out what Mrs. Tuttle put in 'em to season 'em up. Never had better green beans."

Lyla looked at Aunt Marion, expecting her to share her secret for flavorful green beans. But even though her aunt met her gaze, she kept her lips closed. Lyla swallowed a sigh. "Aunt Marion always uses a bit of bacon grease to cook chopped onions and stirs those, along with some brown sugar, into the beans. It does add a nice flavor, doesn't it?"

Mr. Hardwick nodded, chewing.

Aunt Marion patted her mouth with her napkin and rose. "I'll see to that cobbler. I wouldn't want it to burn." She hurried out of the dining room.

Lyla dropped her napkin and stood. "Excuse me. I'll help her." She gave a helpless shrug in response to Jared's questioning expression and darted after her aunt. In the kitchen, she captured Aunt Marion's elbow and held her voice to a whisper. "Is something wrong?"

Aunt Marion opened the oven door and peeked inside. "Of course not. The cobbler is browned perfectly." She grabbed a pair of dish towels to protect her hands and lifted the baking pan from the oven, bringing the wonderful scent of fruit and cinnamon into the room. "But it should cool a bit before I cut it, so—"

"I'm not talking about the cobbler. I'm talking about you. You've hardly said two words the whole meal. Do you dislike"—she gulped—"our guests?"

Her aunt pursed her lips as she placed the pan on the worktable. "Gracious, Lyla, what a question. Of course I don't dislike our neighbors. The Hardwicks are fine, hardworking, God-fearing people. I've always thought highly of the entire family." She flopped the dish towels over her shoulder and began ladling water into the coffeepot. "I'm merely trying not to intrude upon your time with Jared."

Lyla's mouth fell open. "M—my time with. . .with Jared?"

"Yes." Aunt Marion flicked a glance toward the dining room. The mumble of men's voices and the soft click of silverware on china plates drifted through the doorway. A sad smile lifted the corners of her lips. "I realize if you choose to marry you won't live under my roof anymore, but at least you'll still be here in town where—"

"Aunt Marion!" Lyla's voice emerged in a shrill screech. She clapped her hand over her mouth, aimed a frantic look toward the dining room, and then hurried to her aunt's side. She whispered again, this time raspy and breathless. "Jared isn't courting me."

Her aunt's eyebrows rose and she tipped her head, clearly expressing disbelief.

Lyla gripped her arm. "He's not."

Aunt Marion frowned. "Then why is he here?"

Lyla scrambled for a reasonable explanation. "We're friends. We always have been. He. . .and I. . ."

Snippets from the previous night tiptoed through her memory. His warm, possessive hand on her waist as they danced. The sweet, attentive smile on his face as he listened to her talk. The tender, gentlemanly way he escorted her to her wagon and helped her onto the seat. *"Fact is, you're downright beautiful."* The comment whooshed through her mind, bringing a rush of heat.

"I'll let Jared and Mr. Hardwick know dessert is coming." She headed for the dining room. She needed to talk to Jared.

Chapter Six

Lyla marched to Jared's side, gripping her hands so tightly her fingers ached. "Aunt Marion is dishing up the cobbler. While we wait, would you help me with something?"

Without pause he stood and pushed in his chair. "Sure. In the kitchen?"

She pointed to the front door. "Out on the porch."

Jared trailed her outside and glanced around. "Whatcha need done?"

The air held a bite, but her internal fire kept her from shivering. "Nothing. I needed to talk to you alone."

He crossed his arms and gazed at her, attentive. "About what?"

"Aunt Marion has the idea we're courting."

He grimaced. "She and my uncle are a great pair, aren't they?"

Lyla frowned. "What do you mean?"

"He thinks the same thing. I was gonna warn you about it before he and I headed home today."

That explained the man's impish grin. She flapped her hands, fanning her face. "Where did they get such a notion?" But she knew where. From her and Jared. His courtly behavior at the dance, her invitation to dinner, even her dragging him onto the porch for a private chat. . . She fanned harder. "How will we convince them it isn't true?"

Jared gnawed at the corner of his lip, his brows tugged low. "Maybe we shouldn't."

She drew back, her hands stilling. "W–what?"

"Maybe if they think we're courting, it'll give them ideas. Make 'em jealous. Besides, courting couples need chaperonage. What better chaperones than my pa and your aunt? They'll have to spend time together if we—"

"Jared, I won't pretend to be in a courtship!"

He held his hands outward. "Why not? As long as we both know it's pretend, what'll it hurt?"

My heart. She shook her head so adamantly her neck popped. "No. I won't play that kind of game, not even to bring your pa and my aunt together. It's too. . .too. . ."

"Too what?"

"Wrong." As soon as the word escaped, she realized how ridiculous it sounded.

Weren't they already wrong? Their intentions were good—or at least sprang from the good-hearted desire for the ones they loved to be cared for—but their actions were deceitful and manipulative.

He stepped close and lightly gripped her upper arms. A crooked grin creased his face, both teasing and charming at once. "Would it be so awful to be courted by me?"

If he thought she would answer a question like that, he had rocks for brains. She huffed and stepped away from his touch. "That isn't the point, Jared. We agreed to try to get Aunt Marion and your father to consider marrying each other. There has to be a way of accomplishing our goal without the two of us making sheep's eyes at each other."

He frowned and hung his head, scuffing the toe of his boot on the porch floor. "You're right. We have our own plans, don't we?"

Was he talking to her or to himself? She wasn't positive, but she chose to answer. "That's right. You're going to claim a farmstead, and I'm going to teach at a reservation. Neither of us has time to think about a courtship." An unexpected ache settled in the middle of her chest. She stomped her foot, scaring away the odd feeling. "So how do we get the two of them to stop looking at us and to look at each other?"

He scratched his chin. "I dunno. I'm gonna have to think on it some." He gestured to the door, moving in that direction. "But for now, let's head inside and—" He stopped so suddenly it appeared he collided with a barrier. His jaw dropped and his eyes widened. He pointed mutely at the large window that provided a view of the dining room.

Lyla aimed her gaze to the window, and on the other side of the glass she witnessed Mr. Hardwick dipping a spoon into a bowl of cobbler. He seemed happy, but the sight dismayed Lyla. Because he was at the table all alone.

Jared shook his head. "Lithe Legs, unless we're with 'em, the two of them don't stay together. I guess, like it or not, we're gonna have to stick close, or your aunt and my pa will never get to really know each other."

◆　◆　◆

Mrs. Tuttle was a fine cook. But Jared had a hard time swallowing the peach cobbler. It wanted to stick in his craw. Or maybe something else was hard to swallow. *God, Lithe Legs an' me only want what's best for Pa and her aunt. Can't You give 'em a nudge toward each other an' help us out some?*

Mrs. Tuttle offered everyone another cup of coffee when they'd finished their dessert, but Pa pushed away from the table and rose.

"Thank you, ma'am, everything's been real good, but it's time for me to head back to my place—stretch out for my Sunday snooze." He chuckled. "Sunday's are always a good day to catch a nap."

A shy smile formed on the woman's face. "Owen used to nap every Sunday afternoon while I read or stitched on a sampler. Lyla and I were always very quiet so we wouldn't disturb his rest."

Jared exchanged a quick look with Lyla. Her expression mirrored his wonder. They were talking! His pa and her aunt were finally talking to each other!

Pa snorted. "My boys never tried to be quiet for me no matter how many times the missus shushed them. But these days, what with 'em grown up, it's as peaceful as midnight." He turned toward the front door. "It'll be especially quiet if Jared stays over here to visit with—"

Jared leaped into Pa's pathway. "Why don't we both stay? Visit some more? That is, you and Mrs. Tuttle can sit and talk while Lyla an' me wash up these dishes."

Mrs. Tuttle waved her hands. "Now, that isn't necessary."

"It'll let me thank you for treating us to the good dinner." Jared clapped his arm across Pa's shoulders. "Whaddaya say, Pa?"

Pa lowered his head and scratched his cheek. "Maybe Mrs. Tuttle'd rather have some time to herself."

Jared shot a *say something* look in Lyla's direction.

She cleared her throat. "Aunt Marion, would you enjoy company while Jared and I clear the table and clean up?"

The older woman's face was as red as a boiled beet. She glanced at Pa, then at Jared, and finally at Lyla. She shrugged.

She hadn't said no. Jared guided Pa to a chair in the parlor. "You and Mrs. Tuttle have a nice, relaxing chat. Lyla and me'll see to the mess." Without waiting to see what Mrs. Tuttle would do, he bounded to Lyla, gripped her elbow, and steered her into the dining room.

He began stacking plates. Lyla joined him, her lips set in a grim line. He nudged her. "Why aren't you smiling? We got 'em together."

The mutter of voices carried from the parlor. Lyla grimaced. "Subtlety isn't your talent, is it? You might as well have come right out and announced your intention for them to start a courtship. You saw Aunt Marion's face. She's more embarrassed than I've ever seen her, and as soon as you both leave, she's going to be full of questions. What am I supposed to tell her?"

Jared paused for a moment. Pa's chuckle rolled around the corner, and he couldn't resist grinning. Pa wouldn't be laughing that way if he wasn't at ease. "Tell her the truth. My pa's a fine catch who needs a wife, and she's a likely prospect."

She gaped at him. "I'll do no such thing!"

"Might speed things up a bit."

"More likely will send her screaming to the cellar. Women want to be wooed, not rushed into something."

He lifted the stack of plates. "Well, keep two things in mind, Lithe Legs. First, those two folks in the parlor are gettin' up in years, so a lengthy courtship is just a waste of time. And second, you an' me have places to be. That land run starts in April, an' I gotta be in place to make it. So we don't have time to spare." He tipped his head. "Besides, aren't you eager to get started teaching at one of those reservations?"

She swallowed. Longing flooded her expression and brought an expected shaft of jealousy. "Of course I am."

He tamped down the odd reaction and moved toward the kitchen. "Then stop fussin' about leaving the two of them alone in there. Just cross your fingers they'll come to their senses an' hitch up so you an' me can be on our way."

Chapter Seven

Lyla waved good-bye to Jared and his father, then turned to her aunt. Her lips quivered, but she forced them into what she hoped would pass for a realistic smile. "Did you and Mr. Hardwick have a nice chat?"

Aunt Marion slipped her arm around Lyla's waist and tipped her temple to Lyla's. "We did. He's a very dedicated father, and he thoroughly approves Jared pursuing a courtship with you."

Lyla stiffened. "Aunt Marion. . ."

Her aunt stepped away. "Now, I'm not trying to force the issue. You have to choose your own beau. But if you decide to accept Jared's courtship, you can expect my blessing as well as Mr. Hardwick's." She sat in her sewing rocker and reached for the basket that always waited beside the rocker. "I believe your parents would approve of Jared, too, if they had the opportunity to meet the man he's grown to be."

Lyla's vision blurred. She crossed to her aunt and knelt next to her chair. "You really think Mama and Papa would like Jared?"

Aunt Marion cupped Lyla's cheek. "I do." She laughed softly. "Oh, I confess, I thought him something of a scamp when he was a boy, always involving you in unladylike activities."

"C'mon, Lithe Legs, don't get left behind!" Jared's boyish voice blasted from the past, and a smile of fond remembrance grew even while she continued to blink back tears.

"But my opinion of him has changed. It's clear he's become a fine young man, very responsible and strong in his faith. His respectfulness toward his father is also commendable. If I was given the task of choosing a young man from the community for you, Lyla, I would choose Jared."

"I would choose Jared." Aunt Marion's final words seemed to echo through Lyla's heart. In that moment, she realized. . .she would choose Jared, too. If she were seeking a beau.

But she wasn't.

She rose and leaned down to deposit a kiss on her aunt's cheek. "Your approval means a great deal to me, Aunt Marion. But as you know, I intend to travel to Oklahoma Territory and teach. So courtship will have to wait."

Her aunt dipped her head. "So you aren't interested at all in. . . ?"

Lyla bit down on her lower lip. Whether she wanted to admit it or not, saying she had no interest in Jared would be a fib. Aunt Marion's glowing words, Jared's sweet attention over the past days, and memories of their lifelong friendship had stirred the coals of romance in her heart. But confessing her true feelings would only mislead Aunt Marion into thinking there was a chance for her to put aside her intentions to teach. So she chose not to answer.

Aunt Marion sighed. "I'm being pushy. Again. I must bring an end to this self-centeredness." She plucked a torn apron and a needle packet from the basket and then aimed a hope-filled look at Lyla. "I do hope you and Jared will accompany his father and me to next week's church social, however. The first church social of spring. The entire congregation will be there, so your absence would be noted. Besides, if you truly are intent on moving to Oklahoma Territory, you'll want to gather as much time as possible with folks in town. Store up memories of them to carry with you."

She already carried hundreds of memories of Jared, but she wouldn't argue against gathering a few more. Especially when it meant bringing Aunt Marion and Mr. Hardwick in contact with each other. "The social sounds fun. Of course I'll go with you."

"And with the Hardwicks?"

"And with the Hardwicks." Lyla hurried out of the room. The plan she and Jared had hatched seemed to be finding fruition. She should be thrilled. So why did she battle tears?

◆　◆　◆

Nearly every day over the following two weeks, Lyla and Aunt Marion spent time in the company of Jared and Mr. Hardwick. One calm, early March evening they sat on Aunt Marion's porch and sipped the last of the apple cider from the barrel in the cellar. Aunt Marion served it hot and embellished each mug with a cinnamon stick, which Mr. Hardwick brought from his merchandise store, and they chatted and laughed well past the hour when stars dotted the sky. Two other evenings, when rainy weather discouraged them from making use of the porch, they gathered in the parlor, sipped tea, munched cookies, and talked.

On four separate occasions they met for lunch at Sally's Café, and once Aunt Marion graciously accepted Mr. Hardwick's offer to pay the full tab. They attended the church social together, all riding to church in Mr. Hardwick's buggy. On the drive to the church, the two Hardwick men shared the front bench and Lyla and Aunt Marion sat in the back, but on the way home they paired off—Mr. Hardwick and Aunt Marion in front and Jared and Lyla whispering together in the back.

Twice Lyla and Aunt Marion spent an extra hour at Hardwick & Sons General Merchandise, keeping the owner and his youngest son from working by engaging in conversation. Each Sunday, Aunt Marion invited them for dinner, and she and Mr. Hardwick visited in the parlor while Jared and Lyla did the dishes.

On the second Sunday in March, while laughter blasted from the parlor, Jared aimed a smile at Lyla and bumped her with his elbow. "Hear them in there? They're gettin' along just fine. Won't be long now an' Pa will give her a private invitation to supper or a barn dance. Our scheme's workin' the way we hoped, Lithe Legs."

Lyla handed him a wet, slick plate. "It does seem that they enjoy spending time together." She rubbed the dishrag over another plate, casting a glance at Jared. "But they haven't expressed any interest in leaving the two of us behind. I suggested it to Aunt Marion last Thursday—why didn't she meet Mr. Hardwick for lunch at Sally's by herself—and she went red in the face and flustered, so I went, too."

He scowled and plopped the dry plate on the worktable. "She sounds like Pa. I've told him, 'If you wanna have lunch with Mrs. Tuttle, then do it. Why've I gotta come?' He blustered at me and said he wouldn't go if I didn't come."

She giggled. "How funny. Aunt Marion gets flustery and your pa gets blustery."

He snickered, grinning. "They really are a pair, aren't they?"

"Or a well-matched half of a quartet." She sighed and turned a serious look on him. "Honestly, Jared, when will they leave us out of their get-togethers? Not that I haven't enjoyed our excursions, but they're becoming far too dependent on our presence. Somehow we have to push them out of this crowded nest."

He leaned against the dry sink and fiddled with the damp towel. "You're absolutely right, Lithe Legs. We've gotta get them past being flustery and blustery so they're comfortable on their own. Tell you what. . ." He took the wet plate from her and began rubbing it with the towel. "I overheard Pa invite your aunt to next Friday's barn dance out at the Powell place. There's no doubt in my mind he'll insist I go with him, and your aunt'll probably do the same with you."

Lyla nodded. She fully expected the same thing. "Should we refuse to go?"

"No, 'cause then they'll probably find an excuse to stay home, too."

She rolled her eyes, envisioning the battle of wills she'd face with Aunt Marion.

"Let's go, but let's not all ride together. Me an' Pa will go in our buggy, you an' your aunt take your wagon. Then, halfway through the dance, we'll sneak out."

Lyla gaped at him. "It will frighten Aunt Marion if I leave without a word!"

"If you tell her you're leaving, she'll want to go with you. You know she will."

He was right again. Still, she wouldn't intentionally alarm her aunt. "Well then. . .we'll leave a message with someone who can tell Aunt Marion and your pa that we've gone on home."

Jared scowled. "Only if it's someone who won't run and tell them the minute we leave the dance."

Lyla stuck out her hand. "Pact."

"Pact."

They performed their childhood handshake, Lyla transferring a few suds from the dishwater to Jared's palm. He swiped his hand on his pant leg and grinned at her. "Good thing we both have lots of determination, Lithe Legs. We aren't gonna let these two get the best of us, are we?"

"We sure aren't." Lyla spoke staunchly, but secretly she pondered whether she and Jared possessed as much determination as Aunt Marion and Mr. Hardwick. After all, so far the older couple had bent the two of them to their will. She and Jared might be stuck in Friendly forever if something didn't change.

Chapter Eight

If his chest got any lighter, his feet might leave the ground. Jared whirled Lyla around the dance floor while his pa did the same with Lyla's aunt. He couldn't stop grinning. They couldn't have planned a more perfect night.

During the first half hour at the barn dance, the four of them sat to the side sipping mint-spiced well water and munching cookies and cakes. But then he and Lyla joined a dance circle, and Pa and Mrs. Tuttle followed their example. That first dance led to another and then another. The older couple had danced four songs in a row without a break to visit the food table or talk with neighbors. Now, midway through the fifth song, with the two of them having so much fun, he and Lyla could seize the opportunity to sneak out.

Tightening his grip on her waist, he guided her to the outer edge of the circle. When they reached the side of the barn with the doors, which were opened wide to allow in the evening breeze, he whisked her outside.

Lyla stopped at the edge of the yellow path of lamplight flowing from the barn, forcing him to stumble to a halt, too. "Are we leaving?" She gazed in at the dancers.

"Yes." He held up his hand, anticipating her argument. "And I already talked to the Powell's oldest boy. He knows if Pa or your aunt start askin' about us, he's to tell them we got tired an' went on home." He snickered. "If Pa keeps lookin' at Mrs. Tuttle the way he's been doin' for the past two songs, an' she keeps lookin' back at him the same way, they might not notice we're gone until the whole dance is over."

Lyla sighed, still watching the dancers. "I hate to leave. . ."

Jared caught her hand and gave a tug. "They'll be fine, Lithe Legs."

She shot an impatient scowl at him. "I know they will. But I was having fun." All at once her cheeks blazed pink, and she turned away.

Her reaction made his ears buzz. Had she admitted she liked dancing with him? The airy feeling that had carried him around the dance floor returned, and he realized his elation hadn't all been about Pa and Mrs. Tuttle getting along so good. He liked dancing with Lithe Legs Lyla.

He gulped. "Do. . .do you wanna stay then?" He held his breath, half hoping she'd say yes so they could dance some more.

She shook her head. The light brown coils of hair that had escaped the bun at the crown of her head bounced on her slender shoulders. "We made a pact. The idea was to get Aunt Marion and your pa focused on each other, and we accomplished that. So it's time to go."

Regret showed in her blue-green eyes. He wished they'd never made that pact. "It's all right. I don't mind staying. . .if you want to."

She shifted and met his gaze. Determination replaced the longing. "Let's go, Jared. We'll leave your buggy for them. It's more comfortable than Uncle Owen and Aunt Marion's old wagon." She headed across the dark ground.

Jared trailed her, scuffing up dust with his heels. Horses in their traces released snorts as they walked past the row of wagons and buggies. He absently slowed his steps and gave each animal a brief rub on the nose on his way. Lyla reached her family's wagon well ahead of him and was already sitting primly on the seat when he caught up.

He pulled himself into the creaky seat beside her, but he didn't reach for the reins. Fiddle music flowed from the barn, a slow tune that invited a man to hold his partner close and sway gently, like willow tree branches in a breeze. His throat went dry. "It's not too late if you wanna go back in." If they hurried, they could sway together for the last half of the song.

She shook her head again, but he thought he glimpsed regret in her somber expression. "Take me home, Jared."

With a sigh, he picked up the reins, unlocked the brakes, and clicked his tongue on his teeth. The horses strained against the rigging, and the wagon rumbled forward. He guided the team to the road, and they began the three-mile drive to town.

Lyla sat quietly beside him, her hands gripping the tails of her shawl. The night air held a bite, and he considered slipping his arm around her. Just to keep her warm. But he didn't let go of the reins. Something about her formal pose and grim expression made him hesitant to even talk. Had he upset her somehow?

He chewed the inside of his lip and focused on keeping the horses centered on the road—the moon wanted to slide behind clouds and hide the landscape—until they were within a mile of town. Then the moon popped out in full brightness, growing black shadows on the gray ground and bringing Lyla's unsmiling face into view. Curiosity got the best of him.

"What's wrong with you?"

She jumped.

He grimaced. "Sorry, Lithe Legs. Didn't mean to scare you. But I've never seen you so quiet. You're acting mad. Or upset. Or something." He bumped her lightly with his elbow. "What's the matter?"

"I'm not ready to go home."

"You said you wanted to go home."

She huffed and hugged herself, shrinking small on the other side of the bouncing seat. "I know I said it. But I didn't really mean it. I wanted to stay."

Girls could sure be confusing. "So why didn't you say you wanted to stay? I'd have stayed." He battled a wave of regret. "You should've said somethin'. We could've danced some more."

"And if we had, what would we have gained?"

The bitterness in her tone shocked him so much he yanked back on the reins. The horses stopped, and he set the brake in place then shifted on the seat to face her. "I guess we would've gained an enjoyable evening. What's wrong with that?"

She tipped her face to glare directly into his eyes. The moonlight hid the color of her eyes, but fervor glimmered there. Or maybe remorse. "What's wrong is that it puts ideas in my head."

"Ideas about what? You aren't making sense."

She huffed and turned away. "I've already said too much. Let's go on home."

He snorted. She hadn't said enough. Not nearly enough. "I'm not goin' anywhere until you tell me what's got you all in a snit."

Her lips crunched so tight they almost disappeared. If he wasn't mistaken, she was trying not to cry. Lyla was the toughest girl he knew. He must've really done something bad if she was set to cry.

He placed his hand on her shoulder. "I don't like havin' you mad at me. Tell me what I did wrong. If you tell me, then I can promise to never do it again." Her shoulder shook. Yep, she was crying even though she didn't make a sound. He groaned. "Lyla, please. . ."

She pulled loose and wriggled as far away from him as she could. Which wasn't far, because the seat wasn't more than four feet long. If he straightened his arm, he could still catch hold of her. He started reaching.

"You didn't do anything."

He paused, confused and doubtful.

"Well, not on purpose, I guess."

So he'd done something after all. He let his hand drop on her shoulder again and gave a gentle squeeze. "Lithe Legs, stop talkin' in riddles and just tell me what I did. Then I can take it back an' we can be go on bein' friends again."

"We can never be friends again. And I don't want to spend any more time with you. Not alone, and not with your pa and Aunt Marion."

She might as well have punched him in the gut as much as her words hurt. He jerked his hand from her shoulder and gawked at her. "But why? Whaddid I do?"

"Never mind. But I'm done with this game. Now take me home."

Chapter Nine

Lyla shrank into the corner of the seat as Jared yanked the brake handle hard enough to splinter it, grabbed up the reins, and snapped them with a resounding *crack!* The horses lurched into motion, and she held to the side of the seat when the wagon rocked violently.

Jared's hands balled into fists so tight his knuckles glowed in the moonlight. His jaw thrust forward and his eyes narrowed into slits. She'd never seen him so angry, and guilt smacked as hard as he'd applied to reins to the horses' rumps. But how could she answer his question? Could she really admit, *"You made me fall in love with you"*? Of course not. It would do neither of them any good. So she sat in silence, battling tears, until he pulled up to the small barn behind her house.

She started to climb over the edge, but he barked, "Stay put." She waited while he hopped down, rounded the wagon, and then held his hands to her. She blinked back more tears as she allowed him to help her from the high seat. He was a gentleman even in his fury. She wished he'd left her to sit in the wagon and rot.

The moment her feet met the ground, he released her and stomped to the front of the wagon. He grabbed the leather leads securing the horses in their traces. "Go on in. I'll put the team away for you."

She scuttled after him, wringing her hands. "Jared, I—"

"Go inside, Lyla."

Lyla. Not Lithe Legs. She hung her head. "A—all right." She turned to go.

He blasted a huff. "Wait."

She angled her gaze over her shoulder. "What?"

"They're showing interest in each other, but they haven't made a commitment yet. We aren't done."

Lyla closed her eyes. She couldn't continue spending time with Jared. Not knowing she was heading to a reservation and he to a land claim. Not knowing there was no future for the two of them together. She needed time away from him to repair her heart. "Jared, I—"

"Don't worry. We won't be together. Not for this plan."

She cringed. He sounded so harsh. So cold. So unlike Jared. "What then?"

"We'll send letters. Every day for the next week."

She slowly turned to face him. "What kind of letters?"

"The lovey kind of letters." His hard tone didn't match the idea of being lovey. "I'll write to your aunt, you write to my pa. Sign 'em 'Your Secret Admirer.' In the letters we'll arrange a meeting spot. If we do a good job with the writing—fill 'em with mushy talk an' so forth—they oughtta be interested enough to come to the meeting spot. Then when they're face-to-face, they'll figure out they really do care about each other."

Lyla toyed with the idea. Writing letters would mean no contact with Jared, but they would still be guiding Mr. Hardwick and Aunt Marion toward each other. She wished he'd thought of this plan before her foolish heart had plummeted head over heels for him. "It. . .it could work. Where should we have them meet?"

One of the horses poked its nose against Jared's collar. He curled his arm around the horse's neck, giving it a few light pats. It seemed his anger was fading. "Someplace where nobody else'll see. Maybe. . .behind the church. At that bench beneath the willow tree."

"When?"

"Probably better wait until after supper. Let's say seven o'clock next Saturday night."

"All right. I suppose we'll want to slide the letters under each other's front doors rather than using the postal service."

He nodded and headed for the wagon. "That'd be best. Then they'll arrive on time." He heaved himself into the seat. "Since that's set, head on inside. As I said, I'll see to your team, and. . ." He shook his head. Hard. As if dislodging a flea from his ear. "Never mind the 'and.' Good night, Lyla."

Never had a farewell felt so final. Lyla scurried into the house and to her room. She wanted to be sound asleep by the time Aunt Marion returned. Her aunt would likely be full of questions about Lyla's early departure, and she wouldn't be able to answer without bursting into tears, which would open more questioning. It was best to simply go to sleep.

◆　◆　◆

Sunday, by deliberately arising late and lazing in her room, Lyla avoided her aunt's queries. After church, Aunt Marion invited Mr. Hardwick and Jared to lunch. Jared looked past Lyla as if she didn't exist and politely declined. Mr. Hardwick then also thanked Aunt Marion and said he'd better eat at home. Lyla feigned a headache and went straight to her room when they returned to the house, leaving Aunt Marion to eat alone at the kitchen table. Guilt nearly sent Lyla to the kitchen, but instead she retrieved her pot of ink, pen, and writing paper and sat at the little table in the corner of her room to pen the first "secret admirer" letter to Mr. Hardwick.

She dipped her pen, touched its nib to the paper, and wrote, *Dear.* Then she paused. Should she call him Grover or Mr. Hardwick? Aunt Marion never called the merchant by his first name, but surely one who'd fallen in love would not be formal. She couldn't imagine calling Jared by the stilted *Mr. Hardwick.*

"Stop thinking about Jared!" The words emerged in a harsh command. She clapped her hand over her mouth, appalled. Had Aunt Marion heard her? She listened, her heart pounding, but no footsteps sounded in the hall. With relief, she leaned over the page again. Even though Aunt Marion consistently called Jared's father Mr. Hardwick, she would use his given name in the correspondence. Jared had said to make the letters "lovey," and Grover was more lovey than Mr. Hardwick.

> *Dear Grover,*
> *I hope you won't think me forward by calling you Grover. It's how I think of you.*
> *And I think of you often.*

Lyla's face heated. Was she writing to the father or the son? She nibbled the end of the pen for a moment. If she wrote from her heart to Jared, only replacing the father's name, the letter would be lovey. And real. Maybe it would help dispel some of the pent-up feelings coursing through her each time she thought about leaving Friendly and never seeing Jared again.

With Jared's face hovering in her memory, she dipped the pen and continued writing.

> *Although I've never been blatant enough to confess my deepest, fondest feelings for you, they reside within my heart and accompany me every waking moment. Yes, dear, you are on my heart from the moment I arise until the very last moment before I lapse into sleep. Even then, your smiling face enhances my dreams and makes me long for morning when I might hear your voice, inhale your musky scent, gaze into your—*

She gasped, jerking the pen. She'd nearly written sapphire eyes. But Grover Hardwick didn't have Jared's wonderfully rich blue eyes. His were hazel. She scowled. How could she elaborate on hazel? Ah, yes. . .

> *. . .gaze into your eyes of greenish-gold, the colors of sunlight on a sea of grass.*

This lovey letter writing wasn't too difficult when one allowed her imagination free rein. And it was taking the edge off her deep heartache. She bent over the page, new paragraphs already forming in her mind. Then an errant thought flitted through.

Was Jared writing his first lovey letter right now, too?

❖   ❖   ❖

For the first time in his life, Jared wished he had a desk or table in his room where he could write in privacy. Pa had shuffled off to his room for his Sunday nap after a simple lunch of cheese on white bread sandwiches with canned peaches, but knowing that he could emerge at any minute and catch Jared midletter at the dining room table left him edgy and unable to concentrate. This letter wasn't going well at all.

He scowled at what he'd written so far.

> *Dear Marion,*
>
>   *I hope you're having a good day. Mine is fine. It's a little warmer today, more like springtime, and I like that.*

He closed his eyes and groaned. Was he writing to a lover or to a stranger? He'd told Lyla to be lovey. This letter wasn't lovey. It was boring. He wadded up the page. He removed another sheet from the tablet and laid it on the table in front of him. Then he sat for long minutes staring at the thin lines marching across the page. What should he do?

And suddenly he knew. He'd write to Lyla. Being lovey with her wouldn't stretch him at all. He'd been pretty mad at her last night. Was still pretty mad. But only because he'd fallen for her. Fallen so hard it'd left bruises on his heart. But she wasn't interested in him. Not as anything more than a friend. It made him mad that he wouldn't have a chance with her, but being mad didn't erase his feelings. So he'd write them all down. At least if they won her aunt to loving his pa, they'd accomplish something good.

He licked the tip of the pencil lead, aimed the point at the paper, and used his neatest script to start again.

> *Dear Marion,*
>
>   *You're probably going to call me too bold, but I have to say this: I think you're beautiful. . .*

357

Chapter Ten

Aunt Marion's delight at receiving daily missives was contagious. Lyla found herself nearly giddy each morning when she spotted the folded paper tucked between the screen door and its frame. Without planning delivery times, she and Jared chose opposite ends of the day to sneak the letters into place. Jared's notes to Aunt Marion arrived early in the morning, and Lyla ascertained the ones she wrote to his father were waiting when the men returned from work. She often wondered if Jared's heart beat hard and fast when his pa opened her letters. Did Mr. Hardwick read them aloud? Did Jared pretend the words were really for him, the way she pretended his letters were for her?

She would never have suspected her childhood friend possessed the ability to woo a women through flowery words, but she learned otherwise when Aunt Marion shared the contents of the letters with her. He'd found a poetry book somewhere, and he copied the most lovely sonnets, adding his own notes to personalize the poems with additional phrases and thoughts. When Aunt Marion read the words to Lyla at the breakfast table, her heart ached anew with deep longing. If only he meant them for her. If only she accepted them as hers. If only. . .

Daily she reminded herself she had a purpose—to teach. Pining over Jared was useless and childish and foolish. But she pined anyway.

As Saturday neared, Lyla's nervousness grew. What would happen when the two older people came face-to-face and realized they'd been duped? Would they, as Jared speculated, realize they truly did care for each other? Or would anger and embarrassment drive a wedge between them?

◆　◆　◆

Saturday evening Lyla sat down to supper with Aunt Marion, but she couldn't eat. Across the table, Aunt Marion pushed her ham and beans around on her plate with her fork rather than carrying any bites to her mouth. Lyla said, "Are you nervous?"

Aunt Marion shot her a startled look and then sighed. She laid the fork on the table. "Very much so. I've never had a secret admirer. It's an exciting prospect but also rather frightening. I'm half considering not going to the meeting place. What if he turns out to be someone bent on preying on a lonely widow? Or maybe he's a robber who wants to relieve me of my reticule?"

"Would you have your reticule with you?"

Aunt Marion pursed her lips. "I never leave the house without my reticule. You know that, Lyla, as does every other person in town."

Lyla swallowed a giggle, envisioning the fight between her aunt and anyone who dared try to take her little velvet bag containing face powder, a comb, and rarely more than two quarters. "The person who wrote the letters didn't strike me as a common thief. He sounded. . ." An airy sigh left her lips. "Courtly."

"Yes. Yes, he did." Aunt Marion seemed to drift away for a moment. Then she gave a little jolt. "But words can be deceiving."

Heat attacked Lyla's face. The words she'd penned were all true, but the deception lay in whose name she placed in the salutation. She clasped her hands. "So you're not going?" If she didn't go, the entire plan would collapse.

Aunt Marion rose and carried her plate to the dry sink. "I'll go. But I'm leaving my reticule behind. And I'm not going alone." She pinned a stern look on Lyla. "You're coming, too."

Lyla clumsily pushed herself from the chair. "The letters didn't say to bring someone with you."

"I'm aware of what the letters said, but no self-respecting woman would meet a strange man at dusk on her own. So you're coming, too." She brushed nonexistent crumbs from her skirt, her cheeks glowing. "You can hide behind the outhouse. Then, if he proves untrustworthy, I'll call your name, and you can come running. If he knows there's a witness, he'll be less likely to follow through on some unsavory scheme."

Although she knew her aunt's fears were misguided, she couldn't resist the chance to observe their meeting. She nodded. "All right, Aunt Marion. If it will ease your mind, I'll go with you."

◆　◆　◆

Jared pinched his nose to keep from sneezing. Pa'd put on enough cologne to scare off a bear. The scent carried on the breeze across the churchyard to the corner of the building where he hovered in a deep slash of shade. He watched Pa pace back and forth in front of the willow tree, as nervous as he'd ever seen him. But the cologne, the clean shirt, and the new ribbon tie waving in the breeze let Jared know Pa was excited to meet his secret admirer. *God, let this work. . .*

Jared had taken a chance and bought a stage ticket to Arkansas City for next week. He didn't want to leave Pa all alone in that house, but he'd do it if Mrs. Tuttle refused to come. The pull of free land and the chance to build his own farm was too strong. He'd have to trust God to take care of Pa, and he'd have to pray for God to ease the hurt of leaving Lyla behind. He needed a new start worse now than he had before he came up with this scheme. Who'd have thought he'd fall in love with his childhood pal? But he'd done it, and now he'd have to fall out. It'd be easier if he wasn't carrying worry about Pa, too, so he'd double up his trust and head to Oklahoma in faith that Pa would be just fine.

He'd be just fine, too. Eventually. Maybe.

Pa stopped pacing and straightened, his gaze aimed to the west, as alert as a prairie dog on guard duty. Jared held his breath, and then it whooshed out when he spotted Mrs. Tuttle gliding across the brown, flat grass. She'd come! He nearly whooped with glee when Pa stuck out his hands and Lyla's aunt took hold of them without a moment's hesitation.

He gripped the edge of the building and tipped his ear, but to his disappointment he couldn't hear a word they said. They were talking, though. He knew it, because they leaned in close, and their mouths were moving, taking turns. He stared hard at their faces. He had a view of their profiles, so he couldn't be certain, but they seemed pleased then puzzled then pleased again then. . . He frowned? Did Mrs. Tuttle look angry?

The woman turned a bit, appearing to seek the grounds, and he ducked back. Even with the church building blocking him, he heard her strident call.

"Lyla Alice Emerson, you come here right now!"

◆ ◆ ◆

Lyla scurried from her hiding place. At the same time, Jared came trotting from behind the church. She nearly changed direction and raced for home, but her aunt's stern expression advised her not to escape.

She huffed to her aunt's side and managed a tremulous, "Yes, Aunt Marion?"

Aunt Marion held up a stack of familiar letters. "Do you know anything about these?"

She risked a glance at Jared. His panic-stricken face did nothing to help her. She gulped. "Um…yes, ma'am."

"You wrote them?"

Lyla nodded, the motion jerky.

"And signed my name to them?"

"Yes, ma'am."

"Why would you do such a deceptive thing?"

Lyla swallowed a knot of shame. She licked her lips, searching for an appropriate answer.

"It was my idea," Jared spoke up. His tone was bold, his shoulders square, and his chin high. "I convinced her to do it."

The pair of older adults gaped at Jared, and Lyla did, too. His rescue was so noble considering the anger simmering in his father's eyes. She gripped her clasped hands at her throat and trembled as he crossed the grass and stood beside her.

"She wrote letters to you, Pa, and I wrote letters to Mrs. Tuttle."

Mr. Hardwick's face mottled red. "Letters like the ones I got? All sweet an'...an'..."

Jared nodded. "I sure did."

The older man shook his head and blasted out a noisy breath. His gaze narrowed. "Son, you've got some real explaining ahead of you."

Jared had come to her rescue. She would repay in kind. She stepped forward. "Jared and I have been working for weeks to match you two up."

Mr. Hardwick frowned at Lyla, the lines in his forehead deep. "Match us up? You mean..." His jaw dropped.

Aunt Marion began fanning herself.

Jared stepped next to Lyla. "We wanted the two of you to get married. Then I'd know you were being taken care of, Pa, when I headed to claim land in Oklahoma Territory, and Lyla wouldn't worry about her aunt being lonely when she left for the Indian reservation. We figured it was best for both of you."

Mr. Hardwick and Aunt Marion gaped at each other for several silent seconds. Then a grin twitched on the man's lips. Aunt Marion covered her mouth with her hands. Without warning, the two of them broke into hoots of laughter.

Chapter Eleven

Lyla sent a puzzled look at Jared. He met her gaze, confusion evident in his face. The older couple continued laughing. Mr. Hardwick even braced his hand on Aunt Marion's shoulder, and she rested her forehead on his arm.

"Aunt Marion, none of this is funny." Lyla tapped her aunt's arm. "Why are you laughing?" Had the two older people lost their senses?

Aunt Marion removed a handkerchief from her sleeve and dabbed her eyes. "Oh, yes, it is funny, dear. It's very funny when you consider—" Girlish giggles stole the remainder of her sentence.

Jared's father swiped his arm across his face and grinned. "Do you two have any idea why Mrs. Tuttle an' me've been spendin' so much time together?"

Lyla shrugged. "Because Jared and I have manipulated it?"

He snorted. "So we could put the two o' you together. We were tryin' to do some matchmakin'."

Fire flooded Lyla's face. Although Aunt Marion had been very open in her desire for Jared to court Lyla, she hadn't realized Mr. Hardwick was so thoroughly involved. She ducked her head, too embarrassed to meet anyone's gaze. "Oh."

"But you know, Marion. . ." Mr. Hardwick's tone turned musing. Lyla peeked at him from beneath her lashes and caught him pinning Aunt Marion with a boyish half grin. "I've enjoyed spendin' time with you. Enjoyed eatin' your cookin', too, if you don't mind me sayin' so. Maybe these two connivers of ours weren't too far wrong."

A pink blush stole across Aunt Marion's face, erasing years from her appearance. "What are you saying, Grover?"

The man shrugged, his eyes twinkling. "Maybe you an' me should consider spendin' more time together. Without the youngsters. That is, if you don't mind bein' around me."

Aunt Marion giggled. "Why, Grover, I don't mind at all." The two of them linked arms and sauntered off, heads close, whispering.

Lyla clapped her hands together and laughed, too overcome with joy to hold it in. She spun on Jared. "It worked! Jared, our plan worked!" His crestfallen expression squashed her happiness. "What's the matter?"

He gazed after his father. Scuffing his toe in the dried grass, he shrugged. "Our plan worked, but their plan. . ." He flicked a glance at her then looked down. "I reckon I think it would be nice if it had worked, too."

Lyla's heart began a rapid thrum. She pressed her palms to her bodice. "Their plan. . .for us?"

He nodded, still seeming to examine his dust-covered boot toe. "They'll be together. But you an' me, we'll be apart."

Hope fluttered in her chest. "Jared, are you saying you want us to be together?"

A sheepish grin tipped up the corners of his lips. "Sounds kind o' silly, doesn't it, after we made our plans to go separate ways, but. . .yeah. That's what I'm saying."

The flutter of hope took wing and emerged in a happy gasp. "That's what I want, too. It's why I told you I couldn't spend time with you anymore. Our time together was giving me ideas I couldn't allow to grow without risking heartbreak. But if you want it, too, then—" She clapped her hand over her mouth.

He frowned. "What's the matter?"

She shook her head, reality crashing around her. "Jared, we can't be together. You're going to claim land in Oklahoma. I'm going away to teach. Our plans will keep us apart."

He took hold of her upper arms. "But what if I found land near a reservation? Near enough that you could travel there every day and do your lessons?"

Hope swooped in again, stronger than before. "Do you think it would work?"

"It's worth a try, isn't it?"

To be with Jared? To have his company every day? To build a life with him? She smiled. "It's worth a try."

He curled his arm around her shoulders and turned her in the direction of the path his pa and Aunt Marion had taken. "C'mon. Let's go find those matchmakers and tell 'em their plan worked."

◆　◆　◆

Three weeks later. . .

Hand in hand with Jared, Lyla dashed across the churchyard through a shower of rice and good wishes bestowed by members of the congregation. Aunt Marion and Pa Hardwick—because the man insisted she call him Pa rather than Uncle Grover—followed. Halfway across the yard, Jared scooped Lyla into his arms. She squealed in surprise.

He grinned. "Can't carry you over a threshold. Leastwise, not yet. So this'll have to do." He carried her the final few yards to the stagecoach which waited at the edge of the churchyard with their trunks already loaded in the back. He deposited her on the seat and climbed in behind her.

The townsfolk gathered around Aunt Marion and Pa Hardwick, all smiling, laughing, waving, continuing to call out congratulations and blessings. Lyla poked her head out the window and smiled through her tears at Aunt Marion, who stood snug against Pa Hardwick's side with her wedding bouquet still clutched in her hands. They'd said their good-byes that morning before heading to the church for their double wedding, so all that remained was the leave-taking. Driving away would be hard, but knowing Aunt Marion was happy and no longer alone eased the sting of separation. Besides, she had Jared at her side.

Aunt Marion touched her fingers to her lips and blew a kiss. Lyla imitated the gesture.

Pa Hardwick hollered over the throng, "Our prayers go with you! We love you!"

Jared pressed in close behind Lyla. "We love you, too. Be happy."

"We will." He boldly kissed Aunt Marion's cheek right there in the churchyard in front of everyone, and Aunt Marion didn't even blush.

The stagecoach lurched forward, and Jared and Lyla continued waving out the window until the coach turned a corner and hid the church and the joyous throng from sight. Then they settled into the seat with Jared's arm around her waist and her cheek on his shoulder.

Jared tipped his chin against her temple and sighed.

She snuggled closer. "We'll be happy, too."

"Of course we will, Lithe Legs."

"Lithe Legs. . ." Swallowing a chortle, she shifted enough to look into his twinkling blue eyes. "When are you going to stop calling me that ridiculous name?"

He waggled his eyebrows and flicked her veil. "Dunno. It's a pretty good In-di-an name."

The laughter escaped. What a tease he was. And she wouldn't have him any other way.

Kim Vogel Sawyer, a Kansas resident, is a wife, mother, grandmother, teacher, writer, speaker, and lover of cats and chocolate. From the time she was a very little girl, she knew she wanted to be a writer, and seeing her words in print is the culmination of a lifelong dream. Kim relishes her time with family and friends, and stays active in her church by teaching adult Sunday school, singing in the choir, and being a "ding-a-ling" (playing in the bell choir). In her spare time, she enjoys drama, quilting, and calligraphy.

Sing of
the Mercy

by Connie Stevens

Dedication

To all the God-made and God-blessed matches.

To the couples who have worked at their marriage and made it last for the long haul.

To the couples whose love is defined by

"For better or for worse, for richer or poorer, in sickness and in health. . ."

This story is dedicated to couples like Morris and Velma Crumbley,

who know the meaning of commitment.

I will sing of the mercies of the LORD for ever: with my mouth
will I make known thy faithfulness to all generations.
PSALM 89:1 KJV

Chapter One

Prescott, Dakota Territory, 1880

The heat from the cast-iron oven blasted Sarah Trent's face as she bent to retrieve the pan of biscuits while rowdy miners elbowed past each other to get their grub. Even in the midst of their commotion, "How Firm a Foundation" hummed from her heart and lips. Their numbers had dwindled to a fraction of the mob she'd served less than a year ago. How could so much racket come from fewer than twenty men?

The wood-framed tent with the unpainted clapboard front housed more than Sarah's Hash House at the Three Pines mining camp. The makeshift structure also served as a gathering place for men who'd converged on the Black Hills area hoping to fill their pockets with gold. When they all started exchanging opinions over whether any of them would pull more than a few more gold flakes from the sandy creek bottom, she could barely hear herself think. Hymns were her refuge.

Once she'd served all the men and their mouths were occupied with supper, she switched from humming to singing. "'What more can He say than to you He hath said; to you who for refuge to Jesus have fled?'"

Jarvis, one of the men sitting closest to the serving counter, sent her a gap-toothed grin. "Thet there voice o' yourn is so sweet, I don't even need no honey for my biscuit."

Sarah's brother, Lanny, slouched behind the serving counter with his feet propped up on the flour barrel. He snorted at Jarvis's remark. "You might think so, but you don't have to listen to her screech those church songs the whole blessed day."

The remark stung—not because he'd insulted her singing voice, but because her brother had no love for the hymns their mother had taught them in the years before she died. An ache born of guilt and regret assailed. Sarah pressed her lips together so tightly, her teeth pierced the tender flesh. She'd tried to finish the job her mother had begun and raise Lanny to be a fine man who loved the Lord. Tried, but failed. Once again, her inadequacies gnawed on her spirit.

She retrieved the large, graniteware coffeepot and made the rounds, tucking her emotions into her pocket. It wasn't as if she'd never heard Lanny express discontent before. All cups filled, she retreated to the kitchen and lifted the stew-pot lid. "There's plenty more if anyone wants seconds."

Lanny tossed his empty tin plate into the washtub. "Not like it was a few months ago, is it? When Three Pines was overflowing with miners and men had to wait in line to eat." He wiped his mouth on his sleeve. "Every week there's a few less, because the ones who've already left have better sense than the ones still here."

Sarah shifted her gaze to the men sitting at the table closest to Lanny, hoping they'd not take offense to his statement. But Lanny wasn't finished.

"Why are we still sitting here when the Homestake Mine upstream is drilling all the gold out of the rock before it has a chance to come downstream?" His derisive grumble underscored the bitterness of his words. "The creek side claims haven't sifted out more than a few flakes in months. There's no more gold to be had here, not with Homestake's operation grabbing up the gold way up there in the hills. It's not right."

Sarah refilled her brother's coffee mug. "I might remind you that you did, indeed, find some gold, and you spent most of it in the saloons and gambling houses. If you'd saved it like I told you—"

Lanny's boots hit the floor with a thump loud enough to draw the attention of every man in the room, and his coffee sloshed over the edge of his cup. "Get off my back and quit preaching to me. You're not my ma. It's my gold. I'll do what I want with it." He set aside his coffee. "Even the saloons have closed down. Slade's place is the only one left in camp now."

Through gritted teeth, Sarah forced a smile she didn't feel. "It's not a *mining camp* any longer. The miners have voted to establish a town. They've even given it a name—Prescott." She reached to touch his arm, the way their mother used to do. "Lanny, maybe it's time you settle down and become a part of a community."

He shook off her hand, his retort muffled. "I don't intend to be shackled anywhere. Look around, Sarah. This place is dying. I want to go places and see things I've never seen before—things I can't see sitting here panning for a measly few grains of gold."

Before she could form a reply, he stomped out of the kitchen area and found a seat with other men.

Speculating over the places Lanny wanted to go and the things he wanted to see made her stomach knot. But she couldn't let him go without her. Why, he'd get into one scrape after another if she wasn't there to look after him. True, most of the miners had pulled up stakes and moved on. But those who remained weren't in a hurry to leave. Some still held out hope they might hit a rich strike any day, while others were simply tired of the vagabond life, scratching for a grubstake.

The prospect of packing up and moving to wherever Lanny fancied sent a dull ache of dread through her. If Prescott truly did become a town, Sarah dreamed of putting up real walls and a roof instead of canvas and tin, and turning the mining camp's Hash House into a real restaurant where families would come to dine. She pushed the vision away. Simply saying the place was a town didn't make it so, and dreams could turn to ashes overnight.

"Y'know, Miss Sarah, Lanny might have a point." Jarvis and Pete, claim partners for as long as Sarah had been there, stood at the serving counter. Pete rubbed his hand over his scruffy beard. "Me 'n' Jarvis here was talkin' to Bud Welsh yesterday, an' Bud said lots o' camps have shut down. Bud says his freight business is hurtin' 'cause he don't have half the customers he used to."

Jarvis toyed with his coffee mug. "Callin' the place a town and givin' it Grizzly Prescott's name were jest a way to remember the old codger."

Sarah sent her gaze across the tent to the rest of the men who had paused their own conversations to listen to the exchange. Expectant faces waited, and she had a feeling if she followed Lanny to who-knows-where, the rest would leave as well.

"But how can you vote to turn the place into a real town if you have no intention of staying and helping to build the community?" She nodded toward Quinn Walker who sat at one of the far tables. "You even elected a mayor."

The attention of every man in the room shifted.

◆ ◆ ◆

Quinn Walker drained the remainder of the coffee in his mug. When the men appointed him mayor, they all clapped him on the shoulder and said they knew he'd do a fine job. He hadn't gotten the impression then, nor did he get it now, that the men weren't serious about turning Three Pines mining camp into a real town. No, the men all gave the impression they trusted him. How could he let them down?

He slung his leg to the outer edge of the bench and stood. "I'm not one for giving speeches. Guess you all know I didn't really want to be the mayor. But I'm not going to run from the responsibility now that you've placed it on my shoulders."

He cast a quick glance around to every face in the Hash House, including Miss Sarah's. "I remember the town where I grew up—a community where folks got married and raised their families and helped out their neighbors." He tucked his thumbs in his pockets and took a couple of steps forward. "Every man here came from a different walk of life. You all weren't miners when the news first broke about the gold strike hereabouts. All of you left some other occupation to try your hand at being a miner, hoping to get rich."

The men glanced at one another and nodded. Quinn chuckled. "Well, none of us got rich."

Sheepish smiles and a few scowls met his observation. He pointed to the group sitting at the table to his right. "Morris, what did you do before you came here?"

Morris Crumbley swallowed his last bite of biscuit. "I was a tinsmith. Made buckets, washtubs, feedin' troughs, tin plates, and the like."

"Cy, what about you? As I recall, you were a wheelwright, weren't you?"

Cy nodded. "Yep. Wasn't my shop. I worked with my pa."

Quinn stepped from table to table, asking each man his trade before he sought to get rich mining for gold. A breath of hope filled Quinn's lungs, and he gestured all around the Hash House, pointing at each man. "Right here we have a couple of farmers, a blacksmith, a cooper, a boot maker, store clerk, a wheelwright, a tanner, a tinsmith, and Jarvis there worked in a sawmill. I used to work with my uncle who was a builder, and I worked part-time as a county clerk."

Quinn strode to the serving counter where Jarvis and Pete still stood. "Don't you see? We have the makings of a town sitting right here."

A murmur hummed through the group until Jarvis raised his hand. "But, Quinn, none of us have the money it would take to get set up in business. That takes materials and supplies and labor."

The others nodded in agreement, and Miss Sarah's brother crossed his arms and assumed an "I-told-you-so" smirk.

Jarvis's observation rang with truth. He'd just stated moments ago that none of them had pocketfuls of gold. But surely there had to be a way for all of them to come together and return to their former occupations right here in their fledging town of Prescott. "How many of you are interested enough to give me time to come up with a plan?"

Most of the men—except for Lanny Trent—looked to the man at his right and left and shrugged.

Cy leaned to whisper to the men around him, and then nodded. "Don't cost nothin' to listen."

Encouragement ignited in Quinn's chest. "All right. I'll have to spend some time thinking out the details, but what I have in mind is kind of a barter system, except instead of exchanging goods, you exchange labor. I'll have to speak with some folks about materials, but as mayor—and since I have building experience—I'm willing to help any man here."

The men exchanged tentative looks of approval.

Morris Crumbley poked his finger in the air. "I got a question. You said somethin' about marryin' and raisin' families. Don't we need women for that?"

A few guffaws rumbled through the tent. Quinn pulled his brow into a frown, but before he could answer, Miss Sarah stepped forward.

"Can a woman speak at this meeting?"

Quinn didn't think there was a man present who didn't like Miss Sarah. She fed them, she sang to them, and some said her singing was the only religion they got.

"Would you men be willing to marry and settle down?"

Lanny scowled, and a couple of men made crude remarks about the women who worked at the saloons. Sarah's brother responded with a blast of laughter. Red crawled up Miss Sarah's neck and invaded her cheeks.

Quinn stepped forward and pointed to the culprits. "You men will speak respectfully to Miss Sarah."

But when he tried to encourage her to continue, she dipped her head and mumbled something about needing to get back to the kitchen. A few elbows were thrust into ribs, but all smirking ceased when Quinn glared at them.

He followed Sarah into the kitchen. Her sweet voice hummed "Rock of Ages" as she worked at her dishpan.

"Miss Sarah?"

She turned.

The humiliation on her face pierced his heart. "I apologize for those men who can't seem to keep a respectful tongue in their head. I'll deal with them privately. In the meantime, I'd like to hear your idea."

Chapter Two

The aroma of venison cutlets and fried potatoes sizzling in the huge skillet made Sarah's mouth water. She tipped her head and glanced out the front entrance to check the position of the sun. The men would be lining up soon.

At the framed front door of the Hash House, Quinn tapped a tack into the notice they'd written informing the miners of the meeting set to follow the evening meal. All day she'd been singing "O God, Our Help in Ages Past," the words of the hymn forming a prayer on her lips. They needed His help if this plan was to work. When she and Quinn had discussed it, their ideas had sounded workable, even exciting. Now, however, as they prepared to present their plan to the men, doubts tumbled through her. She hoped the suggestions they'd drawn up wouldn't alienate the men. But most of all, she prayed Lanny would agree to go along with their proposal to turn the dying mining camp into a real town, and see it as an opportunity to establish a solid life for himself.

How many prayers had she lifted to heaven for Lanny? For years, she'd longed to see him return to the faith they were taught as children, but her prayers never found God's approval. She couldn't imagine why God didn't want the same things for her brother that she wanted. His Word assured her He listened to her prayers, but for some reason, He didn't seem to agree with her.

Perhaps, if their plan worked, and Prescott grew into the kind of community they envisioned, they could establish a church. Surely having a church and a preacher would impact Lanny's choices.

The apple dumplings she'd made that afternoon sat near the back of the stove. What man couldn't be in a receptive mood while eating warm apple dumplings? She cracked open the oven door to check on the corn bread.

"Want me to ring the bell yet, Miss Sarah?"

She closed the oven and glanced up. Her breath hitched. Quinn's smile had a strange effect on her.

She pulled her attention back to the stove. "Not yet. In a few minutes." She twisted the corner of her apron and glanced at Quinn. "Are you ready to present our ideas to the men?"

He nodded. "Stop worrying. We just have to make them understand how much it will benefit them individually as well as collectively."

She tucked her bottom lip between her teeth and wished she possessed the confidence Quinn seemed to have.

He leveled his hazel eyes at her and held her gaze. "How are you doing, Miss Sarah? I mean, here?" He gestured around the Hash House. "With all the men who've already left, are you making enough to stay in business?"

A shrug lifted her shoulders. "It's a little tight. Sometimes, when I order supplies, I forget I'm not feeding as many men as I was last year. But I'm making do."

Quinn glanced at the carefully-lettered sign above the serving counter that stated breakfast cost twenty-five cents and supper was thirty cents. "You haven't raised your prices since you first opened."

A tiny frown tugged at her brow. "I can't raise my prices when the men are finding less gold." She checked the corn bread again and pulled out the big cast-iron pan. "As soon as I slice this, I'll be ready to ring the bell."

He sent her a grin. "You just keep singing. It makes them smile."

His comment screwed her face in a grimace. "Some of them."

"Most of them." He jerked his thumb over his shoulder toward the door. "They're already starting to line up. Guess the aroma of apple dumplings works better than ringing a bell." He started toward the door, then looked back at her. "Sing something cheery."

The men filed in, dropping their money into the crock sitting beside the stack of clean plates. "What's this meetin' about, Miss Sarah?"

She smiled her sweetest smile. "Enjoy your supper first." As she filled plates with venison cutlets and fried potatoes, she lifted her voice in song. "'My hope is built on nothing less than Jesus' blood and righteousness.'"

Two or three men joined in with her in an off-key harmony, setting off some good-natured banter. Sarah heaped plates with steaming food for the hungry men, but noticed a few silent scowls. She glanced over her shoulder as Lanny reached past her to help himself instead of waiting in line. Sarah shook her head and sent apologetic looks to the other men. Once everyone had a full plate and a seat, Sarah swept her gaze across the Hash House until she found Quinn. Unspoken reassurance from his expression bolstered her. She took the pan of apple dumplings from the stove and went from table to table, scooping them onto each man's plate.

"Mm—mm, Miss Sarah. You spoilin' us."

"I ain't had apple dumplin's since I was a boy."

"Good eatin' tonight, boys."

Sarah smiled her appreciation at their compliments. The men stuffed the dessert into their mouths with gusto.

It was time. She nodded to Quinn.

◆　◆　◆

Quinn stepped forward and pulled the plan he and Sarah had worked on together from his pocket. "Men, can I have your attention?"

Lanny snickered. "Hey, boys, our *mayor* has something he wants to say." He stood. "Well, I don't believe I'm much interested in this little meeting."

"Lanny!" Miss Sarah's voice reflected her annoyance, and the red blush on her face proclaimed her embarrassment.

While Sarah's brother sauntered out, Quinn lifted his hand. "That's all right. Let's get down to business."

The men turned their attention to Quinn.

He unfolded his paper. "The purpose for this meeting is to discuss what we started talking about a couple of days ago."

A miner named Kincaid spoke up. "Quinn, you really think we can be a town?"

"Why not?" Quinn propped one foot on a bench. "We all know four years ago, Deadwood was just a mining camp. By 1877, it became a town. All the tents disappeared and they built wood and brick buildings. They have stores, places of business, houses—"

"And a church."

All eyes turned toward Miss Sarah.

Quinn smiled. "Yes, they do have a church."

Jarvis grinned. "Well, little Miss Sarah there sings to us about God every day."

Pete cackled beside him. "Listenin' to her is about the closest thing you'll ever get to preachin'."

Quinn suppressed a smile. Pete said that every time Sarah sang.

"All right, now." Quinn waited for the men to quiet down. "My point is if Deadwood can go from a mining camp to a real town, so can Prescott. True, a lot more placer gold was found up there, but I believe people who work together to build a town can succeed. Who's to say we can't?"

The men looked at each other and nodded. Quinn's spirits rose a notch. He cleared his throat. "We already know that between all you men, we have a lot of various occupations. So here is my plan.

"Everyone will pitch in and help one another build their place of business. That will begin with teams of men going into the woods and cutting trees for lumber." He tilted his head toward the hills. "It's going to take a lot of trees, so this will be ongoing for the rest of spring and all summer. There are several tents that were left behind when some folks cleared out, so some of you can use those until your place is built."

"But we ain't got no lumber mill."

"I know that," Quinn responded quickly before opposition could fester. "Jarvis here worked in a sawmill, and I know a man I can contact to see if he would be willing to bring equipment in to set up a lumber operation. But he'd be taking a big risk, so before he'll do that, he will need commitments from all of you to see this plan through."

Kincaid folded his arms. "We're listenin'."

Quinn outlined their plan and described how everyone would work toward a common goal, but it would require they barter with labor. Every man who received help building his place would in turn help those who helped him. Quinn glanced at Sarah and knew she was praying.

"The plan is built on a foundation of cooperation and community. Before the end of summer, we can see Prescott with a store, a blacksmith shop, businesses like a cooper, a wheelwright, a tanner, a tinsmith, a harness maker." He nodded toward Sarah. "And a restaurant."

"And a church." Sarah's eyes pleaded. "We need a church."

Kincaid waved from the back. "Speakin' o' churches. You said somethin' the other day about marryin'. Iffen we get us a church, that's fine. But you ain't said how we're gonna find us some wives. We're a little short on gals around here."

Guffaws exploded inside the Hash House. Once Quinn restored order, he beckoned to Sarah. "Since this part of the plan is Miss Sarah's idea, I think I'll let her tell you." He shot a stern look around to each table that warned the men not to step out of line.

Sarah approached and stood next to him—but he noticed, not too closely. With her fingers twisted together, she began explaining how she would draw up notices that Bud Welsh would carry to some of the nearby towns or other dwindling mining camps. "The notices will announce the new town of Prescott, and will include a brief description of what we hope Prescott will be—a community where people can settle and raise families."

She glanced at Quinn, her brows raised as if she sought his approval of what she'd said thus far.

He nodded. "Go on and tell them the rest."

She swallowed. "The notices will invite marriage-minded women to come to Prescott and meet you."

A few varied responses rippled through the group—from grins to snorts. She thanked them for listening and gave the floor back to Quinn.

"Thank you, Miss Sarah." His gaze lingered on her an extra moment, and he realized the men were waiting for him to continue. "Uh, yes. In addition, we will draw up a few extra notices for Bud to drop off at the post office in Rapid City. These notices will be sent to towns to the east."

He rubbed his palms together. "Now, there is another detail to point out. You men have been rubbing shoulders with nobody but other miners for a while. And quite frankly, some of you fellows could do with a bath and a shave. I'll be happy to supply the soap."

Muted complaints rumbled through the men. Pete glared at Jarvis. "Been so long since you've seen a bar of soap, I expect you can't 'member what it's for." A few more hoots of laughter rang out.

"Let me remind you that we have a lady here in Prescott who takes in laundry. I'm sure Mrs. Falk will be happy for your business, and the rest of us will be grateful." Quinn turned toward the kitchen where Sarah stood behind the serving counter. "Also, Miss Sarah has volunteered to give haircuts. You can't meet prospective brides looking like a bunch of grizzly bears."

The men responded with mock protests. He grinned and waited for comments to die down. "You men are pretty rough around the edges. If you're going to attract the women who will be coming, you need to clean yourselves up a little."

As the men rose to leave, a half dozen of them crowded around vying for the privilege of being first in line for a haircut from Miss Sarah. A strange jab poked Quinn's chest. These men were entirely too anxious for a chance to spend time sitting with Sarah while she fussed over them.

Chapter Three

Sarah bent her head over the notice she was writing, keenly aware of Quinn watching over her shoulder. His nearness unnerved her, but she didn't have time to sort through the reasons why. The way he'd jumped to her defense and made sure the men treated her with respect reminded her of the way Papa had always treated Mama.

The Hash House was quiet at this time of day, and she appreciated his help with the signs. Bud Welsh had promised to pick them up on his return trip in a few days, which didn't leave them much time. Scrounging for supplies to write up the notices had been a challenge. Sarah carefully cut labels from tin cans, and Quinn salvaged a piece of damaged canvas and a few scraps of clapboard. Together they worded the notice:

> *ATTENTION*
> *~Women seeking to marry~*
> *The newly established town of Prescott, Dakota Territory*
> *(formerly Three Pines mining camp)*
> *extends an invitation to women*
> *who desire to marry, settle down, and start families.*
> *The men of Prescott are of a mind to take wives and become*
> *   family men.*
> *Opportunities to meet potential husbands and form courting*
> *   agreements.*
> *Bring linens, household items, and such.*
> *See Quinn Walker—mayor*
> *or Sarah Trent at the Hash House.*

Sarah held up the first sign. "What do you think?"

Quinn studied it a moment and gave a nod of approval. "Looks just fine. Writing on the canvas will be a little harder, but Bud gave me a can of black paint to use."

"That was nice of him." She laid the completed sign to one side and prepared to begin a new one.

Quinn's chuckle rumbled. "I think Bud might be in the market for a bride, too."

"Wonderful." Sarah glanced up at him. "What did he say when you talked to him about going into partnership with Crandall to establish a mercantile?"

"He's for it. I think he's tired of sleeping in his freight wagon and rattling his bones back and forth between towns and camps." He drained his coffee cup. "His support will be a big help."

While Quinn cut the salvaged canvas into usable-sized pieces, Sarah retrieved the coffeepot from the back of the stove. "I thought of something this morning. When the brides come, they're going to need a place to stay. What if we took apart two or three of those abandoned tents and built a large one right next door to the Hash House?"

Quinn looked up from his task. "You mean like a dormitory? That's a good idea, and they'd be close by so you could keep an eye out." He gestured toward the signs. "Of course, we're assuming this is going to work and we will have brides pouring in here by the dozens."

Sarah caught the lilt of humor in his voice as she refilled their cups. "I doubt we'll need a three-story hotel, but I am praying for enough ladies to match with all the men who are interested." She set the empty pot on the table.

"Of course, you are." His warm tone pulled her attention away from their project for a moment and she met his gaze.

The corners of Quinn's mouth tipped up. "You know, when some of the men say your hymn singing is the only religion they get, they're wrong. They don't even know about your prayers."

Shyness pulled her back to the work in front of her. "My mother taught me to pray about everything."

The same teasing tone she'd detected in his voice earlier returned. "I can imagine with Lanny around, you get a lot of practice."

Heat rose up her throat and into her face.

"I'm sorry, Sarah." Quinn's voice held a note of chagrin. "I didn't mean that the way it sounded."

"No, you're absolutely right." Regret bled through her. "Lanny certainly gives me a lot to pray about. I just wish—"

Quinn remained quiet, but she didn't fill the void by finishing her thought.

After a time, he prompted. "What do you wish, Sarah?"

"Oh. . ." She waved her hand and hoped the tremble in her middle didn't give her away. "It was nothing. I hope he'll decide to stay here in Prescott. Who knows? Maybe he'll fall in love and settle down with one of the Prescott brides."

"Maybe." He finished cutting the pieces of canvas. "Did you write the letters you were telling me about—to find a preacher?"

"Yes." She patted her apron pocket. "I'll give them to Bud to mail for me. One is to the synod our church belonged to when we lived in Ohio, and the other is to the conclave of churches in Nebraska. Surely someone will be able to recommend a minister for us."

They finished the signs and set them aside to dry. While Sarah cleaned the table, Quinn fidgeted. Worried she'd offended him by taking the liberty to write the letters, she glanced over at him. "Is something wrong?"

"Huh?" He jerked his head up. "Oh, no. I was just wondering. . .did the men come for their haircuts?"

"Three this morning. Two more tomorrow."

"And?"

"And what?"

A sigh hissed from his lips. "Did they. . .behave like gentlemen?"

"I was singing 'Am I a Soldier of the Cross.' How do you suppose they behaved?"

"Hmph. You'll tell me if any of them steps out of line."

"I see these men every day." She plopped her fists on her hips. "Why this sudden concern?"

"Well. . . Because—because—"

She arched her brows and waited.

"Because I'm the mayor." He slapped his hat on his head and strode out the door.

Sarah covered her mouth with her fingertips even though there was no one to hear her chuckle. As she made her way back to the kitchen, another hymn—one of her father's favorites—formed on her lips.

"'Alas, and did my Savior bleed, and did my Sovereign die? Would He devote that sacred head—'"

"Miss Trent?"

She spun. The man standing in the kitchen doorway didn't normally frequent the Hash House, although she was well acquainted with his identity. After all, Lanny had spent many hours and most of his gold in Milton Slade's establishment.

"Mr. Slade. Is there something I can do for you?"

"I wanted to talk to you about *this*." He stabbed his finger toward the drying signs. "This little brainstorm of yours is gonna cut into my business."

If only that were true. In truth, she'd have a hard time feeling sorry if the man had to shut down his saloon for lack of business. "I hardly see how you can blame me for that, Mr. Slade."

He shook his finger at her. "There aren't many miners left here at Three Pines. But you know as well as I do, if you turn the ones who're still here into family men, they'll stop coming in to my place."

She lifted her chin and straightened her shoulders. "And you know, sir, that most of the men who visited your place have already left Prescott. Yes, it's called Prescott, now, not Three Pines. It's not a mining camp anymore. The men who are still here want to see it become a town and they are all in favor of our plan to bring in decent, God-fearing ladies to become wives for them." She crossed her arms. "Furthermore, we've prayed about this. So don't blame me, Mr. Slade. Take it up with God."

Slade growled and stomped out, colliding as he did so with Mrs. Falk, the woman who took in laundry for Sarah and many others in town, including Mr. Slade. Some of her laundry bundles hit the ground, and Sarah ran to help the woman.

Slade barked at Mrs. Falk as he took his leave. "Why don't you watch where you're going?" He stalked away but looked over his shoulder at the chaos he'd caused.

Sarah gasped. "Why, you bully! Come back here and help—"

"No, please." Mrs. Falk stooped and gathered up the bundles of clean laundry, some of which would have to be rewashed. "Let him go."

Sarah helped the slight woman to her feet. "You shouldn't allow him to get away with such rudeness."

Mrs. Falk brushed back mousey brown hair that contained a few strands of gray. "It's all right. I don't want to cause any trouble." She surveyed the dirtied bundles. "I'm sorry, but I'll have to take your laundry back and do some of it over again."

"There's no hurry. Are you sure you're all right?"

"Yes, yes, I'm fine."

Mrs. Falk's mumbled reply left Sarah a bit skeptical.

"At least let me get you a drink of water while you sit and catch your breath."

"Well, a sip of water would be nice."

Sarah dashed back to the kitchen, scooped a cup of water from the barrel, and hurried back to Mrs. Falk. "Here you go."

"Thank you." The woman kept her eyes downcast as she sipped her water, and Sarah studied her for a moment.

"What do you think of the plan to turn the mining camp into a real community?"

Mrs. Falk shrugged. "Married men have wives to do their laundry. I won't be able to make a living here."

Sarah touched her hand. "Why don't you consider becoming one of Prescott's brides?"

The woman blanched and shook her head. "I have to go. Thank you for the water."

As Mrs. Falk grabbed her bundles and scurried away, Sarah wondered about her husband. She'd always assumed the woman was a widow. Had she just made a grave error?

◆　◆　◆

Quinn listened to a couple of the men voice their concerns about the plan to bring in potential brides. Three of the seven men sitting around him had yet to commit to Quinn's plan to establish businesses, and two of them expressed strong doubts—if not dread—over the prospect of marriage.

The man named Duffy scratched his whiskery chin. "Maybe I'll just stay out yonder by the creek side and keep on pannin' for gold. You never can tell. I could strike it rich any day now."

"Aw, Duff, there ain't no more gold. Admit it." Reece elbowed his friend. "It ain't the gold keepin' you out here. And it ain't all the work it'd take to start up a business and help build the town, neither. It's the idea o' gettin' hitched."

"Well, we don't know nothin' about these women comin' to town." Duffy pointed his dirty finger at Quinn. "An' neither do you. What if they ain't perty to look at? What if we don't take a fancy to each other? What then?"

Another man, Leon, bobbed his head. "We don't know nothin' about courtin'."

Quinn held up his hands. "Nobody is going to force you to court or marry. Just don't rule out the idea. Give it a chance. You won't know for sure until the ladies arrive. In the meantime, Miss Sarah and I will teach you what you need to know—how to behave around a lady—so you won't feel awkward. What do you say?"

Duffy and Reece exchanged looks, then they both eyed Leon. "I don't know. . ."

Reece shrugged. "How bad can it be? He said we don't hafta if we don't wanna."

Gradually, the others nodded.

"All right. I'll try."

"Yeah, me, too."

Relief spread through Quinn's belly. A total of fourteen men had committed to the plan. Not a huge number, to be sure. But it was a start. He rose and shook hands with each man before hiking back to let Sarah know.

Sarah. Had he just volunteered her to help refine these men without asking her?

Chapter Four

Sarah sniffed the savory aroma of stewing prairie chickens and gave thanks once again for the gunnysack full of birds Quinn had brought her yesterday. Chicken and dumplings were a treat the men would appreciate. She gave the broth a gentle stir and tapped the ladle on the edge of the pot.

Returning to the worktable, she continued cutting young carrots and greens fresh from the garden. Today marked one week since Bud had taken the carefully printed notices advertising for potential wives to come to Prescott. Impatience nipped at her. She knew better than to urge God to hurry up and answer her prayers, but she was eager to see the brides begin to arrive.

The rat-a-tatting of the hammers next door reminded her the tent dormitory for the brides wasn't yet completed, but she smiled knowing preparations for the women were underway. Quinn promised the shelter would be finished in another day or two. In the meantime, she planned a few feminine touches she hoped would give the tent a more welcoming appearance.

Anticipation bubbled within her, and she raised her voice in yet another hymn. "'Come Thou fount of every blessing, tune my heart to sing Thy grace. Streams of mercy never ceasing, call for songs of loudest praise.'"

The distinctive sound of a freight wagon rattling into town cut her singing short. She fished in her apron pocket for the lengthy list she'd been jotting down all week, waiting for Bud Welsh to arrive. Not only were her larders growing thin, but she also planned some special treats for the brides.

She scurried to the pantry and stood on tiptoe to reach behind the molasses crock on the top shelf for her money box. Her fingers curled around the metal till, and she lifted it toward her.

Something was wrong.

The tin box was too light. She carried it to the table and fumbled in her pocket for the key. But when she tried to insert the key in the lock, the lid opened of its own accord. The broken lock fell away as she pushed the lid back.

An invisible fist punched the air from her body. She tried to gasp, but all she could do was croak. The empty cash box gawked back at her, as if waiting for an explanation. After she'd deposited the proceeds from breakfast this morning, she had nearly sixty dollars in bills, coin, gold dust, and even a few small placer nuggets. Gone.

Nausea rose in her throat. Who would do this?

The list lying on the table beside the empty box begged her attention. Her handwriting on the scrap of paper swam out of focus as tears burned her eyes. What was she going to do?

"Miss Sarah?"

She pulled her gaze toward Bud Welsh's voice. He stood in the doorway of the Hash House, his battered hat twisted in his hands.

"Wondered if you had need of supplies today. I gotta get back on the road right soon, but I wanted to check with you first."

"Bud. Uh, yes, I have a list, but there's a problem."

Bud wove his way through the maze of tables to the kitchen.

Sarah pulled in a deep breath and willed her hands to stop shaking. As she explained her predicament to the freight man, his eyes widened and a scowl carved creases in his face. "Jumpin' catfish, Miss Sarah. What're you gonna do? Got any idea who mighta—"

She waved her hand to cut him off. Entertaining thoughts of who had stolen her money turned her stomach. "I have no idea." It was a lie, and she hoped Bud didn't know it.

"You still need supplies, doncha? I can let you have a few things on credit, but I'd need payment when I come back through next week."

Sarah could have hugged him for his offer, but at the same time hot tears threatened. She'd never purchased anything on credit before. Her parents had always taught her cash on the barrel.

She broke her list down to the bare necessities and offered to let Bud hold her mother's brooch as security.

"Why, Miss Sarah, I'm downright offended. You don't need to give me nothin'. I know you'll pay me." He helped her carry her purchases in from the wagon while she thanked him profusely.

"At least let me fix you some food to take with you on the trail."

He sent her a cockeyed grin. "Now I'd thank you mighty kindly for that."

He lingered by the kitchen door while she fixed thick sandwiches with leftover ham from the smokehouse. She tried to turn the conversation to the notices they'd sent out a week ago, but Bud kept urging her to report the theft to somebody.

"Reckon Quinn oughta know about this, doncha think?"

She bit her lip and shook her head. "Please don't say anything to anybody. It was my own fault. I should have been more careful." She handed him the sack stuffed with sandwiches, three apples, and a bundle of oatmeal cookies. "Thanks again, Bud.

Be careful, and I'll see you next week."

He accepted the food with a doubtful expression. "Leastwise think about it, all right?" He tipped his hat. "You take care, Miss Sarah."

As soon as he was gone, Sarah shoved the empty cash box back into the pantry. Despite telling Bud she had no idea who might have stolen the money, the fact she didn't want to admit was that Lanny was the only other person who knew where she hid the cash box.

◆　◆　◆

Sarah couldn't blame the distant howling of the coyotes for keeping her awake. Even humming "My Faith Looks Up to Thee" all through supper, she couldn't keep her eyes from darting toward the entrance every few minutes. But Lanny never showed up for supper. Even now, as sleep eluded her, he wasn't home yet.

"Lord, it's been dark for hours. He can't still be out at his claim." She rolled to her side and tried to relax. Bud was right, of course. Quinn should be told, but she couldn't bring herself to put Lanny under suspicion.

"There's no proof. It could have been anyone." But her words rang as hollow as the coyotes' howl and as empty as her cash box.

A sharp *thunk* followed by a curse jolted her upright. Off-key singing and slurred words announced Lanny's arrival.

"Roff of dages, clipped for thee, ret me high byself in dee." Another crash sounded like her brother had stumbled over a bench. Sarah yanked back the quilt and scrambled from her cot.

She snatched her robe. "Lanny? Is that you?"

She lit the oil lamp beside her bed and turned up the wick. The glow of the flame lit her way through their tiny living quarters and kitchen to the front of the Hash House.

Her brother lay on the floor, kicking the toppled bench out of his way. When she bent to help him up, he reeked of whiskey.

"Oh, Lanny. Why must you go off drinking? Mama's heart would grieve if—"

Lanny pushed her away and roared to his feet. "Y' think yer my mama, but you ain't. Ah do wha I wanna do." He let loose a string of ear-scorching curses.

Sarah gasped. Mortification nearly choked her to hear her brother use such vile language. She tried to swallow back the tightening in her throat. "Lanny, let me help you to bed. You're drunk."

She took his arm, but he slung her away from him and bellowed at her. "Leef me 'lone. Ah don nee' you an' yer p'eachin'."

He staggered through the Hash House, in the general direction of their living quarters, pushing over tables or anything else in his way.

Hot tears burned her eyes and she squeezed them shut. *"Oh, Lord, why don't You hear my prayers for Lanny?"*

◆　◆　◆

Quinn had tried a dozen different positions on his cot trying to get comfortable, unable to get the picture of Sarah's worried expression out of his mind. He'd stopped short of asking her what was wrong—not because he didn't care, but because he could guess. He suspected it had something to do with her brother, especially since Lanny didn't show up to eat.

A crash and shouting interrupted his weighty thoughts, and he leapt from his bed. The commotion came from the direction of the Hash House. He tugged on his pants and boots and jogged down the path toward Sarah's place. The glow of a lamp threw silhouettes on the canvas walls, and Lanny's cursing echoed through the camp.

Anger hastened his steps. How dare that ungrateful, young hooligan talk to his sister like that. If that lazy, no-good scoundrel laid a hand on her. . .the sound of crashing tables and benches cut into his speculation.

"Lanny, stop it!"

Sarah's distraught voice sliced through Quinn as he propelled himself to the door of the Hash House. Before he could take two strides inside, Lanny's form stumbled against the kitchen doorway and he fell.

Sarah cried out and ran to him. "Lanny! Lanny, are you all right?"

Quinn closed the distance in a few strides. "I don't think he can hear you, Sarah. He's passed out."

Sarah's head jerked up. "Oh, Quinn. You startled me. I didn't realize you were here."

"I heard him bellowing all the way up to my place." He reached down and seized Lanny under his arms. "Show me where to take him."

Sarah led the way past the canvas flap that separated the kitchen from their living quarters. Quinn hefted her unconscious brother, and dumped the boy into his cot.

Sarah pulled a quilt over him and tenderly brushed a shank of hair from his forehead.

Quinn ran his hand through his hair. He wanted to shake Lanny. Instead, he retreated to the dining area and began picking up benches and righting tables. After a couple of minutes, Sarah joined him. Even in the dimly lit room, he could see her hands tremble.

"Sarah, would you like me to stay in case he awakens and gives you any more trouble?" A peculiar longing pierced him—he realized he'd like nothing better than to be around to give Sarah a hand whenever she needed it.

"Thank you for your help, Quinn, but I'll take care of my brother." Sadness defined her words, which only served to fuel Quinn's annoyance.

"If he's old enough to go out and get drunk, isn't it time he took care of himself?"

The lamplight flicked across her face. There was no mistaking her narrowed eyes and set jaw. A hard edge sharpened her tone. "I've been taking care of Lanny since we were children."

"Sarah." He gently touched her shoulder. "Lanny's not a child."

She pushed away from him. "He's my little brother. I'm all he has left in this world. What am I supposed to do, leave him to fend for himself?" Her chin quivered and the lamplight glinted off the moisture collecting in the corners of her eyes.

His fingers itched to draw her to him and let her cry against his chest. Instead, he stuffed his hands into his pockets. "Sarah, do you know what I thought when I heard him yelling and crashing into things? I thought he was hurting you." A chill ran through him.

"Lanny would never do anything to—" She sucked in a ragged breath and looked down, her fingers twisting the edge of her robe. "Thank you for helping me get him to bed. Good night."

He studied her for a long moment. "Good night, Sarah."

As he walked back to his tent, his stomach roiled. Why did she stop in the middle of her defense of her brother? Had the kid already done something to hurt his sister?

Chapter Five

S arah surveyed the finished dormitory tent the men had erected next door to the Hash House. She hoped the women would appreciate the curtains Sarah had made from flour sacks to hang between the cots to provide a bit of privacy, and the wide plank floor the men had nailed in place.

Quinn announced to the men at breakfast that the dormitory was off-limits once the women arrived. At Sarah's request, he reinforced the rule for respectful behavior from the men, adding that "Miss Sarah won't feed you if you don't mind your manners." The warning garnered a chuckle, but the men agreed.

Mrs. Falk approached, her arms laden with bundles of laundry. She looked at the new dormitory. "Is this for the women?"

"Yes. We thought it best to house them all together." Sarah relieved Mrs. Falk of her own laundry bundle. "Would you like to see inside? We've fixed it up a bit so it's as pleasant as we can make it."

Mrs. Falk stepped forward and peered past the door frame. She gave a slight noncommittal shrug. "How many?"

"We aren't sure yet." Sarah adjusted one of the curtains. "We hope for about a dozen to begin. We've sent out quite a few notices."

The woman stood and stared at the tent for a long moment. "Where? Where are they coming from?"

Sarah smiled. She'd never known Mrs. Falk to speak more than a few words, and then only when it pertained to her laundry business. She hoped the prospect of bringing in more women and establishing the town would help the laundress make some friends.

"Well, the notices went to several nearby mining camps, as well as some towns. Bud Welsh delivered some to the post office in Rapid City where they were mailed farther east." As Sarah described where the notices were distributed, a troubled shadow fell over Mrs. Falk's countenance.

"Once the women arrive and settle in, we hope they will agree to pitch in and help the community in different ways."

Mrs. Falk shot a sharp, almost fearful glance at Sarah. "What ways?"

"Helping in the garden, for one thing." Sarah tipped her head toward the rear of the Hash House where her kitchen garden always stood in need of weeding. "If some of the women can sew, perhaps they could help with mending. Of course, I can always use a hand in the Hash House with serving or cleaning up."

Sarah touched Mrs. Falk's arm. "What about you? Could you use some help with your laundry business?"

Several seconds passed before Mrs. Falk responded, but the invitation went unacknowledged. "Be careful of them—the women. You don't know. . . You just don't know."

Sarah frowned. "What do you mean?" But Mrs. Falk was already hurrying away.

◆　◆　◆

Quinn hadn't revisited the topic of Lanny's drunken behavior with Sarah again, but he and God had certainly talked about it. The Lord had prompted him to hold his tongue and let Sarah initiate the conversation. Until then, he continued to pray.

Now, he listened as Sarah explained to Kincaid and several other men how to move their feet in time with the music, and how it was the gentleman's responsibility to lead his partner in a waltz. Quinn had helped push the tables and benches aside, but his insides chafed as he watched her teach the men to dance.

"Now you place your hand like so. . ." She demonstrated. "And hold your part-ner's hand, thus. When the music begins, you move *with* the music." She hummed a lilting tune and nudged Kincaid back and forth. "Don't look down at your feet."

Kincaid halted. "Iffen I don't watch my feet, Miss Sarah, I'm a-feared I'll tromp all over your toes."

Quinn gritted his teeth. The very thought of another man taking Sarah in his arms plowed a furrow into his brow deep enough to plant corn. He stepped forward and tapped Kincaid's shoulder. "May I?"

Kincaid scowled, but the other men hooted. Quinn laid a chaste hand on Sar-ah's side and gathered her other hand in his. He smiled down at her. "Let the music begin."

A delightful shade of pink colored her cheeks and she began to hum. Quinn guided her around the floor in a simple, but smooth pattern. "I like that song. You should sing it more often."

The pink in her cheeks deepened and she dropped her eyes.

"Don't look at your feet."

She snapped her gaze back up at him. He grinned, and couldn't think of any-thing he'd rather be doing. She ended the song prematurely and withdrew her hand before turning to the observers. "See? It's not difficult at all. Who wants to try?"

Quinn clamped his teeth together and worked his jaw muscles. Was it really necessary to teach these clodhoppers how to waltz? He endured a half hour of watching each man by turn follow Sarah's patient instructions.

Just when he thought he couldn't stand another minute, Sarah pronounced the men's dancing skills "passable."

"You all did just fine once you got the hang of it." Sarah glanced at Quinn. "Do you have anything to add?"

Oh, he most certainly did, but he doubted it was the kind of statement she meant. "Nope. What's next?"

"Tomorrow we'll talk about manners, in case any of you feel uncomfortable around a lady." She thanked the men for coming as they filed out. As soon as the last one exited, she sank down on a bench and rubbed her foot.

"If you're free tomorrow, I could use your help showing the men how to open a door for a lady, seating her at the table, some basic table manners, that sort of thing." Her eyes implored him to agree.

"I wouldn't miss it." He pointed to her foot. "How are your toes?"

She winced. "Sore. But it's for a good cause."

"Sarah, be honest. Do you really think this is going to work? Do you believe we can knock the rough edges off these men so they will make suitable husbands?" A tiny niggling of doubt poked him.

She straightened. "Of course. There's nothing wrong with these men that a few reminders of what it means to live in civilized society won't fix."

Quinn laughed. "That and a reminder about the soap. Some of them think they're supposed to wait until the women arrive before they bathe. I'll remind them that no woman wants to be around a man who smells like month-old sweat."

She covered her mouth and giggled. "Oh my, but you're right about that."

She stood and he followed suit. "I might give them a few ideas about how to compliment a lady, as well."

She cocked her head. "How do you mean?"

He reached for her hand. "Miss Sarah, you look lovely today. May I tell you how much I enjoy listening to you sing? Your smile brightens the entire room. Being in your company makes even a rainy day pleasant. Knowing you makes me want to be a better man."

With each sentiment, her eyes grew wider and her mouth formed an O. Should he add that every statement he made was true, and paying her such compliments came easy?

"Most women appreciate having a man say something nice to her." Judging by the blush on Sarah's cheeks, she was no exception.

◆　◆　◆

"'I sing the mighty power of God that makes the mountains rise; that spreads the flowing seas abroad, and built the lofty skies.'"

Sarah gave voice to the hymn and sang to God as she finished tidying the kitchen, but the effort required to open her mouth and give the song freedom wearied her. Truth be told, the music she normally couldn't hold back sounded dull and lifeless to her ears. The fact that Lanny had yet to make an appearance and still snored in his bunk underscored the late hour at which he'd come stumbling in again last night.

She cut the hymn short, and halted her hands from hurrying through their tasks, instead bowing her head. "Oh, God, how long must I pray for Lanny? Have You given up on him? Am I being foolish to keep praying, to keep believing You will change him? Lord, why don't You hear me?"

"Anybody here?"

Sarah leaned to peer past the serving counter. Milton Slade? What did he want?

The saloon owner wound his way through the maze of tables and benches. His shaggy, salt-and-pepper hair stuck out from under his hat.

Sarah stepped to the door of the kitchen to meet him, and bit her lip. She could only suppose the man was coming to harass her further about the plan to bring wives in for the men. She lifted her chin. "Mr. Slade."

"Miss." He cleared his throat and looked around. "I come to tell you somethin' 'cause I think you got a right to know."

Tension stiffened the muscles in her neck, but she worked at keeping her demeanor calm. "Yes?"

Footsteps at the entrance of the Hash House drew both their attention. Quinn's form filled the doorway.

"Slade? I hope you're not here to bother Miss Sarah again."

Slade growled. "I come to tell her somethin', and it don't concern you, *Mayor*."

Sarah sent Quinn a look that she hoped communicated her desire for him to stay. To her relief, he approached and stood nearby, arms crossed.

Reassured by Quinn's presence, she wished for the saloon owner to speak his piece and leave. "What is it you wanted to tell me, Mr. Slade?"

Slade pulled his hat from his head. "It's your brother."

All pretense at appearing composed fled. Her heart hiccupped and her breath caught. "What about him?"

The furrows across his brow deepened. "He's been at my place near every night for the past week, and he's been flashin' nuggets and dust around, buyin' drinks for everybody. And he's been gamblin' a lot. And losin' a lot."

The pain inflicted by his words rent Sarah's heart in two. An ache gathered in her throat, and she blinked back tears. Words refused to form on her tongue.

Slade must have mistaken her silence for indifference. "I ain't complainin' about the business." He blew out a stiff breath. "But I respect what you been tryin' to do, so I thought you oughta know."

She swallowed hard and straightened her shoulders. "I thought you weren't in favor of our plan to bring in wives and establish a town."

Slade shook his head and twisted the brim of his hat. "No, it ain't that. I know you been tryin' to turn your brother into an upstandin' man. Reckon most everybody here knows it. Don't know how he all of a sudden got his hands on that kind o' gold and cash. If anybody has a right to know what he's up to, it's you." He retreated a step or two. "Well, that's all I come to say." He gave Quinn a nod, slapped his hat back on his head, and tipped it to Sarah before he strode out.

Sarah sank down on a nearby bench. Slade's revelation clinched it. She could no longer deny Lanny must have been the one who broke into her cash box. But confronting him would only drive him away.

Quinn eased down beside her. "Sarah?"

He was waiting for an explanation—an explanation she didn't want to give. Her throat tightened.

Quinn's gentle touch on her hand was her undoing. Tears blurred her vision.

"Sarah, where did Lanny get that kind of gold? I know for a fact that he hasn't been out at his claim for over a month."

With a tiny nod, she told Quinn about the broken lock and missing money and gold from her cash box.

"I see." Thankfully, he didn't ask why she hadn't told him immediately, but his next question was even harder.

"Did Lanny know where you kept the cash box?"

Chapter Six

Sarah showed the two new women to the dormitory tent and directed them to pick out any of the available cots. This made seven brides in less than a week. Some were young, others a bit older, some plain, some pretty. As each one was introduced at meal time in the Hash House, the men responded with respect, if not refinement. A girl by the name of Velma appeared to have already caught the attention of Morris Crumbley, and Duffy did a double take when Audrey was introduced. One woman named Hester had appraised the men with the scrutiny of a livestock broker, prompting Sarah to turn her head lest anyone see her giggle. She almost expected the woman to check the men's teeth.

The only thing that dampened Sarah's joy was Lanny's sullenness. Perhaps when she introduced these two new girls—Pamela and Christine—he'd change his mind about wanting to leave.

The first five women had settled in for the most part, and had not minded being asked to pitch in and help with chores at all. That is, except for Florence, who seemed to think she was here to marry a rich miner and was therefore above doing chores. Sarah had pointed out that none of the miners had struck it rich, and if she married one of them, she'd be expected to do all her own chores. Florence had sulked for a day, but when she'd caught a glimpse of Quinn, she decided being helpful might work in her favor.

"When does that deliveryman come around again?" Pamela's question jolted Sarah out of her reverie.

"Deliveryman?" Sarah puzzled a moment. "Oh, you mean Bud?"

Pamela blushed and dipped her lashes. "Yes. He brought us from Sheridan so we wouldn't have to hire a driver. He was very nice."

Sarah smiled. Would Bud and Pamela be Prescott's first romance to bloom?

Before Sarah returned to the kitchen, she made sure the two new arrivals were informed of the schedule. "Supper is at six o'clock. I'd love it if you could help, either with cleanup or in the serving line. We have a ladies' Bible study starting up tomorrow morning at nine."

The Bible study had sounded like a fine idea at first, but with her prayers going unanswered, the zeal she'd once had for reading her Bible had faltered. God must be too busy to hear her. Regardless, she needed to have something ready for the women tomorrow. Perhaps the psalms. Most were short and easy to read.

Sarah scurried to the living quarters at the back of the Hash House and retrieved Mama's Bible. She flipped through the psalms and found one her mother had underlined.

"Psalm 116. 'I love the Lord, because he hath heard my voice and my supplications. Because he hath inclined his ear unto me, therefore will I call upon him as long as I live.'"

Conviction smote her heart. How could she ever think God was too busy to listen to her prayers? He promised right there on the pages of her Bible that He'd hear. "Oh, heavenly Father, I'm so sorry to doubt You. I was wrong. You've been listening all along—it's just my faith that's weak. Father, strengthen my faith."

A faint rap on the front framework of the Hash House drew her attention. "Hello?"

Sarah grabbed an apron and mopped the tears from her face. "Back here in the kitchen."

A dark-haired girl with an apprehensive expression stepped to the doorway of the kitchen. "Are you. . .Sarah Trent?"

"Yes, I'm Sarah." She laid her apron aside.

The girl wore a threadbare, much-mended dress, and held a shabby carpetbag. Her shoes were covered with dust and she released a weary sigh.

The raven-haired girl's tremulous voice was barely above a whisper. "I'm Garnet. The notice said to ask for you."

"Yes, that's right." Judging by the girl's appearance, she must have walked a long way. "You must be hungry. Sit down here." Sarah fixed her a sandwich and set a cup of coffee in front of her.

Garnet dipped her head, almost in a subservient way. "Thank you, kindly, ma'am."

While Garnet ate, Sarah filled in a few details about their new town.

"The dormitory is right next door. C'mon, I'll show you."

In between the two structures, they ran into Mrs. Falk delivering laundry. Sarah made the brief introductions.

"Mrs. Falk, this is Garnet. She has just arrived."

Mrs. Falk barely nodded a greeting and seemed unable to take her eyes off Garnet. Sarah directed Garnet to the dormitory, then turned back to get her money to pay Mrs. Falk. When Sarah returned, Mrs. Falk still stood staring toward the dormitory. Sarah glanced toward the door through which Garnet had disappeared. "She's a quiet one. Seems afraid of her own shadow."

Mrs. Falk thanked Sarah for her payment with a barely perceptible nod and sent another glance to the closed dormitory door. Her eyes spoke something Sarah could not interpret, but the woman's countenance did not invite inquiries. Did Mrs. Falk know something she didn't?

◆ ◆ ◆

Quinn lingered over his coffee and listened to Sarah's sweet voice in the kitchen. He recalled the familiar, old hymn.

"'Praise to the Lord, the Almighty, the King of creation. O my soul, praise Him, for He is thy health and salvation.'"

Sarah joined him at the table, carrying her own mug and the coffeepot. She refilled his cup and set the pot between them.

She cocked her head. "Do you ever go out to your claim anymore?"

He took a tentative slurp of the hot brew. "No. I sold it last month to a fellow who wants to raise sheep out there. He bought up several claims that are no longer producing. He's interested in the grassland and water access."

He shrugged. "I have too much to do here in town now, helping the men organize and get their businesses started. Bud Welsh and Crandall will be ready to open their mercantile in another week. The man I told you about, Ben Morgan, who has the sawmill equipment, has gotten together with Jarvis, and they're felling trees and milling lumber. Morgan is thinking about moving his family here. Kincaid is working on putting a livery and blacksmith business together. Reece and a couple of others are taking turns helping each other build."

Sarah's eyes danced, and her smile pulled a most appealing dimple into her cheek. "It all sounds so exciting." She took a sip of coffee. "I have an idea, and I'd like your opinion. Because if you agree, I'll need your help."

Quinn smiled at the glow she emanated, and listened as she described her plans for a get-together to be held at the Hash House where the men and women could get acquainted. Other than the breakfast introductions as the women arrived, they hadn't truly had much opportunity to get to know one another.

"A few of the women would help me make sandwiches and bake cookies and cakes."

Quinn nodded. "Sounds like just the thing. We can't truthfully call the men refined gentlemen, but at least they are actually *using* the soap I gave them. The next step is to see some couples begin courting."

Sarah clapped her hands like a delighted little girl, and Quinn grinned at her. Did she have any idea how lovely she was?

"Two of the women, Pamela and Christine, know how to make garlands of ivy vines and flowers to decorate the place, and you and Lanny can help me move the tables and benches."

He paused with his coffee cup halfway to his mouth. "Why do you need to move the tables?"

She tented her fingers. "I plan to ask Jarvis to play his fiddle—did you know he played the fiddle?—and Cy his harmonica so couples can try out the men's new waltzing skills."

His gut tightened as he recalled watching her teach the men to dance. Maybe he'd have to be first in line to ask Sarah to be his partner.

◆　◆　◆

The day of the event dawned with excitement humming through the Hash House. Even the men talked about it at breakfast, and Quinn overheard a few of them trading advice on how to ask a woman to dance.

As soon as Sarah shooed everyone out, Quinn poked his head in the kitchen. Two women were busy making cookies, and Sarah smoothed frosting over a cake. He couldn't resist teasing. "I don't suppose I could get a sample in payment for moving all those heavy tables."

Sarah slapped his fingers away from the frosting. "Don't you dare." She retrieved the garlands the ladies had made and beckoned for Quinn to follow her. "If you help me hang these, you can have a cookie."

He threw his head back and laughed. "Sounds like bribery, but I'll take it."

She pointed and directed, and he did her bidding, tacking the garlands around the Hash House. He had to admit they were pretty and added quite the festive touch to the place. As they worked, she sang one hymn after another.

Quinn took the tacks out of his mouth and looked at her. "You know, there's something different about you. You seem happier."

A tiny smile tilted the corners of her lips. "I finally came to an understanding with God. I stopped doubting Him, and He will answer my prayers in His time. It's called trust."

She moved about the room on wings of grace, and Quinn drank in the vision she made. Just when he thought she couldn't be any more beautiful, she proved him wrong.

Sarah picked flower stems from a basket and arranged them in canning jars. "Have any of the men mentioned being interested in a special woman?"

Quinn knew of one man who was more than interested. He was pretty sure he was falling in love with the woman who was now setting little vases of flowers on the tables. "I think maybe Bud likes Pamela. The others haven't been as open, but after tonight, we might see a few of them pairing off."

Sarah fanned herself with her apron. "I invited Mrs. Falk. I hope she comes."

Quinn tacked up another garland. "I don't know anything about her other than she takes in laundry. She pretty much keeps to herself."

Sarah dabbed her brow. "I assume she's a widow, but I've never been able to get her to chat. It's as if she prefers being alone."

She positioned herself at the end of one table and strained to slide it to the wall.

"Hey! What do you think you're doing?" Quinn glared at her with his hands on his hips. "Where's Lanny? I thought he was supposed to help move the tables."

Sarah pressed her lips together, no doubt calling on that newfound trust of which she'd spoken. "He was already up this morning when I got up to cook break-fast. He took a couple of cold biscuits left over from last night's supper, and left. He didn't say when he'd be back."

Quinn narrowed his eyes. "But he knows the party is this evening and you needed his help."

She shrugged. "Lanny doesn't share his plans with me. I don't know where he goes. Maybe he has a new claim he hasn't told anyone about."

Annoyance simmered through Quinn. Lanny knew his sister needed assistance moving the tables today. Wishing he could give the kid what for, he held up his hand for her to stop. "Don't be lifting and shoving these tables. I'll go find one of the men to help me."

"All right. I have pies to bake, anyway." She sent him a knee-buckling smile that robbed him of his good sense. "Thank you, Quinn."

He headed out the door to lasso the nearest man into helping move tables, resolved to move heaven and earth to do whatever Sarah needed.

Chapter Seven

Sarah sang quietly while she pinned up Christine's hair. A flurry of excitement rippled through the dormitory tent. The women giggled like schoolgirls, all except for Garnet, who retreated to her bunk in the corner. The others helped each other dress, loaned hair ribbons and sashes, and shared secrets about the men with whom they hoped to dance that evening.

Sarah hadn't seen Lanny all day. Most of his belongings were still tossed on or under his cot, so she felt certain he hadn't taken off for parts unknown—at least not yet. She sang another verse of "My Faith Looks Up to Thee." Lanny was making it harder and harder to practice the faith she sang about, but she was determined to do so.

A tap at the door sent the ladies scurrying, hiding behind the curtains that separated their cots. Sarah frowned. The men all knew the dormitory was off-limits, and they would see her indignant wrath in all of its glory if they trespassed.

She jerked the door open, ready to berate whoever dared to cross the invisible line, but to her surprise, it was Mrs. Falk.

A rush of pleasure filled Sarah. "Oh, Mrs. Falk. I hope this means you've decided to attend the get-together this evening."

The quiet woman shifted her gaze from Sarah to the partially closed door behind her. "If I'm allowed. Not for me, you understand. But I think I can coax Garnet to go if she has something nice to wear." Mrs. Falk held up a dress draped over her arm.

Sarah stepped all the way outside and closed the door behind her. "That is very nice of you. Garnet is so timid and shy, sometimes I wonder why she came. The others are anxious to get married and settle down, but Garnet..."

Something in Mrs. Falk's eyes halted Sarah's words—a pain with which Sarah could not identify or comprehend, heartache that aged the laundress beyond her years.

Mrs. Falk stared, unblinking at Sarah. The woman's voice dropped so quiet, Sarah had to lean in to hear. "Garnet is one of those women I told you to be careful about. Not because she's a bad person, she's not. But the day she arrived, I knew. I knew what she'd been through and why she ran away."

Sarah widened her eyes. "You know her?"

Mrs. Falk shook her head. "Not until a few days ago. But I know her and a hundred like her. She feels. . .unworthy because of her past. She wants to break away, and that's why she walked for days to get here. But she's scared."

"Scared?" Sarah glanced over her shoulder at the closed dormitory door. "Why?" She touched Mrs. Falk's shoulder. "Tell me."

Moisture collected in the older woman's eyes. "More than anything else she wants to leave her past behind, to find a shred of value within herself. But in her own eyes, she is worthless." A single tear slid down Mrs. Falk's drawn cheek. "Be careful of her. She's already broken. Because her virtue has been stolen."

Sarah couldn't breathe. The ache of compassion tightened her throat. "You mean—"

Mrs. Falk lowered her gaze. "I believe the term is 'soiled dove.'"

"Ohh. . ." Sarah slipped her hand up to cover her mouth. "No wonder she's so withdrawn. I can't imagine the. . ."

"The shame?" Mrs. Falk looked Sarah in the eye once again. "I can." She brushed the tear from her cheek. "I know the torment of desperately trying to make a new life for myself, but constantly looking over my shoulder, wondering when some man might recognize me. And I see the same fear in Garnet." She held the dress out to Sarah. "I will understand if you don't want me to be around the other women. Will you please give this to Garnet?"

"No." Sarah shook her head. "I won't." She stepped away from the door. "You should. Garnet needs a friend. I believe God sent her here to meet you. You will be most welcome—here with the other ladies, and at the party tonight. Please come. We need you, Mrs. Falk."

"It's Miss. I've never been married." She dipped her head again. "Missus made things easier. People accept a widow when they won't accept a—" She bit her lip and then offered Sarah a tight smile. "My name is Deirdre."

"Deirdre." Sarah opened her arms and wrapped Deirdre in a gentle hug.

◆　◆　◆

Sarah slipped into the Hash House and checked one last time to be sure everything was just so. Jarvis was already there, tuning his fiddle, and Cy was looking over the refreshment table with a keen eye. They both looked up when Sarah approached.

"You got the place lookin' mighty festive, Miss Sarah." Cy clasped his hands behind his back.

She smiled and told them to help themselves to a cookie.

Jarvis grinned and licked his lips. "Thank ya, kindly, Miss Sarah." He leaned a little closer, as if sharing a secret. "Do ya think maybe you can do a little singin' tonight with just Cy's harmonica? I hope I can get a dance with that little gal, Christine."

Sarah patted his arm. "I'm sure we can work something out so you and Cy can both have free time."

A few of the men came drifting in, each one scrubbed and spit-shined, sporting a new shirt and fresh shave—evidence the men were serious about meeting a lady and settling down. Sarah's repeated prayer for God to send a preacher to Prescott flitted through her mind and heart once again. If the evening was successful, they'd have need of a preacher before long.

Quinn held the door open for a few of the ladies who entered the Hash House with a blush on their cheeks and anticipation in their eyes. He paid each one a kind compliment, and Florence tittered behind her hand and batted her eyelashes at him.

A strange sensation burned in the pit of Sarah's stomach as she observed Florence openly flirting with Quinn, but she silently berated herself. This party was for the purpose of the men finding potential mates and coming together to help establish their town, not for her to give free rein to foolish emotions. She busied herself fussing over the details and encouraging the men to sit and chat with the ladies before the music started.

Quinn moved to stand next to her. "Everything looks wonderful."

Sarah glanced up at him, but he wasn't looking at the room or the decorations. He captured her gaze and she couldn't pull it away. "Thank you, but you helped, remember?"

"It was nothing. I enjoyed being...here...helping."

What had he been about to say?

Jarvis tapped his foot, counting out the beats, and the strains of "Over the Hills and Far Away" filled the air. For the first minute or two, the men all stood looking at the women, and the women all pretended they didn't notice.

Sarah murmured to Quinn, "Are they just going to stand there?"

Before she knew what was happening, Quinn bowed in front of her. "Shall we show them?"

Heat raced up her neck. She looked up into Quinn's smiling face and was mesmerized by what she saw written there. His eyes spoke silent words she'd missed in all the months she'd known him. When Quinn took her hand, a shiver skittered up her arm and her breath abandoned her.

As he guided her around the floor, carried on the strains of the music, a vague thought tapped her. Why did it feel so right to be in Quinn's arms?

The sound of applause pulled her out of the fog and she realized they'd stopped dancing. The song was over, and Quinn's smile set her pulse to racing. She sucked in a breath and yanked her focus to the women waiting expectantly to be invited onto the dance floor.

This isn't the way she'd planned for the evening to go. The party was for the men and the brides. Flustered, she mumbled a 'thank you' and backed away from Quinn. She needed something to occupy her hands, and she scurried to the serving table and began slicing the cakes.

Deirdre Falk slipped in with Garnet, the girl looking lovely in the deep purple dress Deirdre had brought her. Garnet sent a fearful glance darting around the room. Deirdre spoke quietly to her and they found seats. Sarah lifted a prayer for both of the ladies, and before she whispered 'amen,' one of the men, Reece, shyly stepped over and held out his hand to Garnet.

Sarah paused in mid-slice. "Oh, please, Lord. Give her the courage to say yes."

Garnet's eyes widened and she looked to Deirdre, who gave her a reassuring nod.

Jarvis and Cy struck up another tune and Garnet rose. Reece caught her hand and grinned. He guided her with the music, as if holding something fragile and precious. Sarah's gaze connected with Deirdre's, and they shared a victorious smile.

Couples came together, the self-conscious men remembering to look at their partners instead of their feet. The women smiled in response, attentive to the men with whom they waltzed.

After "Arkansas Traveler" and "Sweet Betsy from Pike," Sarah stepped up and sang an old folk song with Cy's harmonica accompaniment while Jarvis made a beeline to Christine to ask for a dance. When she finished, Quinn leaned toward her and whispered, "It's going even better than we hoped." He nodded toward several couples dancing, or merely sitting and chatting while they sipped punch and ate cookies.

Jarvis drew his bow across the strings in the opening strains of "Reynardine," when angry shouts were heard over the music. Jarvis's fiddle stopped abruptly as gunfire rang out. The women screamed and the men pushed them to safety behind the tables.

Sarah took a few steps toward the door and heard hoof beats thundering away. Quinn grabbed her arm. "Get over behind the tables and stay down." Her heart clenched as Quinn and the other men ran outside, and she lost sight of him. She couldn't make sense of all the shouting.

Sarah scrambled to where the women huddled together. "Is everyone all right?"

Between tears and trembling voices, they assured her they were all fine. Moments later, the door opened and the men carried Milton Slade into the Hash House and laid him on one of the benches. Blood soaked his trouser leg, and he groaned in pain.

Sarah gasped and ran to the kitchen to fill a basin with water. She grabbed some clean dishrags and hurried back, only to find Deirdre Falk had taken charge and was directing one of the men to use his pocket knife to slit Slade's trouser leg, and another to go get a bottle of whiskey.

Sarah handed the basin and rags to her, and stepped back, her hands trembling. Quinn gently pulled her to the other side of the room.

"Sarah." He tipped her chin up to make her look at him. His voice low, he took hold of her arms. "Slade said it was Lanny. He said Lanny was angry because he'd overheard Slade telling you about him spending the gold in the saloon."

Nausea rose in Sarah's throat, and she clapped her hands over her mouth. A sob escaped and she couldn't breathe. Her knees buckled. Quinn caught her and helped her to a bench. He sat beside her and took her hands.

"Mrs. Falk appears to know what she's doing. Hopefully, Slade will be all right. But Sarah. . . I'm the closest thing we have to law enforcement in Prescott. I'm sorry, but I have no choice. I have to go after him."

He thumbed the tears from her cheeks and stood.

"Please understand." He brushed his fingertips across her cheek and strode out the door.

Chapter Eight

The trail back to Prescott stretched northeast. Quinn pulled off his hat and dragged his sleeve across his forehead. He squinted at the sun. Must be near noon. His horse needed a rest as much as he did.

A few cottonwoods provided a shady spot—as good a place as any to rest for a few minutes. Milton Slade's horse—tied to his saddle horn—sidestepped when Quinn dismounted. He tethered both horses to a low-hanging branch and they immediately plunged their noses into clumps of lush grass.

Quinn was glad the sheriff in Chadron had allowed him to take the horse back to Slade, although he didn't imagine Slade would agree getting his horse back was fair recompense for a gunshot wound in the leg.

He patted each horse on the neck and moved to a spot in the shade. He sat and leaned against the tree, enjoying a cooling breeze that rustled the leaves overhead. A jay squawked from a nearby branch.

Quinn glanced up. "Sorry to disturb you, bird. I won't be staying long." He rolled his head from side to side, trying to work the kinks out of his neck. Stiff muscles protested the hours he'd spent in the saddle.

What day was it? The days and nights blurred together into an indistinguishable fog. Not a day passed that he didn't see Sarah's tears in his memory. Nothing could fade the picture in his mind of her anguished eyes when he'd told her he had to go after Lanny. He'd have given anything to remain by her side that night.

As eager as he was to see Sarah again, he also dreaded facing her with what he had to tell her. He prayed God would comfort her. She undoubtedly was praying he'd bring Lanny back to Prescott with him, but that wasn't going to happen. With a deep sigh, he rose. Lingering here only delayed the inevitable.

The sound of babbling water led him to a small stream behind the cottonwoods where he refilled his canteen and watered the horses. He checked the cinch and mounted. Both horses snorted their protest at being denied more grazing time, but he swung north and nudged his horse toward Prescott.

The sun played tag with the clouds all afternoon as it descended until grayness obliterated the rays altogether. The wind picked up and the scent of rain hung heavy in the air. Saddle sore and weary, Quinn rode into Prescott from the south, hoping nobody saw his approach. He had no desire to answer a lot of questions before he had a chance to talk to Sarah.

He led the horses to the lean-to stable behind his tent and proceeded to unsaddle them. Before he finished the task, light footsteps drew his attention. Sarah stood a few feet behind him.

"I've been watching for you for days." Her hands were clasped at her waist and her breathless voice betrayed her emotions. "I'm so grateful you're all right. Did you find him?"

Quinn closed the space between them. Oh, how he longed to take her in his arms and hold her until all the hurtful things in her life retreated. Instead, he reached for her hand, hating what his news might do to her.

"I apologize for being covered with sweat and trail dust." He paused and swallowed. "I have a lot to tell you, but not here. Is there anybody at the Hash House? I sorely need a cup of coffee, and we could speak privately there."

She bit her lip and blinked rapidly. "You finish up here. You must be starved. I'll have something ready for you."

As she turned to go, the sorrow in her voice and the slump of her shoulders sliced through him. He prayed their talk wouldn't add to her torment. He hurried through caring for the horses and went to clean up and put on a fresh shirt.

◆　◆　◆

Sarah poured Quinn a cup of coffee and set a bowl of stew and two slices of fresh bread in front of him. She sat across from him and steeled herself. The way he'd set his jaw when they spoke in the stable forewarned of bad news. She clasped her trembling hands and reminded herself to breathe. If what he had to tell her was the worst, God would see her through it.

Quinn began by telling her how he'd trailed Lanny south into Nebraska. "I remember him talking about California, so I figured he'd head west eventually. I guess he didn't think anyone would follow him because he didn't even try to hide his trail."

He traced the wood grain of the table with his finger. "Lanny's trail led to the settlement of Chadron in Nebraska. I stopped in to the sheriff's office there and told him what had happened. He said he had a young man in their stockade who refused to tell him his name, but he showed me the horse the young fella had come in on. It was Milton Slade's horse."

Tears burned Sarah's eyes and an explosion of relief tangled with the other emotions warring through her chest. If Lanny was in a stockade, that meant he was still alive, but every muscle in her body tensed, waiting for Quinn to fill in the details.

His expression softened into one of compassion and sympathy, as if sensing her impatience. "Lanny was caught breaking into the trading post there in Chadron. He had a sack full of provisions and was trying to pry open a locked drawer when the owner caught him. From what the sheriff said, he put up quite a fight."

Sarah battled for control. She cleared her throat against the tightening that threatened to cut off her words before she had a chance to speak. Her voice faltered. "Is—is h–he all right?"

Before Quinn could reply, her tongue found freedom and the questions that had bombarded her for days broke their shackles. "Did he hurt anyone else? What is he charged with? What will happen to him? Will he—"

Quinn rose and strode around to her side of the table. He sat on the bench beside her and took both her hands in his. His touch released the tenuous grasp she had on her emotions, and she burst into tears.

He pulled her to him and gently pushed her head against his shoulder. She found tender comfort within his embrace, and she let go of all the pent-up anguish she'd been holding back for goodness knew how long. The fear, the failures, the regrets, the feelings of inadequacy—all poured out in the arms of this man who didn't blame her for Lanny's behavior.

He patted her back. "Shh. Don't cry." He pulled out his shirttail and blotted her tears.

She straightened and sniffed. Quinn still held her hand, and she didn't pull away. "What will h–happen now?"

Quinn hesitated, and she could almost see him weighing his reply. "Well, Lanny was caught in the act with the merchandise in his hands, while attempting to break the lock on the cash drawer. The sheriff has sent for the magistrate who should be there in a couple of weeks."

A couple of weeks. But being caught in the act of thievery would result in much worse than two weeks in jail. She curled her fingers within the warmth of Quinn's grip.

She could still detect the strain in his voice. "Meanwhile, Lanny will stay in the stockade there in Chadron. Considering the alternative, at least he has a roof over his head and he's being fed."

His mouth tightened into a straight line—not a smile, not a frown. Likely as encouraging as he could be at this point.

"But did you see him?" Her stomach roiled thinking of the what-ifs.

Quinn nodded. "Yes, I was allowed in to see him twice. He wasn't happy to see me. He was pretty hostile, and he had a few bruises, but he was in one piece."

Her heart ached. She was grateful Lanny was all right, but so grieved that she'd failed him. "Can you take me to see him?"

"No." Quinn shook his head. "That's not a good idea."

"But he needs me. I'm the only one who—"

Quinn tried to shush her, but she yanked her hand away from his.

"You said he has bruises. Is anyone taking care of him? Is there a doctor? He will expect me to—"

Quinn reclaimed her hand and tightened his grip. "No, Sarah. It's a long, rough trip, and it wouldn't be proper for us to be on the trail alone together. I won't damage your reputation." He gave her fingers a little shake. "His bruises weren't that bad. Besides, you have spent nearly your entire life coming to his rescue and getting him out of the scrapes he gets himself into. It's time for him to accept responsibility for his own actions and be a man."

She opened her mouth to protest, but realized she was simply going to make another excuse for Lanny. God reminded her of the vow she'd made to trust Him with her brother. She drew in a slow, deep breath.

Yes, Lord, I trust You.

She had to admit Quinn spoke the truth. "Lanny is his own worst enemy."

"I have to agree."

Sarah rose and went to the kitchen. She returned with the coffeepot and refilled both their cups while Quinn described his second and last meeting with Lanny.

"He did say he never meant to shoot Slade. He thought the gun was empty, and he was just going to scare Slade with it. But Slade thought Lanny was going to rob him and they fought, and the gun went off." He thanked her for the coffee. "Sarah, you know neither you nor I can change the consequences of Lanny's actions. I guess that's the biggest reason I won't take you to Chadron. He has to face this himself."

Sarah released a soft sigh and clasped her hands in her lap. "I'm glad he didn't intentionally shoot Mr. Slade, but you're right. There is nothing I can do for him now, as much as I want to."

Quinn took another sip of coffee. "Before I left, I prayed for him, and invited him to pray with me, but he was pretty sullen."

She tried to smile. "Thank you for praying for him. Maybe all this happened because I didn't pray for him enough."

"Stop it, Sarah." Quinn's voice took on a stern edge. "This isn't your fault." He nudged her chin with his finger. "Nobody could have been a better big sister to Lanny than you've been. I daresay he might have taken a much worse path had it not been for your influence in his life. Maybe when he understands he must be accountable for the choices he makes, and you can't fix the trouble he's in, he will turn his life around."

Despite her best effort to swallow back her sorrow, another tear slipped down her cheek. "I hope so."

Quinn gently thumbed away the tear. She leaned against his shoulder—at the moment, the safest place in her world—and breathed a grateful sigh he was there.

He slid his hand over and captured hers. "How is Milton Slade doing?"

She jerked her head up. "Oh, I almost forgot." A tiny smile tugged the corners of her mouth. "Deirdre Falk has been caring for him. She said the bullet went all the way through." A shudder waffled down her spine. "The night he was shot, she poured whiskey on the wound. He jumped and screamed like she stuck him with a red-hot branding iron. Since then, she's been making special poultices. He's already up and around a little bit, but—" She covered her mouth with her fingertips to suppress a tiny giggle. "Deirdre's been making him behave himself."

Chapter Nine

Quinn tramped up the rutted street toward the Hash House. Pink and pale gold streaked the eastern horizon, and a lone bird chirped nearby. All of Prescott slumbered.

Almost all. The aroma of coffee wafted on the still, dawn air, and Quinn knew Sarah was up and about.

The dark circles he'd noticed under her eyes in recent days bespoke her restless nights, and he wondered if she'd slept at all last night. Even her music had vacated her spirit. He hadn't heard her sing since he'd returned from Chadron.

He entered the Hash House expecting to find her moving about the kitchen, going through her breakfast preparations. The kitchen was empty save for the glow of a lone lantern, but he heard her quiet voice.

"Oh, God, please be with Lanny. Speak to his heart. Remind him how weak he is without You. God, I pray he won't feel I've abandoned him, but he needs Your presence now more than mine. Please, Lord, I pray they will send me word so I'll know what happens. I don't think I could bear not knowing Lanny's fate."

Quinn held his breath. He didn't mean to eavesdrop on Sarah's prayer, but he couldn't help wondering if she could bear knowing what *would* happen to her brother. Some jurisdictions hung men convicted of theft. It was that very possibility that spurred Quinn to the decision he'd made in the predawn hours.

Sarah's heartfelt entreaty rose to heaven, punctuated by a quiet sob that tore Quinn's heart apart. He moved forward, his footsteps alerting Sarah to his presence. She looked up from the place where she knelt by one of the benches. He knelt beside her and added his prayer to hers.

Her soft voice quavered when she whispered 'amen,' and all Quinn wanted to do was assure her everything would be all right. But without knowing himself how things would turn out, he refused to raise her hopes only to possibly have them dashed.

She rose from her place of prayer. "You're up early. It's not even daylight yet. Coffee?"

"Yes, please." He followed her to the kitchen. While she fetched a cup and filled it for him, he told her of his plan.

"I'm leaving this morning to go back to Chadron."

She spun, sloshing coffee over the rim of the mug. "You're going? Oh—" She bit her lip, and Quinn suspected she was about to plead with him again to take her with him.

He leaned against the kitchen worktable. "The magistrate should arrive in a few days."

She wiped up the spilled coffee. "How long will it take you to get there?"

Quinn accepted the cup with a nod of thanks. "About two and a half days."

"Do you think you can get Lanny released?"

Did she know what she was asking? A suspended sentence would take a miracle, especially given that he was caught in the act. Resentment toward Lanny still churned within Quinn for the way the boy had treated Sarah, but for her sake, he'd try to at least put in a word for her brother.

"The magistrate will likely ask if there is anyone present who knows Lanny." He turned all his attention to his coffee cup so he wouldn't have to look her in the eye.

She set about silently mixing ingredients together in a large bowl, and Quinn could only speculate what went through her mind. Her movements were wooden and stiff as she stoked the fire in the stove. After several painfully long and silent minutes, she poured little puddles of batter on a hot griddle. After she flipped the golden circles, she set a stack of flapjacks and a jar of sorghum syrup in front of him with a thump.

Turning her back, she pressed both hands on the dry sink and leaned forward. Whatever was gnawing at her, he wasn't leaving town until she let it out.

"What is it, Sarah?"

She shook her head and her shoulders heaved like she'd just run uphill. "I don't understand why you didn't bring Lanny home with you. Why couldn't you get him out of jail?" She turned to face him, her fists clenched at her sides, and betrayal reflected in her eyes. "You were a county clerk back wherever it is you came from. You know about court things. You could have. . .done something. Why didn't you *do something.*" Her voice cracked on the last two words.

Quinn ran his finger around the edge of his plate and didn't retort. Her accusatory tone stung, but it stemmed from the anguish in her heart. He pulled in a slow deep breath, waiting for her to realize how foolish her charges were. He watched her face contort with the effort to hold back the tears.

She covered her face with her hands. "I'm sorry, Quinn. I had no right to say that." She rubbed her eyes and looked up at the canvas ceiling. "I keep having this battle within my spirit. Every time I think I've trusted everything into God's care, I find myself fighting to grab it all back and fix it my way."

Throwing propriety to the wind, he crossed the kitchen and wrapped her in his arms. "We all deal with circumstances beyond our control, and it's hard to turn loose of those things, especially when it involves someone we love."

Did she have any idea he wasn't talking about Lanny? He battled every day to release his feelings for her to God. Holding her in his arms far exceeded the gesture of a friend. Did she know that? Could she ever feel the same way?

The eastern sky grew brighter by the minute. He needed to be on his way. But he was loathe to leave without letting her know he cared. He bent his head and brushed a soft kiss across her forehead. When he pulled back, she stood within the circle of his arms, eyes closed and all the worry lines and furrows smoothed away from her brow.

She opened her eyes and looked up at him, her whisper so soft, he had to incline his ear to hear.

"God go with you."

◆　◆　◆

How many times would God have to remind her that she'd surrendered Lanny and the guilt she felt over his deeds into His hands? Christine and Garnet volunteered to clean up the kitchen after breakfast, so Sarah went for a walk to think and pray.

She had to admit constantly protecting Lanny had done nothing to change his behavior, but as Quinn had said, she'd tried her best. Maybe she'd tried too hard. Coming to his rescue and making excuses for him had become a habit, one that she now implored God to help her break.

After Quinn rode out, she'd caught herself again rolling over different scenarios in her mind. He'd sidestepped her question about getting Lanny released, which prompted speculation. Had the sheriff summoned Quinn back to Chadron to testify against Lanny? A cold shudder unsettled her. Even if Lanny's circumstances were beyond her control, she could still pray.

And so she did. As she walked down the trail to a grove of cedar trees, she asked God to take care of Lanny, and to prepare her for the outcome. "Whatever happens, God, I know I can rest in Your strength. Hold me, Lord." She sat on a rock in the midst of the cedars. "God, be with Quinn, too. I feel so safe and protected when he's around. My heart ached when he left again, and not just because of Lanny. When Quinn is gone, there is an emptiness and a longing I can't explain."

Speaking the words to God startled her. "God, am I in love with Quinn?" She'd been so focused on other things—looking after Lanny, preparing the men to become proper suitors, the arrival of the brides—she'd had no time to consider her own feelings. She wasn't sure she ought to be entertaining such thoughts now. The plan she and Quinn had developed had nothing to do with her or her feelings. The men and the brides were her priority. Weren't they?

The wind sighed through the cedars, reminding her that over the past three weeks, she'd not sung a single hymn. She closed her eyes and lifted her face to the sun. Singing hymns for the men was one thing, but singing with only God to hear was worship. The soft wind provided accompaniment, and she raised her voice.

"'O for a closer walk with God, a calm and heavenly frame, a light to shine upon the road that leads me to the Lamb. Where is the blessedness I knew when first I saw the Lord? Where is the soul-refreshing view of Jesus and His word?'"

She swallowed and wiped moisture from her eyes. "'The dearest idol I have known, whate'er that idol be; help me to tear it from Thy throne, and worship only Thee.'"

Worship. That's what she needed, and as much as she longed to bring a regular minister to Prescott, she didn't need to sit on a church pew in front of a preacher in order to worship. A rock in the midst of a cedar grove became a cathedral.

Refreshed in her spirit, she walked back to the Hash House. She found the kitchen spotless, and Christine and Garnet sitting with Deirdre Falk sipping coffee. Garnet was still quiet and reserved, but Sarah's heart smiled with gratitude for the progress she'd made, thanks to God's grace and Deirdre's friendship.

"Is there any coffee left?"

The trio turned, and Christine started to rise. "Yes, we made a fresh pot."

Sarah flapped her hand. "Sit down. I'll get it." When she'd filled her cup and joined the other ladies, Garnet looked over at her with a shy blush.

"Miss Sarah, Reece asked me to go on a picnic with him. Is it all right?"

Sarah's heart soared. "That sounds like a lovely idea." She glanced at Deirdre who gave a slight nod.

Garnet dipped her head. "I never learned how to cook much. Could you help me with the food for the picnic?"

"I have a better idea." Sarah set her coffee cup down. "What if we made it a community picnic? Instead of serving supper here in the Hash House one evening, we'll make it a picnic. We can have a bonfire and singing afterwards, and all the ladies can help with the cooking."

The ladies approved of the idea, and the planning would give her something to think about besides Lanny and Quinn. "I'll make an announcement tonight at supper, and we'll plan the picnic for Sunday. How does that sound?"

Garnet's smile lit up the room. "I'd like that a lot."

◆　◆　◆

The proposed Sunday picnic was greeted with enthusiasm, and several of the men wasted no time inviting the lady of their choice. Duffy and Kincaid volunteered to collect wood for the bonfire, and Cy said he'd bring his harmonica.

An air of anticipation buzzed through the town. Sarah suggested to a few of the men that their favorite ladies might appreciate a bouquet of wildflowers, and the women visited the new mercantile for hair ribbons or a bit of lace to adorn their best dress.

If the picnic was as successful as Sarah hoped, she might decide to plan another party at the Hash House for the following week, since the first one was interrupted. Anything to keep her mind occupied and her hands busy. A few of the couples seemed to be making romantic progress—all the more reason to double her efforts to bring a minister to Prescott. Thus far, she'd not received a single response to the letters she'd sent to recruit a preacher. Perhaps it was time to send more letters.

Chapter Ten

The sun hung low in the western sky. After the longest twelve days of his life, Quinn rode into Prescott, anxious to climb out of the saddle, but more anxious to see Sarah. His arms ached to hold her. For the last sixty miles, he'd prayed for God to prepare her heart to hear the news, and that she would accept it as the best possible outcome.

He passed the new mercantile where Les Crandall and Bud Welsh had erected their sign proclaiming the home of Prescott Mercantile. The sight brought a smile. Across the street, Reece Stover's new saddle and harness-making shop stood proudly finished—another addition to their new town. Up and down the entire street, evidence of progress popped up like mushrooms, gladdening his heart. Their plan—his and Sarah's plan—was becoming a reality.

Up ahead, wildflowers in crocks adorned either side of the open door of the Hash House. One of the women—Florence, if Quinn's guess was correct from a distance—stepped out the door, shaded her eyes in his direction, and scampered back in. Moments later, Sarah emerged with Florence on her heels and pointing in his direction.

Sarah's eyes, alight with anticipation, fixed on his as he pulled his tired horse to a halt and dismounted. A half dozen others crowded around the doorway behind her. If he had his way, he'd greet her without an audience.

He tied the horse and stepped toward Sarah, and she toward him.

"I'm so glad you're home. I've missed you." Her welcoming smile almost buckled his knees. The fact that she expressed being glad to see him even before she asked about her brother didn't escape his notice. But the unasked question lingered in her eyes. To make her wait to hear the outcome of the trial would be cruel.

Quinn pulled off his hat. "I'd have been home sooner if the magistrate had shown up on time. He got held up in another town, so he was several days late arriving in Chadron."

"How was Lanny when you got there?" Concern certainly flavored her inquiry, but no worry edged her tone.

"About the same as when I last saw him—grouchy and surly." An understatement to be sure. Quinn had wished he could haul the kid to the woodshed for his unfounded accusations toward his sister, but she didn't need to know that.

"Since we had to wait several days for the magistrate, I used that time to talk to Lanny about the Lord." Quinn shrugged. "At first, he didn't want to hear it." Another understatement.

"But gradually, he realized what kind of deep trouble he was in, and that it was of his own making. He admitted he had nobody to blame but himself. Finally, he broke down and agreed with me that he needed the Lord. He said you and your mother had tried very hard for years to show him that need, but it took landing in jail to make him come to the point of reaching out to God."

"Oh. . ." Sarah's soft exclamation and moisture-brightened eyes underscored her joy—the answer to her prayers. Her eyes slid closed for a moment. "Praise God."

Quinn's hand twitched with longing to reach out to her. "The magistrate was in a foul mood by the time he finally arrived. I just prayed everything would go according to God's plan." He took a deep breath. "Lanny has gotten a reprieve, of sorts. The magistrate agreed sending a young man Lanny's age to prison was a waste. So, in lieu of prison, Lanny will serve in the army for a minimum of ten years."

Sarah clasped her hands under her chin and lifted her face toward heaven. "Oh, thank You, God!"

Onlookers or not, Quinn took her hands, and they whispered their thanks to God together.

◆　◆　◆

Sarah suspected Quinn had something to do with Lanny's sentence. She'd never heard of a convicted thief being sent to the army instead of prison. Her heart overflowed with gratitude—and something else. She could no longer ignore the feelings planted deeply within her heart. Her love for this man went far beyond whatever he may have done for Lanny. Quinn was God's workmanship, created especially for her.

They entered the Hash House, and Sarah hurried to get him something to eat and a cup of coffee. He sat backward on a chair in the kitchen while she filled him in on the progress that had been made in his absence. He grinned as she described last week's picnic and the couples who sat around the bonfire singing all the hymns she'd sung to the men over the past couple of years.

"Sorry I wasn't here for that. It sounds like fun."

She tipped her head and sent him a smile she hoped communicated how much she wished he'd been here as well.

He jerked his thumb over his shoulder. "I noticed the place is all decked out again. What's going on?"

That moment, Garnet came into the kitchen. "Miss Sarah, the tables are all decorated. Do you want me to start putting out the cookie platters?"

"Yes, please. But you'll have to keep Reece from snitching those cinnamon cookies you made. I think they're his favorite."

Garnet blushed the color of her name. "I made extra for him." She picked up two platters and left the kitchen.

Sarah smiled after the girl. "We're having another party, since the one we had a month ago came to such an abrupt end." She glanced at him. "I hope you don't mind that I planned it in your absence. It's just that several of the men and women are beginning to make some progress—romantically, that is—and I think we might see some proposals soon."

His smile nearly robbed her of her good sense. "Don't mind at all. It's a great idea. But—" He angled his chin toward the kitchen door Garnet just exited. "Wasn't that the girl who was so shy when she first arrived she wouldn't even look at any of the men, much less speak to one?"

Sarah laughed. "That's her. Garnet and Reece are one of the couples I'm hoping to see marry."

Quinn polished off his sandwich. "If there is going to be a party, I should really go wash off some of this trail dust and put on a clean shirt."

After so many days being denied his presence, she was willing to take him, trail dust and all, but she nodded. "Hurry back."

"I promise." A short answer, but his eyes said much more.

Sarah watched him stride out the back door, and her heart thumped. She smoothed her hair and checked to make sure her dress was neat and tidy.

She stepped out of the kitchen and surveyed the room. The men had all the tables and benches moved around the perimeter, and the ladies had done a wonderful job with the decorations and refreshments.

Jarvis tuned up his fiddle while Cy sat and chatted with Christine. Mr. Kincaid's former mining partner, Pete, smiled at Hester when she looked up at him, and Morris Crumbley bowed in front of Miss Velma and asked her for a dance later on.

Milton Slade limped in the door with Deirdre Falk on his arm. Sarah went over to greet them. "It's so good to see you up and around Mr. Slade."

He gave a sheepish smile and nodded. "It's all Deirdre's doin'. She took good care o' me."

Sarah bit back a mischievous grin. "You do know, Mr. Slade, that no whiskey or beer is served here."

"I know." He shrugged. "With all my former customers becomin' family men, looks like I'll be turnin' my saloon into another business."

"Oh?" Sarah lifted her eyebrows. "What's that?"

"My pa was in the newspaper business from the time I was a little fella. I used to tag around after him. Guess I still have some ink in my veins."

Sarah's mouth dropped open. "You're going to start a newspaper? That's wonderful."

Mr. Slade pursed his lips. "It'll only be every other week to start, and I talked to Bud Welsh about takin' papers to some of the other camps and towns to sell. Besides..." He glanced at Dierdre. "Guess it's time for me to become a respectable citizen like everyone else if I'm going to stay in Prescott."

Jarvis and Cy struck up "The Last Rose of Summer," and Mr. Slade patted Deirdre's arm. "Don't know if my leg is up to this, but I'm willing to give it a try."

She sent him a confident smile. "We'll take it slow."

Sarah's heart warmed as she watched couple after couple waltz by. The next song was "Long, Long Ago." She glanced toward the door, but Quinn was still absent. She hungered for the sight of him, for the scent of his shaving soap, for the strength of his arms enfolding her close to him.

She busied herself rearranging the refreshment table. The waltz ended and folks stepped up to fill a plate and get something to drink. Someone tapped her shoulder. She turned and caught her breath.

"May I have this dance?" Quinn's hazel eyes twinkled.

She looked over at Jarvis and Cy who grinned back at her. "They aren't playing anything."

Quinn took her hand. "They will."

She hesitated. "This party is for the courting couples."

He tugged her toward the center of the floor. "We're a couple, aren't we?"

Her pulse accelerated and her face warmed. The opening strains of "Down in the Valley" wafted from Jarvis's fiddle. Quinn took her in his arms and glided her around the floor to the haunting melody. She wished the music would never stop.

But the song came to an end, and everyone applauded. It was only then Sarah realized she and Quinn had been the only couple dancing. The heat in her face deepened, but she couldn't keep a smile from her lips.

Quinn raised his hand. "Can I please have everyone's attention. I have an announcement."

Sarah fixed her eyes on him along with everyone else.

"I spoke to a man last week in Chadron. When I told him we were establishing a town here, he was very interested. He is a circuit-riding preacher, and he has agreed to put us on his circuit. He will be coming to Prescott once every six weeks, and we will hold church services here in the Hash House until we can get a church built." He turned to Sarah. "That is, if it's all right with the Hash House's owner."

Sarah gasped. She thought God hadn't heard her prayer, but He'd been working all along. "Oh, Quinn!" She threw her arms around his neck.

Oh, gracious, what was she doing?

She backed up a step, her face flaming and her hand over her mouth. But Quinn didn't appear put off at all. In fact, a Cheshire cat grin spread across his face. He leaned down to whisper to her.

"Our plan is really happening."

Despite her discomfort at her momentary lack of propriety, joy bubbled up in the form of laughter. "Yes, it is."

"In fact. . ." He stroked his chin. "I believe I know who the first couple will be that the new preacher marries."

Sarah glanced from Milton Slade and Deirdre Falk, to Morris and Velma, to Garnet and Reece, to Cy and Christine. "You do?"

"Mm-hmm."

He took her hand and dropped to one knee, right there in the middle of the Hash House. "Miss Sarah Trent, I love you. This isn't our plan, it's God's plan. Will you marry me?"

All breath vacated her body and she swallowed back happy tears. She nodded. "Yes. Yes. Yes."

He stood and picked her up off the floor, and swung her around in his arms to the applause of the citizens of Prescott.

Connie Stevens lives with her husband of forty-plus years in north Georgia, within sight of her beloved mountains. She and her husband are both active in a variety of ministries at their church. A lifelong reader, Connie began creating stories by the time she was ten. Her office manager and writing muse is a cat, but she's never more than a phone call or e-mail away from her critique partners. She enjoys gardening and quilting, but one of her favorite pastimes is browsing antique shops where story ideas often take root in her imagination. Connie has been a member of American Christian Fiction Writers since 2000.

A Match Made in Heaven

by Liz Tolsma

Dedication

To my critique partner and dear friend, Diana. Thank you for sharing in this crazy ride we call authorship. I couldn't have done it without you. You're the best!

Chapter One

Detwiler, Iowa
Spring 1885

Len Montgomery stood and rubbed his aching lower back. He'd spent the night in a ladder-back chair, praying for Mrs. Warren's healing. He allowed himself to gaze at the woman's white face and blue lips. Another soul with the Lord.

At least she didn't pass alone. She had him. Her children went out West years ago to seek their fortunes, leaving the poor widow without nearby family. He buttoned his waistcoat and grabbed his jacket from the chair's finial. He'd best go and telegraph her son and then start making arrangements. His first funeral in his first pastorate.

A soft knock sounded at the door. "Mrs. Warren?"

He recognized that sweet, feminine voice from last Sunday. Too bad he couldn't remember her name. He scurried to the front room.

There she stood, with a tendril of light brown hair escaping its pin, a streak of dirt across her nose, and a bouquet of daffodils in her hand. "Oh, I'm sorry Pastor Montgomery. I've come to bring Mrs. Warren these flowers from my garden. 'When daffodils begin to peer, with heigh! the doxy over the dale, why, then comes in the sweet o' the year.'"

"Pardon me?"

"Shakespeare. Daffodils bring in the best time of the year." Her smile matched the cheeriness of the blooms.

He swallowed hard. Had she been close to the woman? Would the news cause her great upset? "I've been at her bedside all night. I'm afraid I have bad news."

She wilted. "Oh, dear. She had a weak heart, but I prayed the Lord would spare her."

"She shared her testimony with me a few hours ago. We can take comfort that she's now in heaven."

A tear glistened on the woman's long eyelashes. If only he knew her name.

"I guess she won't be needing the flowers."

"You could put them in a pitcher. To decorate the place for those who come to visit."

She wiped away the moisture from her eyes. "What a wonderful idea." With an ease that told him she was familiar with the kitchen, she grabbed a piece of pottery, pumped some water in it, and arranged the flowers, bending one stem one way and another in a different direction.

Once she set the pot on the rough-hewn table, she adjusted her straw bonnet. "I'm glad I ran into you. There's a letter waiting for you in the morning's post."

Why did she know that? Was she a busybody? "Thank you."

"If I'd known I was going to run into you, I would have brought it."

Aha, that's who she was. The postmistress. But her name still eluded him. "There's no rush."

"It might be good news from home. You look like you've had a rough night. Perhaps it will cheer you up."

He attempted to smooth back his always-wild hair. "Maybe."

"Were you headed that way?"

"Yes, to the train station to send a telegram."

"Then stop in. I'll have it ready for you." Just as she breezed in, she floated out, only the scent of fresh air lingering after her.

But what on earth was her name?

◆　◆　◆

"Isn't that just the worst news about Mrs. Warren?" Cora Thomas leaned on the post office counter worn smooth by years' worth of the exchange of coins and letters and gossip.

Annabelle Lewis nodded, her golden curls bouncing in time. "She would have loved the flowers you brought."

"Poor Pastor Montgomery. His hair stood up in every direction, and his waistcoat was buttoned wrong. I'm sure he didn't sleep at all last night."

"I think he's about the most handsome man I've ever met."

"'The Devil hath power to assume a pleasing shape.'"

Annabelle laughed. "You and your Shakespearean quotes. You're going to meet a nice man one day and scare him away with them."

If only they'd sent Max Murdoch running. "If a man can't appreciate the Bard, I can't appreciate him."

"Hush." Color rose in Annabelle's winter-pale cheeks. "Here he comes now."

Pastor Montgomery strode through the general store section of the building, dodging barrels of flour and sugar, almost dumping over several bolts of gingham. He towered over the shelves. In no time at all, he reached the postal counter. "Good afternoon, Miss. . ." He peered around, as if searching for something. His gaze stilled on the postmistress sign, and he squinted. "Miss Thomas." Spoken as a sigh of relief.

Had he forgotten her name? She smoothed down her pink-striped day dress.

"Pastor Montgomery. I suspect you're here about the letter. I'll have it for you in a moment."

Annabelle giggled. She hadn't outgrown her school-girl fantasies yet, though she should have long ago.

Cora turned to the wall of small cubbyholes behind her and drew out the envelope addressed to the pastor. Postmarked from Des Moines. Did he have family there? A sweetheart? But the scrawl across the front was strong and square. And it carried no scent of roses or violets. Written by a man. "Here you are, Pastor."

He raised a single, light brown eyebrow. "Please, call me Len."

Annabelle leaned toward him. "Wouldn't that be too forward?"

"Not at all. We're of similar age. I prefer it. Even though I'm new here, I'd like to feel part of the community. Not the unreachable, untouchable pastor."

And at that, Cora saw him as a man, not just a man of God in a frock coat. And when he smiled a dimpled smile, the urge to giggle like Annabelle overtook her. She tamped it down. "Well, welcome to Detwiler. It's not much as far as towns go, but it's our home." She held the letter to him, her hand shaking.

"It's much bigger than the little one near the farm in Ohio where I grew up."

Annabelle fluffed her dark skirt. "So then, this is like the big city to you?"

He laughed, rich and deep and full. Cora checked herself before she fell under his spell. Max had a laugh like that. It was almost too late before she caught the hard, sinister edge to it.

"Not exactly a big city, but a good place to begin my work as a pastor."

"If you need anything, and I mean anything at all, don't hesitate to ask." Annabelle fluttered her eyelashes. Didn't she realize she was making a fool of herself? "My father owns this store."

"Oh yes." He nodded. "And a very well stocked one, I must say."

"And Cora's father owns the hotel. They serve the best pie there." Annabelle winked. Or did she have an eyelash in her eye?

Cora could almost see Annabelle's mind formulating a plan to woo the new minister and have him to the altar before anyone else snatched him up.

He turned to Cora. "What a nice gesture to bring those flowers to Mrs. Warren."

"I'm sorry I wasn't in time."

"Do you do that often? Bring flowers to the sick, I mean?"

"Other than Shakespeare, I love nothing more than a flower garden."

His crooked grin disappeared. Had she said something wrong? Didn't he like parishioners stepping in like that? Or did he think she should bring something more useful, like a meal?

"I hope your letter brings good news." She nodded at the envelope in his hand.

"Thank you." He tipped his Stetson hat and moved a few steps away before tearing open the seal. He scanned the page, a *V* appearing on his forehead. He smiled, frowned, smiled again, and then shook his head.

Annabelle leaned across the counter and whispered. "Who do you think it's from?"

"It's really none of our business." With a swish of her skirt, she turned back to sorting the mail the train brought that day.

But she caught every word he muttered. "Oh dear. Oh my. He expects me to do what?"

Chapter Two

Len grasped the letter in his hand, afraid he would drop it. He glanced around the store. Someone had to be playing a joke on him. This couldn't be real. He examined the postmark again. Des Moines. Genuine, as far as he could tell.

Dear Pastor,

My name is Mr. William Kimble of Des Moines. I run a large and prosperous farm outside the city. The Lord blessed my wife and myself with seven lusty children. In His good wisdom, He called my wife home to Himself three months ago.

I now have charge of the children, ages six months to nine years, along with the care of the farm. I cannot manage all of this work on my own. It has come to my attention that there might be some young women of fine moral character in your congregation who would be willing to become my bride and take over the household and child-rearing duties.

I ask you to search among these women for one with a spotless reputation, a giving spirit, and a kind heart. She must be good with children and adept at cooking, laundry, and maintaining a home. In return, I will provide her with comfortable accommodations, appropriate clothing, and a generous household budget.

As for me, I am thirty-five years old, in good health, and a pleasant enough sight. I work hard to provide for my family, but I also enjoy spending time with my children in the evenings. Before Fanny went to heaven, she and I often read Shakespeare together. If the woman you choose could have a good intellect, my life would be all the better.

Please understand, this is a rather urgent matter. My children need a mother. I need a wife. I appreciate your prompt attention. You may contact me at the address on the envelope.

Your brother in Christ,
William Kimble

Len steadied himself on the shelf beside him. "He wants me to do what?"

Cora hurried to him, Annabelle trailing her. "Pastor Montgomery, Len, is something the matter?"

How did he even explain? "I'm not sure. This is the most peculiar piece of correspondence I've ever received."

Annabelle stood on her tiptoes. "What's it about?"

He pulled the paper back so she couldn't see it. "Um. . .nothing, really. It's nothing. Must be a mistake."

"But it was addressed to you. I always check twice which box I put each piece of mail in." Cora crinkled her forehead.

"Don't worry. You didn't make the error. The sender is the one with the wrong impression."

"As long as you're sure." Her features relaxed.

He slipped the paper into the envelope. "I am. Thank you."

The bell over the door tinkled as he left the shop and wandered home down the wooden walkway, passing the livery, Mr. Thomas's rather large hotel, the milliner, and the now-quiet saloon. He nodded as he passed Mrs. Jackson and Mr. Wright. At least he remembered their names.

Good thing Cora had a nameplate beside the postal window.

"Pastor. Pastor, do you have a minute?"

Len turned. Rusty Holbrook hurried in his direction. You couldn't miss his shock of red hair in a sea of men. "Sure do."

"Whew." Rusty wiped perspiration from his brow with his ink-stained hand. "What a warm day for April. I heard about Mrs. Warren. What a shame. But Mrs. Alsip said you were with her. I'm sure that will comfort her family."

Word got around fast in a small town. "That's part of my job."

"She said you were making the arrangements. Did you want me to place an obituary in the paper?"

"Would you, please? I'll write up something nice."

"No need. I knew her well enough. She's always lived in the same house. I'll scratch something out before I go to print on Friday."

"Thank you. That's one less worry for me."

"Will it be your first funeral?"

The men fell in step and meandered toward the church and manse. "Yes, the first one on my own."

"Nervous?"

"Should I be?"

Rusty chuckled. "If your homily is anything like your sermons, you'll be fine. What do you have in your hand?"

"A letter from a Mr. Kimble from Des Moines. Apparently he's looking for a wife, and he thinks I can match him with a young lady from the congregation."

This time, Rusty's laughter started deep within. "That's the funniest thing I've heard all week. Let me see the letter, if you don't mind."

"Not at all." Len stopped in front of the manse's white front gate and handed Rusty the envelope.

As he read the letter, Rusty's grin widened until it stretched across his face. "Now, that is remarkable. In a way, I'm sorry for the poor man. But writing to a pastor he doesn't know to find a wife he's never met. . ."

"My guess is that he's contacted every pastor in Iowa."

"You might be right there. Well, after the news about Mrs. Warren, this would cheer up the good people of Detwiler. I have just the spot for it in the paper. Do you mind if I print it?"

"What can it hurt?"

◆　◆　◆

When would she learn to remember things? Cora shook her head as she made her way down the aisle in the now-empty church. All of the congregants were homeward bound to their Sunday dinners. Ma and Pa would be waiting for her, but she didn't want to leave without her Bible. She slid into the pew where her family sat every week and bent to retrieve the tome.

"Can I help you with something?"

Cora jumped and clutched her chest. "Pastor Montgomery, you startled me."

"My apologies. And remember, call me Len."

"I just thought that here, of all places, I should give you the title you're due."

"No need. Did you lose something?"

"I forgot my Bible. Again. It's a regular habit of mine." She grabbed the book from the floor and stood. "See. Right where I left it."

"Let me walk you home. Your parents left several minutes ago."

She pulled her shawl around her shoulders, a little flutter in her chest. Was it acceptable for the pastor to escort one of the church members home from Sunday service? "That would be fine."

He locked the door behind them. "All set."

"I saw the article Rusty printed in the paper about your letter. Was that the one that shocked you the other day?" They kicked up dust as they sauntered down the street toward the center of the small town.

"That was the one. I didn't know what to make of it. Since I'm new here, I don't know the eligible women very well. Rusty thought it was funny and wanted to include it in this week's edition."

"It's so sad that Mr. Kimble's wife passed away and left him with all of those children. I can see his dilemma. Do you have any candidates in mind? Has anyone responded to the article?"

"No on both counts. Then again, I never expected the ladies to line up at my

THE *Matchmaker* BRIDES COLLECTION

office for a chance to wed Mr. Kimble. I allowed Rusty to publish it to put a smile on people's faces."

"'With mirth and laughter let old wrinkles come.'"

"Pardon me?" Len steadied her by the elbow as she lifted her skirts and climbed to the boardwalk.

"'With mirth and laughter let old wrinkles come.' From *The Merchant of Venice*."

He blew out a breath. "*The Merchant of Venice?*"

"Shakespeare. To be a pastor, you must be a well-read man. Didn't you ever pick up one of his plays?"

"Only *Romeo and Juliet,* and only because the schoolmarm made me study it. I much prefer Charles Wesley or Jonathan Edwards."

"Oh." A sour taste filled her mouth. "It means you should laugh enough to get creases around your mouth and eyes."

Like he got when he smiled.

Her hands tingled.

"Well, that I agree with. I'd never heard the expression before."

"You should read a few more of Shakespeare's plays. You might find you like him after all. We could go through them together."

And that boldness? She stopped short. No, she had to be careful. Her outspokenness caused problems with Max. She wouldn't do that again. Wouldn't allow her heart to be smashed another time.

"I don't have much time for that kind of reading. Since I'm new to this calling, I spend my evenings studying everything I can. And working on my sermons." The coolness in Len's voice matched that of the overcast spring day.

"Yes, I can see where you might suffer from a lack of time for pleasure reading." They halted in front of the square, white Italianate house her father built a few years ago. Daffodils swayed in the light breeze. The tulips prepared to put on a great show. "Thank you for walking me home."

"It was my pleasure." He tipped his hat, turned on his heel, and strode away.

Annabelle's prediction came true.

Cora drove off a man with her love of Shakespeare.

Chapter Three

A nd that's when he just about ran down the street, back to the manse." Cora leaned on the postal counter as she spoke to Annabelle.

Her friend tittered. "I'm sure he didn't dash away like that."

"Oh, but he did. He heard Shakespeare and took off like a hunted deer."

"And he didn't mean he wouldn't like to learn. He must be busy, just moving here and getting settled into a new profession. That's time-consuming."

The bell rang, and Mrs. McNultey swished in, the spicy scent of her perfume trailing her. "Has the train arrived yet with the mail? I'm waiting for a letter from my sister. She's too cheap to send me a telegram letting me know when her baby arrived."

Cora glanced at the Regulator clock ticking away on the wall behind her. "The train pulled in a while ago. The mail should have been here by now. I don't know what's keeping Mr. Lewis. He doesn't like to be away from the store for this long."

"The Ladies' Mission Society is meeting at my house in twenty minutes, so I can't wait for it."

"My apologies for the delay. I should have it ready for pickup later this afternoon."

"I suppose I'll have to come back. Or can you send Tommy Yardley to me with it? I'll give him a penny."

"He'd like that."

When all that lingered of Mrs. McNultey was the faintest whiff of her toilet water, Cora escaped from behind the counter and wandered to the bolts of fabric where Annabelle fingered a brown tweed. "I really don't think he's too busy."

"Who?"

"Pastor Montgomery."

"Oh. Well, that's too bad. He's very handsome. I don't care much for Shakespeare, either. Maybe I should bat my eyelashes at him a few times and see what happens."

"Annabelle, you're incorrigible. That's no way for a lady to behave." She had learned that lesson herself.

"We're not all like you. I don't mean to be tied to a postal counter. I want to be married. To a man who will take care of me and maybe even love me."

That version of Cora's life evaporated when Max left her with nothing more than an empty promise of marriage. No, her job didn't disappoint the way he had.

"Cora, Annabelle, come out here and give me a hand with this." Mr. Lewis entered from the back room, red-faced and perspiring, despite the cool temperatures.

Cora hurried to him. "What is it? Is something wrong?"

"I don't know." He dragged the sack of mail behind him.

Dragged it? The town never got more than he could carry. "What's going on?"

"That's what I'd like to find out. Must've been some kind of mix-up at the Des Moines post office." Mr. Lewis rubbed the bald top of his head.

"Great. Now there's lots of sorting to do. I hope Mrs. McNultey's letter is on the top. I don't want to sift through all that to find it."

"Oh, this isn't the half of it."

Annabelle peeked out of the button and notions section. "There's more than that?"

"Two more bags this size."

Cora swallowed hard. "Two more? How am I going to sort it all?"

"I can help you." Annabelle put back the snipping scissors she held. "Looks like we need to get started."

Each of them hauled a bag across the clean-swept wood floor to Cora's section of the store. She untied one of the heavy canvas sacks labeled *U.S. Mail* and drew out a handful of correspondence.

"Pastor Leonard Montgomery. Pastor Montgomery. Reverend Montgomery. The Reverend Montgomery." She glanced at Annabelle. "He's piling up quite a stack of letters. From all over the country. New York, New York, Chicago, Washington, DC."

Annabelle grabbed a handful of letters from her sack, several of them dripping to the floor. "That's strange." She flipped through a few. "All of these are addressed to him as well. Baltimore, Chicago, and New York."

"This can't be." Cora skimmed several more envelopes. Each one of them bore Len's name and were directed to Detwiler, Iowa. "What is going on?"

Mr. Lewis called across the store. "You can't leave those bags standing in the aisle. They're blocking the flour. You're going to have to move them."

Cora shoved the bags behind the counter. "There's only one way to find out why he's receiving all this mail. I'll have to ask him myself."

◆　◆　◆

Len stood wide-mouthed in the middle of Detwiler's general store and post office. He gulped. "All for me?"

Cora nodded. "So far, I've only found one piece that wasn't addressed to you."

He couldn't get over the pile of letters. Three bags of them. "Why?" He'd been reduced to a blathering idiot.

"I don't know. Federal law prohibits me from opening anyone's mail. I tend to avoid actions that lead to prison."

"Yes, of course."

"Are you ill, Pastor Montgomery?" A touch of concern laced Cora's voice.

"No, I'm fine. It's just. . ."

"We've never received so much mail in a single shipment. I'm not sure we've ever received this much in an entire month."

"What am I going to do with it all?"

"Do you know why it's coming here? Or who sent it?"

"I have no idea."

"Maybe you should open a few of them."

"That's a great idea." A schoolboy could have come up with a more intelligent response. He had to get over this shock before she thought him nothing more than the village idiot.

He picked an envelope from the overstuffed mailbag. Cora handed him a silver letter opener, and he slit the seal with it.

> *Dear Rev. Montgomery,*
> *Your article in the New York paper. . .*

"The New York paper?" A headache pricked at his temples. "What about it?"

> *Your article in the New York paper caught my attention. I'm searching for a wife and was wondering if you might be of assistance to me.*

"He wants me to arrange a marriage for him."

Cora's blue eyes widened. "Is that what these are about?"

"Go ahead and open a few. I promise not to tell the sheriff."

She picked up a piece of the mail and slit it open. "'Dear Pastor, I was pleased to learn that you are arranging marriages for young women interested in moving West.'"

He read his next one. "'To Reverend Pastor Montgomery, I'm in need of your matchmaking skills.' My what?" The full-blown pain exploded behind his eyes.

"All of these must be about that letter you got from Mr. Kimble."

She remembered the man's name. Was she interested in him, too? "But how did people from Chicago, Baltimore, and New York learn about it? I doubt any of them read the *Detwiler Recorder*."

"Didn't one of them say they saw it in the New York paper?"

"Somehow, someone in the city read our little newspaper and picked up the story. And printed it." Rusty. A few murderous thoughts flew through Len's mind. "Now what do I do?"

"Etiquette would demand you answer every one of them."

"I'm not in the matchmaking business. I'm nothing more than a small-town pastor. A greenhorn at that." But his mother would agree that he needed to write back to each of these people. "With my other duties, I'll never get through them. How am I supposed to do this?"

"'Wisely, and slow. They stumble that run fast.'" Cora's soft voice tamped down the panic rising inside of him.

"More Shakespeare?"

Her cheeks pinked in a rather becoming fashion. "I forgot you don't care for the Bard."

"That quote, I understand. Work at it a little at a time."

"The best advice for undertaking any project."

"He may have a point. But it's a monumental task. And you should see my handwriting. I didn't earn top marks in penmanship."

"I could help you."

One thing he liked about Cora. She didn't dance around a subject or drop vague hints like many of the other young women he'd met. No, she came right out and said what was on her mind. A much more effective way to communicate. "Would you mind?"

"Not at all. The responses don't have to be lengthy. A line or two will do."

"How am I supposed to afford the stationary, ink, and stamps?"

"Perhaps one of the newspapers in Chicago or New York would help you if you offer to write a follow-up article on how the project goes."

"But I don't want to do any matchmaking." He fiddled with his necktie, trying to loosen it.

"You never know what might come of reading those letters. You could stumble across a couple perfect for each other." She pursed her lips.

"Since I have no other ideas for paying for this, I might have to do it. And thank you. I'll take you up on your offer of help. Do you want to get started this evening?"

"Come to my house at seven. Ma and Pa will be home then. I'll have a piece of pie waiting for you."

He grabbed one of the bags and hoisted it on his shoulder. So long as she didn't rattle off too many Shakespearean lines, this might be an enjoyable venture.

But his own pastor's advice sang in his head. *Don't get involved with any young women you shepherd.*

At the time, easy wisdom to follow.

Then he met Cora.

Chapter Four

Cora smoothed down the skirt of her brown twill suit, picking off a piece of lint. She straightened the fork on the plate of pie and hustled to the kitchen to make sure the coffee was ready. She poured it and sipped. Much too strong. Bitterness bit her tongue. Ick. If only she had a knack for making coffee. Instead, she opened the back door and threw out the nasty brew. Time to start over.

No sooner did she set the pot on the stove than Len arrived. As she went to answer the door, she fanned her burning cheeks. It would do no good to have him see her flustered. "You made it."

"I couldn't resist the offer of pie." The tie around his neck bobbed as he spoke.

"Oh. Well, come in. I have it ready for you. You'll have to wait for the coffee, though."

"Really, Cora, you didn't have to bother for me. To thank you for your assistance, I'm the one who should bring you pie and coffee."

She led him to the parlor where their desserts waited on a marble-topped tea table in the middle of the room. "You can make pie?" And, better yet, coffee?

"I'm sure it's not as good as yours. And I don't make it often." He settled on one of the chairs.

"Let me get that coffee for you." She scurried back to the kitchen where the pot bubbled on the back of the stove. In her haste to grab it and pour it, the towel slipped. Ouch. She put her burned index finger in her mouth. What was wrong with her? She needed to calm down before she made a fool of herself. She took a deep breath before returning to the parlor. "I hope you like it strong."

"To get through all of these letters, it will have to be." He tipped his head, a trace of a smile curving his lips.

She took her place, and they dug into the pie. "So, why did you choose to pastor in Detwiler?"

"Because they hired me."

She craned forward. "That's the only reason?"

"No. When I first came for the church board interview, I found this to be a charming little town. It reminded me of my hometown in Ohio. And the people were kind."

"I've never been to Ohio."

"It's not much different than Iowa." He swallowed his last bite of pie. "That was delicious. Thank you."

"You're welcome. I do have to make a confession."

"I can assure you, it won't go farther than this room."

"But the entire town already knows this."

He quirked an eyebrow.

"Oh, it's nothing like that. I can't bake. The chef at Pa's hotel made it. I'm a horrible cook."

He sipped his coffee, puckering his lips.

"And, I can't make coffee either."

"Thank the cook for excellent pie."

Outspoken and can't cook. What must he think of her?

"Shall we get going on these letters?" He grabbed a handful from the bag beside his chair.

She cleared the plates and cups and brought out pens, ink, and paper. "Before we start, can you remind me of Mr. Kimble's requirements? I want to keep my eye out in case I spot a suitable woman."

"A spotless reputation, a giving spirit, kind, and ready to run a household and raise seven children."

"Well, that should be easy enough."

Len's lips quivered before he broke into full-out laughter. "Oh, and she must love Shakespeare."

"That does narrow the field a bit."

He slit open one of the letters and scanned it. "This young woman is only sixteen but has helped raise her five siblings."

"Too young. We'll tell her we don't wish to take her from her responsibilities. Who's next?"

He opened another piece of mail. "This woman believes that hard work, a firm hand, and a stiff rod are the best ways to bring up little ones. Find a way to turn her down."

"Of course. Let me see." She bit the end of the pen before dipping it in the ink well. "I'll say that we're afraid all of those children would be too taxing for her. What else do you have?"

"Ah, here's a well-read young woman. She fancies Chaucer." He peered over the paper at her.

"No, he said Shakespeare. We'll have to tell her that, unfortunately, their taste in poets doesn't agree."

He sat back and crossed his arms. "But you love his plays and things. Perhaps you should write to Mr. Kimble."

"Me? No, I couldn't. I can't cook, remember?" She laid the pen on the table before it slipped from her perspiring hands.

"We'll never find the perfect woman with all the qualifications he seeks. Besides, you can learn."

"'This above all: to thine own self be true.'"

"See what I mean?"

But she couldn't.

She wouldn't.

Really. What a preposterous idea.

◆   ◆   ◆

Len leaned over the marble-topped table. Cora scripted the replies in her beautiful, teacher-perfect penmanship. "I've never seen anyone write so nicely."

She nodded. "Thank you. Ma and Pa would have skinned my hide if I didn't do my very best in school. Sums weren't my specialty, but handwriting I could manage."

"Much the same way Mr. Kimble wrote. Neat, evenly spaced."

"I don't know about that, but I appreciate the compliment. Now, who's next?"

He ripped open another envelope. "Ah, here's a gentleman wondering if none of the young ladies work out for Mr. Kimble, could I match him with one of them? He likes working with his hands, enjoys a hearty dinner and a clean house, and spends his evening smoking his pipe on his front porch."

Cora studied the ceiling for the moment. "Perhaps we should put that one to the side. Maybe we need a separate pile for those who are interested in other matches and who might be good potential spouses."

"A wise and practical solution, Miss Thomas."

Just a little sparkle glimmered in her eyes. "Let's see if we can find him a suitable helpmeet. Dig through that pile for a lavender envelope addressed in a lovely hand."

He sat back and chuckled. "You're teasing me."

"No more than you teased me."

"Fine. Just to prove you wrong, I'll find the woman God intends for him." He reached over and rifled through the bag, pulling out stacks of letters with each handful. Messy penmanship. He discarded it. Block lettering. Tossed that one aside. Misspelled words. Back into the bag it went.

"Aha." He held up a pale pink envelope and crowed. "This is the one."

"You haven't even opened it."

"I know she's meant for him." He withdrew the single sheet of paper and skimmed the contents. "See, I was right. She can pluck a chicken with the best of them and makes a fricassee that won an award at the county fair. She sews and knits and sings in the church choir. And, to top it off, sunset is her favorite time of the day. Write back to them and share their addresses with each other."

She blinked a couple of times. "I thought you didn't want to play matchmaker."

"I don't. But you challenged me to find him a wife, and I believe I have." He crossed one leg over the other.

"We'll see if this match works out. Don't count this as a victory until they march down the aisle."

They waded through scads more letters until darkness fell, consuming all the light except the small lamp in the middle of the table. Mrs. Thomas came from the kitchen and brought more coffee to keep them going. Several hours later, he rubbed his eyes and yawned. "I can't take much more of this. Everything is blurring in front of my eyes."

Cora flexed her fingers. "I can't feel the pen in my hand anymore." She had taken to writing the replies while he addressed the envelopes.

"It's time to call it a night."

"'Good night, good night! Parting is such sweet sorrow, that I shall say good night till it be morrow.'"

They had almost made it through the evening without any Shakespeare quotes. He stifled a groan and forced himself to grin instead.

"*Romeo and Juliet*. Rather appropriate, seeing the number of couples we're playing Cupid for."

"Oh."

"You really don't care for Shakespeare."

"Maybe one day, I'll appreciate it." Or maybe not.

"Read some of it. You might be surprised at how much you like his plays. They aren't all romance, you know. There are plenty of sword fights and intrigues you might find interesting."

He donned his hat. "Good night, Cora. Thank you again for your help. And the pie and coffee."

"Maybe by the time we're through all this correspondence, I'll have learned to make a decent pot of it."

All the way down the darkened main street of Detwiler, Len tried to keep his mind from the sweet, kind, and all-too-beautiful Cora Thomas. The task proved to be impossible.

Maybe he should take her suggestion under advisement. If nothing else, learning a little about Shakespeare would help him converse with her while they worked their way through the mountains of letters.

Or maybe Mr. Kimble was just the better fit for her.

Chapter Five

Len sat back and rubbed his stomach as he washed down his strawberry pie with a strong cup of coffee. Yes, the Detwiler Hotel's cook made the best pie he'd ever tasted. Next to Mama's, of course.

Across the table, Rusty sipped his brew. "I'm assuming you didn't invite me to meet you for pie to discuss the weather or crops. Is something going on at church?"

"No, everything is fine there. Better than I expected. The people of the congregation have accepted me like I grew up among them. The problem is with Cora Thomas."

"Cora? How so? I never thought much of her engagement to Max, but other than that, she's a sweet girl."

The clinking of silverware against china dimmed in the background. "An engagement? With a young man?" She never mentioned him. He loosened his collar.

"That had to be five years ago. She found out the hard way he was a scoundrel."

Len slumped against the back of the chair, though why the news struck him like a rock in the temple, he had no idea. "That's too bad. No, you're partly to blame for this problem I have."

"Me? How so?"

"You're the one who published that letter in the paper and sent it off to Chicago and New York. Now, notes are flooding in from people countrywide wanting me to either match them with the note's author or with someone else. I have to answer all this correspondence, and Cora is helping me. But she has a fascination with Shakespeare."

Rusty gave a hearty laugh, his green eyes sparkling. "Everyone knows all about that. Yes, Cora can quote him in her sleep. I wouldn't doubt she does. But what does that have to do with me?"

"I need you to help me understand the great poet. You're a writer. You must know something about him you can teach me."

"Me? Teach you? Why?"

"Cora and I will be working together for quite a while on this project. Scads of letters still come in with every train. Please, teach me a few lines, a little bit I can say back to her."

"I have a volume of his plays and another of his sonnets I'd be happy to lend you."

"I don't want to read anything. Just give me a bit so she doesn't think I'm an imbecile."

"You like her." Rusty set his gold-rimmed cup on the matching saucer. "That's why you want to become a Shakespeare expert."

Len leaned forward and hissed. "Absolutely not. I refuse to get involved with a member of my congregation. That leads to problems and awkward situations. This is a working relationship and nothing more. If I could understand a little bit of what Shakespeare wrote, it would help pass the evenings with her better. Give us more to talk about."

"The gentleman doth protest too much, methinks."

He peered sideways at Rusty. "What?"

"It's from *Hamlet*. Actually, the quote is, 'The lady doth protest too much, methinks.' Feel free to use it."

"'The lady doth protest too much, methinks.' From *Hamlet*."

"Correct."

"What does that mean?"

"If you deny your guilt too much, it makes you look guiltier."

Len stuck out his lower lip and nodded. "Not that she's done anything wrong, but it might come in handy. What else do you have?"

"'Now is the winter of our discontent.' That's from *King Richard III*."

"When am I ever going to use that? Don't you have a line a lady like Cora would appreciate?"

"Like a compliment?"

"Yes, that would be perfect."

Rusty fiddled with a spoon. "Let me see. How about this? 'O! she doth teach the torches to burn bright.' That's from *Romeo and Juliet*."

"She does what?"

"Teaches the torches to burn bright. It means she's radiant and the torches in the hall dim in comparison to her."

"Isn't that a bit much? I'm not courting her. I don't want to be her beau." Did he? No, he couldn't.

Rusty rapped him on the knuckles with the spoon. "Here she comes. Might be a good time to try it out."

"Okay." Len cleared his throat, as if he were about to give a sermon. He stood and smoothed down his pants before approaching Cora and Annabelle. "Good afternoon, ladies."

"Good afternoon, Pastor." Cora clasped her gloved hands together. "Are you enjoying another one of our cook's fine creations?"

"Very much so. I'm afraid they'll have to roll me out of here if I eat anymore. And

441

may I say, the lady protests, methinks, like a torch. From *King Richard*, I believe."

She furrowed her forehead. "What did you say?"

Heat rose from his chest. "No, that's not right. Oh, like a torch she thinks." He needed to close his mouth right now.

Cora pursed her lips and pressed a hand to her stomach. Was she trying not to laugh at him? Behind her, Annabelle suppressed a titter.

What a bumbling fool he was.

◆　◆　◆

Cora forced her laughter down her throat. The last thing she wanted to do was to embarrass Len. But what on earth was he doing? What should she say? "Um, you've been trying to learn Shakespeare." That wasn't very bright.

"I'm so sorry. That came out all wrong." The color of his face matched that of her favorite red roses.

"No, it's sweet of you to try."

"I'd better stick to quoting Bible verses." He backed away, bumping into a table and spilling the patron's water. "Oh, do excuse me." He turned and just about ran out the door.

Annabelle pulled Cora by the arm into the kitchen. She broke down into contagious laughter that Cora caught. They giggled and chuckled until tears ran down their faces. Annabelle bent over. "I haven't heard anything so funny since Matthew put a snake in Miss Elgin's drawer, and she ran screaming from the school."

"You have to give him credit for trying." Cora fanned her face from the heat of the stoves. "Poor man. He must be at his wit's end when I start my quoting. I did try last night not to say anything Shakespearean. But one line slipped out as he left. I must have spooked him."

Annabelle tucked a stray curl behind her ear. "He wants to impress you."

"No. That can't be. He doesn't like being in the same room as me because of my silly obsession with the Bard. I'll have to check my tongue from now on before I speak."

"He's sweet on you. Why can't you see it?"

"We had a pleasant time last night, answering the letters, but it was nothing like that." Was it? He was funny and thoughtful, but he didn't moon over her like Max did. Like men in love with women do.

"I wouldn't be so sure."

Cora's father entered through the kitchen's back door and went to her. She pecked him on his round cheek. "Checking up on your staff?"

"Nabbing another pie to feed to the pastor?" He winked.

She winked back. "Coconut cream tonight."

"And how is the letter writing going? I had already retired before you snuffed out the light last night."

"It's going to take us quite a while to go through that stack. There are many more of those evenings in our future. We even have a stack going of possible matches other than with Mr. Kimble."

Annabelle perked up. "Is there anyone who might be good for me? Handsome, wealthy, kind beyond measure?"

Pa chuckled. "Good luck with that." He rubbed Cora's shoulder. "You ladies have a wonderful afternoon. I have to check on reservations for next week."

Once he left, Annabelle elbowed Cora in the ribs. "Come on, there has to be at least one young man in that pile who would be a good candidate for my husband. Do you think you could match us?"

"I don't know. I'm the postmistress, and Len's a pastor. We don't have time to start a matchmaking business."

Annabelle pouted. "I'm not telling you to do this full time. But if you come across a man who sounds interesting, just set him aside for me. That's all I ask. Unless you already know of someone?"

"No." Although, there was the one young man from Wisconsin who owned a general store. He'd sent a photograph of himself, and he was good looking.

"No." Cora gave three big shakes of her head. "You'll just have to keep looking around here."

"Poo. You aren't any fun. Can't I have a peek at a few of those letters? Or maybe you should just marry Mr. Kimble yourself."

"No, I'm not interested in him or in any other man." But heat rose in her neck, and this time, it didn't come from the stoves.

"You do like Len. I can see it in your eyes."

"One nice evening with him doesn't mean we're ready to march down the aisle."

"But you said you'll have many more such nights with him. You never know what will happen."

That may be true, but he would never want her if he found out about her court-ship with Max.

Chapter Six

Len sat back in his office chair and stared out the window at the birds building a nest in the tree outside. What had he stammered in front of Cora? He was useless and hopeless. It was probably a good thing he vowed never to become involved with a church member, because she could never be interested in someone like him.

But he needed to remove the temptation from his path. Make sure he wouldn't do or say something later he would regret.

But how?

"Knock, knock. Anyone in?" Rusty entered.

"Have a seat. What can I do for you?"

Rusty remained standing. "I don't have much time, but I wanted to let you know that I heard back from the Chicago paper. They'll provide the funds for the paper, ink, and postage and such if you write a follow-up article for them on how the matchmaking went."

"Which means I'll have to play Cupid."

"At least you have Cora helping you."

"After today, I'm not sure she'll ever speak to me again."

Rusty smoothed down his curly red beard. "Why not?"

"You heard what I said. I'm sure the entire town knows by now what an illiterate fool their pastor is."

"Naw, they wouldn't think such a thing just because you don't like and don't know Shakespeare. Probably half or more of the people don't know who he is. This isn't the big city. They're country folk around here, just trying to survive."

"Thanks for the encouragement. I don't quite agree with your assessment, but I appreciate it."

"Don't worry about it."

"She was laughing at me. So was her friend."

"You need to laugh at yourself a little bit from time to time. Otherwise, what fun is there in life?"

Len rubbed his hand over the open Bible on his desk. "I'm going to write to Mr. Kimble."

"The man who started this mess?"

"The very man."

"Why?"

"He's perfect for Cora. They can sit and quote Shakespeare to each other all night long."

"You're not interested in her?"

He was, but he shouldn't be. "No. It would never work between us. I'm a disaster when it comes to Renaissance poetry."

"You didn't give it much time."

"Enough."

"So, you're going to try to match Cora and Mr. Kimble? Shouldn't you let her in on the deal?"

"I'll surprise her. See if he has any interest in her first. I wouldn't want to get her hopes up, only to dash them when he doesn't care for her."

Rusty waved away the comment. "Sounds pretty underhanded to me, for a pastor."

"You have to be sneaky when you're planning a surprise."

Rusty adjusted the hat on his head. "Well, I need to get back to work. Hope it goes well for you tonight with Cora."

Len's stomach seized up. That's right. He had to face Cora tonight. What would she say?

When quiet descended again on his little study, he pulled a sheet of crisp white paper from his desk's top drawer. Several ministers before him put the desk to good use. Worn but sturdy, it provided what he needed. He scratched his elbow and tried to bring to mind a good opening for the letter to Kimble.

> *Dear Mr. Kimble,*
>
> *I'm Pastor Len Montgomery. You wrote to me inquiring about a wife for yourself and a mother for your children. I was impressed by your fine attributes. I believe you and our town's postmistress have much in common, especially your love for Shakespeare. She would see it as refreshing to find a man who shares this particular passion with her.*
>
> *She's not afraid of hard work. She's handsome, sweet, and friendly, and has a nephew whom she loves dearly.*
>
> *Please, direct your response to Cora Thomas of Detwiler, Iowa. Don't let her know I was the one to suggest you write to her.*
>
> *Very sincerely yours,*
> *Pastor Len Montgomery*

Len sat back and puffed out his chest. Not bad at all. The letter didn't contain anything that wasn't truthful. He kept his conscience clear. Yes, it would do just fine.

Once the ink dried, he folded the letter and sealed the envelope. He strolled to the post office, hoping Cora would be gone for the day.

She wasn't.

"Len." Her smile almost took up her entire face. "How nice to see you. What can I do for you?" She leaned against the scarred counter.

"I just need postage for this letter." He offered it to her.

She examined it. "To Mr. Kimble. What are you writing him for?"

He swallowed hard. What indeed?

◆　◆　◆

Cora stared at the letter Len intended to send to Mr. Kimble. "What are you writing him for?"

Len wiggled his shoulders. The bell over the store's door jingled. "Well, I'm just writing him about a potential match I found for him."

She studied his face. He didn't quite look her in the eye. Was he lying? No, not a pastor. "Who is it?"

"I really don't want to say at this point. Who knows if it will work out or not."

"It's not Annabelle, is it?"

He gulped. "Annabelle? No, not her. Now, that's all I'm going to say about it. How much do I owe you?"

She accepted his coins and dropped the letter into the mail slot. "Will you come again tonight? I got a coconut cream pie from the hotel."

"Of course. I, uh, I'm sorry about earlier. Rusty tried to teach me some Shakespeare, but I'm afraid I made a mess of it."

"You have nothing to apologize for." She worked to hold back the guffaw that bubbled in her chest. "You don't need to try so hard. Really. I do like people who don't like Shakespeare. If we were all the same, the world would be a very boring place. Don't you agree?"

He relaxed. "You have a point there. God did create us with our own likes and dislikes."

"I'll see you this evening, then."

"Yes, of course." He turned and pretty much bolted out the door.

Annabelle swept in from behind the fabric counter. "Whatever have you done to the good pastor? He looks like he wants the sea to come and swallow him whole."

"I have no idea. Well, maybe he's uncomfortable about his bumble earlier today. We really shouldn't have laughed. He was trying."

"That's because he fancies you. You'll see I'm right."

"I don't think so. I did tell him that I liked people who don't like Shakespeare, but a potential mate would have to be able to put up with my quotes and other ramblings. He would have to understand what I'm talking about."

"You could teach him."

"His lesson with Rusty didn't go very well. I doubt he even wants to try anymore. Well, I'd better get the rest of this mail sorted."

Business at the mercantile was slow, so Annabelle sat on a stool nearby while Cora slid each letter and package into its appropriate slot. Most of the correspondence, however, was addressed to Pastor Montgomery. She tossed those in a separate bag to bring home with her to work on in the coming weeks.

She had almost reached the bottom of the mail bag when she stumbled on a pretty, lavender-colored envelope. The handwriting was neat with a slight flourish. But it was the return address that caught her eye. Parsonage. Evansville, Wisconsin. Parsonage.

She turned to Annabelle. "Look at this. This young lady is a pastor's daughter."

Annabelle raised one eyebrow. "So?"

"So, she might be perfect for our pastor. She knows how to care for a minister and how things run at a church."

"I don't know."

Cora removed a hairpin and slit open the envelope. As she read the note, she restrained herself from clapping. "Yes. Her father has been a pastor all of her life. She's active in the life of the congregation and in charitable causes around the area. She makes meals to bring to the sick, and she has an affinity for small children." She clasped the paper to her chest. If Len wasn't available, her attraction to him would end. And she would never have to reveal her secret. "I'm going to write to her."

"And say what?"

"I'm going to pretend to be Pastor Montgomery."

Annabelle almost fell off her stool. "You're going to do what?"

"Just until I know if she's really all she says she is. I wouldn't want to have him get his hopes up only to have her dash them. When the time is right, I'll tell him what I've done for him and let him take over."

"Are you sure about this?"

Her stomach grumbled, but she lifted her chin. "Yes, I'm sure."

Chapter Seven

The stack of letters from around the country grew until Len thought he and Cora might drown in all of them. They chipped away each night at the replies but made very little in the way of a dent.

Cora leaned back in the chair beside the little marble table in the parlor that was becoming as familiar as his own. "Do you suppose we'll ever get through these?"

"At some point, they'll have to stop pouring in. People will forget about the article, and that will be the end of that. Who's next?"

She slit open the envelope. As she drew out the piece of paper, a scent of roses wafted to him, whether from her or the letter, he didn't know. He forced himself to listen to her words.

"Oh, yes." She sat erect. "Listen to this: 'Thank you so much for introducing me to Henry. We've corresponded a bit, and he's a wonderful man. Even though our letters have been few, I'm making arrangements to travel to Cincinnati to marry him.' We did it. We made a match."

"Getting married? Already?"

"I suppose when you know it's the right one, there's no sense in waiting. I was about to give up on this, but now I can't wait to dig into the pile again."

He groaned. "Wait a minute. Isn't that the first couple I put together on your dare?"

"I believe it is. Fine, Len, I concede. Well done. You appear to be the matchmaker. Are you sure you want to continue your pastoring?"

He chuckled at the teasing tone in her voice but bit back the full laugh that wanted to overflow. Here would be the perfect place to quote a little bit of Shakespeare. If only he knew some.

"'This bud of love, by summer's ripening breath, may prove a beauteous flower when next we meet.'"

Of course, she would have one. He picked up another letter. "Let's see if we can find a match for this lucky person. Maybe it's your turn to give it a try."

The clock ticked away another hour, his coffee now cold. The words blurred on the page in front of him. He was about to take his leave when a furious knocking sounded on the door. Cora went to answer it. A breathless young boy bounded inside. "William Jasper, what are you doing here at this hour?"

"Is the pastor here? It's my pa."

Len scraped his chair back. "What's the matter?"

"I dunno. He grabbed his chest and fell over. And Ma's still in bed after Vera was born. You gotta come quick and help him."

"What about the doctor?"

"Knocked on his door before I came here. He's out somewheres, but I don't know how to find him. Please, Preacher, please come."

Len didn't give the boy a chance to finish his plea before he had his hat in his hand and was out the door. William led the way, Len scurrying to keep up with the boy's pace.

"Len, wait for me."

He glanced over his shoulder. Cora sprinted behind him, clutching her skirts. He didn't slow his pace, though, afraid he'd be too late to help Mr. Jasper.

They came to a shack on the edge of town. A few wilted roses tried to brighten the gray exterior. Len entered through a door that tilted on an angle and scraped the dirt floor as he shut it. The interior of the single room was as dark as the night outside.

"There's my pa, right there at the table." William pointed to the other side of the room.

Mr. Jasper looked like he'd had a bit too much to drink and passed out over his supper. But when Len went to wake him, his skin was cold beneath his touch.

Cora swept into the room and to his side. "What—"

Len shook his head.

The newborn cried, and Mrs. Jasper sat up in bed. "My husband. What's wrong with him? Can you help him, preacher?"

He hated this part of his job. What would he say to the woman? How was he supposed to tell her that she was now a widow, with five small children to raise on her own?

◆　◆　◆

Cora went icy all over when Len shook his head. Poor Mr. Jasper. Poor Mrs. Jasper, with all of these children to take care of and no means of doing so.

Len stood in the dim moonlight shafting through the window. He closed his eyes and sighed. Several times he opened his mouth, but no words came out.

"Pastor Montgomery, will you please take William, Barbara, and Mary to the barn and see if you can find a few blankets for us?"

He turned his head and stared at her out of the corner of his eyes. It was a strange request, but the best she could do on the spur of the moment. "And while you're there, how about collecting a few eggs and making sure the cow was milked this evening?"

He nodded, and the three oldest children, those who were still awake, trooped out after him.

Cora took the infant from Mrs. Jasper and jiggled the baby until she settled down.

"What about my husband?"

"I'm sorry, Mrs. Jasper."

She gasped. "No. Lord, no." She threw back the covers. "Help me up. I have to attend to him."

Cora tucked the now-sleeping Vera into the bed with her youngest sibling. "Please, don't strain yourself. Your children are going to need you."

"I won't. If you lay him out and pump a bucket of water, I'll be able to wash him."

Cora gave Mrs. Jasper a hand and walked with her across the room to the table. Once she was settled, Cora went to the well. Len was there with a bucket and a dipper.

"Did you tell her?"

"I did."

"I'm sorry. I couldn't bring myself to break the news."

"Life will be very difficult for them. I hope they have some family to help them. Where are the other children?"

"In the barn. I'm settling them down for the night. I thought it would be best if they stayed away from the house. Let them get some sleep. There's plenty of time tomorrow to tell them about their father."

"That's sensible."

He touched her hand. "Thank you. I don't know what I'd do right now if you weren't here."

"You'd make out just fine."

"I'm not sure."

Something in the way he said the words struck her heart. Soft. Vulnerable. Almost needy.

"Len?"

"Yes."

But what did she want to say? Too much. Far too much. "Never mind. You'd better get back to the children before they torture one of the barn cats."

She twirled around to return to the house, but he grabbed her by the arm. Heat radiated from his hand through the light cotton material of her shirtwaist. "If. . ."

She almost missed the word for the loud pounding of her heart. "If what?"

"Never mind." He released her then strode back to the barn.

For a moment, she lingered in the yard to catch her breath. What had just happened? Or not happened?

She shook her head in order to concentrate on the awful task in front of her.

By the time the sun rose, she had helped Mrs. Jasper prepare the body, then made her lay down and rest until the baby cried to be nursed. Even then, she burped the little one and walked the floor so Mrs. Jasper could try to sleep. She washed the dishes and swept the floor until she fell exhausted into the rocking chair in the corner.

"Cora."

Someone shook her shoulder. She forced her eyes to open. Len stood over her. "What time is it?"

"About six or so, I think. The sun's just coming up. I'm glad you managed to get some rest."

"Did you?"

"A little."

"Are the kids still sleeping?"

"They are. Let me walk you home? I'll come back to tell them what happened."

She stared at his disheveled coat, straw clinging to it, and his mussed hair. "You need some rest, too."

"I'll get it later."

"We can send Mama over to make breakfast. I know she'll be happy to go."

He touched her cheek, his hand cool. She grasped it. "Didn't you find any blankets?"

"I did, but only enough for the children."

Her insides fluttered. She pushed the feeling away. She'd had it before, with Max. Fluttering didn't mean anything.

Then again, Max wouldn't have gone without a blanket so a couple of fatherless children would be warm at night.

Her legs protested the weight she bore on them, stiff from the couple of hours she slept in the chair. He helped her to her feet. "You'd make a wonderful pastor's wife, Cora."

The fluttering increased.

What did he mean?

Chapter Eight

By later that afternoon, Cora had Mrs. Jasper tucked in bed, the infant Vera sleeping beside her, and a vase of fresh-picked roses on the table. Ma worked over the little stove, stirring a pot of stew, the aroma of meat and broth perfuming the stale air. Len played checkers with the older children at the table.

Ma wiped her hands on her apron. "Go on home now, you two. You've been here all night and most of the day. Get some rest." She shooed them out with a wave of a wooden spoon.

Len handed Cora's straw bonnet to her, the flowers on it as wilted as she. "I'll walk you to your house."

"I have to stop at the post office, just to check on things."

"Then I'll walk you there first."

He took her by the elbow, and as they made their way down the lane, the strange fluttering started up again. Maybe she was coming down with a bug.

"What's so urgent at the office that it can't wait until tomorrow?"

"Nothing. I just want to make sure that Annabelle didn't run into any problems without me." She couldn't tell him she was hoping for a letter addressed to him from a certain Wisconsin pastor's daughter. But two weeks had passed since Cora sent the note off. Plenty of time for Betty to respond.

They chatted about nothing more than the weather as they strolled through town. He never let go of her arm. They passed Mrs. Morris and old Miss Bauer. What did they think was going on? She bent down on the pretense of buttoning her shoe, thankful that he released his grip.

He stopped her from going in when they reached the store. "Thank you again. Mrs. Jasper loved the flowers. It's so thoughtful of you to have brought them to her. I see where they cheer up folks."

"And your prayers and Bible reading helped ease her sorrow, even a little bit."

"Why are you so timid around me?"

"Timid? What do you mean?" No one had ever called her that at any point in her entire life.

"I can't put my finger on it, but I feel like you're holding back. Is there something you need to tell me?"

Oh, if only she could tell him about Max. Then she would be free to give herself to him. Free to tell him all the things her heart longed to share. "No, nothing at all. Thank you for the escort. I don't want to keep you. I may be a while."

He tipped his hat and whistled as he sauntered away in the direction of the church manse.

The jingling of the bell above the shop's door announced her arrival. Annabelle peered up from her station behind the postal counter and waved a piece of paper in the air. "Is this what you've come after?"

"Is it from Betty Demming?"

"It certainly is."

A sudden burst of energy propelled her forward. She snatched the envelope from Annabelle's hand and had it opened in a jiffy. She squealed when she read the contents. "She's interested in him. Said he sounds like just the man God has in store for her, that He's been preparing for her to marry all her life."

"And she's not shy about declaring her feelings, is she?" Annabelle smirked.

"Hush. When that's what this setup is about, why waste time on formalities? I like her. Hand me that pen and the inkwell. I need to write back to her as soon as possible."

Annabelle crossed her arms. "I will not. You can't keep up this charade. Len will be furious when he finds out what you did."

"Nonsense. He'll be grateful. Thanks for the warning, but I'll either write the letter here and now or when I get home. You might as well hand me my pen."

Annabelle huffed but reached to do as Cora asked. "Wait a minute. I forgot. Here's another one addressed to you. This is from the good Mr. Kimble himself."

"Mr. Kimble? From Des Moines?"

"Look for yourself." Annabelle handed over the letter.

The postmark left no doubt that this Mr. Kimble was the original letter writer. Why, though, would he send her a note? Len had written to him, and she imagined that he filled the gentleman in on their wife-finding progress.

Not as fast as she'd opened Betty's letter, she lifted the flap of this one. Strong, square letters flowed across the page.

Dear Miss Thomas,
It has come to my attention that you are a lover of Shakespeare, as am
I. I believe his poetry elevates the mind and instructs the soul. "Love
looks not with the eyes, but with the mind." An evening with the Bard
is second only to an evening with the Lord.

My children are also learning to appreciate his mastery of the
English language. Though they are being raised on a farm, they may
become poets themselves.

Please, write to me and tell me why you love Shakespeare so much
and which are your favorite plays.

Adieu, adieu.
Mr. William Kimble

"Oh, Annabelle, what on earth am I to do?"

◆　◆　◆

Cora sat at the little marble parlor table and racked her brain for a suitable reply to Mr. Kimble's letter. For days, she'd stewed over what to write to him. If truth be told, she didn't want to send a letter back, and she didn't want to start corresponding with the man. Leading him on would be wrong.

But it would be rude if she didn't at least send him one note. Just one. And she needed to hurry up. She expected Len any moment. The stack of letters decreased with each passing day. Only one or two new ones trickled in on each train.

One day soon, they would dry up altogether. They will have answered each letter and made all the matches they could.

And Len wouldn't come anymore.

Why did her heart clench at the thought? She should be happy about it. Glad that she wouldn't have to spend so much time with him when he sent her pulse racing and tied her tongue so she couldn't utter a single intelligible line, except for the Shakespeare he despised.

She tapped the pen on her temple. Time to focus on the job in front of her. How did she reply to him without having him think more than she wanted him to?

Dear Mr. Kimble,
Thank you for your letter dated June 1st. It is true that I enjoy a bit of
Shakespeare from time to time. Hamlet is probably my favorite among
his plays. That is Shakespeare at his best. His writing is brilliant in
that play. And, it gave rise to some of his most popular quotes.

It is refreshing to hear about someone passing on to their children
a love for fine literature. Whatever they do, it will serve them well and
will beautify their lives. I hope that whomever you choose for your wife
will support you in this endeavor and share your love of the Bard.

All the best to you,
Cora Thomas

She reread the missive, blowing the ink dry. She folded the paper and slid it into the envelope before addressing it.

"Good evening, Cora."

She clutched her chest. "Len. I didn't hear you come in."

"You must have been so intent on your letter you never heard me knock. Your mother let me in."

There on the table sat the letter bearing Mr. Kimble's name. She attempted to snatch it away before he saw it, but she wasn't fast enough.

He grabbed it. "Mr. Kimble?"

"Yes. It seems someone informed him of my enjoyment of Shakespeare."

"Really now? How interesting."

Was that a touch of coyness in his voice? "Curious, isn't it?"

"It certainly is. But I'm sure the two of you have much to share, with your common interests and all. Why don't we get to work?"

They labored without saying much for a while. Only the ticking of the clock filled the quietness. After a while, Cora brought out the pie and coffee, and Len sat back, stretching his neck muscles. "Thank you. I'd like to know something."

"What is that?"

"Why don't you have a beau? Rusty mentioned you did once, but it didn't end well."

"I really don't want to talk about Max."

"Whatever you say will never leave this room. You're an attractive young woman. Why hasn't any man caught your eye?"

Her pulse pounded in her neck. "I'm content to work at the post office for the foreseeable future."

"But why?"

"You are persistent, aren't you?" The words she didn't want to tell him bubbled beneath the surface.

"I want to be a friend. Perhaps if I understood your reluctance..."

The words escaped her lips in a whisper. "No man would ever want me."

"What do you mean?"

"I can't tell you." Her mouth went dry.

"You can trust me."

"I allowed my former fiancé too many liberties." Her throat caught in a sob. "I'm a sullied woman."

Chapter Nine

I'm a sullied woman." Cora sobbed out the words and then raced from the room.

"Cora, wait." Len almost knocked over the little table in his haste to go after her. "Cora. Please, let me talk to you." He stood at the bottom of the stairs as she disappeared behind a door.

Mrs. Thomas entered from the kitchen. "What's the matter?"

"I'm afraid I've upset her. Will you please ask her to come down? I need to talk to her." His stomach flip-flopped. What if she wouldn't see him?

"I'll try. She's stubborn, though." Mrs. Thomas ascended the stairs and knocked on Cora's door. He couldn't make out what she said.

But he didn't have any problem hearing Cora's reply. "No. Tell him to go home."

He took the steps two at a time until he arrived beside Mrs. Thomas. "Cora, please, listen to me."

Silence.

"Cora." He knocked. He pounded.

Silence.

"Cora, please answer me."

Again, nothing but silence.

Her mother turned to him. "Maybe it's best you go for now. Once she cools down, you can talk to her. Whatever happened, it might be a good idea to not say anymore in the heat of the moment."

What was this pain in his chest? Why? "You're right, of course. I'll talk to her tomorrow." He spun around to leave then spun back to face the door again. "But I'm not upset with you, Cora."

With that, he marched down the stairs and out the door.

This is why Pastor Sherman told him never to become involved with a church member. And yet, Len had let his heart run away with him. He cared about her.

But what did she mean about allowing her former fiancé too many liberties? How had she sullied herself?

His head pounded by the time he returned to the parsonage. His headache plagued him all night. He couldn't sleep. This was why he needed to get her married to someone else.

Had she told Mr. Kimble what she had done? If she did, would he still have her?

He lit a lamp and sat at his desk until the light came on at the newspaper office. Today was Friday, the day Rusty put the paper out. He always got there before sunup to work. Len dressed and hurried down the street to his friend's office.

Rusty, hands inky, glanced up when Len entered. "What has you up so early this morning? I thought I was the only one crazy enough to work at this hour."

"I haven't slept yet."

"Another call? Do you need me to save space for an obituary?"

Len rubbed his eyes. "What? Oh, no. It's nothing like that. Everyone in town is hale and hearty, as far as I know."

"Then what is it?"

"Do you have a minute?"

"That's about all I have." He motioned for Len to sit.

"I've run into a problem with Cora."

Rusty quirked an eyebrow. "I knew you were sweet on her. You can deny it all you want, but the truth is obvious by the way you look at her."

"And that's the problem. I pushed her to tell me something she didn't want to share, and now she won't talk to me."

Rusty blew out a breath. "But you want her to marry Mr. Kimble."

"Yes. . ."

"Then, her not speaking to you isn't much of a problem."

"She's a member of my congregation, at least until she moves to Des Moines. It's not good if I'm not on speaking terms with one of my parishioners."

"So much so, you can't sleep."

"Exactly. I know how this must look to you, but it's bothering me. We've gotten along so well. I hate for our friendship to end."

"Even though she's moving to Des Moines."

"She's not engaged to Mr. Kimble. At least, not that I know of." Len stood and paced the cluttered room. "I don't know. What should I do?"

Rusty guffawed. "You, Pastor Montgomery, are most certainly in love with Miss Thomas."

"Even if I was, and I'm not, I can't get involved with her."

"It seems to me like you already are."

Len swiveled and stared at his friend. "I can't be. No, the best thing for everyone would be for her to marry Mr. Kimble. As soon as possible."

◆　◆　◆

Cora shuffled into the post office, bleary-eyed from a lack of sleep. The pounding in her head matched Len's pounding on her door last night.

She'd heard him. Heard every word he said. Even when he told her he wasn't upset with her.

But how was that possible? He should be. He had every right to be. She'd just confessed her sin to her pastor. And, she thought, her friend. A good, dear friend.

That's where the trouble lay. She'd let her emotions get the best of her. She'd let her heart feel too much. He was a pastor. He had to say he wasn't upset with her. But her admission changed everything between them. They wouldn't be able to work together anymore.

And that stabbed at her gut more than she expected.

Annabelle waved to Cora from behind the bolts of fabric. "You look worse than Tommy Miller after the horse dragged him through town."

Cora sat on her stool with a thump. "Thanks. That's the kind of cheering up I needed this morning." Her throat burned.

Annabelle left her inventory and went to Cora. "Oh, honey, I'm sorry. I was only teasing. What's wrong?"

"Nothing." Through her eyelashes, she gazed at her friend. "Everything."

"Does it have anything to do with a certain pastor?"

"Yes."

"What did he do?" Annabelle frowned.

"He didn't do anything. I did. I told him about Max."

"He didn't know you were engaged before?"

"No." Cora glanced around the room to be sure Mr. Lewis wasn't around. "About the liberties I allowed him."

"Tosh." Annabelle waved at the air. "I told you before, you did nothing wrong. Kissing a man isn't allowing him liberties."

"We shouldn't have done that. Now, I've kissed a man who will never be my husband."

"Well, I kissed Warren Gebhardt. You don't see me worrying whether or not a man will marry me."

"You were ten."

"So. We're never going to marry each other."

The bell announced a customer.

Len.

Her heart skipped a beat or two. She wasn't ready to talk to him. Never would be ready, for that matter. "Annabelle, tell him I had to excuse myself."

Annabelle held her down by the arm. "I will not. Sooner or later, you're going to have to face him. Might as well be sooner."

Cora tamped down the urge to kick Annabelle and scamper out the back door. "Let go. I'll stay."

Annabelle just smiled. "Good morning, Pastor Montgomery. You're in bright and early today."

"Miss Lewis." He tipped his head at Annabelle. "Miss Thomas." He did the same to Cora.

His hair, always wild, outdid itself, sticking up in every conceivable direction.

"I'll leave you two to talk." Cora's friend pranced off, disappearing into the back storeroom.

Cora held up her hands. "Please, don't say anything. I don't want to talk about it. I heard what you said last night, and it was very kind of you, but it's not true. You must be upset with me. And I understand. So, if you could—"

"I won't push you. I'm the one who was wrong to do so last night. You didn't want to share with me, but I forced the issue. I'm sorry. Please, accept my apology."

"You know what I've done."

"Yes."

"Thank you for the apology. It's not necessary. I'm the one who should be contrite. And I am. God has forgiven me. But man is another matter. 'All that glitters is not gold.'"

His unsteady smile drooped.

"We're not all we appear to be on the outside. I'll continue to help you with the letters, but it's best if we don't work together anymore. You can stop by my house today while I'm here and pick up one of the bags of mail from my mother."

"Cora, that's not what I want at all."

"It is what I want."

"Does this have anything to do with your correspondence with Mr. Kimble?"

"What?"

"I saw your letter to him last night. Do you have an interest in him?"

"What does this have to do with what we were talking about?"

"I don't know. You tell me."

"The two are separate issues. And neither of them your business."

He sucked in his breath. She hated the harsh tone of her own voice. She just wanted to go to bed and pull the covers over her head until she forgot all about Len.

If she ever could.

Another customer entered the store. She brightened her voice. "Thank you for stopping in, Pastor Montgomery. My mother will be home all day. I'll see you on Sunday." She turned from him and busied herself with rearranging the postage cancellation stamps on the counter.

She didn't relax until she heard the bell jingle. And even then, she had to dig her fingernails into the desk's soft wood to keep from crying.

Chapter Ten

L en slammed his office's door shut, the breeze of it ruffling his hair.

"What has you in such a state?"

Len gasped and spun to find Rusty lounging in the chair in front of his desk. "You scared me near to death. What are you doing here?"

"To get the full scoop on your interview with Miss Thomas last week."

"Isn't gossiping women's business?"

"Women's and newspaper reporters'. I'm going to guess you saw her, and it didn't go well."

"Do you call that reporter's intuition?"

"A good guess."

"She doesn't want to work on the letters anymore. She doesn't want to have anything to do with me. All of this nonsense wasn't a good idea from the start. We should never have gotten into this matchmaking business. She'll continue to answer the letters. Just not with me by her side."

Rusty pulled a pencil from behind his ear and tapped the desk with it. "Sit down. It's time for a little pastoral advice."

"You're a newspaperman."

"Semantics."

Len took his seat. If he listened to his friend, maybe he would go and leave him in peace so he could bury himself in his mountain of work.

"You have to come to a decision."

"About what?"

"About Miss Thomas. Do you want her to be part of your life or not?"

"Of course."

"As in a courtship."

Len scrubbed his face. What did he want? The age-old heart-versus-head dilemma warred inside of him. Cora was bright, beautiful, beguiling. And sweeter than the hotel cook's pies. But she was a member of his congregation. And, according to her, a sullied woman. "It would never work. Look what a mess things are already."

"And that's your verdict?"

He didn't want it to be. But there was no other way. "Yes." He croaked out the word.

"Then, it's time to move on. Have you heard from Mr. Kimble recently?"

"He sounded like he might want to pursue a courtship with her. And, I saw she wrote a letter to him."

"And with her out of town, the ship will right itself again."

"Good old Rusty. Ever the optimist."

His friend flashed him a crooked grin. "You don't see me mooning over any of Detwiler's eligible maidens. You have nothing to worry about. You make a mean cup of coffee. I have every confidence you'll do fine on your own."

Chuckling, Len showed Rusty to the door. He slapped him on the back. "Now, there's the way to look at things."

The room fell quiet after Rusty left, only the ticking of the mantel clock on the bookshelf breaking the silence.

He didn't want a wife to make his coffee and press his shirts. No, he wanted Cora in his life to make him laugh, to liven his days, to be his companion.

No, no, no. He couldn't think like that. He had to let her go. And Mr. Kimble was just the man to help him.

The time had come to move his plan to another phase of the operation. Cora and Mr. Kimble corresponded. That much he knew. But letters only told you so much about a person. They needed to meet face-to-face.

How? He paced his tiny office several times. He couldn't very well hand Cora a train ticket for Des Moines. Unless he told her Mr. Kimble sent it.

That reeked too much of deception. And poor Mr. Kimble. What a surprise that would be for him. Shelve that idea. He made several more circuits of the room. What if he convinced Mr. Kimble to come to Detwiler? That had a bit more possibility.

He bit the inside of his cheek. Now, how to get the man into town. Too bad they didn't have the theater or symphony here. He needed an excuse to get Mr. Kimble to visit. Some function that would bring them together. Len rubbed the back of his neck. But what?

When no ideas came, he sat behind his desk. Maybe if he worked for a while, a thought might pop in his head. He shifted the stack of papers. Letters from home. Sermon notes scribbled on various sized sheets of paper.

And then, the list of church announcements caught his eye. He skimmed Mrs. Blanchard's neat writing. The prayer meeting. The Ladies' Aid Society's sewing circle. And the Fourth of July lunch social to raise money for the school.

That was it. Perfect.

Len grabbed a piece of paper from the desk's top drawer and composed his letter to Mr. Kimble.

◆　◆　◆

"Why did you have to pick such a windy day to show me something at the milliner's shop?" Annabelle clamped down on the hat on her head. "I'm going to be forced to buy another one, because this one will be destroyed."

Cora pulled her friend along. "I can't help it that they got a new shipment of gloves. You have to see this black pair with a little button at the wrist. The kid leather of it might as well be silk."

They crossed the muddy street. "Well, if they've cheered you up this much, then they might be worth the loss of this hat. You haven't been this chipper since you and Pastor Montgomery stopped spending time together."

"We were never spending time together in that way. And it was never going to work." Then why did she get such a lump in her throat? She squared her shoulders. "So, I've resigned myself to being an old spinster, and that's just the way I like it. I make my own money that I can spend on gloves and whatever else I like without being accountable to any man."

"Goodness. Susan B. Anthony would be proud of a speech like that."

A gust whipped Cora's skirts around her ankles as she climbed the few steps into the hatmaker's shop. "Maybe I'll even join the women's rights movement."

"Who's joining up with those liberal women?" Gilda Harvey, owner of Harvey's Millinery, maneuvered herself behind the counter.

How did she even fit in the narrow aisle between the display case and the outside wall? "I might, Miss Harvey. I would have thought you would be in favor of them, since you are a shop owner. And an unmarried woman. I admire you for following your dream and never letting a man stand in the way."

Miss Harvey shook her head, her double chin flapping with the motion. "You might be surprised, young lady, to know that I would give this up in a moment if I could go home to a loving husband. My nights and weekends are rather lonely. No children come to visit. Let me tell you, those women's rights ladies are downright dangerous. They tell young girls they should strive to be independent. But it's not all that it appears to be on the outside."

Cora scratched a mosquito bite on her wrist. Miss Harvey had a point. Right now, Cora had Ma and Pa to greet her at the end of the day. But she couldn't live with them forever. It might be nice for a while to be on her own, but she'd get tired of staring across the breakfast table at an empty place.

"I know that if Jimmy Morgan ever asks me to marry him, I'm going to jump at the opportunity." Annabelle unpinned her hat. "Look at this. The wind tore the feather off my favorite bonnet. Could you repair it for me, Miss Harvey?"

"Sure thing, dear. Anything I can do for you, Miss Thomas?"

"Before you go, can you show me those kid gloves you got in last week? I want Annabelle's opinion."

Miss Harvey reached into the case, pulled them out, and set them on the counter. "There you are. You should make your mind up about them soon. Several ladies have been in here eyeing them." She waddled to the back room.

"See, Annabelle, how soft they are?" Cora rubbed them against her cheek. "They would be perfect for Sundays."

"Still trying to impress the pastor?"

"I never wanted to impress him. From the beginning, I knew I wasn't the woman for him." But he did make her stomach flutter in a way Max never did. And he never left her thoughts. "No, Betty is much more suited to him. She's not a fallen woman, like I am."

Annabelle snatched the gloves from her and smacked them against Cora's hand. "Stop it. You are not a fallen woman. You kissed a man. That's all. That is all, right?"

"Of course it is. But I really kissed him." Heat rose in her face. "With passion."

"Because you were in love with him."

"Was I really? Or was I in love with the idea of being in love?" Because what her heart did when she thought of Len was much more than what it did when she'd been engaged to Max. "Anyway, it's time for Len and Betty to meet in person. Letters can only go so far."

"How are you going to manage that?"

"Hmm. We need some reason for her to come to town." Cora leaned against the counter and stared at the ceiling. "Some activity they'll be able to enjoy together. As a couple."

Annabelle clapped. "The Fourth of July box lunch social."

"That's it. Perfect. As soon as I get home, I'm going to write her."

Chapter Eleven

Len drew a large commentary from the shelf behind him, needing to find help with this week's sermon. He sat, opened the tome, and scanned the words on the page. And read them again. And again. But instead of seeing what the scripture passage was teaching, he saw Cora at the moment she all but threw him out of the post office. Lips tight. Hands clenched.

A knock at the door interrupted his musings. "Come in."

The old door creaked open, and one of the church elders, Mr. Franklin, stepped in, his hand shaking as he held his cane. "I hope I'm not taking you away from your work, Pastor, but I'd like a word with you."

Sweat rolled down Len's back, and not from the heat. He stood. "Of course. Please, have a seat." He led the doddering old man to the closest chair. "Would you like a cup of coffee? I have a pot on the stove."

Mr. Franklin rubbed his bald pate. "No, thank you. This isn't a social call."

Len's lunch churned in his stomach. "Is anything amiss?"

"That's what I'm here to discover. As the senior member of the church council, the elders appointed me to come and speak to you about a few matters that are on our minds."

He sat in his chair and clung to the edge of his seat. "I'm sorry if you find my work isn't up to your standards."

"It's not that so much. But we are concerned about you taking on more work than you can handle."

"I don't understand."

"You've been busy answering those letters coming in response to the newspaper article."

Was this what the visit was about? He relaxed his grasp on his chair. "The amount of work it generated for me did concern me as well. But Miss Thomas has been assisting me in writing the responses. And the rate of mail arriving has slowed. We're making great headway. It's actually a nice way to end a busy day."

"We don't want you to neglect the duties to which you were assigned when you took the pastorate."

"I haven't been doing so. I spend the same amount of time each week on my sermons and make the rounds to visit folks on a regular basis. Whenever a need arises in the congregation, I address it right away."

Mr. Franklin stroked his white beard. "I hope that's the case. It's good to hear that Miss Thomas is of some assistance to you. Do you have any interest in the young lady?"

"Miss Thomas? No, not at all. I can assure you that I would never become entangled with a member of my congregation."

Mr. Franklin braced himself against the desk and stood. "Why-ever not?"

As soon as Mr. Franklin left, Len strolled to the mercantile, Mr. Franklin's question rattling in his brain. Why not court a young woman from his congregation? Because it always ended in a mess. But did it always? Pastors often married young ladies from among their membership. So, to say it always ended in disaster was an overstatement.

He needed to pray about it. Seek what the Lord would have him to do. He entered the cool darkness of the store and glanced at the postal counter. Annabelle worked it today instead of Cora.

"Pastor Montgomery. How nice to see you." She nodded her head in welcome.

"Where's Cora?" He ambled to the counter. "I hope she's not ill."

"No. She went home for lunch. I can tell her you stopped by while she was gone."

"I'm not sure what her reaction would be."

She tucked a strand of light-colored hair behind her ear. "If you ask me, she's being foolish."

He staggered backward then scanned the room to be sure no one heard their conversation. Everyone must be home for their midday meal. "What you do mean?"

Her fair cheeks reddened. She leaned across the counter. "I don't want to be a gossip or say anything out of school, but she told me she told you that she's a fallen woman, and that's why she's uncomfortable around you."

Here it came. The death blow to any chance he might have with Cora.

"But she isn't."

He gasped. "She's not? Why, then, would she say she was?"

"In her mind, she believes she is. But she only kissed Max. Nothing more. It's what engaged couples do."

First Mr. Franklin and now Annabelle. What was God trying to tell him?

And what about Mr. Kimble?

◆ ◆ ◆

Cora clutched her bouquet of sunset-red roses as she knocked at Mrs. Layton's blue-painted front door. The poor woman fell and broke her ankle last week. Her married daughter lived close enough to help, but Cora thought that a few flowers might cheer her up.

The curtain fluttered at the sparkling clean window. The middle-aged woman smiled and waved Cora in. "I'm sorry I couldn't get up to greet you. What a silly thing I did, trying to climb the ladder to dust a cobweb in the corner."

"These are for you." Cora held out the arrangement. "I hope they brighten your day. Would you like me to make you a pot of tea?"

"Oh, how sweet of you, dear. Susan only stayed a few minutes this morning. Her youngest has the croup. Can you imagine, at this time of year?"

"That is unusual. I hope he feels better soon." Cora busied herself in the kitchen, stirring up the fire, filling the kettle, and preparing the cups. A few minutes later, the kettle sang, and she carried the tray, complete with some gingersnaps she found, into the parlor.

Mrs. Layton pushed her glasses up her nose and beamed. "Why, thank you, dear. And look who stopped by for a visit while you were occupied."

Cora turned to see Len jumping up from the red, tufted-back sofa across from Mrs. Layton. Her chest tightened, and she struggled to take a breath.

"Miss Thomas. Always good to see you. What a pleasant surprise this is."

The fine china cups rattled on the tray.

"You can set them on the coffee table, dear, and have a seat beside me." Mrs. Layton pointed in the direction she wanted Cora to move, no doubt nervous she'd drop them.

If only her feet would obey. She couldn't follow Mrs. Layton's directive. She could only stand and stare at Len, his hair as wild as ever, his eyes twinkling.

"Cora, dear, is there something troubling you?"

"What? Oh, no. I'm sorry. I didn't know Pastor Montgomery planned to visit you. I'll leave you two alone."

"Mrs. Layton didn't know I was coming. I popped in for a minute on my way home from the Jaspers. They're preparing to move to Pennsylvania, near Mrs. Jasper's sister."

"That will be good for her." Cora set the service on the low table, poured the tea, and took a seat.

Len glanced at his cup then at Cora.

"It's safe to drink. I make a much better cup of tea than I do coffee."

His grin widened until it stretched across his face.

"And I didn't make the cookies."

He guffawed. "Well then." He helped himself to three.

Mrs. Layton fanned herself. "What's so funny?"

"It's a little joke Miss Thomas and I have going."

They had a little joke they shared? That sounded so personal. So. . .intimate. Like they had an understanding or something. He didn't think they did, did he? No, of course not. A pastor wouldn't want anything to do with the likes of her.

"Oh, that's right. The two of you are answering those letters I heard came for you. What a monumental job. How is that project progressing?"

Len set his cup on the table. "Quite well. Miss Thomas and I have managed to make several matches. I hear one wedding is even in the works."

"And what about that poor man who wrote the original letter? Did you find him a suitable wife?"

Len coughed. "Um, I'm not sure. I believe I may have, but it's not definite."

Cora perked up. "You have? Who?"

"Like I said, I'm not sure. The woman may have another interested beau." He reddened until the color of his cheeks resembled a bad sunburn.

"Two men vying for her attention? How did that happen?"

He shrugged and shoved another cookie into his mouth.

"Now, don't you worry, dear." Mrs. Layton patted Cora's knee. "I'm sure there's a wonderful young man out there for you."

Could the earth open up and swallow her right now? "I'm content where the Lord has placed me."

"I believe He has bigger plans for you, dear."

"Yes. Perhaps I'll become postmistress in Des Moines. Maybe even Omaha."

Len grasped his cup in his large hands. "Or maybe He has a husband and a family in store for you."

"Not for me."

"Oh, my dear, you're a lovely young woman."

"I can't." Her throat burned. "I'm sorry. I have to leave." She set her cup down and fled the house.

Len called after her. "Cora, wait. Please."

Chapter Twelve

Len sprinted after Cora as she raced down the street, away from Mrs. Layton's house. "Cora, wait. Please. I have to talk to you."

She didn't turn around or even pause. Thank goodness for women's skirts. Her attire rendered it impossible for her to outrun him. He reached her in short order and grasped her by the elbow.

"Let go of me. Do you want me to make a scene right here in the street?" She struggled against his grip.

"Make all the commotion you want. I won't mind." Though Mr. Franklin's warning rang in his ears.

"You can't have anything to say to me. I said enough for both of us the other week."

"No, you didn't. You didn't share with me the details of how you came to be a fallen woman."

She turned her face from him. "And I don't intend to. You know how to humiliate a woman, don't you?"

He spoke in the softest voice he could and still have her hear him. "Kissing isn't a sin. Your purity is intact."

She stilled. "Who told you that?"

Maybe he shouldn't have shared what Annabelle said. But Cora needed to know. "That's not important. What is important is that you understand you've done nothing wrong. No man would turn away from you because you kissed your fiancé."

"But. . .I. . .you know. . ."

"You had feelings for the man you were about to marry. There's no shame in that. In fact, it's natural." He had those feelings for her. He loved her. Truly. He released his hold on her and kicked at a stone. "God gives us those desires in order that mankind might continue."

She fussed with a bit of lace on the wrist of her dress. "So, you're saying that men will still find me attractive. Perhaps even marriageable?"

"Absolutely." The word squeaked out of his throat. Absolutely. His fingers tingled. "Cora, I. . ."

She opened her mouth just a little. After she licked her lips, they glistened. He leaned in for a kiss.

She stepped back, her mouth now a round O, her eyes wide. "What are you doing?"

Her voice broke the spell. "I, um, thought there was a bug on your shoulder. There isn't."

"I really need to be going." With that, she spun and marched toward the post office.

If he could turn his leg around and kick his own backside, he would. He almost kissed her. After she thought she was a fallen woman because another man kissed her before marriage.

But he loved her.

Was he right to do so?

Who knew love could be so complicated?

◆　◆　◆

Cora paced the wooden train platform, straining to catch the whistle of the coach pulling in from Des Moines.

"Stand still." Annabelle blocked her. "You'll wear a hole clean through the slats, and it won't help Betty arrive sooner."

"I know. But I'm so nervous. What if she doesn't like Len? Then I've disappointed everyone."

"I hope she doesn't care for him."

Cora narrowed her eyes. "Why would you wish that?" Though, deep inside, she wished the same.

"Because you do."

"Keep your voice down." She peered at the small clutch of people at the other end of the platform.

"It's the truth. I see it in the sparkle in your eyes when you look at him and in the softness of your voice when you speak about him."

"I should be angry at you for telling him about my kissing Max."

"But you aren't, because he convinced you of what I've been trying to tell you for five years, my dear, hardheaded friend."

"Is it true?"

"Of course it is, you goose. Kissing doesn't make you impure."

The cry of the train whistle sounded in the distance. Cora fiddled with one of the buttons in the row of them marching down her blue, flounced dress.

Annabelle squeezed her hand. "You can tell me. I'm your very best friend."

And what if she said the words? Would it change anything? He'd never shown any interest in her. She stared at the tracks, which disappeared into the distance. "Yes, I love him. More than I ever loved Max. Or thought I loved him. But that doesn't mean we have a future. His perfect match is about to arrive to meet him. She's the one he should have feelings for. I refuse to interfere with that."

"Even though you interfered with bringing them together in the first place?"

"Oh, pish-posh."

"He stares at you the same way you stare at him. On Sunday, I believe he thought you were the only one in the pews. He gazed at you throughout the entire sermon."

"He did not. That's an exaggeration."

"No, it isn't. Will you trust me on this? I was right about Max, wasn't I?"

"'The fool doth think he is wise, but the wise man knows himself to be a fool.'"

"I'm not sure what that means, but I don't think it's a compliment."

"Just stick to our plan. I'm bringing a box for Betty and one for myself. You're to tell Len to bid on Betty's because there's a surprise for him if he wins it. And you make sure he does."

"How did I get stuck as the auctioneer? There are many men out there better suited to it than me."

"You're far prettier than any of them, that's why." The train whistled again and chugged into the station. With a puff of black coal dust, it came to a stop.

Not many disembarked at their small town on a holiday. A dapper man, his body erect, descended the stairs, scanning the crowd. A round-faced young woman hesitated on the top step. Cora waved to her. That had to be Betty.

My, she was handsome, with soft blue eyes and a slim figure. If she was half as sweet as her appearance indicated, Len would be in love with her by the end of lunch.

Oh, what had she done?

◆　◆　◆

Len pulled up at the station in the phaeton he hired at the livery, spotting Mr. Kimble right away. The man waited on the empty platform, black bowler hat in his hands, dark suit coat pressed, showing no signs of the journey from the city. He tapped his foot as Len reined the brown mare to a halt. "Are you Mr. Kimble of Des Moines?"

"I am."

"My apologies for my late arrival. Mrs. Matthews had a difficult delivery last night. I stayed to pray with the father. I'm glad to report that mother and child are doing well."

"That's good to know."

Why was he spouting such details? The man didn't care. He didn't know Mrs. Matthews from a hole in the wall. "Do you have a trunk?"

"I thank you for your kind offer to spend the night in the manse, but I must return on the late train. I can't leave my children alone for such a long period of time."

"That's understandable."

Mr. Kimble, a full head shorter than him, took his seat, and Len nudged the horse forward. The new arrival pressed his lips into a thin line. Could Cora love such a man? She would be almost as tall as him. Would she laugh her melodic laugh, or would he tell her to be silent?

"This is my first year in Detwiler, but the townsfolk tell me they have the social every Independence Day. The auction proceeds help the school maintain the building and buy books and supplies for the students."

"A worthy cause, then."

"Miss Thomas is a wonderful young woman. She's very bright and caring and loves to talk about Shakespeare."

"I'm glad to hear it. Though, she did mention in her letters she couldn't cook. That does concern me. My children need good, nourishing, filling meals."

"She's a hard worker. What she doesn't know how to do, she'll learn."

People from the town and outlying farms gathered in the school yard. A band played on the platform constructed just for the event. Women's pastel parasols shaded them from the day's intense sun rays. The lemonade would be consumed in short order.

"What do you think of our little town?"

"Rather quaint but very nice. I shouldn't mind visiting here if the match between Miss Thomas and myself works out."

And that's just what Len was afraid of. What if it worked out? Would he miss his only chance at happiness?

But, he hadn't brought Mr. Kimble all this way to back out now. The plan was in motion.

He had to see it through.

Chapter Thirteen

The crowd of Independence Day celebrators pressed around the platform in the school yard as the time for the lunch box auction neared. Cora pushed through the mass, pulling Betty behind her. She'd wanted to freshen up after her long train trip, and now they were on the verge of missing the auction.

"Excuse me. Please, let me through. I have two more boxes." She didn't glance around for Len. Hopefully, he didn't see her.

She arrived, breathless, at the auction table and placed the two lunches among the others. "Annabelle, here they are. Mine is the one in white paper with red and blue ribbons. Betty's is the one in red paper with stars on it. Do you have that straight?"

"Yours is red, white, and blue, and Betty's has stars on it." Annabelle held the school board president's gavel. "Don't worry. I'll get it right."

"And make sure Len bids on Betty's. And wins it. Do whatever you have to do to make that happen."

Annabelle gave one nod. "Okay, ladies and gentlemen. It's time to get started with this year's box lunch auction. Remember, the money we raise today helps our local school, so please, make your offers generous." She picked up one box and held it high. "Who will open the bidding for this lovely box with a large, red ribbon?"

The numbers flew like buzzing bees. Betty squeezed Cora's hand. "Which one is Pastor Montgomery?"

Cora scanned the crowd. It took her a moment to locate him. "He's there, over to the side, with the somewhat wild hair." But he wore a frown instead of his usual grin.

"Ah, yes, I see him. He's very good looking." Betty stood on her tiptoes. "Who's that beside him?"

Cora squinted. "I don't know." She leaned forward. Why, it was the man from the train. What was he doing here? He didn't resemble Len in any way, so it couldn't be his brother or another relative. Perhaps a friend of his. "He must be visiting."

"He's terribly handsome. And rather dapper. It's too bad you don't know him, or you could introduce us."

No. Betty was as good as betrothed to Len. "Maybe you'll meet him when Pastor

Montgomery wins your basket."

The sun beat down on them, and Cora raised her peachy parasol. She might faint from the heat if Annabelle didn't hurry and hold up their boxes. Wanting to be close enough to nudge Len into bidding on Betty's basket when the time came, the two of them inched their way toward the pastor until they stood a few people behind him.

When Cora's legs were about to give out, Annabelle finally lifted Betty's basket in the air. "Who will give me ten cents for this pretty box? And it's very heavy, so there must be many good treats inside."

A man in the back row offered the requested money. Annabelle didn't say anything about the surprise. She leaned over to be closer to Len. "Isn't that a beautiful box, Pastor Montgomery? It looks like someone made it with loving hands. And it's filled with goodies. Perhaps even a pie."

Len nudged the man next to him. "Sounds like a good one, Kimble. One you should try to win."

The man raised his hand. "Fifty cents."

Wait a minute. Kimble? As in Mr. Kimble from Des Moines? "Is this our original letter writer?"

Len nodded. Someone on the other side of the crowd outbid Kimble. He returned the volley. "One dollar."

"What is he doing here?"

Len turned and winked. "It's a surprise. Just you wait and see."

Annabelle held the gavel high. "One dollar is the bid. Going once."

"You have to bid on it." Cora nudged Len in the back.

"No, I think I'll sit this one out. I have my eye on another."

"Going twice."

"But I have it on good authority there's peach cobbler in there."

"No, I prefer blueberry. I think I'll wait."

"Sold to the gentleman in the bowler hat. And who is the lucky lady?"

Behind her, Betty squealed and jumped up and down. "That's mine. He won my box."

Annabelle motioned them forward. What was she doing? She let Mr. Kimble win the box. This wasn't the plan. This wasn't how this was supposed to work out.

◆ ◆ ◆

Len rubbed his hands together as Mr. Kimble and the woman whose box he won meandered off in search of a spot to enjoy their lunch.

What had Annabelle done? She was supposed to make sure Cora's box went to Mr. Kimble. They had a signal. When she said there were many treats inside, that meant it was time for Kimble to bid.

And what was the Lord doing here? Wasn't Mr. Kimble the one Cora was meant to marry? Then, Len could concentrate on pastoring his flock. He glanced at Kimble and the young lady. She leaned toward him and laughed.

His heart jumped around in his chest, much the way his stomach did in his midsection. Not many boxes remained. Annabelle lifted up one wrapped in white paper with red and blue ribbons tied around it. Maybe this funny feeling in his gut was hunger. "Twenty-five cents."

Behind him, Cora gasped. What did that mean?

"Thirty cents." A man in the back bellowed out the bid.

Len raised his hand. "Fifty cents."

Cora sucked in her breath. Was it her box? Maybe, Lord, she was destined for him? "Seventy-five."

Sweat rolled down Len's back. If it was her box, he had to have it. No matter what Mr. Franklin or his mentor thought about the arrangement. "Five dollars."

Cora grabbed him by the shoulders. "No, Len, you can't do that."

"Five dollars it is." Annabelle smacked the gavel on the table.

The deal was sealed.

"Would the couple who will be eating this lunch please come forward?"

Len turned around, his pulse pounding in his neck. "Are you coming, Cora?"

She nodded. "How did you know it was mine?"

"I didn't until you gasped. By the second time, I was sure."

"But—"

"Come on. There are others waiting to eat." He set off, not glancing behind him to check if she followed. They reached the table, Cora huffing up next to him.

"Thank you, Annabelle. You're doing a great job."

Cora shook her head. "No. That wasn't how it was supposed to work."

What did she mean by that?

Light danced in Annabelle's blue eyes. "This is exactly how it was supposed to go. Now, get on with you. I have an auction to finish."

He offered Cora his elbow. "Shall we find a cool spot for our picnic?"

"Yes, that would be fine." She twirled her parasol as they set off.

Down near the riverbank, a birch spread its branches wide. "How's this?"

"It's nice and cool here."

They fanned out the blanket and the feast, and he said grace. "Did you make all of this?"

"With the hotel cook's supervision. It's good. I promise."

He dug into the fried chicken. Nice and crispy. "This is delicious."

She relaxed a bit and munched on a strawberry.

"Do you have something against me?"

She startled. "What do you mean?"

"You weren't thrilled that I won your box. And you said it didn't turn out how it was supposed to go."

She fingered the edge of the blanket. "What is Mr. Kimble doing here?"

He set the chicken down and wiped his fingers on a napkin. "I invited him. With the hopes of matching you with him. I know you've been writing him because, well, I encouraged him to do so."

"You did what?"

"You both love Shakespeare. I can't compete with that."

"You don't need to. I know enough lines from the Bard for the both of us."

The both of us? He chuckled. "I suppose you do. Now, I've come clean. I have a feeling you have a confession of your own to make?"

She drew in a deep breath and released it little by little. "The woman with Mr. Kimble?"

He glanced toward them. They sat, heads almost touching. Could it be that the two of them would get along? "Yes."

"I've been masquerading as you and writing to her. She's here on my invitation. I told Annabelle which box was mine and which was hers. She was supposed to make sure you won Betty's box. But she mixed them up."

He caught Annabelle's attention as she finished the auction. She smiled at him. "Oh, I don't think that was an accident."

"What do you mean?"

His mouth went dry, and his palms sweated. "Annabelle is playing matchmaker today."

"You think she did this on purpose?"

"Not think. I know she did."

"Why?"

Why, indeed? But he listened to his heart. Forget about Mr. Franklin and Pastor Sherman. He needed to listen to God. And God planted this love for Cora deep in his soul. "Listen, Cora, I love you." He grasped her by the hands. "There's no use in denying it anymore. I believe that the Ultimate Matchmaker, the Lord Himself, brought us together for a reason. I love everything about you. Your sweetness, your thoughtfulness, your generosity. Even your terrible coffee and your Shakespearean quotes."

Her hands trembled in his. "What are you saying?"

"Can you find it in your heart to love me?"

She gazed at him, straight in the eyes. Hers brimmed with unshed tears. "I love you, too, Len. More than I thought possible. I've loved you since that night with the Jasper family. You're compassionate and kind, and you put others ahead of yourself. My love for Max was nothing more than a young woman's infatuation. You, Len Montgomery, you I love with all my heart."

Her beautiful words soaked into the very depths of his being. Gooseflesh sprang up on his arms. "Well then, Miss Thomas, there's only one thing we can do about that."

"What?" She whispered, her voice hoarse.

"Will you marry me?"

Her smile outshone the sun. "If you'll have me."

"I will. For the rest of my life." He leaned in to kiss this beautiful woman who would soon be his wife.

She held up her hand to stop him. "Not until we're married."

"Then, let's make it soon." He couldn't wait to spend the rest of his life with her, his one perfect match.

Epilogue

The heat of summer had broken the night before in a wild thunderstorm. This morning, a refreshing breeze stirred the drying cornstalks. Rainwater droplets glistened on the grass.

Pa patted Cora's hand as they walked the couple of blocks from their house to the church. Inside, their friends and family gathered. "Are you nervous, sweetheart?"

"No. Not a tiny bit. Len is the man for me. God brought us together. There's nothing to be worried about."

His mustache danced as he smiled. "Good. Ma and I pray you'll be very happy together."

"I have no doubt we will be."

They entered the church's coat room. Mrs. Yeager worked a tune out of the pump organ.

Cora had eyes for no one else in the church other than Len. She hurried her father along. No need to wait any longer. It was time to get married.

Pastor Sherman came from Ohio to perform the ceremony. As she held hands with Len, she tried to concentrate on the pastor's words. But she could think of nothing other than her almost-husband's warm touch, that heat transferring to her and spreading throughout her body.

"I now pronounce you husband and wife. You may kiss the bride."

Len swept her into his arms and kissed her until she thought her knees would give way. Only his hand behind her back kept her from falling to the floor.

He broke off the kiss to whisper in her ear. "How was that?"

"'Can one desire too much of a good thing?'"

"Not when we're a match made in heaven." And he kissed her again.

Liz Tolsma is a popular speaker and an editor and the owner of the Write Direction Editing. An almost-native Wisconsinite, she resides in a quiet corner of the state with her husband and their two daughters. Her son proudly serves as a US marine. They adopted all of their children internationally, and one has special needs. When she gets a few spare minutes, she enjoys reading, relaxing on the front porch, walking, working in her large perennial garden, and camping with her family.

If You Liked This Book, You'll Also Like...

The Blue Ribbon Brides Collection

Nine inspiring romances heat up at old time state and county fairs. The competition is fierce when nine women between 1889 and 1930 go for the blue ribbon to prove they have something valuable to contribute to society. But who will win the best honor of all—a devoted heart?

Paperback / 978-1-63409-861-8 / $14.99

Seven Brides for Seven Texans Romance Collection

G. W. Hart is tired of waiting for his seven grown sons to marry, and now he may not live long enough to see grandchildren born. So he sets an ultimatum for each son to marry before the end of 1874 or be written out of his will. But can love form on a deadline?

Paperback / 978-1-63409-965-3 / $14.99

The American Heiress Brides Collection

Nine young American women between 1866 and 1905 have been blessed by fortunes made in gold, silver, industry, ranching, and banking. But when it comes to love, each woman struggles to find true love and know who to trust with their greatest treasure—their hearts?

Paperback / 978-1-63409-997-4 / $14.99

Christian Fiction for Women

Christian Fiction for Women is your online home for the latest in Christian fiction.

Check us out online for:

- Giveaways
- Recipes
- Info about Upcoming Releases
- Book Trailers
- News and More!

Find Christian Fiction for Women at Your Favorite Social Media Site:

 Search "Christian Fiction for Women"

 @fictionforwomen
